A QUIET VENDETTA

A
QUIET
VENDETTA

R. J. ELLORY

THE OVERLOOK PRESS
NEW YORK, NY

First published in the United States in 2012 by

The Overlook Press, Peter Mayer Publishers, Inc.
141 Wooster Street
New York, NY 10012
www.overlookpress.com
For bulk and special sales, please contact sales@overlookny.com

First published in Great Britain in 2005 by Orion, an Hachette UK company

Cataloging-in-Publication Data is available from the Library of Congress

Book design by Bernard Schleifer. Typeset by Jackson Typesetting Co.

ISBN 978-1-59020-508-2

Manufactured in the United States of America

ACKNOWLEDGMENTS

TO ALL THOSE at Orion: Malcolm Edwards, Peter Roche, Jane Wood, Gaby Young, Juliet Ewers, Helen Richardson, Dallas Manderson, Debbie Holmes, Kelly Falconer, Kate Mills, Sara O'Keeffe, Genevieve Pegg, Susan Lamb, Susan Howe, Jo Carpenter, Andrew Taylor, Ian Diment, Mark Streatfeild, Michael Goff, Anthony Keates, Mark Stay, Jenny Page, Katherine West, and Frances Wollen. As well to Mark Rusher at Weidenfeld & Nicolson; and to Robyn Karney, my own Thelma Schoonmaker—the embodiment of patience and care.

To Jon Wood, editor and consigliere.

To my agent and friend, Euan Thorneycroft.

To Ali Karim at Shots Magazine and Steve Warne at CHC Books.

To Dave Griffiths at Creative Rights Digital Registry; the crew of BBC Radio WM; Maris Ross at Publishing News; The UK Crime Writers' Association; Daniel, David and Thallia at Goldsboro Books; Richard Reynolds at Heffers in Cambridge and Paul Blezard at One Word Radio.

To Sgt. Steve Miller, Metro-Dade Crime Laboratory Bureau, Miami, FLA, for staying after-hours to answer questions about body parts and the frailty of human beings.

To my brother, Guy.

To my wife of sixteen years, my son of eight.

I owe you all.

Approaching death,
as we think, the death of love,
no distinction,
any more suffices to differentiate
the particulars
of place and condition
with which we have been long
familiar.
All appears
as if seen
wavering through water.

From "Asphodel, That Greeny Flower," Book II
WILLIAM CARLOS WILLIAMS

AUTHOR'S NOTE

THIS IS A work of fiction.

Irrespective of the fact that it is set against historical events and amidst people whose names you will recognize, it is nevertheless a work of fiction. Where actual events have been modified, or perhaps a sequence changed, this was done only to facilitate the telling of the story.

Many of the people herein are long-since dead, and perhaps the world is a better place for it, but they populated my life for some weeks, and in their own way gave generously of themselves. Some of them were funny, some of them disturbing, others just downright crazy. Regardless they came and went, they made their mark, and I acknowledge them for their contribution.

It has been said that the whole is always greater than the sum of its parts, and perhaps in collating and binding these parts together I have made errors. For this I assume complete responsibility, but also plead an element of mitigating circumstance: I was in bad company at the time.

The Author

ONE

THROUGH MEAN STREETS, through smoky alleyways where the pungent smell of raw liquor hangs like the ghost of some long-gone summer; on past these battered frontages where plaster chips and twists of dirty paint in Mardi Gras colors lean out like broken teeth and fall leaves; passing the dregs of humanity who gather here and there amongst brown-papered bottles and steel-drum fires, serving to tap the vein of meager human prosperity where it spills, through good humor or diesel wine, onto the sidewalks of this district . . .

Chalmette, here within the boundaries of New Orleans.

The sound of this place: the jangled switching of interference, the hurried voices, the lilting piano, the radios, the streetwalking, hip-dipping youths playing mesmeric rap.

If you listen, you can hear from porch or stoop the quarreling voices, innocence already bruised, challenged, insulted.

The clustered tenements and apartment blocks, pressed between streets and sidewalks like some secondary consideration, the unwanted reprise of an earlier discarded theme, and running like a strung-together, slipshod archipelago, hopping a block at a time out through Arabi, over the Chef Menteur Highway to Lake Pontchartrain where people seem to stop merely because the earth does.

Visitors perhaps wonder what makes this ripe, malodorous blend of smells and sounds and human rhythms as they pass over the Lake Borgne canal, over the Vieux Carre business district, over Ursuline's and Tortorici's Italian to Gravier Street. For here the sound of voices is strong, rich, vibrant, and there is motion spilling randomly, a pocket of curiosity gathered along the edge of a one-way street, a corridor of downward-sloping entries into parking lots beneath a tenement.

But for the squad car flashes, the alleyway is hot and thick with darkness. The tail-ends of cars—chrome fenders and liquid silk paintwork—catch the kaleidoscope flickers, and wide eyes flash cherry red to sapphire blue as police cars drive a wedge across the street and halt all passage.

To the left and right are hospitals, the Veterans' and LSU Medical Center, and up ahead the South Claiborne Avenue Overpass, but here there is a splinter of activity through the network of arteries and veins that ordinarily flows uninhibited, and what is happening is unknown.

Patrolmen back the sensation-seekers away, herding them behind a hastily erected barrier, and once an arc lamp is hooked to the roof of a car, its beam wide enough to identify each and every vehicle pigeon-holed in the alley, they begin to understand the source of this sudden police presence.

Somewhere a dog barks and, as if in echo, three or four more start up somewhere to the right. They holler in unison for reasons known only to themselves.

Third entrance from the Claiborne end a car is parked at an angle, its fender running a misplaced parallel to the others. Its positioning indicates speed, the rapid arrival and departure of its driver, or perhaps a driver who had not cared to harmonize with perspective and linear conformity, and though the carboy who walked this alleyway—minding automobiles, polishing brights and hoods for a quarter's tip—has seen this car for three days consecutive, he hadn't called the police until he'd looked inside. He'd taken a flashlight, a good one, and, pressing his face against the left rear quarterlight, he'd scanned the luxurious interior, minding he didn't touch the white walls with his dirty, toe-peeping kickers. This wasn't no ordinary car. There was something about it that had drawn him inside.

More people had gathered by then, and down a half a block or so some folks had opened up the doors and windows on a house party and the music was coming down with the smell of fried chicken and roasted pecans, and when a plain Buick showed up and someone from the Medical Examiner's office stepped out and walked toward the alleyway there were quite a few people down there: maybe twenty-five, maybe thirty.

And there was music—our human syncopations—as good tonight as any other.

The smell of chicken reminded the ME's man of some place, some time he couldn't remember now, and then it started raining in that lazy, tail-end-of-summer way that seemed to wet nothing down, the kind of way no one had a mind to complain about.

It'd been a hot summer, a quiet kind of brutality, and everyone could remember how bad the smell got when the storm drains backed up in the last week of July, and how they spilled God-only-knew-what out into the gutters. It steamed, the flies came, and the kids got sick when they played down there. Heat blistered at ninety, tortured through ninety-five, and when a hundred sucked the air from parched lungs they called it a nightmare and stayed home from work to shower, to wrap split ice in a wet towel and lie on the floor with their cool hats pulled down over their eyes.

The Examiner man walked down. Early forties, name was Jim Emerson; he liked to collect baseball cards and watch Marx Brothers movies, but the rest of the time he crouched near dead bodies and tried to put two and two together. He looked as lazy as the rain, and you could sense in the way he moved that he knew he was unwelcome. He knew nothing about cars, but they'd run a sheet through come morning and they'd find—just like the carboy had figured—that this wasn't no ordinary automobile.

Mercury Turnpike Cruiser, built by Ford as the XM in '56, released commercially in '57. V8, 290 horsepower at 4600 revs per minute, Merc-O-Matic transmission, 122-inch wheelbase, 4240 pounds in weight. This one was a hardtop, one of only sixteen thousand ever built, but the plates were Louisiana plates—and should have been on a '69 Chrysler Valiant, last booked for a minor traffic violation in Brookhaven, Mississippi seven years before.

The carboy, released without charge within an hour and a half of his report, had stated emphatically that he'd seen blood on the backseat, a real mess of it all dried up on the leatherwork, clotted in the seams, spilled over the edge of the seats and down on the floor. Looked like a sucking pig had been gutted in there. The Cruiser wore a lot of glass, its retractable rear window, quarter-lights and sides designed to permit full enjoyment of the wide new vistas open to turnpike travellers. Gave the boy a good look at the innards of this thing, because that's what he'd figured was in there, and he wasn't so far from right.

These were the Chalmette and Arabi districts, edge of the French business quarter, New Orleans City, state of Louisiana.

This was a humid August Saturday night, and only later did they clear the sidewalks, haul out that car and lever the trunk.

Assistant Medical Examiner Emerson was there to see a can of worms opened right up, and even the cop who stood beside him— hard-bitten and weatherworn though he was—even he took a raincheck on dinner.

So they levered the trunk, and inside they found some guy, couldn't have been much more than fifty years of age, and Emerson told anyone who'd listen that he'd been there for three, perhaps four days. Car had been there for three if the boy's observation was correct, and there were sections of the trunk's interior, bare metal strips, where the man's skin had adhered in the heat. Emerson had one hell of a job; eventually he decided to freeze the metal strips with some kind of spray and then peeled the skin away with a paint scraper. The trunk vic looked like mystery meat, smelled worse, and the autopsy report would read like an auto smash.

Severe cerebral hemorrhaging; puncture of temporal, sphenoid and mastoid; rupture of pineal gland, thalamus, pituitary gland and pons by standard dimension claw hammer (generic branding, available at any good hardware outlet for between $9.99 and $12.99 depending on which side of town you shopped); heart severed at inferior vena cava through right and left ventricle at base; severed at subclavian veins and arteries, jugular, carotid and pulmonary. Seventy percent minimum blood loss. Bruising to abdomen and coeliac plexus. Lesions to arms, legs, face, hands, shoulders. Rope burns and adhesive marks from duct tape to wrists, left and right. Rope fibers attached to adhesive identified beneath an infrared spectraphotometer as standard nylon type, again available from any good hardware outlet. Estimated time of death Wednesday 20 August, somewhere between ten p.m. and midnight, courtesy of New Orleans District 14 County Coroner's Office, signed this day . . . witness . . . etc, etc.

The vic had been beaten six ways to Christmas. Tied at the wrists and ankles with nylon rope, beaten about the head and neck with a claw hammer, eviscerated, his heart cut away but left inside the chest cavity, wrapped in a regular 60 percent polyester, 35 percent cotton, 5 percent viscose bedsheet, dumped in the backseat of a '57 Mercury Turnpike Cruiser, driven to Gravier Street, moved to the trunk and then left for approximately three days prior to discovery.

There were interns to see to the arrival of the body at the Medical Examiner's office, to watch over it for the couple of hours before it was moved to the County Coroner for full autopsy. Fresh-faced they were, young, and yet already beginning to get that world-weary edge of madness in their eyes, the kind of look that came from spending your life moving the dead from the scene of their misfortunes. They kept thinking *This is no work for a human being* but perhaps had already joined that happy, foolish crowd of folks who believed that, if they were not there to do these things, then no one else would take care of them. There would always be someone to take their place, but they—in their infinite and very mortal wisdom—could never see them. Due, perhaps, to the desperation of looking.

The Crime Scene Security Officer was the man who stood sentinel over the dead to ensure this mortality was not violated further, that no one would walk through the spilled blood, no one would move the torn clothing, the fibers, the fragments, that no one would touch the weapon, the footprint, the microscopic smudge of varicolored mud that could isolate the one thread that would unravel everything; selfishly, with some sense of internal hunger, he would clutch these images and visions to his chest. Like a child protecting a cookie jar, or candies, or threatened innocence, he sought to make permanent the very impermanent, and in such a way lose sight of the real truth of the matter.

But that would be tomorrow, and tomorrow would be another day altogether.

And by the time darkness edged its cautious way toward morning the people who had crowded the sidewalks had forgotten the story, forgotten perhaps why they went down there in the first place, because here—here, of all places in the world—there were better things to think of: jazz festivals in Louis Armstrong Park, the procession from Our Lady of Guadalupe Church, St. Jude Shrine, a fire out on Crozat by Hawthorne Hall above the Saenger Theater that took the lives of six, orphaned some little kids, and killed a fireman called Robert DeAndre who once kissed a girl with a spider tattooed on her breast. New Orleans, home of the Mardi Gras, of little lives, unknown names. Stand. Close your eyes now and inhale this mighty sweating city in one breath. Smell the ammoniac taint of the Medical Center; smell the heat of rare ribs scorching in oiled flames, the flowers, the clam chowder, the pecan pie, the bay leaf and oregano and court bouillon and carbonara from Tortorici's, the gasoline, the moonshine, the diesel wine: the collected perfumes of a thousand million intersecting lives, and then each life intersecting yet another like six degrees of separation, a thousand million beating hearts, all here, beneath the roof of the same sky where the stars are like dark eyes that see everything. See and remember . . .

The image evaporates, as transient as steam through subway grilles or from blackened copper funnels projecting from the back walls of Creole restaurants, steam rising from the floor of the city as it sweltered through the night.

Like steam from the brow of a killer as he'd worked his heart out . . .

Sunday. A hard, bright day. The heat had lifted as if to make room to breathe. Children were stripped to the waist, gathered at the corner of Carroll and Perdido and spraying each other with water from rubber snaking hoses that traipsed from the porches of clapboard houses set back from the street, behind low banks of hickory and water oaks. Their squeals, perhaps more from relief than excitement, scattered like streamers through the low, heady atmosphere. These sounds, of life in its infancy, were there as John Verlaine was woken by the incessant shrilling of the phone; and such a call at that time in the morning meant, more often than not, that someone somewhere was dead.

New Orleans Police Department for eleven years, somewhere in amongst that three and a half years in Vice, the last two years in Homicide; single, mentally sound but emotionally unstable; most often tired, less often smiling.

Dressed quickly. Didn't shave, didn't shower. More than likely there'd be a mess of shit to wade through. You got used to it. Maybe you *convinced* yourself you got used to it.

Heat had been angry the past few days. Closed you up inside it like a fist. Hard to breathe. Sunday morning was cooler; the air lightened a little, the feeling that pressured storm clouds could break through everything now dissipated.

Verlaine drove slowly. Whoever had died was already dead. No point in rushing.

He felt it would rain again, that lazy, tail-end-of-summer rain that no one took a mind to complain about, but it would come later, perhaps during the night. Perhaps while he slept. If he slept . . .

Away from his apartment on Carroll, heading a straight north toward South Loyola Avenue. The streets seemed vacant but for a thin scattering of humanity's lost, and he watched them, their tentative advances, their laughing faces, their hungover redness that spread from the doorways of bars out onto the sidewalk and into the street.

He drove without thought, and somewhere near the De Montluzin Building he hung a right, and then past Loew's State Theater. Twenty minutes, and he stood at the Loyola end of Gravier. Down here there were mimosas and hickory trees, the branches chased of bark, the remnants of their pecan yield stolen weeks before by grimy thieving hands. *Pecan pie,* he thought, and smelled his mother's kitchen, and saw through the window his sister, a cool flannel draped over her head, her thin sapling arms red with the sun, peeling, spotted with calamine and cocoa butter, and thought *If only we could all go backward* . . .

Verlaine looked away leftwards, away from Gravier, through the wisteria that had clung to the walls along this street since he could remember, their pendent racemes like clusters of grape hanging purple and delicate and sweet with perfume; past the grove of mimosas, their cylindrical heads like little spikes of color through the burgeoning light, out toward Dumaine and North Claiborne, the hum of traffic just another voice in this start-of-day humidity. Down among the water oaks and honey locusts, you could hear the cicadas challenging the distant sound of children who ran and played their catch-as-catch-can games on the sidewalks through air that sat tight like a drum, like it was waiting to be breathed.

He knew where the car had been, it was evident by its absence, and strung around the missing-tooth gap were crime scene tapes fluttering in the breeze. The body was found here, some guy beaten to death with a hammer. Ops told him as much as they knew on the phone, said he should go down there and see what he could see, and once he was done he should drive over to the ME's office and speak to Emerson, check the scene report, and then on to the County Coroner to attend the autopsy. So he looked, and he saw what he could see, and he took some shots with his camera, and he walked around the edges of the thing until he felt he'd had enough and returned to his car. He sat in the passenger side with the door open and he smoked a cigarette.

Forty minutes later, the Medical Examiner's office on South Liberty and Cleveland, back of the Medical Center. The day had grown in stature, promised a clear azure sky before lunch was over, promised a mid-afternoon in the high eighties.

Verlaine felt his head stretching as he walked from the car, trying to stay close to the store frontages beneath the awnings and out of the sun. His shirt was glued to his back beneath a too-heavy cotton suit, his feet sweated inside his shoes, his ankles itched.

Jim Emerson, youthful despite entering his early forties, Assistant Medical Examiner and very good at it. Emerson added a certain flair and insight to what would ordinarily have been a dry and factual task. He was sensitive to people, sensitive even when they were rigored and bloated and shattered and dead.

Verlaine stood in the corridor outside Emerson's office for a moment. *Here we go again,* he thought, and then knocked once and walked straight in.

Emerson rose from his desk and reached out his hand. "Short time, plenty see," he said, and smiled. "You up for the trunk job?"

Verlaine nodded. "Seems that way."

"Nasty shit," Emerson said, and glanced to the desk. Ahead of him were three or four pages of detailed notations on a yellow legal pad.

"A surgeon we have here," he went on. "A real surgeon." He looked back at Verlaine, smiled again, nodded his head back and forth in a manner that was neither a yes nor a no. He reached into his coat pocket, took out a packet of bad-smelling Mexican cigarettes and lit one.

"You looked at the body yet?" he asked Verlaine. "We sent it over to the coroner a couple of hours ago."

Verlaine shook his head. "I'm going there in a little while."

Emerson nodded matter-of-factly. "Well, sure as shit it'll spoil your Sunday lunch." He returned to sit at his desk and looked over his own notes. "It's interesting."

"How so?"

Emerson shrugged. "The car maybe. The thing with the heart."

"The car?"

"A '57 Mercury Turnpike Cruiser. That's over at one of the lock-ups. Helluva car."

"And the vic was in the trunk, right?"

"What was left of him, yes."

"They got an ID?" Verlaine asked.

Emerson shook his head. "That's your territory."

"So what can you tell me?" Verlaine reached for a chair against the wall, dragged it close to the desk and sat down.

"Guy got the living hell knocked out of him. Smashed him up with a hammer and cut his freakin' heart out . . . like the betrayal thing, right?"

"That's just rumor. That's a rumor based on one case back in '68."

"One case?"

"Ricki Dvore. You know about that one?"

Emerson shook his head.

"Ricki Dvore was a hustler, a druggist, a pimp, everything. He shipped liquor back and forth out of Orleans with his own trucks, stuff that was stilled someplace out beyond St. Bernard . . . place has grown since then though. You know Evangeline, down south along Lake Borgne?"

Emerson nodded.

"Stilled the stuff down there and brought it in in regular-looking trucks with tanks inside the bodies. He gypped some dealer, someone from one of those crazy families down there, and one by one his wife, his kids, his cousins, they were all beaten on somehow. Three-year-old daughter lost a finger. They sent it to Dvore and he just kept on screwing up. Eventually they dragged him from his truck one night, cut his heart out and sent it to his wife. Cops had Christ knows how many people answering up for that, more crank calls, more confessions than anything I've ever heard of. They didn't have a hope; case folded within a fortnight and stayed that way. They never found Dvore's body— weighted down and sunk in a bayou someplace I'm sure. They just had his heart. That's where the whole thing about betrayal and cutting out people's hearts came from. It's just a story."

"Well, whoever the hell did this, he left the heart inside the chest."

"Seems to me we go with the car," Verlaine said. "The car is good, strong. Maybe it's a red herring, something so out of character it's designed to throw the whole pitch of the invest, but it's such a big part I somehow doubt it. Someone wants to throw the course they do something small, something at the scene, some minor fact that's so minor only an expert would recognize it. The guys who do that kind of thing are smart enough to realize that the people after them are just as smart as they are."

Emerson nodded. "You go down to the coroner's office and take a look yourself. I'll get this typed up and file it."

Verlaine rose from the chair. He set it back against the wall.

He shook Emerson's hand and turned to leave.

"Keep me posted on this," Emerson said as an afterthought.

Verlaine turned back, nodded. "I'll send you an e-mail."

"Wiseass."

Verlaine pushed through the door and made his way down the corridor.

Heat had risen outside and he sweated on the way to his car.

County Coroner Michael Cipliano, fifty-three years old, an irascible and weatherworn veteran. Now only Italian by name, his father from the north, Piacenze, Cremona maybe—even he'd forgotten. Cipliano's eyes were like small black coals burning out of the smooth surface of his face. Gave no shit, expected none in return.

The humid, tight atmosphere that clung to the walls of the coroner's theater defied the air-conditioning and pressed relentlessly in from all sides. Verlaine stepped through the rubber swing doors and nodded silently at Cipliano. Cipliano nodded back. He was hosing down slabs, the sound of the water hitting the metal surface of the autopsy tables almost deafening within the confines of the theater.

Cipliano finished the last table nearest the wall and shut off the hose.

"You here for the heartless one?"

Verlaine nodded again.

"Printed him for you I did, like the blessed patron saint that I am. Paper's over there." He nodded at a stainless steel desk toward the back of the room. "Gopher's sick. Took off day before yesterday, figured he picked something up from one of those John Does over there." Cipliano nodded over his shoulder to a pair of cadavers, floaters from all visible indications, the gray-blue tinge of the flesh, the swollen fingers and toes.

"Found 'em Thursday face down in Bayou Bienvenue. Users both of them, tracks like pepper up and down their arms, in the groin, between the toes, backs of the knees. Gopher figures there's cholera or somesuch in the Bayou. These cats roll in here with it and he contracts. Full of shit, really so full of shit."

Cipliano laughed hoarsely and shook his head.

"So what we got?" Verlaine asked as he walked toward the nearest table. The smell was strong, rank and fetid, and even though he breathed through his mouth he could almost taste it. God only knew what he was inhaling.

"What we got is a fucking mess and then some," Cipliano said. "If my mother only knew where I was on a Sunday morning she'd roll over Beethoven right there in her grave." The lack of reciprocal love between Cipliano and his five-years-dead mother was legend to anyone who knew him. Rumor had it that Cipliano had performed her autopsy himself, just to make sure, to make *really* sure, that she was dead.

"Aperitifs and hors d'oeuvres are done, but at least you arrived in time for the main course," Cipliano stated. "Whoever did your John Doe here knew a little something about surgery. It ain't easy to do that, take the heart right out clean like that. It wasn't no pro job, but there's one helluva lot of veins and arteries connecting that organ, and some of them are the thickness of your thumb. Messy shit, and really quite unusual if I say so myself."

The skin of the corpse was gray, the face distorted and swollen with the heat it must have suffered locked in the trunk of the car. The chest revealed the incisions Cipliano had already made, the hollowness within that had once held the heart. The stomach was bloated, the heap of clothes bloodstained, hair like clumps of matted grass.

"A clean-edged knife," Cipliano stated. "Something like a straight razor but without the flat end, here and here through the left and right ventricles at the base, and here . . . here across the carotid we have a little chafing, a little friction burn where the blade did not immediately pass through the tissue. Subclavian incisions and dissections are clean and straight, swift cuts, quite precise. Perhaps a scalpel was used, or something fashioned to the accuracy of a scalpel."

"Was the whole thing done in one go, or was there time between opening up the chest and severing the heart?" Verlaine asked.

"All in one go. Tied him up, beat his head in, opened him up like a jiffy bag, severed some of the organs to get to the heart. The heart was cut out, replaced inside the chest. The vic was already lying on the sheet, it was wrapped over him, dumped in the car, driven from wherever, and transferred to the trunk, abandoned."

"Lickety-split," Verlaine said.

"Like the proverbial hare," Cipliano replied.

"How long would something like that take, the whole operation thing?"

"Depends. From his accuracy, the fact it was obvious he had some idea of what he was doing, maybe twenty minutes, thirty at best."

Verlaine nodded.

"Seems the body was moved, tilted upwards a couple of times, maybe even propped against something. Blood has laked in different places. Struck with the hammer maybe thirty or forty times, some of the blows direct, others glancing toward the front of the head. Tied initially, and once he was dead he was untied."

"Fingerprints on the body?" Verlaine asked.

"Need to do an iodine gun and silver transfers to be sure, but from what I can tell there seem to be plenty of rubber smudges. He wore surgical gloves, I'm pretty sure of that."

"Can we do helium-cadmium?"

Cipliano nodded. "Sure we can."

Verlaine helped prepare. They scanned the limbs, pressure points, around each incision, the gray-purple flesh a dull black beneath the ambient light. The smears from the gloves showed up as glowing smudges similar to perspiration stains. Where the knife had scratched the surface of the skin there were fine black needle-point streaks. Verlaine helped to roll the body onto its front, a folded body bag tucked into the chest cavity to limit spillage. The back showed nothing of significance, but Verlaine—bringing his line of vision down horizontally with the surface of the skin—noticed some fine and slightly lustrous smears on the skin.

"Ultra-violet?" he asked.

Cipliano wheeled a standard across the linoleum floor, plugged it in and switched it on.

The coal black eyes squinted hard. "Shee-it and Jesus Christ in a gunnysack," he hissed.

Verlaine reached toward the skin, perhaps to touch, to sense what was there. Cipliano's hand closed firmly around his wrist and restrained the motion.

A pattern, a series of joined lines glowing whitish-blue against the colorless skin, drawn carefully from shoulder to shoulder, down the spine, beneath the neck and over the shoulders. It glowed, really glowed, like something alive, something that possessed an energy all its own.

"What the fuck is that, for Christ's sake?" Verlaine asked.

"Get the camera," Cipliano said quietly, as if here he had found something that he did not wish to disturb with the sound of his voice.

Verlaine nodded, fetched the camera from the rack of shelves at the back of the room. Cipliano took a chair, placed it beside the table and stood on it. He angled the camera horizontally as best he could and took several photographs of the body. He came down from the chair and took several more shots across the shoulders and the spine.

"Can we test it?" Verlaine asked once he was done.

"It's fading," Cipliano said quietly, and with that he took several items from a field kit, swabs and analysis strips, and then with a scalpel he removed a hair's-width layer of skin from the upper right shoulder and placed it between two microscope slides.

Less than fifteen minutes later, Cipliano turned with a half-smile tugging at the corners of his mouth. "Formula $C_2H_{24}N_2O_2$. Quinine, or quinine sulphate to be precise. Fluoresces under ultraviolet, glows whitish-blue. Only other things I know of that do that are petroleum jelly smeared on paper and some kinds of detergent powder. But this, this is most definitely quinine."

"Like for malaria, right?" Verlaine asked.

"That's the shit. Much of it's been replaced with chloroquinine, other synthetics. Take too much and it gives you something called cinchoism, makes your ears ring, blurs your vision, stuff like that. Lot of guys from out of Korea and 'Nam took the stuff. Most times comes in bright yellow tablets, can come in a solution of quinine sulphate which is what we have here. Used sometimes as a febrifuge—"

"A what?"

"Febrifuge, something to knock out a fever."

Verlaine shook his head. His eyes were fixed on the faint lines drawn across the dead man's back. Glowed like St. Elmo's fire, the *ignis fatuus* that hung across the bayous, mist reflecting light in every shattered molecule of water. The effect was disquieting.

"I'll get the pictures processed. We'll have more of an idea of what the configuration means."

That word—configuration—stuck in Verlaine's thoughts for as long as he remained at the County Coroner's office, some time beyond that if truth be known.

Verlaine watched as Cipliano picked the body to pieces, searching for grains, threads, hairs, taking samples of dried blood from each injured area. There were two types, the vic's A positive, the other presumably the killer's, AB negative.

The hairs belonged to the dead guy, no others present, and scraping beneath the fingernails Cipliano found the same two types of blood, a skin sample that proved too decayed to be tested effectively, and a grain of burgundy paint that matched the car.

Verlaine left then, took with him the print transfers Cipliano had made, asked him to call when the pictures were processed. Cipliano bade him farewell and Verlaine passed out through the swing doors into the brightly lit corridor.

Outside the air was thick and tainted with the promise of storm, the sun hunkered down behind brooding clouds. The heat breathed through everything, turned the surface of the hot top to molasses, and Verlaine stopped to buy a bottle of mineral water from a store on the way back to his car.

There was something present today, something in the atmosphere, and breathing it he felt invaded, even perhaps abused. He sat in his car for a while and smoked a cigarette. He decided to drive back to the Precinct House and wait there for Cipliano's call.

The call came within an hour of his arrival. He left quickly, as inconspicuously as he could, and drove back across town to the coroner's office.

"Have a make on the pattern," Cipliano stated as Verlaine once again entered the autopsy theater.

"It appears to be a solar configuration, a constellation, a little crude but it's the only thing the computer can get a fix on. It matches well enough, and from the angle it was drawn it would be very close to what you'd see during the winter months from this end of the country. Maybe that holds some significance for you . . ."

Cipliano indicated the computer screen to his right and Verlaine walked toward it.

"The constellation is called Gemini, but this pattern contains all twelve major and minor stars. Gemini is the two-faced sign, the twins. Mean anything to you?"

Verlaine shook his head. He stared at the pattern presented on the screen.

"So, you get anything on the prints?" Cipliano asked.

"Haven't put them through the system yet."

"You can do that today?"

"Sure I can."

"You got me all interested in this one," Cipliano said. "Let me know what you find, okay?"

Verlaine nodded, walked back the way he'd come, drove across once more to the crime scene at the end of Gravier.

The alleyway was silent and thick with shadows, somehow cool. As he moved, those selfsame shadows appeared to move with him, turning their shadow-faces, their shadow-eyes toward him. He felt isolated, and yet somehow not alone.

He stood where the Mercury had been parked, where the killer had pulled into the bay, turned the engine off, heard the cooling clicks of the motor; where he'd perhaps smiled, exhaled, maybe paused to smoke a cigarette before he left. Job done.

Verlaine shuddered and, stepping away from the sidewalk, he moved slowly to the wall that only days before had guarded the side of the Cruiser from view.

He left quickly. It was close to noon. Sunday, the best day perhaps to find a space in the schedule to get the prints checked against the database. Verlaine figured to leave the transfers with Criminalistics and go check out the Cruiser at the pound. He logged the request, left the transfers in an envelope at the desk, scribbled a note for the duty sergeant and left it pinned to his office door just in case they came looking for him.

It was gone lunchtime and Verlaine hadn't yet eaten a thing. He stopped at a deli en route, bought a sandwich and a bottle of root beer. He ate while he drove, more out of necessity than any other consideration.

Twenty minutes later: New Orleans Police Department Vehicle Requisition Compound, corner of Treme and Iberville.

John Verlaine stood with the crisscrossed shadows of the wire mesh fence sectioning his face into squares, and waited patiently. The officer within, name of Jorge D'Addario, had stated emphatically that until he received something official, something *in writing*, he could not permit Verlaine entry to the compound. Verlaine had bitten his tongue, called the duty sergeant at the Precinct and asked him to have Captain Moreau call D'Addario at the pound and make it official. Finding Moreau took a further twenty minutes. Verlaine sat in his car, drank the rest of his root beer, smoked his last cigarette, and finally D'Addario opened the gate and waved him through.

He walked between the rows of symmetrically parked cars, took a wide berth on a jumpsuited black-faced man chasing a fine blue line through the chassis of a Trans Am with an oxyacetylene torch. Copper-colored sparks jetted like Independence Day fireworks from the needle-point flame. Down a half dozen, right, and through another alleyway of vehicles—a Camaro S/Six, a Berlinetta, a Mustang 351 Cleveland backed up against a Ford F250 XLT, and to his left before the Cruiser a GMC Jimmy with half the roof torn away, giving the impression of a can of peas opened up with a pneumatic drill.

Verlaine paused, stood there ahead of the Mercury Turnpike, the yards of burnished chrome, the mirrored wheel shell standing out from the trunk, the indents and dual fresh-air vents, the double tail fins and burgundy paintwork. Sure as shit wasn't no ordinary car. He stepped forward, touched the edged concave runners that swept from the tail to the quarterlights, leaned to look along the base of the vehicle, its white-wall tires muddied a little beneath the chrome underslung chassis and overlapping arches. Requisition Compound wasn't the place for such a car as this.

Moving to the rear of the vehicle, Verlaine took a pair of surgical gloves from his pockets. He snapped them on and lifted the trunk. The night before, a dead guy had been found in there; now it smelled like formaldehyde, like something antiseptic tainted with decay. The image of the body he'd stood over in the autopsy theater crammed into this space was as clear as ever. His stomach turned. He felt the root beer repeating on him like cheap aniseed mouthwash.

He went back and fetched his camera from his car. Took some snaps. Looked inside the back of the Cruiser, saw the thick lake of dried blood across the leatherwork and down onto the carpet. Took some shots of that. Finished the film and rewound it.

Fifteen minutes and he was walking his way out of the compound; paused to sign the visitation docket in D'Addario's kiosk at the gate, turned his car off Iberville and headed back to the Precinct House to check the status of the fingerprint search.

Verlaine, perhaps for no other reason than to kill a little time, took the long route. Back of the French business quarter, along North Claiborne on St. Louis and Basin. Here was Faubourg Treme, city of the dead. There were two cemeteries, both of them called St. Louis, but the one in the French Quarter was the oldest, the first and original burial ground dating back to 1789. Here were the dead of New Orleans—the whites, the blacks, the Creoles, the French, the Spanish, the free—because they all wound up here, every sad and sorry one of them. Death held no prejudice, it seemed. The graves did not reveal their color, their dreams, their fears, their hopes; gave merely their names, when they arrived and when they departed. Crosses of St. Augustine, St. Jude, St. Francis of Assisi, patron saint of travelers who loved nature, who founded the Franciscans, who begged for his meals and died a pauper. And on the other side were the believers, the gris-gris crosses marking their passage into the underworld. Voodoo Queen Marie Laveau, R.I.P. Haitian cathedrals of the soul.

He reached Barrera at Canal by the Trade Mart Observation Tower, asked himself why he was driving so far out of his way, shrugged the question away. He was now ahead of the French Market beyond Vieux Carre Riverview. A good couple of miles of warehouses interspersed with clam joints, jazz clubs, bars, restaurants, diners, sex shops, a movie theater and the landing jetties for the many harbor tours. Despite the heat the streets down there were busy. Groups of Creoles and blacks stood aimlessly at corners and intersections, hurling arrogant and playful remarks at passing women, flying the finger at compadres and amigos, drinking, laughing, talking big, oh so very big, in this smallness of life. Daily you could find them, nothing better to do, persuading themselves that this was the good life, the life to live, where things were easy come easy go, where everyone who wasn't there was a jerkoff, a dumbjohn, a turkey; where the duchesses sailed by, their hands on the arms of trade, making their way to some seedy Maison Joie down the street and back of the next block, and these corner-hugging, street-smart hopefuls were wise to their act and knew not to say anything whatever the trade looked like, for a duchess with a stiletto heel to your throat was no cool scene. Here, the air was haunted forever with the smell of fish, of sweat, of cheap cigar smoke passing itself off as hand-rolled Partageses; here existence seemed to roll itself out endlessly from one dark and humid dream to the next, with no change to spare but daylight in between. Daylight was for scoring, for counting money, for sleeping some, for drinking a little to prep the tongue for the onslaught that would come later. Daylight was something God made so life was not one endless party; something, perhaps, to give the neon tube signs a rest. Places such as this they held cock fights; places such as this the police let them. In the guidebooks it suggested you visit these parts only in groups, directed by an official, never alone.

Verlaine crossed the intersection of Jackson and Tchoupitoulas where the bridge spanned the river and joined 23, where 23 crossed the West Bank Expressway, where the world seemed to end and yet somehow begin again with different colors, different sounds, different senses.

He arrived unnoticed at the Precinct House—the place was almost deserted—and checked status on the prints. They had nothing yet, perhaps wouldn't until someone pulled their finger out Monday morning and got the hell on with what they were paid to do.

It was gone five, the afternoon tailing away into a cooler early evening, and for a little while Verlaine sat at the desk in his office looking out southwards to the Federal Courts and Office complex back of Lafayette Square. Beneath him the street slowly emptied of traffic, and then filled once more with the hubbub of pedestrians making their slow-motion way to Maylies Restaurant, over to Le Pavilion, life travel-ing onwards in its own curious and inimitable way. A man had been butchered, a brutal and sadistic termination, his savaged corpse parked in a beautiful car in an alleyway down off of Gravier. They were all fascinated, horrified, disgusted, and yet each of them could turn and walk away, take dinner, see the theater, meet their friends and talk of small inconsequentialities that possessed their attention to a far greater degree. And then there were others, among whom Verlaine counted himself and Emerson and Cipliano, perhaps themselves as crazy as the perpetrators, given that their involvement in life was limited to tracing and finding and sharing their breath with these people—the sick, the demented, the sociopathic, the disturbed. Someone somewhere had taken a man, hammered in his head, bound his hands behind his back, opened his chest, cut away his heart, driven him into town and left him Alone. That someone was somewhere, perhaps avoiding eyes, avoiding confrontations; perhaps hiding somewhere in the bayous, out past the limits of Chalmette and the Gulf Outlet Canal where the law walked carefully, if at all.

Verlaine, already weary, took a legal pad, balanced it across his knee and jotted down what he knew. The time of death, a few facts regarding the condition of the vic, the name of the car. He drew the constellation of Gemini as best as he could recall, and then stared at it for some time, thinking nothing very much at all. He left the pad there on the desk and called it a day. He drove home. He watched TV for a little while. Then he rose and showered, and when he was done he sat in a chair by the window of his bedroom dressed in a robe.

The warmth of the day, the way his mind had been stretched by its events, took its toll. A little after ten Verlaine lay on his bed. He drifted for a while, the window wide, the sounds and smells of New Orleans drifting back into the room with the faintest of breezes.

You had to live here to understand, you had to stand there in Lafay-ette, out in Toulouse Wharf, there in the French Market as you were jostled and shoved aside, as the ripe odor of humanity and the rich sounds of its brutal rhythms swarmed right through you . . .

You had to do these things to understand. This was the Big Easy, the Big Heartacher. New Orleans, where they buried the dead overground, where everything slid over-easy, sunny-side down.

This was the heart of it, the American Dream, and dreams never really changed, they just became faded and forgotten in the manic slow-motion slide of time.

Sometimes, out there, it was easier to choke than to breathe.

TWO

ORNING OF MONDAY twenty-fifth. Verlaine woke with a head like a bruised watermelon. The sun had broken early and already his bedroom was like a sauna, the feeling in the air that here was a further reprise of the vicious summer New Orleans had somehow endured.

He rose, showered and shaved; he listened to KLMZ-Heavy Jazz out of Baton Rouge playing "Mama Roux" and "Jump Sturdy" by Dr. John. Breakfast was two raw eggs whisked into a glass of milk, two cigarettes, half a cup of coffee. He was out by nine, back to Cipliano's office by nine-forty, and already the traffic was choking up the atmosphere with its own inimitable brand of filth.

"The heart," was the first thing the coroner said as Verlaine walked through the door. Cipliano spoke through a mouthful of something or other. He went through phases of chewing on things, had given up smoking some years back but never lost the need to have something in his mouth—licorice root, chewing gum, a toothpick, whatever.

"This trip with the heart. Kept me awake last night. I come in this morning I got a leaper John, a fucking leaper waiting for me like I got nothin' better to be doin' with my day. Keeping me busy these bastards are, but what can you do, eh? Anyway the leaper can wait. Like I said, this whole routine with the heart is bugging the shit outta me. Used to be the case some years back, not so much now, but used to be that the families out here, the distillery and bootlegging families you know? They would hold their vendettas as close as their liquor. Tight families, inbred, screwed each other, their own kids and sisters, Christ knows what, little 'uns all ended up looking the same, always ugly.

"Anyway, as I was saying, there was a series of different incidents back in the late fifties and early sixties, maybe half a dozen or so, different things, hands cut off, eyes taken out, tongues snipped at the end so the guy couldn't talk properly. Taking the heart was for a betrayal—"

"Like the Dvore thing in '68," Verlaine interjected.

Cipliano nodded. "Sure, the Dvore thing, but that was way after these. That was maybe the last of the line on this kinda thing. Taking the heart was for a betrayal, someone whom the betrayer counted close would have to do it, someone on the edge of the family, a cousin, a mistress, something like that. I'm not saying that this was the case here, but the fact that the heart was cut out is a similar sort of thing to what was happening back then. Usually you'd only get the heart back, the body would be filled up with stones and dumped in the glades or some-such. Here you got the same sort of thing, but the heart is put back inside. It's hard to tell on the blows as well. So many, and all coming at different angles, like whoever did this was walking around the guy in circles while he whacked him.

"I went down to look at the car early this morning, and I figure that maybe the chest was opened up while the guy was on the backseat. And the way the blood ran off the seat was more like splashes, and that made me think that the body lay on the backseat all opened up for the world to see while the guy was driving down to Gravier. Maybe he figured to leave the body on the backseat, but when he got down to the parking lot and saw how well lit it was he decided to stick the vic in the trunk. There were no prints, gloves worn very tight, perhaps surgical, no grain. The sheet, rope and hammer were all like the first report said, standard hardware gear he could have picked up anyplace. Your guy is strong in the arms, a little under six feet though I can't be certain of that. He . . . I say *he* because we don't find many women doing this kind of thing, and also I can only reserve judgement on the possibility of your perp working alone. Whatever, right? Anyway, seems he carried the body out of the backseat, used the rear wing as support, and there are scratches that are consistent with those little rivets they put on denims. If that was what they were, if they were on the top corners of the back pockets and if your man was standing straight as he carried the body, then he's five-ten, maybe five-eleven. There were no hairs or fibers that couldn't have come from the backseat or the floor of the trunk, nothing there worth mentioning. You've got the killer's blood type, if that was in fact his blood, and that's pretty much all you're gonna get out of me on this one."

Verlaine had listened intently, nodding every once in a while as he tried to digest everything Cipliano was telling him.

"You get a make on your prints?"

Verlaine shook his head. "Gonna go check again now."

"Christ, that crew of yours are a lazy bag o' smashers, eh?"

Verlaine smiled.

"So you got any smartass questions for me?"

"Ritual or psycho, whaddya reckon?"

Cipliano hesitated. "This is criminal psychology you're talking here. I'm a coroner, but from what I can see—" He shook his head. "This is not my field. I can't give you anything other than a hunch."

Verlaine nodded. "So give me a hunch."

Cipliano shrugged. "I'd say you have someone who did this for someone else maybe—"

"Why for someone else?"

Cipliano was quiet for a moment. "There's a mentality, a thinking pattern, always some sense of motivation back of these things. If they run into a serial there's always a common thread, and usually it's not until the third or fourth killing that you find it. Then you look back and see that common factor right the way through, like it's an embryonic thought, something that grows, like he's testing something out, putting something there, getting whatever kick he gets out of his own reasoning. He gets a bit adventurous, embellishes the original idea, really makes it obvious, and that's when it comes to light. That's when you have the trademark. This one . . . well, this one's different. If you had a psycho working for himself he'd have maybe left the vic where he killed him, perhaps cut the body up and distributed it someplace. The psycho thing is all about showing everything for the world. Here he wants the thing seen, but he hides it first. He wants it known, but not immediately . . . almost like it's a message to someone."

Cipliano scratched the back of his head. "The majority of actual psychopaths, serial killers, they have the desire for others to share in what they've done, for others to understand, appreciate, sympathize. The killing is an explanation for something—guilt, sadness, rejection, desperation, anger, hate, sometimes just as simple as getting mom and dad's attention. Your man here, he beat the shit out of the vic because he wanted to, but I think the heart was something else entirely. I think the heart was cut out and then left in the chest because he wanted someone to know something. Then you have this shit with the quinine. I mean, what in fuck's name was all that about?"

Verlaine shook his head.

"You gotta understand, I don't really know a thing about this, right?" Cipliano grinned and winked. "All of that I just told you could be complete bullshit and I'm just making out I'm smart. You go check on your prints, and let me know who he was, okay?"

Verlaine nodded. He turned and started toward the door.

"Hey, John."

He turned back to Cipliano.

"Thing to remember, however bad it might get, is it's never as bad for you as it is for these poor suckers."

Verlaine smiled. It was a small mercy indeed.

The image of the constellation drawn on the victim's back haunted Verlaine's thoughts as he drove back to the Precinct House. It was a twist, perhaps significant in the fact that quinine was used, perhaps in the constellation itself. It would all start to open up with the identification of the body. And, figuratively speaking, that was where it had ended as well.

He pulled into the car lot back of the Precinct and went up the steps into the building. Duty sergeant at the desk told him the captain was away for the rest of the day; also told him there'd been one message left for him.

Verlaine took the piece of paper and turned it over.

Always. A single word printed in the duty sergeant's neat script.

Verlaine looked at the sergeant.

The sergeant shrugged his shoulders. "Don't ask me," he said. "Some guy called up, asked for you, I told him you were out and about someplace. He was quiet for a moment, I asked him if there was any message and he said that. Just one word. 'Always.' And then he hung up before I had a chance to ask him who he was."

"You thinking what I'm thinking?" Verlaine asked.

"If you wanna go there that's your choice, John."

"Seems to me I don't have a choice, right?"

The sergeant shrugged his shoulders again.

"Can you call Prints and ask if they have a make on my trunk vic?"

The sergeant lifted the receiver and phoned through. He asked if they had an ID, and then nodded and held out the receiver toward Verlaine. "They wanna speak to you."

Verlaine took the handset. "Yes?"

He was silent for a moment, and then "Okay. Let me know if anything comes up."

The duty sergeant took the receiver and replaced it in its cradle.

"Security tagged," Verlaine said.

"Your prints?"

Verlaine nodded. "It's come up as a security tagged print."

"No shit! So it's a cop or somesuch?"

"Or federal or military or CIA or National Security Agency, who the fuck knows."

"Christ, you got yourself into a wild one there, John Verlaine."

Verlaine said nothing. He looked at the sergeant and then turned back toward the rear exit of the building.

"You gonna head down to Evangeline, gonna go see Always and find out if he knows anything?"

Verlaine slowed and hesitated. He shook his head. "Right now seems the only direction to take."

"Suit yourself, but take care, eh?"

"Call me on the cellphone if Prints come back to you with anything more, would you?"

"Sure, John, sure. You figure you should take someone with you?"

"It'll be alright," Verlaine said. "Me an' Daddy Always haven't crossed paths for a few years."

"Don't mean he'll have forgotten you."

"Thanks," Verlaine said. "That's very reassuring." He walked on to the rear door and returned to his car.

The rain came as he pulled away from the car lot. By the time he reached the intersection it was flooding down in torrents. Verlaine drew to the edge of the road beneath the overhang of a tree and prepared himself to wait until the worst had passed. Down across the sidewalks, petals of wisteria and magnolia, mimosa and Mexican plum littered the way like confetti, scattered pockets of white and cream, yellow and lilac-blue.

When the rain lessened he began moving again. He took the longest route out of Orleans, left across the southwest limits, noticed a highway sign jutting from the ground—*Don't Take A Curve—At Sixty Per—We Hate To Lose—A Customer—BURMA—SHAVE*—an artifact from some bygone age. The further he drove the more the city dissolved away into nothing. The colors were vague and deep, shades of bruising, of bloodshot eyes and wounded flesh. Where he was headed, a small town called Evangeline, was a place to leave, never a place to arrive in or be born into, but to escape from as soon as age and ability permitted. There were dreams, there were nightmares, and somewhere in between was reality, the truly real existence one found not by listening but by looking, by following these strange-colored threads, vague lines that ran from circumstance to coincidence, and from there into the indelible effects of brutal humanity in its most merciless forms. People like the heart-killer were everywhere: standing in stores, waiting for trains, leaving for work, looking no less human, no less real than ourselves, carrying with them the perfect privacy of who they *really* were, their imaginations running riot with the colors and sounds of death and sacrifice, of some urgent necessity to enact their irrevocable maniac nightmares.

The glades unfolded as Verlaine drove, a demarcation point more of sound and smell than vision, for here the undergrowth began to drift from the verges into the road, the asphalt worn and beaten, here and there broken up and allowing small stripes of vegetation to creep through. The air seemed closer, harder to breathe, and the shroud of trees provided a cover that daylight found hard to penetrate. The heat held the rain up, evaporated a good deal of it before it reached the ground, and the mist hung like a pall over everything. The sound of the engine was swallowed, and Verlaine—feeling for perhaps the first time the full weight of his present situation, its possibilities, its potential repercussions—sat uneasily in the driving seat. He slowed the car some and eased through the beginning of this shifting, ever-changing country like someone invading a private and personal territory. He was thankfully unfamiliar with this land, the rise and sweep of verdant plantations, the gaps between the solid ground where the earth would swallow you effortlessly in mud and filth and depthless suffocation. Walk out here with uncertain feet, and those feet would walk you quietly to your death. No one was ever heard out here; however loud they screamed, that sound was snatched away and evaporated by the heat, the solidity, the thick atmosphere. People died out here like it was one moving, living cemetery, and there was no retrieval for burial or cremation. Once this land had you, well, it had you for keeps.

Verlaine's mouth was bitter and dry. He thought of wharfside bars, of cool lemonade, of sweet Louisiana oranges from the French market along North Peters and Decatur.

He drove for close to an hour, and as he felt the beaten dirt road dip beneath the wheels of the car he also felt the intuitive awareness that something was close. He slowed the car, rolled it leftwards and stopped it beneath a deep overhang of head-height branches. But for close inspection—cover afforded by the mist, the trees themselves—the car was almost invisible. Verlaine thought for a moment about what he was doing, whether he would walk out there and never find his way back. As he exited the vehicle his heart hung in his chest like a fist of tense muscle, beating only because his brain dictated it. His pulse was shallow, his head tight and giddy, his hands shaking. He felt nauseous, a little overwhelmed. He felt watched.

From the dash he had taken his gun; he headed on foot the way he'd been driving, sticking to the boundary of the road, careful not to miss the verge and wander into the glades.

Verlaine heard the sound of voices before he saw the house. Imagery again, strange and anachronistic, as he turned through dense branches, through the grasping fingers of thorned and flowered trees. He stopped at the edge of a fence that ran as far as he could see in both directions. He stood there immobile, right within the heart of Feraud family territory, and his heart thudded noisily.

Approaching a turning in the road he found an unlocked gate and, passing through it, he started up the driveway toward the vast frontage of the wooden house. Painted yellow some eternity before, the woodwork had not so much surrendered its color to the heat as absorbed the quality of the environment into itself. It was shadowed and oppressive in some way, the gaudiness of its age-old decoration at variance with its soul. Here was the seat of jurisdiction for this territory; here was the Feraud family with all its many tentacles; here was Daddy Always, the head of this dynasty.

By the time he was twenty yards from the house he could see men standing along the veranda, could hear their voices more clearly, French dialects similar to those found in the wharfside bars, in the Creole gambling haunts, around the cockfight arenas in the harbor houses by Toulouse and Bienville. These men carried carbines, and handguns in belt holsters; they laughed like men with careless minds and careless trigger fingers, absent of compunction, remorse, reason, or responsibility to any law but their own. These men belonged to some bygone age. These men were not the impulsive gun-happy teenagers and gangbangers that Verlaine collided with in his usual line of work.

The hairs on Verlaine's neck rose to attention, his stomach tightened, he felt pearls of sweat break from his hairline and start down his brow.

When the men saw him walking toward the house they fell silent. They stood motionless, almost to attention. They would know who he was. No one but cops came down here in a shirt and tie. They knew well enough not to cause trouble unless it was started by someone else. They would think nothing of killing him, he knew that, but he would have to give them ample provocation first.

"Attendez!" a voice barked somewhere to Verlaine's right.

Verlaine stopped walking.

A man appeared, armed much the same as those on the veranda. He ambled from the trees and came toward Verlaine as if he possessed all the time in the world.

"Vous attendez," he said again as he neared. "You are police, no?" Verlaine nodded.

"What is it you want here?" the man asked, his accent thick, his tone threatening.

"I came to see Mister Feraud," Verlaine said.

"You did, eh?" the man said, and smiled. He turned toward the veranda. His attention seemed to be held for a moment, and then he turned once again to Verlaine.

"He asks you to come?"

Verlaine shook his head.

"So he is not here *peut-être.*"

Verlaine shrugged. "If he's not here I'll come back another time."

The man nodded and looked down. He appeared to be considering his options. *"Vous attendez ici.* I will see if Mister Feraud is in."

Verlaine opened his mouth to thank the man but he had already turned and started walking toward the house. Verlaine watched as he reached the veranda, shared some words with another man by the door, and then passed inside.

He seemed to be gone for an eternity while Verlaine stood on the driveway with a dozen eyes watching him intently. He wanted to turn and run.

Eventually the man returned. He again spoke to one of the men by the door, and then he raised his hand.

"Venez ici!" he shouted, and Verlaine started walking.

Daddy Always Feraud was as Louisiana as they came. A lined and weathered face, creases like ravines running from his eyes, his mouth, the edge of each nostril. His eyes were like washed-out riverbed stones, almost transparent, piercing and haunted. He sat in a deep blue leather armchair, his legs crossed, in his right hand a cigarette. He wore a cream three-piece suit, and held in his left hand a panama hat which he waved every once in a while to cool himself. His hair was fine silver, combed neatly back, but for one unruly spike that protruded from the crown where he had leaned against the chair. He watched Verlaine as he walked toward him from the doorway of the room. His eyes were distant and yet possessive of an expression that said he'd seen too much for too long to let anything slide by. Bruised light filtered through ceiling-high windows graced with the finest organdy curtains. The old man did not speak, and at each shoulder stood two other men, as still as cigar-store Indians, men that could only have been his sons.

Verlaine stopped three or four yards from Feraud. He nodded his head somewhat deferentially. Feraud said a word that Verlaine did not hear and someone appeared with a chair. Verlaine sat without question, cleared his throat, and opened his mouth to speak.

Feraud raised his hand and Verlaine fell silent.

"There is always a price to pay," the old man said, his voice rumbling from his throat and filling the room. "You have come to ask me for something, I imagine, but I must tell you that the principle of exchange holds court in my kingdom. If there is something you wish from me, then you must give me something in return."

Verlaine nodded. He was aware of the rules.

"Someone was found dead in the trunk of a car," Feraud said matter-of-factly. "You believe there is something I might know about this and you have come to ask me."

Verlaine nodded once again. He did not question how Feraud knew who he was or why he had come.

"And what makes you think that I might know something of such a thing?" Feraud asked.

"Because I know who you are, and because I know enough to realize there is nothing that escapes your attention," Verlaine said.

Feraud frowned, raised his right hand and took a draw from his cigarette. He did not exhale through his mouth but allowed the smoke to creep in thin tendrils from each nostril and obscure his face for a second. He wafted the brim of his panama hat and the smoke hurried away revealing his face once more.

"I received a message," Verlaine said.

"A message?"

"It was simply one word: Always."

The old man smiled. "Seems the whole world believes I have something to do with everything," he said.

Verlaine smiled with him.

"So tell me a little about your man in the trunk of his car."

"His heart was cut out," Verlaine said, "and then replaced in his chest. Someone drove him across town in the backseat of a beautiful old car, and then they put him in the trunk and we found him three days later. Right now we have very little to go on, but there was one thing. Whoever killed him drew a pattern on his back, a pattern that looked like the Gemini constellation."

Feraud's expression registered nothing. He was silent for some seconds, seconds that drew themselves into minutes. The feeling within the room was one of breathless tension, anticipatory and oppressive.

"Gemini," he eventually said.

"That's right," Verlaine said. "Gemini."

Feraud shook his head. "The heart was removed, and then replaced in the chest?"

Verlaine nodded.

Feraud leaned forward slightly. He sighed and closed his eyes for a moment. "I think you may have a problem," he said quietly, his voice almost a whisper.

Verlaine frowned.

"If this is who I think it might be . . . well, if this is—" Feraud looked up at Verlaine, his transparent eyes now sharp and direct. "You have a serious problem, and I do not believe there is anything I can do to help you."

"But—" Verlaine started.

"I will tell you this, and then we will not discuss this any more." Feraud stated bluntly. "The man you are looking for does not come from here. He was once one of us, but not now, not for many years. He comes from the outside, and he will bring with him something that is big enough to swallow us all." Feraud leaned back. Once again he closed his eyes for a moment. "Walk away," he said. "Turn and walk away from this quickly and quietly, and if you believe in God then pray that whatever might have been the purpose of this killing has been served. This is not something you should go looking for, you understand?"

Verlaine shook his head. "You must give me something. If there is something you know you must tell me—"

Feraud once again raised his hand. "I am not obligated to tell you anything," he said, his voice edged with irritation. "You will leave now, go back to the city and attend to your business. Do not come here again, and do not ask anything of me regarding this matter. This is not something I am part of, nor is it something I wish to become involved in."

Feraud turned and nodded at the man to his right. The man stepped forward, and without uttering a word made it clear that Verlaine should leave. Confused and disoriented, he was shown to the door, and once out on the veranda he started walking back the way he'd come, again feeling that eyes were burning right through him, his heart thudding in his chest, sweat glistening his forehead—a sensation that he had somehow walked into something that he might seriously regret.

He reached his car and sat for a while until his heart slowed down. He started the engine, turned around, drove back the way he'd come for a good thirty minutes before he finally slowed and stopped. He got out and leaned against the wing of his car. He tried to think in something resembling a straight line, but he could not.

Eventually he climbed back into the car, started the engine, and drove back to the city.

The FBI were waiting for Verlaine when he reached the Precinct House. The dark gray sedan, the dark suits, dark ties, white shirts, clean shoes.

There were two of them, neither of whom looked like they'd smiled since their teens. They knew his name before he reached them, and though they shook his hand and introduced themselves respectively as Agents Luckman and Gabillard there was no humor in their tone, nothing warm or amicable. Whatever this was it was business, straight and direct, and when they expressed their wish to speak with Verlaine "in confidence" he understood that somehow he'd managed to step on the toes of something that he was regretting more and more as each minute passed.

Inside his office it was cramped. Verlaine asked if they wanted coffee; Luckman and Gabillard declined.

"So how can I help you?" he asked them, looking from one to the other as if there really was no discernible difference in their faces.

Gabillard's face was smooth and untroubled. He looked singularly at ease despite the awkwardness of the situation: "In the trunk of a car last Saturday evening a body was discovered. An attempt was made through your Prints Division to identify the victim, and that is the reason we are here."

"The security tag," Verlaine stated.

"The security tag," Luckman repeated. He turned and looked at Gabillard, who nodded in concurrence.

"The identity of the victim cannot be divulged," Luckman went on, "save to say that he was in the employ of a significant political figure, and was here in New Orleans on official business."

"Official business?" Verlaine asked.

Gabillard nodded. "He was here in the capacity of security for someone."

"The significant political figure?"

Luckman shook his head. "The daughter."

Verlaine's eyes widened. "So this guy was babysitting some politician's daughter down here?"

Gabillard cracked his face with a smile that seemed to demand a considerable effort. "This is as much as we can tell you," he said. "And the only reason we are telling you is that you have a very credible and distinguished record here in New Orleans, and we trust you not to communicate anything regarding this matter beyond the confines of this office. The man you discovered in the trunk of the car was attending to a matter of personal security for the daughter of a significant political figure, and with his death the case becomes a matter of federal jurisdiction, and as such your attention to the killing and any subsequent investigation is no longer required."

"Federal?" Verlaine asked. "She must have been kidnapped then, right? You guys wouldn't get involved if it was simply a murder case."

"We can say nothing further," Luckman said. "All we ask of you at this time is to turn over any paperwork, case files, notes and reports that have been made thus far, and we will speak to your captain when he returns and clarify the position we are now in regarding this investigation."

Verlaine frowned. "So we just drop it? We drop the whole thing, just like that?"

"Just like that," Gabillard said.

Verlaine shrugged his shoulders. He didn't know whether to feel frustrated or relieved. "Well, okay. I don't see there's a great deal more we have to talk about then. Medical Examiner and County Coroner will have their reports. You can collect those from the respective offices, and as far as I am concerned I haven't yet filed a report. Hadn't even gotten the thing off the ground."

Gabillard and Luckman nodded in unison. "We appreciate your cooperation," Gabillard said, and rose from his chair.

They shook hands again, and Verlaine directed them to the front exit of the building. He stood on the steps ahead of the Precinct House, watching the generic gray sedan pull away and disappear down the street, and then he turned and walked back to his office.

He wondered why he'd said nothing of the message he'd received, of his visit with Feraud. Perhaps nothing more than the desire to hold onto something, to keep something of this as his own.

John Verlaine stood for a time, thinking nothing at all, and then he remembered the words Feraud had said, and the gravity with which they had been pronounced: *Turn and walk away from this quickly and quietly . . . This is not something you should go looking for, you understand?*

Verlaine understood little of anything at all. This morning he'd woken with a murder case, and now he had nothing. He did not resent the FBI's involvement; he'd been around long enough to know that every once in a while a case could be taken right out of his hands. This was New Orleans, heart of Louisiana, and one thing he knew for sure, as sure as anything in his life: there would never be a shortage of work.

THREE

ROBERT LUCKMAN AND Frank Gabillard had been partners for seven years. Working out of the New Orleans Federal Bureau of Investigation Field Office on Arsenault Street, they believed that between them they had seen it all. Under the aegis of the United States Justice Department they investigated federal offences—espionage, sabotage, kidnapping, bank robbery, drug trafficking, terrorism, civil rights violations and fraud against the government. They also received alerts when security-tagged print identification requests were made by any law enforcement agency in Louisiana. Patched through FBI Coordination Headquarters in Baton Rouge, the ID request was flagged and a report was immediately logged with the local Field Office. Security tags were registered against any official given security clearance within the law enforcement or intelligence community: Police, National Guard, all branches of the military, FBI, CIA, National Security Agency, Department of Justice, any arm of the Attorney General's Office, Office of Naval Intelligence, NASA *et al.* The report was then pursued by the assigned FBI field operatives, and if the case in some way touched their territory they held the right to assume complete control of all files, records, documents, and any subsequent investigation that might be required. They also possessed the authority to clear the ID request and allow the local police to deal with the matter.

In this instance this was not the case.

On the afternoon of Wednesday 20 August, a nineteen-year-old girl called Catherine Ducane left her home in Shreveport, Louisiana. She was not alone. A fifty-one-year-old man called Gerard McCahill had accompanied her, driving the car, attending to her requirements, ensuring that the visit to her mother in New Orleans went without a hitch. Her father, Charles Ducane, had stood on the steps of his vast mansion and waved her goodbye, and once the car had disappeared from view he had returned inside to attend to his business. He did not expect to see his daughter again for a week. He was perhaps a little surprised not to have received a call to say she had arrived safely, but he knew his daughter and his ex-wife sufficiently well to understand that once they were together there would be little time for anything but shopping and fashionable lunches. By the time Saturday rolled around, Charles Ducane was embroiled in a legal complication that devoured every ounce of attention he could summon, for Charles Ducane was an important man, a figurehead in the community, an opinion leader and a voice with which to be reckoned. Charles Mason Ducane was Governor of the State of Louisiana, now in the third of his four-year term, at one time a husband, forever a father, Charles Ducane was always a busy man. Catherine was his only child, and through much of the year she stayed with him in Shreveport. There was little love lost between Charles and Catherine's mother, Eve—so little that Ducane wasn't surprised to learn that Eve had not even called him when Catherine failed to show. But Ducane understood family as well as any man, and also appreciated that the bitterness and resentment that existed between himself and Eve did not also exist in his daughter's world. Her mother was her mother, and what kind of a man would he have been to deny the girl her right to continue that relationship?

The man who'd accompanied his daughter was an ex-cop, before that an ex-Marine, and even before that an Eagle Scout of America. Gerard McCahill was as good as they came, and the times he had driven Catherine Ducane down to New Orleans on such trips numbered close to three dozen.

This trip, however, was different.

The prints flagged through Baton Rouge and passed to the FBI Field Office on Arsenault Street were those of McCahill, and even now that same fifty-one-year-old ex-cop, ex-Marine, ex–Eagle Scout was also serving his time as an ex–human being on the County Coroner's metal slab. It was he who was now heartless, daubed in quinine sulphate, and wearing a paper tag on his toe upon which was inscribed the legend *John Doe #3456–9*.

And Catherine Ducane, she of temperamental moods, of exquisitely expensive taste, she of awkward moments and determined stubbornness, was gone.

Miss Ducane, nineteen years old, beautiful and intelligent and altogether spoiled, had been kidnapped.

This was the situation that faced Robert Luckman and Frank Gabillard as they walked from the Medical Examiner's Office with Jim Emerson's reports, as they crossed town to find Michael Cipliano and tell him as little as they could. This was the situation they confronted when they made the necessary phone calls to have Gerard McCahill's beaten-to-shit cadaver transported from New Orleans to Baton Rouge, where it would be inspected and examined by the FBI's own Criminalistics and Forensics teams.

This was Monday 25 August, and already the world was beginning to collapse.

For these men, though New Orleans was their home, understood all too well that this was a city like no other. Dirty Creole kids in Nikes and grubby shorts, wise-mouths backflashing words that shouldn't have come from the lips of those so young; the smell of a city cooking inside its own sweat; beyond the limits the sprawling outgrowths of Evangeline, domain of the Ferauds and their ilk; gang wars and drug busts and liquor stills, moonshiners brewing twenty-five-cents-a-bottle rotgut that would strip the paint off a car and eat holes in a pair of good shoes; smack addicts and hopheads and folks mainlining amphetamines like there was no time to look for tomorrow; the sounds and smells of all of this, and you just *had* to live inside it to even have an inkling of how it was. New Orleans was the Mardi Gras, it was finding serpents and crosses in the same cemetery on All Saints' Day, the spirit of loa Damballah-wédo walking there beside you as you crossed the street; it was Easter Souvenance, the Festival of the Virgin of Miracles, the celebration of Saint James the Greater and Baron Samedi, it was inscribing the floor of sanctuaries with *vévé* to summon the ritual spirits. New Orleans the beautiful, the majestic, the passionate, the terrifying. And no matter the training programs, no matter criminal profiling and VICAP reports, no matter gun ranges and Quantico and sitting three exams a year, there was nothing that could take into consideration the mores and ethics of the society within which they lived. New Orleans was almost a country all its own.

Cipliano seemed relieved that Luckman and Gabillard were taking his John Doe away. They told him that an FBI vehicle would be arriving within the hour to collect the body.

"Got a freakin' leaper," he told them while chewing a toothpick. "Head like sidewalk pizza if you know what I mean."

They did not, and did not pretend that they did. People like Luckman and Gabillard dealt with serious business, not the inconsequential deaths of junkie suicides.

They left quickly and inconspicuously, as inconspicuously as two dark-suited, white-shirted, clean-cut men could manage, and drove back to the Field Office on Arsenault to begin the unenviable task of profiling the kidnap of Governor Ducane's daughter.

They took their time reading the reports they had collected, and here they learned of such things as the severed vena cava through right and left ventricle at base, severed subclavian veins and arteries, jugular, carotid and pulmonary; of 70 percent minimum blood loss, of hammer-beatings, of lesions and abrasions, of freezing a man's skin in order to scrape it away from the trunk of a stunning burgundy car with rivet scratches on the wing. They learned also of a constellation drawn across Gerard McCahill's back, the constellation of Gemini, the twins Castor and Pollux, the third sign of the zodiac. They read these things, and once again silently marveled at the sheer madness of humanity.

"Where to from here?" Gabillard asked when they were done.

"Kidnap procedure," Luckman said. "Take the fact that she's a governor's daughter out of the loop, that's irrelevant right now, and we run a routine kidnap procedure."

"I don't think that Ducane would be happy with that."

Luckman shook his head. "Don't give a rat's ass what Ducane thinks or doesn't think. Truth of the matter is that there's a standard kidnap procedure and we have to follow it."

Gabillard nodded. "You wanna call it in to Baton Rouge?"

"I call it in to Baton Rouge and they'll take the case as well as the body."

"You got a problem with that?"

Luckman shrugged. "I got no problem with it. You?"

"I got no problem," Gabillard said. He reached forward and lifted the receiver. He called Baton Rouge and spoke to Agent Leland Fraschetti. Agent Fraschetti, a veteran of twenty-six years, a man with a head as hard as a baseball bat, asked that one of them accompany the body from New Orleans and bring all available documentation with them. That, Gabillard said, he would willingly do. He figured it would pretty much kill the day stone-dead; when he got back it would be closing time.

Luckman chose to go with him. They drove back to Cipliano's office and waited for the vehicle from Baton Rouge.

Two miles away John Verlaine looked from his window and tried to erase the image of McCahill's body, the strange glowing lines across the skin, the sensation of disturbance that these recent events had instilled in him. *This is no work for a human being*, he thought, and once again managed to convince himself that were he not there the work would not be done.

It seemed to run its own relay: from Verlaine to Emerson, Emerson to Cipliano, Cipliano to Luckman and Gabillard, and when the body arrived in Baton Rouge, Luckman clutching the files and thinking of the game he would not now miss that evening, Leland Fraschetti was waiting there for them, his eyes wide with anticipation, ready to take his place in this bizarre concatenation of events. Leland Fraschetti was a dark-minded man, a cynic, a natural pessimist. A loner and a failed husband, he was a man who watched Jerry Springer just to remind himself that people—*all* people—were fundamentally crazy. Fraschetti was also a man who went by the letter of the law and, once Gabillard and Luckman had closed the office door behind them, he pored over the reports and summarized his findings, penning extensive notations regarding the errors the local police had made in their handling of the investigation thus far, and when he was done he e-mailed his proposal to the Field Office in Shreveport where local agents would handle the governor's demands to be updated constantly on the progress they were making. The truth was, bluntly, that they had nothing, though Leland Fraschetti, pessimist though he was, would have been the last to admit such a thing.

By the early evening of Monday 25 August, twenty-seven local FBI agents from New Orleans, Baton Rouge and Shreveport were assigned to the standard kidnap protocol. Governor Ducane's phones were tapped, his house was under twenty-four-hour watch; the Mercury Turnpike Cruiser was driven on a flatbed truck to Baton Rouge and housed in a secure lock-up where Criminalistics went over it with infra-red spectrophotometers, ultra-violet, iodine and silver transfers. The plates were traced to the '69 Chrysler Valiant, now rusted and broken and lying on its roof in a wrecker's yard in Natchez, Mississippi, and thirty-eight vehicle storage units—including Jaquier's Lock "N" Leave, Ardren & Bros. Rental Carports Inc., Vehicle Warehousing Corporation (Est. 1953), Safety In Numbers (Unique Combination Vehicle Storage)—were checked to see if any of their respective owners remembered the Cruiser residing there at any time in the past. No one remembered anything. No one, it seemed, *wanted* to remember anything, and by the time Tuesday the twenty-sixth rolled around, a frustrated Leland Fraschetti stood in the doorway of his office in the Baton Rouge FBI Coordination Headquarters and felt his heart sink. He had taken three Excedrin and still a migraine pounded through his skull and threatened to vent itself through his temples. He had unit chiefs calling from Shreveport and Washington DC, he had agents on double shifts and late hours, he had a task force mobilized that was costing something in the region of twenty-three thousand dollars a day, and still he had nothing to take to the High School Show-and-Tell. Criminalistics and Forensics had come back with almost the same report as had been prepared by Emerson and Cipliano, and there seemed to be no links between this case and anything from the past despite rushing a profile through Quantico. The thing sucked, sucked like a whirlpool, and Leland—he of the dark moods and lonely cynicism—was right in the vortex waiting to drown.

They went through McCahill's records with a fine-tooth comb, they checked his ex-wife, his present girlfriend, his drinking buddies, his mother. They searched his apartment in Shreveport and found nothing that in any way indicated he had been forewarned of the events that were to befall him and his charge in New Orleans. There was no shortage of people who would have been more than happy to upset Charles Ducane, but that was standard fare for any politician. The returning Christ would have prompted public protests and harassment lawsuits. That was just the way of the world.

Tuesday afternoon Leland Fraschetti put an A.P.B. through the system for McCahill's car. Every police officer in Louisiana would now be looking for it. A description and photograph of the girl was processed through the same system, and four thousand hard copies of that image were distributed through the ranks. But the truth of the matter was that the kidnapper had already gained six days on them. McCahill had been dead by midnight on Wednesday 20 August. It was now Tuesday 26 August. Catherine Ducane could have been in Paris by now, and they would have been none the wiser.

Leland Fraschetti did not sleep. He was a man who had never suffered from insomnia; it was not in his nature. He knew his place in the grand scheme of things, and he knew everybody else's place too. He did not, as a general rule, take his cases home, but this one was different. It was not merely the fact that Catherine was a governor's daughter. It was not the clamorings of the vulture press. It was not that the upper ranks were hollering all the way from Washington, threatening to send down one of their own details and get this mess fixed up. It was something else entirely. Fraschetti, never one to trust anything so abstract and unreliable as hunch or intuition, nevertheless *felt* that there was something else going on here. He did not think there would be any ransom demands. He did not believe that the tap system now wired into Charles Ducane's house would record the electronically altered voice of any kidnapper. He did not imagine that at any time a single finger belonging to a pretty nineteen-year-old girl would be delivered in a Jiffy bag to the doorstep of Ducane's mansion. Leland, ascribing his perception to nothing other than gut feeling, *knew* that there was a great deal more going on than the evidence suggested.

Had you asked him for his rationale (and oh, how Leland snatched at *any* opportunity to detail such things), he would have shrugged his shoulders, closed his eyes for just a moment, and then looked you dead-square in the face and told you he didn't know, but somehow he *knew*.

Wednesday morning came and went. A little more than twelve hours and it would be four days since the discovery of the body, and though the immediate news flashes and guesswork reports had died their thirty-six-hour death in the journals and on the tube, still the fact remained that a governor's daughter had seemingly vanished from the face of the earth. Ducane was already threatening to come down personally, but had been dissuaded from such a course of action by his advisors and legal briefs. Ducane's presence, more as a father than a politician, would have stirred up the press all over again, and press attention was the very last thing in the world the FBI wanted. Not only would it generate the usual seven and a half thousand crank calls, every single one of them presenting another lead that would have to be followed up, it also—and perhaps more relevantly—would serve to highlight the fact that the most powerful internal investigative body in the country had accomplished nothing.

A little after two that same afternoon, as Leland was once again staring at a detailed map of New Orleans, its brightly colored map pins indicating the route McCahill and Catherine Ducane had taken from the point they entered the city, an agent called Paul Danziger stepped through into the office and told Fraschetti there was a call he should take.

Fraschetti told him to deal with it himself.

Danziger insisted.

Fraschetti, on edge, frustrated more than he could ever remember, turned and snatched at the receiver.

"Yes!" he barked.

"Agent Leland Fraschetti," a voice on the other end stated calmly, matter-of-factly.

"It is. Who is this?"

"Did you know that Ford only ever built sixteen thousand hardtop versions of the Mercury Turnpike Cruiser?"

The hairs on the nape of Fraschetti's neck stood to attention.

"Who is this?" Fraschetti asked again. He inched around the desk and sat down. He looked up at Danziger, raised his eyebrows. Danziger nodded, confirming that they were tracing the call even as he spoke.

"Shame of it is, I really loved that car, I mean I *really* loved that car you know?"

Fraschetti's negotiator training kicked in on automatic. Say nothing negative. Everything positive, everything reassuring. "I can only imagine. It is a truly beautiful car."

"Uh-huh, sure as hell is. I trust you and your colleagues are taking good care of her. You never know, I might need her back someday."

"Yes, we're taking very good care of the car, Mr. . . . .?"

"No names yet, Leland. Not just yet."

Fraschetti could not place the accent. It was American, but there were undertones . . . of where?

"So how can we help you?" Fraschetti asked.

"Be patient," the voice said. "There is a reason for all of this. A very good reason. In a little while, perhaps a day, maybe two, it will all become apparent. You're gonna need the girl back, right?"

"We sure are. She's okay?"

"She's fine, a little temperamental, a little headstrong, but then you only have to look at her background, her family, and you could guess she was gonna be something of a handful." The voice laughed. There was something intensely disturbing about that sound.

"So, as I was saying, in order to get the girl you're gonna have to trade her for something."

"Of course," Fraschetti said. "Of course we understood all along that there would have to be a trade."

"Good enough. So I'll be in touch. I just wanted you to know that you were doing a fine job, and in all honesty I wouldn't feel the same way if someone else was handling things. I'm keeping tabs on everything that's going on. I understand it must be somewhat stressful, but I wouldn't want you guys to be losing any more sleep over this. This is a personal thing, and we're gonna get it all figured out in a personal kind of way."

"Okay, I understand that, but—"

The line went dead.

He waited a second, two, three, and then he was standing in the doorway of his office screaming for the result.

"Call box," Danziger shouted from the other side of the main office. "Call box on Gravier . . . got two units on the way there now."

The same place as the car, Fraschetti thought, and he just *knew* once again that by the time those two units reached Gravier they would find absolutely nothing.

The Washington units arrived a little after seven. It was raining. Leland Fraschetti had not slept for the better part of thirty-six hours. Governor Charles Ducane had called the attorney general himself, figuring, perhaps, that as far as the legal and judicial system was concerned he couldn't get much higher, and the attorney general had called the director of the FBI personally and told him to get his ass in gear.

This is a governor's daughter we're talking about, Bob, Attorney General Richard Seidler had told the director. *A goddamned Louisiana governor's daughter, and we have a bunch of half-assed kindergarten cops meandering all over the countryside with their thumbs up their asses waiting for someone to tell 'em the game is already in the third quarter. This is your nightmare, Bob, and believe me we better wake up in the morning all relieved and ready for breakfast or the shit's gonna fly six ways to Sunday.*

FBI director Bob Dohring listened and acknowledged. He did not retort in an antagonistic or challenging manner. As far as he was concerned, he had already sent two units down to New Orleans and that was as good as it was going to get. Attorney General Richard Seidler could fuck himself right in the ass, but then again Dohring figured the guy's dick was too short.

Fraschetti was thanked for his work and sent home. Agents Luckman and Gabillard were thanked also, and temporarily reassigned to a field office in Metairie. Washington unit chiefs Stanley Schaeffer and Bill Woodroffe relocated everything from Baton Rouge FBI Coordination and set up camp in the New Orleans Field Office on Arsenault Street. They rearranged tables and chairs. They put up whiteboards and city maps. They listened to the call Fraschetti had taken over and over again, until every man present knew it verbatim. They processed every full and partial print from both the phone booth and every coin in it near Gravier, and came away with two minor felons, a guy on parole after four and a half years in Louisiana State Pen. for molesting a fifteen-year-old cheerleader called Emma-Louise Hennessy, and a man called Morris Petri who, in August of 1979, had mailed a box of human feces to the governor of Texas. Every other print was either too incomplete to process, or was a nonperson as far as the federal government was concerned. No one who fitted their profile had used that phone. Woodroffe and Schaeffer had known—even before they'd begun the exercise—that they were doing it for no other reason than protocol. In the final analysis, if everything went tits up and the girl died or was never found, their careers would be on the line for the slightest omission in procedure. They sat up 'til three on Thursday morning brainstorming, and came away with nothing but migraines and caffeine overdoses.

The baton had passed. The new runners were fresh and watered and willing, but the race had no apparent beginning and the end, if indeed there was an end, was nowhere in sight.

Even when Criminalistics came back with a third repetition of the autopsy results, with chemical formulas and blood types and hair samples and fingernail scrapings, it seemed they had all run like fury after their own tails and wound up back at the starter's gate.

It was what it was, and what it was was a bitch.

Morning of Thursday the twenty-eighth. It was now four days and some hours since Jim Emerson had peered down into the darkness of the Cruiser's trunk and spoiled his appetite. The city of New Orleans was going about its business, the press had been shut down on any reports regarding the kidnapping of Catherine Ducane, and folks like Emerson, Michael Cipliano and John Verlaine were spending their daylight hours looking at other bodies and other rap sheets, the car wrecks and Vietnams of entirely different lives.

A voice specialist had been enlisted to analyze the recording made of the call Fraschetti had taken the previous afternoon. His name was Lester Kubis, and though he looked nothing like Gene Hackman he had nevertheless watched *The Conversation* a good two dozen times. He believed that technology would advance to the point where you could listen to the smallest intimacies of anybody's life, and he looked forward to that day immensely. Lester sat in a small, dark room with his large headphones and pored over the brief section of tape for several hours. He came back with a somewhat tentative outline which suggested that the caller had spent time in Italy, New Orleans, Cuba, and somewhere in the southeastern states, perhaps Georgia or Florida. He estimated the caller's age at sixty to seventy years of age. He could not be precise as to his origin, nor any other specific identifying features. This information, though it would prove immeasurably valuable once they apprehended the caller, did not in any significant way assist their current investigation. The age bracket had served to narrow the field, but with a population of something around two hundred and fifty million spread across three and a half million square miles, they were still searching for a molecule in a ballpark. The fact that the call had been made from Gravier meant that the caller, not necessarily the kidnapper, was still in New Orleans, though it was nothing more than a couple of hours to the state line either way. The girl, Woodroffe felt certain, had been spirited out of Louisiana within hours of the kidnapping. Either that or she was already dead. Schaeffer was sure there was more than one man involved. The lifting of McCahill's body from the backseat and into the trunk of the Cruiser would not have been easily done alone, but they both knew they were guessing and fishing. Schaeffer had taken three calls from the head of operations in Washington by lunchtime, and he knew they were as desperate as everyone else. Rare it was to be assigned to a case that had involved Bureau Director Dohring personally, and upon such things a career was exalted or finished. Schaeffer knew little of Governor Ducane himself, but imagined that, much like all governors, senators and congressmen, he would believe the world and all its resources available to him twenty-four seven. Such a case would not die down or disappear. Such a case would be among the highest-profile investigations until it was finished, one way or the other. And he, too, knew it would only be so long before Ducane would appear in person. No matter the life, no matter the pressures, a father was a father when all was said and done. Schaeffer knew Ducane had already threatened to fly down there and kick some FBI ass, but Washington had assured Schaeffer they were doing all they could to keep the governor in Shreveport.

By midafternoon on Thursday tempers were fraying and patience was as thin as rice paper. Woodroffe had taken six men out to Gravier to trawl the area around the site of the car and the call box in search of anything else indicative of the caller's identity or the killer's motivation. Schaeffer held court in the Field Office, he and five men tracking through the entire chain of events since the discovery of McCahill's body. There were many questions, but seemingly no further answers, and by early evening when Woodroffe returned empty-handed, Schaeffer believed they had reached an impasse.

At eight minutes past seven the second call came.

The caller asked for Stanley Schaeffer by name. He told the field agent who took the call that *Stan would know what it was about,* but refused to identify himself.

"Good evening, Agent Schaeffer," were the words that greeted Schaeffer when he took the receiver and identified himself.

It was the same voice, undoubtedly. Schaeffer would have recognized that voice a hundred years from now.

"You are well, I trust?" the voice asked.

"Well enough," Schaeffer replied. He waved his hand to quieten down the murmur of voices around him and took a seat at his desk.

Woodroffe gave him a thumbs-up. The call was being recorded and traced.

"I am calling from a different phone booth," the voice said. "I understand it takes approximately forty-three seconds to locate me, so I won't waste time with asking how the investigation is going."

Schaeffer opened his mouth to speak but the voice continued.

"I told your colleague Agent Fraschetti that a trade would be required. I am now going to give you my terms and conditions, and if they are not met I will shoot the girl in the forehead and leave her body in a public place. Understood?"

"Yes," Schaeffer said.

"Bring Ray Hartmann down to New Orleans. You have twenty-four hours to find him and get him here. I will call at exactly seven p.m. tomorrow evening and he should be ready to take my call. At this time this is all I ask of you."

"Hartmann, Ray Hartmann. Who is Ray Hartmann?"

The voice laughed gently. "That is all part of the game, Agent Schaeffer. Tomorrow evening, seven p.m., and have Ray Hartmann there to take my call or Catherine Ducane is irretrievably dead."

"But—" Schaeffer started.

The line went silent.

Woodroffe was in the doorway before Schaeffer had replaced the receiver in the cradle.

"Two blocks down and east of Gravier," Woodroffe said. "We have a unit three or four minutes away already."

Schaeffer leaned back in his chair and sighed. "Won't find anything," he said quietly.

"You what?"

Schaeffer closed his eyes and shook his head. "You won't find anything down there."

Woodroffe looked momentarily irritated. "You think I don't realize that?"

Schaeffer waved his hand in a conciliatory fashion. "I know, Bill, I know."

"So who the hell is this Ray Hartmann?"

"Fucked if I know," Schaeffer said. He rose from his chair and filled a paper cone from the water cooler. "I don't know who or where he is, but we've got twenty-four hours to find him and get him here or the girl is dead."

"I'll call Washington," Woodroffe said.

"And give the tape to Kubis and see if he can find out anything else about this guy."

"Sure thing," Woodroffe replied. He turned and left the room.

Schaeffer drank his water, crumpled the cone and tossed it into the trashcan.

He returned to his desk and sat down heavily. He sighed and closed his eyes.

Outside it started raining, and a little more than two miles from where Stanley Schaeffer sat an elderly man, perhaps sixty-five or seventy, watched a stream of generic gray sedans invade a street not far from Gravier.

Tucking his hands in his overcoat pockets he turned and walked away. He whistled as he went, a tune called "Chloe," a classic by Kahn and Morret that was popularized by Spike Jones in the '50s, a song that told of a lonely girl searching for her lost love.

The old man had wanted to tell them more, had wanted to tell them everything, but as so many of his friends in the old country used to say, "A temptation resisted is the true measure of character." There was a time and a place for everything. The place was New Orleans, and the time would be tomorrow evening when Ray Hartmann came home.

FOUR

AND HE WOULD say, "But there never was a time when you told me exactly how you felt," and she'd say, "Even if I had told you you wouldn't have listened anyway," and he would close his eyes, sigh deeply, and reply, "How the hell would you have known, Carol . . . I mean, tell me that, how the hell would you have known if I'd been listening?" and then one of them—it didn't matter who—would mention Jess's name, and at that point things would kind of quieten down. Seemed that Jess was perhaps the only real reason Ray Hartmann and Carol talked any more, and maybe because of that there was the hope that somehow, some way, something good might have been salvaged from their thirteen years together. Spend that many years living side by side, breathing the same air, eating the same food, sharing the same bed, and separation felt like losing a limb, and though hours were spent in some vague attempt to convince themselves that the limb was diseased, that it had to be amputated, that they could never have survived leaving it where it was, the truth always haunted them. No one else would ever feel that good, that right, that familiar. And there would always be a standard against which all others were judged, and though the sex might have been better, though the complaints might have been different, they would always be aware of the fact that this new one was not *the one*.

All their conversations went like that these days: recriminatory, bitter, resentful, sharp and to the point. And they would always talk on the phone when Jessica wasn't there, because she was a human being too, all of twelve years old and mindful of what was happening between her parents. Carol Hartmann, separated from her husband now for the better part of eight months, always called when Jessica was out with friends or on a sleepover, or at band practice or down at the gym. And Ray Hartmann—he of the broken heart and bloodied knuckles where he'd put his fist through the kitchen cupboard door that evening of

28 December—would take the call and sit on the edge of his bed, and he would hear her voice and believe that never in his life would he miss anything as much as he missed his wife. Three days after Christmas for God's sake, drunk and loud and screaming some mindless crap at the top of his voice, and Jessica crying and running to her mother because daddy had gone out of the loop once again. And it was never Jessica, and truth be known it was never Carol, whom he'd married one fine February morning in 1990. It was the job, the stress of the job, the way the job carried over into everything you were, everything you ever imagined you could be, and it was a rare and special woman who could have weathered the storms Ray Hartmann brought with him, for sometimes he didn't just bring storms, sometimes he brought Hurricane Ray, loud enough to bring down trees and take the roof right off of the eaves. But for thirteen years she had managed, and though not all of those years had been difficult they nevertheless had had their moments. Prone to mood swings and sudden shifts of temperament, Ray Hartmann had lost count of the number of times his wife had looked at him across the room with an expression of wonder and terror, an underlying sense of panic that this time, *this* time, he might just do something all of them would seriously regret. But he never did, not until that night of 28 December, and then he'd gatecrashed his way through the supposed harmony of their house, and then he'd started up again like a fire siren, and before he knew it he was standing there with blood running out of his knuckles and spotting the linoleum floor, and his wife and his daughter were both screaming at him to get out of the house and not come back. They looked bruised; *spiritually* bruised.

So he left the house that night, more out of shame and an abiding sense of fear about what he might be capable of, and he walked seven blocks in the snow to the ER and they cleaned and bandaged his knuckles and told him to sleep off his drunk on a trolley down the corridor. When he'd woken, his mouth tasting like copper filings and seaweed, he had remembered what he'd done, and when he'd called and got no answer he knew that Carol had taken Jessica to her grandmother's. He'd walked back and taken a few things from the house. He'd checked into a motel for three days and stayed sober. Then he'd rented an apartment in Little Italy, downtown Manhattan, a four-room gray-walled apartment with windows overlooking Sarah Roosevelt Park, and he'd called in sick and spent forty-eight hours asking himself why he was such a goddamned asshole.

Their home, the Hartmann home, was in Stuyvesant Town, and though he drove past the very block where his wife and daughter were, he never set foot on the porch, he never rang the bell and waited for the sound of footsteps in the hall. He was too ashamed, too self-critical of the kind of man he'd been, and he would spend another three or four weeks beating the shit out of himself before he got the nerve to call her.

The first call had been difficult: strained, long silences, ended on a sour note.

The second call, a fortnight later, had been slightly warmer. She had asked him how he was, and he'd said, "Sober, sober since December twenty-eighth," and she had wished him well, told him that she wasn't ready for anything "complicated," that Jessica was fine, she sent her love, and last week she was chosen to lead the gymnastics team for the Homecoming Pageant.

The third call, six days later, Carol let Ray speak to his daughter.

"Hey daddy."

"Hey sweetpea."

"You okay?"

"Sure I am, honey. Your mom says you're leading the gym team for the Homecoming?"

"Yes, sure. Are you gonna be able to come?"

Ray was silent for a moment.

"Daddy?"

"I'm here, Jess, I'm here."

"So you gonna be able to come?"

"I don't know, Jess, I don't know. It kinda depends on what your mom says."

This time it was Jess's turn to be silent, and then she said, "Okay, I'll talk to her."

"You do that, honey, you do that," and then Ray heard the sound of his own voice breaking up with emotion, and he didn't think he could talk to his daughter any more without crying, and so he told her he loved her more than anything in the world and asked to speak to her mom again.

"Don't come to the Homecoming, Ray," Carol had stated matter-of-factly. "It's too soon for me and Jess to see you."

"Too soon for you . . . but what about Jess?"

"Don't start it up again, Ray, just don't start it up again, okay? I gotta go now. I gotta take Jess to get her hair done."

And the call had ended, and Ray Hartmann had hung up and had asked himself why—after things seemed to have been going so well—he just had to be an asshole all over again.

Thirty-seven years old, sick leave from work, holed up in a crappy apartment in Little Italy while his wife of thirteen years took his twelve-year-old daughter to have her hair done.

What he would have given to have taken her himself.

Never did when you were home, the voice inside said, and he cut that short, because he knew from long experience that listening to such voices was the road to madness, and that road led only one way: right down the neck of a bottle, and that was the kind of shit that had gotten him into *this* kind of shit in the first place.

Ray Hartmann was an enigma. Born in New Orleans, 15 March 1966. Younger brother, Danny, born 17 September 1968, the two of them close like flesh and blood should be. Went everywhere together, did everything together, Ray always leading the way, Danny—looking up to him, forgiving all his faults, wide-eyed and wondrous the way that younger brothers always seem to be—and always in trouble, and dreaming like little kids do, and throwing stones and water bombs and skinnydipping, and missing school days to go catching frogs down in the glades . . . all these things, living their lives so fast, so furious, like they wanted nothing left for tomorrow. It was always Danny and Ray, Ray and Danny, like a litany, a mantra to brotherhood.

And then it all ended. 7 July 1980. Danny was eleven years old, eager and enthusiastic and overwhelmed by the magic of everything, and he went down beneath the wheels of a car on South Loyola, and the guy never stopped and Danny got his legs crushed and his head stoved in, and there wasn't even a single breath left in his tiny broken body when Ray got down there and saw his brother was killed.

Ray, fourteen years old, knelt on the sidewalk with his brother's body across his lap, and he didn't say a word, and he didn't shed a tear, and even when the paramedics came down and tried to separate the pair of them there was nothing they could do but carry them both, carry them like they were one, into the back of the Blue Cross ambulance . . . It was Ray and Danny, Danny and Ray, in life, in death, in trouble. Always and forever would be.

They didn't fire up the siren, because they didn't need the siren when the passenger was dead.

The boys' father wasn't there to comfort his eldest because he was gone too, back in the fall of '71 with a coronary that could've leveled a horse. Big man, strong man, a fighter by all accounts, but drank like a buffalo at the desert's last watering hole, and Ray thought maybe that's where his own taste for the liquor came from, but then he told himself no, because *asshole* wasn't genetic. So mom took it all on board, and she held them together, held herself together as well until the little one got rolled by a Pontiac Firebird on South Loyola. They caught the guy later, and he was a drunk too, and they knew it was him because they found the little kid's blood and the little kid's hair caught in the radiator grille on the front. Mom hung in there until after Ray graduated, and then she went too, May of '87. Natural causes, they said. Sure thing. Natural causes like a broken heart and too much losing, and little enough of life to keep the spirit wanting in the face of such adversity.

Ray went into the National Guard, shoveled folks out of snowdrifts and cleaned boots on the weekend; started hitting the bottle a little too often and invalided himself out before he shot himself or someone else. Worked a regular job for six months and then moved to New York in February of 1988. Even now he couldn't understand why he had chosen New York, perhaps for no other reason than it was the one place he could think of that was most unlike New Orleans. He took to studying the law, studied it every hour that God sent, studied it like there was an answer to be found. Didn't find it, but did find a practice that took him as an intern, and he trawled his way through the Circuit Court system, took the bar, became a public defender and tried to make sense of the mistakes that people all too easily made. It was then that the House Judiciary Subcommittee started the integration programs, posting public defenders inside the police precincts, and there they acted as filters for the courts, an attempt to limit the traffic that hit City Hall. It was an economy drive, and to some degree it worked. It was during that program that Ray Hartmann met Luca Visceglia, one of the key investigators who finally nailed Kuklinski. Richard Kuklinski was a star among stars. Recruited by the Gambino family, his audition was a very simple test: he was driven out into New York, driven along regular streets where regular people walked, and with a single word a man was selected at random, a man walking his dog, minding his own business, perhaps thinking about a birthday present he had to buy, maybe his daughter's engagement dinner. The car slowed, Kuklinski climbed out, and with a half dozen steps he faced the man, raised a gun and shot him dead. That was all the Gambinos required of Kuklinski, and Kuklinski was in.

Living on a quiet street with his wife and family in Dumont, Bergen County, Kuklinski took his orders from Roy DeMaio, the Mafia boss whose office was located in the Gemini Lounge in Brooklyn.

Over the next three years the New Jersey Organized Crime Task Force concentrated their efforts on nailing Kuklinski. In the early '80s, when Paul Castellano and the Gambino family instigated a collaboration between the State Organized Crime Task Force and the Bureau of

Alcohol, Tobacco and Firearms, Castellano happened to mention his concern regarding Roy DeMaio. Castellano was worried DeMaio would talk, that he would "go the wrong way." DeMaio was acting increasingly paranoid; and so in 1983 Roy DeMaio's body was found in the trunk of a car. He'd been there a week. Later, much later, when Kuklinski was finally secured in Trenton State Prison, he said of DeMaio's death, "it couldn't have happened to a nicer person . . . If somebody had to die that day, it was a good day for *him* to die."

The New Jersey Task Force employed the assistance of the FBI, and they assigned an undercover agent called Dominick Polifrone to the case. Posing as a fellow hitman, an associate from New York City called Dominick Michael Provanzano, he managed to get Kuklinski talking, and once Kuklinski started talking he was a man who appreciated the sound of his own voice. It was those tapes that finally got him, and whereas the police and the Organized Crime Task Force believe Kuklinski murdered something in the region of forty people, Kuklinski placed his record at something over a hundred. He was a busy boy. As was his younger brother Joey, already serving life in Trenton for raping and strangling a twelve-year-old girl, a girl he dragged across two adjoining rooftops and then hurled, along with her dog, forty feet to the sidewalk below. Maybe such things were in their blood, perhaps—as FBI Criminal Profiling suggested—there were *situational dynamics* that precipitated the direction the Kuklinski brothers took.

Not until 4 July 2002 did Federal and New York State prosecutors finally bring charges against seventeen members and associates of the Gambino crime family. The charges they faced involved racketeering, extortion, loan sharking, wire fraud, money laundering and witness tampering. It was in this miasma of brutality that Ray Hartmann met his baptism of fire. Luca Visceglia had been an insider, one of the few Federal investigators that spoke directly with the crime family members when they came in for questioning. Ray transcribed interviews, he boxed tapes, he checked inventories of evidence, he filed photos and videotapes, and learned a great deal about what these people had done and why they had done it. Fascinated by the underlying causes of such actions, he studied Stone and Deluca's *Investigating Crimes, Fundamentals of Criminal Investigation* by Charles and Gregory O'Hara, and Geberth's *Practical Homicide Investigation*. When Visceglia was made Deputy Investigative Director for the House Judiciary Subcommittee on Organized Crime he was asked to select his own staff. He selected Ray Hartmann, and Ray made himself indispensable. Ironically, though the stress of his work would be the thing that finally drove him and his wife apart, it was in amidst the madness of one of those cases that he met Carol Hill Wiley. Summer of 1989, stationed at the New York District Attorney's Office, Visceglia, Hartmann, and the three others who made up their team were asked to undertake a refiling of all materials relating to the triple murder of Stefano Giovannetti, Matteo Cagnotto and Claudio Rossi. Giovannetti, Cagnotto and Rossi were themselves soldiers for an arm of the Genovese family. They had worked beneath Alessandro Vaccorini, one of Peter Gotti's right-hand men, and under his direction they had carried out at least seventeen known murders between them. They lived together, worked together, and were together in a Lincoln Towncar leaving the outskirts of Brooklyn when tirespikes had brought their vehicle to a shuddering halt. From the verge behind the fence at the side of the highway, witnesses had given varied reports of between four and nine men leveling semi-automatic rifles at the car and turning it into a spaghetti strainer. The driver and his three passengers were blended into mystery meat. The monochrome photographs of the murder scene could in no way have done justice to the actuality of what crime scene investigators found when they closed off the highway and went down there.

Carol Hill Wiley, a twenty-two-year-old New Yorker, brunette, petite, a wicked sense of humor, green eyes, drop-dead-gorgeous smile, had been on assignment under the aegis of the New York State Supreme Court's training program for legal interns and secretaries. She had majored in law herself, had set her heart on a private practice by the time she was thirty, and would have pursued that goal paramount to all else had she not had that same heart stolen by the seemingly reserved and yet somehow strangely fascinating Ray Hartmann. Hartmann, as far as Carol could see, was serviceably handsome, five-foot ten or eleven, sandy-colored hair and blue eyes, with a kind of wasted look about him that told of surviving something bad. Pressed together by duty and obligation, many were the nights that she and Ray Hartmann had stayed late in the dimly lit office on the corner of Adams and Tillary in Brooklyn Heights, right there in the shadow of the Supreme Court building itself. Afternoons they took to walking down to Cadman Plaza to eat their lunch, and there—the Manhattan and Brooklyn Bridges to their right, the Brooklyn-Queens Expressway to their left— they got to talking. It was outside the NYC Transit Museum that Ray Hartmann first kissed her. It was a cold Tuesday in the latter half of December 1989. They were married on 10 February 1990. They moved to an apartment near Lindsay Park in Williamsburg, and there they stayed until Carol got pregnant. Two weeks into her second trimester they moved across the East River and bought a two-bedroomed apartment in Stuyvesant Town. Despite the lengthy journey each day, back and forth across the Williamsburg Bridge, Ray and Carol Hartmann found some small compensation in the fact that her simple request to be assigned to Luca Visceglia's unit was approved. At least they could travel together, work together, go home together.

It stayed that way until Jessica was born, and then Carol decided, without pressure or persuasion, that she would be happier spending her days as a mother rather than examining photographs of dismembered, burned, drowned, decapitated bodies. Money was adequate though not extravagant, and money, lack of, could never have been cited as a contributory factor in the dissolution of the Hartmanns' marriage. Rather, perhaps more accurately, it was a combination of factors on both sides. For Carol, having left the employ of the District Attorney's Office, there was a gradual disassociation from the work that she had done. She began forgetting the way in which the sounds and images and words could haunt your thoughts irrespective of your location. Ray went in to work and dealt with these matters every single day, and it was not hard to become embroiled in the darkness that such work generated. Carol's days were spent looking after Jessica, a remarkably bright and enthusiastic child, and as soon as Ray walked back through the front door she would want to regale him with the many miracles she had witnessed in their daughter that day. Ray, oblivious to the world everyone else inhabited, would often be distracted, curt, brusque and inadequately interested. He started to drink, just that swift half-inch of scotch to smooth off the edges when he came home, the single drink before dinner, and then it became an inch of scotch and a can of beer with his meal, and then sometimes he would shut himself in the den and watch TV, a six-pack on the floor by his feet.

In July of 1996 he shouted at his five-year-old daughter. Wanting to show dad her painting she repeatedly knocked on the door of the den, and Ray—suffering from a migraine which was not surrendering to either Excedrin or Michelob—tore the door open and screamed at the top of his voice: *What in fuck's name do you want for Christ's sake?*

Jessica, shattered, crying, completely unaware of what she might have done to prompt such a reaction, ran to her mother. Carol said nothing. Not a word. Within fifteen minutes she had packed some overnight things into a bag and left the house.

Ray Hartmann fell into the abyss; the abyss populated by all drunks where self-pity, self-loathing and crying are the only footholds marking the way back out. The expression on Carol's face had been as startling and sudden as an epinephrine injection, and it made Ray Hartmann look seriously at what he was becoming. He was becoming someone even *he* didn't like, and that was the worst kind of person of all.

Carol and Jess came back three days later. It was another seven months before Ray Hartmann raised his voice again. This time Carol and Jess went upstate to Carol's mother's place and stayed a week. Ray went to an AA meeting. He began the Twelve Steps. He realized he was perfectly capable of being a scumbag of the lowest order, in fact perfectly capable of becoming the bacteria on the amoeba on the scumbag in question, and he didn't drink again for nigh on a year.

The incident that precipitated the separation of Carol and Ray Hartmann occurred five weeks before her latest departure in December of 2002. Ray had worked late, as was ordinarily the case when a particular investigation was being prepared for the Attorney General's Office. He and Visceglia had secured an inside line on one of the defendant's former girlfriends and she had agreed to testify. She was neither a drug-user, ex-felon, or prostitute, nor an employee of any legal, judicial, police or intelligence agency. She was a star, a perfect and exemplary witness. She could place the defendant in a particular location at a particular time. On the strength of this, he would go down. A stream of fabricated alibis could be undone with her words. She was a woman of substance, a good speaker, and she wasn't afraid.

The evening before Ray Hartmann and Luca Visceglia were to present her as-yet-unsworn affidavit to the Grand Jury, an affidavit that would have earned her federal protection, she was found in a motel room off Hunters Point Avenue near the Calvary Cemetery. This woman, thirty-seven years of age, a respectable background, a good education, who never touched a reefer in her life, had overdosed on cocaine. She was found naked, one hand and one foot bound to the frame of the bed, her mouth gagged, a selection of sex aids scattered across the mattress, and a butt plug in her ass. Once a rape kit had been done there was evidence that she had engaged in vaginal and anal intercourse with at least three different men. The three men were located through their DNA and hair samples. All three were interrogated separately. All three gave exactly the same story. They were male prostitutes, they had all been called and given a motel room address, they had all been promised a thousand dollars if they appeared at a particular time on a particular day. There they would find a woman gagged and tied to the bed. She would have a pillowcase over her face. It was her wish that they fuck her, all three of them one after the other, first in the regular way and then in the ass. She wanted to be slapped around a bit, she wanted them to call her a whore and a bitch, other such things, and once they were done they should leave her exactly where they found her. The money would be in the bedside table drawer. These guys were rent-boys. These guys had seen and done worse every day for most of their adult lives. This was New York. They did what they were asked to do, they took their money, and then they left. No questions asked, no answers required. Whoever had staged this "party" must then have come in and administered the lethal dose of cocaine. There was nothing to suggest that the victim had not administered it herself, after all she had one hand free and could quite easily have scooped a handful out of the clip-top baggie of coke that was right there on the pillow beside her. In fact, there was evidence of cocaine on her hand, under her nails, around her mouth and nostrils. It really could have gone down that way.

Well, however it might have gone down it was enough to invalidate the affidavit and testimony she had given. As far as the Grand Jury was concerned she was a cocaine user who'd hired three male hookers to fuck her in the ass in a motel near Calvary Cemetery. Visceglia was pissed beyond measure. His rage registered somewhere on the Richter Scale. He went out and got drunk. Ray Hartmann—against his better judgment, against the tearful promises he'd made to his wife and daughter—went out too. It was in the early hours of Thursday morning in the first week of December when he rolled in through the front door of his Stuyvesant Town apartment, as drunk as a man could be while still conscious, and collapsed in a heap on the kitchen floor. Thankfully he collapsed onto his side, and not his back, because sometime before his eleven-year-old daughter found him he puked. And when she did find him he was still there, his head resting in a pool of dried vomit on the kitchen linoleum, and she said nothing, did not try to wake him, merely walked back to her mother's room and woke her.

Carol Hill Hartmann, incensed into silence, took a bowl of freezing water and tipped it over her husband's sleeping form. He barely stirred. Finally she woke him by kicking the soles of his shoes, and when he slurred into semi-consciousness, when he opened one sick-caked eye and looked up at her, he mumbled *Leave me the fuck alone, will ya?*

Jessica started crying. She didn't know why, she just did, and though they did not leave the house that day, though they packed nothing for a trip upstate to Carol's mother's place, they agreed that they would not talk to Ray for four days straight. They kept to their word, and despite his begging, his pleading, despite bringing flowers and take-out, despite his promises to stay clean and sober for the rest of eternity, mother and daughter held out.

On the following Monday morning Ray Hartmann found a note on the kitchen counter. Carol had already taken Jessica to school and he was alone in the house. The message was very simple. Carol had written it but it had been countersigned by Jessica.

Ray. We both love you. You are a good husband and a good father. We don't want to be without you. If you get drunk again we will leave you behind. We have lives to get on with, and the man we know and love can come with us or he can get drunk and crazy all by himself. You decide. Carol. Jessica. xxx

When he returned from work that evening both of them were speaking to him. They asked about his day. They chatted between themselves and included him in their conversations as if nothing had happened. The note they had written was in Ray Hartmann's wallet, and he made a practice of looking at it every day and reminding himself of what was important in his life. He held it together, he *really* held it together until Christmas came around and his professional world collapsed once more.

Christmas was tough for Ray Hartmann, always had been, always would be. Christmas was a time for family, and though he had somehow navigated the potential disaster of losing the family he had created, he nevertheless took it hard when December came around. Once upon a time he'd had a father and mother of his own, a younger brother whom he'd loved and adored as much as Danny had loved and adored him. There were four of them, and now there was one. A week couldn't go by without him thinking of Danny at least once. Wide-eyed and mischievous, the pair of them haunting the streets, playing tricks, filling the house with the sound of their laughter and catcalls. Danny would always and forever be a kid in Ray's mind, and that Christmas, the Christmas it all came apart at the seams, it was a kid that started the trouble.

Ray was still living on a promise. He still had the note his wife and daughter had given him, a note he had covered with scotch-tape to prevent it falling apart. But there was something about kids, something that made everything different in the most different kind of way. Many times before Jess had been born he'd spoken to people who were parents. *Do anything for my kids,* they'd say. *Kids are the most important thing in my life. Anything happened to my kids, well . . .* And he'd listened, a degree of interest perhaps, but always objective and somehow separate. When Jess came he knew exactly what they were talking about. Bullet came, well you'd get right in there, no questions asked. You'd kill for your kids, die for them, breathe for them if needs be, and there was no way to share that kind of sentiment with anyone who wasn't a parent.

The photographs came in on Monday 23 December. Ray was on

leave for Christmas but Visceglia called him in. Kid was a bystander, seven years old, walking down Schermerhorn Street with his dad. Kid was carrying a Deluxe Power Rangers Playset. Early present paid for by grandma. Dad said he could have it because he'd helped his mom clean up after grandma had gone home. Dad survived with only a single gunshot to the right thigh to show for his trip to the store. Kid took two in the chest and they broke him like a rag doll. Gang war. Family feud about some smalltime gambling operation that couldn't have turned over more than five or ten grand a week. Gunmen missed their mark and hit the bystanders. No witnesses who had anything helpful to offer. Case was closed before it was even opened.

Ray Hartmann went home from the crime scene with a broken heart. Felt like it could have been him and Jess. Could've been his own mom and Danny. One of those times he started asking himself whether what they were doing was actually making any fucking difference at all. Sure it did, but at times like that all he saw was the kid's body, the anguished and broken-down father, the resigned State prosecutors as they told him there was nothing they could do to help on this one. He didn't drink that day. Didn't drink the next or the one after that. Christmas Eve he had a can of beer at home, and even Carol didn't say a word. Christmas Day itself was good, a day for the family and nothing else, and as Jess opened her gifts she told both her mom and her dad that she loved them more than anyone else in the world, and somehow it seemed like he would come through and out the other side, the kind of man he wanted to be.

Morning of the twenty-eighth he and Carol had a fight. It was nothing really, a stupid thing. She asked him to vacuum the front room. He said he'd do it later. She asked him again after half an hour and he snapped back *I said I'd do it later!* to which she replied *It is later, Ray . . . all I'm asking for is ten minutes' help keeping this goddamned place clean!* Ray got annoyed, there were a few more words, and then he left the house. Just put on his shoes and his jacket and left the house. Later, thinking back, he would wonder if his temper hadn't already been frayed. That morning he'd received an e-mail from Visceglia asking if he could come in for a few hours the following day. He hadn't replied, hadn't wanted to reply, but knew that he would before the day was out. He had no choice. It was one of those kinds of jobs. It was a vocation, an undertaking, it wasn't just a salary. Maybe that was what it was. Or maybe it was because he was still cut up about the little kid, a kid whose name he couldn't get out of his mind, and how he'd lain there two nights after Christmas and all he'd been able to think about was the kid's parents, about how this was a Christmas they would never forget. The dad had taken the Power Rangers Playset in the ambulance with him. Couldn't take his son home, so he took the boy's present from grandma. Wrapping paper had blood on it, paper was torn so you could see what was inside, and there was a narrow spray of blood right across it. Ray had wondered what the father would do with it. How could you keep something like that? What would the boy's mother feel when she saw it? What would Ray say to her if she came and asked what he was going to do about the people who had killed her child?

Hindsight, the cruelest and most astute advisor of all, would be something to which Ray Hartmann looked many times in the subsequent months. He'd stayed away from the house to cool down. This was a rare time, a number of consecutive days when they could be together as a family, and here he was acting like a spoiled child just because Carol had asked him to vacuum. He decided to stop for a single beer at a bar three blocks from home. He lost track of time, he talked with the barman, he caught the tail end of a game on the tube. He even played a couple of games of pool with a guy called Larry, and Larry bought him a beer, and then another, and it would have been nothing short of rude to decline the guy's generosity, and hell it was Christmas, and what was the point of Christmas if you couldn't have a good time?

Ray Hartmann stumbled through the front door of his house and crawled along the hallway a little after one a.m. Carol had waited up for him. So had Jessica. They were both dressed. It was then that he started hollering; it was then that he raised his fist and put it through the kitchen cupboard door. And when Carol pushed past him and he fell to the floor, when both his wife and his daughter started screaming at him, telling him to leave the house and never come back, it was all he could do to raise his bruised and bloodied hand in an effort to silence them. But he heard what they said, and he did leave, and he walked the seven blocks to the ER and got his hand cleaned and bandaged. That night was the end of one thing and the beginning of something else. He took the apartment in Little Italy, Carol and Jess stayed in Stuyvesant Town. That night marked the point at which Ray Hartmann had stopped drinking for life. He didn't go to AA, he didn't even do the first of the Minnesota Twelve Steps, he just decided, and it was perhaps the most certain and solid decision of his life. He'd held to that unrelentingly, and on the evening of Thursday 28 August, separated from his wife and daughter for eight months to the day, Ray Hartmann had been sober for every single one of those days, every single hour, every single minute. He had convinced himself there was a way to get his family back, and that way would be paved with sobriety, hard work, honesty and commitment.

That frame of mind had served him well at work, for work was where he'd buried himself, and his office, narrow and cramped though it was, each wall covered with a pinboard displaying photographs and maps and crime scene details, was where he would ordinarily be found, often late into the night, sometimes in the early hours of the morning.

Morning of Friday 29 August he took a call right there in that same office, at the very same desk.

"Ray?"

"Carol?" In his voice was a tone of surprise, beneath that a sense of concern that something bad might have happened to prompt her call.

"How you doing?" she asked.

"I'm okay, Carol, I'm okay. How's Jess?"

"She's fine, Ray, just fine. She misses you, and that's why I'm calling you."

Ray was silent. He'd learned to speak when he was asked, and the rest of the time keep his asshole mouth shut.

"Saturday, a week on Saturday, September sixth, you can come meet us in Tompkins Square Park at noon. We're gonna have some lunch together and you can see Jess, okay?"

Ray Hartmann was struck dumb for a second.

"Ray? You there?"

"Yes, sure . . . sure I'm here. That's great. Thanks. Thanks, Carol."

"You're coming because of Jess, not because of me. I need more time. I've been grateful for the time I've had, and I've thought about a lot of things. If you and I are gonna make it then we have a number of things to work out. Right now all we're doing is making a little time for Jess, you understand?"

"Yes, sure I understand."

"So you be there, noon a week on Saturday, and if things go fine then maybe you and I will start talking about what we're gonna do."

"Right, of course, of course."

"So we'll see you then, okay?"

"Okay, Carol . . . I'll be there."

And then she hung up, and Ray Hartmann sat there with the receiver burring in his ear, his eyes filled with tears, a kind of idiot grin on his face.

Still looked like that when Luca Visceglia opened the door of his office and stood there with an expression Ray Hartmann had seen all too many times.

New York District Attorney's Office Administrative Annexe B, nine-sixteen a.m., morning of Friday 29 August, and back of Visceglia were three men in dark suits, white shirts, dark ties, and all of them wore that expression: an expression that told Hartmann that he was once again about to collide with the business end of things, though in that moment, lightheaded with the thought that his wife might talk to him again, he had no clue about what they were going to say, and where those words would take him. Whoever these people were they had found him, found him all too easily, it seemed; apparently he had been the only Ray Hartmann in the entirety of the federal employee database system in Washington, and that database had been only the second they had searched.

An hour later and all the colors would be different, the sounds and images too, and Ray Hartmann would be driving along Flatbush Avenue in a generic gray sedan toward the Brooklyn Navy Yard. There he would find a waiting helicopter that would carry him and three New York FBI field agents to the airport. A handful of hours and he would be home, home in New Orleans, and though New Orleans was the last place in the world he would ever have wanted to go, he had no choice in the matter.

The world had come looking for Ray Hartmann, it seemed, and the world had somehow found him.

FIVE

BUSED, DISABUSED, REJECTED, forsworn to some sense of guilt for the way in which these events had transpired, Ray Hartmann stood beside the window of a hotel.

Let the dead be buried, he thought. *Let the dead be afforded whatever degree of respect they deserve, whether they be brother or mother or father, and if they deserve none then at least let them rest. Pax vobiscum.*

The district Ray saw beyond the window was rich with the past, the buildings crouched together, a barrio filled to bursting with Spanish- and French-descent southerners, and the old people, the mothers and fathers, their mothers and fathers where they still lived, stood testament to the fact that tradition and heritage had nothing to do with color or creed. They had built their own, sweated their hands and brows into this earth and grown from it a timeless grapevine of beliefs and ideals that did not change, merely grew with time. This was where Ray had shared the early years of his life with his brother, and coming back here brought with it a storm of emotions that raged right into the present and defied escape. The street where his father fell to his knees as if to pray, his hands clutching his chest, his mouth agape as pecans and avocados and small ripe oranges spilled from his bag across the sidewalk and beneath the wheels of cars; the corners where Ray and Danny had hung out, sweating through many a childhood vacation, escaping chores and whippings, and older kids with stones dropped into long socks that they whirled around their wrists like the old Irish cop with the billy club that used to patrol down here; the alleyway beside the bar where he and Danny used to crouch and wait breathless for some drunk to come falling through the doorway, and when he fell they'd be there to empty his pockets, to take his bottle, a bottle filled with something that coalesced with the warm humid air and knocked them sideways; all of this, these images, forever engraved: indelible.

Ray Hartmann could remember when there was snow on Dumaine.

Snow that hung from the branches of withered wisteria and mimosa and magnolia, and piled against the curb, and dropped from the eaves of houses, and through that whiteness had run the expedient streamers of youthful voices, the mittened and scarved and gloved and galoshed, the hurrying excitement attendant to seasonal novelty that we—in our age, in our reflections, in our bruised hopes and dented dreams—have somehow appeared to lose.

Everything stopped here. Carol. Jess. Luca Visceglia and the manifold legal complications with which he battled each day. The sounds changed, the shadows closed up against him.

The FBI agents had told him next to nothing, merely that his assistance was required in a matter of potential national security. From the plane they had driven him to a hotel and told him to rest for a couple of hours, and yet they had no idea of where they were *really* taking him. Here, a stone's throw from where he stood looking from the window, was Dumaine: a map of his past, a fingerprint he had left behind, the sidewalks where he too had scraped his knees against life and found it rough, unforgiving, coming at him from all sides and never stopping.

After his mother's death he'd vowed never to come back, and yet he realized that his detours had been nothing more than a preternatural rejection of inevitability. He realized New Orleans would once more walk right through him as soon as he crossed its limits, and that sensory invasion was neither willed nor welcome.

Ray Hartmann shuddered in the breeze that found its way through the half-opened window, believed that he would always find this place abhorrent no matter the season—stinking and ripe with the smell of loose and swollen vegetation in summer, and then through fall and winter the frozen brittleness, the ghostly angularity of the trees, the picket fences that ran in non-sequitur patterns through all territories, defiant of whatever authoritarian plutocracy held sway, standing also in defiance of any sense of the aesthetic. This was a mean and hollow country, perhaps its only blessing the people themselves, holding true to the intent and determination of their ancestors who'd dragged whatever life they'd lived out of the clutches of the bayou.

He looked left, turned toward the mimosa grove he could see across the street. On a clear day, standing on a ladder from the garage, he and Danny would look out over such trees, look out over the Mississippi to the Gulf of Mexico, a band of clear dark blue, a stripe through the earth, a vein. Used to dream of sailing away, a paper boat big enough for two, its seams sealed with wax and butter, their pockets filled with nickels and dimes and Susan B. Anthony dollars saved from scrubbing wheel arches and hubcaps, from soaping windscreens and windows and porch stoops for the Rousseaus, the Buies, the Jeromes. Running away, running away with themselves from Dumaine, from the intersection where bigger kids challenged them, tugged their hair, pointed sharpened fingers into their chests and called them weirdos, where they ran until the breath burst from their chests in great whooping asthmatic heaving gusts, turning down alleyways, hiding in shadows, the reality of the world crowding the edges of the safe and insular shell they had created for themselves. Danny and Ray, Ray and Danny, an echo of itself; an echo of childhood.

The distant chatter of children in the street . . .

The indefinable sensation that each time he thinks of these things he's younger for the duration.

And then later, Danny long since gone, coming home from school while his mother was still alive, brief stopovers, passing through . . .

Hi Mom . . .

Ray . . . you gonna stay for dinner, son?

I already ate, Ma, ate on the way down.

She would talk a little of her day, that Mister Koenig had taken her to mass, that she'd prayed for them both and felt all the better for it. She'd talk of a show at the Saenger Theater, of dinner at the Royal Sonesta, and then suddenly she'd be reminded of Mary Rousseau.

You remember Mary Rousseau, down here a block or so when you boys were young . . . pretty little thing you had a crush on?

I remember her, Ma, and I did not have a crush on her.

He would feel the pressure of his mother's hand upon his own.

The smell of the parlor, of chicken cooking, of lavender and ointment for scrapes and burns and bruises, forever ambient of childhood, of growing, losing and learning how to love all over again.

Also leaving, for leaving was the very last thing he did.

So how goes it, son?

It goes, Ma, it goes.

You down here on business?

Sure am . . . wouldn't come down here for any other reason.

Bad business?

Real bad . . . bad as it gets.

She would look at him, this slight and frail-looking woman, though nothing could be further from the truth. One year she was assaulted by a teenager after her purse. She kicked him down an alleyway, cornered him, screamed until someone came to her assistance. Even after that she still walked out alone. She watched everything that happened through pale blue washed-out eyes, and if there was something that went down within four or five blocks from where she sat she could tell you all about it. She could tell you names, dates, places, the lies told, the actual truth. She'd stayed a widow after her husband's death, some said because no man possessed the cojones to question her right to be alone. She was not sorry, she did not regret; she listened, advised, hoped someday to understand all that had happened and make some sense of it.

So what's with you?

Just thinking, Ma.

Always thinking. You don't eat enough vegetables to be thinking so much. Your skin will get pale and you will dry up like a leaf and blow away.

He would turn his head, look out toward the streets where he'd grown up.

Stay and have some lemonade or something, why don'tcha?

Sure Ma, sure . . . I'll stay and have some lemonade . . .

The phone rang. It was as if someone had tied elastic to Ray Hartmann and suddenly snapped him back into the present.

He blinked twice, inhaled deeply, and then reached for the receiver.

"Mr. Hartmann?" someone asked him.

"Yes."

"We're coming up to get you."

"Okay, okay," Hartmann replied, and then he replaced the receiver and walked through to the narrow bathroom to wash his face.

It was just after five p.m., evening of Friday the twenty-ninth. Outside it looked like a storm was coming.

Ray Hartmann's first impression of FBI unit chiefs Stanley Schaeffer and Bill Woodroffe was of their seeming lack of individuality. Both in their mid to late forties, dark suits, white shirts, black ties, hair graying at the temples, furrowed brows and anxious eyes. These guys would spend the entirety of their working lives dressed for a funeral. The two Feds who'd flown out to New York to collect Hartmann had escorted him to the New Orleans FBI Field Office, signed him in without saying a word, walked him through a maze of corridors and then left him outside their door.

"Inside," one of the agents said, and then the pair of them turned and walked away.

When Hartmann knocked it was Schaeffer who told him to come in, who greeted him, shook his hand, asked him to sit down, but it was Woodroffe who started talking.

"Mr. Hartmann," he said quietly. "I understand that you must be feeling some sense of confusion regarding how you were brought here."

Hartmann shrugged.

Woodroffe glanced at Schaeffer; Schaeffer nodded without looking away from Hartmann.

"We have a case here. An unusual situation. A man has been murdered and a girl has been kidnapped, and we find ourselves requiring your services."

Woodroffe waited for Hartmann to speak, but Hartmann had nothing to say.

"The man we believe responsible for both the killing and the kidnapping has asked for you specifically, and this evening at seven he will call and he will speak to you. We believe he will make his demands known."

"What's his name?" Hartmann asked.

"We have no idea," Schaeffer said.

Hartmann frowned. "But he knew my name? He asked for me specifically?"

Schaeffer nodded. "He did."

Hartmann shook his head. "And you think I might be able to tell you who he is from the sound of his voice on the telephone?"

"No, Mr. Hartmann, we don't believe that at all. We have studied your records, we know how busy you have been with the many hundreds of cases that have passed across your desk over the years. But we can't help but think that he might be someone you have dealt with or come across at some point in the past."

Hartmann nodded. "That would be logical, considering he asked for me by name."

"So we want you to take the call, to speak to him," Woodroffe said. "He may identify himself, he may not, but what we are hoping is that he will give us his terms and conditions for the return of the kidnap victim."

"And that would be?" Hartmann asked.

Woodroffe once more glanced sideways at Schaeffer.

"You know Charles Ducane?" Schaeffer asked.

Hartmann nodded. "Sure, Governor Charles Ducane, right?"

Schaeffer nodded. "The kidnap victim is Governor Ducane's daughter, Catherine."

"Holy shit," Hartmann said.

"Holy shit exactly," Schaeffer said.

Hartmann leaned forward and rested his forearms on the edge of the desk. He looked at Woodroffe and Schaeffer, and then he closed his eyes for a moment and sighed.

"You understand I am not a trained negotiator?" Hartmann said.

"We understand that," Woodroffe said, "but we find ourselves in a situation of being able to turn to no one but you. Believe me, if there was some way we could avoid involving you we would. This is a federal matter, and though you are by necessity in the employ of the federal government we also appreciate that this is not the sort of thing you are suited to."

Hartmann frowned. "What, you think I can't take a phone call?"

Schaeffer smiled, but there was nothing warm in his eyes. "No Mr. Hartmann, we know you are perfectly capable of taking a phone call. What we mean is that you are an investigator for the Judiciary Subcommittee on Organized Crime, not a field agent with years of training in hostage negotiation."

"But you guys are, and you figure between us we can get the guy and save the girl?"

Schaeffer and Woodroffe were silent for a moment.

"A flippant attitude is inappropriate for proceedings such as these," Schaeffer said quietly.

Hartmann nodded. "Sorry," he said equally quietly, and wondered how long the call would be, how long he would have to stay afterwards, and whether there would be a late flight back to New York that night.

"So, we do this this evening," Hartmann said.

"Seven o'clock," Schaeffer said.

Hartmann glanced at his watch. "I've got something over an hour to kill."

"You can study these," Woodroffe said, and rising from his chair he crossed the room to a small desk in the corner. He returned with a number of files and placed them in front of Hartmann.

"All the details we have thus far, pictures of the murder victim, pictures of the girl, Forensics and Criminalistics reports, the usual things. Study these now, so when he calls you have some kind of idea of what we are dealing with here."

Woodroffe stayed on his feet as he spoke, and then Schaeffer rose also.

"We'll leave you for a little while. Anything you need?"

Hartmann looked up. "An ashtray. And could someone get me a cup of coffee? Not some of that shit you get out of the machine, but like a real cup of coffee with cream?"

Schaeffer nodded. "We'll see what we can do, Mr. Hartmann."

"Thanks." Hartmann waited until they had left the room before he opened the first file and looked down into the trunk of a '57 Mercury Cruiser with some beat-to-fuck dead guy inside.

It was the constellation that got him. Caught him like a fish on a hook. It meant nothing, at least nothing specific, but the mere fact that whoever had done this had taken the time to draw the constellation of Gemini on the vic's back told Hartmann that here he was dealing with someone a little more sophisticated than the regular kind of thug. And then there was the heart. And then there was the simple fact that the girl who'd been kidnapped was Charles Ducane's daughter. Perhaps it was then, seated in the plain office with the photos, the reports, the transcriptions of the two phone calls that had been made, the collective details of all that had occurred since the night of Wednesday 20 August in front of him, that Ray Hartmann believed he might not get away from this thing tonight.

And if not tonight, then when?

Why did this man wish to speak to him, to *him* in particular, and what would he require of him? Would it be something that would keep him in New Orleans?

And what of Tompkins Square Park at noon on Saturday?

Ray Hartmann sighed and closed his eyes. He leaned forward, his elbows on the table, his forehead against his steepled fingers, and behind his eyes he could see Carol's face, the way she would look at him when he'd done something else to piss her off. And then there was Jess, the way she would greet him when he arrived home, her smile wide, her eyes bright, everything that ever meant anything to him all tied up in the lives of two people he couldn't see . . .

He started when someone knocked on the door.

Ray Hartmann opened his eyes and lowered his hands.

The door opened, and Bill Woodroffe, same expression as before, stepped inside and nodded at Hartmann.

"Ten minutes," he said. "We're gonna take the call out here where we have other agents on additional lines."

Hartmann rose from the chair, walked around the table and followed Woodroffe.

They passed down the corridor and took the second door on the right. The room looked like mission control at Houston: banks of computers, gray freestanding dividers separating dozens of desks one from another, floor-to-ceiling maps on three of the walls, endless rows of file cabinets, and in amongst this a good dozen Bureau men, all of them in white shirts and dark ties.

"Hold up!" Woodroffe shouted over the murmur of voices.

The room fell silent. Could have heard a pin drop.

"This is Special Investigator Ray Hartmann from New York. He is part of the Judiciary Subcommittee on Organized Crime up there. This is the guy that's gonna take the call."

Woodroffe let his words sink in for a moment.

Hartmann felt a dozen pairs of eyes watching him.

"So when the call comes we take it in three stages. Feshbach, Hackley and Levin are gonna take the first pick-up on line one, Landry, Weber and Duggan the second, finally Cassidy, Saxon and Benedict on line three. When all three teams have picked up, Mr. Hartmann will take line four right here. If there is the slightest sound from anyone in the room when the call has been connected through the speakers they will take a two-week unpaid suspension. This is a young girl's life we're talking about, gentlemen, understood?"

There was a hushed series of acknowledgments across the room.

"So that's the game plan. Mr. Kubis will trace the call and record it as per protocol. So take your seats, gentlemen, and wait it out."

Woodroffe indicated that Hartmann should take a seat at the desk ahead of him. Hartmann did so. He glanced at the wall clock. Four minutes to seven. He could feel the tension in his throat and chest. His hands were moist, and beneath his hairline beads of sweat were breaking out. This was not what he had intended to be doing this evening.

At six-fifty-eight someone sneezed. Woodroffe ordered the man from the room.

The place was deathly quiet.

Hartmann could feel his heart thudding in his chest. He wanted to close his eyes for a moment, open them and find that all of this had vanished, that it had been nothing more than some strange non-sequitur dream. He did not dare close his eyes. He could not appear to be unsettled by this in any way. Like Woodroffe had so clearly stated, a young girl's life was at risk.

Six-fifty-nine.

Hartmann glanced up at Woodroffe. Woodroffe looked back dispassionately. This was business, nothing more nor less than business.

Hartmann's presence would naturally be resented. He may have been bound by the same legal and judicial code of practice, but sure as shit he wasn't family.

He looked back at the phone and willed it to ring. He wanted to know. He wanted to hear this man's voice, to know instantly who it was, to turn to Woodroffe and tell them exactly where they would find him and how to rescue the girl . . .

He wanted to be back on a plane to New York knowing that he would see Carol and Jess next Saturday.

He inhaled.

The phone rang and Hartmann nearly left his skin.

"Line one," Woodroffe barked.

"Line two."

Hartmann's heart thudded like a speeding freight train in his chest.

"Line three . . . go!"

A moment's pause, a moment that stretched out forever.

Woodroffe's hand on his shoulder.

Hartmann watching his own hand as it reached for the receiver ahead of him.

Now, Woodroffe mouthed, and Ray Hartmann—he of the broken heart and bitterness, he of the regrets and darker aspects, his mind filled with nothing more than the wish to see his wife and daughter next Saturday noon—lifted the phone.

"Yes?" he said, his voice subdued, almost cracking.

"Mr. Ray Hartmann," the voice at the other end of the line returned. "Welcome home to New Orleans . . ."

SIX

LATER, THE LIGHTS out, through the window from the street the faint glow of New Orleans as it ached in slow motion through the chilled hours of early morning, Ray Hartmann asked himself why he had chosen this life.

A life of crime, if you like; others' crimes, but crimes all the same.

Just as with the police, the FBI, the county coroners and medical examiners, all those whose lot it was to scour the underbelly of America, to turn over the stones, to search out the darker shadows and find what lurked within, he had somehow—through fate or fortune—found himself charged with this duty. The killers, the serial rapists, the hitmen, the murderers, the child molesters, the assassins, the psychopaths, the socio-paths, the guilty, the tormented, the tortured and depraved. Here, in all its resplendent glory, was the worst the world could offer, and he—he of all people, wishing now for nothing more than safety and sanity for himself and his family—was once again walking along the edge of the abyss, looking down, tempting equilibrium, challenging his own sense of balance to see if this time, *this* time, he would fall.

Back in New York, in the office complex he shared with Luca Visce-glia and the crew, were the details of a hundred thousand lives wrecked by a collection of truly crazy people. Even the FBI's January 1997 release of fifteen thousand pages of documents relating to the Mafia, the death of Kennedy, of Jimmy Hoffa, the workings of the Teamsters' Union and the killing of their associates and cohorts, gave no indication of the extent to which the government and its many systems had been infected by corruption and Machiavellian dishonesty. Even Hoover, perhaps the most shrewd and conniving hypocrite of them all, had once commented, "I never saw so much skullduggery . . ."

Ray Hartmann had spent hundreds of hours immersed in the history and heritage of these people. He remembered vividly the conversations he and Visceglia had started and never seemed to finish in the small office they had first shared. Back then Hartmann had believed himself cognizant of the methods and motives of these people, but Visceglia had illustrated his naiveté.

"Never really been anything other than the Gambino and Genovese crime families," Visceglia had told him. "Those families were established many generations before any of the stuff we have to deal with. Those people divided New York like it'd always belonged to them . . . like it had always been their own."

Visceglia chain-smoked, he drank too much coffee. He possessed an air of philosophical resignation regarding his place in life. He seemed to carry the weight of this darkened world on his shoulders, and those shoulders would bow and strain beneath the pressure, but they would never give.

"Stressed?" Hartmann had asked him one time, and Visceglia had smiled wryly, nodded his head as if such a thing was the understatement to shame all understatements, and said, "Stressed? Like the Brooklyn fucking Bridge, Ray."

Hartmann had acknowledged him but hadn't known what else to say. In the face of what they were dealing with what *could* one say?

"Billions of dollars," Visceglia said. "And these people own territories that cross the fucking world, and all of it gained within a handful of decades. It just beggars fucking belief. Lives are lost with no more concern than a five-dollar hand of poker. This whole thing goes back forever . . . and this is where the names you have heard come from, people like Lucky Luciano, Bugsy Siegel, Meyer Lansky and Al Capone."

Visceglia would shake his head and exhale. There was something about the way he did it that sounded like he would empty out and vanish.

"The Genovese family was where Joseph Valachi came from, and he threw everyone a left-handed curve when he testified at the Senate Permanent Investigations Committee in September and October of 1963. Valachi was the one who used the term 'Cosa Nostra,' 'This Thing of Ours,' and the things he told the Committee freaked the living shit out of everyone who heard him. Bottom line was that what he had to say didn't directly incriminate anyone enough to charge them, but it did turn things around for the families."

"I've read about that stuff," Hartmann said. "The whole code of silence thing—"

"Omerta," Visceglia said. "Valachi violated omerta . . . one of the few family members ever to do so, and he opened up a can of worms that gave more insight into the power struggles and rank-and-file operations of the Mafia than any other man."

"You know why he did that?" Hartmann asked.

Visceglia shook his head. "I know something of it, yes."

Hartmann raised his eyebrows expectantly. It was late, he should have been on his way home, but there was something about the subject that both intrigued and appalled him.

Visceglia shrugged his shoulders. "Valachi had joined Salvatore Maranzano's organization in the late '20s, and he served beneath Maranzano until Maranzano was assassinated in '31. Thereafter Valachi served beneath Vito Genovese within the Luciano family. He was nothing more than a button man, a soldier. He was a hit man, an enforcer, a numbers operator and a drug pusher, and he did whatever he was told to do. They got him in '59 and he went down on a fifteen to twenty for trafficking. Sent him to Atlanta Penitentiary in Georgia, and there he kind of lost his mind—maybe the lock-up, maybe the loneliness, but he got it into his head that Vito Genovese had named him as an informer and ordered his death. He mistook another prisoner called Joe Saupp for a hitman called Joe Beck. Valachi killed Saupp with an iron pipe and was given a life sentence. It was only at that point that he decided to turn informer. He wanted federal protection and that was the only way he could buy it. The only thing he had of any value at all was what was inside his head."

Visceglia smiled, again that expression of philosophical resignation. "Ironic," he said, "but by the time Valachi reached the Senate Permanent Investigations Committee hearings he was guarded by no less than two hundred US marshals. More bodyguards than the fucking president. The Mafia put a $100,000 tap on his head. Regardless, Valachi went on to name more than three hundred Mafia family members and present a more detailed and concise history and structure of the Mafia than had been available before. Valachi named Lucky Luciano as the most important voice within the Mafia. He told them about the Havana conference and how, even in exile, Luciano had still controlled the business relentlessly. He gave up Meyer Lansky as Luciano's second-in-command. The family started to call Valachi Joe Cargo. That was bastardized to Cago, the Italian dialect expression for shit."

Visceglia laughed and lit another cigarette.

"Valachi wasn't no fucking Einstein. He was just muscle, and most of what came out of his mouth during those hearings was later discredited. Seems that members of Valachi's crew knew Valachi well enough. They told him a whole heap of bullshit, things that Valachi actually thought were the truth. Nevertheless the words of Joseph Valachi and the subsequent Valachi Papers proved devastating to the Mafia. That was the point at which it all started to come apart at the seams. If Vala-chi hadn't gone down and sung like a fucking canary who knows what the fuck might have happened."

Visceglia paused and shook his head. "Truth was that after Valachi's testimony the New York City Police Department released a very significant statistic. More family members in the tri-state area had been jailed in the subsequent three years than in the previous thirty. The guy did what he did, right or wrong, as far as the federal people were concerned, and though not one word actually served to finger anyone directly it still raised public and political awareness of what was really going on and what these people were capable of."

"And now?" Hartmann asked.

"Now? Well it ain't what it used to be," Visceglia said. "Things ain't never the same as they was in the old country . . . whaddya know, huh? Give it a name, forgeddaboudit, right?"

Hartmann had laughed. Visceglia, despite everything, despite the pictures, the stories, the lives lost, the deaths witnessed, despite everything he carried on his shoulders, somehow managed to retain an element of dry humor. Visceglia wasn't married, and one time Hartmann had asked him why.

"Married? Someone like me? Wouldn't be fair to drag someone into this who hadn't asked to be part of it."

Hartmann had appreciated the sentiment, and believed—perhaps—that he possessed sufficient strength of character to maintain an air of separation and objectivity. He believed he could live two lives, one at work and one at home, and it would only be in time that he would see how insidiously one could silently invade and unsettle the other.

Complex and almost indecipherable, incestuous and nepotistic, the Mafia was a many-headed Hydra that had survived all attempts to wipe it out. It was not something that existed in any real or tangible sense. It was a spectre, a series of interconnecting and yet separate shadows. Grasp for one facet and another would slip irretrievably out of reach. It was *This Thing of Ours*, and those whose thing it was were perhaps more loyal than any officially recognized body that faced them.

And Hartmann, despite the hours of reading files and transcripts, despite the tapes he'd listened to, the court reports he'd fallen asleep over, had never really managed to grasp the true meaning of this "family." These people did indeed seem to be the worst the world could offer, and many were the times he'd asked himself if he shouldn't just step away from the edge, take three paces back and turn the other way. And yet even in his darkest times, even when he understood that carrying the weight of this was a major contributory factor to his drinking, and understood also that drinking would be the thing that could irretrievably take his wife and his child away from him, he nevertheless found himself unable to avert his eyes. Morbid interest became fascination became obsession became addiction.

And so he lay there on his hotel bed, the echo of the conversation he'd held earlier that evening still echoing in his mind, and the thoughts that came with it were shadowed and oppressive and almost too heavy to bear.

"You're here for the duration, my friend," Schaeffer had told him with a simple matter-of-factness that allowed for no rebuttal. "You are an employee of the federal government whichever way this comes, and as such you are now working within our jurisdiction. What we say goes, and that is the *only* way it can be. We are dealing with a girl's life, not *just* a girl, but the daughter of one of the country's most significant politicians. Charles Ducane has been a personal friend of the vice president since they attended college together, and there is no way in the world any of us would say *No* to the vice president. You understand this, Mr. Hartmann?"

Ray Hartmann had nodded. Yes, he understood, understood that he had no choice in the matter. He watched Schaeffer's face as he talked, as the words issued from his lips, and yet all he could see were the faces of his wife and child when they appeared at Tompkins Square Park the following Saturday and he was not there. That was *all* he could see. He could hear something as well, and what he heard was Jess's voice as she asked *Where's daddy gone? Why isn't he here? He said he'd be here, didn't he, Mommy?*

And Carol would have to explain once more how *daddy* wasn't really running with the same program as them, that *daddy* had a very important job to do, that *daddy* never meant to not be there and there had to be a good explanation for his absence. But in her mind Carol would be cursing him, telling herself that she'd been a fool to believe he would ever keep his word, that despite being apart for these months nothing had changed, that Ray Hartmann was still the same self-centered, disorganized, alcoholic loser that he'd always been.

But that wasn't the truth. He hadn't always been self-centered, hadn't always been disorganized, and sure as hell he hadn't been, and *wasn't*, an alcoholic. It was this that had made him this way, this life, these people, and now he was falling right back into the same patterns all over again despite promising himself that this year, *this* year, would be the one he left this crazy bad business behind.

Hartmann turned over and buried his face in the pillow. New

Orleans was out there, the same New Orleans he had left with a vow never to return. But return he had, and in returning he'd carried with him all the suitcases he believed he'd left behind. He had never really set them down, that was the truth, and whatever was inside them, whatever it was that scared him so much he dared not look, had been right there all along. You never really let things go, you just fooled yourself into believing that you had grown out of them. How could you grow *out* of them when they were, always had been, and always would be an intrinsic part of exactly who you were?

He felt the tension in his chest, a difficulty in breathing. He turned over and stared at the ceiling, watched the trace-lines of car headlights as they turned at the end of the street beneath his window and wound their way out into the darkness. Out there he would find simpler people with simpler lives. Yes, they told lies, they cheated, they failed one another and possessed their regrets, but those things *belonged* to them; they were not so crazy as to try to carry their own burdens and the burdens of the rest of the world as well.

No one had ever told him it would be easy. But sure as hell they'd never let on it was going to be this hard.

Hartmann sat up and reached for his cigarettes. He lit one and flicked on the TV with the remote. He let the sounds and images blur together in his mind until he had no idea what he was watching or why. It worked for a minute, perhaps two, but always present was the sound at the other end of the phone, the way the voice had seemed to crawl down the wire and invade his head right through his ear.

And the way those first words sounded, and how they could not have been worse.

"Mr. Ray Hartmann . . . welcome home to New Orleans . . ."

A chill edge of fear crawled along his spine. It settled at the base of his neck. He reached up with his right hand and massaged the muscles that were knotting into small fists.

Hartmann opened his mouth. He looked sideways at Schaeffer. Nothing came forth. Not a word.

"You are well, Mr. Hartmann?"

Schaeffer nudged him in the shoulder.

"As can be," Hartmann replied.

"I understand that you have been dragged all the way home from New York . . . or did you manage to convince yourself that New York was now your home?"

Hartmann was silent.

Schaeffer nudged him again. Hartmann wanted to lunge from the desk and drive the receiver right into Schaeffer's face. He didn't. He sat stock-still and felt the sweat break out on the palms of his hands.

"I don't think I did that," Hartmann said.

"Then you and I have something in common, Mr. Hartmann. Despite everything, all these years, all the places I have been, I am like you . . . I could never get New Orleans out of my blood."

Hartmann didn't reply.

"Anyway, I can imagine Mr. Schaeffer and his federal agents are busy trying to trace this call. Tell them it doesn't matter. Tell them that I am coming in. I am coming in to speak with you, Mr. Hartmann, to tell you some things."

"Some things?"

The man at the other end of the line laughed gently. "You and I, we shall be like Robert Harrison and Howard Rushmore."

Hartmann frowned. "Like who?"

"Harrison and Rushmore . . . you do not recall those names?"

"No, I don't. Should I?"

"Robert Harrison and Howard Rushmore were the men who published *Confidential* magazine. You know, 'Uncensored and off the record,' 'Tells the facts and names the names.' You have heard of *Confidential* magazine?"

"Yes," Hartmann said. "I've heard of it."

"That's what we are going to do, you and I. We are going to spend some time together, and I will tell you some things that perhaps your federal people won't want to hear. And this is the deal. I'm coming in. I want to be treated with dignity and respect. I will tell you what I want you to know. You can do anything you wish with the information I give you, and then when we are done I will tell you where you can find the girl."

"Catherine Ducane."

"No Mr. Hartmann, Marilyn Monroe. Of course Catherine Ducane. Catherine Ducane is what this is all about."

"And she is okay?"

"She's as okay as could be expected under the circumstances, Mr. Hartmann, and that is all the information you will get from me this evening. As I said, I will be coming in, and when I am there I will tell you what you need to know, and that will be our business."

"How will we know you when you come?" Hartmann asked.

The man laughed. "Oh you will know who I am, Mr. Hartmann. That, I can assure you, will be the least of your worries."

"And when will you come?"

"Soon," the man said. "Very soon."

"And what about—"

The line suddenly went dead. Hartmann held the receiver against his ear even though he could hear the burring sound of a disconnected line through the speakers in the room.

He shuddered. He closed his eyes. He slowly replaced the receiver in the cradle and turned to look at Schaeffer.

Kubis appeared in the doorway, his face flushed, his eyes those of an agitated man. "Two blocks down," he shouted. "He was calling from two blocks down."

Schaeffer moved far faster than his size should have permitted, but he was out of the room with three other agents running after him, and though they went out through the front doors of the Field Office at a run, though they would charge down Arsenault Street and nearly lose their lives as they cut through the traffic at the intersection, though they would within three minutes stand at the very box from where the call had been made, they would find nothing. Schaeffer knew there would be no prints. He knew the impression of the caller's ear, as telling as DNA, as individual as retina scans and fingerprints, would have been wiped from the receiver, and though he knew these things he nevertheless ordered the phone booth taped and cordoned, he instructed the deployment of Criminalistics to go over the thing with a microscope, and yet in his heart of hearts he knew he was achieving nothing more than the exercise of protocol.

And then he returned. He shared words with Hartmann. He gave him his marching orders and instructed one of the agents to sequester Hartmann in the nearby Marriott Hotel.

And there Hartmann would be found, lying on the bed, smoking a cigarette and watching TV in the early hours of Saturday 30 August, a week to the day from when he was supposed to meet Carol and Jess. A week from the first real chance to rebuild his life.

Way to go, he would think. *Way to go, Ray Hartmann.*

And after a while he would turn the volume right down and lie there watching the light from the screen flickering on the walls, and he would feel the tension in his chest, the sense of breathlessness and claustrophobia, and he would know—above all else he would know—that you never actually escaped from these things, because these things always came from within.

Such was the way of his world.

SEVEN

BRUTALLY EARLY HOURS of Saturday morning.

Hartmann drove through the Arabi District below the Canal Bayou Bienvenue and above the 39 Highway that followed the Mississippi all the way down to St. Bernard. Here it became Highway 46 and took a straight route east toward Evangeline. With Lake Borgne to the south he pulled off the main freeway, slowed for a while with the window of his car open wide, and felt the breeze that came down off the water. Still New Orleans, but—as with all the districts inside the city limits—Arabi possessed a flavor and tempo all its own. A string of seedy and run-down clam bars and restaurants hunkered low along the shorefront, down where the warehousemen and yardhands split their palms on packing crates and drank their dreams through bottles without labels that came from beneath counters, half a dollar at a time. There were girls down there too, girls who walked from their waists and hips, not from their legs, girls with too much lipstick and too much liquor, brassy acts teetering in precarious heels and shamelessly bearing a resemblance to the men they serviced, twenty or thirty dollars a time.

Hartmann drove on. Rain coming down now. Escaped for a little while from the Marriott, while the world and all its cousins slept soundly in the knowledge that the madness that same world offered would still be there come daylight.

Found himself out near the airport. Left the car and stood near the fence that separated the fields from the runways, hands in his pockets, his collar turned up against the bitter slant of rain that seemed to razor slices from his skin. He watched as a damp piece of paper was caught by the wind and tossed toward the fence. It clung desperately to the wire for a moment and then, as if moving across a chessboard, it shifted an inch or two to the left. Pawn to bishop three, and through the gap it went like a rocket, spinning out over the tarmac like it was late for some life-or-death appointment. A sound pulled at Hartmann's attention, and he turned to watch an aircraft slide upwards from the far runway like a silver bullet. The clouds swallowed it effortlessly, so effortlessly there was nothing but a thin breath of slipstream to remind him that it was ever there at all.

He tried to light a cigarette but it was useless. He turned his back on the runway and started walking toward the Louis Armstrong International Terminal, and in that moment felt like he was turning his back on a watershed.

He could have run.

Renting the car had been easy enough. A single call to room service. A credit card number. Forty-three minutes later a car appeared outside the front of the hotel. And then he was inside, had started the engine, felt the thing turn over as he changed gear and pulled away. Could've just kept on going. Could've taken 39 or 46 or any other highway. And Schaeffer and Woodroffe wouldn't have realized he was gone for a good two or three hours. They would've found him. Only so many places he could've gone. Would have *definitely* found him. No question about it.

He walked back from the Terminal to his car and climbed in. Sat there for a while with the engine running, asking himself why he had already decided to stay. Perhaps for the girl, for Catherine Ducane. But then weren't his own wife and daughter far more important than Catherine Ducane would ever be? Of course they were. So why was he staying? Duty? Because these people could take away his job, his livelihood? Hadn't he been waiting for something to do just that? To give him no choice but to walk out into the big wide world and find something else to do? Sure he had.

So why was he staying?

He closed his eyes, leaned back against the headrest and exhaled. Truth was he didn't know.

An hour later Ray Hartmann was back in his room at the Marriott. He had taken off his wet clothes, showered, dressed once again, and by the time he called room service for coffee it was close to six in the morning.

Soon they would come, and when they came they would bring with them the worst the world could offer.

Schaeffer and Woodroffe didn't even have the decency to come themselves. They sent one of their agents, a young Ivy League–looking kid of no more than twenty-two or three, pressed white shirt, immaculately knotted tie, shoes Hartmann could see his reflection in. He possessed the bold brass of naïve self-importance, the brightness of eye that told

Hartmann this kid had yet to see what was out there. Stand over the bloodied and battered corpse of some eight-year-old kid, walk through the aftermath of a fast food restaurant drive-by shooting, smell the rank odor that emanated from a drowned cadaver, hear the sound of gases erupting from a swollen stomach as the ME sliced it open like an over-ripe watermelon . . . Walk a mile or two in Ray Hartmann's shoes and that bold brass and bright eye would grow tarnished and blunted and cynical and dark.

"Mr. Hartmann, they're ready," the kid said.

Hartmann nodded, and rose from where he'd been sitting on the edge of the mattress.

He followed the kid out to the front of the hotel where a dark gray sedan sat like a well-behaved animal.

"You want me to drive?" Hartmann asked, and truth be told he asked merely to see the flash of anxiety and uncertainty in the kid's eyes.

"I'm here to drive you, Mr. Hartmann," the kid said, and Hartmann smiled and shook his head, and said, "My name is Ray . . . you can just call me Ray."

The kid smiled, seemed to relax a little. "I'm Sheldon," he said. "Sheldon Ross."

"Well Sheldon, let's get the fuck outta here and find the bad guy, eh?"

Hartmann got in the passenger side.

"Belt," Sheldon said as he climbed into the driver's seat.

Hartmann didn't argue. He reached behind his shoulder for the belt and buckled in. Sure as shit the kid wouldn't drive more than forty miles an hour; the law was the law, and as far as Sheldon Ross was concerned the law was all there was. For now.

Schaeffer and Woodroffe were present and correct when Hartmann arrived. They were seated in an office off the furthermost corner of the main room. Agent Ross walked Hartmann down, left him standing there at the door and seemed to disappear without a sound. Schaeffer looked up, smiled as best he could, and waved Hartmann in.

"So we wait," Schaeffer said. "We wait for your caller to show his face, it seems."

Hartmann pulled a chair from against the wall and sat down. "Just a thought," he said, "but I don't think it would do any harm for me to speak to the people that dealt with this from the beginning. A new viewpoint perhaps."

Woodroffe shook his head. "I don't see that such a thing would really serve any purpose," he said, and in his tone was the defensive territoriality that came with agencies crossing each other's paths. He would in no way be pleased for Hartmann to find something they might have missed.

Hartmann shrugged nonchalantly. "Just figured it would be better than sitting around with nothing to do," he said. He turned and looked absentmindedly out of the small window to his right. He assumed the manner of one who could not have cared less. The rain had stopped some while back but there were dark thunderheads along the horizon. He couldn't tell if they were coming or going.

Schaeffer leaned forward and rested his forearms on the table. "I don't see that it would do any harm. Was there anyone in particular you felt you should speak to?"

Hartmann shrugged again. "I don't know, the ME perhaps, what was his name?"

"Emerson," Woodroffe said. "Jim Emerson, the assistant medical examiner."

"Right, right," Hartmann replied. "And then there's the coroner and the Homicide guy as well."

"Cipliano, Michael Cipliano, and the detective was John Verlaine."

Hartmann nodded. "Yes, those three. Figured I should at least go over their reports with them and see if there's anything else they remember."

Schaeffer rose from the table and walked to the open doorway. "Agent Ross!"

Sheldon Ross came hurrying down the room and stopped just short of the door.

"Get hold of the assistant ME Jim Emerson, County Coroner Cipliano and John Verlaine from Homicide. Pull whatever strings you have to and get them down here."

Ross nodded. "Sir," he said, and turned to hurry away.

Schaeffer came back and sat facing Hartmann. "So—you have any thoughts about our caller, Mr. Hartmann?"

Hartmann shook his head. "Nothing comes to mind, no. Can't say I place his voice, and there's nothing about what he said that makes me feel I know him."

"But he knows you," Woodroffe interjected.

"And you guys as well," Hartmann replied. "Seems he knows an awful lot more about us than we do about him."

For a moment there was an awkward silence.

Hartmann could sense the reaction to what he'd implied: that information was making its way out of their office. Such a thing was very unlikely indeed, but if these assholes wanted to play hardball then he would give them a run for their money.

"The names of agents in most branches of law enforcement are not withheld from the public," Woodroffe said matter-of-factly. Again there was that element of defense in his tone. Here was a man who'd perhaps violated protocol a few too many times and taken a rap from someone upstairs. Here was a man destined to be careful for the rest of his life.

"True," Hartmann said, "but there must have been a specific reason for him to request my presence."

"No question about that," Schaeffer said. "And if he comes in, or should I say *when* he comes in, perhaps he will tell us."

Hartmann looked up. Ross stood in the doorway.

"Here within half an hour, all three of them," he told Schaeffer and Woodroffe.

Schaeffer nodded. "Good work, Ross."

Ross did not smile, merely nodded and left the room once more. Hartmann watched him go and felt a sense of sympathy, even *empathy*, with the kid. One day Sheldon Ross would wake up and realize he was like the rest of them, and within *them* Hartmann included himself. One day he would wake up, and find that no matter how hard he rubbed his eyes, no matter how many times he sluiced his face with cold water in the bathroom, it would seem as if he was looking at the world through a gray film. Colors were duller, less bright and vivid; sounds always gave off an element of alarm; meeting people became a game of guessing what their motive or intent might be, and whether you were prepared to risk your own life, the well-being of your family, by getting to know them; all these darker aspects and shadows crept up on you insidiously, and then they were there; they were as much a part of you as the sound of your own voice, the color of your eyes, your own darkest secrets.

He closed his eyes for a moment.

"Tired, Mr. Hartmann?" Woodroffe asked.

Hartmann opened his eyes and looked back at the man. "Of life? Yes I am, Agent Woodroffe. Aren't you?"

Emerson and Cipliano were straightforward enough, as were the vast majority of those in Forensics and Criminalistics. They were scientists, doctors, morticians with an insatiable appetite for facts. The physical evidence was what it was. The condition of the body, the map of lines on the back, the knife wounds and adhesive tape, the rope burns and hammer blows. All these things had been investigated as thoroughly as could be, and the documents were typed and copied and filed and numbered.

Verlaine, however, was a different story. In John Verlaine, Hartmann recognized a little of himself.

"Sit down, Detective," Hartmann said, and Verlaine shed his coat and hung it over the back of the chair before he complied.

"Any coffee around here?" Verlaine asked. "Can we smoke?"

"I can get you some coffee," Hartmann replied, "and yes, you can smoke." He retrieved the ashtray from the floor beneath his own chair and set it on the table in front of Verlaine.

Hartmann left, returned within moments with a fresh cup of coffee. Woodroffe had been sufficiently cooperative to send out for a cafetière and some half-decent grounds.

"Intriguing, eh?" Verlaine asked.

"It is."

"What's your position on this then?"

Always the detective, Hartmann thought. *This guy probably questions all the parents at his own kids' PTA meeting.*

"My position?"

"Sure," Verlaine said, and smiled. "You're not a Fed, right?"

Hartmann shook his head. "No, I'm not a Fed."

"So what's your position in this circus?"

Hartmann smiled. He appreciated Verlaine's honest cynicism. This was a man he could have worked with in New York.

"My position, Detective, is that I am officially employed within federal jurisdiction. I work for the Deputy Investigative Director for the House Judiciary Subcommittee on Organized Crime."

Verlaine smiled. "You must have one helluvan office."

Hartmann frowned. "What d'you mean?"

"Well, title like that you'd need one helluva door to put the sign on."

Hartmann laughed. The man was hiding something. Humor was always the last line of defense.

Hartmann lit a cigarette and let the silence between them return.

"So you went down there?" he asked.

"Where? Gravier? Sure, I went down there."

"And the pound too. You saw the car, right?"

Verlaine nodded. "Beautiful car. Never seen a car like that before, and more than likely never will."

Hartmann nodded. He was watching Verlaine's eyes. Next question was important. Eyes were key. People always looked to the right when they were remembering something, to the left when they were imagining something or lying.

"So you wrote everything up, or at least relayed everything you found out to the Feds here . . . who was that? Luckman and Gabillard, right?"

Verlaine smiled. "Sure," he said, and his eyes went left.

Hartmann smiled too. "So what else was there?"

"Else?" Verlaine said, sounding genuinely surprised.

Hartmann nodded. "Something else. You know, the little thing we always keep back from the suits, just in case it winds up back on our desks and we want to get a head start? You're a veteran at this shit, Detective. You know exactly what I mean."

Verlaine shrugged. "Came to nothing."

"You wanna let me be the judge of that?"

"It was just a message."

"A message?"

"Someone called the Precinct House and left me a message."

Hartmann leaned forward.

"Someone called and left me a message of one word."

Hartmann raised his eyebrows, questioning.

"Always," Verlaine stated matter-of-factly.

"Always?"

"Right. Always. That was the message. Just that one word."

"And that meant something to you?"

Verlaine leaned back in his chair. He took another cigarette from the packet on the table and lit it. "Rumor has it that you're from New Orleans originally."

"Word gets around fast."

"However big New Orleans might appear to be it ain't ever big enough to lose a secret inside."

"So?"

"So anyone from New Orleans must have run by the Ferauds."

"Always Feraud," said Hartmann.

"That's the man. Daddy Always. That's what I figured the message meant."

"You follow it up?"

"You mean did I go talk to him? Sure I did."

"And what did he have to say for himself?"

"He said that I had a problem, a serious problem. He said there was nothing he could do to help me."

"Anything else?" Hartmann asked.

"A little. He said that the man I was looking for didn't come from here, that he was once one of us, but not now, not for many years. He said that he came from the outside, and that he would bring with him something that was big enough to swallow us all. That was the exact phrase he used, that it would swallow us all."

Hartmann didn't speak. The tension in the room was tangible.

"He told me to walk away. He told me that if I believed in God then I should pray that this killing had served its purpose." Verlaine shook his head and sighed. "Always Feraud told me that this was not something I should go looking for."

"And this you didn't report to Luckman or Gabillard?"

Verlaine shook his head. "What the hell purpose would it have served?"

Hartmann shook his head resignedly. He knew exactly what might have gone down. Luckman and Gabillard would have instigated a raid on Feraud's place, and if they had somehow avoided a stand-off and gotten to see Feraud himself, then they would have come away none the wiser than when they went in. There was nothing in the world that would have prompted Feraud to give the FBI anything at all.

"He told you to walk away from this," Hartmann reiterated.

"Yes. Told me to walk away. Told me not to go looking. Also told me not to go to his place again, and not to ask anything of him regarding it. He said it wasn't something he was part of, nor was it something he wished to become involved in."

"And he said nothing about Catherine Ducane? Mentioned nothing about the kidnapping?"

The detective shook his head. "He didn't say anything, no, but that doesn't mean he knew nothing about it, right? He's familiar with the way this works. He answers only what he's asked. He doesn't talk about anything without it being brought up by someone else first."

"And that was the end of your meeting with Feraud?"

Verlaine nodded. "Sure was. You don't go outstaying your welcome down there, you know that."

"So what do you make of it?" Hartmann asked.

"Out of school?"

"Yes, out of school."

"Whoever the hell it was got the girl, right?"

"Yes, Catherine Ducane."

"And right now she's either been hidden somewhere or she's dead?"

Hartmann nodded agreement.

"I figure it has to be something personal between the kidnapper and Charles Ducane. Man like that doesn't get to be a man like that unless he's walked alongside a few dangerous people on the way. If it wasn't personal there would have been a ransom demand by now, or maybe a call to let us know where we could find her body."

"You know anything specific about Ducane?" Hartmann asked.

Verlaine shook his head. "No more than anyone else would know who lives in New Orleans and gets on the rumor lines."

Hartmann reflected on this for a moment. He'd heard his own things about Ducane but wanted to hear it from someone else's point of view. "Such as?"

"The gambling licenses, the kickbacks, the campaign slush funds, all the shit that goes with the territory. A governor doesn't get to be a governor without greasing some palms and silencing some tongues, you know? I've never followed anything up on him, never had the need to, nor the interest for that matter, but evidently he's gotten someone mightily pissed along the way and now the shit has hit the fan."

"Evidently," Hartmann said.

"So you need anything else from me?" Verlaine asked.

Hartmann shook his head. "I don't think so."

"And none of this goes any further, right?"

Hartmann shrugged. "Why would that matter to you?"

Verlaine smiled wryly. "I got parents, and then I got the Feds and whoever the fuck else on the other. You drag me into this any further and you endanger either my professional reputation or my life. You know the deal, Mr. Hartmann."

"I do, and no, this won't go any further—"

A sound outside. The sudden hubbub of voices. Hartmann rose from the desk as someone knocked sharply on the door and opened it.

Stanley Schaeffer stood there, his face flushed, his eyes wide. "You got someone here," he said, urgency in his tone.

Hartmann frowned. "I got someone?"

"Your caller, we think it's your caller."

Verlaine looked at Hartmann. His face was grave.

Hartmann came out from behind the desk and followed Schaeffer at a near-run.

EIGHT

THERE WERE THREE of them, and they all looked the same, and they all wore the same expression of confusion, anxiety, the tension of the moment, and all three of them had their hands on their guns, but had not drawn them, for they were uncertain of what they were dealing with. And one of the three agents was Sheldon Ross, and when he turned and saw Hartmann burst through the door at the far end of the entrance foyer there was a momentary yet very evident flicker of relief in his eyes.

For a handful of seconds, couldn't have been more than six or seven, everyone stood silent and immobile. Three agents surrounded the man, and on the other side of the foyer Hartmann stood next to Schaeffer, and when Hartmann looked at Schaeffer there was something about the way he looked that communicated the same sense of disbelief as Hartmann himself felt.

The man who had walked into the foyer of the FBI office had to have been at least sixty or sixty-five. He was dressed immaculately: an overcoat, a three-piece suit, white shirt, a deep burgundy tie, patent leather shoes, leather gloves, a black cashmere scarf around his neck. His face was a network of symmetrical lines—creases and wrinkles and crow's feet like origami unwrapped—and beneath his heavyset brows his eyes were the most piercing green—emerald almost—intense, somehow possessed.

The old man broke the silence, and the words that came from his lips were spoken with the same unmistakable dialectic tones that Hartmann had listened to on the phone, and yet again many times on the tapes they had made.

"Mr. Hartmann," the man said. "And Mr. Schaeffer." He paused and smiled, and then he looked at the three younger agents facing him and said, "Gentlemen, please don't feel any necessity to draw your guns. I am here of my own volition, and I assure you I am quite unarmed."

Hartmann felt his heart thudding in his chest. His throat was tight, as if someone had gripped it and was damned if they were going to let go.

The man took one step forward, and the three agents—armed though they were—each simultaneously took one step back.

"My name," the man said, "is Ernesto Perez." He smiled, a broad and genuine smile. "And I have come to talk about the girl."

It was Schaeffer who moved first, and as he moved so did two others beside him. Who started shouting was uncertain in Hartmann's mind, but there was no doubt as to the contagious effect a single raised voice had on the proceedings. Schaeffer pushed past the agents in front of him, and before Hartmann could react he was holding a gun, a gun that he aimed directly between Perez's eyes.

"On the floor!" Schaeffer was commanding.

Pandemonium broke out instantly. It seemed that there were twice as many people in the foyer all of a sudden. Schaeffer was at the head of them, and at one point he turned and looked at Hartmann, his face white, his eyes wide, and it seemed that all the frustration and pressure he'd been feeling since this began were encapsulated within that split-second glance.

Perez looked back at Schaeffer implacably. He raised his right hand slowly, then his left; he too looked at Hartmann, in his eyes a sense of resigned disbelief that such behavior was necessary.

"Down!" Schaeffer commanded once more, and then there were three or four of them, guns drawn and leveled, and Perez went slowly to his knees.

"Hands behind your head! Get your hands behind your fucking head!"

Hartmann took a step backward and looked down at the floor. For some reason he felt awkward, almost embarrassed, and when he looked up he saw Perez was staring right back at him.

Hartmann tried to look away but he could not. He felt transfixed, pinned to the spot, and when Ross went forward and handcuffed Perez it seemed that the whole world slowed down to ensure that this moment lasted forever. Hartmann sensed the breathless tension in those present, and he was aware of the tremendous pressure such a confrontation would create. He closed his eyes for a second; he prayed with everything he possessed that a sudden movement wouldn't prompt a reaction, an unsteady hand, a moment's nervousness, a dead kidnapper . . .

After a moment everything went quiet.

Perez, his upturned face visible to all, smiled at Stanley Schaeffer.

"I have come of my own accord, Agent Schaeffer," he said quietly.

The two agents to Schaeffer's right were visibly shaken and on edge. Hartmann prayed that one of them wouldn't pull the trigger in a moment of agitation and uncertainty.

"I don't believe that this is altogether necessary," Perez went on. His voice was steady, as were his hands, his eyes, everything about him. Kneeling there on the floor of the foyer he appeared just as calm as when Hartmann had first seen him.

"This is a good suit," Perez said, and he smiled with his eyes. "A very good suit, and it is such a shame to dirty it by kneeling here on the floor."

Schaeffer turned and looked at Hartmann.

Hartmann didn't move, didn't make a sound. He thought of John Verlaine, reminded that he had left him in the back office. He wondered where Verlaine was, if he had somehow managed to leave the building amidst the confusion generated by Perez's arrival.

Perez shook his head. "It seems that we have reached an impasse. I remain here on the floor and we accomplish nothing at all. I stand up, you release these quite unnecessary handcuffs, and I shall tell you what it is you have been waiting for."

Again Schaeffer turned and looked at Hartmann. Hartmann did not know what was expected of him; here he possessed no authority at all. Schaeffer was in charge of the investigation and was the one who'd believed it necessary to put Perez on his knees and handcuff him.

"You stand slowly," Schaeffer said. His voice broke midsentence and he repeated himself. There was the slightest waver in his tone, as if he was unsettled by this man even though he was now cuffed and almost prostrate.

Perez nodded but did not speak. He rose slowly to his feet, and even as he did so the men behind him, the men who had been so quick to draw and aim their guns, stepped back and looked awkward. One of them lowered his gun and the others quickly followed suit.

Hartmann watched, slightly amazed at how Perez seemed to have effortlessly taken control of the situation with barely a word.

Perez stood facing Schaeffer with his hands behind his head. He merely nodded and Schaeffer motioned for Ross to unlock the cuffs. Perez lowered his hands and massaged each wrist in turn. He nodded at Schaeffer and smiled courteously.

Schaeffer turned and nodded at Hartmann.

Hartmann paused for a second, and then he came forward with his heart thundering in his chest and his throat tight like a tourniquet.

Later, because thoughts that came after the fact always seemed more incisive and relevant than those born in the moment, Ray Hartmann would recall the tension of that moment, the way everything had unfolded, the way the old man had come forward to greet him, how the collective body of agents had withdrawn, and how—when he opened his mouth and spoke—it seemed that everything that had gone before, everything that had brought them to that point, seemed so insignificant. This man, calling himself Ernesto Perez, had appeared without fanfare, without armed escorts, without blaring sirens and flashing cherry-bars; had appeared in the foyer of the Bureau's office in New Orleans, perhaps the FBI's most wanted man, coming of his own accord, coming without demand or warrant. He had appeared quietly and politely, and yet somehow commanded the attention of all who were there with his unmistakable charisma and presence.

Ernesto Perez, whoever he might have been, had arrived before them, and for the moments it took for everyone to register what he was saying, it seemed the world had stopped.

Hartmann spoke first; opened his mouth and said, "Mr. Perez . . . thank you for coming."

Perez smiled. He stepped back and gave a courteous bow of his head. He slowly removed his overcoat, his scarf also, and then—without seeming in the least presumptuous—handed them to Sheldon Ross. Ross turned and glanced at Hartmann, Hartmann nodded, and Ross took the scarf and gloves.

Perez took another step forward.

Schaeffer raised his hand. "Stop right there," he said.

Perez looked at Hartmann, his expression one of slight bemusement.

"It's okay," Hartmann said. He stepped ahead of Schaeffer, crossed the room to where Perez stood, and reached out his hand.

Perez took it, and for a moment the two of them stood there immobile.

"Seems we have a great deal to discuss, Mr. Perez," Hartmann said.

Perez smiled. "It seems we do, Mr. Hartmann."

There was a moment's silence, and as Hartmann looked at the old man he saw nothing more than the reason he might once again lose his family. Had it not been for this man he would still be in New York, nothing to concern him but making it to Tompkins Square Park on time . . .

"I have a proposition," Ernesto Perez stated matter-of-factly.

Hartmann's train of thought was derailed.

Perez smiled again. "But perhaps it is not so much a proposition as a presentation of incontrovertible fact. I have the girl. I have her somewhere safe. I can guarantee that no matter how many federal agents you bring down here you will never find her."

From the inside pocket of his jacket he withdrew a single color photograph. Catherine Ducane—strained, exhausted-looking, standing against a blank and featureless wall, in her hands a copy of the *New Orleans Herald* from the previous day. The *Herald* meant nothing; the paper could be bought all across Louisiana and in some of the adjoining states as well.

Hartmann stood silent, watching every move the man made, his body language, the way his turn of phrase emphasized certain points. Hartmann knew two things from watching him: that there was indeed *no* possibility of finding Catherine Ducane without this man's direction, and secondly, perhaps more importantly, that he was in no way afraid. He had either done this before, or was free of any concern regarding his own welfare.

Hartmann sensed Schaeffer beside him. He sensed his thoughts, the kaleidoscope of emotions that would be running through him, the anxiety he would be feeling about how to explain this situation to his superiors in Washington. All these things, and underlying them the conviction that a man such as Schaeffer would feel: that Ernesto Perez was beneath him, that Ernesto Perez was the sort who was always better dead.

Hartmann willed Schaeffer to stay silent, to say and do nothing. Perez was used to being in control, and he would merely rise to any provocation by making their predicament all the more dangerous.

"My terms, if terms is an appropriate description, are simple, if perhaps a little peculiar," Perez continued. He seemed relaxed, unhurried. "I have some things to say, a great many things, and thus my request that Mr. Hartmann be present."

Hartmann looked up at the sound of his name.

Perez smiled, and once again nodded his head. "Perhaps I feel I owe you something, Mr. Hartmann."

Hartmann frowned. "Owe me?"

"Indeed. We have crossed paths before, indirectly, never face-to-face, but in some small way our lives connected some little while ago."

Hartmann shook his head. There was nothing about the man that struck a chord with him.

Perez smiled. His eyes were dark and intense. He seemed to be speaking of something for which he held fond memories.

Hartmann clenched his fists. He bit his tongue. He said nothing.

Perez lowered his head, and then looked up once more and scanned the faces of the men looking back at him. "I think it was Pinochet perhaps, yes it was Pinochet who said that sometimes democracy must be bathed in blood."

Perez shook his head, and turned once more to Hartmann. "But that is past," he said, "and we must talk of the present. As I said, I feel that there is a small matter for which I owe you a debt, and thus I have asked for you to be here. There are a good many things of which I wish to speak, and Mr. Hartmann will be present to hear them. Once I am done, once I have said all I wish to say, then I will tell you where you can find the girl and she can be returned to her father. Is that understood?"

There was silence, perhaps for no more than ten or fifteen seconds, but those seconds drew out infinitely, and it seemed that everyone present was waiting for another to speak.

Finally it was Hartmann. "Do we have a choice?" he asked.

Perez shook his head slowly and smiled. "If the life of Catherine Ducane carries any importance at all then no, Mr. Hartmann, you do not have a choice."

"And if we concur with your wishes, if we give you the time to say what you have to say, then what guarantee can you give us that Catherine Ducane will be found alive?"

"No guarantee, Mr. Hartmann. No guarantee at all save my word."

"And once we have her back, what will you ask for yourself?"

Perez was silent for some time. He once more surveyed the faces that looked back at him, and it was as if he was taking a mental note, a series of snapshots of his surroundings, the people present, so as to always have them to view in hindsight. Hartmann sensed that here was both the beginning and the end of something for Ernesto Perez.

"For myself?" he asked. "I will stand and face whatever justice is deemed fitting for a man in my position."

"You will give yourself up?" Hartmann asked suspiciously.

Perez shook his head again. "A man like me never gives up, Mr. Hartmann, and that is perhaps where you and I share a little in common. No, I will merely be relinquishing my power of choice regarding my own fate."

Hartmann said nothing. He turned and looked at Schaeffer, whose expression was one of total incredulity. There were things he wanted to say, questions he wanted to ask, but in some fashion his mind and his mouth failed to connect.

"So be it," Hartmann said finally. "It seems we've been placed in a situation where we have no choice."

"So be it indeed," Perez replied. "I would ask for safe housing in a nearby hotel. We shall conduct our discussions either there or here in this office, that is up to you. You can escort me from one building to another under armed guard. You can place me under arrest and keep me watched twenty-four hours a day, but I would ask for sufficient time to sleep and for adequate food. You can record our discussions or have them transcribed by someone else in the room, again that is your choice. I make no conditions as to the security or retention of those things I tell you, and I will trust Mr. Hartmann to make a decision as to whether or not any action is taken against any other person whose name I might divulge. Those are the parameters within which we shall work."

Perez turned to Sheldon Ross and extended his hand. Ross looked at Hartmann, Hartmann nodded and Ross returned the overcoat and scarf to Perez.

"Shall we?" Perez asked Hartmann.

Hartmann turned and started walking, Perez following him, and after Perez the collective federal body moved slowly and in single file like schoolchildren crossing the street.

They walked through the main offices and entered the room at the rear, and here Ray Hartmann and Ernesto Perez sat facing each other.

"If I could perhaps have a cup of strong coffee, without sugar but with ample cream, and also a glass of water, Mr. Schaeffer," Perez stated. "And while you are attending to that, perhaps you could have one of your people arrange for whatever recording facility might be required?"

Schaeffer nodded in the affirmative, and walked away, neither questioning nor challenging Perez's right to ask these things of him.

A few minutes later Lester Kubis appeared in the doorway, carrying a case from which he produced desk mikes and cables. He was fast and efficient, and within ten minutes he gave a thumbs-up from a desk situated six feet from the doorway. On it was a large reel-to-reel tape recorder and additional cables running into a PC that would record the discussions directly to CD.

Schaeffer returned with coffee for both Perez and Hartmann, also a glass of water and a clean ashtray.

"So," he said as he paused in the doorway. "I'll be here if you require anything further."

"Thank you, Mr. Schaeffer," Perez said quietly, and then with his right hand he reached out and gently pushed the door to.

Hartmann looked at the old man; his lined face, his intense eyes, his heavyset brows. The old man looked back and smiled.

"So here we are, Mr. Hartmann," he said, and his voice possessed a rhythm and timbre that seemed both relaxed and direct. "You are ready for this?"

Hartmann shrugged. "I'm ready," he replied. "For what, I don't know, but I am ready."

"Good enough," Perez said. "I have a great deal to say, and not a great deal of time to say it, so pay attention. That is all I can ask of you."

"My attention you have," Hartmann replied. He wanted to ask the man what he meant. How much did he want to say, and how much time *did* he possess? He wanted to know the answer to these questions, and he knew that it was not because of Catherine Ducane, not for fear of the girl's life or what her father might think, it was because of Carol and Jess, the fact that what this man had done might make it impossible for him to be there come Saturday . . .

"Okay." Perez smiled. He leaned back in his chair, and before he spoke again he took the glass of water and drank from it. "So . . . we shall begin."

Hartmann raised his hand.

Perez tilted his head to the right and frowned.

"I must ask you something," Hartmann said.

Perez nodded. "Ask away, Mr. Hartmann."

"It's just . . . well, you said that there was some debt you owed me, that we had crossed paths before—"

Perez smiled. "Later," he said quietly. "It is not important now, Mr. Hartmann. What is important here is the life of the girl, and the fact that until this matter is resolved you and I will be sharing one another's company, and that is something that can be either straightforward or complicated. I have no wish to prolong this matter any more than is entirely necessary, and I am quite sure you have matters to attend to that are an awful lot more pressing than the well-being of the governor's daughter. You have your own family, I understand?"

Hartmann's eyes visibly widened.

Perez nodded. "You have your own family to go back to, and I can imagine this whole affair has been somewhat of an inconvenience to you already."

Hartmann didn't speak. He thought again of his wife and daughter; he thought of their appointed meeting. He felt once again the frustration of being brought to Orleans, of now being committed to staying, and all of this because of the man facing him.

"You are a dedicated and patient man, Mr. Hartmann. I understand the nature of the work you do, and the degree of commitment required to continue spending your days dealing with the sort of things you have to deal with. Perhaps you and I are more alike than you imagine."

"Alike?" Hartmann asked, a tone of antagonism in his voice,

antagonism toward not only the man himself, but the sheer nerve he possessed to make any kind of comparison between them. "How could you think we were alike?"

Perez leaned back and smiled, relaxed and unhurried. "The things we see, the things we know about, the sort of people that populate our lives. They are the same people, you know. You and I are walking along different sides of the same track, and though we might look at something from a different perspective we nevertheless are still looking at the same thing."

"I don't—" Hartmann started, a feeling of anger rising inside him.

"Don't what?" Perez asked, and his tone was one of worldly knowing and self-assurance that Hartmann found not only unnerving, but galling beyond belief. Perez might indeed have seen the same things as him, might even have been directly or indirectly involved, but here, at least in this situation, Perez was entirely and effortlessly in control. Somehow—despite being the perpetrator of one of the most important federal cases Hartmann had been connected to—he had managed to walk in amongst them and wrest control. He had the upper hand; he knew he had it, and he was going to bet everything he owned on how his cards fell. Irrespective of whatever sense of self-possession Perez maintained, he was still capable of preventing Hartmann from seeing his family at the end of the week. For this, for this alone, Hartmann could feel nothing but anger, even hatred.

"You don't believe we share a similarity of nature and viewpoint, Mr. Hartmann?" Perez asked. "I can assure you right here and now that there is a very narrow dividing line between the path you have walked and the one I myself chose. A religious man would perhaps speak of the dualist concept, where for every part of man that could be considered good there is also an opposed and equal part that is evil. How a man turns is dependent solely upon the events and circumstances of his life, but I can guarantee you that there is no difference when it comes to ethical and moral standpoints."

Hartmann shook his head. He did not understand what Perez was saying; perhaps his emotional reaction to this situation prevented him from *wanting* to understand the man.

"Dependent upon the individual himself there is no difference between right and wrong. What I might consider right is entirely dependent upon what I consider to be the most constructive stance to take. The fact that you disagree with that stance doesn't make you any more right than I. One man's ceiling is another man's floor. I believe that is a common saying here in the United States of America."

"But the law?" Hartmann asked. "What you have done is a violation of the law." He heard the edge in his own voice, the same edge that would surface when he'd been drinking, when unacceptable circumstances had managed to invade his life and upset him.

"What law would that be then, Mr. Hartmann?"

"The law established by the people."

"And what people would that be? Certainly not me. I never agreed to any such laws being established. Were you ever consulted? Did your government ever take the time to ask you what you considered to be the right and wrong thing to do in any given situation?"

Hartmann shook his head. "No, of course not . . . but we're talking of guidelines that have been laid down for centuries about what is generally considered to be right and wrong behavior. These laws are based on what has been proven to be the most survival-oriented action in any given situation."

"Survival-oriented for whom?" Perez asked. "And if that is the case then why is the vast majority of law in this society considered a perverse travesty of justice? Ask any man in the street and he considers the police and the courts corrupt, ruled by special consent, by legal technicalities, by nepotism and graft. Ask the average man in the street if he believes that justice can be attained here in your peace-loving and democratic society and he will laugh in your face."

Hartmann could not respond. Angry and agitated though he was, he knew Perez was right.

"So what do we have, Mr. Hartmann? We have you and I, nothing more nor less than that. I have come here to speak my mind, to be listened to, and when I am done I will tell you what you want to know about the girl. That is the deal here, and there is no other offer."

Hartmann nodded. Perez had seemingly orchestrated this scenario, had drawn Hartmann into it regardless of Hartmann's power of choice, and that was as complicated as it could become. It was a black-and-white situation, no shades of gray between.

"So once more," Perez said. "I shall begin?"

Hartmann nodded in the affirmative and leaned back in his chair.

"Very well," Perez said quietly, and started to speak.

NINE

AND SO I tell you of these things, not because I believe they are important, though in some ways they are, but because I am tired, I am growing old, and I feel that this is perhaps the last time that my voice will be heard. These things go back a great many years, back almost to the start of the last century, and the way these things began perhaps contributed to the way they ended. Cause and effect, no?

These words from my mother. My mother. The sound of her voice even now resonant in my ears. It was she who told me of my father's land, and his father before him; how the history of that land had borne a people that were strong-willed and unafraid of dying. Death was as much a part of life as anything else, she would say, and it was because of this lineage that I became who I am. Of this I am sure, but to comprehend all I will tell you, it is necessary that we retrace steps that were made by people long before I was born.

I was a small child, and she sat with me, and this story she told me to help me understand some of the passion and violence that were held inside my father. I would listen to the sound of her voice, and when she paused I could hear her heart beating as I laid my head against her chest. Through the window I would feel the breeze from outside, the warmth of the air, and believe that never could someone feel so secure and safe.

"It was a day that began much the same as any other," she said, "and yet—almost as if history itself had wrenched open a wound—the blood of men would be spilled before the sun set. Voices would be raised, families would be ruined, and amidst all of this something would begin that has influenced and directed so much of your father's life. Your father, Ernesto. He comes from these people I speak of, and because of these things he is a strong-willed and decisive man."

She paused and stroked my hair. I listened to her heart.

"*¡Hijos de Puta!* they screamed," she said. "*¡Hijos de Puta!* But the words all blurred together like they were one word, and that one word carried hatred and venom and despair and anguish, and beneath that a sense of frustrated desperation, and beneath even that there seemed to be a sense of abject hopelessness, because they knew—each and every one of them—that no matter how many times they shouted, and no matter how loud their collective voice, and no matter how much spirit they managed to muster as they gathered in a raggle-tag disheveled crowd, they couldn't change the inevitable.

"There were men on horses, Ernesto . . . men with guns on horses. Smoke billowing out from the narrow wooden huts that gathered along the edge of the trees like children crowding for warmth.

"It was in a place called Mayari in Cuba, out near Biran in the Oriente Province. Immigrant laborers lived there, one of them a man called Ruz, hailing originally from Galicia in Spain. He came to Cuba for the future it promised. Grew sugar, harvested it, sold it for meager profits, and watched while government men came down to rout out the instigators of a local protest and burned their houses to the ground.

"February of 1926, and Ruz stood on the border of his land and prayed to a God he barely believed existed, and trusted that his faith would stop the government men from burning his property too. His prayers were heard, it seemed, for within an hour the government men rounded their horses and carried away toward the horizon, and left behind them families without livelihoods, families who knew nothing of the protests, and had they known would not have had the strength to raise their voices. But when it came to their own homes, well then they did find the strength, but it did no good. No good at all.

"Ruz turned and walked back the way he'd come, and when he reached his own house his wife was waiting for him. Concern lined her face, and when he pulled her close, when he pressed his hand gently against her belly, when he told her that nothing, *nothing in this or any other world*, would come to harm her or their child, she believed that she could not have made a better choice in marrying this man.

"For Ruz was a good man, a man of honor, of principle, and come August he would watch as his wife bore a son, and they would watch that son grow, and the son's name was Fidel Castro Ruz, and he would work alongside his father in the sugar cane, and when he was six years old he would convince his parents to send him to school. And they would talk in hushed voices when Fidel Castro Ruz was sleeping, and they would agree that an education gave a child a future. So they sent him—this brave, bright, wide-eyed child—and Colegio Lasalle would take him in Santiago, and then Colegio Dolores, and through the years to come, as Hitler came, as Franco declared victory against the Republicans in

Catalonia, as the Nazis marched on into Czechoslovakia, the child Ruz would study hard and well."

My mother paused. I looked up at her, her face passionate, but with a passion so different from that of my father. My mother was passionate about living, about making everything good for us, whereas my father was somehow frightening and violent and angry. It was as if he carried all the burdens of the world upon his shoulders and the weight of those burdens was killing him.

"He was a fine student," my mother went on. "There didn't seem to be anything he didn't want to know. He worked hard through those years that saw Europe at war. In January of '39 Franco entered Barcelona. He was allied to General Yague's Moors, and from the north the Nationalist troops moved forward and cornered the Republicans. By March Franco had taken Madrid and ended the Spanish Civil War. Six months later Germany and Russia invaded Poland, and within forty-eight hours the war had begun. Hitler invaded Denmark and Norway and France, Trotsky was murdered in Mexico City, the Japanese attacked Pearl Harbor . . . and Fidel Castro Ruz, now a young man of sixteen entering the Jesuit School of Colegio Belen, would watch the world in turmoil. It was as if a hurricane rose up from the heart of Europe, and somehow it drew the rest of the world into its own breed of madness. Castro would survive all of this, and he would eventually give Cuba back to her people. He is an important man, Ernesto, a man you should learn about. You have it in you to be as powerful and wise as Fidel Castro Ruz."

My mother stopped. She pulled me tight. "And what of you? You were alive even then, Ernesto Cabrera Perez. Born not in Cuba, though that was your father's homeland, and even though you and Fidel Castro Ruz had the same date of birth, 13 August, you were all of five years old, oblivious to what was happening on the other side of the earth. You were here in America, in New Orleans, state of Louisiana . . ."

She turned away then and smiled, as if remembering me as a small child gave her some sense of comfort and solace. I listened to every word she said. She had been the child of a poor family, but she was intelligent and perceptive, reading all she could find, listening to her own parents as they told her about the world. Time and again she instructed me to pay attention to everything around me, to learn to read, to read everything as she had done, and to recognize that life was there to be understood. She wanted me to survive. She wanted me to escape the world within which she had found herself, and make something of my future.

My father was a boxer, a fighter born and bred, a man who had for some reason left Cuba behind him for the bright lights and brash shallow promise of the New World. My father, the "Havana Hurricane." A powerful man, both in physique and temperament; his wife, my mother, a Southern American–Hispanic girl from the poorest of backgrounds, and between these two—the wild fury of manhood that was always my father, and she the brooding, dark-haired, emerald-eyed southerner who tempted all men like Delilah—I was caught between a rock and a hard place. I was an only child, and perhaps suffered for it. If there was violence to be displayed it was displayed toward me and me alone. If there was affection and sympathy, then I was there also, and between these wild swings of emotional exuberance I began my life understanding that nothing was certain save uncertainty itself. Within a moment my father could turn into a rage of punishment, sweeping his bruised knuckles wide and flooring both my mother and me. He would drink, drink like a man from the desert, and when he won a fight, when he carried home fistfuls of sweat-stained dollars, we knew that those same dollars would disappear through the neck of a bottle of cheap sourmash, or between the legs of some seventeen-year-old hooker.

Only later would I see those girls for what they were. These girls were like no other girls in the world. They possessed that wide-mouthed inbred look, chewing gum, slutting some illegitimate Creole twist when they walked, and when they talked their voices came up through their legs, their hips, their swollen breasts. They acted cheap and trashy, believing perhaps that this was the way they were supposed to act, and when they slanted by, tilting their eyes out beneath thick brunette bangs, you could sense in their expression how they felt about you. They ate you with their eyes, sucked your root with their arrogant and conceited lips, rolled you over backward across wide rhythmic shoulders and buried you in the belief that to lie with them beneath some clammy, sweated sheet was the closest you would ever come to Heaven. Perhaps they were fathered in Hell, fathered by brothers and cousins, and abused before they realized there were differences between men and women.

This was a town called Evangeline, down south along Lake Borgne, and it was a small broken-up town that ran by its own rules, and those rules were branded in iron, and it would have taken more than any number of men to change them. The people were strong-willed, resentful of strangers; they clutched their secrets to their chests like unwanted gifts, things they wished to shed but could not. They carried a myriad burdens, and even as a small and frightened child I could read it in their cracked faces, their sun-bleached hair, their worn hands, their open hearts. For this, for me, was where life began and ended; this was where I found all that was significant about life—fear, anger, hatred, power and pain. Love and betrayal too, for love and betrayal walked hand-in-hand, cater-cousins, blood-brothers, echoes of the soul. My father, the Hurricane, did not sleep with these women because he did not love my mother; he loved her the only way he knew how. He loved her enough to beat her when she bad-mouthed him, to hold her afterwards as her eye bruised, to wrap cracked ice from the cooler in a towel and hold it against her swelling face, to calm her tears, to whisper his gentle platitudes, and then to coax her into taking his cock into her mouth, breathing life into him sufficient that he could turn her onto her side and bury himself inside her, to hold her shoulders hard against the floor while he emptied his rage out the best way he knew how. And she would scream his name, and shed tears as he hurt her, but she was blind enough to believe that now he would love her like the man she wanted, and not the man she had married.

Later I would think of my father. Later I would dream. Even as a child I dreamed, but my dreams were not of cotton candy and fair-grounds, of childhood as some warm and secure hiatus before adulthood . . . No, no such things as these. My dreams were of my father, and how one day I would see him undone.

He continued to fight, his bare-knuckle madness displayed for the world to see most every Friday and Saturday night, and by the time I was eight, as I heard of the death of Roosevelt, as the Second World War finally collapsed beneath the weight of its own insanity, I would go with him to the brutal and sadistic tournaments held in backlots and car parks behind sleazy bars and pool halls, where for twenty-five dollars a time grown men would beat each other senseless and bloody. I was given no choice in the matter. My father said I should go, and so I did. On the single occasion that my mother expressed some vague disagreement in the matter he merely had to raise his hand and she was silenced, never to protest again.

So, as Fidel Castro Ruz graduated from Colegio Belen in Havana with a Ph.D in Law, as he went on to enter the University of Havana, I stood and squinted, with barely opened eyes, through the chicken-wire fencing that separated the backyard behind some broken-down moon-shine haunt, squinted and grimaced and dared myself to go on looking as my alcohol-reddened father brought his callused and brown fists down repeatedly on some poor challenger's head. He was the Hurricane, the Havana Hurricane, and there was no one, not one single man, who ever walked unaided from a fight with my father. On three occasions—once when I was nine, the second time when I was eleven, the third when I was twenty-one—I saw him beat men to death, and once the death was confirmed I saw money exchange hands, the body drawn up tight in a hessian sack, and then dark-faced men with leather coats lifted the cadavers and carried them to the back of waiting flatbed trucks. I heard those bodies were sawed up like a jigsaw and hurled piece by piece into Lake Borgne. There the fish and the snakes and the alligators would remove any evidence that those men had existed. Their names were left unspoken, their faces forgotten, their prayers unanswered. One time I asked my father about them, and he turned to me and breathed some whiskey-fueled challenge that included the phrase *comer el coco*. I understood little Spanish at that time, and did not know what he meant by "eating his head." I asked my mother, and she told me that he did not wish to be interrogated and brow-beaten.

Later, I would think that the saddest thing about my father's death was his life.

Later, I would think a great many things, but as a child growing up in a small run-down four-room adobe house on the edge of Evangeline, the sour smell of Lake Borgne ever present in my nostrils, I believed the world to be nothing more than a bruised and bloody nightmare spewed from the dark imagination of a crazy God.

To understand me, both as a child and man, is to understand some things of yourself that you could not bear to face. You shy away from such revelation, for to see it is to relinquish ignorance, and to relinquish ignorance is to know that you yourself are guilty of the recognition of possibility. We all possess our darker aspects; we are all capable of acts of inhumanity and degradation; we all possess a dark light in our eyes that, when ignited, can incite murder and betrayal and infidelity and hatred.

Perhaps I was such a child, one of those who walked, who looked, who reached toward the promise of the unseen, only to find myself without equilibrium and grasping the air ahead of me, feeling the tightness in my chest as fear erupted throughout my fragile body, and then the sense of certainty that all was lost as my feet slid from beneath me and I began to fall . . .

And fall I did, all the way down, and even now—these many years later—I have yet to reach the lowest depths.

I was born out of poverty and grew beneath the shadow of drunken brawls between the two people who I believed should have loved one another the most. It was a birth of regret, both my mother and father believing until the very last moment that I should have been aborted, and though this was not for the lack of trying—she on her knees, he kneeling behind her holding her shoulders, giving all his strength and support, with Lysol douches, with orangewood spikes, with prayers *In nomine patris et filii et spiritus sancti Mary Mother of God it hurts . . . Lord forgive me, it huuuurts . . . Oh God, look at all this blood . . .* Still I came.

There, among the bloodied and dirty sheets, within the crowded and broken shell of a Ford trailer home, the windows cracked, along their edges the filth and grease of a hundred years, and the whole frame tilting to the left where the tires had sagged, finally believing that to protest decay and dilapidation was to protest the passage of time itself, and that was something that could not be done, I was born.

And screaming voices moving from broken trailers to tarpaper shacks to this battered and religiously dirty adobe and plank-wood house on Zachary Road. And later, sometimes having to carry my mother, barely able to make it to the small and shadowy bedroom, but I did carry her, cautiously, knowing that if I lost my balance then she would fall too, and in falling would shatter like a porcelain doll.

Such things as these are my life, my memories, my past. I walked these steps, one foot patiently following the other, and sometimes slowing to ask myself if perhaps there was another way I could have walked, but realizing that I would never know, and even if I did what point was there in asking such a question, for I would never be able to take it. I had made my choice.

The world went by me unnoticed. Gandhi was assassinated, Truman became president of the United States, the North Koreans invaded the south, and Fidel Castro Ruz graduated Havana University's Faculty of Law and went into practice in the city of my father's birth. My father talked of the life he could have led. He told me names like Sugar Ray Robinson and "The Bronx Bull" Jake La Motta, spoke of Randolph Turpin and Joe Louis, of Rocky Marciano and a dozen more that even now I cannot remember.

He told me also of his homeland, the Cuba that he had left behind. He told me stories of Castro, of his intention to campaign for parliament in the election of '52, how General Fulgencio Batista overthrew the government of President Carlos Prio Socarras in a coup d'état. Castro went to court and charged the dictator Batista with violation of the Cuban Constitution, but the court rejected Castro's petition, and then before the fall of 1953 Castro organized an armed attack with one hundred and sixty loyal followers against the Moncada Barracks in Oriente Province. This attack, alongside a second against the Bayamo Garrison, failed. Half of Castro's men were killed, and Castro and his brother Raul were taken prisoner.

I listened to these things, listened to them with half my mind elsewhere, for I did not care for my father and even less for the history of his country. I was an American, born and bred. I was no more Cuban than Eisenhower, or so I believed.

But violence was in my blood, it seemed, perhaps hereditary, carried in some airborne virus that my father exhaled, and though many years later I would see a pattern, a series of smaller, less significant events that preordained what was to come, it was a single defining event that ultimately dictated the course of my life.

The month was September of 1952. I was home alone. My father was drunk in some bar, wagering what little money he had on some senseless harm he intended to do to someone, my mother in the market collecting provisions, and the man came to our house. The salesman. He stood there on the porch, his yellow-checkered pants, his short-sleeved shirt, his tie hanging around his midriff, his hat in his hand.

"Hi there," he said as I drew out from within the shadows of the hallway. "My name is Carryl Chevron. Know that sounds like a lady's name, but it ain't, young man. Is your folks home?"

I shook my head, all of fifteen years old, standing there in shorts and shoes, my chest bare, my head wrapped in a damp towel. The spring had been a bitch, the summer worse, and even as it dragged its sorry ass toward fall the heat was still oppressive.

"I'm lookin' for some folks who's int'rested in learnin' here," Carryl Chevron said, and then he turned his head back toward the road as if he was looking for something. His eyes glinted, glimmered like the moon, and I wiped my hand beneath my nose and leaned against the door jamb in the shady porch of that beat-to-shit house.

"Lookin' for some folks that might be tempted toward wisdom, know what I mean?" Again the tilted head, the glimmering eyes, his face glowing something that I had only seen in my father's face when he sat in his chair, his bottle in his hand. Somewhere a dog started barking. I glanced toward the sound, but even as I turned I knew I was interested in what this man was saying.

I turned back. The man smiled.

"Is that real gold in your teeth?" I asked, as I peered into the shadow that filled the man's mouth.

Carryl Chevron—a man who'd spent much of his life telling folks that he didn't have a girl's name, who'd been bruised and burned emotionally for this one parental curse, yet who'd never had the foresight and logic to change it—laughed suddenly, nodded his head and reddened his face. "Why yes, sure it's real gold. You think someone such as me, someone who carries such wisdom across the world, would have anything but real gold and diamonds in his teeth?" And then he leaned forward, and with the hand that wasn't balancing him against the jamb, he tugged back his lip and showed me a gleaming gold canine, in its center a small glassy stud that seemed to shine with the same light that beamed from his eyes.

"Gold and diamonds," he managed to say with half his mouth moving. "Real gold and real diamonds and real wisdom right there in the back of my car. You wanna see them?"

"See them?" I asked. "See what?"

"My 'cyclopedias, my 'cyclopedias, young man. Books so filled with wisdom and learnin' you'll never need to look any other place than right between the leather covers, right there, packed like smart marching soldiers in the back of my vee-cule. You wanna see?"

"You're selling books?" I asked, and for a moment I could see my mother's face, the way she pleaded with me to read, to learn, to absorb everything that the world could offer.

The man stepped back, looked suddenly amazed, offended even. "Books!" he exclaimed. "Books? You call them volumes of genius books? Boy, where the hell did you get yourself growed up?"

"Zachary Road, Evangeline . . . why, where did you grow up?"

Chevron just smiled. "I'll bring one," he said. "I'll bring one right up here and show you."

He walked back to the dirt road, to his car, and from the rear seat he lifted out a box and balanced it on the edge of the fender. From the box he took a large black book that appeared to weigh many pounds, and even as I saw it, all of fifteen years old, I knew that that was the kind of place where folks got their smarts. I watched Carryl Chevron walk right up onto the porch carrying that book, and though I couldn't really read worth a damn, could only just manage to write my name, and even then some of the letters being backward, I just knew I had to have them. *Had* to. I believed it was what my mother would have wanted. She would be proud if I managed to obtain and own such things.

"Here we are," Chevron said. "Volume One. Aardvark through Aix-La-Chapelle to Canteloupe. In here we find Abacus, Acapulco, the Aegean Sea, Appalachian Mountains, Athlete's Foot, Milton Babbitt, the Bayeux Tapestry, the Congress of Berlin, Boccherini, Cadiz, Catherine De Medici, Cherokee Indians, China . . . everything, just everything right here that a young man such as yourself might ever wish to know." He leaned forward, held out the opened book, the smell of crisp paper, the tang of new leather, the print, the pictures, the wisdom of it all. "Everything," Chevron whispered, "and it could all be yours."

And me, standing there with my skinny arms and my bare chest, the damp towel wrapped around my head like a turban, reached out to touch the understanding that seemed to ooze from the pages. The book was snapped shut, withdrawn immediately as if on elastic.

"Buy . . . or be stupid for the rest of your life. Wisdom is priceless, young man, but here we have wisdom going for nothing, driven here from the heart of the world for you. For *you*, young man."

I heard what the man was saying, and in some way it could really have been my mother. The world was there to be understood, she had told me, and this man appeared to have brought that world to my doorstep.

Chevron held the book tightly between his hands and leaned toward me. "You know where your folks keep the money, huh? You know how mad they'd be if they learned I'd been out here giving such things away and they missed the opportunity of a lifetime. Where are they? Out working?"

"They're out," I said. "Won't be back for a little while, I reckon." I kept glancing at the book Chevron held in his hands. There was something magnetic about it, something that *drew* me toward it. "My dad has money, but I don't figure he'd be interested in some books though," I said, and already I was trying to work out what I was going to do, how I was going to make these books my own.

"Aah," Chevron sighed, as if he understood something that could only be understood by the two of us. "We know, don't we? Young man . . . we know what's here even if no one else has the brains to figure it out. This can be our little secret, our little secret, just you and me. Maybe you should just go get some money and then you and I can make a deal, okay? You and I can make a deal, I'll drive away, and then when your folks come back they'll be so grateful that you took advantage of the opportunity that I'm giving you here."

I hesitated for a moment, closed one eye and looked at Carryl Chevron, looked once more at the book he held in his hands. I could hear the sound of my mind working overtime; I didn't know what to do, but I *had* to do something.

"How many are there?" I asked.

"Nine," he said. "Nine books in all. All of them just like this one, right there in the box in the back of my car."

Again I hesitated, not because I was in doubt about what I wanted but because I was uncertain of what I was going to do to get it. "Okay," I said, "bring them in. I'll get you some money, but you're not to tell anyone, right? You don't tell anyone you came here and gave me the books."

Chevron smiled. A dream, he thought, another dream; the right place, the right time of day, another dumbfuck kid who knew where the money was kept and could be worked like a bellows.

Chevron walked back to the car and retrieved the box from the rear seat. He lumbered back, his cheap shirt chafing his shoulders and elbows, sweat running down his chest like a river. Times like this he didn't care, times like this it was worth it. The trip had been good. Here a week in this Godforsaken shithole of a territory, and this would be his fifth sale, one of them to an old guy who seemed too blind to read, and sure as hell hadn't managed to see the difference between a ten-dollar and a hundred-dollar bill, the rest to kids such as this one, kids old enough to know where the cash was stashed, young enough to be fascinated and think nothing of consequences. Work fast, dump this crap, drive on, lose yourself out there in another worn-out dustbowl of a town where no one knew who he was or would ever see him again. He'd be back in New Orleans within three or four days, out of the state inside a week: fat through a goose.

He reached the porch, stood there for a moment, and then shoved on the screen door, stepping through it before it banged back against the jamb. He stood in the cool darkness of the hallway, his nostrils twitching at the rank undercurrent of alcohol and piss and body odor. It never ceased to amaze him how people could actually live like this. He dropped the box of books on the floor, nothing more than a deadweight meal-ticket as far as he was concerned, and waited for the kid.

"Hey!" I called from out back, and already I had decided that there was no possibility I could *not* have those books. With those books, with everything inside them, I could be the boy my mother wanted me to be, and then—one day—I'd be a man like Fidel Castro Ruz, a man who made a difference. "Money's here . . . come get it."

Chevron stepped through the hallway into a small corridor that led to the back of the house. *The kitchen*, he thought. *Always the kitchen, inside a kettle, in a sock inside a pan buried at the bottom of a cupboard. Jesus, I'd make a helluva thief. These people are so goddamned predictable.*

Into the kitchen indeed, and there he found me shuffling through a drawer.

"Come help me," I said. "Hey, maybe you wanna beer or something?"

"Well, that's mighty fine of you offerin' there, young man, but I really must be on my way, have a lot of folks to see before I leave this here town of yours."

Chevron could hear the shit oozing from his own mouth, talking like some hick farmhand laborer, and tonight he'd be holed up in some dusty highway roadhouse, some brassy act who could suck the chrome off of a trailer hitch doing her thing in his lap, in his hand a bottle of something cool and sweet, laughing to himself about this here routine he'd pulled so many times it'd gotten to be corny.

He crossed the room and stood a foot or so behind me and waited for the money to show its pretty face.

"Suit yourself," I said. "Anyways, how much d'you want? You want all of this?"

"That'd be fine," Chevron said. "You just find all you got in there, just keep it comin' and we'll make out just fine an' dandy."

"Think I got all of it here," I said.

I turned then, and Chevron stood there, his hand out ahead of him, his eyes glinting greedily, and the strength of my grip as I held his wrist surprised him, and the power that pulled him suddenly forward into a handful of kitchen knives, tugged him all the way forward until his cheap cotton-covered belly met the handles of those blades, seemed to surprise him more than the pain they delivered.

The shirt perforated effortlessly, as did the man's gut, and from his midriff, through his pinioned tie, out over his belt and down the front of his pants, came a river of blood more suited to the slaughter of a pig.

And then the knives were twisting, and through his gaping gold and diamond-decorated mouth came a desperate sound, a sound like rattling, as if his lungs were attempting escape through the tortured confines of his throat, lodging somewhere against his trachea, against the palate and the roof of his mouth. Blood came with that sound, I could smell its earthy bitterness, and when his bulging eyes cast downward he saw my face, the face of a child, white and deathly pale, and I was leaning up toward him, smiling, twisting away out of his line of vision as his eyes rolled up to their whites in the back of his head.

He staggered back against the edge of the table. The table rocked, but didn't give, and when I released his wrist he just continued to stand there, off-balance, everything gone wild inside his head, colors and sounds and the bursting sensation in his lower gut all rolled up tight into something indefinable. I'm sure he felt his bladder give, felt the warm issuance tracing a narrow and rapid line down the inside of his leg, and then he toppled forward onto his knees, his face now beneath mine, the knives exiting his flesh like the slow grinding teeth of some huge mechanical cog, spitting sideways across the dirty linoleum as his life bled out before him. Inside he slumped, his innards twisted up and glued together, his hands scratching frantically on the greasy floor . . . and I stepped away, picked up one of the knives from the floor, and then took a handful of hair at the back of Chevron's head, tugged hard until I could feel the muscles straining in his neck, and then with one movement, a movement so deft it seemed natural, I sliced his throat from ear to ear.

This was my first kill. My first real human being, and to feel that sudden warmth bursting between my fingers, across my wrist, my forearm, to hear the spattering of life as it showered from mortality into dust was something unreal, something profound, disturbing.

Something almost perfect.

I was my father perhaps. For some brief moment I was my father, and afterwards I stood there and looked at what had happened. I looked at this strange man lying on the floor of the kitchen, and then I knelt down beside him. I reached out my hand and touched the skin of his face—his cheek, his lips, his eyelids, his nose. I felt the moisture of sweat on his brow, the coarseness of his hair, the rough unshaven folds of skin above the wound in his neck.

There was a smell, something earthy, like rust and damp corn, like . . . like someone had died. That was the smell. Unique. Unmistakable. Once you inhaled that smell there was nothing else it could be. I believed, perhaps, that this would be a defining moment, that this would be the point where I became the man my mother wished me to be, where I would take these books and read and study and learn all there was to learn about this world, and with that knowledge I would step forward with confidence, and become something. Become some*one*.

I was not aware of how much the killing of the salesman would change me. During those seconds that I kneeled beside his slowly cooling body, I imagined that all I had done was engineer a way to obtain something that I would have otherwise been deprived of. That was how I rationalized and justified my action. But there was more, much more, and it would only be later that I understood the insidious shadow such an action would cast across my entire life. Wanting to please my mother I had become my father. Only for a moment, perhaps, but nevertheless I had become him. Desiring of the one true thing in my life, I had become the one thing I could never have hoped to understand. I felt panic, apprehension, confusion, a sense of imbalance, and yet at the same time I believed that I had accomplished something of which my mother would have been proud. My father killed people for no reason at all. I had killed someone for a good reason, a very good reason, and with the knowledge that was now going to be mine I would become the person she wished me to be.

Perhaps. Perhaps not. I was a child then, possessing a child's eyes and a child's mind. I had done something I did not fully understand, but *I* had done it, and thus *I* was someone.

I washed up first, and then I carried the books two at a time from the box on the floor to my small bedroom. I stacked them on a blanket, folded the blanket over them, and then pushed them all the way to the wall beneath my cot.

I returned to the kitchen, stood there for a moment with a sense of mild frustration. How could something so brief be so damned messy?

I removed all the money from Carryl Chevron's jacket, the bills thankfully unsoiled with his blood. I took cloths from the cupboard beneath the sink, wet them beneath the faucet, and then started working along the linoleum floor from the door toward the prostrate body. When I had reached the body from all sides and cleaned up the blood I returned to my room. I took a sheet from the bed, carried it back to the kitchen and spread it out on the floor. I rolled Chevron sideways until he lay awkwardly in the middle, and then I folded the edges over his legs and arms, over his torso and his dumb, senseless face. I tied the sheet at each end, knotted it well, and then dragged the body out of the kitchen and along the hall toward the front door. The man was heavy, he moved inch by incredible inch, and I heaved and gagged with the exertion. I convinced myself that it had been worth it, worth every struggling, breathless, choking moment it took to haul the carcass to the inner porch. I acted swiftly, mechanically almost, and with an almost complete absence of emotion. The thing was done. It could not be undone. I did not see the point of being any more afraid or confused.

I took Chevron's keys and walked out to his car. I opened it, released the handbrake, started the engine, and then reversed the vehicle back toward the front of the house. From there it was a mere three or four steps to where the body lay inside the front door. The man's weight was remarkable to me, but once I had lifted the upper half of his body over the lip of the trunk the impetus folded him in all the way.

I drove east no more than a mile or so, parked the car at the edge of a deserted and narrow road that ran out toward the swamplands beyond Lake Borgne and the canal intersections, family territory I was familiar with. For a while I rested. The heat pressed in at me from all sides. I even turned on the radio and listened to some Creole music from a station out of Chalmette District. It came to me after about half an hour of no thought. I knew that that was the best way—to think nothing at all, just to plant the idea right there in the middle of my mind and let it grow of its own accord. It took seed, it grew, it blossomed like wisteria in the vague breathless humidity. I backed the car up and let it roll in amongst the hickorys and water oaks. A hundred yards, the tires already shredding up the loose fermented undergrowth, spitting it out in healthy brown gobs like chewing tobacco from beneath the chassis, and then I killed the engine. From the back seat I took a jack, and with something akin to Herculean effort I hitched the rear end of the car a good foot high. With the trunk now close to chest height I had some difficulty rolling out Chevron's body, but I managed it, sweating furiously, my fingers stuck together with the man's blood, my hair stuck to my face like paint. I let the body drop, removed the sheet, and then with the side of my foot I shoved the body back beneath the rear wheels, the head directly under the right, the waist and upper legs beneath the left. I stepped back, kicked the jack, and heard the crunching demolition of bone and feature as the heavy rubber tires ground their way back to earth through Carryl Chevron's mortal frame. I cleaned my hands off on the sheet, threw it into the trunk, and once inside the car I started the engine and rolled the car back and forth over the body a few times for good measure. I wound up the windows, locked the door, returned to where Chevron's battered body lay half-buried in the loose earth inside the boundary of the trees. I took each hand in turn, and using the jack lever I smashed Chevron's fingers against a rock so no fingerprint identification would ever be possible. I did the same with his jaw and lower face. The jack, the rock, the sheet, even the shirt I was wearing— I took all of them and walked until the waterlogged earth started to suck at my feet. I pushed these things beneath the surface and felt the ground hungrily devour them. I watched them disappear, the mud closing over them like slow-motion oil, and then I turned and ran back toward the road. Ran like a kid to a birthday party.

I stopped beside the unidentifiable body of Carryl Chevron, a forty-seven-year-old confidence trickster, born in Anamosa, flunked out of high school, dishonorably discharged from the army for theft, survivor of two wives, three ulcers, a suspected coronary condition that turned out to be a gargantuan case of heartburn, and I smiled.

It had been different—the killing, the disposing of the body, the small moments of chilling panic, the cleverness, the deceit, the perfection of it all. I kicked the battered head once more, watched an angry arc of gray-scarlet matter jet from the toe of my shoe, and then I walked back to the car. There was a certain magic to it all, a certain power, its beauty and simplicity matched only by the stars I could see from the narrow window of my room during clear-skied winter nights.

That was my first and original sin; a sin I committed in an effort to become something of which my mother would approve, and in doing so I had perhaps allowed my father to infect and inhabit my soul.

Carryl Chevron was never found, never reported missing, perhaps— truth be known—never even missed. Maybe some brassy act in high heels with too much rouge and too little class was still waiting for him in a dusty roadhouse someplace down the stateline. And maybe some of the kids who bought his books were still sore from their beatings.

Who the hell knew, and who the hell cared?

The car I drove a mile further into the swamplands, and then I watched as it slid effortlessly, silently, gracefully into the bayou, never to surface.

I had my books, and I learned to read them, and I read as if my life depended on it. Hard-earned volumes of wisdom where I found the heart, its workings, the subclavian and vena cava, where I found da Vinci, Einstein, Michaelangelo, Dillinger, Capone: the many geniuses the world had offered and then greedily taken away. They were my one true possession, all my own, worshipped and tended with care, for they had cost me dearly, both me and the man who had brought them. And my father, too drunk or too bruised to see what was there in front of him most of the time, and my mother, cowed and quiet in his presence, never thought to ask or inquire how I had come by such things. I kept them safe, there beneath my bed, and I walked through every word on every page and then started over again.

Those nights, cool and loose, the sky clear, peppered with stars and constellations I could identify and name, the heat somehow eased by the breeze that came north from the river, feeling alive, anxious . . .

Feeling there was so much I wanted—*needed*—to know.

Later, many years later, when time had unfolded and I had learned so much more of the world beyond my home, I would think these things:

Perhaps if I had been someone, if I had *really* been someone, then these events would not have happened.

Perhaps if I had fought in Vietnam and come home a hero, my breast painted with ribbons, the girls from Montalvo's Diner crowding my arms as if they could all be enveloped in one fell swoop. And bearing a scar across the cheek, above the eye maybe—visible, but not so visible as to be ugly.

Perhaps if I had walked out through the mud and blood and shit of Da Nang or Quang Ngai or Qui Nhon, shouldering a rucksack heavy with C-Rations, Kool-Aid, salt tablets, ammunition, lucky mascots, a flak jacket rolled tightly between my burden and my spine. Things you could close your eyes and still feel the weight of.

Perhaps if I had been there to carry some wounded comrade through the thigh-deep water of a raining napalm nightmare, the vegetation crumpling around me, falling, dissolving, staggering breathless and burned, my hair scorched to my scalp, my arms bloody with the red sweat of my load.

Perhaps if I had walked a hundred miles to the back-lines, the rear, where the medic tents stood white and clean and filled with the smell of anaesthetic and morphine, where fresh-faced first tour medical students turned their eyes away from the carnage, where I had to stand and bind and weave and amputate and stem the heavy flow of blood from the gutted stomach, the jagged wound, the missing eye, the greenstick fracture leaping from the surface of the skin like some winter-silhouetted teeter-totter . . .

Perhaps then, only then, could I have possessed something of which to speak.

And thus would not have felt empty.

It was I—who wished folks would called me Six or Lineman or Doc, or some other well-earned nickname, a name that people would hear and ask of its origin, and in being told they would understand what a deep and perfect human being I was, flawed, yet brave and bold, and experienced, and rich in something few possessed—it was I who was in some way nothing, and yet so afraid of being nothing I imagined that everything I wanted could be taken from others.

And so I did.

I remembered times I would sit back in the corner of Evangeline's only diner, Montalvo's, popping peanut M&Ms, snapping them back against the roof of my mouth and feeling them *thunk* against my teeth, and grinding up their bitty sweetness, and finding the candy shrapnel tucked down inside my gums . . . and it was late evening, and soon Montalvo's would close, the warm-faced Creole-Irish halfbreed cook whose name I could never recall would turn me out into the depth of the night, wishing me well, laughing in that broken Americanized twang that sounded like no accent I had ever heard, or would ever hear again. He rolled, that man did, rolled across the greasy linoleum floor, rubbing his hands through a greasy towel, wiping the back of his greasy hand across the lower half of his greasy face, and he smelled of fried onions and fried eggs, of fried fries and tobacco. Like a roadhouse on fire. A unique smell that no human being should ever have to carry, but he did, and he carried it effortlessly, the smell a part of him in everything he said and did and thought.

But for the time being I was safe, there at the back of the diner, watching the three or four regular kids dance to the jukebox, the two girls, their wide mouths popping the spearmint tang of gum, their rah-rah skirts over firm brown thighs, their flats and ponytails and rubber bands and the men's wristwatches they wore, and me wondering what it would be like to fuck one of them, wondering what it would be like to dissolve my tongue in that spearmint tang, or maybe to fuck two of them together, to lose my hands beneath those spinning skirts, to touch the very heart of whatever they believed their lives really were.

For now, they were safe.

I believed that if I had read novels I could have talked, but I did not read novels, merely facts from encyclopedias.

To talk of such things would have made it all too obvious that I had no life at all.

And so I killed things.

What else could a poor boy do?

I watched the tight-thighed girls, their whirling skirts, the way they glanced at me arrogantly, the way they dared each other to *speak to the weird kid in the corner with the M&Ms* when they first started coming here an age ago. They took the dare, one or two of them, and I was shy and pleasant, and I blushed, and they giggled, but now they have grown some and they don't bother with dares, they just think I'm weird, and they dance all the more with their thighs and their skirts and their peppermint tang.

I hated them for their smooth brown skin. I wondered what their sweat would taste like straight from the skin. Beads like condensation down the glass walls of chilled bottles. Like rain against glass.

I sat alone, there in Montalvo's Diner, and perhaps the only person who did not think I was weird was the crazy halfbreed cook with the forgotten name who carried a smell that should not have had to be carried by any human being.

He did not worry that I had nothing to say, for I bought my Cokes, popped my M&Ms, sat and looked and breathed and existed.

I did not speak.

I would think to speak, but all I could come up with was "Well-uh-I-kinda-killed-some-things-one-time . . . ," but seeing as how that wasn't really the polite kind of talk folks were looking for, I did not say it.

And, as such, had nothing to say.

Perhaps if I had been caught . . .

Perhaps then, and only then, would I have had something of which to speak.

Sometimes I would challenge myself, dare myself to walk up to one of those girls, those tight-skinned teenage tornadoes, and ask their name, and say "Hi, I'm Bill" or "Doc" or "Lineman" or "Swamper," and feel them blush a little, and smile, and say "I'm Carol or Janie or Holly-Beth," and ask me how I came to be called something such as that. I would shrug noncommittally, as if it didn't really matter, and tell them it was the war, *back a long time, honey, a long time ago that you wouldn't want to be hearing about.* And we would dance then, and she would give me gum, play some records I liked maybe, and then later as I walked her home, she would ask me again how I came by my name, and I would tell her, in small, measured emotional phrases, and through the spaces between my words she would feel the depth, the strength, the power of self-control needed for someone to return from such a place and still be able to smile, to laugh, to say "Hi" and dance in Montalvo's Diner with someone such as herself.

She would fall in love, and I would feel the pressure of her hand in mine, the way her shoulder rubbed the side of my chest as she leaned to stroke my cheek, to kiss my face, to ask me if maybe, somehow, possibly I might consider seeing her again . . .

And I would have said, "Sure honey, sure thing," and I would have felt her heart leap.

Or maybe not. Maybe I would hold a Coke bottle in my hand, and as they pulled me close I would break the base of the bottle against the wall, and then turn to face Bobby-Sue or Marquita or Sherise or Kimberley, and say, "Here, a little of something cool and hard for the pleasure of your company . . . ," and grind the glass teeth deep into the solar plexus, through the vagus nerves, and feel them tighten and twitch, dancing like a headless chicken through the scrubbed backlot behind a busted trailer, feeling them close up against the broken shards like the hands of hungry, shit-faced kids, the blood pumping, sweating out through the aperture, glowing over my hands, warming them, filling the pores, finding my prints like narrow channels and filling them . . .

And then lean them against the wall, fuck them in the ass, comb my hair and go home.

Perhaps then, and only then, would there be something of which I could speak.

Before Carryl Chevron I had killed a dog. Before that I had set a cat in a pen with three chickens and watched them run their little hearts out. Before that I killed some other things, but now I cannot remember what they were.

Time rolled onwards like some unspoken darkness, and within it there were sounds and motions that even now I cannot bring myself to recall.

Eisenhower was inaugurated as president.

Julius and Ethel Rosenberg went to the electric chair in Sing Sing.

Fidel Castro Ruz was jailed after a failed coup.

Rocky Marciano retained his world heavyweight title when he KO'd Jersey Joe Walcott. My father said he could have done the same. My father was a drunk. A liar. A failure of a man.

I was sixteen years old, and New Orleans was in my blood.

St. James the Greater, Ougou Feray, the African spirit of war and iron. The driving rhythm of drums and chants and people pouring red wine, rice and beans, meat, rum and soft drinks into a pond, and then those same people writhing in the mud and sharing their special powers by touching bystanders. Serpent and cross in the same cemetery on All Saints' Day, and summoning the most powerful of all spirits, loa-Damballah-wédo, the spirited festival of Vyéj Mirak, the Virgin of Miracles, and her voodoo counterpart Ezili, the goddess of love. Washing a bull, applying perfume, dressing it in a cape, and then slaughtering it, its blood collected in a gourd and passed to those possessed by the loa. They drank to feed the spirit. Sacrificing white pigeons to the Petro loa, a spirit that demanded birds and hogs, goats and bulls, sometimes bodies from tombs. All Souls' Day, Baron Samedi, loa of the dead.

I was sixteen years old. I was almost a man, but still I couldn't stand and take the beatings my father delivered. Not only to me, but to my mother—she of the graceful, artless, silent hope.

It was the end of 1953.

I think back and images merge and blend together, faces become the same, voices carry a similar tone and timbre, and I find it difficult to place events in their correct chronological sequence. I think of Cuba, my father's homeland, the things that happened there, and then realize that those things came later, much later. My own past challenges me with forgetfulness, and this scares me, for to forget my past is to forget who I am, how I became such a person, and to forget such things challenges the very reason for living.

Perhaps the saddest thing about my own death will be my life.

Some of us live to remember; some of us live to forget; some of us, even now, make ourselves believe that there is some greater purpose worth working for. Let me tell you, there isn't. It isn't complicated, it is almost too simple to be believed. Like faith. Faith in what? Faith in God? Greatest thing God ever did was fool the world into thinking that He existed. Look into a man's eyes as he dies and you'll see that there's nothing there. Just blackness reflecting your own face. It's that simple.

I will tell you now about the death of my mother. Though it would not come for another four years I will tell you of it now.

Through 1954, through the eras of McCarthy, the Viet Minh occupation of Hanoi and the very inception of the Vietnam War, through the release of Castro and his brother Raul on General Amnesty in May of 1955, through all these things.

Beyond Castro's departure to Mexico where he organized his exiles into the 26 July Revolutionary Movement, how he led eighty-two men to the north coast of Oriente Province, where they landed at Playa Las Coloradas in December of '56, how all but twelve survived who retreated to the Sierra Maestra mountains and waged a continuous guerrilla war against the Batista government, how those twelve became eight hundred and scored victory after victory against the dictator in the hot madness of revolution and spilled blood that was as much a part of history as anything that might have happened in Europe . . .

Until finally Batista was defeated and fled to the Dominican Republic on New Year's Day 1959, and we were there—my father and I—there in Havana when the victorious Castro entered the city, and the people believed, the people *really* believed that things would be different now.

And all I could think of was how my mother should have been with us, but by then she was dead, and how we had fled America, land of my birth, and made our way here to the country of my father's birth.

So I will tell you about that night—a Friday night, 19 December 1958—and you can ask yourself if what happened to my father could really be called anything but justice.

When the men came down to drag the body from the yard I remember thinking something.

What will happen to his wife? What will happen to his children?

For I knew all of these men had wives and children, just like my own father. Just like the Havana Hurricane.

Less than a week to Christmas, and the dead man's wife and children would be home even then, waiting for him to return. But that night he would not come stumbling through the door, red-faced, his fists bloody, his vest drenched with sweat. That night he would be dragged from a yard by three men, his body hefted with no more grace or respect than if it had been a side of beef, and bound tightly within a length of torn sacking, and thrown into the back of a flatbed truck. And men with callused hands and callous faces, men with no more soul than a stone, no more mercy or compunction than a lizard bathing itself on a sun-bleached rock, would drive that truck away, and for ten dollars, maybe less, they would strip the body and burn the clothes, cut the flesh and let it bleed some, and then sink it into the bayou where alligators would swiftly dissemble everything that could be identified.

And my father, the Hurricane, staggering home, his own vest

spattered with a dead man's blood, and roaring drunk in the doorway, and challenging the world to defy him, to tell him he was not the master of his own house, and my mother scared, pleading with him not to hold her so roughly, not to be so angry, so violent, so insatiable . . .

And me, crouching there behind the doorway of my own room, tears in my eyes as I heard her scream, and listening as she rallied all the prayers she could muster, and hearing her voice and knowing that such sounds would only incense him further, and feeling that somewhere in amongst all this madness there must be something that made sense.

But I didn't find it—not then, not even now.

And then the silence.

Silence that seemed to bleed out from beneath the doorway of their room, and walk its soundless footsteps down toward me, and feeling with it the shadow of cold that could only be translated one way.

And the silence seemed to last for something close to an eternity, perhaps longer, and knowing that something was wrong.

Dead awful wrong.

And then the wailing scream of my father as he burst from the door of their room, and how he staggered down the corridor as if something had taken ahold of his soul and twisted it by its nerves into torment.

The vacancy of his eyes, the whiteness of his drawn, sweat-varnished skin, the way his hands gripped and relaxed, gripped and relaxed. Killer's fists. And waiting for him to open my door, to look down at me, and recognizing something in his eyes that I had seen only an hour before as he stood over the beaten body of a slain man, and seeing something else, something far worse, something akin to guilt and blame and regret and shame, and horror and despair and madness, molded into one unholy indescribable emotion that said everything that could ever need saying without a single word.

I rose to my feet and pushed past him.

I ran down the corridor and heaved through the door of my mother's room.

I saw her naked, more naked than I had seen her since my birth, and the blackened hollowness of her eyes, the way her head was twisted back upon itself at the most unnatural, awkward angle, and knowing . . .

Knowing that he had killed her.

Something rose inside me. Alongside the hatred and panic, alongside the revulsion and hysteria, something came that was close to a base impulse for survival. Something that told me that no matter what had happened here, no matter how this thing had come about, I had to escape. Murder had been committed, murder of my mother by my own father's violent hand, and irrespective of my feeling toward him in that moment I was certain that to stay would have been the end of my life as I knew it.

Perhaps, in some dark way, it was everything I had been waiting for; something that was sufficiently powerful to drive me away.

I stepped forward.

I looked down at her.

Even as I stared at her cold and lifeless face I could hear her voice.

Could hear the songs she sang to me as a baby.

I turned back toward my father, his back toward me, his body rigid and yet shaking uncontrollably, his fists clenched, every muscle inside of him taut and stretched and painful, and I knew that I had to leave. Had to leave and take him with me.

I ran from the house. The street was deserted. I ran back without any comprehension of why I had left.

I shouted something at him and he looked at me with the eyes of an old man. A weak and defeated man. I hurried to my room and gathered some clothes, stuffed them into a hessian sack; from the kitchen I took what few provisions remained, wrapped them in a cloth and buried those in the sack also, and then I took a shirt and forced my father's arms through the sleeves, buttoned it to the neck, and then walked him out, walked him as if I was marching with two bodies, and I took him down to the side of the road and left him standing there, gaunt and speechless.

I returned to the house, and after standing over the dead form of my mother for a minute further, after kneeling and touching her face, after leaning close and whispering to her that I loved her, I backed up and returned to the kitchen. I took a kerosene lamp and emptied its contents in a wide arc across the floor and the table, trailed it out through the doorway and down the hall, and with the last inch and a half of fuel I doused my mother's body. I backed up, I closed my eyes, and then took a box of matches from my pocket and lit one. I stood there for a moment, the smell of sulphur and kerosene and death in my nostrils, and then I dropped the match and ran.

We had run a quarter of a mile before I saw the flames make their way to the sky.

We kept on running, and ever present was the urge to run back, to douse the flames and drag her charred body from the ruins, to tell the world what had happened, and ask a God I didn't believe in for forgiveness and sanctuary. But I did not stop, nor did my father beside me, and in some strange way I believed that that was the closest I had ever been to him, the closest I would ever come.

It was December of 1958, a week before Christmas, and we headed east toward the Mississippi state line, and when we reached it we headed still east toward Alabama, knowing full well that to stop was to see our destiny slip from our hands.

Seventeen days we walked, stopping only to lie at the edge of some field and snatch a broken handful of hours' rest, to share the few mouthfuls of food that remained, to rise and ache through yet another day of passage.

Into Florida: Pensacola, Cape San Bias, Apalachee Bay; into Florida, where you could see the island of Cuba, the Keys, the Straits and the lights of Havana from the tip of Cape Sable. And knowing that we were merely a handful of miles from my father's homeland.

We hid for three days straight. My father said nothing. Each day I would creep away at night and walk down to the beaches. I talked with people who spoke in broken-up Spanish, people who told me they could not help me time and time again, until finally, on the third night, I found a fisherman who would take us.

I will not tell you how I traded for our passage, but I closed my eyes and I paid the price, and I still believe that I carry the scars of my own fingernails in the flesh of my palms.

But we were away, the wind in our hair, the sea air like some cleansing absolution for the past, and I watched my father as he clung to the edge of the small craft, his eyes wide, his face haunted, his spirit broken.

That was my mother.

Her life and her death.

I was twenty-one years old, and in some way I believed my own life had come to an end. A chapter had closed with a sense of finality, and if ever I believed I could recover from what had happened, if ever I believed that there was some way back from the events of my childhood, from not only the murder that I had now committed, but also the murder I had witnessed, then I was mistaken.

My soul was lost; my destiny was closed and sealed and irreversibly decided; the world and all its madness had challenged me and I had succumbed.

If ever there was a Devil, I had accepted him as my compadre, my blood brother.

I had at first followed in my father's footsteps, and then rescued him from justice for the killing of my mother.

In my mind was a darkness, and through my eyes I saw that same darkness everywhere I looked.

What was once within now became all that was without.

We landed at Cardenas. I brought with me a shadow that I carry to this day.

TEN

OF ALL THE things he had learned, Ray Hartmann knew one thing for certain: that it was not possible to apply reason to an unreasonable action.

Perhaps in some dark and shadowed corner of his mind he could find some measure of understanding for these things that had been done—the killing of Perez's mother, the burning of the body, the escape to Cardenas in Cuba, even the death of the salesman—but he could not begin to understand the man who had done them. Hartmann did not believe evil was hereditary, but just as he had studied before, just as he had learned in books by Stone and Deluca, the O'Haras and Geberth, he believed there were indeed *situational dynamics*. This was the territory of criminal profiling, and here he was, lost and without anchor, hurled headlong into something that he could never believe real.

"You are somewhat introspective, Mr. Hartmann," Perez said quietly, and leaning forward he took a cigarette from the packet on the table and lit it.

"Introspective?" Hartmann echoed.

Perez smiled. He drew on his cigarette and then issued two fine streams of smoke from his nostrils.

Like a dragon, Hartmann thought. *Soulless.*

Perez shook his head. "You find such things difficult to comprehend?"

"Yes, perhaps," Hartmann replied. "I have read thousands of pages, seen hundreds and hundreds of pictures of such things, the things men can do, but I don't know that I am any the wiser as to motive and rationale."

"Survival," Perez stated matter-of-factly. "It always comes down to nothing more fundamental than survival."

Hartmann shook his head. "That's something I can't agree with."

"I see," Perez replied.

Hartmann leaned forward. "You truly believe that all the things that have been done have been in the name of survival?"

"I do."

"How could survival ever justify murder?"

"That is easy, Mr. Hartmann, because more often than not it is simply a matter of yourself or them. Faced with such a situation there are few that would be willing to sacrifice their own lives."

Hartmann looked at Perez, looked right at him, and believed that this man was more animal than human being. "But what about paid killers . . . what about people who murder complete strangers simply for money?"

"Or for knowledge?" Perez asked, perhaps making reference to the death of Carryl Chevron.

"Or for knowledge, yes."

"Knowledge is survival. Money is survival. The truth is that motive can never be truly appreciated by another. Motive is a personal thing, perhaps as personal and individual as the killer himself. He kills for some reason understood only by himself, and that reason can always be explained by the individual's own perception of what will enable him to survive in the best manner at the time. Later, perhaps, in hindsight, a different viewpoint will lend itself to the situation and the perpetrator may believe that he has done wrong, but in the moment of the killing I can guarantee that it was adjudicated to be the most contributive to his own survival, or the survival of that which owned his loyalty."

Hartmann was shaking his head. He could not stretch his mind wide enough to encompass what Perez was saying. Truth be known he was horrified by the man, and there was nothing he wished for more than to leave the room and never return.

He looked up, half-expecting Perez to continue, but Perez had finished talking. Hartmann was aware of the fact that every word the man had spoken was being recorded behind closed doors. Lester Kubis would be there, headphones clamped to his head, and over his shoulder would be Stanley Schaeffer and Bill Woodroffe, their brows sweating, listening to every word Perez uttered in the vain hope that it would give them some indication of where they might find Catherine Ducane.

But Perez had given them nothing but himself, and all of himself. Hartmann did not doubt that what Perez was telling him was the truth, and already he believed there was no easy way to understand the man's motivation for his actions. How this man was connected to Charles Ducane Hartmann could only guess, but the corridors of power were lined with victims of men such as Ernesto Perez. Time would tell, of course it would, but Hartmann was aware that he had little time at all. A week from then, noon of Saturday 6 September, he was supposed to meet his wife and daughter. This event would be swept aside as irrelevant compared to what he was dealing with now. His own personal affairs were of no concern to either Schaeffer or Woodroffe or, least of all, to Attorney General Richard Seidler, FBI Director Bob Dohring and Governor Charles Ducane. Their sole concern, understandably, was the whereabouts and welfare of Catherine Ducane.

Later, lying on his bed at the Marriott Hotel, Hartmann would close his eyes and recall the man he had faced for the better part of two hours. Ernesto Perez, an old man who had begun his life confronting the destructive nature of his own father and the violence he had wreaked through every aspect of his childhood. Perez was now sequestered on the top floor of the Royal Sonesta Hotel, the remainder of the lower four floors having been cleared of guests by the FBI. The Sonesta now housed in excess of fifty Bureau operatives, security could not have been tighter for the president himself, and in the penthouse suite Perez himself was guarded by twelve armed men. He had asked for a music system, CDs of Schubert, Shostakovich, Ravel, Louis Prima and Frank Sinatra, also for clean shirts and nightwear; and for his supper he'd requested fresh marlin, Viennese potatoes, a green salad and a bottle of Cabernet Sauvignon. These things had been arranged, because for the brief while that he was the guest of the FBI as opposed to the Federal Penitentiary system, Ernesto Cabrera Perez would be given every accommodation and granted every wish. And then the girl would be found—dead or alive—and the party would be over. Hartmann felt certain Perez was aware of this fact, and thus he was sure he would take every advantage he could. The man, whoever he was, was evidently wise in the ways of the world, and that included the FBI and what they could provide.

Schaeffer and Woodroffe met with Hartmann after Perez had been escorted away.

"What d'you think?" Schaeffer asked him.

"About what?"

Schaeffer rolled his eyes and looked discouragingly at Woodroffe.

"About the New York Knicks' chances this fucking season, Hartmann . . . what the fuck do you think I'm talking about?"

"Perez or the girl?"

"Okay, Perez," he said. "First Perez."

Hartmann said nothing for a time. "I think he knows exactly what he's doing. I think he's planned this down to the last detail. I think day by day he will tell us only so much as he wants us to know, that he will give us little bits and pieces of this and make us work very hard to see the whole picture. His motives? I have no idea. Perhaps that won't come until the very last piece falls into place. Right now he has the upper hand. He has something we very much want, and he knows we will cater to him in every way we can in order to find that out."

Woodroffe was nodding in the affirmative. "That's my take on it," he said. "I've got people working on him already. We have his prints. We know what he looks like. They will trawl through every file and document we've got. They'll go through CODIS, to VICAP Criminal Profiling at Quantico. Transcripts of what he tells us will be passed to the best people we have and if there's anything to discover they'll find it."

Hartmann was not so sure there would be anything to find. He believed that Perez knew exactly what he was saying and how he was going to keep them running until the very last moment. For a second he even considered the possibility that the girl was already dead.

"So motivation we don't know, and are not likely to know until he tells us," Schaeffer said. "Until we have some kind of a handle on that there is nothing we can do but follow exact protocol. We have sufficient resources to follow any lead we might find, realistic or otherwise. If anything comes up from other areas we'll go with it, but right now our main task is to keep this man talking, keep him on the subject as best we can—"

Hartmann smiled drily. "I believe he intends to tell us his entire life story. This is his unwritten autobiography, the opportunity of a lifetime to tell us everything that he's done, everywhere he's been, and everything he knows about everyone else. It would surprise me if we didn't encounter Governor Charles Ducane at some point along the line."

There was silence for a moment from both Woodroffe and Schaeffer, and then Woodroffe leaned forward, rested his hands on the table and assumed a very serious expression.

"I do not need to tell you that everything you hear both inside and outside this office is governed by the jurisdiction of the FBI. Not a word, not a single word will go out of here, you understand?"

Hartmann raised his hand. "I'm not in kindergarten, Agent Woodroffe—"

Woodroffe smiled. "I am well aware of that fact, Mr. Hartmann, but I am also aware that you have had your own troubles in the past, a small area of difficulty regarding the way you have handled your own personal affairs, and it is not unknown to us that you have been registered with Alcoholics Anonymous, and have run into some significant difficulty with your wife and daughter as a result."

Hartmann was incensed. He opened his mouth to speak but Woodroffe raised his hand.

"It is of no matter to us," he said. "We understand that you have performed in an exemplary fashion for a considerable time in your job, and we also understand that you are here at the specific request of Perez and there is nothing we can do about that. All we are saying is that this is a matter of the highest national priority right now, and we need everyone on the same side and running after the same ball."

Hartmann sighed inside. He did not wish to be there, having this conversation with these people. His native human instinct cared about Catherine Ducane as a human being and he did feel a certain sense of responsibility and duty to see this through. He would do what he had been asked to do, he would get it done as quickly as was possible, for every day that elapsed brought him a day closer to the possible resolution of the *difficulty with his wife and daughter* that Woodroffe had alluded to.

This was not a game, this was real life—rough edges, sharp corners and all. Hartmann had no mind to run up against these people, or to have them dictate his life and time any more than they absolutely had to.

"You won't have any difficulty with me," Hartmann said, willing himself not to lunge across the table and punch Woodroffe. "I am here to do this, and when it's done I will disappear and you will never hear from me again. Now, if you don't mind, I'm tired and I would like to go back to my hotel, because I imagine that we will all be gathered here once again tomorrow morning for the second chapter in this most fascinating story."

"Less of the attitude," Schaeffer said.

Hartmann nodded. He did not tell them *Fuck you and the horse you rode in on.* He refrained from asking them *Who the fuck do you people think you are?* He bit his tongue, held his temper, and rose slowly from his chair. There was a quiet and unspoken sense of pride in knowing that he would come through this and never have to speak to these people again.

And so he left—walked from the New Orleans FBI Field Office on Arsenault Street to the Marriott Hotel. Here there were no armed Bureau agents to watch over him. Here there was nothing more than a simple functional hotel room, a comfortable bed, a TV he could watch with the sound turned off as the day closed down around him.

He thought of Carol and Jess and Saturday 6 September. He thought of Ernesto Cabrera Perez and how a man like that would see this world. Not through the same eyes, and not with the same emotions. However polite and cultured and erudite the man might have seemed, he was as crazy as the rest of the sick bastards that seemed to have populated Hartmann's life. Such was the life he had chosen, and such was the life he lived.

His sleeping hours were crowded with images, angular and disturbed. He imagined that it was Jess who had been kidnapped by this man, that Carol had been the one found in the trunk of the Mercury Turnpike Cruiser on Gravier Street only a week before. He imagined all manner of things, and when he was woken by a call from room service a little after eight he felt as if he had not slept at all.

He went down for breakfast and found Sheldon Ross waiting for him.

"Take your time Mr. Hartmann," Ross said. "They'll be bringing Perez over to the office at about ten."

"Come have a cup of coffee with me," Hartmann said, and Ross sat with him, shared some coffee, and said nothing of why they were there.

"You married?" Hartmann asked.

Ross shook his head.

"Any particular reason?"

"I've got time."

"You should," Hartmann said. He reached for a piece of toast and buttered it.

"Special kind of girl who would want to be married to the FBI," Ross said.

Hartmann smiled. "Don't I know it."

"You're married, right?"

Hartmann nodded. "Married, and still trying to stay married."

"Pressures of work?"

"Indirectly, yes," Hartmann replied. "More the pressure of being a complete asshole fifty percent of the time."

Ross laughed. "It's good that you can be honest about it, but as far as I can see it cuts both ways."

"Sure it does, but like you said it's a special kind of person who wants to spend their time married to the sort of thing we do." Hartmann looked across the table at Ross. "You live with someone or you live alone?"

"I live with my mom."

"And your dad?"

Ross shook his head. "Dead a good few years now."

"I'm sorry."

Ross waved the condolence away.

"So you go home and tell your mom the kind of things you've had to look at all day?"

Ross laughed. "She'd have a freakin' coronary."

"That's the point, isn't it? And with a wife, someone who's even closer to you in some ways, and then add kids on top of that, and you got a somewhat untenable situation."

"So there's no hope for me?" Ross asked.

Hartmann smiled. "Maybe you should marry an FBI girl."

"Brutal," Ross said. "You seen the sort of girls that join the Bureau? Not exactly Meg Ryan."

Hartmann laughed and ate his toast.

Half an hour later they walked together to Arsenault Street.

Woodroffe and Schaeffer were waiting. They said their respective good mornings, and then Hartmann was shown once more into the small rear office where he had sat with Perez the day before.

A small coffeemaker had been installed, as had a wheeled trolley upon which sat cigarettes, ashtrays, clean cups and saucers, a bag of jelly beans and a box of Cuban cigars.

"What the man wants the man gets, right?" Hartmann had commented to Schaeffer, who nodded and said, "Right to the point we nail his ass for the girl, and then he's gonna get an eight-by-eight in gray steel-reinforced concrete and two hours of daylight a week."

Hartmann sat down. He waited patiently. He knew when Perez had arrived in the building because he was accompanied by a good dozen or more FBI operatives, all of them awkward and nervous.

Perez appeared in the doorway of the small office and Hartmann instinctively rose from his chair.

Perez extended his hand. Hartmann took it and they shook.

"You slept well, Mr. Perez?" Hartmann asked, at once feeling a sense of apprehension around the man, but at the same time a considerable degree of disdain.

"Like the proverbial baby," Perez replied as he sat down.

Hartmann sat down also, reached for a packet of cigarettes on the trolley, offered one to Perez, took one himself, and then lit them both. He felt an unusual conflict of emotions—the necessity to treat the man with some degree of respect, and at the same time he hated him for what he had done, what he represented, and the fact that he had single-handedly jeopardized the only real chance Hartmann had to salvage his marriage. He looked at Perez closely; he believed there was nothing in his eyes, no light of humanity at all.

"I have a question," Hartmann asked.

Perez nodded.

"Why am I here?"

Perez smiled, and then he started laughing. "Because I asked you to be here, Mr. Hartmann, and right now I have all the aces and none of the jokers."

"But why me of all people?"

Perez sighed and leaned back in his chair. "Did you ever read Shakespeare, Mr. Hartmann?"

Hartmann shook his head. "I can't say that I did."

"You should read him, as much as you can. The truth of the matter is that Shakespeare said that there were seven ages of man, and apparently just as there are seven ages of man, there are also only seven real stories."

Hartmann frowned. "I don't understand."

"Everything you read, every movie you might see, everything that happens in life is one of these seven stories. Things like love and revenge, betrayal, such things as this. Only seven of them, and each of those seven stories can be found in every one of William Shakespeare's plays."

"And the connection?" Hartmann asked.

"The connection, as you so call it, Mr. Hartmann, is that everything you could ever wish to know about me, about why I am here, about what has happened to Catherine Ducane and why I chose you to come home to New Orleans and listen to my story . . . all of the answers can be found in the words of William Shakespeare. Now pour us some coffee and we shall talk, yes?"

Hartmann paused for a moment and then he looked directly at Perez. He had been right. There was not the slightest spark of humanity in the man's eyes. He was a killer. Hartmann reminded himself of what had been done to Gerard McCahill; he remembered Cipliano's words, *It's hard to tell on the blows as well. So many, and all coming at different angles, like whoever did this was walking around the guy in circles while he whacked him.* He pictured Ernesto Perez doing just that: walking around a bound and gagged man, hammer in his hand, raining blow after merciless blow down on the defenseless victim until shock and blood loss brought his life to an end.

Inside he shuddered.

"You're not going to give us anything, are you, Mr. Perez?" he asked.

Perez smiled. "On the contrary, Mr. Hartmann, I am going to give you everything."

"About the girl though," Hartmann said. "You're not going to give us anything about the girl."

"All in good time," Perez replied.

"And you can assure us she is safe and well, and that no harm will come to her?"

Perez looked away toward the corner of the room. His face was implacable, and Hartmann believed a man such as this must have spent the greater part of his life withholding as much as he could from everyone around him. A man like this would stand on a subway platform, in a queue at a coffee shop, biding his time patiently as he waited in line at a supermarket checkout, and no one would have had an inkling of who he was.

"I can guarantee nothing, Mr. Hartmann. Even as we speak Catherine Ducane might be choking to death on the ropes that have been used to tie her. She may have attempted to work herself free and be suffocating even as we speak. She does not have a lot of time, and thus any time you spend attempting to solicit information from me is indirectly contributing to her demise. It's the rule of threes, Mr. Hartmann—"

"The what?"

"The rule of threes. Three minutes without air, three days without water, three weeks without food. Catherine Ducane has already been in my possession since Wednesday the twentieth . . . that's the better part of a week and a half already."

In his possession, Hartmann thought. *That's the way he thinks of her.* Hartmann closed his eyes for a moment. He tried not to think of her. He tried not to comprehend the combined frustration of every federal operative that was now directly, and indirectly, involved in this situation. He tried to focus his mind, but no matter how hard he concentrated he could not pull away from the image of a starved and frightened young woman tied somewhere to a chair, all the while believing that this man would return only to kill her.

"So we should waste no more time, Mr. Hartmann," Perez said matter-of-factly. "We should talk, should we not?"

"Yes," Hartmann said.

He poured the coffee. He set the cups on the table along with an ashtray and, as Ernesto Cabrera Perez began to speak once more, Ray Hartmann leaned to his left and gently closed the office door.

ELEVEN

"LO *CUBANA—ESTÁ AQUÍ*" The real Cuba—it's here!
Havana.
Stalinism and palm trees.
The crumbling façade of Spanish colonialism.

Barrio di Colón, the tattered remnants of the red light district from Batista's dictatorship.

San Isidro, once beautiful, stately, awe-inspiring, now ramshackle and desperate, hunkering around Havana's railway district like a dirty and discarded coat.

Later, much later, there was a boy who would become as close to me as a brother, and we would remember this time.

"You remember January of '59?" he would say. "When there was a strike of all the working people, and Havana came to a standstill. Batista was president then, and his secret police were fighting with the rebels in the streets. It was then that Castro's guerrillas came from the mountains, and they ran through the streets and took this city. There was no one left to fight them, no one at all. You remember that time, Ernesto?"

The boy would smile, and in that smile was a memory of something that would forever remain a part of our lives.

"When Castro made Manuel Urrutia the president after Batista fled, and he swore in the new government at Oriente University in Santiago de Cuba, yes? They made Castro Delegate of the President for the Armed Forces and Jose Rubido as Chief of the Army. And Castro? He drove like a conquering Caesar along the length of the island toward Havana! We celebrated everywhere he went, and that evening we heard that those who'd stood against Castro in Las Villas Province, Colonel Lumpay and Major Mirabel, had been executed."

The boy had smiled again. "I saw them executed, Ernesto . . . I saw them plead for their lives, but Castro was like a king returned to his homeland and he allowed no mercy. He put Che Guevara in charge of Havana itself, and we went through the streets, thousands of us, and we burned flags and we set buildings on fire, and there were men drinking wine and singing and fucking women in the street. Down Calzada de Zapata we went, our voices raised, and out along Avenida Salvador Allende and through Coppelia Park to the Cristobal Colón Cemetery . . .”

I laughed with him. I remembered these things. I had been there too. Ernesto Cabrera Perez. We were amongst them, me and my ghost of a father, caught in the whirlwind of revolution and passion and gunfire.

My father was all of forty-six years old, but he carried himself as if he were sixty or seventy. The Havana Hurricane had come home, back to a place whose name he had used with self-aggrandized pride, but in the face of everything, the age and history and significance of this place, he was nothing more than what he truly was: a fighter, a whiskey-fueled brawler, a bare-knuckle madman possessing neither sufficient sense nor sanity to work a trade alongside his Friday night thunderings. And yet he was even less than that—weaker and more broken and less substantial than I had ever believed, and he carried inside of him a guilt so burdensome that the strength remaining in his bones and frame could not have borne it for long. He had killed his own wife. In a fit of insatiable sexual fury he had broken his own wife's neck as he forced her against the wall. That was what he was, and that was all he ever would be: a stupid man, old before his time, who in some moment of drunken madness had killed the only person who'd ever really loved him. Loved him not for what he was, but loved him for what she believed he might become. In the end she was wrong, for he became nothing, and I walked with that nothing, the shell of a man that was my father, through the streets of Old Havana, down along Calle Obispo to the Plaza de Armas, and as he walked he whispered in his hoarse and fatigued voice, *No es fácil . . . no es fácil. . .* It's not easy . . . it's not easy.

"I know, Father, I know," I would reply, and though my words bore the face of sympathetic understanding, they carried behind their backs the grim steel of vengeance.

The Sicilians—years, so many years later—would tell me of vengeance. "*Quando fai i piani per la vendetta, scava due tombe—una per la tua vittima e una per te stesso,*" they would say. You head out for vengeance, you dig two graves . . . one for your victim and one for yourself. And then they would smile with their mouth but not with their eyes, and in that expression you could see a thousand years of understanding about the darker elements of man and the shadows that he carried.

But during those first few weeks, as we found our feet, as I discovered the land of my father, as Cuba gave birth to something inside of me that made me believe that wherever I might have been born, wherever I might have been raised, this place—this impassioned, heated, sweating, writhing confusion of humanity and inhumanity, sprawling out from west to east, a punctuation mark between the Atlantic and the Caribbean, the Gulf of Mexico, the Florida Straits, the Windward Passage—was so much more than I had ever believed or imagined.

Such romance, such fiction! Names such as Sancti Spiritus, Santiago de Cuba, a stone's throw from Haiti and Jamaica, from Puerto Rico and the Bahamas; St. James the Apostle Carnival, the African-Catholic faith of Santeria, and rumba and salsa and cha-cha-cha, and lazy island days out of Cayo Largo, and here is where Hemingway would live at *Papa's Place*, Finca la Vigia, and after his death his family would give his home to the people of Cuba for carrying the dreams of their son for the better part of twenty years.

And it would only be later, much later, years behind me once I had returned to the United States, that I would look back and believe that Cuba had always been in my heart and soul, that had I stayed there all the terrible things to come would perhaps never have happened. But by then it was too late, and by then I would be looking at my life with the mind and eyes of an older man, not the man I was then, the young man walking my father through those self-same streets, believing that here I had found nothing more than a sanctuary from the justice that my father would inevitably meet . . .

Though not the way I then believed.

And not from my own hand.

For now my hand did nothing more than lead the way for him, show him where he would lie down in the dark one-room hovel we rented for a single American dollar a week—the same hand that gripped the sill of the window as I looked out toward the lights of Florida while my mind believed that if I could only make it back there alone, if I could only find my way, there would be something waiting for me that would give everything else some sense.

But then it did not, and would not for a great many years to come. The New Year of 1959 I was nothing more than my father's keeper, and as he lay on his mattress, as he mumbled unintelligible words interspersed with the sound of my mother's name, as his mind slowly dissolved into the final darkness of guilt for who he was and what he had done, I knew I had to escape from this life any way I could.

My eyes were open, my heart was willing, and I had long since realized that the pathway to freedom was bought with dollars. Hard-earned or not, there was only one way out, and that way carried a price.

I'll tell you something now: in the 1950s it was different. Seemed to me a man was a man and a girl was a girl. None of this free love, men holding hands with men in public kind of thing. Guy wanted to take it up the ass then he did it in the privacy of his own home, or maybe he rented a hotel room by the hour. At the time I figured people like that were crazy, not the *Jesus told me to stay home and clean my guns* crazy, but just a little short on whatever it took to make a hundred cents spend like a dollar. Maybe I don't seem to be the truthful kind of person, but I'll let you in on one other thing: I say something, well you can take it to the bank, and I'll tell you what happened in 1959 with the old guys and the rent boys and the promise of a dollar.

The room I rented for me and my father was on the outskirts of Old Havana, *La Habana Vieja*, and back behind the Plaza de la Catedral there was a street called Empedrado. The house we inhabited was shared by the better part of six or seven families, some with kids no taller than my knee, and some with babies who would cry at night when the heat was fierce, or who would cry from hunger or from thirst, or from the croup when it came and infected them, all of them at once.

Met a boy there; seventeen he was, maybe eighteen or nineteen, but he smoked cigarettes like he'd been doing it for a thousand years. His family name was Cienfuegos, his given name Ruben, and Ruben Cienfuegos became as close to me as any other human being. It was with him that I spoke of the revolution, of Castro overthrowing Batista and taking Cuba back for the people. It was he who taught me how to smoke the cigarettes, he who showed me pictures of girls with wide mouths and wider legs that made me so horny I could've fucked a cracked plate given a little lubrication, and when he told me of his cousin, a sixteen-year-old called Sabina, when he told me she would *do me* for two American dollars, I went like a lamb to the slaughter. A narrow mattress in the corner of a darkened room, and Sabina—whose hair was longer than any girl's I'd ever seen, whose eyes were wide and bright and eager, and yet somehow wary like a feral thing; a girl who pulled down my pants and massaged my cock until it was stiff and aching, who took me by the hand and laid me down, and then lifted her skirt and sat astride me, who then lowered herself onto me until I felt I would disappear completely between those muscled brown thighs, and who rolled over me like a wave of something terrible and magical and profound, and who later would take my two American dollars and tuck them into the waistband of her panties, and lean forward and kiss my face, and tell me that she could feel my warmth inside her, and then had laughed and told me that what had just happened was as necessary and vital as being christened by the Pope himself in the Vatican, and told me then that if I had left it any longer I might very well have drowned her. And then she showed me to the door and down the stairs to where Ruben stood smoking and smiling and satisfied . . . When Ruben Cienfuegos told me of these things, and then made his promise that it would happen, and then brought me to the place where it did happen, well Ruben became perhaps the most important person in my life.

And she, she whose name I would never forget, and yet met only once, became something that existed only in my mind and my heart. In years to come I would think of her, Sabina, and make-believe that she was somewhere thinking also of me. In some way that moment with her was as meaningful as the moment I stood over the dead body of Carryl Chevron such a long time before. A defining moment. A moment that would stand as a testimony of my life, evidence that I had in fact walked the earth, that, at least once, perhaps twice, I had truly been *someone*.

I thought of her often, but never spoke her name, because to speak of her would have been to break the spell and let the world know something of who I was. Who I was belonged to no one but me, and that was the way I wished it.

It was Ruben who told me of the Italians. He told me of the Hotel Nacional and how a black man called Nat King Cole—who was not a real king and did not possess a kingdom—had sung there for the Italians and yet could not stay in the hotel that night because he was *negroid*, and how the Italians had come here to Cuba when they had been forced out of Florida by the authorities, forced out because they had killed so many people and taken so much money, and how the law could do nothing to stop them. Cuba was their salvation, Cuba was their home from home, and in ten-thousand-dollar apartments they would drink Folger's Coffee and smoke Cohibas and Montecristos and Bolivars and Partagases.

"Up there," he told me, "near where they live, you will find the little birds."

"The little birds?"

Ruben smiled. "Yes, Ernesto, the little birds . . . the faggots, the queers, the homos, the young men who will take it up the ass for a dollar and a pack o' smokes."

I closed my eyes. I thought of that night as I waited for the tide to turn, as I buried my fingernails into the palms of my hands and paid the ferryman his price of passage. I knew what Ruben Cienfuegos was talking about, and with that knowledge came a sense of hatred and loathing for whosoever would support such a terrible trade.

"The rich guys go down there, the ones with all the dollars, some of them Italians, some of them Cuban businessmen who have a taste for such things." Ruben smiled and winked and lit another cigarette. "And I have an idea, my little Ernesto," he said, even though I was older than him by a year or two, and then he smiled and winked again and told me of his plan.

Three nights later, dressed in a clean white shirt Ruben had borrowed from his cousin on his mother's side, Araujo Limonta, with pressed pants made of thick cotton, with canvas shoes similar to those worn by the boatmen who haunted the bars along Avenida Carlos M. Céspedes, I stood with my heart in my mouth and an American cigarette in my hand near the corner of Jesús Pergerino Street. I stood there patiently as the cars drove by, some of them slowing down as they cruised along the curb, and I waited for as long as I believed it possible to wait. Later Ruben told me it was no more than ten minutes before a car pulled to a stop ahead of me, as the window came down, as a greasy-haired man with a gold tooth like Carryl Chevron the salesman leaned out toward me and asked me how much.

"Two dollars," I told him, for this is what Ruben Cienfuegos had directed me to say, and the man with the gold tooth and the greasy hair had smiled and nodded and reached his hand through the window and waved me over. I climbed into the car just as Ruben had said, my heart thundering enough to burst right there in my chest, my teeth gritted, sweat breaking free of my hairline and itching my skin. I sat silently as the man drove a half block further and slowed to a dead stop in a dark pool between the streetlights. Ruben said he would be waiting. Ruben said he knew where the men would take me, and as he told me these things he told me that I was to act naturally, to act as if I had done such things a thousand times before, for he would be there—my savior, my benefactor—and he would ensure no harm came to me.

The greasy-haired man placed his left hand on my knee.

I flinched, I could not help it.

The hand with its fat fingers, with its single gold ring with a blue stone set within, traced a line from my knee toward my crotch. I could feel the pressure against my leg, could feel the weight of sin that was intended, and I closed my eyes as that same hand reached between my legs and started rubbing me, just as Sabina had done, but this time different, this time with a motion that made me sick inside.

What Ruben hit the man with I do not know. But he hit him hard. I didn't even see him coming, but through the open window on the other side of the car a dark shape came rocketing in toward us, and collided with the back of the man's head.

His anticipatory leer became a wide-mouthed expression of shock—but just for a second, nothing more than a heartbeat—for he swayed backward suddenly, and then his head rolled sideways on his shoulders and he fell against the dash.

I came out of the passenger door as if I had been ejected with great force. I fell to the road, fell to my hands and knees, and though I wanted to puke I could manage nothing more than a dry choking cough. My instinct told me to drag the greasy-haired gold-toothed man out of the car and kick him, to kick him hard and fast, to kick him in the head until he would never wake up, but Ruben was then beside me, lifting me from the road, standing there to support me, to start me laughing as he pointed at the unconscious form of the man in his tailored suit, in his expensive car, the sickening pervert smile wiped from his face with one swift blow to the head.

"Quick!" Ruben said, and together we entered the car.

We took the man's ring, his pocketbook, his watch, even his shoes. We took his leather belt, his keys, his cigarettes and a half bottle of whiskey we found beneath the driver's seat. We ran from the side of the car laughing like schoolgirls, and we kept on running—down San Miguel and across Gonzalez, across Padre Valera and Campanario—and we kept on running until I felt my lungs would implode with the pressure.

Later that night, as we smoked the man's American cigarettes, as we drank his whiskey, as we counted once more the sixty-seven American dollars we had found tucked into the back of his pocketbook, I realized that everything I could ever wish for could be taken with violence.

Back so many years before—in deciding to kill a man for the knowledge he had brought, deciding to do something that would make my mother proud of me, but in some way had made me a reflection of my father—I had taken my first step down a lonely road. There were those, people such as Ruben, who would walk with me for some time, but even Ruben Cienfuegos, with his wide smile and riotous laughter, with his whiskey-fueled bravado that night in *La Habana Vieja*, was not among those willing to take the necessary extra step. I could have killed the man, could have dragged him from his car and beaten him just as my father had beaten so many men before. But my father had only ever killed a man out of passion, out of the fury born of his sport, whereas I had killed a man for something I believed I could own. I believed then that such things were in my blood, and it would only be another two weeks before the blood rose once more, before I realized that what I was doing was not simply a matter of ability, but more a matter of *necessity*. I could kill, and so I did, and the more such killing I carried out the more necessary it became. It was like a virus that gripped me, but it came from the mind and the heart and the soul, not from the cells or the nerves or the brain. It was there within me, perhaps had always been, and it was merely an issue of eventual provocation, the force majeure, and Cuba—its lights, its heat, its promise, its emotion— seemed to fuel that provocation without effort.

I became a man in Havana. I became my own hurricane. Seemed to me that every life I extinguished was in some way a repayment to God for how He had mistreated me. I was not so naïve as to consider myself piteous or worthy of special vindication, but I was not so ignorant as to believe that what I possessed was anything but valuable. There were men who would pay for what I could do. Rare is the soul who will take another's life, and then walk home, his hands steady, his heart quiet in his chest, taking only sufficient time to consider how well he had exe- cuted the act, how professional he had been. It became the semblance of a vocation, and I followed the calling with a degree of natural response that served to excite me.

Ernesto Cabrera Perez was a killer by nature and by choosing.

I made my choice. I wore it well. It suited me, and I suited it.

I consummated my craft in the first week of February of 1960.

The intervening year was one of real life. During those months, as Cuba stretched through her growing pains, as Havana reestablished itself beneath the new regime, Ruben Cienfuegos and I lived life like there was no tomorrow. We stole and cheated and conned our way through many hundreds of American dollars, much of it finding its way between the legs of hookers, down the necks of bottles, and out at the bloody mid- afternoon cockfights and nightly jai-alai contests. We believed we were men; we believed that this was how *real* men behaved, and we felt little responsibility for our actions and significantly less scruples.

Castro was the Premier of Cuba, *el Comandante en Jefe*, and with his own breed of communistic vision he had ousted the Batista-owned and run casinos. He was not blind to the ravages of hedonism that had raddled his homeland, and even on the eve of his assumption of power the people of that same homeland had stormed the multi-million-dollar hotels that had once served the tourist trade and lined the pockets of

Batista's family and the organized crime cohorts. In downtown Havana the crowds were frenzied and enraged. They stormed in their hundreds to the doors of the casinos and hotels, and broke their way into the empty air-conditioned, plush-carpeted foyers to wreak havoc. Inside they found roulette, dice and card tables, bars and slot machines, ten thousand of which had been controlled by Batista's brother-in-law. Batista's Mafia-financed palaces were destroyed. The military and the police stayed in their barracks, senior officers knowing all too well that their own troops would merely join the mobs, and no one stepped forward to prevent the people from tearing the hotels and gambling joints apart.

Castro abolished gambling as one of his first decrees as the new dictator. Even as the decree was passed, even as the boats bringing tourists from Florida and the Keys sat idle and empty against the jetties and docks, Castro knew he could not win. That money, the same money that had been creamed as graft from these dens of iniquity, was the finance that had kept Cuba alive. Castro also knew that the Syndicate possessed the only people who could make the casinos and hotels run at a profit, and thus he retracted his decree and gambling was legalized once more. Now state-run and overseen, where Batista had charged $250,000 for each license, and more again beneath the table, Castro's regime levied a fee of $25,000 plus 20 percent of the profits from each casino. He made it illegal for anyone other than naturalized Cubans to act as croupiers, and the Americans came in as "official teachers." Castro hired advertising agencies to promote the high-life of Havana; the hotels were rebuilt and refurbished after the ravages of his people on the eve of his assumption; the tourists came back in their thousands, and with them a reputed annual revenue exceeding fifty million dollars.

A little more than twenty years earlier a different sequence of events had begun that would bring to Havana one of the most influential organized crime figures in history. In January 1936 a government special prosecutor named Thomas E. Dewey began a series of raids on New York's brothels. The raids continued until March when a ninety-count indictment was brought against Charles "Lucky" Luciano. Luciano fled New York to a gambling club in Hot Springs, Arkansas, and this was where he was arrested. He was extradited to New York City, and on 13 May 1936 his trial began. On 7 June of the same year a jury found Luciano guilty of sixty-two counts of prostitution, and he was sentenced to thirty to fifty years in Dannemora Prison in upstate New York. On 7 May 1945, a petition for executive clemency and freedom was made to the now governor, Thomas Dewey, and Dewey agreed to a reduction of sentence. On 3 January 1946, Dewey announced that Luciano would be freed, but he was to be deported to his native Sicily. Luciano was released from Great Meadow and taken to Ellis Island. Here he boarded the vessel *Laura Keene*, which set sail on its two-week voyage to Genoa. Between February and October Luciano moved from his hometown of Lercara Friddi to Palermo, thence to Naples and on to Rome. Here he obtained two passports, and aboard a freighter he made his way to Caracas in Venezuela. He flew from Caracas to Mexico City, where he chartered a private aircraft for his flight to Havana, Cuba. He was ninety miles from the coast of Florida, a stopover on his planned return to the United States.

In Havana Luciano was met by his childhood friend and ally Meyer Lansky and taken to the Hotel Nacional. It was in that same hotel that Luciano and Lansky arranged what would later be known as the Havana Conference for the third week of December 1946. Luciano moved into a plush and extravagant home in the Miramar suburb. Lansky traveled back and forth between Miami and Havana, keeping Luciano informed of the arrangements for the Conference.

On Christmas Eve the Conference took a break. Wives and girlfriends arrived and a party in honor of Frank Sinatra—an up-and-coming star who had arrived with the Fischetti brothers—was held.

The Havana casinos flourished, even under Castro's regime, and Meyer Lansky, the man Batista had employed to make Cuba the place for America to gamble away its hard-earned millions, now made those millions for Castro. He had cleaned up the Sans Souci and Montmartre clubs, had leaned on major operators like Norman Rothman and forced them to straighten up their acts, had had many of the crooked American casino managers deported, and instigated the practice of dealing blackjack from a six-deck shoe, a practice which stacked the odds heavily in favor of the casinos and prevented cheating by both players and dealers.

The Italians carried gambling in their blood and bones, they were the most proven and successful impresarios in the business, and their willingness to pay government officials for the right to operate their business was legend. Lansky brought with him the cream of the crop from Vegas, Reno and New York. At his right hand was his own brother, Jake, installed as the floor manager in the Nacional's casino. From Florida came Santo Trafficante who was given an interest in the Sans Souci, the Comodoro and the Capri. Joseph Silesi and the actor George Raft bought pieces of the business, along with Fat the Butch from New York's Westchester County and Thomas Jefferson McGinty from

Cleveland. There was no opposition, and thus there was no need for the heavy-handed tactics employed on the mainland. The tourists had no worry about loaded dice, stacked decks or magnetic clips beneath the roulette wheels. The business was as clean as it could get, and with decades of experience behind them the Syndicate established Cuba as the place to be. Pit bosses, dealers and stick-men were ferried in from the States, and they trained the Cuban croupiers and house-staffs in the ways of the world. Castro's denunciation of gambling had at one time sent the tourists out to the La Concha Hotel in San Juan or the Arawak Hotel in Jamaica, but his reversal had brought them home once more, and it was into this world that Ruben and I stepped unknowingly in the beginning of 1960.

The scam still ran, the "little bird" scam for the queer businessmen and switch-hitter Cubans, and while Fidel Castro Ruz curried favor with the USSR, while he instigated agreements to buy Russian oil, while he generated friction with the US by taking American-owned properties and giving insufficient compensation, Ruben and I were busy making our mark and loading our own dice.

It was a Friday night, 5 February, and it was Ruben's idea that we head up to the car lot back of the Nacional and check out the trade. It was new territory, but Ruben had heard that the tricks up there were prepared to pay upwards of twenty dollars a time to get their balls emptied by some young Cuban stud. If they carried that much for a blow-job, Ruben said, then what kind of bankroll had they pocketed when they went out for the night?

I was twenty-two years old, I looked no more than eighteen or nineteen, and when I walked from the car to the edge of the lot, when I stood leaning against the railing that separated the lot from the walkway, dressed in white linen pants, an oversized ivory-colored shirt and canvas boat shoes, when I lit my cigarette and flicked the hair from my eyes, I could tell that there weren't many of those old boys that could have resisted me. It was an act, a performance, a face I wore for the world, and I wore it well. Like a professional.

The car that drew alongside me was a deep burgundy Mercury Turnpike Cruiser, a hardtop, and the way the silk paintwork shined, the way the chrome runners and wheel-hubs reflected a million lights from the Nacional behind me, I knew I was right up there with the players.

The driver was no Cuban. His manner, his voice, his clothes— everything about him told me he was Italian. He smiled wide. He winked. He told me "Hi there," asked if I was waiting for someone in particular, if he could give me a ride somewhere.

"Kind of ride would you be speaking about?" I asked him.

"Any kind of ride you might be interested in," he said.

"Kind that pays maybe twenty dollars?" I asked.

"Maybe," the man said, and again he smiled, and then he winked, and I walked around back of the car and slid in through the passenger side door.

"I got a little place," the man said, and then he placed his hand on my knee.

I pressed myself against the seat, and there in the rear waistband of my pants I could feel the handle of my shiv. I smiled to myself. He was not a big man. He dressed too well to be a heavy hitter for the mob. Dressed well enough to carry a handsome bankroll for his night out on the town.

"Where we going?" I asked.

"See when we get there," he said, and I watched as his hands tightened on the steering wheel. He had on a wedding band, a plain gold hoop, and I wondered where his wife was, what his children were doing right that second, and I asked myself how these sick-minded mother-fuckers ever believed there wouldn't be some night when they would be nailed for what they were doing.

We drove for no more than five or six minutes, and then we turned left down a driveway ahead of a roadside motel. I could feel the tension in every sinew, every nerve, could feel the muscles tensing in the backs of my legs and my shoulders. I was frightened, I cannot deny it, but I was also excited. How many times we had pulled this scam I could not recall, and experience had proved that I could do this thing alone. Ruben was somewhere back near the Nacional; he would wait for me there, wait for me to return with as many dollars as I could take from this trick, and then we would party. On my side was fear. It was that simple. These guys were frightened of discovery, frightened that something would be said, frightened that they would be found out for what they were, and it was that fear that caused them not only to give in when faced with a youth with a knife, but also to say nothing of what had happened. Where would they go? Who would they report this to? The police? Their Mafia contacts? Somehow I didn't think so.

The man drew the car to a halt back of a motel cabin. He killed the engine, took the keys and tucked them inside his jacket pocket, and before he exited he offered me a cigarette from a gold cigarette case. I took one and the man lit it for me, one for himself also. I followed him as he walked from the car to the front door of the cabin. With the same key chain he unlocked the door, stepped aside to let me enter, and then followed me in. It was a plainly decorated room, the lights dimmed, ahead of me a double bed, a dresser with an oval mirror on top of it, and to the right a deep armchair facing a small table with a TV on top.

The man removed his jacket. "What shall I call you?" he asked.

I shrugged. "Anything you like," I replied.

"Francisco," he said matter-of-factly. "I shall call you Francisco."

I nodded, but inside I was smiling. I thought of the next five minutes, perhaps the five minutes after that, and how much money I would run from this motel cabin with and the night that would follow.

"And what shall I call you?" I asked.

The man smiled. "You can call me 'Daddy,'" he said quietly.

In that second I felt sick to my stomach. I could only begin to imagine what kind of crazy fuck would request such a thing. I wanted to stab him through the heart right there and then. I wanted to make him kneel on the floor and beg for his life before I drove my shiv through his eye. I wanted to make him pay for all the many times he must have done this before.

And then I thought of my own father, the expression on his face as he staggered through the door after a night of fighting, the deadlight eyes, black and emotionless, with which he looked at my mother. Give them a name, give them a nationality—it didn't matter. These animals were all the same.

The man kicked off his shoes and then, unbuttoning the top of his pants, he let them drop to the floor. He stood there in his socks and shorts, and then he loosened his tie and took off his shirt.

I looked at his face. He had that same hollow emptiness of expression. The expression that would so frighten my mother.

I could see the man's erection straining its way out of the middle of his body, and when he eased down his shorts and let them drop to his ankles, when he started to massage his own cock until it stood upright, when he looked across at me and smiled and opened his mouth, and said "Come to Daddy, Francisco . . . come and take care of your daddy . . ." it was all I could do to take a step toward him.

Revulsion filled my chest, revulsion and anger and hatred for him and his kind. I eased my right hand around to the back of my pants, I felt the handle of the shiv between my fingers, and even as I reached him, even as he raised his hand and placed it on my shoulder, as I felt the pressure he applied to bring me down to my knees so he could force his cock into my mouth, I remembered that night on the beach in Florida, the price I had paid for my passage to Havana.

I was quick, quicker than his eye could follow, and with my right hand clenched tight I brought the shiv around like a tornado and drove it forward into his balls.

His eyes wide, sudden, unexpected, his body instinctively arched, a rapid and shocking rigidity that crushed him back against the dresser, and then down onto the floor as he tried to force himself away. I felt the man's hand grip my waist, my shoulders, the tops of my legs, felt them relax as I pulled out the blade and once more brought it home into the side of his neck. He opened his mouth to scream, and his mouth was filled with the taste of blood, his nostrils with the smell of sweat. And then he could not breathe as his throat filled up, could not think, and the ceaseless grinding motion of the steel in his neck brought bright splashes of gray and scarlet into his eyes. He struggled, kicked his legs, his elbows flapping, but I had a hold on his throat, and I tightened that hold until he knew he would suffocate.

Images against his face, right up against him as if forcing their way inside. His breathing halted, he tried to say something, choked, eyes filled with water, with pain, with colors, his ears screaming with sounds, with pressure, the unrelenting violence of each fractured maniac second. He could not move, and then I sensed the moment he realized that his body was giving up, and in that moment of nervous relaxation I pushed him back onto the floor.

I punctured his throat once more with one swift and silent sweep of the knife. He felt the last moist warmth of his life enter the back of his throat, the top of his chest, felt his heart choking up whatever laid inside him and give it up to the world, this place, this dark and hollow cabin room, the strange crazy eyes that pressed against him from all sides.

His body shuddered violently, it shook in rapid consecutive motions, his throat pumping jagged red slashes across his chest, across the carpet, his stomach, the front of the dresser. I looked down as he rock-and-rolled through spasm after spasm of reluctant death, as he shivered and clawed and arched his back away from the blood-soaked matting.

I closed my hands over my ears, I bit my bottom lip until I too could taste blood, and then he collapsed.

Still and silent.

Like someone had deflated him.

His hand swung wide and banged against my knee. It rested there, its weight against my own sweated leg, and for some moments I just stared at it, at the blood-covered fingers, at the way they curled up accusingly, pointing toward me, the tension of the skin, the manicured nails, the sheen of polish, the lines in his palm—heartlines, lovelines, lifelines . . .

I moved my leg and the hand hit the carpet soundlessly.

Somewhere a dog barked, and then the sweep of brights as a car passed in the street, seeing everything for a split second and then disappearing into the night.

There was silence but for my own labored breathing, the sound of something building in my chest, the sound of some huge emotional release as I surveyed what I had done.

Condensation ran its fingerprints down the inside of the windows. I could smell cigar smoke, old and bitter, the tang of cheap alcohol, of diesel wine brewed in oil cans and gasoline drums, the ethyl haunt of late nights, gagging, retching into nowhere, into blind-eyed foolish wisdom, thinking that life begins at the base of a bottle or between a hooker's thighs. I would be reminded of that smell the better part of four decades later, a warm night in Chalmette district, heart of New Orleans.

I was somewhere aloft, somewhere outside of myself looking down. Up there was Aix-La-Chapelle to Canteloupe, Cantata to Equation of Time, Equator to Heraclitus, Heraldry to Kansas, Kant to Marciano, Marconi to Ordovician Period, Oregon to Rameau, Rameses to UFO, Unified Theories to Zurich. Up there was wisdom, the very heart of hearts. Who was I really? The child of a lesser God? I thought not. More so a God from some lesser child.

I leaned back on my haunches and breathed deeply. I closed my eyes and centered myself. What I had done was right there in front of me. What I had done was indelibly painted across the carpet, across the dresser, across the back wall of the cabin. I thought of all those who had been here before me and I asked myself if justice had not been seen to be done.

I smiled.

An eye for an eye.

I had done this. *I* had made this happen. Was I not now someone? Surely I was; surely I was something that so many others were incapable of being. I was Ernesto Cabrera Perez, a man capable of killing other men, a gifted man, a dangerous man. I was someone special.

I breathed deeply. For a moment I felt dizzy, a little sick. I raised my hands and looked at the blood that was drying on my skin. I could feel the tension it created, and when I clenched my fists I believed I could hear the blood cracking and splitting in the pores and wrinkles of my fingers. I turned them over. These were the hands that had lifted my mother when she could not walk by herself. These were the hands that had defended me against the railing fists of my father.

I was scared. I asked myself what was inside me that made it possible for me to do these things.

I looked into nothing—an abyss, a hollow—and when I closed my eyes I felt the dizziness and disorientation grow even worse. I opened my eyes and shuddered. Whatever was there I did not want to know.

I stood up, stripped off my clothes, and hurried through into the small adjoining bathroom to wash the blood from my hands.

I dressed in the man's shirt and suit, put on his shoes, bundled my own clothes together and tied them in a ball. In the inside pocket of his jacket I found the car keys. In the other pocket I found a bankroll close on a thousand American dollars. I looked down once more, and as to serve no purpose other than adding insult to injury, I raised my right foot and stamped down hard on the man's face.

I turned and walked to the cabin door. I glanced back one more time.

"Sleep tight, Daddy," I whispered, and stepped out into the night.

I climbed into the car, started the engine, and drove out into the town, a town known only by those who lived there, a town that was none the wiser and would not be for some hours.

And those hours passed in a haze of alcohol-induced lust and heated passion. With the better part of a thousand dollars between us, Ruben Cienfuegos and I trawled the lower-life end of *La Habana Vieja*, and there we found girls who would do indescribable things for less than ten bucks Americano. We drank as if we had walked from the desert, and as morning ached its bruised and sallow way toward the horizon and color returned to the monochrome haunts of the darker underbelly of the city, we staggered half-blind and incoherent to our rooming house where I found my father sleeping the sleep of the dead. I remember stepping over him, hearing him slur and mumble unintelligibly, and I thought for a moment how easy it would have been to kneel across his chest, wrap my hands around his throat, and choke the last pathetic breath from his body as payment for what he had done to my mother. I stood over him for some time, the walls bending every which way they could, and I withheld myself. I believed it would have been too easy to kill him then, for the penance he had delivered to himself, of a broken-spirited man, a shell of whatever he once was, was far worse. I decided to let him suffer his own pains a while longer, and I crossed the room and lay down on my own mattress.

When I awoke it was late afternoon. I thought to call on Ruben and venture out once more into our hedonist's paradise, but I stayed a while and spoke with my father. I gave him some money and told him to go out and get himself cleaned up, to buy some new clothes, to find some seventeen-year-old hooker and do his worst. He took my advice, once again pathetic and obsequious, and from the window of our room I watched him stumble away from the building toward the end of the street. I cleared my throat and spat after him. I turned my face in disgust. I could not bear to think that he had been the one to bring me into this world. I was better than him. I was Ernesto Cabrera Perez, son of my mother and of no one else.

As the sun slipped beneath the skyline I left my room and walked down the stairwell to Ruben's room. I knocked loudly, waited for a while, and then noticed that the door was not only unlocked but off its latch. I stepped inside. The lights were out, and where Ruben should have been, lying on his mattress, there was nothing but the sweat-stained tussle of sheets.

Perhaps he had come up to find me, and seeing me asleep had left. I knew where he would be. Down the block and across the intersection was a narrow-fronted bar where he and I would meet when we became separated. I wandered down there, appreciating the feeling of freedom that so many dollars in my pocket produced, sufficient to fuel me through another week of such a lifestyle. Not a care in the world.

When I found no evidence of Ruben in the bar I became puzzled. I considered where he might have gone. I asked one or two of the older men if they had seen him.

"He had many dollars," one of them said. "He was here some time ago, an hour, perhaps two, and then he left. He did not say where he was going. I didn't ask. What you people do is none of my business."

I left the bar and walked toward downtown. Perhaps he had gotten drunk and made his own way out to find some entertainment for the evening. I did not really care. Ruben could take care of himself. I thought to go back and get the car, the Mercury Cruiser I had driven from the motel the night before, and parade my way through the old city, pick up some girls, maybe drive out to the coast and make out on the beach. I decided against it. It was a conspicuous car, quite unlike any I had seen down here, and I did not wish to draw attention to myself.

For three hours I wandered through Old Havana. I paid a hooker to give me a blowjob in a back street but my body was so tired and replete with liquor I could not respond. I gave her money anyway, and she asked me to come visit her next time I was around. I said I would, but minutes after she had walked away I would have been unable to recognize her face. After a while they all started to look the same.

It was close to midnight when I turned back and headed home. I was angry, frustrated; irritated that Ruben had left without me, but in some way relieved. I needed to sleep. I felt poisoned with whiskey and cheap rum. I had eaten nothing since I'd woken and my body pained me greatly.

It took me the better part of an hour to reach the rooming house. The place was dark, my father had evidently not returned, and when I started up the stairs toward my room I thought to call in and check if Ruben had returned and was sleeping off his drunk.

The lights were out, the door was still open, and when I pushed it wide and stepped inside I knew that something was wrong.

The light that shone directly into my face blinded me. It was almost painful in its intensity, and before I had a chance to shout, to say something, there were hands on my shoulders. Terror, absolute breathless terror, grabbed me from behind and would not let me go. I was forced to my knees, and even as I opened my eyes once more a rough hessian bag was forced over my head and something was tied around my neck. My hands were tied, so tight I could feel the blood swelling at my wrists. My feet were behind me, and before I could move them or attempt to stand, I felt the pressure of something hard and unyielding against my forehead.

The click of the hammer was almost deafening.

The voice was unmistakably Italian.

"You are Ernesto Perez?" the voice asked.

I said nothing. I felt urine escape from my crotch and soak my pants. I could see the darkness that had faced me in the motel room. I could see whatever was inside me and it terrified me.

Somewhere to my left I heard a struggle. I heard a muffled voice, someone suppressing a howl of pain, and then there was silence for a heartbeat.

"You are Ernesto Perez?" the voice asked again.

I nodded once.

"You killed a man in a motel last night," the voice stated matter-of-factly.

I didn't move, didn't say a word. I had lost all sensation in my hands. I could feel the veins in my neck swelling and pulsing.

"You killed a very good friend of mine in a motel last night, and now we are going to repay his death."

I felt the barrel of the gun stabbing at my forehead. I wanted to scream, wanted to lash out any which way I could, but with my hands tied, and the men behind me standing on my ankles, any movement was impossible.

"Stand up," the voice said.

I was dragged roughly to my feet.

I could still sense the bright light shining directly toward my face even through the sacking over my head.

The light moved, back and to the left, and then with one swift motion the bag was snatched from over my face and I stood facing the man with the gun. That gun was now aimed squarely at my stomach.

I felt everything inside lurch upwards into my chest. It took every ounce of will I possessed to stop myself from screaming.

I looked to my left, and there, roped to a chair, gagged and bound like an animal waiting for slaughter, was Ruben Cienfuegos. He had been beaten within an inch of his life. His eyes were so swollen he could barely open them, his hair was matted with blood, his shirt had been torn from his shoulders and there were cigarette burns all over his skin.

I looked back at the man facing me, unquestionably an Italian. He was my father's age, but his eyes were darker, and when he smiled and nodded there was something truly unnerving in his expression.

"You know this man?" he asked. He glanced toward Ruben.

I shook my head.

The man smiled and raised the gun. He aimed it directly between my eyes. I could almost hear the sound of his finger muscles tensing as he increased the pressure on the trigger.

"You know this man?"

Once again I shook my head. I believed it would not have been possible for me to speak even had I wanted to. My throat was tight, as if a hand gripped it relentlessly, and as I tried to breathe I felt a fear so profound I believed it would stop my heart right where I stood.

The Italian shrugged. "Seems to me one of you is lying then," he said. "He says he knows you. He says your name is Ernesto Perez and you don't deny it. How come he knows your name?"

I shook my head. I looked directly at the man, past the gun and straight into his eyes. "I-I do not know," I stuttered. I tried to sound certain. I tried to sound like a man speaking the truth. "He is a liar," I said.

Ruben Cienfuegos groaned painfully. He started to shake his head.

I tried to move my head, tried to look back over my shoulder. I was aware of two men standing behind me. I turned back to face the Italian once more. He had eyes like a shark, dead and without reflections. I knew that black, lightless expression would be the very last thing I saw.

I decided I would die. In that moment I decided that I would die, and if I did not die then this point would be a catharsis. If I survived this test then it would prove to me that all I had done was not wrong. This would be the confirmation of my life's direction, and if not . . . well, if not, I would not have to concern myself with it any more.

I decided not to be afraid.

I thought of my mother, and the pride she would feel in my strength.

I decided that I would not be afraid, and if this man with the dead eyes killed me then I would find my mother and tell her that everything had not been in vain.

I would live, or I would see my mother again; that was my choice.

"One of you is lying," the man said. "You admit your name is Ernesto Perez?"

"Yes," I replied. "I am Ernesto Perez."

"And this one here?" he asked, indicating Ruben with a sweep of the gun.

"Is someone I have never seen before."

Ruben groaned once more. I could feel his pain, but in feeling it I also began to feel nothing at all. Whatever capacity for sympathy I might have possessed had dissolved and vanished. I realized then that, in being confronted with my own death, the lives of everyone else around me became truly insignificant. This moment would be the exorcism of whatever shred of conscience and compassion I might still have owned.

"So if this is someone you have never seen before it will mean nothing to you if he dies?"

I looked at the man. I did not flinch. Not a single muscle moved in my face. "Nothing at all," I said quietly, and then I smiled.

"And of this man that was killed last night in the motel? This one here says that you were guilty of his murder, that he was not there and you were the one who killed him."

I shook my head. "If he was not there then how does he know anything about it?" I asked.

"You are saying he is a liar?"

"I am," I replied. I felt my heart slow. I felt my pulse in my neck. I felt the tension in my head and heart start to ease. I believed that I had never lied so well in my life.

"And what does that say about you . . . you can stand there and let another man defame and slander your name? Let a man call you a murderer and you do nothing?"

I stared back at the Italian. "I will exact my vengeance at the appropriate time."

The Italian laughed, threw his head back and laughed out loud. *"Quando fai i piani per la vendetta,"* he said, and the two men behind me started laughing also.

"You exact your vengeance now," he said, "or both of you die here in this room."

I looked at Ruben, could see that he was straining to make eye contact with me out of the swollen wreck of his face.

"You pay for the death of my friend and you clear your own name with this killing," the Italian said. "You prove yourself a man, my little Cuban friend, and you preserve your own life." He smiled once more. "We have a deal?"

"We do," I said, and I glanced once more toward Ruben.

The Italian stepped back, lowered his gun, and moved to the side of the room. The two men behind me untied my hands and I stood there, my heart thundering in my chest, sweat running down my entire body, my hands shaking violently as the blood rushed back into them and gave them feeling once more.

The Italian nodded. One of the men behind me stepped forward and handed me a tire lever.

"There are two hundred and six bones in the human body," the Italian said. "I want to hear you break every single one."

Later, much later, seated on the floor in my own room, the Italian told me his name.

"Giancarlo Ceriano," he stated, and he lit two cigarettes, one of which he passed to me. I looked at him then, looked at him for the first time without death staring back at me. He was dressed immaculately, everything about him precise and exact and tailored. His hands were manicured, his hair smooth, his every movement somehow graceful but in no way anything but masculine. Ceriano seemed like something feral, something between a man and an animal, and yet elegant and discerning and very intelligent.

"I know you killed the man in the motel room," he went on. "Do not question how I know this, and do not deny it. You will offend me greatly if you lie to me now." He looked at me with his black deadlight eyes. "I am right, no?"

"You are right," I said.

Ceriano nodded and smiled. "His name was Pietro Silvino. He worked for a man called Trafficante. You have heard of Trafficante?"

I shook my head.

"Trafficante is a very important man, a very good friend of mine. He possesses interests in some of the casinos out here, the Sans Souci, the Comodoro and the Capri. He believes in family, he believes in honor and integrity, and it would break his heart to learn that his friend, a member of his own family, a man with a wife and three beautiful children, was out here paying boys for sex . . . you understand?"

"I understand."

Ceriano flicked the ash of his cigarette on the floor. "In some way you have spared Don Trafficante's family a great deal of heartbreak by killing Silvino before such a thing was discovered, and though I can in no way condone your action, I am nevertheless impressed by your unwillingness to stand down in the face of your own death. You have a brave spirit, my little Cuban friend. I am impressed by your performance, and there is perhaps some work you might be interested in."

"Some work?"

"We are the foreigners here. We stand out in the crowd. People know who we are and what we are doing here. We do not speak your language, and nor do we understand well your customs and rituals. But a native—"

"I am from New Orleans," I said. "I am an American, and I was born in New Orleans."

Ceriano widened his eyes and smiled. He started laughing. "From New Orleans?" he asked, in his voice a tone of surprise.

I nodded. "Yes. My father is Cuban, but my mother was from America. He went there and married her. I was born over there, but we came here recently after my mother died."

Ceriano shook his head. "I am sorry for the death of your mother, Ernesto Perez."

"As am I," I replied.

"So, New Orleans," Ceriano said. "You have heard of Louis Prima?"

I shrugged.

"Louis Prima was born in Storyville, Louisiana. The singer. Plays with Sam Buttera and the Witnesses? You know . . . 'Buona Sera,' 'Lazy River,' 'Banana Split For My Baby' . . . and what was that other one?" Ceriano looked at one of his henchmen. "Aah," he said, and with a wide smile on his face he started singing, "I eat antipasta twice just because she is so nice . . . Angelina . . . Angelina, waitress at the pizzeria . . . Angelina zooma-zooma, Angelina zooma-zooma . . ."

I smiled with him. The man seemed as crazy as a shithouse rat.

He waved his hand aside nonchalantly. "Whatever . . . so you are an American, eh?"

"I am."

"But you speak like a Cuban."

"I do."

"Then, for us, you shall be a Cuban, you understand?"

I nodded. "I understand."

"And you shall do some work for us here in Havana, and we shall pay you well and protect you, and if you serve us we shall perhaps let you keep Pietro Silvino's beautiful car, right?"

"Right," I said, because I believed I had no choice, but more than that I truly believed that here I had been presented with an opportunity to fulfil my vocation, to find my place in the world, to return to America with enough money and power to make my mark. I remembered a sign I had seen over the Alvarez School. *Sin education no hay revolucion posible.* Without education, revolution is not possible.

Here was my education. Here was a way into a world I could only ever have dreamed about.

Here was my escape route, and with people such as these behind, beside and ahead of me I foresaw no repercussions, no consequences, no obstacles.

Here was the American Dream, its darker edges, yes, its blackened underbelly, but a dream all the same, and I wanted that dream so much I could taste it.

They left that night, Giancarlo Ceriano and his henchmen, and with them they took the broken remains of my blood brother, Ruben Cienfuegos. Where they took him and what they did with his devastated body I do not know. I did not ask. I had learned already that with people such as this you answered, but you did not ask. They frightened me, but I found that I respected them as much as any people I had ever known. I recognized their brutality, their passion, their seeming ability to swiftly dispatch both the living and the dead. Theirs was a different world, a greater world, a world of violence and love, of family and greater fortune.

As he left Don Ceriano said, "We shall tell Don Trafficante and Pietro Silvino's family that he was murdered by a Cuban thief. We shall tell them also that you were the one to identify the thief and to kill him. You will earn yourself a name, a small name, my little Cuban friend, but a name nevertheless. We will call on you again, and we will talk of business together, you understand?"

"I understand," I replied, and believed—perhaps for the first time in my life—that I had walked into something that *could be* understood.

I did not sleep that night. I lay awake on my mattress, and out through the window I could see the stars punctuating the blackness of the night sky.

In my mind circles turned and within each circle a shadow, and behind each shadow the face of my mother. She said nothing; she merely looked back at me with a sense of wonder and of awe.

"I have become someone," I whispered to her, and though she did not reply I knew—I just knew—that *someone* was all she had ever wished me to be.

TWELVE

"THE MAN DOES not exist," Schaeffer said matter-of-factly. "Right now we have used all the resources at our disposal, we have trawled through every database we have access to, and this Ernesto Cabrera Perez does not technically exist. There is no record of anyone by that name ever having entered, exited or resided in the mainland United States. There are no Social Security numbers, no passports, no work permits or visas . . . absolutely nothing."

Woodroffe sat beside Schaeffer, silent and expressionless.

"Silvino's death, however, we can verify," Schaeffer said, as if this was some sort of consolation prize.

Hartmann leaned back in his chair and folded his hands behind his head. Back of his eyes a narrow pain threatened to become a migraine and he was using much of his concentration to make it disappear. He believed he would not succeed. It was late in the afternoon, and Perez had spoken almost continuously. They had stopped to eat around one o'clock and, in between the questions, Perez had commented on the quality of the food.

Later, when he was done talking, he was once again escorted to the Royal Sonesta with his two dozen bodyguards.

"But I don't get the Shakespeare connection," Schaeffer said.

Hartmann shrugged. "I believe he is merely showing us that he is not an ignorant man. Christ knows what it might mean, but sure as hell it will keep your Quantico guys busy for the rest of next week."

Schaeffer smiled drily. Hartmann was surprised to see the man did indeed have a sense of humor.

"So what now?" Hartmann asked.

Schaeffer shrugged. "Hell, what the fuck do I know? We all take the rest of the day off, go see a movie or something? I got God knows how many people available to me and I don't know where to send them. I got phone calls coming on the hour every hour from everyone in the Senate and half the fucking United States Congress. I tell 'em what we're doing. I tell 'em we're listening to the guy, we're working through every word he says to see if we can't get some kind of fix on where he might have put her. I've got agents going back through DMV records to try and find some record of this car and where it's been all these years. Jesus, I've got people re-fingerprinting every phone booth he used, going through his clothes for trace fibers and samples of dirt he might have picked up on his shoes. I'm doing every goddamned thing I can think of, and right now, as we speak, I have zip."

Hartmann rose from his chair. "I gotta get outta here, get some fresh air or something. That okay with you?"

"Sure," Schaeffer said. "Get a pager from Kubis so we can call you if we need you. Seems to me that there ain't one helluva lot that you can do until tomorrow."

Schaeffer stepped away from the doorway and let him pass. Hartmann went to see Lester Kubis, who gave him a pager and checked that it was working.

Hartmann nodded at Ross as he left, and passing out through the front door onto Arsenault Street he was at once surprised by the clear blue of the sky, the warmth of the sunshine. There was a tangible difference between here and New York, a difference he had missed in some ways, but beneath that there was the awareness of all that New Orleans represented. He thought about Danny, and thoughts of Danny became thoughts of Jess which, in turn, became thoughts of Carol and what would happen come Saturday. Right now it was not a problem. This matter could conclude tomorrow, perhaps the day after, and he decided that he would not concern himself with it until the latter part of Friday. It was Sunday evening. He had five days to hear what Perez had to say.

Ray Hartmann walked for the sake of walking, no other reason. He took a left at the end of Arsenault and headed downtown. He looked at the façades of buildings he had not seen since early 1988, the better part of fifteen years before. *Plus ça change,* he thought. The more things change the more they stay the same.

He kept on walking, trying to keep his mind absent of anything specific, and before he could take stock of where he was he found himself at Verlaine's Precinct House. He went up the steps and passed through the double doors. It was quiet inside. Seemed as though nothing moved. The duty sergeant didn't even look up from his paperwork, not until Hartmann reached the desk and cleared his throat to attract the man's attention.

The sergeant, his brass-colored name tag identifying him as one

Walter Gerritty, looked up, peered over the rim of his horn-rimmed glasses and raised his eyebrows.

"I was after John Verlaine," Hartmann said.

"And I should imagine you are not the only one," Gerritty said. "And who might you be?"

"Ray Hartmann . . . Special Investigator Ray Hartmann."

Gerritty nodded sagely. "And would that mean you are a special person, or that you only investigate special things?"

Hartmann smiled; the guy was a wisecracker. "It would mean both, of course," Hartmann said.

"Good enough for me," Gerritty said, and reached for the telephone at the edge of the high desk. He dialed a number, waited for a second, and then said, "Trouble awaits you in the foyer." He did not wait for a response and hung up. "He'll be down in just a moment or so." Gerritty resumed his paperwork.

Hartmann nodded and took a step back from the desk.

Gerritty peered over the rim of his glasses again and scrutinized Hartmann. "Problem?"

Hartmann shook his head.

"Good enough then," Gerritty said, and once more his head went down and he started writing on the sheet before him.

Verlaine appeared within a minute, perhaps less.

Gerritty watched him come down the stairs. "Figured it was a pissed-off husband, didn't you?" he asked Verlaine.

The cop smiled. "You are an asshole of the first order, Gerritty," he said.

Gerritty nodded. "We all have our chosen station in life," he replied, "and we do our best to keep up standards."

Verlaine looked at Hartmann. Perhaps there was a moment of uncertainty, and then he reached the bottom of the stairwell and came toward Hartmann with his hand outstretched.

"Mr. Hartmann," he said. "Good to see you."

Hartmann shook the other man's hand. "Likewise," he said. "I wondered if you were free for a while. If you're busy we could meet up another time."

Verlaine shook his head. "Now is good. I'm done with this shift in a little less than an hour."

"Figured you were done with your shift half an hour after you arrived," Gerritty interjected.

"Wiseass," Verlaine said, and then turned and started back up the stairs. "Come on," he said to Hartmann. "My office is up here."

Hartmann followed Verlaine to the top, where they turned left. Three doors down and they were in a narrow office with a small window. There was barely sufficient space for the desk and two chairs. Against the wall stood a three-drawer file cabinet, and it was positioned in such a way as to prevent the door from opening to its full extent.

"They give me the smallest office in the building . . . one day I hope to be promoted and I'll get the broom cupboard."

Hartmann smiled and took a seat.

"You want some coffee or something?" Verlaine asked.

"Any good?"

"Fucking awful . . . like stewed raccoon piss and molasses."

Hartmann shook his head. "I'll take a raincheck then if you don't mind," he said.

Verlaine edged his way around the desk and took a seat facing Hartmann. A cool breeze sneaked through the inched-open window as if it had no business entering. Evening was on its way and for this Hartmann felt grateful. With darkness there were fewer reminders, fewer things he recognized. With the darkness he could excuse himself from the world, retire to his hotel room to watch TV and pretend he was back in New York.

"So what can I do for you?" Verlaine asked.

Hartmann shrugged his shoulders. "I don't know that you can do anything specific," he said. "We got the guy, you know?"

Verlaine nodded. "So I understand. How is he?"

"Old," Hartmann said. "Late sixties, loves the sound of his own voice. Listened to him talk for the better part of two days and still I have no fucking idea why he took the girl or where she might be."

"And you have half the FBI all over you like a bad rash."

"A very bad rash."

"Why you?" Verlaine asked. "You got some connection with this guy?"

Hartmann shook his head. "No idea . . . no idea at all."

"And that makes you feel real good," Verlaine said.

Hartmann nodded. "Sure as hell does."

"So what happens now?"

"Out of school?"

Verlaine nodded. "Not a word passes beyond this door."

"He's here . . . seems he wants to tell us his life story. We listen, we take notes, we make tapes, we have three dozen criminal profilers sweating blood up in Quantico, God knows how many agents down here running around in ever-decreasing circles, and we take it as it comes."

"So why come see me? You lonely down here in New Orleans?"

Hartmann smiled and shook his head. "You were the one who started this. You've been around some years, right?"

"Here in Orleans, or in the Department?"

"The latter."

"Eleven years all told," Verlaine said. "Three and a half in Vice, last couple in Homicide."

"You're not married?"

Verlaine shook his head. "No, and never have been. I have one brother and one sister but they keep themselves pretty much to themselves . . . end of a fucking dynasty, that's me."

Hartmann looked toward the window, southwards to the Federal Courts back of Lafayette Square. "The thing I can't get out of my head is this connection to Feraud," he said. "I can't help but think that Feraud is the one man who might know a great deal more than he's willing to say."

"I don't doubt it," Verlaine replied.

"And what did he say when you went down to see him? I know you told me already, but tell me again."

Verlaine opened the drawer on the right-hand side of his desk. From it he took a reporter's notebook and flipped through several pages until he found the one he wanted. "I made a note of it," he said. " 'Fess me up to the Feds if you like, but there was something about what Feraud said that really got to me. Why, I don't know, but after I told you about this I felt I needed to be clear about what he'd said, and so I wrote it down as best as I could remember." Verlaine leaned back in his chair and cleared his throat. "He said that I had a problem. He said I had a serious problem and that there was nothing he could do to help me. He said that the man I was looking for didn't come from here, by which I presumed he meant New Orleans, that he was once one of us, but not for many years. Feraud said that this man came from the outside, and that he would bring with him something that was big enough to swallow us all."

Verlaine looked at Hartmann.

Hartmann didn't speak.

"Feraud said I should walk away, that this was not something I should go looking for."

"And there was no mention of the kidnapping, and nothing about Gemini . . . no reference to either of those?"

Verlaine shook his head. "I didn't ask, and he didn't venture anything. Feraud is not the sort of person you push for answers."

Hartmann nodded. "I haven't been here for fifteen years, and I am aware of the man's reputation."

"So that was that. He said what he had to say and I left."

Hartmann leaned forward and looked directly at Verlaine. "I want to go back there to see him."

Verlaine laughed suddenly, unnaturally. "You're fucking joking, right?"

Hartmann shook his head. "I wanna go out there and talk to the man . . . I wanna find out how much he knows about this. I want to see if he knows this man, see if it doesn't prompt him to tell us a little more."

"And compromise the entirety of the federal investigation?"

Hartmann nodded. "That, yes . . . I have considered that, but nevertheless, right now he's the only person who seems to have any kind of an understanding of who this man is and what he might have done."

"All due respects for your cojones, but you can leave me the fuck out of that," Verlaine said. He looked nervous, agitated.

"I'm not going to get anywhere near him without you," Hartmann said.

"So you're not going to get anywhere near him then," Verlaine said, "because you sure as hell ain't dragging me into this. This is a federal jurisdiction investigation for Christ's sake! You seen how many people they've brought down here? This is Catherine Ducane, daughter of Louisiana's governor, and you wanna go do something that could jeopardize the entire operation?"

Hartmann shook his head slowly. "They don't have an operation. They have one helluva lot of men and horsepower. They have radios and tape recorders and voice experts and criminal profilers, but the fact of the matter is they actually don't have a plan between them. They are just waiting this out, hoping to hell that Perez will say something that gives them a clue as to where the girl might be."

Verlaine was quiet for a moment. "That's his name . . . the old guy? Perez?"

Hartmann nodded. "Ernesto Perez."

"What the fuck is that? Spanish or Mexican or something?"

"Cuban."

"Mafia?"

Hartmann glanced toward the window. He was saying too much and he knew it. "Indirectly, yes . . . connections with the Mafia in Cuba."

"And he's just sitting there telling you his whole life story, like his autobiography or something?"

"Yes, seems that way," Hartmann said. "Man's singing like a canary."

"And right now he's given you nothing that indicates why he took the girl and where he's hidden her?"

"Or if she's even still alive," Hartmann said. "He challenged me when I was talking to him. He made mention of something called the rule of threes."

Verlaine nodded. "Air, water and food, right?"

"That's right. By implication he suggested that she was somewhere with no food and every moment I wasted time in talking to him was a direct threat to her life."

"You believe him? You reckon he's got her somewhere and she's starving to death?"

"Christ only knows . . . I don't know what to believe any more. He knows what he's doing, and he's obviously very organized. Despite all the power of the federal government we're still no further forward in finding the actual location of this girl."

Verlaine said nothing for a little while. "This means something to you." It was not a question, more a simple statement of fact.

Hartmann looked back at Verlaine. He frowned.

"Something personal . . . I get the idea that this is in some way personal for you."

Hartmann shook his head. "Personal is personal . . . that's why it's called personal."

Verlaine smiled. "I understand that, but you're asking me to do something here that is very personal to me."

"To you . . . whaddya mean?"

"The fact that I might wanna stay alive a little longer. Feraud is not a man you cross. He's not a man you ignore. He asked me to walk away from this, to not go looking, and to never speak of it to him again."

"And you're gonna do what he says?" Hartmann asked, a sense of challenge in his tone.

Verlaine smiled and shook his head. "Don't come that shift with me . . . you wanna play your stupid mind games you go play it on the Feds. I got better things to do than fuck with something that ain't my business."

Hartmann was lost for words. He looked at the man facing him, the only man that could perhaps be an ally in this thing he had somehow managed to create for himself, and he realized that if he was to have any chance at all of getting some help he would have to tell the truth.

"You wanna know why I want this to end?"

Verlaine nodded. "Try me, and if it's good enough then I might consider giving you a hand."

Hartmann felt as if he would collapse inside. He realized how tired he was, how worn around the edges, and despite all that had taken place, all that he had heard from Perez, the one thing there at the forefront of his mind was what would happen if he missed his Saturday meeting with Carol and Jess.

And so, understanding that there was nothing further he could tell Verlaine, he told him the truth.

And Verlaine listened, and did not interrupt, and did not ask questions, and when Hartmann was done Verlaine leaned back in his chair and folded his arms behind his head. "So you're in the crap up to your fucking neck and you need me to bail you out?"

Hartmann nodded. "In the crap with this thing, with my wife and my kid, with my fucking job and everything else that matters a damn. I gotta see this through to the end. I gotta see it through, and on the one hand I cannot rush it, but on the other hand what happens with my wife and my daughter is one fuck of a lot more important to me than what happens to Catherine Ducane. I wanna see it done, I wanna see the girl back safe, but I need to get back to New York and see my wife before she gives up on me completely."

Verlaine was quiet for a time. He looked at the wall above Hartmann's head and seemed to be completely lost.

Hartmann could feel his heart beating in his chest.

Verlaine shook his head slowly and looked at Hartmann. "I get killed doing this and I am gonna be so fucking pissed you won't believe it."

Hartmann smiled. "You're a cop first and foremost, John Verlaine, and I know that you might have some sense of willingness to help me out, but above and beneath everything else you're in this to get the bad guys, right?"

Verlaine smiled. "Not just to get 'em," he said. "Wanna get the chance to shoot some motherfucker as well."

Hartmann laughed. "So you're gonna do this?"

"Against my intuition, against every shred of better judgment, against every rule in the fucking book . . . but yes, I will do this."

Hartmann, expecting to feel relief, felt instead a sense of fear gnawing at him. What was he doing? What the hell did he expect to happen when he went out there to see Antoine Feraud? He reminded himself of the reason for his action, and though this did nothing to assuage his apprehension, it nevertheless served to focus his mind. The intention was to get through this as fast as possible, to find the girl, to put the bad guy in the joint, to get the hell back to New York and salvage what he could of his marriage and his life.

"Tomorrow evening?" Hartmann asked.

Verlaine nodded. "Tomorrow evening it is."

"Time?"

"Come for six . . . we'll see what we can do."

Later, alone once more in the Marriott Hotel, Hartmann watched TV with the sound up. Anything to drown out his thoughts. He understood that he was ignorant of the full consequences of his actions, but he believed in the inherent balance of the universe: that if one approached something with a good intention then that could often turn the tide in one's favor. Had he believed sufficiently in the existence of God, he would have prayed. But he had seen far too much of the dark underbelly of humanity to consider that there was anyone out there taking any kind of responsibility for what was going on down here.

Some hours passed, and as New Orleans greeted midnight Hartmann fell asleep fully clothed. He dreamed of Carol and Jess, he dreamed of himself and Danny running through the streets of New Orleans; dreamed of sailing away in a paper boat big enough for two, its seams sealed with wax and butter, their pockets filled with nickels and dimes and Susan B. Anthony dollars . . .

Dreamed of these things, and yet beneath them, crawling in the shadows and the darker corners of his mind, he dreamed of a man lying dead in a pool of blood in a Havana motel cabin.

Monday morning, the first day of September. Incipient fall, and soon the wind would chill, the leaves would turn, and winter would make its gradual way toward even this part of America.

Hartmann arrived at the FBI office a good half an hour early. The tension was almost tangible, something perceivable from the street. They were all aware of the fact that they were together for no other reason than Perez and the kidnapping of Catherine Ducane, and they were acutely aware that Perez could be so easily wasting their time. The girl could be dead already.

"We got the facts on this Pietro Silvino," Schaeffer told Hartmann, but Hartmann was of the belief that Perez was telling them nothing more or less than the facts as he knew them. He believed that Perez was here for his own catharsis, for the cleansing and absolution of his own conscience. It would serve no purpose to tell them lies, at least no purpose he could discern.

"Found dead in a Havana motel room in February of 1960," Schaeffer said. "No one was ever charged or convicted of the killing."

Woodroffe nodded slowly. "I reckon there's gonna be an awful lot more like that," he said. "He's started right at the beginning and we've gotta listen to all of it before we even get an idea of what he's done with Catherine Ducane."

"And for what?" Schaeffer asked, the frustration evident in his tone. "Only to find out that the girl was dead a half hour after he took her?"

"You cannot think that way," Woodroffe said, but in his voice Hartmann could tell that he had thought that way also. All of them had. It was inevitable and inescapable. They really had no idea who they were dealing with, and no real indication of which way this would go.

"I'll tell you something—" Hartmann began, but suddenly there was a hubbub behind them, and looking down the length of the open-plan office he saw the first of the FBI escort team that would bring Perez in.

"Well, we'll see what he has to say for himself today," Hartmann said, and he turned and made his way toward the small office at the back of the building.

Perez seemed subdued when he sat down. He looked at Hartmann but said nothing at first. He reached for a polystyrene cup and filled it with water from a jug on the trolley. He drank slowly as if quenching his thirst, and then he set the cup down on the table and leaned back in his chair.

"It is different now," he said. "You live this life, you do these things, and it is only when you talk about them that you feel anything at all. I have never spoken of these things before, and now I am hearing them I am beginning to understand that there were so many choices, so many directions I could have taken."

"Is it not the same with all of us?" Hartmann asked, thinking at once of his own brother, of Carol and Jess.

Perez smiled. He took a deep breath and exhaled slowly. "I think I am tired. I think I am old and tired, and I will be relieved when this comes to an end."

"We could end it now," Hartmann said. "You could tell us where you have hidden Catherine Ducane, and then you would have all the time in the world to confess."

Perez laughed. "Confess? Is that what you think I am doing here, Mr. Hartmann? You think I have come to confess to you like a priest?" He shook his head. "I am not the penitent one, Mr. Hartmann. I have not come here to tell the world of my own sins, but to tell of the sins of others."

Hartmann frowned. "I don't understand, Mr. Perez."

"You will, Mr. Hartmann, you will. But everything will come in its own time."

"But will you give us no indication of how much time we have?"

"You have as much time as I am prepared to give you," Perez replied.

"That is all you will say?"

"It is."

"You understand the importance of this girl's life?"

Perez smiled. "It is all leverage, Mr. Hartmann. If I had taken a New Orleans restaurant waitress then you and I would not be sitting here in this room. I know who Catherine Ducane is. I have not done this without thought or planning—"

Perez fell silent.

Hartmann looked up.

"She is not somewhere where she will easily be found, Mr. Hartmann. She will be found when I decide to have her found. Where she is she will not be heard even if she screams continuously at the top of her voice. And if she does that she will only wear herself out and shorten her own lifespan. The road is long, Mr. Hartmann, and she is already at the very end of it. We play this game the way I wish it to be played. We follow my rules . . . and perhaps, just perhaps, the Ducane girl might see daylight again."

Perez paused for a moment, and then he looked up and smiled. "So we shall continue, eh?"

Hartmann nodded, and closed the door once again.

THIRTEEN

MIAMI IS A noise: a perpetual thundering noise trapped against the coast of Florida between Biscayne Bay and Hialeah; beneath it Coral Gables, above it Fort Lauderdale; everywhere the smell of the Everglades—rank, swollen and fetid in summer, cracked and featureless and unforgiving in winter.

Miami is a promise and an automatic betrayal; a catastrophe by the sea; perched there upon a finger of land that points accusingly at something that is altogether not to blame. And never was. And never will be.

Miami is a punctuation mark of dirt on a peninsula of misfortune; an appendage.

And now—of all places—my home.

Cuba was behind me, and with it the trials and tribulations of a land that still wrestled with its own conscience. 1960 folded up behind us, and looking back I saw events that somehow scarred a people's history, Castro vacillating indecisively between the promise of a dollar-rich hedonistic west and the validation of political ideology presented by the USSR. Castro seized US-owned properties and made further agreements with communist governments. He agreed to buy Soviet oil, even as John Fitzgerald Kennedy assumed the presidency of the United States in January of 1961 and sanctioned the cessation of diplomatic relations with Cuba. On 16 April 1961 Fidel Castro Ruz declared Cuba a socialist state. Three days later, backed by CIA funding and US military support, one thousand three hundred Cuban exiles invaded Cuba at a southern coastal region called the Bay of Pigs. Khrushchev promised Castro all necessary aid. The United States government incorrectly assumed the invasion would inspire the people of Cuba to rise up and seize power from Castro, to instigate a coup d'état, but they assumed wrong. The Cuban populace supported Castro without question. The invaders were captured, and each of them was sentenced to thirty years in jail.

The United States, in its continued infinite wisdom, went on pouring the nation's hard-earned dollars into military support for South Vietnam.

In February of '62 Kennedy imposed a full trade embargo on Cuba. Two months later Castro offered to ransom one thousand, one hundred and seventy-nine of the Bay of Pigs invaders for sixty-two million dollars. Kennedy sent the Marines into Laos. Sonny Liston KO'd Floyd Patterson in two minutes and six seconds.

October brought the discovery that Castro was permitting the Soviets to establish long-range missile launch sites in Cuba, ninety miles from the American mainland. A blockade of Cuba was instigated that Jack Kennedy had every intention of maintaining until Khrushchev agreed to remove the missiles. Castro announced his commitment to a Marxist-Leninist ethos; he nationalized industry, confiscated property owned by non-Cuban nationals, collectivized agriculture and enacted policies designed to benefit the common man. Many of the middle classes fled Cuba and established a large anti-Castro community in Miami.

On 28 October, after thirteen days during which the entire world dared not to blink, Khrushchev announced that all missile-launching sites on the island would be dismantled and returned to the USSR. On 2 November Kennedy lifted the Cuban blockade.

In December, the United States paid a fifty-three-million-dollar ransom and the Bay of Pigs invaders were freed.

I watched the events of those months unfold from a house in downtown Miami. I was twenty-five years old by the time the world exhaled once more, and though I had paid attention to these things it was as if they were merely moments of radio interference interrupting the soundtrack of my life.

And this *was* now my life. I had arrived here with no more mention than I deserved. In some small way I was myself an appendage, an addition to something so much bigger than myself, and though I was absorbed into the extant operation that existed in Miami, there was always the awareness that I was different. These people—people with names like Maurizio, Alberto, Giorgio and Federico, who all seemed to have secondary names like Jimmy the Aspirin (because he made Don Ceriano's "headaches" go away), Johnny the Limpet and Slapsie Maxie Rosenbloom—were part of a crew nicknamed the Alcatraz Swimming Team. They drank plenty, they laughed more, they spoke in broken Italian-American, and every other phrase seemed to be *"Chi se ne frega,"* which meant "Who gives a damn!," and I believed they didn't, and never had, and never would.

By the time I arrived it was March of 1962. January had seen the death of Lucky Luciano, a man whose name I heard quoted more times than perhaps any other. In some small way his death had played a part in Don Ceriano's return to the United States, for there were "family matters" to attend to that seemed pressing and urgent. His return was met with great enthusiasm, and those who were there to greet him as we arrived at a palatial three-story house in downtown Miami seemed to ask nothing of me. I was taken in without question, and on the two or three occasions Don Ceriano was asked about me he merely said, "This is my friend Ernesto. Ernesto has taken care of some things for me, some very important things, and his loyalty is beyond question." This seemed enough, for I was given a room in that house, a house where I would live with Don Ceriano and members of his family for a little more than six years. Don Ceriano let me keep the car, the Mercury Cruiser that had once belonged to Pietro Silvino, and money was available whenever I needed it. I felt at once part of this family, but yet so much an outsider. I did not feel afraid, only perhaps a little overawed by the people that I met, the seeming magnitude of their personalities, and I tried my best to be a part of whatever I had been inducted into. Once again it was merely a matter of self-preservation and survival. I had left Cuba, I had come to America; I possessed nothing but those things afforded me by Don Ceriano and his people. I had made a bed perhaps, and it was not difficult to lie in it. The world went about its business and I went with it.

The "important things" I had taken care of were simple enough. Don Ceriano would give me a name, sometimes show me a photograph, and I would be dispatched. I would not return until the man that bore the name was dead, no matter how long it took. Between the death of Pietro Silvino and my departure from Cuba I had taken care of eleven "important things." Each of them was unique, each of them special, the last one of which was my father.

Killing your own father is a truly spiritual experience: such a thing cannot exclude killing a little of yourself, yet at the same time it is an exorcism. There are some I have spoken with who talk of carrying the faces of the dead, as if some small part of their spirit enters you as they die, and from that point forward they will always be there. If I close my eyes and think hard enough I can remember all their faces. Perhaps, just perhaps, I can look in the mirror long enough and see their reflections in my own eyes. Imagination plays a part I am sure, but I believe there is some truth in what I have been told. We carry them all, but I—at least—carry the image of my father the most.

When he died he was all of forty-six years old. I had arranged a job for him at one of the smaller nightclubs in Old Havana, a club owned by Don Ceriano's brother-in-law, a wild-eyed and aggressive gambler called Enzio Scribani. Scribani had married Don Ceriano's youngest sister three or four years before, and though his promiscuity and perverse sexual tastes were legend, there was something about the way in which such things were handled that denied the possibility that he would be anything but family. Later, six or seven years after I had left Havana, Don Ceriano's sister, Lucia, a beautiful, innocent-looking girl, killed her husband by driving a pair of pinking shears through his right eye. She had then taken her own life.

My father, his reputation as the Havana Hurricane still to some degree intact, was employed as a doorman at the Starboard Club, a relatively minor concern in the grand scheme of things. Here the walk-on players and bit-piece actors in the grander theater of Havana's Mafia operations came to flirt with the hostesses, to gamble hundreds instead of thousands of dollars, to sometimes wander through the rear curtains where worn-out Cuban housewives would dance and take their clothes off for ten or fifteen dollars a time. It was a shabby place in reality, and though Enzio Scribani was the owner and proprietor of the establishment he seemed to make it his business to be there as infrequently as possible.

My father did his job. He turfed out the drunken Cubans; he protected the dancers from their irate brothers and lovers and husbands; he escorted the money couriers from the club to the bank; he made little noise, he did not complain, he took his dollars at the end of each week and he drank them away before Monday rolled around again. With the money I earned from my Havana work with Don Ceriano I had rented a five-room apartment off Bernaza near the Old Wall Ruins. Here, my father had a room where he would sleep off his drunk until it was time to wake and return to work. I saw little of him, and with this arrangement I was satisfied. He spoke little, and when he did there was always an underlying apologetic tone, and as the months drew on I became less and less interested in what he had to say, and more intent that at some point soon he would cease to be my responsibility. I did not hate him. Hate was too strong an emotion for someone toward whom I felt nothing. Less than nothing. I often imagined that, in attempting to eject an undesirable from the Starboard, he would embroil himself in a fight that would get him shot or stabbed or beaten to death. But there was no such event. It seemed that my father, in relinquishing his arrogance and conceit, had also relinquished his right to be involved in anything of moment at all.

In the latter part of August 1961, a few days after another engagement had been organized for myself and an adversary of Don Ceriano's, after another small matter had been perfunctorily dispatched, I received a visit at my apartment from Giorgio Vaccorini. To me he was known as Max or Maxie, short for Slapsie Maxie Rosenbloom the boxer. The nickname had been earned as a result of an incident outside the Hotel Nacional when a parking attendant had tried to take Giorgio's keys from him in order to park and valet the car. Giorgio, drunk and incoherent, had believed he was being robbed, and he turned and let fly with a roundhouse that broke the kid's neck. One punch and the teenager was dead. The matter was closed within half an hour with the delivery of ten thousand US dollars to the home of the Cuban National Chief of Police. So Maxie came to see me late afternoon. He looked serious, a little tense, and he asked me to sit down as he had some news for me.

"A little problem," he started, and again he assumed a serious expression. When these guys got serious then life was serious.

"Your father," he went on. "There seems to be some kind of problem with your father."

I leaned back in my chair and crossed my legs. I looked around for my cigarettes but could not see them.

"He went with the delivery guy to the bank this morning," Maxie said, his voice hushed, a little hesitant. "They took the usual kind of money, maybe five or six grand, and they went off to the bank just like regular."

I sat patiently, waiting for the problem to be voiced.

"Seems they never reached the bank, Ernesto. Seems that your father and the courier never arrived at all, and we got to thinking that perhaps they did a runner with the money."

I nodded understandingly.

"An hour or so ago we found the courier. You know Anselmo, young guy with the scar on his face here—" Maxie raised his right hand and indicated a point above his left eyebrow.

I knew Anselmo Gamba; had fucked his sister one time.

"We found Anselmo with his throat cut down an alleyway off of one of the sidestreets near the Starboard, maybe two or three blocks away. There was no sign of your father. Not the money neither. So Don Ceriano . . . Don Ceriano said I should come down here and speak with you and see if you couldn't take a look for your father and take care of things, you know?"

I nodded.

"So that's what I came to tell you," Maxie said, rising awkwardly from the chair. "See if you can't find him, sort out what happened, okay?"

I smiled. "Okay Maxie, I'll sort things out. Tell Don Ceriano that whatever the problem is isn't a problem any more."

Maxie smiled back. He seemed relieved to be going. I showed him to the door, placed my hand on his shoulder as he stepped into the hall-way, and noticed that he flinched. I noted this inside. Even Slapsie Maxie, a man who had hit a kid with a roundhouse and busted his neck, was a little scared of the Cuban. This pleased me, confirmed once again that I had become someone.

I waited until Maxie was out of sight and then collected my coat and my cigarettes. I left the apartment and started toward Old Havana and the watering holes where I knew my father would be hiding.

It took me three hours to find him, and by then it was evening. The sky was black, almost starless.

Even as he saw me coming toward him across the floor of a beat-to-shit rundown joint on the coast side of the quarter he started to cry. I felt nothing. This was business pure and simple, and I had no time for overemotional performances.

"The money?" I asked him as I slid in beside him on the seat.

"They robbed it," he slurred. "Robbed the money and killed the kid . . . I tried, Ernesto, I tried to stop them, but there were three of them and they were quick—"

I raised my hand.

"Ernesto . . . they came out of nowhere, three of them, and there was nothing I could do . . ."

"You were supposed to protect the courier," I said matter-of-factly. "That's your job, Father. They send you along to protect the courier, to make sure that the money gets to the bank, that nothing happens to him on the way."

My father raised his hands as if in prayer. "I know, I know, I know," he whined. "I know why they send me, and every time I have done my job, every time I have protected him and nothing has happened—"

"You have the money with you?"

My father opened his eyes in shock. "The money? You think I took the money? You think I would kill someone for money? I am your father, Ernesto, you know I would never do something like that."

I nodded. "Yes, I know you, Father. I know you would kill someone for no money at all."

He did not reply. There was nothing he could have said. All these past years the death of my mother, his wife, had sat between us like a third person. It had always been there, spoken of or not, it had *always* been there.

My father shook his head. "You have to tell them . . . you have to tell them what happened. You have to make them believe that I did not steal the money and kill the boy. I didn't do it, Ernesto, I *couldn't* . . ."

"You have to tell them, Father. You have to stop running away and hiding. The longer you stay away the more they will believe that you took the money. If you come with me now and tell them what happened, how these men robbed you and killed Anselmo, I will support you, I will make them understand that there was nothing you could have done."

My father nodded. He started smiling. He was already rising to his feet. He reached out and gripped my arm. "You are my son," he said quietly. "I will never forget what you have done to help me. You brought me here, you got me a job, a place to live, and I will remember this for the rest of my life."

My father, the Havana Hurricane, did not have to remember how much he owed me for very long at all. A little more than twenty minutes later he lay dead in an alleyway two blocks from the Starboard Club. He did not question me when I turned right and walked him down that alleyway, which he would have known went nowhere at all. He did not cry out when I hit him across the back of the head and he fell awkwardly to the ground. He lay there for a moment, stunned and speechless, and in his eyes was an expression of such resigned inevitability that I knew he was aware of his own death coming fast like a freight train.

From the ground I took a brick, and squatting down with one knee on his chest I raised the brick above my head.

"For your wife," I told him quietly. "For your wife and my mother this is long overdue."

He closed his eyes. No sounds. No tears. Nothing at all.

I think he was dead after I hit him the first time. The corner of the brick destroyed much of the right-hand side of his face. I imagined the subsequent repeated blows to his head and neck would not have been felt at all. It was like killing a dog. Less than a dog.

Three days later it was discovered that Anselmo Gamba and my father had been robbed on the way to the bank. They had been robbed by three Cuban brothers—Osmany, Valdés and Vicente Torres. I was not dispatched to attend to them, for such things as the killing of three small-time Cuban hoodlums was considered beneath my talents, but someone was dispatched and the money was recovered, and a month and a half later an oil drum was recovered from the Canal de Entrada with three heads and six hands inside.

Don Ceriano had been the one to tell me that my father had not lied, that they had in fact been robbed on the way to the bank.

"I sent you to attend to this matter for my own reasons," he told me. "I sent Maxie over to tell you so that you could help us find your father and discover what had happened."

I did not reply.

"I wondered what you would do when you found him," he went on. "I wanted to know what action you would take."

Again I said nothing. I was asking myself if there was a point to what he was saying.

"And you killed your own father," Don Ceriano said.

I nodded my head.

"You have nothing to say, Ernesto?" he asked.

"What do you want me to say, Don Ceriano?"

Don Ceriano looked both surprised and perplexed. "You killed your own father, Ernesto, and you have nothing to say?"

I smiled. "I will say three things, Don Ceriano."

Don Ceriano raised his eyebrows.

"Firstly, my father murdered his own wife, my mother. Secondly, his punishment was both appropriate and overdue." I paused for a moment.

"And the third thing?" Don Ceriano asked.

"We shall not talk about it again as it deserves no importance."

Don Ceriano nodded. "As you wish, Ernesto, as you wish."

It was not mentioned again. Not a single word came from Don Ceriano's lips, nor any of those who worked with us while we were in Havana. My father's murder was as effortlessly forgotten as his life.

During the coming months I was to understand more of the connections between Florida and Cuba than I had believed existed. Of these things Don Ceriano spoke, but it was also from conversations between the members of his family and those who attended the house in Miami that I learned much of the background. Mafia money had been moving into Florida since the 1930s, with investments in such places as the Tropical Park Race Track in Coral Gables and Meyer Lansky's Colonial Inn. During the 1940s the Wofford Hotel had been a base for both

Lansky and Frank Costello, Costello having close ties with a man called Richard Nixon who would later become president of the United States. Ironically, during the Watergate investigation some years later, an outfit called the Keyes Realty Company was identified as having been the intermediary between organized crime and Miami–Dade County officials. In 1948 Keyes Realty had transferred ownership of a property to a Cuba-Mafia investment group called ANSAN. Later, that same real estate interest passed in ownership to the Teamsters' Union Pension Fund and Meyer Lansky's Miami National Bank. Subsequently, in 1967, ownership was signed over to Richard Nixon, and it was discovered that one of the Watergate burglars, a Cuban exile, was a vice president of that same Keyes Realty Company. Lou Poller, one of Meyer Lansky's trusted confederates, had taken over control of the Miami National Bank in 1958, and it was through this bank that Mafia money was laundered, often used to purchase apartment buildings, hotels, motels and mobile home companies. The house in which I stayed during those six years in Miami was one of those real estate interests, and it was to here that many of Don Ceriano's people would come to talk business, to pass details on about who "needed their ticket punched," or who should "get a letter on the Chicago typewriter."

I heard word of Santo Trafficante Jr. again. His name had been mentioned in Cuba, but I had not appreciated that he had in fact been born right there in Florida. Trafficante had operated the Sans Souci and Casino International operations in Havana, and possessed interests and influence in the Riviera, the Tropicana, the Sevilla Biltmore, the Capri Hotel Casino and the Havana Hilton. In Tampa he controlled the Columbia Restaurant, the Nebraska, the Tangerine and the Sands Bars. Trafficante had fled to Havana in 1957 after Grand Jury subpoenas were issued for his arrest and questioning. In the early part of 1958 he had been questioned by the Cuban National Police regarding the Apalachin Meeting, which he denied having attended. He was still wanted in New York for his alleged involvement in the killing of Albert Anastasia, but the Cuban National Police were interested in his manipulation of the bolita numbers for Cuban operatives on behalf of Fidel Castro.

Whatever may have been the allegations against him, Don Ceriano said enough for me to understand that Santo Trafficante Jr. had overseen all Mafia-related operations in Florida since the death of his father in August 1954. As far back as 1948 and 1949 Trafficante had been involved with Frank Zarate, the principal defendant in a case instigated by the Federal Bureau of Narcotics, who collaborated with US Customs and the New York City Police Department to break a Peruvian cocaine supply coming into the US through Cuba. Irrespective of this matter, Trafficante was granted resident status by the Cuban Immigration Department in October 1957. In a memo issued by a narcotics agent called Eugene Marshall in July 1961, it was made clear that Castro had operatives working in Tampa and Miami who made significant bets on Cuba's bolita through Trafficante's organization. Trafficante himself was observed meeting several times with a man called Oscar Echemendia. Echemendia was not only a part-owner of the Tropicana Night Club in Havana, but also one of the most influential controllers of the bolita in Dade County, Miami. It was rumored that after Castro's seizure of power, after he ousted organized crime from the casinos and hotels in Cuba, he kept Santo Trafficante Jr. in jail as he so disliked the man. This was a cause for amusement among the families in Miami, for they knew that Trafficante was an agent for Castro, and he was influential in establishing the terms upon which the Mafia could return to Cuba.

Thus there was a connection between Florida and Cuba, and thus I was accepted as a member of their family. Ceriano was a main player, a heavy hitter, and I played my part for Ceriano. I consorted with an organization called Cuban Americans in Miami; I relayed inside information from employees of Radio Martí, a US-government sponsored station, and soon I could utter the words *Chi se ne frega* with as much conviction as the rest of them. I was young, I was willing, I could wear a silk Italian suit with as much panache and style as anyone, and I felt no compunction. I believed these people, I believed their motives and rationale, and if the instruction came that someone needed to be excommunicated from the world, I executed that request with punctuality and professionalism. To me it was a job that had to be done. I did not ask questions. I did not need answers. In some small way I wanted for nothing.

I believed I had arrived, that there was a purpose to my life, and considering my natural ability to do things that no one else was prepared to do, I was afforded a degree of respect and camaraderie that was ordinarily reserved only for blood relatives. I was Ernesto Cabrera Perez, adoptive son of Don Giancarlo Ceriano, soldier of Santo Trafficante Jr., head of the Mafia in Miami. There were people here who would figure more prominently as the months became years. It was an era of tension and political subterfuge. Anti-Castro feelings were high amongst some factions of the families, and it was in Miami that wealthy Cuban exiles collaborated with Sam Giancana to oust Castro from

Cuba. From what little I could gather, both the CIA and the FBI were instrumental in funding such operations. A man called Robert Maheu, apparently ex-CIA, had hired Sam Giancana to form assassination squads to go after Castro, and Giancana had put his Los Angeles lieutenant, Johnny Roselli, in charge of the operation. Years later, in 1978, when the House Select Committee questioned Roselli he said that those teams were trained for the Kennedy assassination as well. That was all but part of the truth. Kennedy was a different story, a story that would not emerge for more than a year. From Roselli the Select Committee never established any further details. His body was found floating in an oil drum off the Florida coast. Sam Giancana was shot in Chicago. There were three different assassination teams in Dallas on the day Kennedy was killed, and only one was known by Roselli. The other two came from within the United States Intelligence community, and those that filed reports for the Warren Commission, those that handled the legal implications of all subsequent investigations, were far more informed as to what actually occurred than they ever said. They had their own *cosa nostra,* and they kept their mouths shut and their thoughts to themselves, and have done to this day.

I did not understand the politics, and I did not pretend to. I knew that people visited with Santo Trafficante, and from Trafficante would come messages to Don Ceriano, and some of those messages would find their way to me and I would be sent forth to see to things in the best way I knew how. Connections between Miami and New York were tight, also with Los Angeles, but when I heard of Don Ceriano's intended move into the casinos and clubs of New Orleans, I felt that an aspect of my own past was in danger of surfacing. I believed I had disconnected, but—through my loyalty and allegiance to those who'd brought me back from Havana—I was to be obliged to return to my own homeland, the place of my birth, the beginning of all these things.

It was soon after the murder of Marilyn Monroe, August of 1962. Found dead in her Hollywood bungalow after taking an overdose of Nembutal, Marilyn Monroe was a casualty of war, it seemed. Jack Kennedy's sexual preferences were not unknown within the Mafia community, for it was Jack Kennedy who'd had an affair with Judith Exner, a girl who had also slept with Sam Giancana, the most influential Chicago mob boss. Exner had been introduced to Kennedy and Giancana by Frank Sinatra, who had entertained the likes of Albert Anastasia, Joseph Bonanno, Frank Costello and Santo Trafficante on Christmas Eve 1946 during a break in the infamous Havana Conference, a conference which had resulted in the contract to kill Bugsy Siegel for the theft of several million dollars from the Flamingo operation in Las Vegas. Besides Judith Exner, it was known that Kennedy had had an affair with Mary Pinchot Meyer, a fact recorded in the memoirs of White House assistant Barbara Gamarekian. The Meyer girl wound up dead only months after Kennedy himself, and it certainly wasn't from natural causes. Another girl, only eighteen when she went to the White House to interview Jackie Kennedy for a school newspaper, was Marion Fahnestock, known at the time as Mimi Beardsley. After Kennedy met her she was rapidly assigned a post as a White House intern, and from then until days before Kennedy's assassination she continued an affair with the most powerful man in the world. Marilyn was a different story. Interns, secretaries, legal aides and internal White House staff—these people could be hushed up and paid off. But Marilyn Monroe? Marilyn had to die, and die she did. On 5 August 1962, a little more than a year before Kennedy got his own cranium ventilated in Dealey Plaza, Marilyn was obliged to take a few more Nembutal than she really needed to get herself off to sleep. Don Ceriano knew the details. I asked him one time, and he said, "You know enough to know that she is dead." He said nothing beyond that, and I didn't ask again.

It was in the latter part of that month that I was asked to visit a man called Feraud in New Orleans. I had been away the better part of four years, and in my expression Don Ceriano saw that I did not wish to go.

He asked me why.

"I have my own reasons," I replied.

"Reasons enough to dissuade you from doing something I need you to do?"

"There would never be enough reasons to dissuade me, but I can ask you only once if there is someone else who can be sent."

Don Ceriano leaned forward. He rested his elbows on his knees and steepled his hands together. "This man, this Antoine Feraud, is a very powerful man. He has much influence and importance in New Orleans. New Orleans is like Havana of old, it is a gambling city, a city filled with prostitution and drugs and great potential. We need to work out a cooperative agreement with these people, and as a gesture of goodwill I wish you to go to see this man and do something for him, you understand?"

I nodded. "I have asked, and you have answered."

"You are a good man, Ernesto, a true friend. I would not ask you if there was someone else I could trust as much, but there is not. I am not prepared to risk the possibility of losing the business that will come our way because of this man by sending someone who may make a mistake."

"With your blessing I will go and do this thing," I said.

Ceriano rose to his feet. He placed the flat of his hand on my head. "If only my own sons were of your caliber and ability," he whispered, and then he leaned and kissed my cheek.

I rose. He gripped my shoulders. "I will be with you," he said quietly, and I believed he would be—if in spirit alone—for he had become more a father to me than the Havana Hurricane had ever been.

Louisiana came back to me like a cancer, once benign, now malignant.

Louisiana came back to me like a nightmare I believed I had forgotten.

Times were that the law would walk these tracks: the Revenue men driving their unmarked cars along these winding roads, out here amongst the bayous, the intersecting canals that cut some fine-drawn line between the swamps and stagnant tributaries. Times were that they would bring their city prayers down here and fight for what they believed was equitable and just. They would find distilleries, dynamite them, arrest the families' men and bring them to trial before the peripatetic circuit court judges who traveled these quarters dispensing law and judicial expertise. The families would retaliate the only way they knew how, returning justice in true eye-to-eye manner, killing and maiming and returning wounded Revenue men back to the city. For many years this process continued, until statisticians with sharp pencils and white collars proved that these search-and-destroy missions were fruitless. They lost as many men as they arrested. The belief in the law changed, civilization seemed to grow around the family territories, and people were no longer interested in what was done beyond their limits. The police did not so much concede defeat as adopt a live-and-let-live attitude. This itself wore these agreements into the earth, a path cut through by the passage of many feet rather than any conscious decision, and the territory stayed the territory, the law that applied to these people quite the opposite to any law known and followed elsewhere.

I entered this country with the degree of respect ordinarily reserved for the dead, but I also understood that the dead could perceive nothing, and thus deserved no respect. Don Ceriano had spoken to me of Antoine Feraud. Daddy Always, he called him, for this was the name he was given in these parts. To take the law into your own hands down here was to play into the hands of Feraud, and his authority was close to autocratic. Those who followed him, Don Ceriano told me, followed him reverentially. Those who did not walked a fine line between his compassion and his own form of brutal and indifferent justice.

A bridge spanned a small tributary close to the limits of Feraud's land. His property ran a good mile from the large colonial house that had passed down the family line for many generations, and where the swamps began his necessity to guard his boundaries ceased. The bridge was stationed at all times by at least two of Feraud's men, tall, invariably ugly, and they carried carbines or pump actions with no threat of unlawful possession. The police knew, and they understood a man's desire to protect his land and his family, and concessions had been granted.

It was 1962, but here time had stopped somewhere in the 1930s.

One afternoon, with the threat of imminent rain darkening the sky as if evening had already begun, I approached the bridge with a deepening sense of desperation. I did not want to be here, but I had no choice. To return to Don Ceriano with this thing undone would be to return with betrayal. There was work to be done, and as an act of good faith between Feraud and Ceriano I had been sent to complete the work. This I would do, but this thing scared me. This was my own homeland, a place where I had witnessed the death of my mother, and though my father had paid the price for his actions, though I had exacted my own justice for what he had done, I still harbored a memory of this place in the darkest recess of my heart.

At the bridge I was greeted by Feraud's men. They spoke in broken New Orleans French, and they directed me up toward the house. I started through the banks of swollen, fetid undergrowth that infested this land like spreading sores. Perhaps the water was bad, stagnant and oily; perhaps the density of foliage denied sufficient light; perhaps the earth was deficient in nitrogen and minerals, for the trees down here were twisted and gnarled, and the branches that leered over the foot-worn pathways were like beckoning arthritic fingers, summoning harsh words and harsher actions. When darkness drifted through these groves and banks, there could be no man who didn't feel some sense of unease, the shadows pressing against the face, the hands, the humidity exaggerated, the vision blurred and limited to ten or fifteen feet. Years ago I had walked near this territory. Years ago I had driven a dead man out here and crushed his head beneath the wheel of a car. I could recall that journey, fine lines of condensation chasing tracks down the car windows, the smell of the bayou, the intensity of it all . . .

I walked out toward Feraud's house, paused at the end of a wide, churned-up driveway, its mud ridged and dried where the tires of arriving and departing cars had twisted the earth into patterns of progress. I stood with my hands buried in the pockets of my coat. I was apprehensive, tight in the stomach, and when I walked on I felt my heart beat a little faster with every step. It was not the prospect of meeting Feraud that scared me, nor the promise of whatever he might ask of me, but the fact that this territory—after all these years—still aroused feelings that I could not comprehend.

Ahead of the house's wide frontage, a cream-colored sedan was parked, the rear door opened toward me and an elderly man seated inside was smoking a long cigar. Up on the wooden-balustraded veranda a swing hammock rocked gently back and forth. On it sat two small dark-skinned children who said nothing, who just looked at me as I approached.

The man in the back of the car watched me also, drawing on his cigar every once in a while and issuing a fine pall of silvery smoke out into the darkening atmosphere. The breeze came up from Borgne, the trees shifted with the breathless vacuum it created, and the sound of cicadas punctuated the static silence with a regularity that seemed unnatural.

The hollow echo of my feet on the wooden planking at the front of the house, the screen door creaking as I reached for the handle and drew it open, the wire mesh casting fine checkered patterns on my skin, sweat breaking out across my forehead; nervous tension sat in the base of my gut like something awful sleeping.

The house smelled of roasted pecans, freshly squeezed orange juice and, beneath these vague aromas, the bittersweet tang of alcohol and cigar smoke, the haunt of old leather and wood, the ghosts of the bayou that invaded every room, every hallway and corridor.

I took my left hand out of my pocket. I stood there silently. I heard footsteps approaching from the rear of the house and instinctively took a step backward.

A domestic, an ancient Creole with a face like warped, sun-bleached leather appeared through a doorway alongside the stairs. A wide grin creased the lower half of his face.

"Mr. Perez," he said, his voice like a deep ache coming from some-where within his bones. "Mr. Feraud is waitin' for ya . . . come this way."

The old man turned and walked back through the doorway. I started after him, the sound of my footsteps resounding in triplicate through the vastness of the house's interior.

We walked for minutes, it seemed, and then a door appeared as if from nowhere on the side of the hallway, and I waited while the old man opened it and indicated I should pass through.

Feraud stood there, immobile. He looked out through the ceiling-high windows that seemed to span the entire length of the room, and when he turned, he turned slowly, all the way round to face me.

He smiled. He was not an old man, perhaps no more than forty or forty-five, but etched into his parchment skin were lines that spoke of a thousand years of living. Don Ceriano had told me that this man was responsible for many killings, people shot and hanged and garrotted and drowned in the bayous, and even as I looked into his eyes I imagined that this man was perhaps responsible for the fights that my father had attended; that a man such as this would have money and influence to not only arrange such things, but also take care of any misfortune that might befall one of the fighters.

"To make a man a myth determines his stature," Don Ceriano had told me before I'd left. "For despite the rumors, some of which have been exaggerated, there are still many stories that are factual in their origin. When he was thirteen Feraud killed his own father—opened his throat with a straight razor, cut his tongue away and sent it to his mother in a handmade mother-of-pearl box. With his father silenced, Antoine Feraud became the child Napoleon. There were many who refused allegiance, more from their revulsion at his merciless lack of respect for his forebears than his age, but a few examples brought opinions around. Feraud was renowned for one unerring quality. In his favor you were protected. If you crossed him you followed the advice of those who knew him: you left the county, the state, even the country, or you killed yourself. By the time he was twenty, Feraud was credited with more than ten suicides, people who had apparently killed themselves as a result of his dissatisfaction. Better to die fast with a bullet in your head than to suffer the penalty that Feraud would inflict. He took the law away, and everything ran by his word. He created a territory, and within that territory everything was his and his alone."

"Mr. Perez, *venez ici*—" Feraud said. His voice was rich and deep; it echoed within the huge room.

I stepped forward, apprehension flooding my body. I approached him. He smelled of lemons, of some vague and haunting spice, of smoke and ancient armagnac.

"You have come from my friend Don Ceriano," Feraud said. *"Il dit que vous avez un coeur de fer* . . . an iron heart?"

Feraud stepped back. He reached up and held my shoulders. I could not move, could barely breathe, and then he steered me gently toward a high wing-backed chair in front of the window. He took the chair beside it, lowering himself slowly, tugging the creases of his pants before he sat.

"I know of Don Ceriano," Feraud said. "He is a powerful man, a man of spirit and virtue. He possesses ambitions and dreams, and this is good. A man who does not possess dreams is an empty shell. He believes that we can conspire in business, that we can serve each other well, and I am inclined to agree. In order to initiate what I believe will be a mutually beneficial relationship, he has offered me your services in a small matter that needs to be addressed. *Comprenez-vous?*"

I nodded. I was here not for Feraud but for Don Ceriano. I did not need to understand anything but the details of what had to be done.

"Very good," he said. "We shall have dinner here. You shall stay with us, and then tomorrow we will discuss this business and see what is to be done."

It was late afternoon of the following day when Antoine Feraud sent Innocent to fetch me from my room. I once again followed the old Creole through the corridors of the vast house and was shown into a room where Feraud stood talking with another man. He was perhaps the same age as myself, somewhere in his midtwenties, though any similarity between us stopped there. He was Louisiana-born and bred—not the Louisiana of my mother and father, but that of old Orleans money, the kind of money that wanted for nothing, and thus was unaware of any such notion as absence.

Antoine Feraud introduced the man as Ducane, Charles Ducane, and when he shook my hand he gave that impression of worldly confidence that comes from having sufficient family money to make anything go away. He was a handsome man, perhaps a little taller than I; dark-haired, his features almost aquiline. He appeared to me as a man who knew that anything could be obtained with enough money or violence, and yet his features told me that he understood neither. His looks would gain him the attention of women, and yet the lack of compassion behind those looks would ultimately drive them away. His position and connections would gain him associates and "friends," but such people would remain loyal only so long as his position served their own ends. I was there to make something go away, and where most men would have believed me dangerous, at least a man to be wary of, this Charles Ducane seemed to register nothing. It was only as I watched him that I saw the seams and joins that defined him. He was somehow awkward in his manner, and as he spoke he seemed to be seeking Feraud's approval for each word he uttered. Feraud was the Devil, and this man, this young and inexperienced man, was perhaps his acolyte. I imagined there was some arrangement between them, that Feraud was orchestrating the execution of some necessity, and for this thing Ducane would be forever in his debt. For all the world Charles Ducane wanted people to believe he was someone important, someone special, but in all truth I believed that whatever was happening was going to take place solely and exclusively because of Antoine Feraud. A Faustian pact had been engineered, and though Ducane appeared to be of significance in this matter, it was Feraud who had created the reality.

We three—the head of the Feraud family, his old-Orleans-money friend and myself, the crazy Cuban-American—sat in a room not dissimilar to the one where I had first met Feraud. Feraud and I said almost nothing throughout the whole exchange, and Ducane spoke with me as if we were close, had always been close, and would remain so for the rest of our lives. He was pretending that I had entered his world, that I had been granted an audience with Lucifer and should be appreciative. But Charles Ducane, unknown to himself, was in truth talking to Satan.

"Politics is Machiavellian," he began, "and where once a concession might have been made for territorial indiscretions, we have an indiscretion here that cannot be forgiven. My family owns a great many businesses, many interests right across the state, and behind those interests are people whose names must never be questioned or sullied, and whose pockets must be kept fat with enough dollars to make them feel they need no more. You understand, Mr. Perez?"

I nodded. I didn't need the précis, merely the name, the place, the manner in which the job needed to be done.

"My father owns a factory where canned goods are processed. There is a senior manager there, a man of little significance, but his brother is the head of the workers' union, and the workers are restless and agitated. This, in and of itself, is of no great importance, but the company is to be sold, and if there is the slightest hint of unrest within the ranks the deal could be soured. The union man is a voice for the workers, he is their guiding force, and with a few words he could march those men right out of there and collapse this sale. We are not interested in the union. They can fight amongst themselves until Kingdom come after the factory has been sold, but for the next two weeks we require nothing but silence, compliance and hard work."

Charles Ducane, a young man, a man perhaps asked to "take care of this small matter" by his father, leaned back in the deep leather armchair and sighed.

"The union man we will not touch. He is too visible. We have spoken with him but his head is as hard as rock. He has no wife, no children, and thus the closest person to him is his brother, the manager. Tonight, a little after nine, the manager will take a young woman to a motel off the highway down here, perhaps three or four miles away, and he will stay the night. We require a message to be carried to the union man, a message he will not misinterpret, and how this is done we do not care. There is to be no connection to me or my family. It must appear to be the work of some crazy person, a vagabond or an opportunist thief perhaps, and we will ensure that the message is received loud and clear. We need this to be unmistakable but unconnectable, you understand, Mr. Perez?"

"The name of the motel?" I asked.

"The Shell Beach Motel," Ducane said. He paused for a moment and then withdrew a single monochrome photograph from his inside breast pocket. He handed it to me. I studied the man's face, and then I returned the picture to Ducane.

Ducane smiled; he turned and looked at Feraud. Feraud nodded as if granting Papal indulgence.

I believed then that I understood what was happening. Ducane, perhaps his family, needed this man killed. They could not do it themselves, such a thing would have been too great a risk, but more importantly it seemed that such a thing had to be sanctioned by Feraud. Ducane, important though he considered himself to be, had been sent as the negotiator. I wondered what price these people had had to pay in order for this execution to have been granted.

Feraud looked at me. "Any further questions?"

I shook my head. "Consider it done."

Ducane smiled and rose to his feet. He shook Antoine Feraud by the hand, and then me. He said something in French to Feraud which I did not understand, and Feraud laughed.

He looked once more directly at me, and in that second I saw the fear manifest in his eyes, and then he started toward the door. Innocent appeared and escorted him to the front of the house.

"This is important enough," Feraud said once Ducane had disappeared.

"I understand," I replied.

Feraud smiled. "You do not care for details, do you, Ernesto Perez?"

I frowned.

"The whys and wherefores of all of this business we are involved in."

"I ask when I need to ask, and when I do not I keep my thoughts to myself."

"Which is the way it should be," Feraud said. "Now we will eat, and when we are done you will do this thing. Then you will return to see Don Ceriano and tell him that he and I will do some business of our own."

It was close, the air thick with the smell of verdant growth. Out there I was alone. Out there the sky pressed down on me between the thick overlapping branches of the trees, and between the gaps I could see the stars watching me in silence.

To my left the highway ran a straight line back toward Chalmette and the Arabi District, and every once in a while the faint hum of some traveler drifted through. From where I lay in the mud, from beneath the ankle-deep water that stuck to my skin, I could see the vague haunt of lights in the distance. I lay quiet for some time, and then I rose slowly and stripped naked. I became one with everything around me; I became truly, seamlessly invisible. I stood there in the swollen heat of night, and then I shifted back and disappeared into the silence and darkness of the bayou. Sometimes I went under, walking out along the bottom of some stagnant riverbed, and then I surfaced, my hair slicked to my skull, my eyes white against the blackness of my face. Around me the trees stretched their roots through the soft and forgiving earth, teasing their gnarled fingers into the weed-infested water as if to test it for temperature, and everywhere, inside every breath, was the smell of decay, the strong odor of a country dying—inborn, inbred, slime-caked boles crumbling into the ground, and from the mulch of their stinking graves a new land would be born. The ground was thick with this amniotic pulp, the effort of life attempting escape, the stench heady and enervating, a high like smoking something dead.

Sometimes I paused to kneel, the sensation of undergrowth between my legs, and I leaned back, my head angled away from my body, and I closed my eyes. I could smell burning, like gasoline, oil, cordite, wood. I could smell gasoline on my skin, see the colors that grew and spread across my arms, my chest. I imagined my face in deep rainbow hues, blackened at the nose and chin, and above this the frightening starkness of white eyes. I bared my teeth, and wondered how much like a nightmare I looked. I smiled, I crouched and crawled back to the water and sank beneath the filth.

I walked a mile, perhaps more, and above me the stars watched all the way. They bore witness, they understood, but they did not judge. They saw us all as children, because compared to them we came and went in one brief twinkling, and if I understood this I understood how we were all truly nothing. Nothing mattered. Nothing bore any significance in comparison to that. Nothing meant anything any more.

I eventually tired, and lying at the side of some swollen tributary, the dank and stinking water overlapping my chest, I closed my eyes and rested. After an hour or so I rose once more and started out toward the highway.

Lights were ahead of me. Something stirred within, something excited, something indefinable, and I stepped into the depth of the trees and watched. A car turned off the highway and slid silently into the forecourt of a semicircular arrangement of small cabins. A motel. Lights from a cabin. People. My heart beat beautifully, had never worked better, and I understood that I was loved by the stars, loved by the earth, loved by everything, for that's what I was, wasn't I? I *was* everything.

Again I sank to my hands and knees, and from where I hid within the dank and humid woods I started out through the undergrowth toward the lights. I was one with the darkness. I was unseen, unheard, unknown. I was everything and nothing. My thoughts were hollow and weightless, and they turned in invisible circles, back and forth within the bounds of some limitless and empathetic mind. Ghosts, you see. I haunted the world.

I reached the edge of the road. I crouched in silence. I held my breath. There was nothing out there, nothing but me and the lights, and I slipped across the surface of the highway, my feet never touching the ground, it seemed. I was perfect. More than perfect. I *was* somebody.

There were twelve cabins, five with lights, seven without. I was within speaking distance of the first but I said nothing. There was nothing to say.

In my hand I held a knife I had carried all the way without thinking, as if a natural appendage to my arm. Its blade was blackened with mud and filth, and wiping it clean between my fingers, I turned it beneath the light of the neon sign. It flickered brilliantly, colored like gasoline on water—indigo, purple, blue, indigo once more.

I slipped through the shadows that clung to the walls of the cabin. I edged up against the back door, and crouching low beneath the window I peered over the edge.

People I did not recognize.

I moved away, once more slipping between the cabins as if I was a shadow myself.

I found them in the fourth lighted cabin.

I crept to the back of the low building, and leaned up against the wall. I slipped the edge of the knife in between the latch and the striker plate of the rear door. I heard the snick of the metal as it clicked back. The door eased open effortlessly, and I slipped into the room, gliding like air, like slow-motion fire.

The woman was asleep on the bed, her bottle-blond hair spread out over the pillow. Her hand had slipped free of the covers, dangled from the edge of the mattress as if she had forgotten its ownership.

I could smell sex in the air, and I breathed in the bitter tang of liquor mingled with the raw stench of sweat. I leaned closer as she exhaled. I could hear him. He was talking to himself, mumbling something incomprehensible as he stood in the bathroom doorway watching her. I waited until he turned out the bathroom light, slipped off his robe, and slid beneath the sheets beside her. She turned toward him, toward me, and in the flickering light of the neon sign through the thin curtains I could see her mascara was smeared, her hair tousled, dark roots creeping out from the surface of her scalp and giving it all away.

I watched these nothing people, and I thought of the man's name, his age, where he came from, where the world believed he was. There was no one here but people who meant nothing, said nothing of consequence, listened to themselves speaking as if they possessed the only voice in the universe. They have been watched, from the moment of their inception, by the stars. They did not understand. I understood.

I leaned back. I smiled. With my left hand I grasped my erection, with my right hand the knife, and then, sliding across the floor on all fours I approached the edge of the bed. I lay right beneath the man. He could have reached out and touched me, but he heard nothing. I rose slowly, as if I had grown from the carpet, and then I raised the knife and held it a foot above his heart. I pushed forward with all my weight, felt the knife puncture, and then with greater force than even I believed I possessed I drove that blade home. I felt it slide through flesh and cartilage and muscle. I felt it stop against the back of his ribcage.

The sound from his lips was almost nothing.

She did not wake.

I frowned, and wondered how much she had drunk before she lay down on the bed. The man was dead. Blood ran across his chest like a rivulet of black. Light like that turned blood the color of crude oil. I touched it with my fingertips. I raised my head, and then leaning gently forward I painted a cross on the woman's forehead. She stirred and murmured. I touched my finger to her lips. She murmured again, sounded like someone's name but I did not hear it clearly.

"Huh?" I whispered. "What was that you said, sweetheart?"

She murmured again, a breathless whisper, a distant nothingness.

From the side of the bed I rolled the man down onto the floor. I lowered him without a sound, and then I climbed in where he had lain, the sheets warm, the mattress imbued with the heat of his body. I felt the dampness, could smell the raw earthiness of what had happened here before I arrived, and moving my hand down I slid it across her stomach, over her ample heavy breasts, down across her navel and between her legs. I stroked my fingers through her pubic hair, she smiled in her sleep, her lips slightly parted, her eyelids flickering, and then when she spoke I could feel my heart thundering in my chest. I felt the emotion and power of that moment rising to my throat.

I closed up against her, aware of the filth that had dried to my skin, the smell of the bayou, the sweat I had bled in the miles I had walked to this place.

I thought of the dead man who lay on the floor beside us. I thought of the reasons why Feraud and Ducane had to have him killed. Reasons were inconsequential. Reasons were history.

Perhaps it was such thoughts that woke her. Alien thoughts. Strange sensations as she reached out her hands to touch me, to feel for my stomach, my legs, the memory of something she had found there that once had her scratching the walls, gasping for air, crying with pleasure . . .

She opened her eyes.

So did I.

Her eyes were rimmed with sleep, bloodshot and unfocused.

Mine were stark, brilliant white against the blackness of my face. I looked like a nightmare.

She opened her mouth to scream, and with one hand I forced her jaw closed. Gripping the base of her throat with my other hand I rolled over and on top of her. I could feel the pressure of my erection against her stomach. She struggled, she was heavy, strong almost, and it was some moments before I could push myself inside her. I thrust hard. I hurt her. Her eyes widened, and even as she felt me thrusting up inside her again, even as she struggled to breathe at all, she knew from the expression in my eyes that she was going to die. My hand tightened relentlessly around her throat. And then it was as if she resigned herself to it. She seemed to fall silent inside, and even though I knew she was still alive there was nothing left within her with which to fight. I thrust again, again, again, and then I sensed the moment that her life gave way beneath her. I released her throat. She lay still and silent. I thrust once more, and as I came I kissed her hard and full on the mouth.

I lay there for some time. There was no hurry. Where I was going would wait forever, it seemed. I teased her bleached-blond curls around in my fingers. Her eyes were open. I closed them. I kissed her lids in turn. Her mouth was open, gasping for air that would now never come. I moved against her, felt her fading warmth, felt the softness of her flesh turn cool and unyielding, and after an hour, perhaps more, I grew from the bed like some angular tree and padded barefoot into the bathroom.

I showered, scrubbed the dirt from my skin. I washed my hair with shampoo from a bottle labeled *Compliments of the Shell Beach Motel*. I soaped myself with a small ivory tablet that smelled of children and clean bathrooms. I stood beneath the running water, my face upturned, my eyes closed, and I sang some tune I remembered from years back.

I dried myself with clean towels, dressed slowly in the man's garments, much as I had done after Pietro Silvino had died. The clothes were large. I turned up the cuffs of the pants, left the shirt unbuttoned at the neck and did not wear his tie. His shoes were two or three sizes too big so I stuffed the toes with the woman's silk stockings. The jacket was cut wide at the shoulders, ample in the waist, and when I stood before the small copper-spotted mirror I looked like a child dressed in his father's clothes.

Hell, we were all children beneath the stars.

I smiled.

Nothing mattered any more.

I spent a minute at the doorway of the cabin. I breathed in the swollen air, the raw earthy ambience, and then I inhaled again and the whole world came with it.

I took the man's cigarette lighter from his jacket pocket. I walked to the edge of the bed. The tiny flame that started climbing from the edge of the bedsheet toward the spread-eagled form of the woman looked like a ghost. I watched until the sound of burning cotton was audible within the silence. I leaned sideways; I lit the lower edge of the curtain. The cabin was nothing more than wood and paint and felt. It would burn well on a hot airless night like this.

I closed my eyes.

The past was the past.

Now this was the future.

I dreamed my dreams, I lived my nightmares, and sometimes I chose guests to stay a little while.

I left the cabin and did not look back. I walked toward the highway, the stars above me, my ears filled with silence.

Word had gone ahead of me to Don Ceriano. He greeted me like a long-lost son. There was much drinking and talking. Afterwards I slept for the better part of a day, and when I woke Don Ceriano told me that Antoine Feraud and he were working together exactly as he had planned.

"Whatever you did," he said, "it was a good thing, and I thank you for it." Don Ceriano smiled and gripped my shoulder. "Though I think perhaps you scared these people a little."

I looked at him and frowned.

Ceriano shook his head. "Possibly they are not used to things being dealt with so swiftly and with so little difficulty. I think Antoine Feraud and his friend . . . what was his name?"

"Ducane," I said. "Charles Ducane."

"Right, right . . . I think they are a little concerned that if they cross me you will visit them in the night, eh?" He laughed loudly. "Now they know your name, Ernesto, and they will not wish to upset you."

I did not hear Antoine Feraud's name again, not directly, for some time. I did what I was asked to do. I stayed with Don Ceriano in the house in Miami, and from there I watched the world unfold through another year.

I remember the fall of 1963 with great clarity. I remember conversations that were held into the early hours of the morning. I remember the names of Luciano and Lansky, of Robert Maheu, Sam Giancana and Johnny Roselli. I remember feeling that there were things beyond the confines of those walls that were of greater significance than all of us combined.

In September of the year a man called Joseph Valachi revealed the key names in organized crime to the Senate Committee. Don Ceriano spoke of Jack Kennedy's father, how he had been in with the families, how family money had put Jack Kennedy in the White House with the promise that concessions and allowances would be made for New York, for Vegas, for Florida and the other family strongholds. Once Kennedy was in, however, he had reneged, and with the assistance of his brother Bobby they had announced their intention to oust the families from all illegal businesses and rackets countrywide.

"We have to do something," Don Ceriano told me one time, and this was after Valachi's testimony, and the way he spoke of it made me feel that something had already been done.

November twenty-second I realized what had been done. I believed that the family had consorted not only with the wealthy Cuban-American exiles, but also with the big conglomerates who paid for the Vietnam War. It was ironic, to me at least, that the only criminal case ever brought against any man for the assassination of Kennedy took place in New Orleans, the trial of Clay Shaw overseen by District Attorney Garrison.

I did not ask questions. Who had killed Jack Kennedy and why was of no consequence to me.

On 24 November Jack Ruby, a man I knew by name and face, a man who had been to the Ceriano house on more than three or four occasions in the previous three months alone, shot and killed Lee Harvey Oswald on television.

"Eight bullets," Don Ceriano told me later. "They found a total of eight bullets down there in Dealey Plaza, and not one of them matched the rifling of the weapon Oswald was supposed to have fired." And with that he laughed, and said something in Italian, and then he added *Chi se ne frega!* and laughed again.

It was as if I had stepped back to watch the world commit itself to madness during those subsequent years. I was down in Miami. The weather was good, the girls were beautiful, and I had all the money I needed. Every once in a while Don Ceriano would call for me, and with a name, a face, I would walk out into the world and do what I was asked to do. Sometimes they were Italians, other times Americans, even Cubans and Mexicans. Miami was a cosmopolitan place, and I had no prejudice when it came to killing a man.

In early 1965 I heard of Che Guevara again. He had left Cuba to form guerrilla groups in Latin America. A handful of months later I would see a photograph of him dead. He looked no different than any other man. Castro still held sway in Cuba, but I did not care. Cuba was not my home, and I believed never would be again. America was a drug, and I was addicted.

I was twenty-nine years old when Richard Nixon said he would run for president. On same day I killed a man called Chester Wintergreen. I garrotted him with a length of wire in an alleyway behind a pool hall. Now I do not remember why he died, and now it does not matter.

In March Robert Kennedy, the same man who had orchestrated the reversal of agreement between his own father and the heads of the families, announced he would run for president.

Don Ceriano spoke to me of this man, how he was the first attorney general of the United States to make any serious attempt to destabilize the hold of the families on organized crime and the labor unions. He mentioned a man called Harry Anslinger, referred to him as "Asslicker," one-time US Commissioner of Narcotics, and how Anslinger believed that Robert Kennedy would hound the families until they were undone.

"Asslicker speaks about Robert Kennedy like he's a crazy man," Don Ceriano said. "He says that Kennedy holds these meetings, and where previous attorney generals have felt that their job was done if they merely called attention to the families, Kennedy goes down the list, one by one, and he names each and every significant figure in organized crime and asks the relevant officials what progress has been made in bringing them down. Asslicker doesn't see eye to eye with Hoover. Hoover would always run the party line, tell the press and the government that there was no such thing as the Mafia, but after the Apalachin Conference in '57 he had to change his tune."

Robert Kennedy went on to win the first Primary in Indiana and the second in Nebraska. In June, after similar meetings in similar houses with similar gatherings as those in the fall of '63, Robert Kennedy was shot dead in the Los Angeles Ambassador Hotel after winning the Californian Democratic Primary. The Kennedy era was over, the Nixon era was to begin, and Don Ceriano—with him Jimmy the Aspirin, Slapsie Maxie Vaccorini, others who had become part of the Alcatraz Swimming Team—well, Don Ceriano decided it was time for a change.

"We're going to Vegas," he told me in July of 1968, "where the money comes down on you like rain, where the girls stay beautiful forever, and where people like us can't break the rules because we were the ones who made them in the first place. And if anyone complains, well *chi se ne frega,* 'cause we've got Ernesto to take care of business, right?"

I nodded. I smiled. I felt a quiet sense of importance.

We didn't drive. We went out to the airport in Tampa and we flew. The car, the Mercury Turnpike Cruiser that had once belonged to Pietro Silvino, was housed in a lock-up owned by the family. It would stay there for as long as it was necessary. I had no idea then that it would be more than thirty years before I would see it again.

I would follow Don Ceriano to the ends of the earth, and Las Vegas . . . well, Las Vegas was only half as far.

FOURTEEN

AT FIRST THEY spoke of nothing but Charles Ducane, how the present governor of Louisiana may have been instrumental in ordering the brutal killing of two people so many years before.

Schaeffer challenged Woodroffe and Hartmann, challenged them to say nothing beyond the confines of the FBI Office, but challenged also the veracity of the information given by Perez.

"The guy's a killer . . . not only a killer, but a psychopath, a homophobic fucking death machine," Schaeffer said, more venom and anger evident in his voice than Hartmann had ever heard before.

"But he knows shit," Woodroffe said. "He knows about Ducane—"

"And he knows who killed Kennedy," Hartmann said, and later he would think that he'd said it just to throw a further curve into the proceedings.

"Aah fuck off!" Schaeffer snapped at him, and tempers were thinner than ever, and emotions were frayed at the edges, and it seemed like all it would take was a single wrong word and everything would fall apart at the seams.

"Why the hell not?" Woodroffe said. "Someone knows who killed Kennedy . . . why not our man?"

"Yes," Hartmann added. "Perez knows who killed John F. Kennedy."

Schaeffer rose from his chair. "Enough!" he snapped. "Enough already. We're dealing with the present, the facts . . . we're dealing with the kidnapping of Catherine Ducane. We're dealing with nothing but those things that relate directly to what has happened to Catherine Ducane."

Hartmann and Woodroffe looked at one another, and then at Schaeffer. There was something unspoken between the three of them—the knowledge that Ducane was in this as much as Perez himself, the belief that unless someone way up high curtailed it there would be an in-depth inquiry into Ducane once his daughter had been found . . .

It was there. No one said a word. It didn't need to be said.

"I don't wanna hear another word about Charles Ducane and what he might or might not have done or been involved in God knows how many years ago," Schaeffer said, "and I sure as fuck don't wanna hear *anything* about John Kennedy or Marilyn fucking Monroe, or anyone else for that matter, okay?"

He glared at both Hartmann and Woodroffe. Neither of them challenged him.

"Now will someone get Kubis in here?" Schaeffer said, his teeth gritted, his fists clenched.

Woodroffe rose and left the room.

A moment later Kubis stood beside the desk.

"Exactly," Schaeffer said. "What did he say *exactly*?"

Kubis looked down at the sheaf of papers in his hand. He cleared his throat. "The road is long, Mr. Hartmann, and she is already at the very end of it. We play this game the way I wish it to be played. We follow my rules . . . and perhaps, just perhaps, the Ducane girl might see daylight again," Kubis said.

Schaeffer turned toward the larger office behind him and shouted for Sheldon Ross.

Ross appeared within moments.

"Ross, get me a map of New Orleans, something that covers all the roads and highways. I mean every road and every goddamned highway running into, through and out of the city."

Ross nodded and disappeared.

"You reckon he's given us something?" Woodroffe asked.

Schaeffer shrugged. "Christ almighty knows. Seems to me he's the sort of person who only says something if he means to say it. He said that she would not be heard even if she screamed continuously at the top of her voice, and then he says this thing about the road being long and that she was at the very end of it, and that if we follow his rules she might see daylight again."

"Buried?" Hartmann asked. "You figure he's hidden her underground?"

"Could be nothing more than an expression," Woodroffe said.

"We check it out," Schaeffer said. "Whatever the fuck it is we check it out."

Ross returned, in his hand a map which he passed to Schaeffer. Schaeffer spread the map out before them, took a pen from his shirt pocket and began to scrutinize the network of lines that indicated every road in and out of New Orleans.

"What makes you think she's even in the state?" Hartmann asked.

Schaeffer waved his question away as inconsequential. He had his mind on something, and he would not be diverted.

"Write these down," Schaeffer said to Woodroffe, and Woodroffe took a sheet of paper, his pen suspended over it, and waited for Schaeffer to speak.

"From where we sit we go north," Schaeffer said. "You got Highway 18 out through Mid City, becomes Pontchartrain Boulevard and goes all the way out to Lakeshore West. Cutting across that and heading west you got Highway 10 out toward Metairie. Southeast you got the Pontchartrain Expressway to the Greater New Orleans Bridge, heading across the river into Algiers and McDonoghville. East you got Florida Avenue. South you've got the Claiborne Avenue which cuts back up toward Carrollton, but you gotta take into consideration the area all the way down through the University district and as far as Audubon Park. That's five zones in all."

Schaeffer looked up at Woodroffe. "You got that?"

Woodroffe nodded.

"So how many people we got altogether?"

"Fifty, maybe sixty at a push," Woodroffe replied.

"Divide them up equal, ten or twelve men to a unit. Separate them into twos. Section each of the five zones equally and map out every road and highway, every dirt track and footpath that heads out toward the Mississippi River or Lake Pontchartrain, everything that takes you as far as the land will let you go. Have them drive the routes, check out every empty house, every motel and truckstop, anything that could be considered the end of the road, so to speak. And tell them to look in basements and outhouses, anyplace that looks like it might go underground."

"You really think—" Hartmann started, but stopped dead when Schaeffer raised a warning hand.

There was a moment's silent tension as Schaeffer looked first at Hartmann, then at Woodroffe.

"Yes I do, Mr. Hartmann. Whatever you were gonna say, yes I do. You don't take the calls from the director of the FBI, who is all too eager to tell me what Governor Ducane is telling him every hour on the hour. You don't have to file reports at the end of every six-hour shift detailing what we are actually doing. Not what we are *thinking* about doing, but what we are *actually* doing. If you wanna take the calls, if you wanna explain yourself, then fine, you come back to me with something better. Seems to me that in this situation we can either wait for Perez to tell us or we can do something proactive."

Schaeffer once again looked at them both in turn, and then added, "So, any questions, or do we do something effective?"

"We do this," Woodroffe said, and rose from his chair.

Hartmann nodded and leaned back.

"Right. No more fucking about," Schaeffer said. He rose also, and before he left the table he turned and looked at Hartmann.

"There isn't a great deal more you can do," he said. "I'd go back to the hotel if I were you and sit tight."

Hartmann nodded. "Maybe you should ask for some more people. Seems to me sixty men ain't an awful lot to cover the kind of territory you're talking about."

"I got what I got," Schaeffer replied. "If they send me some more then so be it. Right now I gotta use what resources have been assigned and that's just the way it is."

Hartmann nodded. He felt for the man. He stood up slowly and silently thanked God he was not in Stanley Schaeffer's shoes. "If you need me, if there's anything I can do, you know where I am."

"Appreciated, Mr. Hartmann."

Schaeffer turned and walked away. Already Hartmann could hear the hubbub of voices gathering in the corridors as Woodroffe organized the briefing that would take place.

Hartmann left as inconspicuously as he could. He went on foot, walked down to the intersection and turned right. No one, as far as he knew, saw the way he went, and for this he was grateful.

He reached Verlaine's Precinct at five after six. The evening was swollen with humidity; evidence of a storm on the way. Across the horizon loomed an ominous wide band of gray-green cloud. The atmosphere reflected Hartmann's state of mind. He had listened to Perez speak of things he'd done here in New Orleans. He knew the Shell Beach Motel, no more than a mile or two from where he now stood, and the thought that this man had walked through this country just a handful of years before Hartmann himself was born, years when his mother was alive and within walking distance of what had happened, unnerved and disturbed him. Perhaps the reason Perez had chosen him was because they had both been born here, because they both understood something of the nature of Louisiana, for this country was owned by nothing but itself. Whatever was built here could be sucked right back into the filthy earth if Louisiana so desired.

Verlaine was waiting in the foyer.

Hartmann opened his mouth to speak and Verlaine shook his head.

He crossed the foyer and showed Hartmann out of the building and down the steps. Only when they reached the sidewalk did he speak.

"This isn't happening," he said quietly. "You never came here and we never did this, understand?"

Hartmann nodded.

Verlaine took Hartmann's arm and hurried him across the road and down half a block to where his car was parked. He climbed inside, released the catch for Hartmann to get in the passenger side, and then started the engine and pulled away. Twice he looked back over his shoulder, as if he was ensuring he wasn't being followed.

"You got your audience with Feraud," Verlaine said, "but I had to pay a tribute."

"A tribute?"

Verlaine nodded. There was tension in his voice, fear in his tone. "I had to make something disappear quietly, you get me?"

Hartmann realized what had happened: Verlaine had made a trade with Feraud.

"Better that I don't know anything," he said.

"Too damned right," Verlaine replied, and eased the car off the main freeway and down a slip road that would take them toward Feraud's territory.

Within half a mile Hartmann felt it: Feraud's presence. *Smells like Cipliano's office*, he thought. *Smells like dead bodies, bloated and rank, and no matter if the air-con has been running all night it's a smell that you can't escape. Even when you leave it's there on your clothes.*

A quarter-mile from Feraud's house and Hartmann felt a sudden and necessary urge to turn back, to tell Verlaine that he had been wrong, that he didn't want to do this, that he'd decided it wouldn't be a good idea to do anything that might jeopardize the federal investigation. The thought was there but the words didn't come . . . and later he would think that even though he felt these things he also knew, in his heart of hearts, that he was prepared to do almost anything to see this come to an end.

And so he said nothing, and Verlaine kept driving, and before long they were slowing down and shuddering to a halt at the side of the mud-rutted road that ran alongside the edge of Feraud's property.

"You ready for this?" Verlaine asked.

Hartmann shook his head. "No, and I don't think I ever will be."

"Feeling's mutual."

Hartmann opened the door and stepped out. The clouds he'd seen on the horizon were now directly overhead. He shivered at the feeling that came with the smell, the breathlessness around him, the feeling that everything was tightening claustrophobically. This place had the power to invade the senses, to invade the mind and the heart. This place provoked images and sounds and memories that he had believed gone, but they were not gone, never had been, and he knew that Louisiana and all it represented would be eternally a part of who he was. Like a fingerprint on the soul. This was his past, and however hard and fast he might run from it, it would never leave him. The simplicity was that it was always one step ahead, and wherever he might turn it was there waiting.

"You first," Hartmann said. "He knows you."

"Lucky for me," Verlaine cracked, but there was no humor in his tone. Once again Hartmann recognized that his companion was as scared as he was.

They took the path and cut through the trees. The light was bad, dense and forbidding, and Hartmann carried with him the image of Ernesto Perez sliding through this undergrowth on his way to the Shell Beach Motel.

. . . *Sometimes I went under, walking out along the bottom of some stagnant riverbed, and then I surfaced, my hair slicked to my skull, my eyes white against the blackness of my face . . . such a high . . . like smoking something dead . . .*

Hartmann felt a wave of nausea in his chest and clamped his hand to his mouth. He believed he had never been so afraid in his life.

And then Feraud's place was ahead of them, a vast colonial mansion. There was a single lighted window visible on the ground floor, and up on the veranda a group of men stood talking and smoking. They carried carbines, they talked in low guttural Creole French, and when they saw Verlaine and Hartmann they stopped.

Half a dozen pairs of eyes watched them as they made their way up to the house.

None of them said a word, and this was in some way worse than being challenged. It meant that they were expected. That simple: he and Verlaine were expected.

One of the men stepped forward and held out his hand.

Verlaine turned to Hartmann. "My gun," he said quietly, and Hartmann didn't even consider questioning him. Verlaine reached around back of his waist and released the catch on his holster. He handed over his .38 and waited patiently for their next instruction.

Another man stepped forward and frisked both of them, and then he turned and nodded.

The man who held Verlaine's gun stepped forward and opened the front door of the house. He indicated with a swift nod of his head that they should go inside.

Rock and a hard place, Hartmann thought, and walked into the house behind Verlaine.

They waited for minutes that appeared to stretch into hours. Somewhere the sound of a grandfather clock, its ticking like the beating of some heart, echoed through the seeming emptiness of the house. It was all dark wood and thick rugs, and even Hartmann's breathing seemed to come back at him in triplicate.

Eventually, even as Hartmann believed he couldn't take a second more of the tension, there was the sound of footsteps. Coincidentally, the sky above them seemed to swell and rumble. Thunder was starting up somewhere, perhaps a mile, perhaps two, from where they stood. Soon the rain would come, the lightning illuminating the surrounding countryside in bright flashes of monochrome, the trees set in stark white silhouette like skeletons against the blackness of the horizon.

A Creole appeared, middle-aged, his hair graying at the temples, and stood for a moment at the end of the hall that ran from the main entranceway.

Hartmann remembered Perez speaking of an old man called Innocent, a man that must have been dead a considerable number of years by now. Perhaps this was his son. Perhaps employment in this particular line was inherited.

"Come," the Creole said, and though his voice was barely a whisper it carried through the building and reached Hartmann as if the man had been standing right beside him.

The entire ambience of the place was enough to make his skin crawl.

They followed the man and were shown into a room that Hartmann guessed must have been at the front of the building. It was from here that came the only light in the house, and that light stood in the corner and barely illuminated the place enough for them to see Feraud.

But he was there, no doubt of it. Hartmann sensed the man.

His eyes adjusted to the gloom, and then he caught the shape of a ghost rising from behind a high-backed chair. It was cigarette smoke, a plume of cigarette smoke that arabesqued in curlicues toward the ceiling.

The Creole nodded toward the chair, and then turned and left the room.

"Gentlemen," Feraud said, and his voice was like something dead and buried and now crawling its way up through damp gravel.

Verlaine went first, walking slowly toward the window, Hartmann a step or two behind him. When they reached the end of the room

Hartmann could see that two chairs had been set against the wall, evidently for their audience with Feraud. The man was like Lucifer's Pope.

Verlaine sat down first, Hartmann followed suit, and when he looked up he was shocked by the appearance of the old man before him. Feraud's skin was almost translucent, paper-thin and yellowed. His hair, what little there was, was thin and frail, like strands of damp cotton adhering to his skull. The wrinkles on his face gave the impression of a man burned and healed, the lines deep and irregular and almost painful to see.

"I asked you not to come back," Feraud said, and as he spoke smoke issued from his nose and his mouth.

Verlaine nodded. He glanced at Hartmann but Hartmann was transfixed by Feraud.

"You did this thing for me?" Feraud asked.

"I did," Verlaine said. "The case will never reach the Circuit."

Feraud nodded. "An eye for an eye."

"This is Ray Hartmann," Verlaine started.

Feraud raised his hand and smiled. "I know who it is, Mr. Verlaine. I know exactly who Ray Hartmann is."

Feraud turned his eyes toward Hartmann, eyes like small dark stones set into his face. "You have come home, I understand," Feraud said, which was the second time someone had made that comment. The first time it had been Perez, right there on the telephone while Hartmann was in the FBI Field Office.

"It doesn't leave you, does it, Mr. Hartmann?"

Hartmann raised his eyebrows.

"New Orleans . . . the sounds and the smells, the colors, the people, the language. It is a place all its own, eh?"

Hartmann nodded. The man was voicing thoughts he had possessed only a little while before. He felt as if Feraud could see right through him, that the man had an ability to wear his skin, to see what he was thinking, to know what he was feeling right in that very moment. Antoine Feraud and Ernesto Perez were perhaps more like brothers than he and Danny had ever been.

"So you have come with your ironic name to find out what I know," Feraud said.

Hartmann frowned and shook his head.

"Hartmann," Feraud said. "Hart-man . . . your name. You have come down here to find our heart man." Feraud laughed at his own play on words. Ray Hartmann felt ready to puke.

"And what makes you think I know any more than what I have already told Mr. Verlaine?"

Hartmann took his heart in his hands. "Because we have spoken with Mr. Perez . . . Ernesto Perez. You remember him, Mr. Feraud?"

Feraud smiled. "Perhaps, perhaps not. I am a very old man. I have met a very great many people throughout my life and I cannot be expected to recall every single one."

"But this one I think you do remember, Mr. Feraud . . . because he came down here many years ago and did some things for you and Charles Ducane that it would be difficult to forget."

Feraud nodded. He seemed to be acknowledging the fact that what Hartmann was saying was true.

"And what is it that you think I can tell you?" Feraud asked.

"Why he's come back," Hartmann said. "Why he's done this . . . kidnapped Charles Ducane's daughter, what he has done with her."

Feraud shook his head. "What he has done with her I do not know. Why he has done this? That is an altogether simpler question."

"And the answer?" Hartmann asked.

"The answer you will have to get from Mr. Perez."

"Mr. Perez is taking a great deal of time arriving at that answer, Mr. Feraud, and I am not sure we have that much time."

Feraud smiled. "I am sure that if Mr. Perez is anything close to the man you think he is he knows exactly what he is doing and how it will transpire. Perhaps Mr. Perez has already killed the girl . . . perhaps he has already sunk her body into the bayou and he is just biding his time, seeing how long he can keep you people interested before he tells you what he's done. I understand that he has killed someone else already, a man found in the trunk of a car some days ago."

Hartmann nodded. "Yes, that's right . . . well, as far as we can gather Perez was the one who killed this man."

"Don't underestimate him, Mr. Hartmann. That is all I am able and willing to tell you. You have a dangerous man here in New Orleans, and I am sure that if his reputation is anything to go by he is capable of an awful lot more than just the killing of one man."

"And you are not willing to help us?" Hartmann asked.

Feraud waved Hartmann's question aside as if it was of no significance at all. "And for what reason? What reason on God's green earth could I have for wanting to help you and your Federal people?"

"Because he might have come down here to seek an audience with you also?" Hartmann asked.

Feraud laughed. "This man of yours, he would not get within a hundred yards of me."

"Anyone can be killed, Mr. Feraud . . . anyone at all, even the president of the United States can be killed if the killer is willing to stake everything on such a venture."

"I am sure, Mr. Hartmann, that if your Mr. Perez had it in his mind to kill me he would have made his attempt before turning himself over to you. I understand that you have him safe and secure in the city, that he is guarded at all times by a significant number of federal agents. First of all he would have to find his way out of there, and then he would have to come through my people to reach me. The likelihood of Mr. Perez accomplishing such a thing is a matter for dreams, not for reality."

"So you are not willing to divulge any further information, Mr. Feraud?"

"You speak as if you believe I know more than I am telling you."

"I am convinced of it."

"Be convinced," Feraud said. "Be as convinced as you like. They are your thoughts and you are more than welcome to them . . . now, if you don't mind, I am very tired. I am an old man, I know nothing more of this man Perez, and even if I did I can imagine that you would be the very last people on the earth I would want to share such information with."

"And what about Ducane himself?" Hartmann asked.

Feraud turned and looked at him. He blinked slowly, like a lizard, and he pinned Hartmann to the spot with an unerring gaze. "What about Charles Ducane?"

"Your involvement with him," Hartmann said matter-of-factly. "The fact that you and he have known each other for a great many years, that you have transacted certain business arrangements . . . that certain favors have been granted."

"You assume a great deal, Mr. Hartmann," Feraud said.

"I assume nothing, Mr. Feraud. I merely make reference to certain things that have been forthcoming in my conversations with Mr. Perez."

"And you believe everything he is telling you?"

Hartmann nodded. "I believe something unless it is challenged or proven wrong."

"That is a very trusting attitude, Mr. Hartmann . . . and an attitude that will accomplish little but your own downfall if you apply it to Ernesto Perez."

"And Charles Ducane?"

Feraud shook his head. "I have nothing further to say."

"You think I should apply my trusting attitude to him, Mr. Feraud? You know him, have known him for all these years . . . you're probably more qualified to make a judgement on Charles Ducane's trustworthiness and honesty than anyone else, right?"

Feraud smiled and nodded his head. He raised his right hand and pressed his index finger against his lips.

"We made a deal," Verlaine said suddenly. "We made a deal that I would take care of this thing you asked of me, something that jeopardizes my job, and you would speak with us."

Feraud lowered his finger from his lips. His smile rapidly vanished. "What are we doing right now, Mr. Verlaine? We are speaking, are we not? I said I would speak with you, and as always I have kept my word to the letter. Now again, if you don't mind, I would like to rest."

Thunder rolled outwards above the house. Somewhere to Hartmann's right he heard the sound of footsteps, and when he turned he saw the Creole standing there waiting for them to leave.

"I will not forget that you have failed to keep your word, Mr. Feraud," Verlaine said.

Feraud looked at Verlaine, his eyes cold and hard and unforgiving. "Be careful, Mr. Verlaine . . . be careful or I might choose not to forget you."

Hartmann felt the skin crawl up his back and tighten at the base of his neck. His hands were sweating, his whole body was sweating, and he wanted nothing more than to leave the house, to make it safely to the car, to drive back to the city and never once look over his shoulder.

They walked back the way they had come, the Creole ahead of them, and once they were again on the veranda Verlaine's gun was returned.

Neither of them said a word as they walked to the car, and only when they had finally reached the sliproad that ran to the freeway did Verlaine say something.

"Never again," he said, and his voice was almost a whisper.

Hartmann opened the passenger door and climbed inside.

Verlaine started the engine and pulled away.

"Guy scares the living fucking Jesus outta me," Verlaine said. His voice was hoarse. It cracked midsentence and Hartmann noticed how tightly he was holding the steering wheel. His knuckles were white and stretched.

"Not a man I would like to upset," Hartmann said.

"That's the problem," Verlaine replied. "I think I just did."

"He won't do anything," Hartmann said. "A warning is not the same as a threat."

"I hope to fuck not," Verlaine replied, and then they gained the freeway, and the lights of New Orleans were ahead of them.

They did not speak again until Verlaine pulled to a stop two blocks from Hartmann's hotel. He did not wish to have any of the federal agents see that they had been together.

"You need any other favors," Verlaine said, "you can forget about them before you even think it."

Hartmann smiled. "Thank you for your help," he said. He reached over and gripped Verlaine's hand where it rested on the steering wheel. "Go home," he said. "Have a couple of shots of bourbon and hit the sack. Forget about this . . . it isn't your problem, okay?"

Verlaine nodded. "Thank fucking God."

Hartmann climbed out of the car and watched as Verlaine drove away. He turned right and started walking, and within a minute or so had reached the Marriott. He glanced at his watch. It was a little before nine, and already he felt as if he hadn't slept for three weeks.

In his room he undressed and showered. He called room service and ordered coffee. He turned on the radio and listened to nothing in particular, and then he lay on his bed and wished this had never begun.

And then the storm began—suddenly, violently—and the sound of rain rushing down from the sky and hammering against the roof of the hotel was almost deafening. Hartmann turned over and buried his head beneath the pillow. Still the noise was there, ceaseless and unrelenting. The whiplash snap of lightning, and back of that the rolling mountain of thunder that escalated until it seemed the whole sky was charged with its force and momentum.

The sound was perhaps some help, for within it Hartmann found it difficult to think. He recalled these same storms from his early childhood, both he and Danny as tiny children crouched beneath the covers while their father told them that somewhere God was angry, but not with them, and so there was no need to be afraid, and from the landing the sound of their mother's voice telling them that big boys weren't afraid of storms. Hartmann closed his eyes, closed everything down, and somehow managed a brief respite from what was happening to his life.

Within twenty minutes he was asleep—quietly, gratefully asleep—and he did not wake until the telephone rang with his alarm call on Tuesday morning.

It was 2 September, and he had only four days until his life reached yet another watershed.

He rose without delay, he showered and dressed, but his mind was elsewhere, unable to find any real point of anchorage, and only when Sheldon Ross came to get him did he realize he was on his way back to the Field Office.

Another day, another handful of hours seated in the cramped and airless room.

Another dark catastrophe of visions courtesy of Ernesto Cabrera Perez.

When he arrived he was acutely aware of how empty the place was in comparison to the previous days. Schaeffer was present, as was Woodroffe, but apart from them he saw only two or three additional agents.

On each wall of the main outer office Schaeffer had positioned a large monochrome photograph of Catherine Ducane. Hartmann paused and looked at the face staring back at him. The picture showed Catherine at perhaps fourteen or fifteen years old. She was a pretty girl, but innocent and vulnerable.

"Looks like my brother's daughter," Woodroffe said, and Hartmann started nervously. He had been miles away, thinking that when Jess was such an age she would look perhaps very similar. Maybe that was Schaeffer's intention: to give them all something, to keep it there in their minds at all times. They were looking for someone, a real person, not only a real person but a frightened and confused teenage girl who had no idea why she'd been taken.

Hartmann said nothing. He turned and made his way through to where Schaeffer was waiting. In the man's eyes he could see the question that didn't need to be verbalized.

Schaeffer shook his head. "Nothing yet," he said. "I got sixty men putting hundreds of miles on their wheels and between them they have come back with nothing."

Hartmann merely nodded and took a seat at the table beyond the small office where he would sit with Perez.

Perez was controlling them all, like some sort of chess grand master. Everything they were doing had been predicted by him, every eventuality had been taken into consideration, and—in all honesty—Hartmann believed that whatever they did, whatever effective action Schaeffer might instigate, they would be seated there for as long as it took for Perez to finish what he had to say.

And then the man came, and Hartmann turned and saw him

walking down the length of the open plan office, an agent on each side of him. He was going nowhere—they all knew that, and he was going nowhere merely because he intended it to be that way.

Hartmann rose to his feet. He nodded at Perez as Perez walked past him. Perez smiled, entered the narrow room at the end and Hartmann walked in behind him.

Once seated, Perez steepled his fingers together and closed his eyes. He seemed to inhale deeply, exhale once more, as if performing some kind of ritual.

"Mr. Perez?" Hartmann asked.

Perez opened his eyes. Hartmann imagined he heard a dry clicking sound, like a lizard sunbathing on a rock.

"Mr. Hartmann," Perez whispered.

Hartmann felt his skin crawl. There was something tremendously unnerving about the mere presence of the man.

"I have been thinking," Perez said. "Considering the possibility that we may run out of time."

Hartmann frowned.

"It seems that the more I tell you of my life the more there is to tell. I was thinking only last night of another aspect of how these things have come about, and though I had never intended to tell you of them I feel they are integral to obtaining a full understanding of the situation within which we find ourselves."

"I'm listening," Hartmann said, "but I must urge you to tell me whatever you wish as quickly as possible. It would seem to be a pointless exercise if the girl dies."

Perez laughed. "Not at all, Mr. Hartmann. She is alive as long as I tell you she is alive. She could be dead even now. The beauty of this situation is that I am the only person who knows where she is . . . even Catherine Ducane herself has no idea where she is imprisoned. Until I tell you where to find her you will have to hear me out."

"So start talking," Hartmann said. He clenched his fists beneath the edge of the table, out of view. He willed himself not to lose patience. He was tired. He knew Schaeffer and Woodroffe and the other sixty agents assigned to this were tired also. They were all here, every last one of them, because of this man, and this man—this animal—was playing games with them.

"Speak," Hartmann said. "Tell me what you want me to hear and let's get this done, okay?"

Perez nodded. "You are fatigued, Mr. Hartmann, no?"

Hartmann nodded. "I am fatigued, yes, Mr. Perez. I am so dog-tired you have no idea. I am here because you insisted that I be here. I am willing to hear everything you have to say, and though everything you have told me so far makes me feel nothing but revulsion for what you have done, I am nevertheless obligated by duty and by loyalty to continue this charade."

"Emotions are strong," Perez said. "Revulsion? Duty? Loyalty? These are powerful words, Mr. Hartmann. I would ask you not to lose your connection to reality until I am finished . . . I believe that is the very least I can ask of you, considering what I have done for you."

"For me?" Hartmann asked, his tone incredulous. "What you have done for me? What the hell are you talking about?"

"Your perception of yourself," Perez replied. "Already I perceive that your own view of yourself has shifted. You have come to realize that you are in fact solely and exclusively responsible for the situation within which you find yourself. You have been a troubled man, Mr. Hartmann, and if nothing else my presence here has assisted you to put such things into perspective."

Hartmann shook his head. He couldn't believe what he was hearing, and yet at the same time there was a dark shadow of something that told him that the man was somehow right.

Had his perspective changed? And if so, had it been because of Perez?

"Whatever," Hartmann said, simply because there was nothing appropriate he could think of to say. He would not be played by this man. He would sit and listen. He would do his part in helping to locate Catherine Ducane, and then he would go home and do his best to straighten out the Vietnam of his own existence.

"So talk to me," Hartmann said. "I want to hear what you have to say, Mr. Perez . . . I really do."

"Very well," Perez said. "Because you asked, and asked politely, I will tell you."

"Okay," Hartmann said, and reached out to close the door behind him.

FIFTEEN

LAS VEGAS WAS the promised land.

One time a jerkwater nothing of a place somewhere in the desert—gas stations, truckstops, a scattering of run-down and ramshackle slot-machine emporiums and greasy diners where the *Blue Plate Special* was the kind of mystery meat you wouldn't serve to a dog— but envisioned as a glittering opportunity going to waste by Meyer Lansky. Lansky kept hounding Bugsy Siegel to see the possibilities, to open his mind and let it run wild—the legalized gambling, the unconquered territory—and finally, in 1941, Siegel sent a trusted lieutenant, Moe Sedway, to see if he couldn't figure out what Lansky was talking about.

After the war was over, Siegel, far more interested in his Hollywood playboy lifestyle, finally looked for himself and got a glimpse of the Las Vegas that Lansky had conceived of. Las Vegas, and the six million dollars that Siegel ploughed not only into building The Flamingo but also into his own Swiss accounts, became the legacy that would not only memorialize his life, but also instigate his death.

Meyer Lansky, never a man to capitulate on his own vision, assumed control of The Flamingo, and within a year it turned a profit. Las Vegas became a honeypot for the wasps. Las Vegas State officials levied stringent rules and regulations to keep the families out, but it was futile. Lansky controlled The Thunderbird; Moe Dalitz and the Cleveland mob assumed autonomy over The Desert Inn; The Sands was controlled jointly by Lansky, Joe Adonis, Frank Costello and Doc Stacher. George Raft, the Hollywood actor, came in on the deal, and even Frank Sinatra was sold a 9 percent share. The Fischetti brothers—the same brothers who took Sinatra to provide entertainment at the Havana Conference, Christmas Eve of 1946—controlled The Sahara and The Riviera, alongside Tony Accardo and Sam Giancana. New England's head honcho, Raymond Patriarca, moved in and took possession of The Dunes.

And then there was Caesars Palace. Back of Caesars were Accardo,

Giancana, Patriarca, Jerry Catena from Vito Genovese's outfit, and Vincent "Jimmy Blue Eyes" Alo. Conversations with Don Ceriano never failed to include the legendary Jimmy Hoffa, leader of the Teamsters' Union, a man who orchestrated the investment of ten million into the Palace and another forty million around Vegas's other numerous hotspots. The money masqueraded as loans, but those loans were as good as permanent and no one ever thought to return a dime. No one thought, either, of the hundreds of thousands of over-the-hill truck drivers who never did get their pension checks as they'd been promised.

I went to Caesars soon after the Alcatraz Swimming Team arrived in Vegas. It was vast and extravagant, a place guested by those who, some decades before, might have guested the *Titanic*. I had never seen anything like it before. The hotels we had frequented in Havana, places like The Nacional and The Riviera, paled in comparison. I walked barefoot on a carpet that almost reached my ankles. I took a bath in a tub in which I could have effortlessly drowned. I lay on a bed, wide like a football field, and when I called room service they were there within minutes. Las Vegas seemed to be everything I could never have imagined it to be, and though I was there in Caesars no more than forty-eight hours, I felt I had—at last—truly arrived.

Once Don Ceriano's business at the hotel was done, I and the rest of the crew moved to the outskirts of the city. We took a house on Alvarado Street. Don Ceriano came down the following morning and he gathered us together.

"People here," he said, "ain't nothing like the people back in Miami. This is where the real deal lives. This is where we get the running orders, and we run just like they say. Job needs doing we do it, no questions asked, no answers expected."

He smiled, leaned back in his chair. "We ain't smalltime, never have been, never will be, but this is earned territory. Lot of blood got spilled to make Las Vegas, and that blood belonged to men like us, men who were better than us truth be known, and we keep our hands in our pockets and our eyes going both ways at once if we wanna stay alive. You get me?"

There was a consensual affirmative from the gathered crew.

"Down here you got politics and kickbacks and folks in high places who wanna stay high. They don't wanna get their shoes dirty kicking shit down the sidewalk. That's where we come in, and if we do what we're asked then there'll never be a shortage of money or girls or respect. Key to all of this is knowing your place on the totem pole, and while we may not be feeling sand between our toes we sure as shit ain't the fancy bit on top."

Where we were on the totem pole was the hired hands, the wet crew, the guys that got a call in the early hours of the morning to go down to The Sands, come in quiet through the back kitchen doorway, turn left, left again, and there in the meat locker find some poor dumb schmuck who figured he could take the place with a blindside hand fat with Schaffners; figured he could get the dealer to catch the eye of some pretty cigarette girl and slip a jack where it shouldn't have been; where we were was hammering that poor schmooze's thumbs to a pulp and then kicking his ass six ways to Sunday so he and his confederates got the message loud and clear; where we were was driving a trailer jammed to the gunnels with stolen liquor and Luckies out of the desert at three a.m., parking it up behind a cheap bordello, unloading those cases into a lockdown garage, slipping away quietly and losing the trailer down a ravine near Devil's Eyelid, and walking four miles back on foot as the sun rose and the heat got mighty and the shirt you were wearing stuck to your back like a second skin.

Where we were was things like that, and though there was always an element of edge to such things, though the fun you got out of it was never more than the fun you made, there were times I believed that I was destined for so much more. And that's why I spoke to Carlo Evangelisti, and that's how I ended up involved in the death of Don Ceriano and taking an audience with Sam Giancana's cousin, Fabio Calligaris.

Early part of 1970. Six months and I would be thirty-four years old. I was all grown up in some ways, other ways still like the kid from way back when. Watched the people around me, watched them well, saw them married, having kids, and then walking out on their wives and screwing some two-bit floozy who shifted smokes from a tray at one of the smaller casinos. Never made a deal of sense to me, but then I don't know it was ever supposed to. Couldn't understand how a man could have a family and then do such a thing. Taking a wife and children was the farthest thing from my mind at the time, but right back to my father and the way he treated my mother I could never really understand the seeming absence of loyalty that these people demonstrated. I spoke with Don Ceriano. He took me aside, and quietly he said, "There are some things you see, some things not. Likewise, there are some things you hear, and just as many you don't. A wise man knows which is which, Ernesto," and we never spoke of it again.

Business was varied but good. There were younger men earning their scars in my place. Days came when I would be dispatching one man to make collections, another for enforcement of an agreement made with the Ceriano crew. I would spend most of my time with Don Ceriano himself, there at his right hand, listening to him, speaking with him, learning more of the ways of the world. Only once during that year was I directly involved in the death of a man. A mile or so from the house, back of the intersection that split that quarter of the city in half, we ran a bookmaker's shop out of a factory warehouse. Warehouse fronted for some frozen orange juice exporting scam, good-sized operation turning over something in the region of five million a year. Warehouse was owned by one of Slapsie Maxie's cousins, man by the name of Roberto Albarelli. Fat guy, too fat by too much, and the way he'd lumber across the yard shouting and badmouthing the Ricans and niggers who worked the joint made me smile. Asshole was a good enough guy, but sure as hell he looked like a gunnysack full of shit tied at the neck and busting in the middle. Rumor had it when he fucked his wife she always had to ride on top, otherwise he would've suffocated the poor bitch.

Weekend came around. Me and Slapsie, and another pair from the Alcatraz Swimming Team, went down there to make some book, to collect some dues for Don Ceriano. Found Roberto sweating like a stuck pig on barbecue day in the trailer office he managed on the back-lot. Those days I was old enough to do the talking when Slapsie didn't feel like it so the conversation went down between me and the lard-ass.

"Jeez, stinks like a Turkish sauna bath in here, Roberto. What the fuck you been doin'?"

"Got trouble," he started, and his voice went high-pitched at the end and I knew there was something he was excited about.

"Trouble? Kinda trouble?"

"Got skinned by some asshole Puerto Rican motherfucker for eight grand and change," Roberto said.

Slapsie pulled me up a chair and I sat down facing the fat guy. "Eight grand? What the fuck you talkin' about? What Puerto Rican mother-fucker?"

"Puerto Rican motherfucker who skinned me for eight grand this morning," Roberto said. "That Puerto Rican motherfucker."

"Whoa there, slow the fuck down, Roberto. What the hell you talkin' about?"

Roberto took several deep breaths. He murmured some Italian prayer under his breath. His shirt was black beneath the armpits and he smelled ripe like a sour watermelon.

"Took a long shot on a mare that should've made it no further than the boneyard," he said. "Thing was nothing more than three pints of glue and a handbag. Took a thousand dollars and knew I had it made . . . dumb stupid motherfuckin' Puerto Rican asshole wouldn't know one end of a horse from the next. So anyways and whatever, I took the fucking bet, okay? I took the goddamned stupid fucking bet and the boneyard mule came in just before a pony that'd lost its rider halfway down the lane. Figured I had it made. Cut for Don Ceriano, cut for me, and we's all happy as Larry for the weekend. Puerto Rican motherfucker comes down with his tab and claims an eight-to-one payback placing first in the line-up. I tells him he's got a mouth full of shit and a head full of piss, and then in comes three of his asshole Puerto Rican motherfucker friends, and they got heat on them, one's got a lead pipe and whatever the fuck. He shows me the ticket, and even my blind grandmother, may her soul rest in peace amen, coulda seen that they scratched out the name of the boneyarder and wrote in the name of the winning horse."

I was watching Roberto with both my eyes going the same way. Roberto was family, as good as family got, but he had a reputation for varnishing the lies with a gloss of truth. He knew well enough that any lie around this place walked with mighty short legs, but that wouldn't have stopped him hitting on the race winnings for a few grand. From what I could see he was telling the truth, and already my mind was asking premature questions.

"So these assholes demanded a payback of eight grand, and shit I didn't wanna die, Ernesto, I really didn't wanna die today, so what the fuck was I gonna do? There was four of them and one of me, and you know I don't move so fast these days, and they had heat and they had a freakin' lead pipe, and it was right there in their eyes that they didn't give one single scrawny rat's ass about whacking me and taking everything I got."

Roberto started blubbering then, shaking like Jell-O near a drum roll, and I gripped his shoulder and held it firm and made him look in my eyes and tell that what he was saying was the truth so help him God.

"Sure as shit is brown and the Pope ain't never got laid," he said. "It's the fucking truth, Ernesto . . . those asshole Puerto Rican motherfuckers took eight grand off of me and Don Ceriano, and I don't know what the fuck I'm gonna do."

"Where're they at, Roberto?"

He looked surprised. "Who?"

"The goddamned Puerto Ricans, Roberto, who the fuck d'ya think I mean? Jeez, goddammit, Roberto, sometimes you are the dumbest motherfucker ever to walk the face of God's green earth."

"The bowling alley down on southside, you know?"

I shook my head. "No, I don't fucking know, Roberto. What bowling alley?"

"Near Seventh and Stinson—"

"I know where he means," Slapsie said quietly.

"So I'm gonna go down there, Roberto, and I'm gonna find me some Puerto Ricans living the high-life with eight grand and change, and I'm gonna sort this thing out. But I'll tell you once and once only . . . I go down there and you've pissed down my back and told me it's rainin' then I'm gonna come back and cut your goddamned pecker off and make you eat it, you get it?"

"It's true, all of it's true," Roberto said, and then he started crying and blubbering again.

I stood up. I looked at Slapsie. "You come with me, and you," I said pointing to another of the crew. I turned back to Roberto. "I'm gonna leave one of the boys here to take care of you 'til we get back, okay? You try any weird shit and he's gonna ventilate your fucking head, you understand?"

Roberto nodded. He nodded between one sobbing wretched sound and the next.

Me and Slapsie and the younger guy, kid with bad skin and crooked teeth called Marco who was related to Johnny the Limpet in some way or other—we took the car and headed southside. Slapsie drove, he knew the way, and within twenty-five minutes we'd pulled up outside some beat-to-shit bowling alley with a small greasy-looking diner attached to the side like a malignant tumor. Outside there was one teenager, couldn't have been more than fifteen or sixteen, and from the look of him he was as high as Vesuvius on some filthy-smelling shit these assholes always smoked.

I nodded at Marco. He got out of the car and walked straight toward the kid. A handful of words. The kid nodded and sat down on the ground. He pulled his knees up to his chest and wrapped his arms around them, lowered his head until his chin touched his chest and he stayed there like a sleeping Mexican outside a five-dollar bordello.

Me and Slapsie came from the front of the car. Slapsie carried a baseball bat, a good solid wooden thing with a four-inch nail hammered through the head. See him coming like that and you'd piss your pants and reaffirm your belief in the baby Jesus. I smiled to myself. Adrenaline pumped like a jailhouse bodybuilder.

The door wasn't locked. Me and Slapsie went through quietly. Could hear voices as soon as we were inside, that and the thunder of a bowling ball making its way down one of the lanes, the clatter of pins as the ball made its target, the whoops and hollers of three or four dumbass Puerto Rican motherfuckers who'd figured their luck was in when they took down Roberto Albarelli for eight grand and change.

They saw Slapsie first. The one nearest us couldn't have been more than twenty years old. He looked for a second like someone had asked him to cut his own pecker off, and then he started screaming at us in Spanish. The second Rican came up behind him. He looked pissed, real pissed, and then the third one came, and the third one was reaching in back of his pants waistband for what could only have been his heat.

Slapsie was a big guy, big like Joe Louis, yet when he decided to run he ran like one of those small greyhound niggers, all stick-bones and painted-on muscles and not an ounce of fat to share around.

He came alongside the first guy and pushed him aside, the second one too, and then he let fly with his bat and caught the gun-puller in the upper arm with the four-inch nail.

Can't remember a scream that ever sounded quite like that before or after. Later I figured it must have been the acoustics of that place, for the sound that erupted from his mouth was like some strange prehistoric bird. He went down like a bag of bricks and lay there for some time. Slapsie kicked him sideways into the bowling lane and he didn't move. I don't know whether he was out cold or frightened stiff, but whichever it was it was fine by me.

I approached the taller of the Ricans. In my hand I held a .38, just loose at my side but enough so they both could see it.

"Eight grand and change, please," I said.

The taller one looked at me kind of weird. I shot him in the left foot. He went down silent, didn't even utter a sound, and but for the scrabbling of his foot on the glossed surface of the floor you wouldn't have known he was there.

"Eight grand and change, please . . . and don't make me ask you again or you'll be leaking out through a hole in your fucking head."

The shorter one made a move. Slapsie had him gripped by the back of his neck before he went a foot.

"You wanna play a ball or two?" I asked Slapsie.

Slapsie grinned. "Sure . . . ain't played this shit for years."

"Put his head in there," I told Slapsie, and Slapsie dragged the kid across the floor and pushed his head down into the bowling ball return chute. I could hear him screaming. Sound echoed out from the chute like he was calling me long-distance from Pough-keepsie.

The first ball Slapsie threw went like a rocket along the lane and would've broken any number of pins had his aim been any good.

"Throw like a bitch," I said, and Slapsie laughed.

I heard the ball go back over the far edge and drop into the return runway. I listened as it was projected back upwards and started its rapidly accelerating journey home.

The kid screamed. He knew what was coming.

The sound as that bowling ball hammered into the top of his skull was like Slapsie's baseball bat colliding with a side of beef. The kid didn't utter a sound.

I turned and looked at the kid with the bullet in his foot. His eyes were wide, his skin white like a nun in wintertime.

"Try again," I told Slapsie, and he let another ball fly down the lane. Bang on target. Strike.

The pins caterwauled away like frightened children, every last one of them.

"Motherfucker!" Slapsie shouted, and he did this little dance from one foot to the other.

We waited. We quietened down. The ball dropped down the back and started its way home.

The sound of contact was wet and crunching. Whatever tension may have existed in the kid's body dropped out of him completely. I hauled him up and let him slide to the ground. The top of his head was little more than mush as far down as the bridge of his nose. One of his eyes lolled drunkenly out of its socket and dangled against his blood-spattered cheek.

I turned and looked at the kid on the floor.

"Eight grand and change, please," I said quietly.

The kid raised his hand and pointed to a bag on the seats behind us. Slapsie walked over and opened it up. He smiled. He nodded. He picked up the bag with his left hand, and then he took one step backward, another, and with his right hand he raised his bat way over his shoulder and brought it down like Thor's hammer. The four-inch nail punctured the kid's forehead. His eyes bugged out like they were on springs, and then there was nothing but the nail through the bat holding him up off the ground. Slapsie wrenched sideways and the nail tore free. The kid slumped to the ground and rolled onto his side.

I looked at Slapsie. Slapsie looked at me.

"Figure the fat guy is off the hook," he said quietly.

"Figure he is," I replied.

We left as quietly as we had entered. The teenager outside still sat there with his head on his knees. Back of his neck showed a dark black bruise just above his shoulders. Marco had more than likely stamped on him and just broken his neck.

Business done, we went back to see Albarelli. We gave him the money. He would've sucked my dick if I'd asked him. Told him not to say a word. Way it worked was that you just dealt with the bad news, but you never passed it up the line. Albarelli wouldn't have said a word anyway, would've shot his reputation to pieces, but despite that there was a form and a protocol to these things. Don Ceriano never knew what Don Ceriano didn't need to know. Like he'd told me himself, *There are some things you see, some things not. Likewise there are some things you hear, and just as many you don't. A wise man knows which is which.*

That was business, the kind of business that needed sorting out every once in a while, and me and Slapsie and Johnny the Limpet, all of us who made up the Alcatraz Swimming Team, well, we were there to take care of such things, and take care of them we did.

A couple of years later a ghost of Miami came back to haunt us. Irony itself. June of 1972 five men were arrested at the Watergate Complex in Washington: James McCord, security co-ordinator of the Republican Committee to re-elect Nixon, some other ex-CIA goon, and three Cubans. Remembered the Wofford Hotel, the base for Lansky and Frank Costello in the '40s, how Costello had possessed strong ties with Nixon. One of those self-same Watergate burglars, a Cuban exile, was vice president of the Keyes Realty Company, the outfit that mediated between the families and Miami–Dade County officialdom. When the shit hit the fan for the Nixon administration Don Ceriano knew more about what was going down in Washington than most of the Washington insiders. He was the one who told me about the White House informant, the guy that was later referred to as "Deep Throat."

"Some FBI big shot," he said. "He was the one who gave the inside track to those two Washington newspaper hacks. Hell, maybe if they hadn't made such a mess with Kennedy, they would have whacked Nixon, instead of all this complicated legal bullshit they've had to go through."

Second irony, and one that was much closer to home, was that Nixon's fall from grace was instrumental in the death of Don Giancarlo Ceriano the better part of two years later.

Nixon held on for dear life throughout that time. He fought the only way he knew how. Guy was as crazy as a bug on a hotplate, but he was a politician so we didn't expect much else.

Don Ceriano kept his house in good order. He worked hard. He collected dues for the family and made good on their agreements. But there was word from Chicago, always the quiet word from Chicago. History in Chicago went way back to Capone, Don Ceriano told me, and when Capone was jailed for tax evasion his mantle was assumed by Frank Nitti. Nitti ran the business the way the National Commission of *la Cosa Nostra* wanted, quiet yet powerful, and right until the time he and a handful of others were indicted for extortion of the Hollywood studios he was considered one of the best. Rather than face trial, Frank Nitti shot himself in the head and the Chicago mob was taken over by Tony Accardo. Accardo brought affluence to the family down there. They moved into Vegas and Reno. They ran a street tax on everything that went down in Chicago, and then in 1957 Accardo decided to step down in favor of Sam Giancana. Giancana was Frank Nitti's opposite. He was an extravagant man, with a high-profile lifestyle, and he stayed in power until he was jailed for a year in '66. When he was released he resumed his position, and despite the ill-favor that was felt toward him by others in the families he stayed there. Ironically, a year or so later, by which time I had long since moved to New York, Sam Giancana was shot eight times. They shot him in the basement of his own house, as if murder wasn't insult and ignominy enough.

It was New Year 1974. Christmas had been good. Don Ceriano's three sisters and their families had come out to Vegas to spend time with him. They brought with them eleven children, the smallest no more than eighteen months old, the eldest a pretty girl of nineteen called Amelia. For those two or three weeks, perhaps even as far back as Thanksgiving, things had quietened down. 1973 had been fortuitous for Don Ceriano. He had sent all of eight and a half million dollars in paybacks to the bosses and they were pleased with him. Besides the Flamingo and Caesars Palace there were the dozens of smaller casinos and bars, whorehouses and bookmakers that Don Ceriano oversaw. These places provided the vegetables to run alongside the main course. As the New Year crept into the second week of January, as our minds turned back toward the business at hand, there was word from Chicago that Sam Giancana wanted a hand in what Vegas had to offer. Don Ceriano heard it along the grapevine, and when he mentioned it he spoke in words that were condescending and contemptuous.

"Giancana . . . a fucking playboy," he would say. "Nothing more than six feet of shit in a five-hundred-dollar suit. Asshole thinks he can come down here and muscle in on this he can take a real long walk off of a short harbor, know what I mean?"

But for all the words, all the bravura, Giancana was a very powerful man. Chicago, everything that Capone and Nitti had established before him, was a major part of the family's concerns. If Giancana wanted something he usually got it, and it was he who sent his right-hand man, Carlo Evangelisti, and his own cousin, Fabio Calligaris, to speak with Don Ceriano in the third week of that new year.

I remember them coming. I remember the limousine that pulled up on Alvarado Street and the way they looked as they exited the vehicle and made their way toward the house. They had come with someone's blessing, I knew that much, and whatever Don Ceriano might have wanted, the fact was that when it came to family decisions he was not a general but a lieutenant.

Calligaris and Evangelisti sat with Don Ceriano in the main room of the house. I brought them whiskey sours and ashtrays. I remember the way Fabio Calligaris spoke, his voice like something dead being dragged across the floor of a mortuary, and when he looked at me there was something in his eyes that seemed to command both respect and fear. Perhaps, looking back, there was something in him that reflected an aspect of myself. Perhaps, for the first time in many years, I recognized a little of what I had become, and beside that an understanding that I was nothing to these people. I was not family; I was not blood; I was not even Italian.

They stopped to eat at some point, and as Calligaris rose from his chair he looked at me and smiled. He turned to Don Ceriano and he said, "Don Ceriano . . . who is this man?"

Don Ceriano turned to me. He held out his hand and I walked toward him. He placed his arm around my shoulders and hugged me tight.

"This, Don Calligaris, is Ernesto Cabrera Perez."

"Aah," Calligaris said. "The Cuban."

He registered my surprise, and then smiled knowingly. "We have a mutual friend, Ernesto Perez . . . a man called Antoine Feraud from way down south in Louisiana."

My surprise was even greater.

Calligaris reached out his hand toward me. I reached back. He gripped my hand and shook it firmly. "To know Mr. Feraud is to know half the world," he said, and then he laughed. "He is a force to be reckoned with, certainly as far as the southern States are concerned. He has one or two politicians in his pocket, and to have earned a reputation with him will serve us well . . . perhaps more and more as time goes on." Calligaris paused; he looked me up and down for a moment.

"I understand from what I hear that you are a man of decisive action and few words."

I didn't speak.

Calligaris laughed. "Evidently this is true, I see," he said, and he and Don Ceriano looked at one another and smiled.

Calligaris nodded. "Good, so we eat, and then we will talk some more."

Don Ceriano released me and I went out back to the kitchen. I sat there while people rushed around me carrying food through to the dining room. My mouth was as dry as copper filings. I felt a burning tension in my chest. There were people out there in the world who knew my name, knew of the things I had done, and these were people I would not have recognized had I walked past them in the street, had I sat beside them in a bar. The thought frightened me, and since I had become a stranger to fear it was a moment that I would think of for many years to come. It was a moment that marked a change for me, a change of direction, a change of lifestyle, but only later would I realize how significant it was. For now, for that brief time, I sat silently in the kitchen while Don Ceriano, Fabio Calligaris and Carlo Evangelisti, perhaps the three most powerful men I had ever known, sat and ate antipasta no more than ten feet away.

That night, darkness pressing against the walls of my room, the sound from the street beyond nothing more than a murmur of endless traffic through the city of Las Vegas, I looked back and asked myself what I had become. I thought of my mother, how cruelly and unnecessarily she had died, and also of my father, the Havana Hurricane, and the way he had looked at me in that alleyway when he knew his death had arrived by the hand of his own son. I did not cry for him. I *could* not. But for her, for everything she was before my father, for everything she would have become had she not chosen to marry him . . . for her I shed a tear. It came back to family. Always to family. It came back to blood and loyalty and the strength of a promise. These people, these Italians, were not my family. I was all that existed of my own bloodline, and with my death would come the death of everything that my mother had wanted for me. It was perhaps then that my thoughts turned to a family of my own, and how family was strength and passion and a sense of pride in creating something that was an extension of one's self. I went to sleep with that thought, and though the next day would augur greater change than ever I could have imagined, nevertheless the seed had been planted. And it would grow; with time it would grow, and the more it grew the less space I had left to allow for any other thoughts. What happened in the coming weeks I allowed to happen for that reason, for never once did I believe that I would find what I was looking for in that house on Alvarado.

Now, in hindsight, I seem to remember the following day with greater and greater clarity, as if such hindsight has given me the advantage of perspective. Sometimes Don Ceriano would say *Ernesto, you say too little and think too much,* but closer to the truth was that I thought rarely, if at all. I was not then, and never have been, an introspective man. Perhaps my life did not permit me the luxury of contemplation, for to consider the things that I had done, the people I had killed, the path I had chosen, would have been too painful. Now—older, perhaps a little wiser—I possibly would have made different choices. Certainly not the killing of my father, for even with older, wiser eyes I can see there was no other way. I could not have stood by and let someone else kill him. That would not have been justice. Guilty of the death of my mother, guilty of torturing her for so many years before, I had to kill him myself. And the others? Well, I was a good soldier, a member of the Italian family, but perhaps no more than some inbred distant cousin who appeared only when there was work to do that no one else would undertake. I do not know, and now I do not care to know. By the time I was old enough to see these things for what they were I was too old to do anything about them. It was what it was. The past was the past, and there was nothing I could say or do to change it.

That day, the day after the arrival of Fabio Calligaris and Carlo Evangelisti, was a watershed. As I came down to the breakfast table that morning I perceived a presence in the room that I had felt before. It was the presence of death. Death carries a shadow. It waits, it lingers for some certain moment, and then it takes what it has come for swiftly, most often silently, always completely. Don Giancarlo Ceriano, a man who had been my father since February 1960 and the death of Don Pietro Silvino, a man who had schooled me in the ways of the world for the better part of fifteen years, carried about him that shadow of death.

"Ernesto . . . you slept well?" he asked.

I nodded. "Yes, Don Ceriano . . . I slept well."

He smiled. "So today is a big day, a day for the future," he said. He buttered a crust of ciabatta and proceeded to dip it in a bowl of espresso. Don Ceriano was a man of some urgency; often he would scan the newspaper while eating, to his right an ashtray with a burning cigarette which he would retrieve and draw from periodically; in front of him the TV would be playing, and in the background someone would be discussing with him the details of some aspect of their work. He could do these things simultaneously, as if he possessed insufficient time to do each of them in turn. As a younger man I believed he had a mind the size of America; in later years I realized that this was the only way he could crowd out the sound of his conscience.

"My friends Don Carlo and Don Fabio will return shortly. We will once more go over the details of the Chicago family's interests in our business here in Las Vegas. This will be a fortuitous year for us, I believe, a very fortuitous year indeed."

I didn't want to eat; I could not eat. I poured a cup of coffee, I lit a cigarette, I listened patiently while Don Ceriano spoke of how things would be better once Sam Giancana's people were here to assist in the management of the business. I did not believe a word of it. I cannot explain how, but somehow all of Don Ceriano's words, words that he had been given by Don Calligaris and Don Evangelisti, seemed transparent. They seemed of a different color to the air in the room, or perhaps they carried beneath them the shadow of death. I did not try to understand why I knew what would happen, but I knew it, knew it with all my heart. I understood, even then, that I would take whatever action I had to in order to preserve my own life. I believed that it was not only for myself that I wished to survive, but for the memory of my mother. If I died, then there would be nothing left of her. Nothing at all. This I could not allow to happen, and so I decided—against all judgment and loyalty, against all conscience and honor—that I would walk from this day regardless of what might happen to Don Ceriano. He was not my family. *I* was my family. Myself and the memory of my mother.

Later, an hour perhaps, Don Calligaris and Don Evangelisti returned. They came with boxes of cigars, with bottles of vintage armagnac, and flowers for Don Ceriano's house. Soon the place was rich with the aroma of smoke and spirit and summer. I went to the kitchen and attended to nothing but my own sense of unease and anticipation, and it was not long before Don Ceriano came through, already half-drunk before noon, and told me that he would be going out with Fabio and Carlo to see some of the business enterprises and casinos. Calligaris was behind him in a second. He insisted I accompany them, and once again his voice, like something dead being dragged across the floor, and his eyes, that seemed to command both respect and fear, left nothing I could do to refuse his insistence.

We took Don Ceriano's car. Don Ceriano drove, beside him Carlo Evangelisti, myself and Don Calligaris in the back. We drove for an endless time, it seemed, but the streets were still familiar and so we could not have traveled for very long. Don Ceriano spoke incessantly. I wanted to tell him to shut up, that he would need all his energy to fight against what would inevitably come, and when he asked questions of me there was nothing I could do but murmur an affirmative or a denial.

"Once again you think too much and say too little, Ernesto," he said, to which Don Calligaris interjected, "Seems that would be a good attitude for a whole lot more of our people," and they all laughed, and they were laughing in the face of something terrible, and it seemed that Don Ceriano was the only one who could not see it. Perhaps he was blinded by greed, the promise of money or reputation or acknowledgment from the family, but he was blind whatever the reason, and inside I had already done my grieving because I knew there was nothing I could do to save him.

Don Ceriano was dead even in the moment that he had awoken that morning, perhaps earlier, perhaps in some brief exchange of words that had taken place between his visitors from Chicago the night before. Only later would I understand the weeks and months of prelude to his death. Only later would I understand that the decision had been made by someone he had never even met.

We pulled over at the back of a warehouse downtown. We were close to the edge of the desert. The sun was high, the air heated and dry, and there was a breathless tension in the atmosphere.

"Here we can do anything to a car that you can do to a car," Don Ceriano said. "Here we have a crew who can steal cars to order, who can strip and remove chassis numbers, change plates and log books and whatever the hell else in a handful of hours. We run maybe six to a dozen vehicles through here a week, many of them winding up in the midwest and the northern states." He was lighthearted, proud even, and he sat back in the driver's seat with the window open, in his hand one of the expensive cigars that had been delivered that very morning.

It was in that moment, as he raised the cigar to his lips, that Don Fabio Calligaris whipped the wire over Don Ceriano's head and pulled it back again with every ounce of strength he possessed. Caught between the wire and his neck was Don Ceriano's right wrist, and I watched with a sense of abject and disconnected horror as the wire cut into the flesh and the cigar he was holding was crushed into his face.

Even as instinct urged me forward, urged me to do something to help Don Ceriano, I glanced to my left and saw Don Evangelisti looking at me. His eyes challenged me to move. The way he held his body, the way he leaned against the back of the seat, I knew he held a gun that was aimed directly at some part of my body.

Everything seemed to slide away into a vague unreality. I felt the urgency of Don Ceriano's helplessness. I felt the need to do something to help him. I was aware of my loyalty to him, the agreements that had been made, and against all of these things the necessity to preserve my own life and the memory of my family.

"Aah fuck, fuck, fuck," Don Calligaris was saying, and then Don Ceriano started thrashing and screaming.

Don Calligaris leaned back and placed the bottom of his right foot against the back of the driver's seat. He clenched his fists, and started jerking the wire back again and again. Don Ceriano screamed louder. Blood poured from the gash in his wrist, a gash that grew deeper with every sudden movement.

I watched in horror. I could not move. Everything inside me told me to do something, *anything*, but I seemed unable to move.

Don Ceriano, his eyes wide, his mouth open—screaming in agony as the pain increased—looked at me.

I looked back at him—blank, feeling nothing.

I was oblivious of the gun that Don Evangelisti held. I had gone beyond the point of concerning myself with what might happen if I reacted. All I knew was that this was not my time to die. It could not be.

"For Christ's sake shut the fuck up!" Evangelisti was shouting, as if Don Ceriano had a choice, and it was in that second, as I watched the blood pumping from his wrist, as I watched the muscles straining in Fabio Calligaris's face, as I saw the sudden panic that registered on the face of the man beside Ceriano, that I knew I had to do something.

I looked to my left. I remember that. I looked to my left out through the window, looked out toward the desert, the sheer absence of anything recognizable against the horizon, and I asked myself if this could be the end of my life also.

My mother looked back at me. I had to survive, if only for her. That was my decision. The decision prompted action, and I clenched my fist. I leaned forward, past Don Calligaris, and with my right hand I hammered sideways into Don Ceriano's temple.

He stopped screaming for a split second.

He looked back at me over his shoulder. He realized in that moment that I was not going to help him, that I had made a decision to let him die in that car.

He started screaming again.

I pushed Don Calligaris aside, the wire loosened from its hold, and awkwardly thrusting myself between the two front seats I gripped Don Ceriano's throat with my hands. Again his screaming ceased. I pushed his arms down, removed the obstruction to the wire, and then I fell back into my seat.

Calligaris looked at me for a heartbeat moment, and then, once more and with force, he jerked the wire back. I heard it slide through the flesh of Don Ceriano's neck. I heard his breath fighting to escape through the sudden rush of blood, heard his feet as they kicked against the pedals in the well of the car, and within seconds he slumped back.

Don Ceriano was dead. He, who had been spoken of weeks before in New York; he, whose death warrant was signed, sealed and delivered before Christmas; he, whose name had already passed into the vast and forgotten memory of the National Commission of *la Cosa Nostra,* was dead.

Don Ceriano, his head lolled back against the headrest, bled out into his own lap while Fabio Calligaris and Carlo Evangelisti closed their eyes and regained their balance.

I said nothing. Not a word.

After some minutes Don Calligaris opened the door and stepped out of the car. I followed him and walked a good ten or fifteen yards away from the vehicle. Don Evangelisti followed suit, but then he turned back toward the warehouse and made his way toward it swiftly. Somewhere I heard an engine revving, a heavy diesel engine. From the back doors of the warehouse a wide tractor with a loading scoop on the front emerged. We three watched as the tractor rumbled across the dirt and neared the car. Within a minute or two the tractor had lifted the car as if it were made of nothing but paper, and turning slowly, lumbering like some vast prehistoric creature with prey in its jaws, the tractor made its way back toward the warehouse, toward the car crusher that sat idling and patient on the other side of the lot.

I watched it go. My heart beat slowly. This was life and death in Las Vegas, family-style.

Don Calligaris walked toward me and offered me a cigarette. He lit it for me, and then with the same dead stare he fixed me to the ground. He smiled coldly. "What did you see here, Ernesto Cabrera Perez?"

I shook my head. "Here? I didn't see anything here, Don Calligaris."

I saw then, as he raised his cigarette to his lips, the blood on his hands. I looked down and saw blood on my own. There was blood on Carlo Evangelisti's five-hundred-dollar suit. Don Giancarlo Ceriano's blood.

"You saw nothing here," Don Calligaris stated matter-of-factly.

I shook my head. "There was nothing to see."

He nodded and looked down at the ground. "You ever seen New York, Ernesto?"

I shrugged.

"No?" he asked.

I shrugged again, shook my head. "No, I've never seen New York."

"There could be a place in New York for a man such as yourself, a man who sees little and speaks less."

"There could be," I said.

"Man like you could make some money in New York, have a position of influence . . . have the time of his life, in fact." He laughed as if remembering some personal experience.

I looked across at Don Evangelisti. He was smiling too.

"You're not from Chicago, are you?" I asked.

Don Calligaris shook his head. "No, we're not from Chicago."

"You don't work for Sam Giancana, and you are not his cousin?"

Calligaris smiled once again. "Sam Giancana is an asshole, a shoe-shine boy in a five-hundred-dollar suit. Sam Giancana will be dead before the year is out. No, we do not work for him, and no I am not his cousin. We work for people who are an awful lot more powerful than Sam Giancana, and you can come work for us if you wish."

I was quiet for a moment. With the death of Don Ceriano there was nothing for me here. I was the hired hand, part of the wet-job crew, and for all I knew Slapsie Maxie, Johnny the Limpet and the rest of the Alcatraz Swimming Team were as dead as Don Ceriano somewhere in Vegas.

"There is nothing for me here," I said. "I can come to New York."

They both smiled. Don Evangelisti said something in Italian and they laughed some more.

Don Calligaris walked toward me. He reached out his blood-spattered hand and I shook it. "Welcome to the real world, Ernesto Perez," he said quietly, and then he released my hand, and started walking, and I followed him back to the warehouse where a car was waiting for us.

I looked back as we drove away, saw the tractor as it raised Don Ceriano's car high above the ground and then let it fall into the crusher. I closed my eyes and said a prayer for his soul, even now on its swift and inevitable passage into Hell.

I turned around and looked forward, because forward was the only way I could look, and if New York was my destination then so be it.

I was thirty-six years old. I was alone. I was no longer part of this family. I took what was given to me and there seemed no choice.

By the time I boarded an aircraft, in my hand a single case holding all my possessions, I had separated myself from all that had come before, and prepared to start over again.

This was how it had to be done, for to look back was to see the past, and the past was too painful to see.

New York beckoned; I flew out of Las Vegas toward it with hope in my heart.

SIXTEEN

"**W**E HAVE THE salesman . . . we don't have a body, but we have a confession," Woodroffe said.

They were seated in the main office of the building, he and Hartmann and Schaeffer; it was early evening, an hour or so after Perez had been escorted back to the Royal Sonesta.

Hartmann had a headache the size of Nebraska. He was drinking too much coffee, smoking too many cigarettes; felt as if he had been cornered in a nightmare of his own worst devising.

"We have the murders of Gerard McCahill, Pietro Silvino, this guy McLuhan, two people in the Shell Beach Motel and this Chester Wintergreen, whoever the fuck that might be. Now there's the three Puerto Ricans and Giancarlo Ceriano in Vegas. We believe that we can verify at least six of these killings, and we have no reason at all to suspect that Perez is not guilty."

Hartmann looked across the table at Schaeffer. Schaeffer's expression was black, the expression of a tired and desperate man, and Hartmann believed that there was nothing in the world that could help him. They were all in the same predicament, the same tortured reality that Perez had so effortlessly created, and at the same time the three of them were ultimately responsible for what might happen as a result.

"So?" Hartmann asked.

Woodroffe looked at Schaeffer; Schaeffer nodded and Woodroffe turned back to Hartmann.

"The men we sent out have still found nothing."

Hartmann looked down. "Perhaps she is not even in New Orleans," he suggested, a thought that he imagined had been present in all their minds from the very start. Perez had been ahead of them by days, and he could have driven the girl halfway across the United States and they would have been none the wiser.

"So we have the authority to make a deal with him," Woodroffe said, and even before he had explained his rationale Hartmann started to smile. He smiled like the similarly tired and desperate man he was.

"We have authority from both FBI Director Dohring and the attorney general himself, Richard Seidler, to make a deal with Perez," Woodroffe went on. "And we want you to go over to the Sonesta and speak with Perez and see if he is willing to trade."

"And what would the proposal be?" Hartmann asked.

Once again Woodroffe glanced at Schaeffer.

"At least six counts of murder," Schaeffer said. "Six counts of murder that Perez has confessed to and that we can find evidence to corroborate, and in exchange for information on the whereabouts of the girl and her safe return—" Schaeffer looked down at his hands. He paused for a moment and then looked up once more. "In exchange for the girl he walks."

"He *walks*?" Hartmann was astounded.

"Well, he walks as far as the United States justice community is concerned. He will be extradited back to Cuba, and if the Cuban government wants to make something of whatever crimes were committed on Cuban soil, then that's their business. We would not be willing . . . well, let's just say that we would not put ourselves in a cooperative position as far as forwarding any evidence to them is concerned."

"And if she's already dead?" Hartmann asked. "If she's already dead, and this wasn't just a kidnapping but a seventh murder you can corroborate?"

Schaeffer shook his head. "That is a gamble we are prepared to take."

"We?" Hartmann asked, his tone a little accusatory. "Don't you mean you, or Dohring and Seidler, and back of them Charles Ducane with whatever pressure he's brought to bear through his political connections?"

Woodroffe leaned forward. He rested his hands flat on the table. "We are operating on the assumption that the girl is still alive," he said. "We have simply been granted the authority to put this proposal forward to Perez, and seeing as how he chose you to come down and hear him out we are choosing you to go over and tell him what we are prepared to do."

"You're wasting your time," Hartmann said, "and in all honesty I don't think you'll accomplish anything but pissing him off. Don't you see, this isn't about the girl? It isn't even about the kidnapping, and it sure as hell ain't about Perez murdering Gerard McCahill or anyone else. This is about Perez's life . . . it's about the things he's done and the people who told him to do them—"

"Aah for Christ's sake Hartmann, you're talking out of your ass," Woodroffe snapped.

"Am I?" Hartmann interjected. "You really think you understand what's going on inside this man's head?"

"No . . . but I suppose you do," Schaeffer said.

Hartmann sighed; this was going to be a circular and pointless confrontation. "I believe I do," he said. "At least a little of it."

"Then please enlighten us," Schaeffer said, "because right now it seems we are no closer to understanding anything about what happened to Catherine Ducane than we were a week last Saturday."

"It's about being someone," Hartmann said. "It's about being no one at all, and then becoming someone, and then realizing that you're no one at all once more."

"Come again?" Woodroffe said.

"Ernesto Perez was a nobody . . . some beaten-to-shit kid with a crazy father, and then his father kills his mother and he's gotta get out of the US. So he heads to Cuba, and there he meets people with money, people who want him to be whatever he is, and he does these things and he has money, reputation, he has people afraid of him, and now I believe he has been excommunicated from that life. He has found himself in a situation where the people who were supposed to be his friends, his family if you like . . . well, they've turned their backs on him and he finds himself alone."

"What the fuck is that all about?" Woodroffe asked. "You're a fully qualified criminal profiler all of a sudden?"

"It's a gut feeling," Hartmann said. "I've sat in there for God only knows how many hours listening to this man tell the story of his life, and there is a lot we don't know, that is for sure, but there is a great deal we can surmise. What I can see, what I have read in what he has told us so far, is that he has come to realize he has been the pawn of more powerful men, and now he is in a position, for what reason we don't know, where perhaps he has needed something and they have not been willing to help him."

"Hypothesize all you like," Woodroffe said, "but the truth of the matter is that we follow protocol, and protocol is established by senior authority, and that senior authority is directing us to put forward a proposal and see if a deal can be struck."

Hartmann didn't reply.

"We need you to get behind this, Hartmann," Schaeffer said. "We need you to be on the same team as us. We got something to do here—"

"So do it yourself," Hartmann interjected.

Schaeffer sighed audibly. He closed his eyes and leaned his head back. He spoke again without moving his head and Hartmann could tell how utterly and completely frustrated he was. "We need you to do this," he said slowly. "We need you to handle whatever doubts and reservations you might have about this and go over there and talk to this wacko. We need you to give it your best shot, and who the hell knows . . . it might not come to anything, but right now everything you're saying, everything *any* of us are saying, is merely supposition and assumption. Perez might go for the deal, he might not—"

"He won't be interested," Hartmann said.

"And why the fuck are you so sure of that?" Woodroffe asked.

"Because he's a murderer and a psychopath. He's an old man who's spent the whole of his life killing people, right from his teens. We didn't know anything about him. He could have stayed wherever he was and never made a sound, and none of us would have been any the wiser. He's kidnapped the girl for a reason. He hasn't just turned himself in to confess all these things to make himself feel better. He has an agenda, a rationale, and however fucking crazy that might be, it's still a reason, right? He never had a jail sentence to begin with . . . why on earth would he go about creating one?"

Woodroffe shook his head and looked at Schaeffer. "He's right. Why has he turned himself in at all? Why didn't he just stay wherever the hell he was and die quietly?"

"Because he's fucking crazy, and crazy people do crazy things all the time," Schaeffer said. "You cannot apply reason to an unreasonable action."

Hartmann raised his eyebrows. He remembered having that exact thought himself.

"So what the fuck do you propose?" Woodroffe asked Schaeffer.

Schaeffer shook his head. "We don't have a choice. We have been asked to put a proposal to this man, and that's what we're gonna do. We're gonna give it our best shot. Hartmann is gonna go over to the Royal Sonesta Hotel, and with a hundred federal agents present, he's gonna sit in a room with Ernesto Perez and ask him if he wants to make a trade for the life of the girl. We'll see what Perez has to say, and if he tells us to go fuck ourselves then we're in no worse a situation than we are right now."

"Good point," Woodroffe said. "Mr. Hartmann?"

Hartmann shrugged his shoulders. "You guys are in charge here . . . I'm just the ex-alcoholic who drove a twelve-wheeler through his life and then got dragged down here against his will and wants nothing more than to go home. But don't blame me if he gets so pissed off he decides he's *never* gonna tell us where the girl is."

"That's a risk we'll have to take," Woodroffe said.

"Agreed," Schaeffer said. "I ain't gonna be the one to call the FBI director and tell him go shove his proposal up his ass."

"It's your call, boys," Hartmann said, and he rose to his feet. "But I ain't doing it tonight."

Schaeffer frowned. "Whaddya mean, you ain't doing it tonight?"

"I have a migraine the size of most of Louisiana and then some. I didn't sleep good last night. I am not in the best frame of mind to negotiate a trade for Catherine Ducane's life. You want me to do this then you gotta cut me some slack on how it's done. I need some time to think about this, to work out how I should best speak to him. I think it's a fucking waste of everybody's time, but I also understand that if he says no then we haven't really lost anything either. I have more reasons not to be here right now than you guys could ever imagine, and the last thing I wanna do is blow my only chance of leaving here as soon as possible by going at this in completely the wrong frame of mind."

"I agree with Hartmann," Woodroffe said.

"You wanna call Bob Dohring and tell him we ain't doing this right now? If we ain't doing it now then when the fuck are we gonna do it?"

"Tomorrow," Hartmann said.

"Every twenty-four hours is another twenty-four hours of Catherine Ducane's life. You understand that, right?"

Hartmann nodded. "I understand that . . . of course I understand that, but if she's dead then another twenty-four hours ain't gonna make the slightest bit of difference, and if she's alive then she's alive because Perez wants her alive, and if that's the case then she'll stay alive until he's got to the end of whatever the fuck it is he's decided to tell us."

"So what do we tell Dohring?" Schaeffer asked. "You have any bright ideas for that one?"

"Tell him Perez refused to speak to us 'til tomorrow. Tell them that he wants to tell us all about New York before he discusses anything else. Tell him whatever the fuck you like. I'm getting out of here. This place is driving me fucking nuts, and the last thing I'm gonna do right now is go over to the Royal Sonesta and barter with Ernesto Perez. And if whatever you tell Dohring doesn't work, tell him I'll quit unless he gives us some flexibility on this . . . and he can come down and work *his* charm on Perez and see what the fuck happens then, okay?"

"Have you been drinking?" Woodroffe asked. "Is this getting to you so much that you've fallen off the wagon, Mr. Hartmann?"

Hartmann closed his eyes and clenched his fists. It took everything he possessed to restrain himself from lunging across the table and belting Woodroffe.

"No, Mr. Woodroffe, I have not been drinking . . . apart from the poisonous fucking coffee that you people have somehow managed to concoct."

"It's okay," Schaeffer said, "I'll handle Dohring. There's a good deal of sense to what you're saying. You go back to the Marriott. Get some rest. We'll hear Perez out tomorrow, and then we'll put our proposal to him. We're all agreed, right?"

Hartmann nodded. Woodroffe grunted noncommittally.

Schaeffer rose from his chair. "Then it's settled. Tomorrow we listen to what the man has to say, and when he's done Mr. Hartmann will go to the Sonesta and speak with him alone."

Hartmann nodded his thanks to Schaeffer and walked across the office to the exit. He glanced back when he reached the door and saw both Woodroffe and Schaeffer standing silently, neither of them looking anywhere in particular, each of them lost somewhere within their own thoughts. Perhaps they had families too, Hartmann thought, and for a second he realized that he had paid no mind at all to what either of them might be going through as a result of this. But the fact of the matter was that they had chosen this life, this line of work, and he— Ray Hartmann—had seemed to wind up here by nothing but default.

He shook his head and went out through the doorway. The images of Catherine Ducane looked back at him from each wall as he walked. The effect unnerved him greatly.

Schaeffer watched him disappear into the corridor and turned to Woodroffe. "You think he took it?"

Woodroffe shrugged. "Maybe, maybe not. Seems to have done."

Schaeffer nodded. "It's important that he thinks we're actually going to make this deal with Perez. If he doesn't believe that this is our position then he will not communicate it with any conviction."

"I think he'll give it his best shot, but I think he probably knows Perez better than both of us. I think Perez won't take it . . . think he'll tell us to go fuck ourselves."

"And I think Ernesto Perez is going to die," Schaeffer said. "Regardless of whether he agrees to a deal or not, regardless of whether he tells us where the girl is, or if we find out she's been dead from day one . . . whatever the hell happens he's going to die."

"I know," Woodroffe said. "I know."

"So we go with this. We let Hartmann think we're making the deal. We let them both believe that we will let Perez walk, right up to the point where he tells us about the girl, and then we fuck him, okay?"

"That's the brief we've been given, that's what we do."

Schaeffer nodded and reached for his jacket.

"And Hartmann?" Woodroffe asked.

Schaeffer turned and looked at his partner. "What about Hartmann?"

"He will not be happy to find that he's been cut out of the loop."

Schaeffer seemed to sneer for a moment. "You really think anyone gives a rat's ass about whether Ray Hartmann is happy or not? Come on, Bill, get real. This thing is gonna go forward regardless of who gets stepped on. This is Ducane's daughter for Christ's sake. You really think how anyone feels is gonna be taken into consideration?"

Woodroffe shook his head. "I know," he said quietly. "It's okay, we go with it whichever way it's supposed to go. We'll do a body count later and clean up the battlefield."

"Always the way," Schaeffer said. "Always the way."

"And Ducane? When do we start knocking on his door and asking who's home?"

"Right now we don't," Schaeffer replied. "That is not part of our gameplan, and as far as I know it never will be. It's our job to find the girl, and once the girl's found then whatever happens to Charles Ducane is gonna be someone else's business."

"What d'you think?" Woodroffe asked.

Schaeffer shook his head. "I don't think anything. I cannot afford to think anything. I start sidetracking into whether or not Charles Ducane is in some way involved in all the shit we've been hearing then I'm gonna get into discussions I don't want with people I don't want to meet. You understand what I'm saying?"

Woodroffe nodded. "As clear as daylight."

"So until we're invited we don't show up, because whatever the hell kind of garden party that is I can guarantee you we'll not be welcome." He rolled down his shirtsleeves, put on his jacket, and then held the door open for Woodroffe.

Woodroffe rose from his chair. "One day it'll make sense," he said.

"Who told you that?" Schaeffer asked.

Woodroffe smiled sardonically. "The patron saint of liars."

"There you have it," Schaeffer said, and smiled. "Only man that can be trusted in this line of work."

Two blocks down Hartmann stopped at a phone booth. He called information for the number of Verlaine's Precinct House. When he was put through he found Gerritty once again on the desk.

"He's out somewhere," Gerritty said when Hartmann asked for Verlaine. "You want his cellphone number?"

Hartmann took it, hung up, dialed the cellphone number and found Verlaine in transit.

"Where are you?" Hartmann asked.

"About three blocks from the Precinct. Why? This isn't another one of your insane fucking ideas, is it?"

"No," Hartmann said. "I wanna ask if you'll do something for me. Don't worry, it's harmless enough . . . it's something personal."

"Meet you on the corner of Iberville," Verlaine said. "You know where that is?"

"Sure."

Hartmann drove over there and pulled up. He waited no more than three or four minutes and then saw Verlaine's car approaching.

Verlaine parked up against the curb and Hartmann made his way over there.

"Shoot," Verlaine said.

"Thursday night—if we're still in this on Thursday night—I want you to call my wife in New York."

Verlaine didn't say anything.

"I want you to call her and tell her I'm on an official thing. Obviously you can't tell her where I am, but I want you to tell her I'm on an official thing, and there might be a chance I won't make it back to New York for Saturday."

"Sure," Verlaine said. "I can call her, but why don't you call and tell her yourself?"

Hartmann shook his head. "Let's say there's a possibility she will read it as a cop-out or something. There's a good possibility she won't believe me, but if you call and tell her there will at least be a shred of credence to it."

"Trouble?" Verlaine asked.

"You could say that."

"Things gonna work out for you?"

"I hope so."

"I'll call her," Verlaine said. "You tell me what to say and I'll say it, okay?"

Hartmann nodded and smiled. "Thanks, John . . . much appreciated."

"Not a problem, Ray. You okay?"

"Sure," Hartmann said, and reached for the door lever.

"Where you headed now?"

"The Marriott," Hartmann said. "Got one bitch of a headache and I gotta get some sleep."

"Sure thing. You take it easy, okay?"

Hartmann made his way across the street to his own vehicle and drove slowly back to the Marriott. From his room he called for a sandwich and a glass of milk to be sent up. By the time they arrived he wondered if he had the strength to eat. He did anyway, the better part of half of it, and then he pulled off his clothes and collapsed on the bed like deadweight. He slept, slept like deadweight too, and even the alarm call didn't manage to wake him.

He did wake though when Sheldon Ross got a passkey and let himself into the room.

It was a quarter of eight, morning of Wednesday 3 September, and Ross waited patiently outside the door while Hartmann showered and dressed.

They left together, drove across to Arsenault Street, and once there Hartmann found Schaeffer and Woodroffe seated exactly where they had been the evening before.

"You boys even go home?" Hartmann asked.

Schaeffer smiled and rolled his eyes. "Don't fucking remember," he said, and before he could say another word there were voices and people, and Ernesto Perez, two men ahead of him, two men behind, and for all the world to see it appeared that he had become someone of importance all over again.

Once they were again seated across from one another, Hartmann looked at Perez and wondered if what he had said hadn't been the truth. Had he in fact started to re-evaluate his own life? Had he started to truly accept that he was exclusively responsible for the situation he was in?

Hartmann shrugged the thought away. How could someone such as Perez precipitate anything of any worth? The man was an unconscionable psychopath, a hired killer, a brutal and unforgiving murderer. Surely there was nothing about him that could provoke any sense of mitigation or temper. Hartmann—despite himself—even considered the possibility that there might be something vaguely human within this individual, and then he closed such a thought down.

"You are okay, Mr. Hartmann?" Perez asked.

Hartmann nodded. He tried to think of nothing at all. "You were going to tell us about New York."

"I was indeed," Perez replied. "In fact I was listening to Mr. Frank Sinatra only last night in my hotel room, singing about that very same city. You care for Mr. Sinatra?"

"A little. My wife likes him a great deal."

Perez smiled. "Then, Mr. Hartmann, you have a wife with exceptional taste."

Hartmann looked up. For a moment he was angry, felt invaded almost, as if mention of his wife from Perez's lips was a personal affront.

Perez preempted any possibility that Hartmann could speak by smiling, raising his hand in an almost conciliatory fashion, and saying, "Enough, Mr. Hartmann . . . we shall speak of New York, yes?"

For some reason Ray Hartmann went cool and quiet inside. "Yes," he said. "New York . . . tell me what happened in New York."

SEVENTEEN

"**Y**OU GONNA STAY here with these people then you gotta get it right," Don Calligaris told me.

My head hurt. I had smoked too many cigarettes and drunk too much strong espresso. All these people ever seemed to do was smoke and drink, eat rich Italian food, pasta and meatballs and sauces made with red wine and sweet-tasting herbs. Seemed to me their food looked like the aftermath of a multiple homicide.

"Five families, and it really ain't no different from remembering all the players in a football team or somethin'," Don Calligaris went on. "Five and five only, and each of them have their names, their bosses, their underbosses, names that you need to know if you're gonna mix with these people and have them take you seriously. You need to think Italian, you need to speak the language, you need to wear the right clothes and say the right words. You need to address people in the correct manner or they're gonna think you're some poor dumb fuck from the countryside."

New York was cold. It was confusing. I had figured New York to be a single place, but it was made up of islands, each of them with different names, and where we were seated—in a small diner called Salvatore's on the corner of Elizabeth and Hester in Little Italy—was a district on an island called Manhattan. The images, the names, the words that surrounded me were as new as the people who accompanied them: Bowery and the Lower East Side, Delancey Street and the Williamsburg Bridge, the East River and Wallabout Bay—places I had read about in my encyclopedias, places I had imagined so different from how they appeared in reality.

I believed Vegas to be the backstop of the world, the place where everything began and ended; New York disabused me of all I had believed. Compared to this Vegas was nothing more than its origin: a small nothing of a place hunkering at the edge of the desert.

The sounds and images dwarfed me; they frightened me a little; they created a tension within that I had not experienced before. Crazy people wandered the streets asking for change. Men were dressed as women. The walls were painted with crude garish symbology, and every other word uttered was *fucker* or *motherfucker* or *assfucker.* The people were different, their clothes, their mannerisms, their bodies. People looked worn-out or beaten or bruised or swollen-headed from some late-night jag that had poisoned them with too much liquor or cocaine or marijuana. I had seen these things in Vegas, they were not new to me, but in New York everything seemed magnified and exaggerated, as if here everything was done twice as hard, twice as fast and for twice as long.

"So there's the Gambino family," Don Calligaris said, interrupting my thoughts. "Albert Anastasia was boss from '51 to '57. He started something you might hear of around here, a little club called Murder Incorporated. After Anastasia was killed the family was taken over by Carlo Gambino, and he's been the boss since '57. Then you have the Genovese, and these guys are Lucky Luciano's family. After him came Frank Costello, and then Vito Genovese was boss until '59. After Vito came a three-man council until 1972, and now the Genovese family is run by Frank Tieri. The third family, our family, is the Lucheses. Long history, lot o' names, but all you gotta know is that Tony Corallo is the boss now. You'll hear people refer to him as Tony Ducks." Calligaris laughed. "Gave him that name 'cause of all the times he ducked out from under the Feds and the cops and whoever the fuck else might have been after him. Then you got the Colombos, and they're headed up by Thomas DiBella. Lastly you got the Bonanno family. They got Carmine Galante in charge, and if you ever meet him you don't look him straight in the eye or he'll have someone whack you just for the sheer fucking thrill of it."

Calligaris drank some more coffee. He ground his cigarette out in the ashtray and lit another.

"You got your New Jersey factions down here as well. Family has always been stronger in New York and Philly, but they got an established outfit in Newark, New Jersey, and the boss down there until '57 was a guy called Filippo Amari. Nicky Delmore ran from '57 to '64, and now they got Samuel De Cavalcante—"

I was looking at Don Calligaris with a blank expression.

He started laughing again. "Hell, kid . . . think you better take a bundle of serviettes here and make some fuckin' notes. You look like your face was a blackboard and someone just wiped you clean."

Calligaris raised his hand and attracted the attention of the guy behind the diner counter. "More coffee," he said, and the guy nodded and hurried away.

"Anyways, all you gotta remember is you're here so's we can use some of your special talents." Calligaris smiled broadly. "You got yourself somethin' of a rep for the work you did for ol' Giancarlo Ceriano, dumb fuck though he was."

I looked up, raised my eyebrows.

"Stupid fucker thinks he can rake off the cream from the milk and get away with it, you know?"

I shook my head.

Calligaris shook his head and sighed.

"Don Ceriano—" Calligaris crossed himself. "May he rest in peace . . . Don Ceriano, wise in the ways of the world he might have been, but he was given a specific instruction of how the Vegas business was supposed to be handled. He was only supposed to use certain men for certain things, he was supposed to pay over certain percentages to certain officials at certain times of the year. This is the way things work, and they've always been that way. Don Ceriano was an underboss for the Gambinos. Historically there's always been a good relationship between the Gambinos and the Lucheses, and that's why I was asked to go down and sort things out with Don Ceriano, make sure he understood who he was working for and why. Anyway, we sorted that little thing out, and now the Gambinos and the Lucheses have a part-share in the whole thing in Vegas, and it's gonna get done right. You can't run a business without a few dollars getting shared out between the right people at the right time, you know?"

Calligaris paused while the diner guy brought coffee for us both. He reached into his pocket and took out a twenty-dollar bill. "Hey kid," he said. "Buy your girl a necklace or something, eh?"

The kid took the twenty, stuffed it into the front pocket of his apron, and then he looked momentarily dejected and said, "Thanks, but I ain't got a girl right now."

Calligaris started to smile, and then he frowned. "What the fuck is this? What the fuck you bustin' my balls about, you dumb schmuck? You want me to go out and get you a freakin' girl or what? Get the fuck outta here!"

The kid stepped backward, a flicker of fear in his eyes.

"Hey!" Calligaris snapped. "Gimme the fuckin' twenty back, ya little fuck!"

The kid snatched the twenty-dollar bill from his apron pocket and threw it toward the table. Don Calligaris snatched it from the air, and then rose and started after the kid. He made to kick him and the kid started to run. I watched with amusement as the kid hurried down the length of the diner and disappeared through a door at the back.

Don Calligaris sat down. "Jesus Mary Mother of God, what the fuck is all this shit? Kid can't even be grateful for a tip, has to get all smart-mouth and wiseguy with me."

He reached for his coffee, lit another cigarette.

"Anyways, as I was saying, all you gotta do is keep your eyes open and your ears closed. You work for me now. You get an order to clip some fuck, then you go clip the fuck, right? Things is done right and clean and simple here . . . and none of that weird shit like what went down in New Orleans, okay?"

I tilted my head to the side.

"That freaky shit with the heart, you know? Whatever the fuck his name was, Devo or something, right? Dvore, that was the fucker! That thing that you did when the guy's heart was cut out."

I shook my head. "I didn't cut anybody's heart out," I said.

"Sure you did. You went down there and did some work for Feraud and his politician buddy. Cleaned up some shit a few years ago. Word got out that you whacked that Dvore fucker for some shit he was pulling and took his heart out."

"I never heard of anyone called Dvore, and I never cut anybody's heart out. I did something for Feraud because Don Ceriano asked me to, but that was back in '62, and I ain't been down there since."

Calligaris laughed. "Well, shit, kid . . . seems someone has been using your name to make a mark on the landscape. I got word that you whacked this guy Dvore for the Ferauds and this politician buddy of theirs, and just to make the fucking point you cut his heart out."

I shook my head. "Not me, Don Calligaris, not me."

Calligaris shrugged. "Aah what the hell . . . you should see the things they got my name down for. Never did any harm, helps to build your reputation, right?"

I listened to what Don Calligaris was saying, but my thoughts were back in Louisiana. From what I was being told it seemed that Feraud and his old-money buddy Ducane had taken care of some things and attributed them to me. That did not sit well. The feeling was as if some-one was walking around in my skin.

"So what the fuck, eh?" Calligaris said, interrupting me. "You gotta do whatever you gotta do, and if there's something to be gained by sayin' it's someone else then fair enough. Can't say I haven't done the same thing myself a couple or three times."

Don Calligaris changed the subject. He spoke of people we would see, things he had to do. From what I could gather it appeared I would be with him all the time, that I was to take care of the business end of things as he dictated. He had his minders, his own consigliere, but when it came to dealing with something that required a more terminal remedy, then I was to be called upon. It would really be no different from my relationship with Don Ceriano, and though there were nearly fifteen years behind me, though Don Ceriano had been there through everything, it seemed I had disconnected from that life. Florida and Vegas, even Havana and all that had happened, were behind me. There seemed no purpose to hold onto such things. Nevertheless, the fact that Antoine Feraud and his politician friend were down in Louisiana taking care of their business and attributing it to me concerned me greatly. At some point the matter would have to be addressed.

Don Calligaris lived in a tall narrow house on Mulberry Street. Back a half block and over the street was a second house, a small place, and it was here that he brought me after we left the diner. He introduced me to two people, a young man called Joe Giacalone, the son of someone Don Calligaris referred to as "Tony Jacks," and a second man, a little older.

"Ten Cent Sammy," Don Calligaris said, "but people just call him Ten Cent. Comes from his calling card, see? Leaves a dime behind whenever someone gets clipped, like that was all their life was worth."

Ten Cent rose from his chair in the small room at the front of the house. He was a big man, bigger than me by a head, and when he reached out his hand and shook mine I could feel sufficient tension in his grip to relieve my arm of its socket with one swift tug.

"Joe's just here hangin' out," Ten Cent said. "He comes down here when his girl is bustin' his balls, right Joey?"

"Screw you, Ten Cent," Joe said. "I come down here to remind myself how fuckin' smart I am in comparison to a dumb fuck like you."

Ten Cent laughed and sat down again.

"You'll stay here with Ten Cent," Don Calligaris said. "He'll give you the straight shoot on what goes down and when. Don't deal with anyone but him an' me, you understand?"

I nodded.

"You got a room upstairs and Ten Cent will help bring your stuff in. Take a rest, have a siesta, eh? We got a party tonight at the Blue Flame and you can meet some of the guys. I gotta go take care of somethin' but I'll be around if you need me. Just tell Ten Cent, and if he can't figure somethin' out he can call me."

Don Calligaris turned and gripped my shoulders. He pulled me close, and kissed my cheeks in turn. "Welcome, Ernesto Perez, and whether you whacked Ricki Dvore and cut his freakin' heart out or not you still gonna come in useful up here in Manhattan. You enjoy yourself while you can, 'cause you never know what shit might be waitin' for you around the corner, right Ten Cent?"

"Right as fuckin' rain, boss."

Don Calligaris left, and for a minute I stood there in the front room of that house feeling like the world had closed a chapter on me and started another.

"You gonna take a weight off or what?" Joe Giacalone said.

I nodded and sat down.

"Hey, don't be so uptight, kid," Ten Cent said. "You got a new family now, and if there's one thing about this family they sure as shit know how to take care of their own, right Joey?"

"Sure as shit."

I leaned back in the chair. Ten Cent offered me a cigarette and I lit it. Joey put the TV on, surfed channels until he found a game, and within a few minutes I had stopped questioning why I was there and what would happen. It was what it was. I had made my choice in a split second in Don Ceriano's car. Ceriano was dead. I was not. That was the way of this world.

The Blue Flame was a strip joint and nightclub on Kenmare Street. First thing I was aware of was how dark it was inside. A wide stage ran the length of the building on the right-hand side, and across this stage three or four girls in tasselled bras and panties no bigger than dental floss gyrated and ground their hips to a bass-heavy music that came from speakers along the floor beneath them. Over to the left three or four long tables had been pulled together, and seated around them were perhaps fifteen or twenty men, all of them dressed in suits and ties, all of them drinking and laughing, all of them red-faced and loud and trying to outdo one another.

Ten Cent took me down there. Don Calligaris rose as we approached and with a flourish of his hand he silenced the gathered crew.

"Ladies, ladies, ladies . . . we have a new guy in town."

The gathering cheered.

"This is Ernesto Perez, one of Don Ceriano's boys, and though Don Ceriano cannot be with us this evening of course, I'm sure he would appreciate the fact that one of his people got wised up and came to Manhattan to work for us."

There was a round of applause. I smiled. I reached out and shook hands. I took a glass of beer that someone handed me. I felt good.

"Ernesto . . . shit, we gotta do something about your freakin' name!" Don Calligaris said. "Anyways, this is Matteo Rossi, and here we have Michael Luciano, no relation, and Joey Giacalone, you know, and this is his father Tony Jacks, and over there is Tony Provenzano, Tony Pro to you and me, and to his right you got Stefano Cagnotto, and next to him you got Angelo Cova, and the skinny fuck down the bottom is Don Alessandro's kid, Giovanni. This crowd over here," he said, indicating the other side of the table. "Well, this sorry shower of saps and wasters is just some bunch of homeless fucks we picked up in the street."

Don Calligaris laughed. He raised his hands and clenched his fists. "This is your family, legitimate in some cases, the rest of them a bunch of bastards!"

Calligaris sat down. He indicated a chair beside his and I took it. Someone passed me a bowl of bread slices, and before I knew it I was surrounded by plates of meatballs and salami, and other things I didn't recognize.

They talked, these people, and their words were like one vast rush of noise in my ears. They spoke of "things" they were taking care of, "things" that needed taking care of, and at some point the girls were gone, the music went down low, and Tony Pro was leaning forward with everyone's attention rapt and he was talking about someone I had heard of once before.

"Cocksucker," he was saying. "Guy's a freakin' cocksucker. Hard bastard, I'll give him that, but we don't need him back now we got Fitzsimmons. Frank Fitzsimmons toes the line an awful lot more than Hoffa ever did, and seems to me we should keep it that way."

Don Calligaris was shaking his head. "Sure, sure, sure, but what the fuck're we gonna do, eh? Guy's a name, a big fucking name. You can't just whack someone like Jimmy Hoffa and expect to walk away with nothin' more than dust on your shoes."

"Anyone can get whacked," Joey Giacalone said. "Kennedy said that . . . that anyone could whack the fucking president if he was determined enough."

"Sure, anyone can get whacked," Don Calligaris said, "but there's whacking someone and whacking someone, and they ain't necessarily the same fucking thing, are they?"

Another man further down the table, Stefano Cagnotto if I remember rightly, said, "So what's the fucking difference . . . You do it right, who gives a fuck who it is? It's not who it is but how it's done that matters."

Tony Pro nodded his head. "He's right, Fabio. It's not who it is but who does it and how it's done that matters . . . hey, Ernesto, whaddya reckon?"

I shook my head. "I don't know who you're talkin' about," I said. I had heard the name Jimmy Hoffa before, but I was ignorant of his significance in this game.

Tony Pro laughed. "Hey, Fabio, where d'you get this kid? You go collect him from the farm?"

Calligaris laughed. He turned to me. "You heard of the Teamsters?"

I shook my head.

"Labor organization sorta thing . . . unions and truckers and construction crews an' all that sorta stuff. Hell, I heard the Teamsters even got a union for the hookers and the strippers."

"No shit?" Tony Pro said. "Hell, ain't we movin' with the times."

"Anyways," Calligaris went on. "Teamsters, International Brotherhood of Teamsters, they're a big fucking organization, handle all the unions and the pension funds and all manner of shit." He turned to his left. "Hey, Matteo, you deal with this thing enough, what's the word on the Teamsters?"

Matteo Rossi cleared his throat. "Organizes the unorganized, makes workers' voices heard in the corridors of power, negotiates contracts that make the American dream a reality for millions, protects workers' health and safety, and fights to keep jobs in North America."

There was a ripple of applause amongst the crowd.

"Seems to me," Tony Pro said, "that someone should look out for Jimmy fuckin' Hoffa's health and fuckin' safety."

The crew laughed. They talked some more, and then there was more food coming and the music got louder, and a girl with breasts the size of basketballs came out and showed the family how she could make the tassels on her nipples spin in two different directions at the same time.

We ate, we drank, and the name of Jimmy Hoffa was not mentioned again that night. Had I been aware of what would happen I would have asked questions, but I was new, it was not my place, and I didn't wish to alienate myself from these people before I even got to know them.

It was three days later that I saw her.

Her name was Angelina Maria Tiacoli.

I saw her in a fruit market on Mott Street, a block over from Mulberry. She had on a summer print dress, over it a camel-colored overcoat and in her hand she carried a brown paper grocery bag loaded with oranges and lemons.

Her hair was rich and dark, her complexion olive and smooth, and her eyes, hell, her eyes were the color of warm creamy coffee. I held my breath when she looked at me and I looked away quickly. Ten Cent was with me and he told her "Hi Angel," and the girl smiled and blushed a little and mouthed "Hi" back.

I watched her go, watched her intently, and Ten Cent nudged me and told me to put my eyes back in my head.

"Who is she?" I asked.

"Angel," he said. "Angelina Tiacoli. Sweet girl, sad story."

I looked at Ten Cent. He shook his head. "Don't be getting any fucked-up ideas, ya Cuban fruitcake. She's strictly out of bounds."

"Out of bounds?"

Ten Cent shook his head. "Jesus, you ain't fuckin' listenin' to me . . . I say she's no go then she's no go, okay?"

"Okay," I said, "but just tell me who she is."

"You remember the other night at the Blue Flame?"

I nodded.

"Guy down at the end, guy called Giovanni Alessandro?"

I didn't remember, but then there had been so many people, so many names.

"His father is Don Alessandro. Big boss. No fucking about. Don Alessandro has a brother . . . well, he *had* a brother called Louis. Louis was a mad fuck, a real mad fuck at the best of times, little left of center if you know what I mean. Anyways, he was married to some girl, a good Italian girl, and he went out on her, you know?"

"Went out?" I asked.

"Christ, kid, you really is from the farm, ain'tcha? He went out . . . you know, he went and fucked some other broad. You know what that means?"

"Yes, I know what that means."

"Lord God, the kid's a fucking genius! Anyways, Don Alessandro's brother goes and fucks some other broad and this broad has a kid . . . and the kid is Angelina. Everyone knows she ain't exactly blood, but hell she's a good kid and she's sure as hell pretty, so Don Alessandro keeps her here around the family."

"And her mother?"

"That's the sad part. Her mother was some hooker or stripper from someplace, crazy junkie bitch, and she and Don Alessandro's brother got to fighting one night when Angelina was about eight or nine years old, and they ended up shooting each other. Don Alessandro had already told his brother not to see her any more, that he would make sure everything was taken care of for the kid if he just promised to stop fucking the hooker, but Louis Alessandro was a crazy bastard, and he went on seeing this junkie bitch for years, and then all hell broke loose and this pair of fruitcakes ended up whacking each other, and Angelina ends up losing her father and her birth mother, and she ain't got nothin' left but her dad's wife who ain't her real mother, you follow me?"

"Yes," I said.

"Anyway, her father's wife, the woman who shoulda been her mother but wasn't, she don't want anything to do with Angelina, and so she tells Don Alessandro that he better take care of the girl seein' as how the girl is his niece, and she's gonna go someplace upstate and start her life over again away from her dead husband's crazy good-for-nothin' family. So Don Alessandro gave her some money, and then he made sure Angelina was looked after until she was all growed up, and then he bought her a place. That's where she lives now, all by herself."

"And how come she's out of bounds?" I asked.

"Because it just ain't done, you know? The girl's mother wasn't Italian, she wasn't part of the family . . . the poor kid's mother was some half-crazy fucked-up junkie bitch from no place special who put her pussy where it shouldn't have been. Now get the fucking oranges would ya for Christ's sake . . . what the fuck is this with the third fuckin' degree anyway?"

I saw her again a week later. Same store. Was down there by myself collecting groceries for Ten Cent. I made a point of saying "Hi" to her, and though she said nothing in response she did look at me for a heartbeat, and in that heartbeat there was the ghost of a smile, and in that smile I saw the promise of everything else that might lie behind it.

The day after I saw her in the street. She was leaving a hairstyling salon on Hester. She wore the same summer print dress and camel-colored overcoat. She carried her purse tight in both her hands as if afraid someone would snatch it from her. I approached her, and ten or twelve feet away I sensed that she was aware of my presence. I slowed down and stopped on the sidewalk. She slowed down also. She glanced to her right as if wondering whether to cross the street to avoid me, but she hesitated, hesitated long enough for me to raise my hand and smile at her.

She tried to smile back, but it was as if the muscles of her face were denying her the right. Her hands did not move; they clutched the purse tightly, as if the purse was the only thing she could be sure of in that moment.

"Miss Tiacoli," I said quietly, because I knew her name from Ten

Cent, and would not have forgotten that name even if forgetting had been a life-and-death matter.

She tried to smile again but could not. She opened her mouth as if she planned to say something, but not a word came forth. She looked to her right again, and then once back at me, and then she stepped suddenly from the sidewalk to the street and hurried across Hester.

I watched her go. I followed her a good fifteen yards on the other side of the road.

She stopped suddenly. She turned toward me. Cars went by unnoticed between us. She let go of the purse with her right hand and raised it, palm facing me as if to stop me coming any further, and then as quickly as she had stopped she started walking again, faster this time. I let her go. I wanted to follow her but I let her go. At the corner of Hester and Elizabeth she glanced back once, just for a split second, and then she turned and was gone.

I walked back to the house empty-handed. Ten Cent called me a "dumb fuckin' Cuban," and sent me out once again to get cigarettes.

In April of 1974 we moved house. Apparently where we were had been marked by the Feds and it was no longer safe. Don Calligaris stayed in his tall narrow house on Mulberry but me and Ten Cent went over Canal Street to Baxter on the edge of Chinatown. The house was bigger, I had three rooms to myself, my own bathroom, and a small kitchenette where I could cook the food I wanted when we weren't eating together. I bought a record player and started listening to Louis Prima and Al Martino, and when Ten Cent was out of the house I would take a suit on a hanger from my wardrobe, hold it close like a partner, and pretend I was dancing with Angelina Maria Tiacoli. I had not seen her since that day on Hester when she came out of the salon, and most nights I thought of her, of how it would be to lie beside her in the cool half light of morning, the warmth of my body against hers, the words we would share, of how important everything would become if she were with me. I felt like a child with a schoolyard crush, and there was a passion and promise that lay within that feeling that were new to me.

In June me and Ten Cent had to go uptown to Tompkins Square Park and meet with a man called John Delancey. Delancey was a Clerk of the Court on the Fifth Circuit. He told us that there was a pending investigation coming to a head. The target was Don Fabio Calligaris and Tony Provenzano.

"Tony Pro had someone killed," John Delancey told us. "I don't know why, I don't know what it was all about, but the guy was a cop's brother.

Cop's name was Albert Young, a sergeant at the 11th Precinct. They cut his brother's balls off and put them in his mouth for God's sake, and the cop has been shouting long enough for someone to take notice."

Ten Cent was nodding. He looked intent. "So how come this falls on Calligaris?" he asked.

"Because the Feds have been after Calligaris for years but they never got anything on him. Calligaris is hand-in-glove with Tony Ducks, and Tony Ducks is boss of the Luchese family, and if anything happens to Calligaris then the Feds reckon it will bring down the Lucheses. They wanna make it seem like the Lucheses welched on Tony Pro and start another faction war."

Ten Cent laughed. "Shit, these people work for the government and they must be the dumbest motherfuckers ever to walk the face of the earth."

"Maybe so," Delancey said, "but they got wires and circumstantial evidence, fabricated or otherwise, that puts Calligaris in a room with Tony Pro saying as how they're gonna whack the cop's brother."

"That's bullshit," Ten Cent said. He looked like he was going to get angry.

Delancey shrugged. "Just tellin' ya how it is, Ten Cent. You gotta get Calligaris to sort out the cop, make him shut his mouth, and then you gotta plug the leak that's inside your family."

"You gotta name?"

Delancey shook his head. "No, I don't gotta name, Ten Cent, and if I did you'd have it, but all I know is that someone inside your camp, someone who comes close to Calligaris, has given the Feds what they need and they're gonna use him as a witness."

Later, after a fat brown envelope was passed discreetly from Ten Cent to Delancey, we walked back to the car.

"Not a word of this to anyone," Ten Cent warned me.

"A word of what?" I asked.

Ten Cent winked and smiled. "That's my man."

Three nights later on a dark corner—East 12th near Stuyvesant Park—I picked up on Sergeant Albert Young of the 11th Precinct leaving a wine store and crossing the road to his car.

Four minutes later Sergeant Albert Young of the 11th Precinct—twice decorated for valor, three times commended by the Office of the Mayor for bravery above and beyond the call of duty, seven times recipient of a 118 citation for excessive force—was slumped in the driver's seat with a .22 caliber hole back of his left ear. He wouldn't shout about his brother any more. More likely than not he'd get to speak with him real soon in cop heaven.

Four days subsequent Don Calligaris came to our house and spoke with me and Ten Cent.

"You guys gotta plug the leak," he said matter-of-factly. "We watched what happened after the cop got clipped, and we know who spent too much time away from home. We had him followed and he met some suits in Cooper Square up near the Village yesterday morning."

Ten Cent leaned forward.

"This name goes out of this room and there's gonna be hell to pay. You gotta do it quick and quiet. Send Ernesto. He did good with the cop, very good indeed, and we need the same kind of thing here. We need it to look like he was into something bad so they don't parade him round like some sort of martyr, okay?"

"Who?" Ten Cent said.

Calligaris shook his head and sighed. "Cagnotto . . . Stefano Cagnotto, the dumbass sorry excuse for a piece of motherfuckin' shit."

"Aah fuck, I liked him," Ten Cent said.

"Well, you ain't gonna get to like him any more, Ten Cent. Asshole got himself picked up on a speeding ticket, they searched his car, found a bag of coke and a .38. He was looking at a year, two tops if he screwed up the trial, and he's talking about turning States and walking if he gives up me and Tony Pro for the cop's brother."

Ten Cent turned and looked at me. "You remember him from the Blue Flame?"

"No," I said, "but you can show me who he is . . . and he sure as hell is gonna remember me, right?"

Calligaris smiled. "You're a good one, Ernesto, and it sure as shit is a shame you ain't from back home otherwise you'd be getting yourself made before fuckin' Christmas."

Don Calligaris left then. Me and Ten Cent sat for a while in silence, and then he turned to me and said, "Sooner the better, kid. Let's go check out where the motherfucker is and see how we're gonna do this, okay?"

I nodded. I stood up. I asked if I had time to clean my shoes before we left.

That night, middle of a hot June in New York, I sat in the back room of Stefano Cagnotto's overnight apartment in Cleveland Place. A block away was the Police Headquarters building. I appreciated the sense of irony. I had been waiting for the better part of two hours before I heard the sound of feet on the risers below. The tension felt good in my gut. I wanted to take a piss but it was too late to move.

The apartment was dark but for a thin film of light that seeped through the curtains to my right. In my hand I felt the weight of a silenced .38. I was dressed in a good five-hundred-dollar suit. I had on a white shirt and a knitted silk tie. Had you seen me at the Blue Flame with the Luchese crew you wouldn't have thought twice. I was part of their family, Cuban blood regardless, I was part of the Lucheses, I was someone, and that someone felt good.

Stefano Cagnotto wasn't drunk, but he carried a skinful, and when he came through the apartment door he fumbled and dropped his keys. He swore twice and searched around in the darkness to retrieve them. I heard the jangle of metal as he picked them up. He closed and dead-bolted the door. That was instinct. In this business you always dead-bolted even if you'd only come back 'cause you'd forgotten your pocketbook.

Once inside he flicked on the light. I heard him sit down. Heard his shoes scuttle along the floor as he kicked them off. He started singing to himself. "Fly me to the moon, and let me play among the stars . . ."

Anytime now, I thought. *Anytime now, motherfucker, your wish is gonna come true.*

I worked my feet around in circles until I heard the ankle bones pop. I eased myself forward in the chair and took the weight of my body in my knees and my feet. I rose carefully, soundlessly, and I took a step toward the front room. By the time I reached the doorway Cagnotto had walked out back to the kitchen. I heard the rush of the faucet.

I held my breath and waited for him to come back.

In his hand he held a glass. He saw me. He dropped the glass.

"What the fu—"

I raised my hand.

"Ernesto," he said. "Jesus fucking Christ, Ernesto, you gave me the scare of my fucking life! What the living fuck are you doing here?"

I brought my right hand out from my side.

Cagnotto's eye fixed on the gun.

"Aah Jesus Christ, Ernesto, what the fuck is this shit?" He looked down at the ground. "Look what the fuck you made me do," he said, indicating the shattered glass at his feet. He stepped over the broken shards carefully and took a couple of steps into the room.

"Put the fucking gun away Ernesto. You're giving me the fucking creeps. What the fuck're you doing here? What d'ya want this time of night?"

"Sit down," I said quietly. My voice sounded gentle, almost sympathetic.

"Sit down? I don't wanna sit the fuck down."

"Sit down," I said again, and then I raised the gun and aimed it squarely at his gut.

"You must be fucking kidding," he said. "Who the fuck put you up to this? Is this that fat fuck Ten Cent? Jesus, what the fuck does he think this is . . . April fucking Fools' Day?"

I took a step forward and raised the gun so it leveled with Cagnotto's eyes. "Sit down," I ordered.

"You don't come down here and tell me what the fuck to do, you guinea fuck . . . Who in fuck's name d'you think you are?"

Cagnotto's fists were clenched tight. He took another step forward and I went for him without a moment's hesitation.

Thirty seconds later, no more, Stefano Cagnotto was seated on the edge of a two-thousand-dollar Italian leather sofa nursing a wide cut on the side of his head. He was still stunned, so whatever the hell came out of his mouth didn't make a great deal of sense. He was a little incoherent, but he didn't have any difficulty understanding what was going to happen when I placed a bag of coke on the glass table ahead of him and told him to get busy.

He knew he was going to go out one way or the other. He didn't even protest, didn't even try to defend his actions or himself. Came down to it he had some degree of honor, and there was something I could respect in that regardless of the situation.

Four lines and he was having a hard time concentrating on what he was doing. I set my gun aside and helped him a little, holding his head back while he pushed cocaine into his own nostrils. I opened his mouth and threw some in there myself, and when he started gagging I put my forearm against his chest and pushed him back against the sofa. He started puking then, and every time he retched I pushed his head down so he didn't puke over me. I never did coke, never would, and I didn't know how much these assholes would stick up their noses at a time. I had brought a bag with me that Ten Cent had gotten from somewhere, maybe a cupful all told, and by the time we were done more than half of it was down Cagnotto's throat or up his nose.

I didn't need to shoot the motherfucker. Had never intended to. He died after about ten minutes.

The Feds case never resurfaced. June closed up, as did July and August, and I never heard another word. Don Calligaris just told me *Good job kid*, and that was the end of that.

September I followed Angelina Maria Tiacoli three blocks before she realized I was behind her.

She looked mad. She turned on her heels and walked back toward me.

"What are you doing?" she snapped accusingly, but there was something heated and passionate in her voice that sounded a great deal more purposeful than just anger.

"Following you," I told her.

"I know you're following me," she said. She took a step backward and pulled her coat tight around her. This one was black, like a heavy woollen fabric, and on the edges it had a silk trim. "But what are you following me for?"

"I wanted to speak with you," I said. I felt brave and bold, like the schoolyard boss.

"About what?"

"About whether I could take you to go see a movie or maybe have something to eat, or maybe just a cup of coffee in a diner or something."

Angelina Maria Tiacoli looked dumbstruck. "You can't ask me that," she said. "You understand that you can't follow me down the street and ask me that."

I frowned. "How come?"

"Do you know who I am?" she asked.

"Angelina Maria Tiacoli," I replied.

"Yes, that's my name, but d'you know who my father was?"

I nodded. "Sure I do. Ten Cent told me."

"Ten Cent?"

"He's a guy, just a guy I know."

"And he told you all about me?"

"No, not all about you. I'm sure he doesn't know a great deal about you at all. He told me your name, who your father was, and the rest I figured out for myself."

"The rest? The rest of what?"

"Aah, you know, like how pretty you are, and how you look like the sort of person it would be great to know, and how good you and me would look if we dressed up smart and went somewhere nice, like a restaurant or a show or something."

"And you figured that all out by yourself, did you?"

I nodded. "Sure I did."

"Well," she said, "I don't know who you are, but if you have a friend called Ten Cent then I can only imagine what kind of people you might mix with, and if you mix with them then any one of them can very quickly tell you that I am not the sort of person that men in the family mix with, and I sure am not the kind of girl you take to a restaurant or out to a show."

I shook my head. "Why, what's wrong with you . . . you sick or something? You got like a terminal illness?"

Angelina Tiacoli looked like someone had slapped her face. "You are such a smart guy," she said, and she took a step toward me. "You talk to your stupid friends with their stupid names, and they tell you who I am, that I'm nothing but some hooker's daughter, and maybe if you follow me down the street I might take you home and fuck you or something. Is that how it happened? Is that the kind of conversation you had back there with your family?"

I was stunned. I didn't know what to say. I fought with the words in my head but I lost. I opened my mouth and nothing but silence came out.

"Go back to wherever the hell you came from and tell your friends that if your goddamned family hadn't cursed me to this life then I would have long since gone. You tell them that from me, and if you come down here again, or if you stop me in the street or follow me, then sure as hell I'll get someone to clip you, you poor dumb stupid Italian thug."

She glared at me.

I opened my mouth.

"Not another word," she said, and then she turned and hurried away.

"I . . . I'm not . . . I'm not Italian," I stammered, but the sound of my voice was lost in the clatter of her heels on the asphalt, and before I could say another word, before I could raise my head or get my brain in gear sufficiently to take a step after her, she had reached the corner of the street and turned.

Another thirty seconds and I snapped out of it. I went after her at a dead run, but even as I turned the corner I knew she would have disappeared.

I was right. She had vanished. Not a sound.

I stood there for some time with my heart in my mouth, and then I swallowed it with difficulty and started back home.

Christmas came and went. New Year also. I didn't see Angelina save for a fleeting glimpse near the bus station as I drove past with Ten Cent and Don Calligaris. I couldn't be sure it was her, but even seeing someone who *might* have been her was enough to make me realize how much I longed for her. All the time I had been in New York I had not slept with any girl—no hookers, no strippers, no one—and I believed that back of my celibacy was the belief that I was saving myself for Angelina. I wanted to be with her. I wanted to hear that voice, once so filled with venom and anger; I wanted to hear that same voice as she spoke words of love and passion, and spoke them for me.

The spring unfolded. Winter lost its bitter grip on New York, and with the change of seasons came a change of temperament and mood in the Luchese camp. There was discussion once more of the Teamsters, of this man Hoffa whom I had heard mention of so many months before in the Blue Flame.

"Has to go, has to fucking go," Don Calligaris said. "He's a short fat fuck, a nothing, a piece of shit arrogant cocksucker. Just 'cause he was Teamsters' president he thinks he owns the fucking country. They sent him down on this jury tampering and wire fraud bullshit but that asshole Nixon grants him clemency and we got him back like a fucking cancer. Jeez, why can't he just leave the fucking thing alone? We're doing fine with Frank Fitzsimmons, hell, he's a pussycat compared to Hoffa. But no, Hoffa's got to stick his nose in where it ain't fucking wanted, and he's giving everyone ball-ache by the truckload. We gotta do something about this motherfucker . . . gotta make him get the fuck outta here and not come back."

July of 1975 there were meetings, long meetings. I saw people come and go through the house, Don Calligaris's place also—people like Tony Provenzano and Anthony Giacalone. I learned that Tony Pro was the current vice president of the Teamsters, and whenever he spoke of Jimmy Hoffa he spoke like he was talking about something he'd picked up on his shoe from the sidewalk.

"Whenever we want Frank to look the other way we find he ain't even on the same block, and that's just the fucking way we want it," Tony Pro would say. "Nixon told Hoffa to stay out of the unions for ten years, that was part of the deal on this clemency thing. He comes back and we got the Feds breathing down our necks like you wouldn't fucking believe. The guy . . . Jesus, we tell the guy time and time a-fucking-gain to keep his face out of the business, but this guy is so hard of fucking hearing I don't think he got no ears at all."

July twenty-eighth, a Monday, and Don Calligaris called me over with Ten Cent. When I arrived at the Mulberry house the place seemed packed with people, some I knew, some I had never seen before. No names were given, but later Ten Cent told me that the guy sitting next to Joey Giacalone was Charles "Chuckie" O'Brien, a very close friend of Jimmy Hoffa's, someone Hoffa referred to as his "adopted son."

"We're gonna kill this motherfucker," Joey Giacalone said. "Vote's been taken and he's been voted a dead fuckin' loser. We all had enough of this ball-ache he's been dishin' out."

A meeting had been arranged in Michigan, place called the Machus Red Fox Restaurant in Bloomfield Township. Hoffa was going to meet with Tony Provenzano, Tony Giacalone and a Detroit labor leader to discuss Hoffa's intention to run for presidency of the Teamsters again. Hoffa wanted to know if the heavy hitters would back him if he challenged Frank Fitzsimmons.

Tony Pro and Tony Jacks would never arrive. Tony Jacks would go to his usual appointment at the Southfield Athletic Club to work out, and Tony Pro would be over in Hoboken, New Jersey, visiting local Teamsters' offices. He would make sure he shook lots of hands and spoke to lots of people who wouldn't forget him being there. The labor leader would be suitably delayed and would arrive at the Machus Red Fox sometime after three. Joey Giacalone had a maroon-colored Mercury he was going to lend to Chuckie O'Brien. Chuckie would arrive at the restaurant and tell Hoffa the meeting place had been changed. Hoffa would trust Chuckie without question. He would get in the car. He would leave his own Pontiac Grand Ville right there in the Machus Red Fox car lot. He would never get out of the Mercury alive.

There was another element that caught me off-guard.

"You gotta understand that it also comes back to this thing with Feraud and his connection with Vegas and the Luchese family," Tony Pro said. "You wanna keep this going with New Orleans, and believe me there is a great deal more money to come out of there than is coming right now, then you gotta understand that we're doing this not only because we wanna keep Frank Fitzsimmons as president of the Teamsters, but also to keep the south states happy. Who's the guy we got down there?"

"Ducane . . . Congressman Charles Ducane," Tony Jacks said.

"Right, Ducane. He's the lead figure down there right now, he's the one who has the say on the Teamsters' contributions, where the money goes, who gets what. Feraud has him in his pocket, and if we don't keep Ducane happy by doing this then we stand a chance of losing all the southern states' funding as well. These guys have got their fingers in everyone's fucking pies, and if we upset them then there's gonna be some bloodshed and warfare. This is a necessary thing for everyone concerned, and it cannot, it *must not*, go wrong."

"That's why I want your blessing to send Ernesto," Don Calligaris said.

Tony Provenzano looked across at Calligaris and then at me. "Right . . . this is what we gotta talk about. This Ducane has one of his own people, some ex-military guy or something." He turned and looked at Joey Giacalone. "What the fuck was this guy's name?"

"McCahill, something-or-other McCahill."

"Right . . . so Ducane wanted to send this guy down here to do this thing with Hoffa, but we wanna use our own people."

"Definitely," Don Calligaris said. "This is family business and it stays within the family. Like I said, I wanna send Ernesto."

Tony Pro raised his eyebrows. "How so?"

"Ernesto is from New Orleans originally, he did some work for Feraud and Ducane through Don Ceriano back in the early '60s. I wanna send him and then I want word to get back to Feraud that we used one of his own on this thing. This fixes any difficulty these boys might have with us not using this McCahill guy, right?"

Tony Provenzano nodded. "Makes sense to me. Ernesto?"

I nodded. I said nothing.

Tony Pro smiled. "He ever speak?"

Calligaris smiled. He put his hand on my shoulder and squeezed it. "Only when he has to, and only when it's people he likes, right?"

I smiled.

"Shit, I better do something nice for him then," Tony Pro said.

"He ain't the sort of guy I want disliking me."

They laughed. I felt good inside. It was a feeling I was getting used to. I thought also of Feraud and Ducane, people whose names recurred time and again in my business dealings, people who seemed to have become more and more significant as time had passed. Where once I had believed this Charles Ducane a small and nervous man in the employ of Antoine Feraud, it now seemed that he had mastered his own territory. He had become someone, just as I had, but in a necessarily different way.

"So this thing goes down on Wednesday," Tony Jacks said. "From now on it's called Gemini. That's all, just one word. I don't wanna hear no names or dates or places. I just wanna hear one word when you guys refer to this thing, and that word is Gemini."

"What the fuck does that mean?" Tony Pro asked.

"It's a fucking star sign, you dumbass motherfucker. It's a zodiac thing, and there's a picture of a guy with two heads or some fucking thing. It's just a fucking word, okay?"

"So why that?" Tony Pro asked.

"'Cause I said so," Tony Jacks said, "And because Jimmy fucking Hoffa is a two-faced motherfucker who's gonna lose them both come Wednesday."

So I went to Michigan and I met with Jimmy Hoffa on a warm Wednesday afternoon in Bloomfield Township. He was a big guy. Big hands.

Big voice. But he was nervous. I think he knew he was going to die. He got in the Mercury when Chuckie O'Brien turned up at the Machus Red Fox, and though I sat in back he didn't ask me who I was. He was talking too fast, asking why the meet had been changed, if Provenzano and Giacalone were already there, if Chuckie had heard any rumor about whether or not they would back him in his attempt to be Teamsters president again.

He kicked a lot when I put the wire around his neck from in back of the car. He kicked like Don Ceriano, but I felt nothing at all. Chuckie had to hold his arms in his lap, and it took some doing because he wasn't no hundred-and-forty-pound sapling. Jimmy Hoffa had some fight in him, right until the end, and there was one fuck of a lot of blood. It was just a business thing this time, and there was very little to say about it. He had pissed my employers off something serious, and that was all there was to it. President of the Teamsters he might once have been, but the look in his eyes in the rearview, the look I saw as he choked up his last breath, was the very same as all of them. Didn't matter whether they were the Pope or a labor leader or the second coming of Christ, when they saw the light behind their eyes going out they all looked like frightened schoolteachers.

Figured I might look like that one day, but I would jump off that bridge when I got there.

A little more than twenty minutes later I stepped from the car with a bloody piano wire in my coat pocket. Jimmy Hoffa, sixty-two years old, was driven south to a family-owned fat rendering plant and he was blended into soap. I walked back toward the Red Fox. I caught a bus into Bloomfield. From there I took another bus to the train station. I arrived back in Manhattan on Thursday 31 July. Thirteen days later it was my thirty-seventh birthday. Don Fabio Calligaris and Tony Provenzano threw me a party at the Blue Flame, a party I will never forget.

It was Tony Giacalone who asked me, asked me what I wanted for my birthday, told me I could have anything I wanted in the world.

"Your blessing," I told him. "The blessing of the family."

"Blessing for what, Ernesto?"

"To marry a girl, Don Giacalone . . . that's what I want for my birthday."

"Of course, of course . . . and who do you want to marry?"

"Angelina Maria Tiacoli."

They gave me the blessing, reservedly perhaps, but they gave it, and though it would be another four months before I saw her again it was on that day that my life changed irreversibly.

Later many other things would change also. In August Nixon would finally concede defeat and resign, taking with him the spider's web of connections that ran throughout the families right across the United States. On 15 October the following year Carlo Gambino would die of a heart attack while watching a Yankees game on the TV in his Long Island summer home. He would be succeeded, not by Aniello Dellacroce as everyone believed would be the case, but by Paul Castellano, a man who built a replica of the White House on Todd Hill, Staten Island; a man who negotiated a truce with the Irish–New York Mafia and offered their leaders—Nicky Featherstone and Jimmy Coonan—permission to use the Gambino name in their dealings for a 10 percent cut of all their earnings from Hell's Kitchen on the West Side; a man who would ultimately contribute to the relinquishing of power the Italian crime families held in New York. Carmine Persico would depose Thomas DiBella as head of the Colombo family in 1978; Carmine Galante would hold sway in the Bonanno family until 1979 when he was murdered at Joe and Mary's Italian Restaurant in Brooklyn, and he was replaced by Caesar Bonaventre, the youngest ever capo, merely twenty-four years old. By then my time in New York would be coming to a close; by then I would have long since graduated from the clip jobs and shootings where I had earned my reputation, and my apprenticeship would have ended.

I believed I came to New York to find something. What it was I was looking for I did not know then, and even now cannot be sure. What I found was something I could never have anticipated, and that is something I will share a little of with you now.

It was close to Thanksgiving, and though Thanksgiving was not a particularly significant event in the Italian calendar, it was nevertheless a reason to eat more, to drink more, have parties at the Blue Flame and make wisecracks about one another.

I borrowed Ten Cent's car, took it to an autoshop and had them valet it. God almighty only knows what they found inside, but they were family people and wouldn't have cared anyway. I parked the car a block from the house so Ten Cent wouldn't forget he'd lent it to me and drive off someplace, and I walked home. I dressed nice, like for church or something, and I cleaned my shoes and knotted my tie. It was early evening, a Saturday, and by seven I was leaving again with a spring in my step and two thousand bucks in my pocket.

When she opened the door she was dressed in nothing but slippers and a housecoat. Her hair was tied back of her head like she'd been cleaning or something, and when she saw me standing there with a thousand-dollar suit and a thirty-five-dollar bouquet it was all she could do to keep her eyes in her head. I was not a spectacularly handsome man, I mean hell, I couldn't have modeled for magazines or whatever, but I scrubbed up clean and you could have taken me anyplace and not felt ashamed.

"Yes?" she said.

"There's a show at the Metropolitan Opera," I said. I handed her the flowers. She looked at them like I was handing her a bag with a dead rat inside. "Anyway, there's a music show at the Met—"

"You said that already . . . you better hurry now or you're gonna miss the start."

I looked at her. "I worked hard to look this good, and you look good even in your housecoat and your slippers. You get happy just being mean to people, or is it because you're sick in the mind or something?"

She laughed then, and the sound was like something better than anyone might ever hear at the Met.

"No, I'm sick in the mind, and I can't help but be mean to people," she said. "Now go away with your stupid flowers and whatever. Go find some pretty blonde with legs to her neck and take her to the opera house."

"I came to take you."

Angelina Maria Tiacoli looked aghast. "I seem to remember seeing you in the street. That was you, wasn't it?"

"On Hester Street when you came from the hairstyling salon."

Angelina frowned, was momentarily taken aback. "What, you take notes or something?"

I shook my head. "No, I don't take notes . . . I just have a knack for remembering important stuff."

"And where I get my hair done is important?"

"No, not where you get your hair done . . . the fact that it was you was what was important."

"You're serious, aren't you?"

"Serious enough to ask for Don Giacalone's blessing, and for the blessing of the family."

"Blessing for what?"

"To marry you, Angelina Maria Tiacoli . . . to marry you and make you my wife."

"To marry me *and* to make me your wife, is that so?"

"Yes, that's so."

"I see," she said. "And you know who I am?"

"I know enough about you to want to take you out, and I don't know enough about you to find you very interesting indeed."

"So I'm interesting, eh?"

"Yes," I said. "Interesting and beautiful, and when you speak I can hear everything in your voice that makes me think I could love you for the rest of your life."

"Did you practice this before you came over, or did you get a Hollywood screenwriter to make this stuff up?"

I nodded my head. "You got me there. I got a Hollywood writer to put it all down on paper for me, and I told him if it didn't work then I was gonna go over to his house and shoot him in the knee."

She laughed again. I was getting through.

"So you went and dressed up all smart and you bought some flowers and you came over here with no invitation to ask me if I would go to the Metropolitan Opera with you?"

"I did."

"I can't come."

I frowned. "Why?"

"Because I can't go out with you, or anyone like you, so you're gonna have to get over it real quick and find someone else to harass."

Angelina Tiacoli smiled once more, but it wasn't a warm or well-meaning smile, and then she closed the door hard and fast and left me standing on the stoop.

I waited for thirty seconds or so until I heard her footsteps disappear inside, and then I stepped back, laid the bouquet against the door and drove home.

I went back the following afternoon after lunch.

"You're back again?"

"Yes."

"You're not gonna give up, are you?"

I shook my head.

"How was the music show?"

"I didn't go."

"You want me to pay for the tickets, is that it?"

"No, I don't want you to pay for the tickets."

"So what *do* you want?"

"I want to take you out someplace nice, maybe see a movie—"

"Or a show at the Met."

"Right," I said, "a show at the Met, or maybe just have a cup of coffee someplace and talk for a while."

"Just a cup of coffee."

"Sure, if that's what you want."

"No, it's not what I want, but I'm thinking if I go for a cup of coffee with you then you might leave me alone. Is that hoping too much?"

"Yes, that's hoping too much. If you come for a cup of coffee with me then I'm gonna want to come back and go someplace else next time."

Angelina said nothing for a moment, and then she nodded. "Okay," she said. "Come back at four."

She closed the door.

I went back at four. I beat on the door until someone in the adjacent house leaned out of the window and told me to *shut the fuck up, asshole.*

Angelina was either out, or she was hiding inside.

I wasn't mad, not then, not ever; I was just determined.

I left it 'til Tuesday evening, a little after seven and I called at her house again.

She came to the door. She was dressed smart, a skirt, a woollen jacket, a pretty pink blouse that made her complexion warm and inviting.

"I was ready last night and you didn't come," she said.

"I didn't say I would come last night."

"You're right, you didn't, but seeing as how you came the day before and the day before that I figured you were gonna come every day until I gave in."

"If you'd said you were gonna be ready last night I would have come last night. You just shut the door on me and then when I came back on Sunday you weren't here."

"I was here, I just didn't come to the door."

"How come?"

"I wanted to see how persistent you were."

"And?"

"And you're very persistent, though I'm still surprised you didn't come yesterday."

"I'm sorry."

"Apology accepted," she said. "So where you gonna take me?"

"Where d'you wanna go?"

"Over to Sixth Ave on the subway, and find the most expensive restaurant and eat stuff I've never eaten before."

"We can do that."

She paused for a moment as if contemplating something, and then she nodded. "Okay, give me five minutes and I'll be down."

"You're not gonna shut the door and then go hide inside the house?"

She laughed. "No . . . give me five minutes."

I gave her five minutes. She didn't come down. She left me standing there a further two minutes and then I heard her footsteps behind the door.

She opened up and came out. She looked great; she smelled great, something like violets or honeysuckles or something, and when I gave her my arm she took it and I walked her to the car. I opened the door for her and drove her to the subway station. I didn't ask her why she didn't want to drive. She wanted the subway, she got the subway. Had she asked me to *buy* the subway for her I would have found a way.

I took her to Sixth Avenue. We found a restaurant, and whether it was the most expensive one on the Avenue I don't know, didn't care, but I spent two hundred and eleven dollars on dinner and left a fifty-dollar tip.

I didn't drive her back from the subway station to the house when we returned. I wanted to spend as much time with her as I could. I walked with her, it took a good twenty minutes, and when I stood on the stoop and told her I'd had the greatest night of my life she reached out and touched my face.

She did not kiss me, but that was okay. She did say I could call on her again, and I said I would.

I saw her most every day, except for those few days I was out of town on business, for the better part of eight months. In July of 1976 I asked her to marry me.

"You want me to marry you?" she asked.

I nodded. My throat was tight. I found it hard to breathe. The girl did the same thing to me as Ten Cent would do to someone who welched on a payback.

"And why d'you wanna marry me?"

"Because I love you," I said, and I meant it.

"You love me?"

I nodded. "I do."

"And you understand that if I say no then you can't ever come round here again. That's the way it goes in this business . . . you ask a girl to marry you and she says no, then that's the end of the matter. You know that right then it's dead and gone to Hell. You understand that, Ernesto Perez?"

"I understand that."

"So ask me properly."

I frowned. "Whaddya mean, ask you properly? I just did ask you properly. I gotta ring here in my jacket pocket and everything."

Angelina turned her mouth down at the edges and nodded her head approvingly. "You gotta ring?"

"Sure. You didn't think I'd come down here and ask you to marry me if I didn't have a ring?"

"Let me see it."

"Eh?"

"Let me see the ring you brought."

"You're serious?" I asked.

She nodded. "Sure I'm serious."

I shook my head. This wasn't going according to plan; this was getting an awful lot more awkward and complicated than I'd imagined. I reached into my jacket pocket and took out the ring. It was in a small black velvet box.

I handed it to Angelina.

She took it, opened it, removed the ring and held it up to the light. "Real diamonds?" she asked.

I scowled. Now I was beginning to get pissed. "Sure it's real diamonds. You think I'd bring something to get engaged that was some cheap piece of shit—"

"Language, Ernesto."

I nodded. "Sorry."

"And it's legit?"

"Angelina, for Christ's sake—"

"I gotta ask, right? I gotta ask. I've been living around people like you all my life. Don't think there can be more than three or four things given to me in my life that weren't stolen. Getting engaged is important, getting married even more so, and I wouldn't wanna be making any vows to God and the Virgin Mary on something that was stolen from some poor widow down on 9th Street—"

"Angelina, for fuck's sake—"

"Language—"

"Screw the fucking language. Give me the fucking ring back. I'm going home. I'm gonna come back tomorrow when you're a little less crazy."

Angelina held the ring in her hand. She closed her fist around it. "But I thought you came down here to ask me to marry you?"

"I did. I came down here to ask you to marry me, but you're just standing there busting my goddamned balls for no reason."

"So do it properly," she said.

"I just did for Christ's sake!"

"Down on one knee, Ernesto Perez . . . down on one knee and ask me properly with no cursing or taking the Lord's name in vain."

I sighed. I shook my head. I kneeled down on the stoop and looked up at her. I opened my mouth to speak.

"Yes," she said, before I had a chance to say a word.

"Yes what?"

"Yes, Ernesto Perez . . . I will marry you."

"But I haven't even asked you yet!" I said.

"But I *knew* you were gonna ask me and I didn't want to waste any more time."

"Aah Jesus, Angelina—"

"Enough cursing Ernesto, enough cursing."

"Okay, okay . . . enough already."

In November I suggested we get married in January of the following year. She put it off until May as she wanted to be married outside.

Three hundred people came to the party. It went on for two days. We took a honeymoon in California. We went to Disneyland. I did not have to learn to love her. I had loved her from a distance for a very long time. She was everything to me, and she knew it. Apart from the children she was the most important thing in my life. She made me important, that was how I felt, and that was a feeling I never believed possible.

In July of '76 I had heard of Castro, how he had declared himself Head of State, President of the Council of State, also of the Council of Ministers. Word of him came from TV reports regarding the Senate Select Committee in Intelligence under Senator Frank Church and their investigations and inquiries regarding the alleged CIA involvement in the attempted assassination of Castro. It made me think of Cuba, of Havana, of my mother and father and all that had gone before. Of these things I said nothing to Angel, for that was what I called her, and that's what she was.

In a way she was my salvation, and in some way my undoing, and but for the children there would have been nothing to show for any of it. But those things were later, so much later, and now is not the time to talk about such things.

By the time we talked about leaving New York I was forty-three years old. A second-rate B-movie actor had become president of the United States, and Angel Perez was pregnant. She did not want our children to grow up in New York, and with the family's blessing we thought of moving to California, where the sun shone twenty-three hours of the day, three hundred and sixty-three days of the year. I cannot say that we existed together in a halcyon haze of contentment; I do not believe such a thing would be possible for a man with work such as mine, but the images and memories of my parents' relationship were so far removed from what Angel and I had created that I was happy.

I did not believe, not for a heartbeat, that anything would go wrong, but then—in hindsight—I can honestly say that I was not a man who lived my life on the basis of belief.

New York became a closed chapter. We flew out in March of 1982, Angel was six months pregnant, and though it would be another fifteen years before I returned to New York I would never again look at that city with the same eyes.

The world changed, I changed with it, and if there was one thing I had learned it was that you could never go back.

EIGHTEEN

THE STORM HAD not abated. Rain hammered down relentlessly, and when Hartmann was escorted from the FBI Field Office across town to the Royal Sonesta—a convoy of three cars, himself in the central vehicle with Woodroffe, Schaeffer and Sheldon Ross—he imagined himself more the guilty party than the confessor. For that's what he was being, was he not? Confessor to Ernesto Perez, a man who had filled his life with as many nightmares as was perhaps possible for one human being.

"I cannot believe this," Woodroffe had kept repeating, and was even now saying it again as they drove. "Jimmy Hoffa's murder must be one of the most significant unsolved murders of all time—"

"Apart from Kennedy," Ross had interjected, a comment that provoked scowls of disapproval from both Woodroffe and Schaeffer. Hartmann imagined that the party line in and amongst the Bureau was that J. Edgar Hoover and the Warren Commission had been right all along. It was, he could only suppose, one of those topics of conversation that did not occur among these people. They believed what they believed, but what they believed stayed inside their heads and did not venture from their lips.

"Jimmy fucking Hoffa . . . Christ al-fucking-mighty," Woodroffe said. "I remember it. I remember it happening. I remember all the speculation, the newspaper reports, the theories about what had happened to him."

"You must have been in your teens," Schaeffer said.

"Regardless," Woodroffe said. "I remember it well. And when I came into the Bureau and started reading files that related to organized crime that name came up again and again. That was the big question . . . what the hell happened to Jimmy Hoffa? I can't believe that Perez was the one who actually killed him. And that Charles Ducane, the fucking governor of Louisiana, knew about it . . . in effect sanctioned it—"

"And was gonna send Gerard McCahill down to do it," Hartmann said, which seemed to him the most relevant point, and the one everyone seemed to be unwilling to face.

"Enough," Schaeffer said. "We have no evidence of that."

"But we know that pretty much everything Perez has said so far has proven to be true," Woodroffe retorted.

"Supposition," Schaeffer replied. "We do not know that everything he has said is true, and right now we are investigating Ernesto Perez, not Charles Ducane. As far as I am concerned Charles Ducane and his daughter are the victims of a crime, as is Gerard McCahill, and I don't want to hear another word about it."

"There's also the fact of how McCahill's body was found," Hartmann said.

"How so?" Woodroffe asked.

"The drawing on his back . . . the constellation of Gemini. That was the word they used when they referred to the hit on Hoffa . . . they referred to it as Gemini. I figure that must have been done to remind Ducane that his involvement had not been forgotten."

"Again supposition," Schaeffer said. "We don't know anything for a fact. All we have to go on is the word of one man, and he's as crazy as they come."

"Well shit," Hartmann said. "There goes one of life's great mysteries," and that seemed to kill the subject stone-dead. There was silence for a moment. Hartmann looked out of the window. In the back of his mind he could see the image of the constellation glowing on McCahill's back, and then he thought of Ernesto Perez standing over the dead body of Stefano Cagnotto. For a heartbeat he was back in the motel with Luca Visceglia, a motel out near Calvary Cemetery the night before an affidavit was due to be sworn. He knew how someone looked when they'd been forcibly overdosed.

"Now we gotta find the wife," Schaeffer said. He looked over at Hartmann in the back seat. "See if you can't get him to tell you something more about the wife. She's gotta be around somewhere."

"And the kid . . . boy, girl, whatever, they've gotta be in their early twenties now," Woodroffe said.

"I've got FBI Trace alerted," Schaeffer added. "They'll find her, we just don't have a realistic estimate on how long it will take. They'll go back as far as they need to. Fact of the matter is that there's no one in this country who can't be traced eventually."

"Except for Perez himself," Woodroffe said, and Schaeffer cut him a look that silenced him immediately.

"I don't think we can rely on Perez's wife being any part of this," Hartmann said.

"And what brings you to that conclusion?" Schaeffer asked.

"Perez is too smart to involve his own family. That would be too close to home."

"Regardless, it's something," Schaeffer said, "and in this situation we follow everything, no matter how unrelated it might seem right now."

"And that includes Charles Ducane?" Hartmann asked, and though it was a question it was as good as rhetoric because he knew how Schaeffer would respond.

Schaeffer just turned and looked at him. The expression on the man's face was cold and aloof, but beneath that there was something tired and beaten. "You wanna get into this again?" he asked Hartmann.

"Do I *want* to?" Hartmann asked. "No, I sure as hell don't. I don't *want* to get into any of it. In fact I'd much prefer to just step away from the whole thing and go back to New York right now."

"We find the girl," Schaeffer said.

"And then?"

Schaeffer raised his eyebrows.

"And then someone is talking to Ducane?" Hartmann asked.

Schaeffer closed his eyes and sighed. "Whether or not someone talks to Ducane is entirely up to someone else," he replied.

"And none of us here are gonna take any responsibility for that at all, right? You've heard what I've heard—"

Schaeffer raised his hand. "Enough already," he said. "I'm doing one thing at a time, I'm following the brief I've been given . . . and right now the only thing that bears any relevance to anything is Catherine Ducane."

"So we're gonna let it all slide once we find the girl?"

Woodroffe leaned forward. "Ray . . . just drop it for now, okay? We go do this meeting with Perez, we do everything we have to do until we've got the girl back, and then—"

Hartmann interjected. "It's okay. I'm not saying anything else. It isn't my job to decide who runs this country anyway."

Schaeffer didn't respond; figured it was better that he didn't. This was a circular conversation, and right in the middle of it was a great number of things that none of them really wanted to know.

The journey was brief, made longer simply by the rainfall; the streets were flooding against the storm drains, and here and there Hartmann saw people hurrying through the downpour in some vain effort to avoid the worst of it. It was hopeless, the heavens had opened wide, and everything that was available was being focused on New Orleans. Perhaps God, in His infinite wisdom, was attempting to clean the place up. It wouldn't work: too much blood had been spilled on this land for it to be anything other than a small reflection of Hell.

The convoy pulled up outside the Royal Sonesta. Hartmann was out and running toward the front entrance, and there he was met by three federal agents. Inside there were four more, all of them armed, all of them clones of one another, and Hartmann realized how much attention and money was being devoted to this operation.

Now he was being placed in a supremely untenable position. He knew, with more certainty than most other things in his life, that Perez was not here to barter for the life of the girl. That was the very least of his interests. Perez was not here to avoid jail or the death sentence or anything else the justice community could throw at him. Perez was here to tell a story and to make a point. What that point was, well that was anybody's guess. Hartmann had reconciled himself to giving it the best he had, and if the best wasn't good enough then they could have someone else come in and do the job.

One of the agents took his overcoat and handed him a towel.

"Fucked-up weather," Hartmann said and started to dry his hair and the back of his neck.

The agent just looked back at him implacably and said nothing.

Where the fuck do they get these people? Hartmann wondered. *Maybe they have a factory out near Quantico where they just breed them from the same stem cells.*

Hartmann returned the towel and straightened his hair.

Woodroffe appeared beside him, Schaeffer close behind.

"You gonna give me a wire?" Hartmann asked.

"The entire fucking hotel is wired," Schaeffer said. "There are five floors to this place and Perez is up on top. We have to use the stairs because the elevators have been immobilized. The first four floors are locked at all exits and entries. All the windows are sealed from within, and up on the fifth there are something in the region of twenty agents spread out in the corridors and the rooms on either side of Perez. Inside Perez's room there are three agents who keep watch from the main room. Perez uses the bedroom, the bathroom adjacent to it, and sometimes he comes into the front to watch TV and play cards with our people. Food is brought to him from the kitchens in the basement, and it goes up the stairs just like everything else."

"You have created a fortress for him," Hartmann said.

"Well, he sure as hell ain't gonna get out . . . and no one is gonna come in to get him."

Hartmann frowned. "And who might want to come in?"

Woodroffe glanced at Schaeffer. Schaeffer shook his head. "I have no idea, Mr. Hartmann, but this guy has been full of enough surprises so far that we just ain't taking any risks."

"So it's up the stairs we go," Hartmann said, and made his way across the foyer to the base of the well.

"Mr. Hartmann?" Schaeffer called after him.

Hartmann slowed and turned.

"I understand your reservations about this, and I can't say that I believe this will accomplish anything, but we got a girl out there, a teenage girl who could be still alive, and until we know for sure what the hell happened to her we still have to do everything we can."

Hartmann nodded. "I know," he said quietly. "I know that as well as anyone here, and I will do everything I can. The truth is that I feel this won't accomplish anything for us . . . won't accomplish anything for her."

"Just do your best, eh?" Schaeffer said.

"Sure," Hartmann said, and with that he turned and started up the stairs, two of the Feds from the foyer with him, and it wasn't until he reached the fifth floor, wasn't until he stood three feet from Perez's door, that he understood the significance of what he was about to do. What he said now could serve to turn Perez against them, to make him unwilling to speak, and if he did not speak he would never finish telling them of his life, and Hartmann believed that that had been the entire purpose of kidnapping the girl in the first place.

From wanting to be somebody to believing he was somebody to a sense of loss that he was nobody once again.

Was this now nothing more than the last-ditch attempt of an old man, albeit crazy, to make something of himself before the lights went down for the last time?

Hartmann glanced at the expressionless agent beside him. "Let's do it," he said quietly, and the agent leaned forward and knocked on the door.

From the bedroom came the lilting sound of a piano.

Hartmann frowned.

Inside the first room were three more of Schaeffer's crew, all of them seasoned veterans by the look of them. The one nearest the door greeted Hartmann, shook his hand, introduced himself as Jack Dauncey.

Dauncey seemed genuinely pleased to see someone from the outside world, perhaps someone who was not part of the FBI.

"He's inside," Dauncey said. "We told him you were coming over . . . you know what he asked us?"

Hartmann shook his head.

"If you'd be staying for supper."

Hartmann smiled. "A character, huh?"

"A character? He's one in a million, Mr. Hartmann." Dauncey smiled and crossed the room. He knocked on the door and within a moment the music was lowered in volume.

"Come!" Perez commanded, and Dauncey opened the door.

The room had been assembled as both a sitting area and bedroom. The bed was pushed against the left-hand wall, and over on the right was a table, two chairs, a sofa and a music system. It was from this that the lilting piano was coming.

"Shostakovich," Perez said as he rose from his chair and walked toward Hartmann. "You know Shostakovich?"

Hartmann shook his head. "Not personally, no."

Perez smiled. "You people defend ignorance with humor. Shostakovich was a Russian composer. He died a long time ago. This piece is entitled 'Assault On Beautiful Gorky,' and it was written in commemoration of the storming of the Winter Palace. It is beautiful, no? Beautiful, and very sad."

Hartmann nodded. He walked across to the table and sat down at one of the chairs.

Perez followed him, sat facing him, and but for the music they could have been seated once more in the FBI Field Office.

"Perhaps we should conduct our interviews here from now on," Perez said. "It would save all the trouble of ferrying me back and forth surrounded by all these federal people, none of whom, I can assure you, have the slightest shred of humor, and it would be so much more comfortable, no?"

Hartmann nodded. "It would. I'll suggest it to Schaeffer and Woodroffe."

Perez smiled and reached for his cigarettes. He offered one to Hartmann. Hartmann took it, retrieved his lighter from his jacket pocket and lit them both.

"How are they bearing up?" Perez asked.

"Who?"

"Mr. Schaeffer and Mr. Woodroffe."

Hartmann frowned. "Bearing up?"

"Sure. They must be feeling the stress of the situation, yes? They have found themselves in perhaps the most uncomfortable set of circumstances of their collective careers. They must be feeling a tremendous amount of pressure, with the girl gone and all manner of high and mighty people breathing down their necks demanding results, results, results. I can only begin to imagine how they must feel."

"Stressed," Hartmann said, "like the Brooklyn Bridge."

Perez laughed. "You are good, Mr. Hartmann. I knew very little of you before we met, very little indeed, but since we have been spending this time together I have grown to like you."

"I'm flattered."

"And so you should be . . . there are very few people I can say that I honestly like in this world. I have seen too many crazy things in my time, things people have done for no apparent reason at all, to make me believe that human beings are all as equally lost as one another."

"Why me?" Hartmann asked.

Perez leaned back and looked at Hartmann. "This question intrigues you. I have seen it playing amongst your thoughts from the first day. You want to know why it was that I asked you to come down here and listen to me when I could have asked any number of people and any one of them would have come?"

Hartmann nodded. "Yes," he said. "Why did you choose me?"

"Three reasons," Perez stated matter-of-factly. "First and foremost, because you are from New Orleans. You are a Louisianan, just like me. I am of Cuban descent, granted, but irrespective of that I was born here in New Orleans. New Orleans, like it or not, has always been my original home. And there is something about this place that only those who were born here, only those who have spent their formative years here, can truly understand. It has a voice and a color and an atmosphere all its own. It is like no other place on earth. There is such a blend of people here, faiths and beliefs, languages and ethnic strains, that makes it truly unique. In a way it possesses no singular identifying characteristic, and thus it cannot be easily identified. It is a paradox, a puzzle, and people who visit can never really grasp what makes it so different. It is a place you either love or hate, and once you have decided your feelings for it there is nothing that can change them."

"And you?" Hartmann asked. "Do you love it or hate it?"

Perez laughed. "I am an anachronism. I am the exception that proves the rule. I have no feeling for it at all. Now, having seen all I have seen, there is almost nothing to love or to hate in this world."

"And the second reason?"

"Family," Perez said, and he spoke quietly, but there was such intention and emphasis behind this single word that it hit Hartmann forcibly.

"Family?" he asked.

Perez nodded. He reached forward and flicked his cigarette ash in the tray.

Hartmann shook his head. "I don't understand."

"You do," Perez said, "perhaps better than anyone who's involved in this. You understand the strength and power of family."

"How so?"

"Come on, Mr. Hartmann, you cannot deny what you know is true. What about your mother and father? What about Danny?"

Hartmann's eyes opened wide. "Danny?" he asked. "How the fuck d'you know about Danny?"

"The same way I know about Carol and Jessica."

Hartmann was speechless. He looked at Perez with an expression of abject incredulity.

"Come, come, Mr. Hartmann, don't act so surprised. I am not a stupid man. You do not live the life I have lived and survive by being stupid. I may have done some things that you find difficult to comprehend, but that does not make me crazy or ignorant or unprepared. I am a planner, a thinker. I may have worked with my hands, but the work I have done has been for the greater part cerebral in its execution."

"A suitable turn of phrase," Hartmann said.

"Execution? No pun intended," Perez said. "There are some people who are born for particular things, Mr. Hartmann, things such as politics and art, even Shostakovich who managed to combine the two and have something of worth to say, and then there are some who fall into a path which is somehow not of their own choosing."

"And where would you place yourself?"

"The latter, of course," Perez replied. He ground his cigarette out and lit another. "Events conspired perhaps, I am not sure. Perhaps when I die it will all become plain and evident and I will understand everything. Possibly events conspire to make us who we are, but then again I sometimes think that subconsciously we possess the power to influence events and circumstances around us, and in this way we actually determine, for the greater part, exactly what happens to us."

"I can't say I have that philosophic a viewpoint about it," Hartmann said.

"Well, consider it from this perspective." Perez leaned back in his chair. He seemed as relaxed as he could be. "Your own situation is a perfect example. Your father's death, the death of your younger brother, the work you have done for most of your adult life. Are these things the factors that contributed to your difficulty, or was the difficulty there all along merely waiting for the necessary force majeure to cause it to surface?"

"My difficulty?"

"The drinking," Perez stated.

"The drinking?" Hartmann asked, once again unsettled by the degree to which Perez knew the details of his life.

"The drinking, yes. The difficulty that you have struggled with for so many years, and the thing that finally prompted the departure of your wife and daughter."

Hartmann felt disturbed and tense. "What do you know about them?"

Perez shook his head and smiled. "Do not worry yourself, Mr. Hartmann. Your wife and daughter have absolutely nothing to do with this matter. I understand the sense of responsibility you feel toward them—"

"Like your own wife and child, Mr. Perez?" Hartmann interjected, realizing that here was an appropriate opportunity to pursue this line of inquiry.

"My wife and child?" Perez asked. "We were not talking about my wife and child, Mr. Hartmann, we were talking about yours."

Hartmann nodded. "I know, but considering we are discussing this area I find the fact that you have a wife and child tremendously fascinating."

Perez frowned.

"Your line of work, the things that you did . . . how could you go home and look your wife in the face knowing that only hours before you had murdered someone?"

"I imagine much the same way you managed it," Perez said.

"Me? What do you mean? I never murdered anyone."

"But you lied and you deceived her, and you pretended to be something you were not. You made promises and then you broke them, I am sure. It is the same with anyone who carries a shadow, Mr. Hartmann, whether it be alcoholism or gambling or infidelity. Whatever the shadow that might haunt them, they are still effectively leading a double life."

"But you killed people. You went out with the intention to murder and you did so. I think that is very different from having a drinking problem."

Perez shrugged. "Depends on your personal philosophy . . . whether you consider that events conspire to make you who you are, or if you are someone who believes that Man possesses the ability to determine events by his own power of mind."

"We are getting off the subject," Hartmann said, at once intrigued and very uncomfortable.

"Indeed we are," Perez said, "though I must admit that I believe family to be as important a subject of discussion as you do."

"Okay then," Hartmann said. "What about the girl?"

Perez looked up. "What *about* the girl?"

"She is part of someone's family. She has a mother and a father."

"And a cat and a dog. And she can play the piano, and she likes talking to her girlfriends about boys and clothes and cosmetics."

"Right . . . what about her? What about *her* family?"

"What about them?"

"You profess to believe in the necessity and importance of family. Have you considered how they must feel?"

Perez smiled once more and leaned forward. He rested his hands on the table and steepled his fingers together. "Mr. Hartmann, I have considered everything."

"So?"

Perez raised his eyebrows.

"So is how they feel important?"

"Of vital importance, yes," Perez replied.

"So is what you are doing perhaps not the most disturbing and upsetting thing that you could do?"

Perez laughed, but there was seemingly nothing malicious in his tone. "That, Mr. Hartmann, is precisely the point of the exercise."

"To upset Charles Ducane and his ex-wife as much as possible?"

Perez waved his hand. "The wife, Eve I believe her name is, how she feels is of no significance to me. But Charles Ducane . . . he is a different story altogether."

"How so?"

"Because he is as guilty as I, and yet here he is, governor of Louisiana, sitting up there in his mansion with the world protecting him, and I am here, ensconced within a small fortress, protected from the world by the might of the FBI, and having to justify my existence to you, an alcoholic paralegal who is ashamed of the fact that he was born in New Orleans."

Hartmann reached for another cigarette. He believed he needed to change the pitch of the discussion before Perez became angry. "I find it remarkable that you were responsible for the death of Jimmy Hoffa."

Perez nodded. "Someone had to have killed him. Why not me?"

"Did you shoot Kennedy as well?"

"Which one?"

Hartmann smiled. "You did them both?"

"Neither, though I believe that I would have gotten away with it, unlike Oswald and Sirhan Sirhan, neither of whom were ultimately responsible whatever J. Edgar Vacuum and the Warren Commission might have reported. The assassination of John Kennedy, the resultant mystery that has surrounded his death for the last forty years, has to be the most spectacular and successful example of government disinformation propaganda that has ever been achieved. Adolf Hitler would have been proud of what your government has accomplished with that. Wasn't it he who said that the greater the lie the more easily it will be believed?"

"It's your government too," Hartmann said.

"I am selective . . . it is the lesser of two evils. The United States or Fidel Castro. I am still trying to make a decision as to which one I would prefer to be allied to."

Hartmann was quiet for a moment. He smoked his cigarette.

Perez broke the silence between them. "So you did not come here to visit or to have supper, or to smoke my cigarettes, Mr. Hartmann. I believe you came here with a proposal."

"How do you know that?"

"It is about time for the attorney general to play his best hand, and like I said before, you do not live the life I have lived and survive by being stupid. So out with it. What is it they are prepared to offer me?"

"Clemency," Hartmann said, believing that the entire conversation had been predicted and determined by Perez from the off. This was not the way Hartmann had wanted to handle it, but it had become something out of his control. He had believed his cards were hidden, but he had sat down at the table unaware that his cards had been chosen for him by his opponent.

"Clemency?" Perez asked. "Mercy? You think this is what I came here to ask for?"

Hartmann shook his head. "No," he said. "I don't."

"I came here of my own volition. I handed myself in to you people with no resistance. I could have continued to live my life, could have done nothing. Had I not called the FBI, had I not spoken with these people, had I not asked for you to come here, then we would not be having this conversation. I could have taken the girl, I could have killed her, and no one would ever have been any the wiser."

"They would have found you," Hartmann interjected.

Perez started laughing. "You think so, Mr. Hartmann? You really think they would have found me? I am nearly seventy years old. I have been doing this for the better part of five and a half decades. I was the man who killed your Jimmy Hoffa. I put a piano wire around his neck and pulled so hard I could feel where the wire stopped against the vertebrae of his neck. I did these things, and I did them all over this country, and these people didn't even know my name."

Hartmann knew Perez was right. He had not lived this life and survived by being stupid. If he had wanted to kill Catherine Ducane he would have done, and Hartmann imagined the murder would have gone unsolved.

"Okay," Hartmann said. "So this is the deal . . . you give us the girl, you are extradited to Cuba, and the United States Federal Government will not further any information about your past to the Cuban Justice Department. That's the deal, take it or leave it."

Perez leaned back in his chair. He looked pensive for some time, said nothing, and when he turned his eyes toward Hartmann there was something cold and aloof in them that Hartmann had not seen before. "You will come back tomorrow night," he said. "We will meet in the morning as planned. I will tell you some more things of myself and my life, and when we are done we will return here for dinner, you and I, and I will give you my answer."

Hartmann nodded. "Can you tell us one thing?"

Perez raised his eyebrows.

"The girl. Can you assure us she is still alive?"

Perez shook his head. "No, I cannot."

"She is dead?"

"I didn't say that."

"You are saying nothing?"

"That is right, I am saying nothing."

"If she is dead it makes this whole thing rather pointless," Hartmann said.

"It is only pointless to those who do not yet understand the point," Perez replied. "Now, if you don't mind, I am tired. I would like to rest. I have an appointment in the morning, and if I am tired I do not concentrate well."

Hartmann nodded and started to rise from his chair.

"It has been a pleasure, Mr. Hartmann," Perez said. "And I trust that things work out for yourself and your family."

"Thank you, Mr. Perez, though I do not necessarily feel I can reciprocate the sentiment."

Perez waved Hartmann's comment aside. "It is of no matter to me what you think, Mr. Hartmann. Some of us are more than capable of making our own decisions and allowing life to intervene as little as possible."

Hartmann did not reply. There was nothing more he could say. He walked back to the door of the bedroom and let himself out.

Behind him the music increased in volume—Shostakovich's "Assault On Beautiful Gorky"—and Hartmann looked at Dauncey with a somewhat bemused and mystified expression.

"Like I said before, a real character," Dauncey said, and opened the hotel suite door to let Hartmann out into the corridor.

The rain finally stopped around ten. Hartmann sat on the edge of his bed in the Marriott Hotel and considered the awkward slow-motion war-zone of his life. Carol and Jess were not happy with him; Schaeffer and Woodroffe, Attorney General Richard Seidler and FBI Director Bob Dohring were not happy with him either. By now Charles Ducane would surely know Hartmann's name, and believe him to be the man responsible for the safe return of his daughter. And what *about* Charles Ducane? Had he really been involved with these people? Organized crime? The murder of Jimmy Hoffa? The killing of McLuhan and the two people in the Shell Beach Motel back in the fall of '62? Was Charles Ducane as much a part of this as Ernesto Perez?

Hartmann undressed and took a shower. He stood beneath the water, as hot as he could bear, and stayed there for some time. He thought of Carol and Jess, of how much he would have given to hear their voices now, to know they were safe, to say he was sorry, to tell them that he was in some way undergoing a catharsis, an exorcism of who he had once been, and that from this point forward it would be different. It would all be *so* different.

Ray Hartmann, for a short while, was overcome with a sense of desperation and despondency. Was this now his life? Alone? Hotel rooms? Government inquiries and investigations? Spending his days listening to the worst that people had to offer and trying to make deals with them?

He sat in the base of the unit. The water flooded over him. He could hear his own heart beating. He felt afraid.

Later, lying on the bed, he fought with a sense of restless agitation and did not sleep until the early hours of Thursday morning. His mind was punctuated with strange images, images of Ernesto Perez carrying Jess's lifeless body out of a swamp while Shostakovich played the piano in the background.

And then morning invaded his room, and he rose, he dressed, he drank two cups of strong black coffee, and he and Sheldon Ross—who now looked ten years older than the young fresh-faced recruit he had first seen only a handful of days before—made their way back to the office on Arsenault Street to hear what the world and all its madness had to offer them today.

And it was only as he passed through the narrow doorway into the all-too-familiar office that he remembered that there were three reasons. Three reasons Perez had chosen to bring him here to New Orleans. Perez had told him two of them, and Hartmann—amid all that had been said—had forgotten to ask for the third.

It was the first thing he asked Perez when they were seated.

Perez smiled with that knowing expression in his eyes.

"Later," he said quietly. "I will tell you the last reason later . . . perhaps when we are done, Mr. Hartmann."

When we are done, Hartmann echoed. It sounded so utterly conclusive.

"So we shall share a little of California," Perez said. "Because I believe that sharing is a truly Californian trait, is it not?" Perez smiled at his own dry humor and leaned back in his chair. "And when we are done we will return to the hotel. We will share some supper and then I will give you the answer to your proposal."

Hartmann nodded.

He closed his eyes for a moment and tried to see his daughter's face.

He struggled but it did not come.

NINETEEN

ANGEL AND I, we went out to the West Coast of America; to California, named after an island in the Spanish novel *Las Sergas de Esplandian* by García Ordónez de Montalvo.

The Land of Happily Ever After; the Big Sur coastline where the Santa Lucia mountains rise straight out of the sea; the northern coast, rugged and desolate, deep banks of impenetrable fog; the dormant volcano Mount Shasta; beyond this, vast groves of one- and two-thousand-year-old redwood trees.

Los Angeles, The Angels, surrounded to the north and east by the Mojave Desert and Death Valley, but despite the vision and the apparent romance of this place, despite the promise of sun, of twenty miles of white sand and warmth at the Santa Monica beachfront, we came to this city in March of 1982 as immigrants and strangers.

Our welcome was no welcome at all. We moved into a third-floor walk-up on Olive Street by Pershing Square in downtown LA. We paid for the place in cash and registered under Angelina's maiden name, and though we had been people in New York, though we had possessed faces and characters and personalities, in LA we possessed nothing. We were swallowed silently, effortlessly, into the great maw of humanity within that pinpoint microcosm of America.

It was three weeks before I saw our neighbor. I came back from a meeting with Don Fabio Calligaris's cousin who ran a chop-shop on Boyd Street. I saw a man leaving the house adjacent to my own, I raised my hand, I called out *Hello*, and he turned and looked at me with a sense of distrust and resentment. He said nothing in return, did not even acknowledge my presence but hurried away, glancing back only once to repeat the look of hostility. I wondered for a moment if my sins were painted on my face for all the world to see. They were not. It was not me; it was Los Angeles that did it to them, relentlessly and irreversibly.

We came here for Angelina, for the children also.

"The sun shines here," she said. "It is always dull and gray in New York. There are too many people who know of me back there. I wanted to get away, Nesto. I *had* to get away."

I could empathize with her. I felt the same way for New Orleans, perhaps for Havana, but the coldness of the city, the absence of feeling and family in California was disturbing.

There was no shortage of work, however. Through Fabio Calligaris's son I met Angelo Cova's brother, Michael. Michael was a man unlike any I had met before. He was a big man, in stature—much the same as Ten Cent—but more so in personality. We met in the first week of May, and he explained to me that there were matters of business that I could attend to in Los Angeles that would be gratefully acknowledged by New York.

"LA is Lucifer's asshole," he said. We sat in a small diner back of Spring Street. The narrow building seemed to rumble constantly with the traffic running along the Santa Ana Freeway. Ahead of us was the Hall of Justice, behind us the US Courts, around the corner the Criminal Courts Building. I felt cornered in a way, fenced in by the presence of authority and federal residence. "LA is what God created for human beings to exercise their depravity. Here you got hookers with faces like a bulldog licking piss off of a lemon tree. You got thirteen-year-old boys peddling their asses for barbiturates and amphetamines. You got drugs the like of which you wouldn't give a dying man to ease his pain. You got gambling and murder and extortion, all the shit you'll find in New York and Chicago, but in LA there's a difference. Here you'll find something missing, and the thing that's missing is a basic respect for the value of human life."

"What do you mean?" I asked.

"Take last week," Michael Cova said. He leaned back in his chair and crossed his legs. He held a small espresso cup in his hand despite the fact it was empty. "Last week I went down to see a guy who runs a few girls. They ain't bad-looking girls, little rough around the edges, but slap some face paint on them 'n' they look halfway decent. Sort of girl you'd slip the old salami and have a pretty good time, you know? So, I went down there to see him. He wanted some help dealing with some assholes that were trying to muscle in on the turf, and there was this girl down there, couldn'ta been more 'n' twenty-one or two and she had half her face banged up so bad she couldn't see out of her eye. Her lips was all swelled like a punchbag, and across her neck and throat were these dark black welts like some motherfucker had tried to strangle her."

Michael cleared his throat.

"I says to this guy, I says, 'Hey . . . what the fuck happened to her?' and he says, 'Oh, take no notice of the bitch,' 'n' I says, 'What the fuck happened, man? She get hit by one of these assholes you tellin' me about?' 'n' he laughs 'n' he says, 'No, she got herself teached a good lesson.'"

Michael uncrossed his legs and leaned forward.

"So I says, 'What the fuck is that all about? She got a lesson about what?' and this dumb fuck he says, 'Bitch tried to hold out on me, bitch tried to hold out on me for fifty bucks she got off some rich asshole from uptown so I had to teach her a lesson, right?' and he started laughing."

Michael shook his head and frowned.

"I was shocked, man, I can tell you without any problem. This asshole beats the living crap outta this poor girl for the sake of fifty bucks. Never seemed to occur to him that she wasn't gonna be entertainin' anyone with her face all smashed up. Never thought to occur to him how much money he would lose with her out of business 'n' all. And that's the kinda thing I see every day down here. Basic lack of respect for the value of human life. It's like they's all lost their own self-respect and dignity, and sometimes it can't help but stick in my craw."

Michael put his empty cup on the table.

"So things is a little different down here, and though we didn't wanna have you involved with any of this kinda shit I'm afraid that you're gonna come across it whether you look for it or not."

"So what d'you want me to do?" I asked.

"A bit of this, a bit of that. Angelo told me something about the kind of work you were doing for Fabio Calligaris, and we figured we could always use a little help in that quarter, you know what I mean?"

I nodded; I knew what Michael Cova meant. "So is there something specific?"

Michael smiled. "Well, that little story I told ya just then, I didn't tell ya just for the sake o' shootin' the breeze and passin' the time of day. I told you because the guy, the hitter, you know? The one who slapped the girl around?"

I nodded; I knew what was coming.

"Well, seems she's not the only one who's been holdin' out on fifty bucks here and fifty bucks there. Seems he's as guilty as any of those girls of his, and we need you to go down and have a few words with him, sort of words he will thoroughly understand and never have the chance to repeat."

"You want him clipped?"

Michael looked surprised, and then he started laughing. "Shit, Angelo was right about you. You don't fuck around, do you?"

I shrugged. "What's the point? You want him clipped then say you want him clipped. We'll save all the nice things about the weather and whatever the fuck else for sometime when I come over to yours for a barbecue."

Michael dropped the friendly face. I heard it hit the floor of the narrow diner near the Santa Ana Freeway.

"Sure, so we want him clipped. You can handle that?"

"Consider it done. Any particular *way* you want it done?"

Michael frowned. "Whaddya mean?"

"There's as many different ways to clip someone as there are different people. Sometimes it needs to be fast and quiet, like the guy disappears for a holiday and never comes back, other times it's because someone needs an example made to anyone else who might have the same idea—"

Michael brightened up. "That's the baby. You got it there. We want him done like he's an example to any of the other smalltime lowlife scumbags who might be getting the wrong idea about who they're working for."

"When?" I asked.

"When what?"

"When d'you want him done?"

Michael shook his head. "Today?"

"Okay," I said. "Today's as good as any other. What's the address?"

Michael gave me the address, a house on Miramar and Third near the Harbor Freeway.

I rose from my chair.

"Now?" he said, seeming surprised.

"Any reason not to?"

Michael shook his head. "S'pose not. Why the hurry?"

"I gotta pregnant wife back home . . . said I wouldn't be out late."

Michael laughed suddenly, coarsely. He looked at me like he expected me to start laughing as well. I didn't.

"You're serious," he said.

I nodded.

"Okay. Fair's fair. You gotta do what you gotta do."

"Not a problem," I said, "You want me to call you and let you know when I'm finished?"

"Sure, Ernesto, you call me."

"You gonna be here?"

Michael shook his head. "I'll be home more than likely."

"Gimme your number."

He gave me his number and I wrote it down alongside the address he gave me. I looked at the address and the number until I was certain I would remember them, and then I lit the piece of paper and let it burn in the ashtray.

"And the guy's name?"

"Clarence Hill," he said. "Buttfuck's name is Clarence Hill."

I took a route avoiding the main freeways—Spring down to Fourth, along Fourth and beneath the Harbor Freeway to Beaudry, and there on the corner of Miramar and Third I found the place.

I backed up and parked the car two blocks south, got out and walked back on foot. By that time it was early evening, the sun was down and the lights inside told me where the girls were working.

I went up the front steps and knocked on the door, knocked three times before it was opened, and when I stepped inside, the smell of the place assaulted my nostrils violently.

"You want?" some ugly rash-faced Hispanic asked.

"Need to see Clarence," I said.

The Hispanic frowned. "Whassup wit' you? You gotta cold or some-thin'? Don't be comin' down here infectin' everyone wit' no goddamned flu."

"I ain't got the flu," I said. "I ain't gonna breathe through my nose . . . this place stinks like no place I ever been before," which was not true, because as soon as I had walked inside the door I was reminded of some late night, staggering through the doorway of the house where I had lived with Ruben Cienfuegos so many years before.

The Hispanic made a sneering noise, and said, "What you want wit" Clarence?"

"I got to see him," I said, "I gotta deliver something from Michael."

The Hispanic smiled broadly. "Shee-it, why in the fuckin' hell you not say you was here from Michael? I know Michael, me an' Michael we go ways back and then some more. Me an' Michael sometimes just sit down and have a beer, make some face-time, you know?"

I nodded. I smiled, I could imagine that Michael Cova sitting down and having beer with the Hispanic was as likely as me shooting the breeze with Capone.

"So where is he?"

The Hispanic nodded toward the stairs. "Up on the first, third door on the left, but for fuck's sake knock on the door 'fore you go in 'cause he's more than likely getting his hardware polished if you know what I mean."

I shook my head, but I smiled for the Hispanic. Clarence wasn't only beating the crap out of the trade, he was stealing from the cookie jar as well.

I went up quickly and quietly, along the upper hallway until I reached the door. I knocked once, heard a voice inside, and I went in.

Clarence Hill was a fat fuck useless sack of nothing worthwhile. He sat back in a deep armchair dressed in nothing but shorts and a filthy tee-shirt. In his right hand he held a TV remote, in his left a can of beer. On the floor ahead of him were three more empty cans.

"Yo!" he said. "Think maybe you're in the wrong room, mister."

I shook my head. "Michael sent me."

Clarence tilted his head to the right and squinted at me. "Ain't never seen you before. How the fuck d'you know Michael?"

"We're family."

Clarence smiled wide and cheerful. "Well hell, if you're family with Michael then you're family with me . . . come on in, take a load off."

"I will," I said. I took a .38 from the waistband of my pants and pointed it directly at his head.

Clarence dropped the remote and the beer can simultaneously. He opened his mouth to say something, something loud and worthless no doubt, and I raised my left hand and pressed my finger to my lips. "Ssshhh," I whispered, and Clarence fell silent before a single word had escaped his trembling lips.

"The guy downstairs . . . what's his name?"

"L-L-Lourdes."

I frowned. "Lourdes? What the fuck kinda name is that?"

"Tha-that's hi-his n-name," Clarence mumbled. "That's his name . . . Lourdes."

I leaned back toward the door and shouted the Hispanic's name.

"What?" he hollered up from below.

"Up here," I shouted.

"Up here what?"

I looked at Clarence. Clarence nodded.

"L-Lourdes, get the fuck up here right now!" Clarence shouted, like he believed that cooperating with me would make the damndest bit of difference.

Lourdes came up the stairs. I stepped behind the door, and when he walked in I shoved him hard and he went sprawling across the floor.

"What the fu—" he started, and then he turned and saw me standing there with a .38 and he shut up real quick.

From my inside pocket I took a knife, small and sharp. "Take this," I said, "and cut Clarence's tee-shirt off."

"Wha—"

"Do it." My voice was direct and firm. "Do what I say real quick and real quiet and maybe someone's gonna walk out of here alive."

Lourdes took the knife. He cut Clarence's tee-shirt off at the shoulders, and within a few moments stood there with the filthy rag in his hand.

"Now cut it in strips and tie Clarence to the chair over there." I indicated to the left where a plain deal chair stood against the wall.

They didn't need prompting; the pair of them cooperated and said nothing.

Three or four minutes and Clarence Hill, shaking and sweating profusely, sat tied to the chair in the middle of the room.

"Take the cover off the cushion and jam it in his mouth," I said.

Clarence's eyes were wide and white; looked like two ping-pong balls balancing on his great fat face.

Lourdes did as he was told, and then he stood there with the small, sharp knife in his hand and waited for me to say something.

"Now cut his pecker off."

Lourdes dropped the knife.

Clarence started screaming, but with the material in his mouth he made barely a sound. He was thrashing wildly in the chair, every ounce of his strength fighting against the restraints that held him.

"Lourdes . . . pick up the goddamned knife and cut that fat fuck's pecker off or I'm coming over there and do you first."

Lourdes, his whole body rigid with terror, leaned down to pick up the knife. He held it gingerly in his hand. He looked at me. I nodded in the affirmative.

Clarence passed out before the blade reached him. That was a good thing for him. Lourdes did what I told him to do, but it took a good five or ten minutes because he stopped to retch and heave about once every thirty seconds. The blood was unreal. It flooded out and soaked the chair, ran in rivulets onto the floor beneath, and soon Lourdes was nothing more than a gibbering wreck of a man, kneeling there on the floor in Clarence's blood, in his right hand the knife, in his left Clarence's pecker.

At one point Clarence seemed to come round, his eyes opened for a split-second, and when he looked down at his own lap he passed out once more. Ten minutes, maybe less, Clarence would be dead from blood loss if he hadn't had a coronary seizure already.

"You did good, Lourdes," I said, and then I took the cushion, pressed it down against the back of his head as he knelt on the floor, and I shot him.

Lourdes collapsed forward, and within a moment you couldn't tell whose blood was whose.

I tucked the gun into the waistband of my pants. I stepped out of the room and closed the door quietly behind me. I went down the corridor, passed a door through which I could hear some guy hollering *Baby baby baby,* and went down the risers two at a time to the lower hall.

I paused for a moment, breathed once through my nose to remind myself of how goddamned awful the place smelled, and then I went out through the front door and closed it tight behind me.

Later, after dinner, I called Michael Cova at home.

"Done," I said quietly.

"Already?"

"Yes."

"Okay, Ernesto, okay. Hey, how's the wife?"

"She's good, Michael, thanks for asking."

"When's the baby coming?"

"June . . . should be June."

"Well, God bless you both, eh?"

"Thank you, Michael . . . appreciated."

"You're welcome. Tell her 'Hi' from me."

"I will, Michael."

"See ya tomorrow."

"Tomorrow," I said, and hung up the phone.

"Nesto?" Angelina called from the front.

"Sweetheart?"

"Come massage my feet for me, would you, honey? I ache all over."

"Sure thing, sweetheart. Just gonna lock up the front."

I locked the door, flipped the deadbolt, and walked back in front to see my wife.

June seventeenth 1982, St. Mary Magdalene Hospital on Hope Street near the park, Angelina Maria Perez gave birth to twins. A boy and a girl. I cannot begin to describe what I felt, and so I will not attempt to, save to say that there had never been anything before and nothing since that could even come close to what I experienced in that operating theater.

We had no idea there were two. I knew she was big, but big compared to what? I had expected one child. We were blessed with two. I counted their fingers, their toes. I held one within each arm. I walked around in circles looking down at them until I believed I would fall over with the sheer weight of joy and emotion and pride and love.

My babies. My blood. *My* family.

At that time I did not question whether I would be caught in some conflict between the family of my business and the family of my blood. I questioned nothing. I asked for nothing. In that moment I believed that whatever God may have existed, whatever power was out there beyond the parameters of my understanding, I had been blessed with something priceless and beyond measure.

Three days later we took Victor and Lucia home. They cried, they were forever hungry; they woke us with their pleadings in the cool half-light of nascent morning, and we went from our bed with something in our hearts that had never been there before; something that we had once believed unattainable.

For six weeks, right until the end of July of that year, I made no attempt to contact anyone. In some way I was grateful for this. I received one call from Michael Cova. He expressed his good wishes and sent the blessings of his family. Ten times, perhaps more, we would wake, we would go outside the front door, and there on the porch we would find baskets of fruit, wickerwork jars of dried meats and salami. I understood then that whatever kind of people they were, whatever blood may have been spilled in the name of greed, of vengeance, of hatred and possession, they were still human beings. They respected blood and family and the ties that bound such things more than anything else. They respected me, and in this way they gave me the time I needed to be with my wife and my children.

Angelina and I—like teenagers caught with the first enthusiastic sweep of love—could find no wrong with the world. Each day dawned with a brighter sun, a bluer sky, a sweeter smell in the air. Angelina did not ask why there was no business to attend to, and it was perhaps for the first time during those weeks that I began to question why she had never asked me what I had done, what business I would leave to attend to in the days before the birth of our children. At first I imagined it was because of her heritage, the fact that she had been born herself within the confines of this world, that her father, her father's brother—all these people surrounding her as a child—had been there inside the dark underbelly of American organized crime. Later, as I watched her play with Victor and Lucia, as I caught her watching me from the doorway of the kitchen when I pulled faces and made them smile, I realized that she did not *want* to know. She asked no questions because she already knew the answers, and thus she stayed silent, even as the telephone calls started in the first week of August; silent as I stood in the hallway, my words hushed to a whisper, as I explained to the world beyond our door that I needed a little more time: another week, perhaps two.

After the calls ended I would walk back in to see her.

"Everything okay?" she would ask.

I would nod and smile and tell her everything was fine.

"They want you back?"

"Sure they do, Angelina, sure they do."

"And you're going?"

"Not yet . . . a little while longer."

Silence for a brief while, and then, "Ernesto?"

"Yes?"

"You have a family now—"

"Angelina . . . we have spoken of this before. Everyone I know has a family. All of these people have families. Their families are the most important things in their lives. They still have things to attend to, business still goes on and it has to be dealt with. Just because I now have a family doesn't change the fact that I am responsible for my agreements."

"Agreements? Is that what you call them?"

"Yes, Angelina, agreements. We are here because people helped us be here. I have a duty to return the favors that are granted. This is a long-term thing, Angelina . . . you have been part of this life even longer than I. You understand the way these things work, and there's nothing that can be done to change it."

"But Ernesto—"

"Angelina, enough. Seriously, enough for now. This is the way that our life is—"

"But I don't want this life any more, Ernesto."

"I know, Angel, I know," and then I would hold her and she would say nothing, and I would be afraid to look at her because I knew she would see right through me, and understand that I also did not want this life any more.

On Monday 9 August 1982, the same day that John Hinckley was detained indefinitely for the attempted assassination of President Ronald Reagan, Samuel Pagliaro, a man I had known as Ten Cent in another life, came to the door of our house and asked for an audience with me.

I greeted him warmly, I had not seen him for the better part of five months and I was happy to see his face, happy as he gripped my shoulders and hugged me, and kissed Angelina, and then lifted my children from the carpet as if they were nothing more than feathers, and complimented their beauty, their bright eyes. It was good to see Ten Cent, but beneath my superficial welcome there was a sense of darkness and foreboding that warned me of what was to come.

Later, after we had eaten, he took me aside. We sat in the room at the front of the house. Angelina was upstairs with Victor and Lucia attempting to get them to sleep.

"Don Calligaris is pleased for your good fortune," Ten Cent began. "He is very pleased with the work you have done out here, and good words have come back home from Michael Cova also. But this time has come to an end—"

He looked at me with a flash of anxiety in his eyes. He knew me well enough to understand that I could be capable of violence and passion. He was—despite his size—perhaps a little concerned about my potential reaction.

I said nothing. I merely nodded. I understood enough of the way these things worked to know that, with a word, all that I had could be taken from me in a heartbeat. These people, fiercely loyal to their own, would nevertheless see me as an outsider if I chose to cross them. I had no intention of doing such a thing, but I was aware that there was indeed a conflict within me. Perhaps what I felt was a reflection of some earlier part of my life. I had never possessed an introspective mind; I had never questioned things deeply. I could relate the sense of conflict I was experiencing to two other events in my life: the killing of Don Ceriano, how my loyalty to him was challenged by my necessity and will to survive; and the death of the salesman in Louisiana. Wishing so hard to become something my mother would have wanted me to be, I became something that was so much like my father. It was not a good thing for me to experience, but I felt it again in the presence of Ten Cent as he reminded me of who I had been, who I was now expected to be once again.

"There is something that needs to be done," he went on. "Something that Don Calligaris feels would be most suited to your abilities, and he asked for me to come here and ask this of you."

I nodded. "Go on."

"There has been an injustice done, a grave injustice. For many years the ties between New York and Los Angeles have been strong. Don Calligaris has family here, and they have always looked out for each other." Ten Cent shook his head and looked at his own hands in his lap. There was a tension and an awkwardness in his manner that were new to me.

"Ten Cent?"

He looked up.

"Tell me what it is that Don Calligaris wants."

Ten Cent cleared his throat. For a moment he looked away toward the window, toward the night sky, the lights of the city. "Don Calligaris's wife has a sister. She is married to an American. They have a daughter, a good girl, a fine and pretty girl, and she came out here to Los Angeles to be an actress. Last month they received word that she had been drugged and raped at some party in Hollywood, that she had been violated in the worst manner possible . . . things too wicked to describe." Ten Cent paused, as though it was difficult for him to talk about such things. "The girl's parents, they spoke with the police, but the police know who the mother is, that she is the sister-in-law of Fabio Calligaris, and they tell her that there is no real evidence that their daughter did not consent to the things that were done. I understand it was some movie actor's house, someone who is well known out here, and his father is an influential man in this business. The movie actor was not the one who did these things, but some other man, a clothing designer or something, and he has done this thing and there is no justice for what has happened. Don Calligaris asks if you will act on his behalf and see to this matter. He does not wish for there to be any further trouble beyond whatever justice you see fit, but he wishes this to be done or he will lose honor within the family. He told me to show you the pictures of what they did to his niece, and for you to make a judgment regarding what you felt would be appropriate justice."

I nodded. I looked back toward the half-open doorway. I could see the light coming down from the upper landing and I knew that no more than twenty feet away my wife lay with my children as they slept. I understood blood, I understood family, and I respected and loved Don Fabio Calligaris enough to take care of his business. But my sense of responsibility to Don Calligaris did not lessen my inner conflict. As always, I had no choice in the matter, and as time would go on it would become more and more difficult to reconcile those situations where choice was not an option. I went out of duty, that was the truth, but for the first time in my life I questioned it.

The girl must have been beaten half-dead. Her face was swollen to twice its normal size. There were cuts on her upper arms and her breasts, as if someone had beaten her with a wire. Her hair was matted with blood, one eyed closed completely due to the swelling of her cheek. Her buttocks were the same, and around her lower stomach and the tops of her thighs there were marks as if ropes had been used to burn her.

"These are police photographs?" I asked.

Ten Cent nodded.

"And how did Don Calligaris get them?"

"He has friends in the New York police department. He had them send copies."

"And there were no questions as to why New York would need them?"

"His friend in New York told the LAPD that he'd heard of the case, that he believed there may have been a link between this and some outstanding investigation there. They didn't ask questions. They just sent them, and Don Calligaris gave them to me to show you."

Never women and children . . . you never hurt the women and children. That was the thought that came to me. Unspoken, as if by tacit consent, and here—a member of my patron's family—beaten within an inch of her life by a clothes designer from Hollywood.

"His name?" I asked.

"Richard Ricardo is the name he uses," Ten Cent said. "It is not his real name, but that is the name he uses, the name he is known by."

"And he lives where?"

"He lives in an apartment not far from Hollywood Boulevard, the third floor of a building on the corner of Wilcox and Selma. The apartment number is 3B."

I did not write down the address. My memory was good for small details, and carrying written names and addresses was never good practice.

"Tell Don Calligaris that this matter will be very swiftly resolved," I said.

Ten Cent rose from his chair. "I will, and I know he will be appreciative, Ernesto."

"You are leaving already?" I asked.

Ten Cent nodded. "There are many things I have to do before I leave Los Angeles. It is late. You must see to your children."

Once again the dichotomy of my life; black and white, no shades of gray between.

I saw Ten Cent leave. I held his hand for a moment at the door.

"We will meet again soon," he said quietly. "Give my best wishes to your family, Ernesto."

"And mine to yours," I replied.

I watched him walk down the steps to the street, walk to the end of the block. He did not turn back, he did not glance over his shoulder, and I closed the door quietly and locked it.

That night I could not sleep. It was the early hours of the morning when Angelina stirred and woke, perhaps sensing my internal disturbance.

She lay there quietly for a moment or two, and then turned and snaked her arm across my chest. She pulled me tight and kissed my shoulder.

"Your friend," she said. "He has something for you to do?"

I nodded. "Yes."

She did not speak for a minute. "Take care," she said, "Now you have not only yourself to think of."

And she said nothing more, and when morning came she said nothing of Ten Cent, nothing of the business that he had brought for my attention. She made breakfast as always, tending to the children—all of seven weeks old, innocent and wordless, wide-eyed and wondering at the ways of this new world they had entered—and in my heart I felt for them, felt for who I had become, and what they would feel if they ever knew.

I left that evening. It was dark and the children were sleeping. I told Angelina I would be no more than a few hours, and for a while she held me close, and then she reached up and kissed my forehead. "Take care," she said once more, and stood at the door to watch as I walked down the street. At the corner I glanced back. She stood there, illuminated in silhouette from the light inside the house, and I felt something in my heart, something that should have pulled me back, but I did not slow or stop or retrace my steps with second thoughts; I simply raised my hand and waved, and carried on my way.

I took the subway as far as Vine. I made my way down Hollywood Boulevard and the Walk of Fame, turned left on Cahuenga, right onto Selma, and there at the corner of Wilcox I found the building of which Ten Cent had spoken. I could see lights right across the third floor, also the second below, and I could hear the faint sound of music coming from the windows.

Entrance was easy. I went in through the back exit out of which the garbage and tradesmen would come. I found the base of a narrow stairwell that appeared to climb the height of the building, and up I went—silently, two risers at a time—until I reached the third floor.

I stood silently in the doorway at the top of the well, held it open no more than an inch or two, and it was there I heard the music louder. It came from the apartment facing me, from behind a door with 3B clearly visible on it, and I stayed there for some minutes ensuring that there was no coming and going along the hallway. When I was sure there was no one entering or leaving any of the upper apartments I crossed the hallway. From my inside jacket pocket I took a thin sliver of metal and eased it between the door jamb and the striker plate. I nudged it down until I felt it touch the latch, and then with silent hair's-breadth motions I started to wedge the blade into the lock. The lock sprang without difficulty. I turned the handle and the door gave way. I inched it open a fraction and waited for any sound inside. I heard nothing but the music, louder now, and realized that whoever was there would not have a hope of hearing me as I entered.

The hallway carpet was thick and dark. Along the walls hung black-and-white photographs, some of them clearly identifiable as images of cityscapes from many years before, others more abstract and undefined as to subject matter. I closed the door behind me, slid the chain across and flipped the deadbolt. Richard Ricardo evidently believed that once he was within the confines of his own home he was safe. Nothing, but nothing, could have been farther from the truth.

I went along the hallway without a sound. My breathing was low and shallow, and when I reached the end and pressed myself against the corner of the wall I could tilt my head and see into the main warehouse apartment.

Through a half-open door on the other side of the room I could see the end of a bed. The figure of a man, apparently naked, flitted across my line of vision and I shrank back. I waited for a second and then looked again. I could see no one.

I stayed close to the wall and went into the main room, pressing my body against the plasterwork and circumventing the entire width until I came around on the other side and stood at the rear edge of the bed-room door. I could hear voices, at first one and then a second, and with my heart thundering in my chest I withdrew my .38 from the waist-band of my pants.

The sight that greeted me as I peered around the doorframe and looked into the room surprised me. There were two men, both naked, one of them lying back on the bed with his hands cuffed to the stead. The second man was kneeling between the spread-eagled man's legs, his head going up and down at a furious rate. I watched them for a little while, my mind turning back to Ruben Cienfuegos and the men we had robbed in Havana, the death of Pietro Silvino, the things he had said to me before I killed him.

The man lying down was moaning and writhing. The second man continued energetically for some thirty seconds or so, and then he kneeled back on his haunches, pulled the other man's legs together, and then sat astride them. Shuffling forward he moved upwards until he sat across the man's chest, and then using his hand to hold the cock of the man beneath him he gently eased backward. I watched as the man's cock slid inside him. The two of them were laughing together, and then the man on top started to rock back and forth, gently increasing his speed as he went.

I stepped away from the wall, crossed the room behind them, and with a single swipe of the gun handle I swept the music player off the table. The music stopped dead. The two men stopped also.

"What the hell—" the upper man exclaimed, and then he turned, and then he saw me standing there with a gun in my hand, and there was an expression in his eyes that said everything that could ever be said without a single word.

"Oh my God . . . oh my God," he started, but the man beneath him was pale, in shock. Not a word came from his mouth as he lay there, with his hands cuffed to the frame of the bed, as naked as the day he was born, his cock inside someone's ass and feeling like the world was ready to end.

The man on top fell sideways and started to his feet.

"Sit the fuck down," I said.

He did as he was told.

"You want money?" he started whimpering, and then there were tears in his eyes. "We have money here, a lot of money . . . you can have all the money—"

"No money," I said, and it was in that second that both of them realized what was going to happen.

The handcuffed man began crying, and pulled his knees up to his chest and tried to turn his body away so I could not see him naked.

"What d'you want?" the seated man asked.

"Which one of you is Ricardo?" I asked.

The seated man looked at me with horror. "I . . . I am Richard Ricardo," he said, and his voice cracked with fear.

"You're traveling both ways then?" I said, and I smiled.

Ricardo frowned.

"Girls and boys, whichever takes your fancy, right?"

He shook his head. "I don't know what you mean . . . what do you want?"

"Retribution," I said, and from the inside jacket of my pocket I took one of the photographs that Ten Cent had shown me.

I held it up so it could be clearly seen.

Ricardo stared silently at the picture, and then he closed his eyes.

"What's his name?" I asked, and indicated the other man lying on the bed.

Ricardo glanced sideways at him. "His name?"

I nodded. "His name."

"Leonard . . . this is Leonard."

"Well, tell Leonard he ain't a fucking ostrich. Just because he ain't looking at me doesn't mean he's invisible."

Ricardo reached over and put his hand on Leonard's shoulder. Leonard tried to shrug it off. He buried his face deeper into the pillow, and though the sound was muffled I could still hear him sobbing.

"Undo the cuffs, Richard," I said.

Ricardo reached for the key on a small table beside the bed and unlocked the cuffs. Leonard tugged the bedsheet up and covered himself.

"Leonard?"

Leonard didn't move.

"Leonard . . . turn this way and look at me or I'm gonna come over there and shove this gun so far up your ass you won't stop hurting 'til Sunday."

Leonard turned onto his side, and then eased himself upright. He clung onto the sheet as if he believed it would protect him against a bullet.

I held up the photograph so he could clearly see it. "You he might love for eternity," I said, "but your friend Richard has a certain way with the ladies that they don't appreciate."

"You . . . you don't understand—" Ricardo started.

I raised my gun, pointed it directly between Ricardo's eyes, and took three steps forward until the barrel touched the bridge of his nose.

"Shut the fuck up," I said. With my other hand I held the photograph and waited until he was looking directly at it. "You know this girl?" I asked.

Ricardo tried to frown, tried to make out like he was remembering whether or not he knew her.

"We're not playing games here," I said. "I know and you know, so don't waste my time telling me anything else. You know this girl?"

Ricardo nodded. He closed his eyes. Tears were running down his cheeks.

"You did this to her?"

"She . . . she wanted me to . . . wanted me to hurt her . . . you gotta understand she's a crazy fucking bitch. She wanted me to hurt her . . ."

"She wanted you to hurt her," I said matter-of-factly.

Ricardo was nodding furiously.

"She wanted you to beat the crap out of her, wanted you to hit her so hard she couldn't see straight for days, wanted you to whip her with a wire coat hanger until she'd screamed so much she lost her voice? She wanted you to do that?"

Leonard was looking over Ricardo's shoulder at the photograph, his eyes wide and incredulous.

"Ricky . . . Ricky? You did this to that girl?"

Ricardo turned suddenly. "Shut the fuck up, Lenny."

"Yes," I interjected. "Shut the fuck up, Lenny."

Lenny closed his open mouth and turned away. He looked like he was going to puke. I figured he wouldn't want to fuck Richard Ricardo in the ass again.

"So seems to me that whatever the hell went down between you and this girl, well she got a little more than she asked for . . . would that be somewhere close to the truth, Ricky?"

Ricardo didn't move a muscle, didn't say a word. I jabbed the barrel of the gun into his forehead. He winced with the pain.

"You reckon that's somewhere close to the truth?"

Ricardo nodded.

"You sorry for what you did to her?"

"Oh Jesus . . . oh Jesus God, I'm sorry. I never meant for it to be that way . . . I promise I never meant for it to turn out like it did . . . it was a wild night, it was crazy, there were all these people and we drank too much and took too much coke, and things just got out of hand—"

"Ssshhh," I whispered. "Ssshhh now, Ricky, it's okay . . . it really is okay."

Richard Ricardo opened his eyes and looked up at me. There was a pleading expression in his eyes—pleading for understanding, for mercy, for his life.

"Never again," he mumbled. "Never again . . ."

"Too right," I said, and with all the force I could muster I raised the gun and brought it down on the top of his head.

The sound was indescribable, as if his whole body had collapsed from within—"Nyuuuggghhhh." He fell sideways and rolled off the edge of the bed onto the floor. Blood started to ooze from the split in his skull and soak into the carpet.

Lenny started screaming. I reached across the bed and grabbed him by the hair. I forced him face down into the mattress to muffle the sound, and then I warned him that if he didn't shut the hell up he was going to get a bullet in the back of his neck. He stopped immediately.

I dragged him off the bed, and threw him to the floor next to his friend.

In my hand I held a pillow.

I looked down at Lenny, his tear-streaked face, his wide and horrified eyes.

"When was your birthday?" I asked him.

He looked at me in dismay.

"Your birthday?" I repeated.

"Jan-January," he stuttered.

I nodded. I held up the pillow. I pressed the gun into it. "Last fucking birthday you're ever gonna have," I said, and I pulled the trigger.

The bullet hit him in the throat. His hands grasped his neck. He clawed at his own flesh as if believing that he could pull the bullet out. Blood erupted from the wound and spattered across his chest, his legs, across Ricardo, and then he fell sideways and lay on the floor. His body shook for some time. I stood there and watched him until he stopped.

Ricardo stirred.

I let fly with a mighty kick to his chest and he went still. I leaned down, pressed the pillow against the side of his head, and shot him through the temple.

An hour and a half later I stood in my bedroom looking down at the sleeping forms of my wife and my children. I leaned forward and kissed them—all three in turn—gently on their foreheads. I held my breath. I did not wish to make a sound that might wake them.

I left the room. I walked downstairs. I washed my hands and face at the kitchen sink, and then I sat for a while in the darkness smoking a cigarette. When I was done I went through to the front and lay down on the sofa. I fell asleep there, slept like the dead, and when Angelina woke me it was gone seven in the morning. I was still fully dressed apart from my jacket and shoes.

"Come and have breakfast with us," she said quietly. She leaned down and kissed me. I rose and stood for a moment, and then I placed my arms around her and pulled her close.

In the kitchen the TV was playing silently. I said nothing when Richard Ricardo's face appeared on the screen, and also the face of his friend Leonard. I made no sound, I didn't even flinch, and when the anchorwoman reappeared I reached out and switched it off.

I ate my breakfast. I talked to my children even though I knew they could not understand a word I said. I felt unsettled, anxious. I did not feel good.

An hour or so later, having shaved and showered, and dressed in a clean shirt and a different suit, I left my house and walked three blocks to a diner. There I sat in silence, and with a cup of coffee in front of me and a cigarette in my hand, I watched people as they walked by the window and out into their lives.

Two of those lives were closed last night. Two of those lives—people of whom I knew nothing—were terminally closed. I did not question what I had done, nor why I had done it. I was asked to do something and I complied. This was the way of my world; the only world I knew.

It was the following day that I saw the newspaper. It was a day old, lying there innocuously on a chair at the back of Michael Cova's cousin's barbershop where I had stopped to have a haircut. I picked it up and turned it to the front page.

▪ TWO SLAIN IN BRUTAL HOLLYWOOD MURDER ▪

Son of Los Angeles Deputy Mayor shot

My breath stopped for a moment.
I looked at the images of the two men I had killed in the apartment.

Last night, in Hollywood, the son of Deputy Mayor John Alexander was murdered in a double slaying that has rocked the city of Los Angeles. Leonard Alexander, 22, was found murdered at the home of well-known celebrity fashion designer Richard Ricardo. Police Chief Karl Erickson was present at the scene, and made the following statement—

I read no further. I closed the paper and tossed it back onto the chair.
I got up and left the barbershop, walked two blocks with no particular purpose in mind, and then I turned around and retraced my steps.
For the first time in my life I imagined people were looking at me.
I found a phone booth on the next intersection, and I called long distance to New York. I reached Ten Cent with no difficulty.
"Ernesto?" he said, surprise evident in his voice.
"You heard what happened?"
"I did, yes . . . is there a problem?"
"A problem? The other man was the son of the Los Angeles deputy mayor."
There was silence at the other end of the line.
"Ten Cent?"
"I'm here, Ernesto."
"You heard what I said?"
"Yes, I heard you . . . what's the problem? Did someone see you at the building?"
"No, no one saw me at the building. Of course they didn't. But the kid was the son of the deputy mayor. They won't let this thing lie down."

"We know, we know Ernesto . . . but don't worry."

"Don't worry? Whaddya mean?"

"We're gonna take you out and send you someplace safe."

"Take me out?"

Ten Cent laughed. "Take you out . . . yes, take you out of LA, not *take you out* for Christ's sake! Don't worry, Don Calligaris understands the situation, and he's not gonna leave you there."

"He is upset about the other man?"

Ten Cent laughed again. "Upset? He's as happy as I've ever seen him. You know what he said? . . . he said, 'Two assholes for the price of one.' That's what he said."

I was quiet for a moment.

"Ernesto?"

"Yes."

"It's gonna be okay . . . I ain't never heard you scared before. It's gonna be fine . . . we'll have you outta there just as soon as Don Calligaris figures out where to put you. You sit tight. Do nothing, say nothing . . . we're gonna make it right, okay?"

"Okay, okay . . . don't let me down."

"I give you my word, Ernesto. You're as much family as anyone else."

I closed my eyes, I breathed deeply, I said "Okay," and then I hung up the phone.

I walked home like a man lost. I walked home scared. Ten Cent had been right; this was a new feeling, and the feeling was difficult to comprehend.

It came back to family. Now there wasn't just me, now I was a responsible man, a man who carried the burden of a wife and children, carried it willingly, yes, there was no question about that, but it made everything so different.

Angel was waiting when I arrived home.

"The children are asleep," she said, and then she turned and walked through to the kitchen. It was obvious she wished me to follow her, and I did without question.

I sat at the table while she made coffee. I smoked a cigarette, something I had refrained from doing at home since the children had been there, but in that moment there was a sense of nausea and tension within me that it was hard to assuage.

Angelina placed the coffee in front of me and sat opposite.

She reached out and took my hand. She held it for a moment, and then she looked directly at me and smiled.

"Something has changed, hasn't it?" she asked.

I nodded but did not speak.

"I'm not going to ask about it, Ernesto . . . I trust you, always have done, and I know you wouldn't have done something unless there had been a very good reason for it. But I am not crazy, and I am not stupid, and I understand enough about the way our family is to know that whatever might have happened it isn't something you will talk about."

I opened my mouth to speak.

"No, Ernesto, you will listen to what I have to say."

I closed my mouth and looked down at the table.

"Whatever this thing is," she said, "I want you to tell me if it has endangered the lives of our children."

I shook my head. "No Angelina, it has not."

"You would not lie to me Ernesto, I know that, but this time I am going to ask you to give me an answer, and whatever the truth might be I want to know. Tell me now if this thing will endanger the lives of our children."

"No," I said quietly, and I shook my head once more. "It will not."

"Okay," she said, and her very being communicated her relief. "So, what does it mean for us?"

"It means we will have to move soon," I said. "We will have to go to another city and make our home all over again."

Angelina did not say anything for some time, and then once again she squeezed my hand. I looked up and there were tears in her eyes. "I married you because I loved you," she said. "I knew who you were, I knew enough about the people you worked with to know how this life would be, and if we have to move then I will come with you, but I will ask one thing of you and I want you to give me your word."

"Ask it, Angel, ask it."

"I want you to promise me that nothing will ever happen to Victor and Lucia . . . that is the only thing I ask of you, and I want you to promise me that."

I reached out and took both her hands. I held them for a moment, and then I touched her cheek, with my fingers, wiped away the streaked tears that were trailing down it.

"I promise," I said. "I promise on my life that nothing will ever happen to them."

She smiled. She bowed her head, and when she looked up she was smiling. "I wanted to stay here, Ernesto . . . in California. I wanted the children to feel sunshine on their faces and swim in the sea—"

She stifled her tears and was quiet for some moments.

She looked up at me again.

I felt my heart like a dead fist in my chest.

"How long do we have?" she asked.

"I don't know. They will tell me when they have a place for us."

"Not New York again, Ernesto . . . anywhere but New York, okay?"

"Okay," I said. "Okay."

We waited three months. The worst three months of my life. There was nothing for me to do. I was told to stay home, to be "a family man," and Ten Cent would call me to make arrangements when things were in place.

Three times, seated there at the window in the front of the house, I saw squad cars pass by slowly. I imagined they knew who I was, where they could find me, and they were just waiting for me to leave the house so they could follow me and make their arrest.

They never did. I left the house very infrequently, and by the time November arrived, by the time Ten Cent finally called and told me where we were going, I believed that I could not have stood another day in that place.

Angelina was the soul of patience. She became the perfect mother, investing every ounce of her attention, every second of her time, in the children. I watched her, I envied her ability to lose herself entirely in what she was doing, but I also realized that this was the only way she could cope with the situation I had created. I could have given her such a life, but I brought her to this. I felt bad for that, guilty, and I cursed the day I had been so eager to please Don Calligaris. He had said to kill one, but I had killed them both. That was my mistake, and I paid for it dearly.

"Chicago," the voice said at the end of the line. "Don Calligaris is moving to Chicago and taking a large part of our operation there. He wants you to be there with him, you understand?"

"I understand."

"You leave the day after tomorrow. Make your way out to O'Hare and I will meet you there."

I said nothing.

"Ernesto?"

"Yes?"

Ten Cent smiled; I could hear it in his voice. "Tell Angelina to pack some warm things for the kids . . . Chicago is a fucking icebox this time of year." He laughed and hung up the phone. I stood there with the burring sound in my ear and a cold stone inside my heart.

TWENTY

"WE HAVE NOTHING on the wife," Schaeffer said. "Not a single fucking thing."

"It's been twenty-four hours," Hartmann replied. "Even you guys can't expect miracles."

"And now we have two kids to find, not one. I cannot believe that with the most advanced, state-of-the-art security database systems in the world we cannot find any evidence of this woman having existed."

"But you're going off one name," Hartmann said. "And who's to say that the name he's using is actually his real name?"

Schaeffer didn't reply. He looked awkward for a moment. The most complex and advanced security database in the world was only as effective as the information given to it. Bullshit in, bullshit out—wasn't that the technical phrase?

Woodroffe stood up from the table in the main office. It was five of seven. Perez had been returned to the Royal Sonesta a little after six. Hartmann was aware of the fact that he had an appointment to keep with the man.

"So we get our answer tonight," Schaeffer said, and in his voice was a tone of philosophical resignation. Though it had not been discussed further, there was no doubt in Hartmann's mind that they were all fully aware of what that answer would be. Perez was not interested in a trade-off, and that had never been his purpose. It was that simple. Perez was here to make himself heard, and right now it seemed the whole world was listening.

"You guys are now looking into Ducane's involvement in these things, right?" Hartmann asked, and—truth be known—he believed he was asking it merely to stir up dissent.

Schaeffer shook his head. "Transcripts of everything Perez has said have been passed directly to the attorney general and the director of the FBI. It's their decision, not ours. Like I said before, and I'll say again, we are here to get the girl, not to involve ourselves in the comings and goings of corrupt politicians."

"Allegedly corrupt politicians," Hartmann said, his tone a little sarcastic.

Schaeffer nodded. "*Allegedly* corrupt politicians, right."

"Whaddya reckon?" Hartmann asked.

"About Ducane?" Schaeffer shook his head. "I've been too long in the FBI to be surprised about anything, Mr. Hartmann . . . and that's all I'm gonna say on the matter."

"So where from here?" Woodroffe asked.

"I go have some dinner with Perez," Hartmann said. "I hear him tell me how we can go stick our proposal up our collective asses, and then I go back to my hotel and get some sleep. I got a busy day tomorrow."

Woodroffe shook his head and sighed.

"Let's get it done then," Schaeffer said, and rose from his chair.

"Filet mignon," Perez said, and indicated a chair at the table in his room at the Sonesta. "It appears they have done a serviceable job. I shall perhaps recommend this hotel to some of my friends."

Hartmann removed his jacket and took a seat at the table. A cloth had been laid, there were candles, warm plates already in place and on a trolley beside them covered dishes emitted a number of very pleasant aromas.

Perez remained standing as he served dinner, as he offered vegetables, as he poured the wine, and when he too was seated he unfolded a napkin and laid it across his lap.

"I have considered your proposal," he said quietly, "and though I am in no way ungrateful for the concern of the attorney general and the director of the FBI about my welfare, I have decided, after long consideration, that I shall decline their offer."

"Long consideration?" Hartmann asked. He smiled knowingly. "You knew the answer to the question before it was even asked."

Perez shrugged. "Perhaps my consideration of the proposal served no other purpose than to enable us to spend a little time together this evening, Mr. Hartmann. We are both in the best company we can find at this particular juncture in our lives, and I felt it would be good to take advantage of it. I believe that we are both humble enough to realize that something mutually educational and beneficial can be gained from this relationship."

"I have learned something," Hartmann said.

Perez looked up. "Pray tell."

"That no matter the situation a person might find himself in there is always a choice, and dependent on that choice his life will advance or decline."

"You believe, of course, that I perpetually made the wrong decisions?"

"Yes, I do. I accept that you made your decisions based on what you believed at the time, but I consider that your beliefs were fundamentally wrong. Hindsight is a tremendously effective tool for determining the correctness of a man's decisions, but unfortunately it is always too late by the time you have that advantage."

"You are a closet philosopher, Mr. Hartmann."

"I am a closet realist, Mr. Perez."

Perez smiled. He speared a piece of steak and ate it. "And now?"

Hartmann raised his eyebrows.

"You have made a decision about your life from this point forward?"

"I have."

"And that is?"

Hartmann was quiet for a second. "I have come to the conclusion that there is no such thing as the perfect answer, Mr. Perez. I do not believe Man is capable of always selecting the perfect answer. What may be perfect in that moment will not necessarily be perfect five minutes later. There is always the ultimate variable."

"Variable?"

"People," Hartmann said. "The variable of people. The choices you made were, by their very nature, inherently connected to the people in your life. You believe you understand them well enough, especially if they are the people you live with, and you make choices based on what you consider will be not only the best for yourself, but also the best for them. The problem is that people change, people are unpredictable, and they have other factors that influence their opinions and viewpoints, and opinions and viewpoints are subject to change. The connections and interrelationships between people are tenuous and fickle, Mr. Perez, and thus I don't believe there will ever be a solution which is right for everyone involved simultaneously."

"You have made a decision about your own family?" Perez asked.

"I have."

"And?"

"To make it work . . . to do everything in my power to make it work."

"And you believe you can do that?"

"I *have* to believe it, or everything else becomes sort of pointless."

"And there is action that you can take?"

Hartmann did not speak.

"Mr. Hartmann?"

Hartmann looked up. "There was an action I was planning to take, but events have conspired to make that action perhaps impossible."

"Tell me."

"I was supposed to meet with my wife and daughter."

"Here?"

"No, in New York."

"When?"

"This Saturday at noon."

Perez paused for a second. He leaned back. He set his knife and fork down, took the napkin from his lap and wiped his mouth.

"And I have been the event that has conspired against you," he said quietly, almost sympathetically.

"You have . . . though I understand that there is significance to our meetings. Of course these events may not be as important to me as they are to you, but I have nevertheless made an agreement, and that is something I will stand by."

"There is your realist, Mr. Hartmann, the very thing that you are afraid of becoming."

"Afraid? How so?"

"To accept the fact that you can do nothing about this because of me is fatalist. A realist would take action regardless of other causes."

"I will take action."

"Action sufficient to repair whatever damage might be done by failing to meet your wife and daughter on Saturday?"

"I believe so, yes."

Perez nodded. He placed the napkin on his lap once more and lifted his knife and fork. "So be it," he said. "I believe you will take whatever action is necessary and deal with the situation effectively."

Hartmann looked at Perez and saw that this line of conversation would go no further. He continued to eat, though eating was the last thing on his mind, and when he was done they spoke more—of music, of art, of philosophy—but Hartmann knew that it was all a pretense, a face Perez was wearing for the world, a means by which he could talk without saying anything at all. He wished to reserve his revelations for the FBI office. This was the way he wanted it, and this was what he accomplished.

Hartmann left a little before eight-thirty. He met Woodroffe and Schaeffer in the downstairs foyer. They had been party to all that had been discussed in Perez's hotel room, and already Perez's response had been relayed to the attorney general and the director of the FBI.

"Still nothing on the wife," Woodroffe told Hartmann. "We can only assume that both the names, Perez and Tiacoli, are assumed. There is no record of any woman with those names ever having been born, resident, married, divorced or anything else in the mainland United States. But we keep looking," he added, "and we keep looking until we have something better to look for."

"And Criminalistics and Forensics have come up with nothing else to help us? And the teams of people you sent out to search the different routes in and out of the city?" Hartmann asked. "Nothing that gives any kind of indication of where he might have her?"

Woodroffe shook his head. "Absolutely zip."

"You got people tearing their hair out."

"I got people tearing *my* hair out," Woodroffe said, and for the first time Hartmann saw how utterly exhausted these people were— mentally, physically, emotionally. Upon this their entire futures could rest, and that was something Hartmann had never really taken into consideration. He had only considered how this affected him. Perhaps here he had found another lesson worth learning.

"I'm going," Hartmann said. "Gotta get some rest."

"I didn't know this thing about your wife," Schaeffer commented.

Hartmann shrugged. "What's there to tell? I screwed it up . . . up to me to un-screw it up as best I can."

"Good luck," Schaeffer said.

Hartmann nodded. "Need as much as I can get."

"Don't we all?" Schaeffer replied, and then he smiled, and as Hartmann turned toward the door he said, "Sleep good, eh?" and Hartmann realized that when he saw Schaeffer the following morning the man would probably have not slept at all.

From the Royal Sonesta he drove across town to Verlaine's Precinct. Verlaine was off-shift but the desk sergeant called his mobile and put Hartmann on the line.

"You ready for this?" Hartmann asked.

"As ever," Verlaine replied. "You wanna meet me somewhere?"

"Where?"

"You know the Orleans Star? Bar in the Vieux Carre near Tortorici's Italian."

"Yes, I can find it."

"Meet you there in about twenty minutes. I can call her from my cellphone . . . that way she can't get Information to track the landline back to New Orleans."

"See you there," Hartmann said, and he hung up.

"So whaddya want me to say?" Verlaine asked.

They were seated in Verlaine's car across the street from the bar. Hartmann hadn't wanted to go inside, firstly because Carol would have heard the music in the background and figured him to be somewhere where he shouldn't have been, and secondly because Hartmann did not want to tempt himself with liquor. What was it Perez had said: a temptation resisted is the true measure of character? Something such as that.

"Tell her you're a police officer, that you're not from New York, that there's a federal investigation ongoing and I am a very necessary part of it. Tell her I am quite some distance away and there's a very strong possibility that I might not make it back to New York for Saturday."

"You gonna want to talk to her?" Verlaine asked.

"Don't reckon she'll wanna talk to me," Hartmann said.

"Gimme the number."

Hartmann gave him the number. Verlaine dialed it.

Hartmann sat there with a sweat breaking out on his forehead. His hands were shaking, he could feel his heart hammering through his chest. He felt like a teenager all over again.

"Carol Hartmann? Hi, my name is John. I am a detective with the police department.

"No ma'am, there's nothing wrong, I'm actually calling on a personal matter.

"Yes, about your husband. He's actually away from New York right now, quite a distance away, and he's become involved in a very important federal investigation, and—"

Verlaine glanced at Hartmann. "Yes ma'am, he is."

Verlaine nodded, looked at Hartmann again. "She wants to talk to you."

Hartmann could not contain his surprise. Verlaine passed him the phone and Hartmann took it. His hand was visibly shaking.

"Carol?"

No Ray, it's the Archangel bloody Gabriel. What the hell is this all about?

"Like John said. I got myself into something down here—"

Down where?

"I can't tell you, Carol . . . but there's a federal investigation going on—"

Since when?

"Since a few days ago . . . and I'm away from New York right now and I wanted to call you and tell you that I might not be able to make it back before Saturday."

So why the hell didn't you call me? Why are you getting some guy I never heard of to call me?

"Because I was afraid you might not believe me, Carol."

Aah come on Ray, you know me better than that. A drunk you might be—

"*Been*, Carol . . . a drunk I might have *bee—*"

Well, that remains to be seen. Anyway, a drunk you might have been but you were never a liar. We've been married a good many years, Ray, and I know you better than anyone on the face of the earth. So what's the deal then? When are you coming back?

"I don't know."

You must have some idea . . . a week, two, a month?

"No, no idea . . . I don't think it will be as long as that but right now it's unknown."

And you can't tell me anything about it, obviously.

"Right."

Well, okay then . . . it is what it is. You do whatever you have to do, and when you get back to New York call me and I'll see how I feel. I had my doubts about us meeting anyway—

"Doubts?" Hartmann said, anxiety tripping his voice. "What doubts?"

I'm not going to do this now, Ray . . . not on the phone while you've got some guy sitting next to you. You call me when you get back to New York and if we meet . . . well, we'll see how things are when you call, okay? You want to speak to Jess?

Hartmann nearly dropped the phone. "Hell yes . . . Jesus Carol . . . thanks."

Christ Ray, what the hell is up with you? You act like I've forgotten you're her father. Hang on there . . . I'll go get her.

Hartmann looked at Verlaine. "My daughter," he said, and Verlaine nodded and smiled.

Daddy?

"Hi sweetpea . . . how are you?"

I'm fine, Daddy. How are you doing?

"I'm okay, honey . . . you looking after Mom for me?"

That's not my job, Daddy, that's yours. So when you coming home?

"Soon I hope, Jess, real soon. I called to say that I couldn't get there for Saturday, but I'm gonna call Mom as soon as I get back to New York and we'll meet up, okay?"

You're not coming Saturday?

"I can't, honey." Hartmann felt his voice cracking with emotion.

Oh Dad, we were gonna have a picnic an' everything.

"I know sweetheart, but I gotta do something and I don't think it will take long, and when it's done I'll come back to New York and we can see each other."

Tell whoever it is that they should give you a day off so you can come and see us.

"I would if I could, you know that, Jess . . . but right now there's this thing I gotta finish and I'll be right back, okay?"

I miss you, Dad.

"I miss you too, sweetpea, but it won't be long, I promise."

You mean it this time?

"I mean it, Jess . . . I *really* do mean it."

Okay Dad. Don't be long, okay? Here's Mom.

"Okay Jess . . . I love you, honey. Daddy really, really loves you."

Ray?

"Carol."

We gotta go . . . I got to get her to bed.

"Okay Carol . . . and thanks."

Whatever . . .

"I love you, Carol."

I don't doubt it, Ray, and never have . . . but the old saying is true.

"The old saying?"

Yes, Ray, the one about actions speaking louder than words. Whichever way you look at it we made an agreement for Saturday, and that ain't gonna happen right now. I'm pissed with you about that and I know Jess is upset. That makes me pissed twice as much. I know whatever I say ain't gonna change what you've decided to do, and the fact of the matter is that the more I think about it the more I feel that most of our married life went on that prem-ise. You have a think about that, and if you decide that what we've got is worth salvaging enough then I believe you'll make it here on Saturday. If not, well you won't, right?

Hartmann was struck dumb.

I'll tell Jess goodnight for you, okay?

"Carol—"

I'm taking her to bed, Ray . . . I don't have anything else to say.

The line went dead and Hartmann sat there with the cellphone pressed against his ear for some seconds. There were tears in his eyes, a fist of emotion in his throat, and when he turned and handed the phone back to Verlaine he said nothing.

"It's gonna be okay," Verlaine said. "Hell, she let you talk to your kid, right?"

Hartmann nodded. He wiped his eyes with the ball of his thumb. He reached for the lever and opened the door.

"Thanks John," he said as he started to climb out of the car.

"Hey," Verlaine called after him.

Hartmann looked back over his shoulder.

"You're gonna come out of this fine," Verlaine said. "Believe me, I've seen worse. The trick is to keep breathing, right?"

Hartmann smiled. "Right," he said. "The trick is to just keep breathing."

He slept better. That much at least. And he did not dream. And when Ross came to collect him in the morning Ray Hartmann just held onto the memory of his daughter's voice. Amidst everything—the madness, the killing, the brutality of everything he was hearing, everything he was witness to—that memory seemed like his only anchor in the storm.

Schaeffer and Woodroffe were no further forward on identifying Perez's wife and children, and all of them—even if unspoken—knew that that line of investigation was a hide into nowhere. None of them voiced it because none of them wanted to lose any more hope. There was little enough to go around. First twenty-four hours were the most important in a missing persons case. They knew that as well as they knew their own names. Within another twenty-four hours Catherine Ducane would have been gone for two weeks.

Her time was running out.

Perhaps it had vanished already.

And then Perez arrived with his escort, and he was shown down to the office where Hartmann was already waiting for him. He removed his coat and handed it to Sheldon Ross, and Ross closed the door gently behind him.

"Mr. Hartmann," Perez said quietly as he sat down in the small office at the back of the building. "Have a cup of coffee and let me tell you what happened in Chicago."

"I have had two cups of coffee already, Mr. Perez."

"To stay awake?" Perez asked.

Hartmann waved the question aside. "You need to tell us what is happening here, Mr. Perez," he said.

Perez frowned. "Happening here, Mr. Hartmann? What is happening here is that I am going to tell you about Chicago—"

"You understand what I mean—" Hartmann started.

Perez leaned forward. His expression was cold and aloof. "You will listen to me," he said quietly. "You will listen to what I have to say and then I will tell you where she is."

Hartmann shook his head. "We need to know that she is at least alive, Mr. Perez."

"*We* need to know?" Perez asked. "And who would *we* be, Mr. Hartmann? Is this simply a matter of your own situation—"

"Enough," Hartmann interjected. He could sense Schaeffer beyond the door. He knew that there was nothing he could say to impress upon Perez the frustration and anger he was feeling. Everything was closed up inside, everything tight and breathless, and he knew that whatever he said there was no way around this. Perez would tell them what he wanted *when* he wanted, and that was the bottom line.

"So tell me," Hartmann said. "Tell me what happened in Chicago."

Perez nodded and leaned back in his chair. "Okay," he said, and for a moment he closed his eyes as if in concentration.

When he opened them he looked back at Ray Hartmann, and for the first time in all the hours they had spent together Hartmann believed there was a spark of real emotion inside the man, like something had welled up inside him and was ready to burst.

"Family," he started. "It was, and always will be, everything to do with family."

TWENTY-ONE

"**N**OW HERE," DON Calligaris said, "*here* you got some fucking history." He laughed. He seemed in good humor. Three days we had been in Chicago, Angelina and me, the kids, all of us installed in a house on Amundson Street. Don Calligaris, Ten Cent, a couple of other guys who were part of the original Alcatraz Swimming Team back in Miami, were in a house across the street. *We got our own little neighborhood*, Don Calligaris kept saying, like he was trying to convince himself that whatever he had left behind in New York wasn't as good as this. I did not ask why he had left; I did not care to know; all that mattered was that my family was out of Los Angeles, and Chicago—bitterly cold, its vicious wind that rushed in from the edge of Lake Michigan seeming to find you wherever you hid—was an awful lot better than living with your eyes in the back of your head.

"So here, here in Chicago," Don Calligaris went on, "is where a great deal of American people get their ideas about the family. The whole prohibition thing, and the way that politics ran down here at the beginning of the century, you know? Big Bill Thompson and Mont Tennes, and then out of New York the man himself, Al Capone. You heard of Al Capone?"

"Sure I heard of Al Capone," I said.

Don Calligaris smiled.

I thought of Angelina and the children. She was out somewhere, walking them in the park or some such. I was here, in Don Calligaris's house, when I wanted to be with them. I felt more and more that I was leading two separate and irreconcilable lives.

"Capone was born in Brooklyn, was part of a street gang called the Five Pointers," Don Calligaris said. "One of the gang bosses back then, a guy called Frankie Yale, he recognized a certain quality in Al and put him to work as a meeter and greeter at this dime-a-dance club called the Harvard Inn on Coney Island. Then Al Capone starts to get ideas of his own. He starts to act outside his authority, and he kills one of

Wild Bill Lovett's White Hand Gang. He knows he's gotta get out of there before Frankie Yale gets him whacked so he leaves New York. He was twenty then, maybe twenty-one, and he comes to Chicago to work for Big Jim Colosimo. Big Jim was the heaviest operator of hookers in Chicago, made a shitload of money, but he didn't wanna get into the liquor business. Someone shot him in the Wabash Avenue Cafe, and word has it that it may have been Capone who did that."

I watched Don Calligaris as he talked. He was speaking of his ancestors, if not by blood then by trade and reputation. Fabio Calligaris wanted to be ranked alongside these people; I could tell by the tone of pride in his voice as he spoke. He wanted to be remembered, for what I didn't know, but he wanted his name alongside Capone and Luciano and Giancana. Don Calligaris would never be anything but an underboss, powerful in his own way and with his own reputation and recognition, but he lacked the necessary ruthlessness to take him to the top.

"Johnny Torrio took over Colosimo's rackets, and with Capone's help they established breweries in preparation for the big thirst. They knew what was coming, they saw the opportunity, and they took it with both hands. Smart guy, Johnny Torrio . . . he worked to stop all the Chicago gangs fighting between themselves and gave them individual turfs. He gave the northside to Dion O'Banion, but the majority of the city belonged to Torrio and Capone, and by 1924 they were carving up the better part of a hundred grand between them every single goddamned week."

Don Calligaris laughed. I wanted to use the head but I didn't want to interrupt him in full flow. He was in his element; he seemed more at ease than I ever remembered him. Maybe there was something in New York that was shadowing him and he had escaped, just as I had from Los Angeles.

"Capone put someone up for Mayor of Cicero, and Cicero became the power base for the liquor operations. Things had never been as smooth as silk between Torrio and Capone and O'Banion, and then in late 1924 O'Banion gave the word on a brewery operation. The police raided the place, arrested Torrio, and he was fined five grand and sentenced to nine months. O'Banion got himself whacked in his flower shop a little while later. Northside gang took a new boss, a Polack called Hymie Weiss, and they went back for Capone and tried to off him and Torrio. They escaped, but Weiss wasn't a man to quit, and they went after Torrio again the same day and shot him five times. Torrio didn't die, but he was all fucked up, and he went to jail to do his nine months looking like the fucking invisible man. Couple of weeks after Torrio got out they hit Weiss and killed him. Guy called Bugs Moran came in to run the northside after Weiss was killed. He ran the operation from a garage on Clark Street. Capone sent a couple of his people, guys by the name of Albert Anselmi and John Scalisi, down there. He dressed them up as police officers. They had seven of Moran's crew lined up against the wall and they killed 'em. St Valentine's Day Massacre they called it, and later on Capone got Anselmi and Scalisi whacked.

Bunch of businessmen went to see President Hoover at the end of the '20s. They asked him to repeal prohibition and take out Capone. Hoover assigned a guy called Elliot Ness to the Chicago PD. Ness was a Treasury Department guy, but he was a tough bastard by all accounts. He went after Capone, but he never actually got him. That was when they came up with the idea of hitting him for tax evasion, and finally they arrested him in 1931. Capone did a couple of years in Atlanta and then they shipped him to Alcatraz."

Don Calligaris sipped his coffee and lit another cigarette. The room seemed full of smoke, and each time I looked toward the window I thought of Angelina and the children. I wanted to be away from here, outside with the people I cared for, not trapped inside this house listening to old war stories.

"Capone's gang . . . hell of a gang, you know? That's where people like the Fischetti brothers, Frank Nitti and Sam Giancana came from. Nitti was the one who took over control when Capone went down, and he and a bunch of others were indicted for extorting money out of some studios in Hollywood. Frank didn't wanna go down, he didn't wanna testify against his family, so he shoots himself in the fucking head with a .38. Then Tony Accardo took over and moved Chicago's interests into Vegas and Reno, and he stayed until '57 when he stepped down in favor of Giancana. Giancana was boss 'til '66, did a year in jail, and then he came out and was living the high life until '75 by which time everyone had gotten sick of his bullshit. He got himself whacked, and then there was a whole bunch of assholes fighting over who should be boss so Tony Accardo comes back. He's boss here now, and he's who we're gonna be working with. He's an old-timer, a very smart guy, and he wants us to keep some areas of his operations in line so he can spend his time making new friends and gaining some territories. That's where you and I come in. I had to come down here, and I wanted some people with me who I could trust to do the necessary things, right?"

"Right," I said.

Don Calligaris smiled. "So how's it goin' with you and Angelina? How's it to be a father now, Ernesto?"

I smiled back. Every time I thought of Angelina and the children there was a feeling of warmth and certainty. "It's good, very good. It's a helluva thing."

"Tell me about it. Nothing more important than family, you know? Nothing in this world is more important than family, but you gotta keep your priorities right, you gotta keep your head straight and your eyes going both the same way. You gotta remember how you came by what you got and that you owe your dues."

He was speaking of Don Alessandro, Don Giacalone and Tony Provenzano, the people who had given their blessing for me to marry inside the family, albeit an unspoken connection; the fact that Angelina Tiacoli was born out of a relationship that brought the death of her parents and a sense of shame to the Alessandros, but family all the same.

Don Calligaris was warning me that whatever might have been given me could just as easily be taken away. I heard what he said and I understood it. I had no intention of displeasing these people; they were an awful lot more powerful than me, and wherever I might have run to, wherever I might have taken Angelina and the kids, the influence and communication lines of this family spanned the entirety of the United States, even as far as the Florida Keys and Cuba, and they would have found us. A man alone, perhaps just myself, I could have become lost. But with a wife and two small children there wasn't a prayer. The simple truth was that there was nothing I would knowingly do to jeopardize what I had created with Angelina and the children. They were everything; they were my life.

"I know the score, Don Calligaris . . . I understand the way things work. That thing in LA turned out a mess, but it got done."

Calligaris nodded. "It got done, Ernesto, that's the main thing, and I appreciate it. All of that is behind us now. We all have things we would change if we were given the time again, but it's all water under the bridge, you know? We deal with whatever we have to, and then we move on. This is why coming here to Chicago is a good thing. It gives both of us a chance to make things better. There are important things happening here. It is a new start. We make it work for ourselves and for the family, and we do what we have to do."

Once again I recognized the unspoken in his words. Something had happened in New York to prompt his departure. He would not tell me; Don Calligaris was a man who gave out information only when it was needed. I did not ask, it was not my place to ask, and had I done so he would have been both offended and annoyed.

Ten Cent came into the room. It was good to see him. We had years behind us, and though he was much more part of this family than I was, he was nevertheless a man I felt I could trust. He treated me as an equal, as much a part of this as himself, and I believed that whatever might happen he could always be depended upon.

"So we relax for a few days," Don Calligaris said. "We take it easy. I go see a couple of folks, we get some things worked out, and then we wait and see what kind of work they're gonna require of us."

I stayed a little while longer. I talked with them of nothing consequential. Ten Cent asked about the children, said he would come down later that day and have some dinner with us. I was happy for him to come. Angelina liked him, the children just seemed to laugh when he was around, and with him in my house I always felt a sense of reassurance that nothing would come to harm us. That was the way it was then— knowing who would stand beside you, who would stand behind. Always present, even as you slept, was the certainty that no one was defensible, there was no one who could not be reached. These people took out their own if it served the purpose of the family, and though I had my connections, though I had given them loyalty and support for the better part of twenty-five years, my life would be gone in a second if I crossed the lines. I did not intend to do such a thing. It was the furthest thing from my mind. But I was not naïve, I was learned and wise in the customs and mores of this business. Business was business, and clipping someone was as significant as giving him a haircut if requirements dictated.

The first call came on Monday 22 November, three days before Thanksgiving.

"It's time," Ten Cent said. "Come to the house."

I walked back from the front hallway to where Angelina sat in the kitchen with the children. They were six months old by then, growing by inches each day, it seemed, and only the previous day Lucia had uttered her first barely identifiable word.

"Da . . . da . . . da," she'd said, and reached out her arms toward me. That simple action, the sound that had accompanied it, had brought tears to my eyes.

"You away for long?" Angelina asked.

I shook my head. "I don't know."

She looked distressed. "You tell Fabio Calligaris from me that you are a husband and a father now, and he shouldn't be involving you in anything that will cause trouble."

What she meant, though she could never have brought herself to say it, was that I should tell Don Calligaris to leave me in an office somewhere counting stacks of dollar bills, that he shouldn't be sending me out to engage in actions that would risk my life.

I told her I would pass on her message, but I knew, and she knew also, that no such message would ever reach him.

I reached over and touched the side of her face. She turned her face and kissed my palm.

"It will be okay," I whispered.

"Will it?" she asked. "You promise?"

I nodded. "I promise."

"On the lives of your children, Ernesto?"

"Don't ask me that, Angel."

"Then give me your word, as my husband and as their father."

"I give you my word."

"Then go, do whatever you have to do . . . I will see you when you come home."

I kissed my children. I went upstairs. I put on a clean shirt and tie, a suit, an overcoat. I took my .38 from a bundle of socks at the bottom of the dresser, and I tucked it into the waistband of my pants. I lit a cigarette and stood there for a moment looking out through the window into the street. Cars went by, carrying people who knew nothing of my world and all it entailed. They were blissful in their ignorance, and I envied them that.

Downstairs once more, I stood on the lowest riser from where I could see through into the kitchen. Angelina busied herself around the children, feeding them, cleaning up after them, and there was an emotion I felt as I watched her that could never have been defined. It was beyond love. It was beyond the physical and emotional. I believed that it was something spiritual. I thought of something happening that might take all of this away, and for the first time in as long as I could recall I experienced a moment of such deep, profound panic that I had to hold onto the banister so as not to lose my balance. I closed my eyes and breathed deeply. I willed myself to think of nothing negative.

I shook my head, and once more looked down into the kitchen. Angelina had moved out of sight, but the children were there, both of them wide-eyed and smiling. Neither of them could see me, but in their expressions was something that I believed I would never achieve for myself. A sense of true happiness, of peace perhaps, and I wondered if ever there would be a time I could escape this life and take them away from my past.

I breathed deeply. I stepped down and walked along the hallway to the front door. I let myself out quietly, and closed the door behind me.

Don Calligaris was waiting for me in the kitchen of his house. With him were two men I had not seen before. The older man had red hair speckled with gray at the temples, the other, jet-black eyes that looked like the coals one would use to make a snowman.

Ten Cent came into the room behind me and we all sat at the table near the window.

"There's a lot of history here," Don Calligaris said, "and a great deal of it goes back to Dion O'Banion. There was bad blood back then in Prohibition, but bad blood runs good with time, and the northside, the turf that Johnny Torrio gave to O'Banion and the Irish gangs, is still a good part Irish. We are here to work out some things, because Tony Accardo wants us to work with the Irish and make the northside more profitable. You got hookers down there, right?"

The older, redheaded man nodded.

"And there's the narcotics and gambling, even the slot machines are owned by the Irish, and they need a little help handling some details that are jeopardizing their territory."

The two men signaled agreement but said nothing.

"This man," Don Calligaris said, indicating the older of the two, "is Gerry McGowan, and this man here is his son-in-law Daniel Ryan. Mr. McGowan—"

"It's Gerry," McGowan said. "No one calls me Mr. McGowan save the fuckin' priest." He laughed. His accent was Irish-American, a thick brogue, and when he smiled I could see that three of his front teeth were half-capped with gold.

"Gerry works for a man called Kyle Brennan, and Mr. Brennan is the boss of the Irish family."

"Known as the Cicero Gang," Gerry McGowan said, "seein' as how Mr. Brennan's family comes from Cicero, see."

"Mr. Brennan owns most of the land that verges on the business quarter," Don Calligaris explained, "and there are some Chicago business people who have applied to the Mayor's Office to have the land claimed back as part of Chicago city territory. They wanna make some developments, tear down the old buildings where much of Mr. Brennan's business is transacted, and Mr. Brennan needs some help sorting these matters out. We have been asked, as a show of good faith and friendship, to help work out these problems and make them go away."

"Who's back of it?" I asked.

"Asshole goes by the name of Paul Kaufman," McGowan said venomously. "Jew motherfucker from back east who's come down here to make waves. He's some bigshot city business type, no wife, no kids, maybe forty-five years old, and he's got all the dollars in the world behind him. He's into stocks and bonds and investment things, figures he can force Chicago City Council to flatten the back end of the northside so's he can put up a shitload of office blocks and apartment buildings."

"And who's his contact in the City?"

"Senior Development Officer he is . . . goes by the name of David Hackley. The plans that Kaufman has submitted have to go through him, but he doesn't get the final say-so. That comes to a board meeting of the Chicago City Council in January of next year, but Hackley is a serious contender, and whatever he advises is what the board is gonna recommend. If he says go then they'll go, and there ain't gonna be a thing we can do about it."

"So Hackley's the man," I said. "You remove the connection between Kaufman and the City Council and he'll be back at square one."

"Well, maybe," Daniel Ryan interjected. "It ain't so simple as just whacking Hackley. You take Hackley out of the picture and they'll just dust themselves down and get someone else in there who'll give the word. What you gotta do is make sure that Hackley advises against the redevelopment plans . . . and he has to *really* advise against them, like he has to tell the Council that redeveloping the area would be a bad thing for Chicago."

"But he ain't gonna do that, is he?" I asked; a rhetorical question.

Gerry McGowan smiled. "Not unless he's got a very good reason to do what we want, right?"

"Right," I said. "But I don't think this is gonna be a matter of breaking into his house and beating the crap outta him . . . this ain't gonna fly with strong-arm tactics. This is politics, right? Politics is what got him where he is and politics has to be the thing that takes him out."

"Whichever way it goes, but we need Hackley silenced before the middle of next month, because that's when he puts his final case before the Council. They'll be away through Christmas sure, but when they meet again in January they'll have had all the time in the world to consider the proposal, and I'm sure there's gonna be plenty of sweeteners for these folks courtesy of Jewish hospitality."

"We know anything useful about Hackley?" Don Calligaris asked.

"Seems clean as driven fucking snow. Wife, three kids, married only once. Doesn't use drugs or hookers, doesn't gamble, doesn't drink liquor by all accounts. Real hardworking all-American fucking genius from what I gather."

"Everyone has their Achilles heel," I said.

McGowan smiled with his gold teeth. "Sure as shit they do, but we been looking around this guy for the better part of three months and we ain't found nothin'."

I shrugged. "Man doesn't have an Achilles heel, then you make one for him."

McGowan nodded. "Well, that's what we're here for, and if you sort this matter out then the Irishers and the Ities are gonna get along just fine."

"You go back to Mr. Brennan," I said. "Go back with our blessing and goodwill. Tell him he sent you to see the right people, that we will take care of this matter for you, and that by the middle of next month Hackley will stand up before the Chicago City Council Board and tell them that redeveloping the northside would be the very worst thing that they could do."

McGowan smiled. "I have your word on that?"

I stood up. I extended my hand. McGowan rose also and shook with me. "You have my word," I said. "You have the word of Don Calligaris's family it will be done."

McGowan grinned from ear to ear. "This," he said, "is the kind of business we like to do."

Don Calligaris rose also. "So," he said, "let's eat."

That night, McGowan and Ryan long since gone, I sat with Don Calligaris in the back room and we spoke.

"You gave the word of the family," he said. "I understand why you did that, and that is what they came here for, but now you have said this you cannot go back to them and tell them it cannot be done."

"It will be done, Don Calligaris."

"You're so sure?"

"I am."

"How? How can you be so sure, Ernesto?"

"Because when I say I'm gonna do something I'll do it."

"I have to trust you," Don Calligaris said.

"Yes, you have to trust me . . . and have I ever let you down?"

He shook his head. "No, you have never let me down."

"This is important, right?"

Don Calligaris leaned back in his chair. "I left New York for a reason," he said. "I am not going to tell you the reason because it is not important now, but the fact of the matter is that something that should have been done was not done and it caused some trouble for the family. In a way I am lucky to be alive . . . but then I never believed in luck. I am alive because I am valuable, because I am a made man, and once you are made there is no way you can be removed without the express permission of the head of the family. Tony Ducks, Don Corallo, did not want me out of the family, but he sent me here to make things good, to pay my dues." Don Calligaris looked away for a moment, and then looked back at me. "Sometimes we all arrive at a point where we have to make something good, where we have to pay the dues, you know. Anyway, this thing, this thing with the Irish family, we will make this work and I will have paid my dues, I will have served my time in the wilderness if you like. You say you can do this then I need you to do it. I need you to carry through with your word and the word of the family and make this happen. If you do this then I will owe you my life in a way, and there will come a time when you need something from me and I will make it happen. You understand, Ernesto?"

"Yes, I understand, and I will make this happen, and the Irish family will keep the northside, and you will be able to go home."

Don Calligaris rose and stretched out his arms. I rose also and he hugged me tight.

"You do this, and in my eyes you will be a made man, Ernesto Perez, crazy Cuban motherfucker or not."

He laughed. I laughed also.

I left after a little while, and even though I would now have to dedicate myself to ruining someone's reputation, to ruining someone's life more than likely, there was a sense of exhilaration in my heart. I did not have to kill anyone. That was the reason I had given my word. I would never have spoken such a thing, would never have told Don Calligaris my reason, but the fact of the matter was that I *wanted* to do this, to make this thing right, because I would walk away without any more blood on my hands.

That night I slept soundly. I did not dream. I did not fear for the safety of my family. And when I rose the next morning even Angelina noticed a difference in my manner.

"Things went well yesterday?" she asked.

"Yes, Angelina, they went well."

"You have some work to do?"

"Yes, there is some work to do."

"But it is safe," she said matter-of-factly.

"Yes, it is safe . . . you needn't worry for yourself or the children."

"And you? Need I worry for you, Ernesto?"

"No, nor for me. I have some things to do but it is business that can be done with words. You understand?"

"I understand."

She did not mention it again; she asked me no more questions. The subject was closed, and I sensed in her attitude a deep relief and confidence that everything, just *everything*, was going to be alright. What she could never know, and never hope to understand, was the significance of this situation for me. I would perform an action, I would resolve this matter, and the simple truth was that no one would die. I, Ernesto Cabrera Perez, would go out to fix something and kill no one.

It seemed that Gerry McGowan had been right; I watched the comings and goings of David Hackley for the better part of a week and he seemed the model American citizen. I hated him for it. I had given my word. I had little more than two weeks, and before five days had passed I wondered what in fuck's name I was gonna do.

I remembered then something Don Ceriano had told me many years before, about heading out for vengeance and digging two graves.

This matter was not one of vengeance, but one of territory, and with the word of the family and Don Calligaris's position in the balance, I could not do anything but make this work. If David Hackley did not possess an Achilles heel, then perhaps his son did.

I switched my attention to the young man. I staked out his office and his apartment. I watched him leave his work late at night and go home. I believed him for a while to be a younger version of his father, and there seemed to be nothing to identify any weak point in his life.

It was the beginning of December. I sat in my car a half block away from the exit of the apartment building where James Hackley lived, and I was set to start up the engine and go home when the door opened and the man himself appeared. He was dressed for the weather in a long overcoat, a scarf and gloves, and he hurried across the street to where his car was parked and climbed in.

I followed him a good two miles downtown, through the less wealthy areas of the city to the edge of the northside. Here he slowed, stopped on Machin Street, and after spending a few moments looking for something in his car he climbed out and started down the street. I followed him on foot a good fifteen yards behind, ever alert for the moment he would turn and glance back over his shoulder. He did not, and I watched as he crossed at the intersection and entered at the side door of a porn cinema on Penn Street. He was in the Cicero Gang's territory, right there in the heart of the area his own father was planning to demolish, and he was frequenting one of the cinemas more than likely owned by Kyle Brennan. Irony put a smile on my face. It did not give me what I wanted—hell, half of America's model citizens went to porn shows and strip clubs, and there wasn't a thing in the world that could be considered illegal about it, but it was something, it was a start, and a start, however small, was better than nothing at all.

I went into the cinema after him. I walked to the counter and asked after the young man that had just entered.

"And what the fuck business is it of yours?" an overweight greasy-vested man behind the counter said.

"Important business," I said. "I'm here on behalf of Gerry McGowan, and I need your assistance."

"Oh shit," the man said. "Oh shit, I'm sorry, mister . . . I didn't know Mr. McGowan was sending anyone down here tonight. I think we're all paid up . . . in fact I'm sure we are . . . let me call the boss down and you can have a word with him. Hell, what the fuck am I thinking? Come with me, come through here and up the stairs and you can speak with him yourself."

I followed the overweight guy as he heaved his vast girth up a narrow flight of stairs. We turned right at the top, and he knocked on a door.

"Come!" Someone shouted from within.

The fat guy went in. I followed him. We stood in a small but neatly decorated office, plain walls, a wide mahogany desk, behind it a smartly dressed man with the same dark hair and bright eyes as Daniel Ryan.

"Julie, what the fuck is this?" the man behind the desk said. "I'm busy up here . . . you should be on the desk downstairs making sure those asshole kids don't sneak in without payin'."

"Someone here," the fat guy said. "Someone from Mr. McGowan."

I stepped around Julie and faced the man behind the desk. He smiled. He came around and reached out his hand. "Hey, how goes it there?" he said. "Name's Michael Doyle . . . what can we do for you and Mr. McGowan?"

"I told him we were all paid up, Mr. Doyle . . . soon as he said he was from Mr. McGowan I told him we were all paid up," the fat guy said, nervousness evident in his voice.

"Okay Julie, okay . . . you don't mind yourself with this, you go on back down and tend to the desk, okay?"

"Okay Mr. Doyle," Julie said, and worked his width out through the doorway and thundered down the stairs.

"Not so easy to find good help these days, eh?" Michael Doyle said. He indicated a chair other side of the desk and asked me to sit down. I did so, and Doyle resumed his chair opposite. "So what can we be doin' for you an' Mr. McGowan?" he asked.

"You have a customer here, a man by the name of James Hackley."

Doyle shrugged. "Christ, I wouldn't know . . . sure as hell ain't my hobby to go associatin' with the people that come here to watch this stuff."

"He is the son of a very important Chicago real estate developer called David Hackley. Mr. McGowan needs your help to make something go away, and there's a good possibility it may involve putting his son in a somewhat embarrassing position."

Doyle laughed. "Well, I'd consider being found with your pants round your ankles in a joint like this somewhat embarrassing."

I shook my head. "Something a little closer to the bone," I said.

Doyle leaned back in his chair. "Something he wouldn't walk away from without it dirtying the family name a little?" he said.

"A lot," I replied. "Something that could be held in limbo, something that could come out of the woodwork if the developer doesn't see eye to eye with Mr. McGowan."

"And if this could be done, then I'm sure it would mean a good word in Mr. McGowan's ear for me, right?"

"And a good word in Mr. McGowan's ear is a good word to Kyle Brennan," I said. "I figure you might find yourself working somewhere a little more upmarket if this goes the way we want it to go."

Doyle grinned. "I think we can fix something up, Mr—?"

"Perez," I said. "My name is Perez."

"I think Mr. James Hackley will be gettin' a polite invitation to see something a little more colorful than whatever the hell he might be watching tonight."

It was that simple.

Three days later James Hackley was arrested in the back room of a small cinema on Penn Street. Three other "clients" were arrested with him. They were charged with "solicitation to view minors engaged in illegal sexual activities." Michael Doyle had organized a private showing of some kiddie porn. James Hackley was arraigned and bound over, bailed for thirty thousand dollars, and scheduled to appear for further questioning on 11 December.

On 9 December a brief conversation took place between the captain of the Chicago Police Precinct where Hackley had been charged and two of Kyle Brennan's trusted consiglieres. A deal was made. A contribution of an undisclosed sum would be willed to the 13th Precinct Widows and Orphans Fund within the week if the charges against Hackley were dropped for lack of evidence.

Two hours later, one of those same consiglieres met with a reputable and upstanding member of the Chicago Rejuvenation Council on a park bench near Howard Street. The conversation lasted no more than fifteen minutes. The men, one of them a crestfallen and dejected-looking David Hackley, walked away without a word.

On Thursday 16 December, 1982, David Hackley rose before the Chicago City Council Board Meeting and presented his case. He advised in the most determined and unreasonable words that planning permission to redevelop the northside of Chicago at this time be denied. He presented a good case, even issued an eleven-page proposal as to why such a move would be detrimental to the history and character of the city.

The Council came back with a unanimous decision on the twenty-second, three weeks ahead of schedule. Permission to redevelop was denied. Paul Kaufman was sent home with his tail between his legs.

The following day, 23 December, just in time for Christmas, all charges against James Hackley were dropped due to lack of sufficient evidence.

The Cicero Gang were joyous, as was Don Calligaris. We had an Irish-Italian party at a club on Plymouth Street on the northside, and I met Kyle Brennan. He gave Angelina five hundred dollars *for toys and things for the babies, you know?* and I believed that here in Chicago— despite the bitter wind and often vicious rain from Lake Michigan, among the itinerants and stragglers, the Irish gangsters with their brogue and brash manner—we had perhaps found a home.

For the subsequent eight years, as we watched our children grow, heard them speak their first words, saw them learn their first alphabet and write their first sentences, we stayed in Chicago. We kept the same house down the street from Don Calligaris and his own extended family. I cannot say that there weren't times that I was required to go back to my old trade, to exercise my muscles and consign some miscreant to the hereafter, but those times were few and far between. It was approaching the end of the decade, the world had grown up also, and as I reached my fifty-third birthday in August of 1990—as I stood at the doorway of my house and watched as Victor and Lucia, now eight years old, came running down the street from where the schoolbus had let them off— my mind turned to thoughts of where I would go when I became too old for such things. The world was changing. Influences from Eastern Europe were cutting across the family's business in America. Street-gangs of teenage youths were killing one another with no more mercy than one would kill an insect. Russians and Poles and Jamaicans were all providing supply lines for weapons and drugs and hookers, and they had the manpower and artillery to command and maintain their place at the table. We were aware of what was happening, and we believed that the generation following ours would have to fight so much harder than we did to keep any part of our operations alive. But we also knew that, just as you could never resign from such a life as this, so you could not retire. You were permitted to see out your latter days in Florida perhaps, even California near the mountains, but you were always there, always remembered, and if there was some action that needed to be taken and your presence was required, then so be it.

Don Calligaris himself was close to sixty-five, and though Chicago had served him well I could see his thoughts also turning to where he might go and what he might become when working was no longer an option.

"Time has closed up on us," he said one time. "It comes and goes in an instant, it seems. I can remember running down the street as a child, thinking that a day lasted forever. Now most of the day has gone by the time I have eaten my breakfast."

We sat in the kitchen of his house. Ten Cent was in front watching TV.

"My children keep me thinking like a teenager," I said.

"How old are they now?"

"Eight last June."

Calligaris shook his head. "Eight years old . . . I remember when Ten Cent used to carry both of them in one arm."

I laughed. "Now my son Victor, he could probably wrestle Ten Cent to the ground. He is a tough little man, the head of the house as far as he is concerned."

"But his sister, she is smart like most girls," Don Calligaris said. "The men are the head of the house, but the girls, they are the neck, and they can turn the head any which way they please."

I heard the phone then, and with it came a sense of foreboding. Business had been without trouble for some time, and there had been no calls for the better part of a month.

I heard Ten Cent shut down the TV and walk out into the front hall.

"*Si*," I heard him say, and then he set down the receiver on the table and he walked to the kitchen.

"Don Calligaris, it is for you, from upstairs."

"Upstairs" was the word we used for the boss and his people; "upstairs" meant that something was going to happen, something that would require us.

I listened for words I could understand in Don Calligaris's conversation, brief though it was, but despite all my years with these people I had never taken the time to learn Italian. I tried to speak Spanish as often as I could, even to myself, but Italian, though similar in many ways, just seemed too difficult to manage.

Don Calligaris was no more than a minute, and then he returned to the kitchen and looked at me.

"We have a sit-down," he said.

"Now?" I asked.

"Tonight." He glanced at his watch. "Three hours from now at Don Accardo's restaurant. He wants all three of us, and there will be a good few more, I think."

I raised my eyebrows.

"I don't know, Ernesto, so don't ask me. We do not discuss details on the telephone. All I know is that we meet at seven at the trattoria."

I went home to dress. I spoke with Angel, told her not to wait up for me. The children were away with some friends and would return later. I told her to say goodnight to them for me, to tell them I would see them in the morning.

I looked at her, a woman of forty-four, but still in her eyes that difficult and awkward young woman I had first met in New York.

"You have made my life something of which to be proud," I told her.

She frowned. "What is this? Why are you talking like that?"

I shrugged. "I don't know. I have been thinking the past few days that I am becoming an old man—"

She laughed. "There are few old men who have as much energy as you, Ernesto Perez."

I raised my hand. "Seriously," I said. "I have been thinking that soon it will be time to make some changes, to find somewhere to live where the children will be away from all this."

Angelina looked at me then. There was an expression in her eyes that told me she had been waiting to hear these words for as long as she had known me. She shook her head, perhaps with an element of disbelief. "Go to your meeting, Ernesto. We will talk about such things another time."

I leaned forward, I held her face in my hands and I kissed her.

"I love you, Angelina."

"And I you, Ernesto. Now be gone with you—"

Then I saw tears in her eyes, welling up in the corners. I brushed the hair back from her cheeks and frowned. "What?" I asked.

She shook her head. She closed her eyes and looked down at the floor.

I lowered my hand and raised her chin. She opened her eyes and looked back at me.

"What?" I asked again. "What is it?"

For a second there was a flash of anger in her expression, and then it softened. She shook her head once more and said, "Go Ernesto, go now. I have things to do before the children come home."

I did not move. I waited until she looked at me once again and I opened my mouth to ask her what was happening.

She shifted to the left and rose to her feet. I stepped back for a moment, puzzled at first, and then I recognized the fire inside her.

"You know what it is, Ernesto," she said, and in her voice was the edge of defiant independence that had so attracted me when I first knew her. "You go to your meeting now. I will not question what you are doing, and when you come back I will not ask what you have done. You are a good man, Ernesto. I know this, and if I did not believe that there was more good in you than evil I would never have stayed. You are who you are, and I am wise enough to know that I will never change that . . . but I will not have you risk my life or the lives of our children—"

I raised my hand. I was shocked, not at what she said, for these were words I had perhaps been expecting for many years, but the vehemence and anger with which she uttered them.

"Do not tell me to quieten my voice," she said. "I want you to say nothing, Ernesto, nothing at all. I don't want to hear you explain or defend yourself or the people for whom you work. Go and speak with them. Go and do whatever you have to do, and when you are done I will still be here with your children. Whatever madness lies out there, I wish you to keep it from our door, because if anything happens that hurts my family I will kill you myself."

I could not speak, I dared not say a word.

She crossed the room and took my overcoat from the back of a chair. She held it out for me and I walked toward her. She even lifted it up for me to put my arms into the sleeves.

I turned to face her and she raised her hand and pressed her finger to my lips.

"Go," she said. "I have said everything I needed to say. I am empty, Ernesto."

I started to think of how I should respond and she read my thoughts.

"No," she whispered. "Go finish whatever business you have to finish and then we will talk of the future."

I left the house and walked back across the street. My mind was like a hollow gourd.

We talked for a little while, Don Calligaris and I; we ventured ideas on what the sit-down could be about, but in truth we knew nothing. I could not concentrate. I could see Angelina's face, the flash of anger in her eyes, the fear she felt for our children.

At six-thirty we left, and at the end of the street I looked back toward my house, toward where my wife and children would be while I was at Don Accardo's restaurant, and I wished I could step out of the car and go back.

I had a premonition of something dark walking those sidewalks, pausing in front of my house. I swept such thoughts away. My wife and children were safe. There was nothing to be concerned about. I forced myself to believe that this was the truth.

The restaurant itself was packed to the walls every which way. We maneuvered our way between tables and chairs, waited while waiters performed circus balancing acts with antipasta and steaming plates of carbonara and made it through to the back behind the main room. Here we were greeted by Don Accardo's men, heavyset Sicilians with unresponsive faces, and were shown to a table where a good dozen men were seated.

We did not wait long for Don Accardo to appear, and as he entered the room everyone rose and clapped. He quietened them down with a gesture and then he sat also. A few minutes passed while people lit cigarettes, while introductions were made, and then Don Accardo spoke.

"I appreciate that you have all come to see me on such short notice. I understand that you are busy people, you have families and things to attend to, and the fact that everyone I asked to come is here has been duly noted."

He paused for a moment and took a sip of water from a glass to his right.

"Were it not a matter of some importance I would not have called you here, but there is a matter of some grave concern to myself and others that will require our immediate attention."

Don Accardo looked around the faces at the table. No one spoke.

"Some years ago, we dealt with a matter on behalf of our Irish cousins. Don Calligaris took some action which paved the way for a relationship which has grown from strength to strength these past years, and for this we are grateful to Don Calligaris and his people."

There was a murmur of consent and acknowledgment around the table.

"Now it seems our Irish cousins are faced with a more serious threat to their operations, not here in Chicago, but in New York, and they have asked for our assistance once again."

The room was silent.

"For several years there has been a relationship between the families in New York, specifically the Lucheses, and a man called Antoine Feraud from New Orleans."

I looked up suddenly. I thought for a moment that I had imagined what I heard.

"You have all heard of this man. You all know what he is capable of. We helped him with a small matter some time ago, a little difficulty we had with the Teamsters."

Eyes around the table turned toward me. There were a few nods of respect, all of which I returned. I had not realized how many people knew who I was and of my history.

"So now we have a situation with this Feraud. He has strong ties with the French and the Hispanics here in Chicago, and he is muscling in on Brennan's northside territory. Brennan is a strong man, he will not tolerate such things, but with the French and the Hispanics behind Feraud he is strong in some areas. Feraud has no concern regarding who he works with . . . the Polish, the Eastern Europeans, and he will use these people to take whatever he wants. Brennan has again asked us for our help, and we are here to make a local vote on this matter."

"This will be a war," a man to the right of Accardo said.

Accardo nodded. "This is something we have to be aware of. A war it may become, and though I am the last man in the world who would care for war right now, it is nevertheless a situation of loyalty and honor. For the past many years we have worked close with the Irish. They are not as strong as we are, and therefore we have the upper hand. There are concessions made for us that would otherwise be worthless, and it is not without its benefits that the vast majority of senior officials within the police department are Irish. This is a strong tie, a tie we do not have with the French or the Hispanic people, and I would be very aggrieved if we lost the foothold we possess in this city. This is, after all, Big Jim Colosimo's city, and we would not want it taken away from him."

Again a murmur of agreement from the gathering around the table.

"So speak amongst yourselves for a little while. We will take a vote, and when we have decided, we will send word to Brennan and his people and wait for a strategy to be outlined."

Don Accardo raised his right hand. "Proceed," he said.

I turned to Don Calligaris. "I cannot believe this . . . after all these years, these same people."

Don Calligaris smiled. "It's the way it works. These people put each other in positions of power, and then they work to keep all their friends where they are. This is a political arrangement that has been present since Machiavelli."

"There is no question," I said. "Our ties with the Irish are so much stronger than those with Feraud and his people."

"But Feraud has people in Vegas, also in New York. There aren't many, but then it doesn't necessarily take an army to win a war."

I shook my head. "I know where my loyalties would lie," I said. "And I have my own view regarding Feraud and his politician friend."

Calligaris nodded. "I think you will find the opinion here agreeable with yours."

Don Accardo raised his hand again and the hubbub ceased.

"So we have a vote to take. All those in favor of working again with Brennan and the Cicero Gang to oust these French and Hispanics, raise your hand."

The vote was unanimous. No question. These people knew who they wanted close, and it was not Feraud's organization.

We stayed a couple of hours. We ate well, we drank many bottles of rioja, and when we left we believed that we had been party to a small matter of politics. Even Don Calligaris waved his hand aside when I mentioned it, saying, "This is nothing of great consequence . . . I imagine we will hear a few words in the coming weeks, and then it will be gone. The Irish will be Irish and keep the whole thing within their quarter."

Don Calligaris's words could not have been further from the truth.

Within a week thirty-seven men had been killed, eleven from within the Chicago family, one young man the son of Don Accardo's own cousin. Though whatever battles raged on the northside did not directly involve us, we were nevertheless aware that at any moment the telephone could ring and we could be dispatched to take care of something.

By the time September arrived Chicago had fallen silent. The call we expected never came. We waited still, but there was no further word of what had happened between the Irish and Feraud's people, save that Feraud had withdrawn his French and Hispanic soldiers from Chicago and gone home.

Don Calligaris believed the thing was done.

Christmas came and went.

We celebrated the New Year with a trip to Niagara Falls. We went— Angelina, myself, Victor and Lucia—like a real American family. We were not, had never been and never would be, but for all appearances that was what we were.

Again I broached the subject of where we would go when I ceased to work, and once more Angelina changed the subject tactfully. It seemed she did not want to mention this, as if ceasing to be part of what we had in Chicago would signal the end of something else. Perhaps she saw some sense of balance had been attained, and she did not wish to tempt fate by unsettling it. Perhaps she was doing nothing more than working out what she really wanted, because she knew that the decisions we made at this time would determine the rest of our lives. I did not know; Angelina would come to me when she was ready, and when she was ready she would tell me what she wanted to do.

In March of 1991 Don Accardo died. For a brief while the family was in disarray. Don Calligaris spent more and more time away from the house, and it became a rare occasion when I would see him.

On the sixteenth of that month Ten Cent called at my house.

"Don Calligaris is coming tonight," he said. "He has been away dealing with family matters, but tonight he is coming back and he wants to take you and your family out for the evening. Get yourselves dressed and ready. He will bring gifts for Angelina and the children. He is very happy. Things have worked very well for him."

I spoke with Angelina. She seemed excited, the children too, for all the children knew of Don Calligaris was that he spoke to them as if they were grown-ups, but he spoiled them like eight-year-olds.

By the time Don Calligaris came we were dressed as if for church. The children were uncontrollable, and we had to shut them in the kitchen until Don Calligaris was ready to meet them in the front.

We drove together, all of us—Don Calligaris up front with Ten Cent, me and Angelina with the children in the back. It was a warm evening for the time of year, and we went right into the heart of Chicago to the finest restaurant in the city. Out of respect for Angelina and the children Don Calligaris had chosen a place that had no family connections. For this I was grateful; I knew that my children were old enough and wise enough to hear everything that was said around them.

We ate well, we talked of inconsequential things. The children told tales of their trip to Niagara, and Don Calligaris told them a story of a visit he made to Naples when he was a boy.

My children were well-behaved and polite, interested in everything Don Calligaris had to say, and more than once he looked at me and smiled. He knew how special my family was; he understood, above all else, the importance of family, and as he spoke with them, as Angelina leaned forward to refill their glasses I watched all three of them—my wife, my son, my daughter—and I was truly aware of how I had been blessed, and I believed in that moment that I had somehow shrugged off the weight of the past, the death of my own mother and father, the things that had taken place in New Orleans and Havana. I was now a man.

The evening drew on. The children were tiring, and before I knew it we were calling for the check, gathering coats and hats, preparing ourselves to leave.

Don Calligaris gave the keys to his car to Ten Cent. "Take Angelina and the children," he said. "Pull the car out front. Ernesto and I will be no more than a minute."

"There will be changes now that Don Accardo has passed away," he said once we were alone. "We have elected a new boss, a good man, a friend of Don Alessandro's, a man called Tomas Giovannetti. You will do well with him." Don Calligaris leaned back in his chair and smiled. "For me things will change too. I will be returning to Italy at the end of the month, and I will be staying there."

I opened my mouth to speak.

Don Calligaris raised his hand. "I am an old man now, much older than you. I did not have a wife and children to keep me young . . . such a wife you have, Ernesto, and your children!" He raised his hands and clenched his fists. He laughed. "You have such a special family, and even though they are not mine I am proud of them." He lowered his hands and reached out to grip my forearm. "The time has come for me to make a move to pasture. You will stay here with Ten Cent, and Don Giovannetti will ensure that things are taken care of for you . . . like I said, he is a good man, believes greatly in the importance of family, and he knows of all the things you have done to assist, both here in Chicago, also in New York and Miami. I spoke well of you, but he knew already of your reputation."

I shook my head. I did not know what to say.

"Change is inevitable," Don Calligaris said. "Everything changes. We take the changes, we change with them, or we lose everything."

I heard Victor calling for me at the door. I turned and saw him standing beside Ten Cent. They walked across the room toward us.

"Angelina and Lucia are in the car out front," Ten Cent said. "We're ready to go. The children want to go home and play with their toys."

"To go to bed more likely," I said, and started to rise from my chair.

Victor pulled a face at me, the spoiled-child face he had somehow mastered to perfection.

"Perhaps ten minutes," I said. "Ten minutes and then bed for you, young man."

"Twenty," Victor replied.

Don Calligaris laughed and ruffled Victor's hair. "That attitude I have seen before, eh Ernesto?"

"We shall see," I said. "Now we go . . . come on." I took his hand and turned away from the table where we had been seated.

"So we shall stay in touch once I am home," Don Calligaris said, "and perhaps when you are too old to keep a job in the city you will come out and see me."

I laughed. It was a pleasant thought. The image of myself and Don Calligaris as old men sitting beneath the olive trees in the warm evening sunshine.

I looked ahead at Victor and Ten Cent. Victor reached no higher than Ten Cent's elbow, but Ten Cent was leaning down to listen to something Victor was telling him. I could hear the sound of laughter, of people sharing one another's company, I felt the warmth of the atmosphere, the feeling that things were going to change, but change for the better; the feeling that despite everything that had gone before us we were still alive, we had made it through this far, and we were going to make it all the way. A sense of accomplishment perhaps; a sense of pride; of certainty that somehow all was well with the world.

Later, all I could remember was the light. The way the room seemed suddenly bathed in light. The sound did not come until much later, or at least that was the way it seemed at the time, but when it came it was ferocious, like a tidal wave inside my head, and then there was the glass, and then there were people screaming, and then I felt the slow-dawning realization of what had happened.

The sensation was one of something trying to escape through my ears and eyes, as if everything inside my head had built to such a pressure there was nothing for it to do but burst outwards.

I remember climbing over spread-eagled people as I ran to the door.

I remember shouting at Ten Cent to hold onto Victor.

I remember wondering if the children would be too excited to sleep once we arrived home.

Colors rushed together in a confusion and my eyes could not focus. I fell sideways and felt a sharp pain rushing through the upper part of my leg. Instinctively my hand reached for the gun in back of my waistband, but it was not there. This had been a time for my family. That's all it had been. Surely something was wrong; surely these things—these sounds and feelings, the awareness of pain and destruction—belonged to someone else's life?

I remember a man bleeding from the head, a sharp jag of glass jutting from his cheek, screaming for help at the top of his lungs. I remember all these things, but even those things faded when I fell out through the front doorway and saw the burned and obliterated wreck that was once Don Calligaris's car.

Black and twisted metal, the smell of cordite and seared paint. The wave of disbelief as I realized I had somehow been thrown into someone else's reality, for this was not happening, this was not how the evening was supposed to end, this was wrong . . . so wrong . . .

The heat was unbearable, and even as I tried to approach what was left of the vehicle I knew there was nothing I could do.

The sense of hopelessness was overwhelming. The sound inside my own head as my life collapsed.

My wife and my daughter.

Angelina and Lucia.

I fell to my knees on the sidewalk, and from my throat came a sound that was inhuman.

That sound went on forever.

It seemed to be all I could hear for hours.

Even now I cannot recall how I made it away from that place, nor what happened to me that night.

"I am sorry," Don Calligaris was saying. "I have pleaded with them. I have told them that I was the intended victim of this terrible thing, but there is nothing I can do."

My head in my hands, my elbows on my knees, Ten Cent standing behind me with his hand on my shoulder, Don Calligaris ahead of me, his face white and drawn, tears in his eyes, his hands shaking as he reached out toward me.

"I know that you have been with us all these years, and there is no question of your loyalty, and perhaps if Don Accardo was still alive he would have done something . . . but things have changed. I am no longer in possession of the influence I once had. Don Giovannetti is now in control. He does not feel that he can take an action so soon—"

Don Calligaris leaned forward and buried his face in his hands. "I hurt for you, Ernesto. I have done all I can. I have spoken with Don Giovannetti, and though he understands that you have been a loyal part of this family he feels that he cannot violate adherence to tradition. He is the new boss. He also has to earn his reputation and loyalties. Tradition says that we cannot avenge the death of someone who is not blood. You are Cuban, Ernesto, and your wife was the daughter of someone who was not part of this family, and though I have argued your case for hours there is nothing further I can do."

I raised my head.

"I have done everything I can, Ernesto . . . everything."

I looked at Don Calligaris as if he was a stranger. "And me? What of me and Victor?" I asked.

"I have money . . . we have money, more money than you could need, but it is time for change, Ernesto, and you must make whatever decision you feel is best for yourself and your son."

I heard his words. They were swallowed into the vast dark silence that was my mind. I said nothing in return, for there was nothing to say.

Some days later I buried my wife and my daughter. Beside me stood my son, so in shock he had not spoken since the explosion. His sister and his mother had been murdered, by whom we did not know, but whoever it was had set their heart on killing Don Fabio Calligaris and had failed. Had Don Calligaris died there would have been retribution. Had Don Accardo still been boss perhaps he would have redressed the balance, because he knew who I was and would have made a case for me before the Council of *la Cosa Nostra*. But things had changed; there was a new godfather, and he believed that justice would be seen to be done in time. He was not a rash man; he was a strategist and a politician, and so early in his position he believed it would not be right to act on my behalf.

I never saw Don Giovannetti. I believed, and believe to this day, that he would not have been able to look me in the eye and tell me the lives of my wife and daughter meant nothing.

The following day, two days before Don Calligaris—fearing for his life—would leave for Italy, I boarded a family-owned ship bound for Havana. With me I took a suitcase crammed with fifty-dollar bills, how much in all I did not know, and beside me as we slipped away from the harbor was my eight-year-old son Victor.

He asked me only one question as we watched the land disappear behind us.

"Will we ever come back home?"

I turned to look at him. I reached out my hand and finger-tipped away the tears from his cheeks.

"Someday, Victor," I whispered. "Someday we will come home."

TWENTY-TWO

"**A**ND THAT," HARTMANN said, "is possibly the best reason for not having been able to find the wife. Now we know that not only is she dead, but the daughter as well."

"But the son," Woodroffe said. "The son is still alive. Well, we can assume that he's still alive. He would be what, born in June 1982 . . . he would be twenty-one by now?"

"You thinking what I'm thinking?" Hartmann asked.

"That the killing of Gerard McCahill, at least the lifting of the body itself, could not have been done by Perez alone?" Woodroffe asked.

"Right," Hartmann said. "It has always bothered me that this whole thing was arranged and executed by one man . . . now there's a good possibility that there were two of them."

"Speculation," Schaeffer interjected. "It's nothing but another guess on our part. We don't know anything about the son. He could be dead as well for all we know."

"I don't disagree," Hartmann said, "but right now we have something to follow up on. We can assume from what Criminalistics and Forensics have told us that McCahill's body could not have been lifted into the back of the car, and then again from the rear seat of the car to the trunk by someone alone."

"We can *assume* that, yes," Woodroffe stated.

"And there was this thing about the scratches on the rear wing of the vehicle. Where's the report?"

Schaeffer stood up and walked across the main room to a stack of bank boxes against the wall. He opened one, leafed through the pile of papers inside, and returned with Cipliano's report.

"Here," he said. "He says that there were some scratches on the rear wing of the car. He says they could be consistent with the rivets they put on jeans . . . you see Ernesto Perez wearing jeans?"

Woodroffe smiled. "Somehow I don't think so."

"And the height?" Hartmann asked.

"Says that if the person who carried the body had used the rear wing for support, and if he'd been standing straight at the time, then his height would have been estimated at five-ten or -eleven."

"How tall is Perez?" Woodroffe asked.

"About that height . . . but that tells us that his son could be about the same height as well."

"Maybe, maybe not," Schaeffer said. "I'm five-nine and my son is six-one-and-a-half."

"It's something," Hartmann said. "It takes me in the direction of the son . . . well, at least someone other than Perez also being involved, and the son seems the most likely possibility."

"We ain't gonna know until we know, that's the real truth," Schaeffer said.

"And we still have the wrong name—or what we can consider to be the wrong name. If the wife and daughter were called Perez then that name would have come up," Woodroffe said.

"I'm having people follow up on the car bombing. Chicago, March of '91. If it happened, there will be details—names, reports, documents that we can access. I imagine we will have word on it within the hour." Schaeffer leaned back in his chair and stretched his arms out beside him. He looked exhausted. "Don't know about you guys, but I could manage a steak and whatever else comes with it. Feel like I haven't had a decent meal in a week."

"Sounds good," Woodroffe said. He stood up and retrieved his jacket from the back of his chair.

Hartmann rose also. He figured no harm could be done. What else would he do? Head back to the Marriott, watch TV, fall asleep in his clothes thinking about Jess and Carol and wake in the early hours of the morning with a bitch of a headache?

"Any suggestions?" Schaeffer asked. "This is more your town than ours."

"Vieux Carre . . . old New Orleans side of the city. They have some great restaurants."

"Good enough," Woodroffe said. "We'll leave Ross here. I'll make sure he has all the numbers and tell him to call as soon as he gets word back on the Chicago bombing."

The three of them left by the front entrance. Ross was located and briefed on the situation, the information that was expected. He and three other agents stayed behind in the office to take calls, to inform Schaeffer and Woodroffe if anything came up that would require their attention. Once again, the obvious absence of so many of the field operatives reminded Hartmann of the money and manpower that were being devoted to this. Those teams had been out for days, and not one of them had come back with anything substantial.

"Bring me a take-out or something, eh?" Sheldon Ross called after Hartmann, and Hartmann turned and raised his hand.

"Next time you come with us," Hartmann called from the doorway. "And we'll talk about how to find you an FBI girl that looks like Meg Ryan!"

Ross laughed and waved as Hartmann disappeared. He turned back and headed for the central office within the complex.

They took Schaeffer's nondescript gray sedan, as much an advertisement for the Bureau as a red Pontiac Firebird, but still they insisted on using them. Hartmann sat up front, Woodroffe in the back, and Hartmann directed Schaeffer away from Arsenault toward the old side of the city.

There was much for him to remember, although he tried his best not to. Thoughts came thick and fast, with them images: he and Danny, his mother, even a memory of his father that he believed he'd forgotten. It was close to the bone, always had been perhaps, but Hartmann had somehow managed to bury it in the believed importances of his own life. Roots were roots, weren't they? *Everybody has roots,* he thought, and then remembered that that had been a line from a poem by William Carlos Williams that Carol had been so fond of. He believed there was a fragment of hope for his marriage, and certainly there was no lack of love from his daughter. She missed him. She had said that, as clear as daylight. She *missed* him. His heart soared when he thought of her, the sound of her voice still echoing inside his head. But Carol had *doubts.* She'd said that. She said he should call her when he got back to New York, and then she would see how she felt. Looking from the window along the streets of his past, he could hear her voice as if she had been sitting right behind him, almost as if he could have turned and looked right back at her in that very moment . . .

The memory of her voice and the image of her face were broken up then, and at first it seemed that he was imagining something. They had just taken a left turn toward Iberville and Treme, and the sound that came up behind them was like a tidal wave. There was no way to describe it, but it took Hartmann's attention by surprise, and he turned suddenly and involuntarily to look out of the rear window.

Woodroffe was looking too. They saw it together, and though there might have been words to describe what they saw those words were never voiced.

Smoke seemed to rush upwards from the ground like a tornado in reverse. And then there was another sound, like a hundred thousand cannons going off at once, and Schaeffer slammed on the brakes and hit the curb with force.

"What the living fu—" he started, and then there was something like a slow-motion dawning realization, and after that came a sense of recognition, and close on the heels of everything came an awareness that none of them could even begin to comprehend.

"Ross," Schaeffer said, but it was more like a sound than someone's name, and he slowed the car, pulled it into reverse, skidded one hundred and eighty degrees in the middle of the street and started back the way they had come. He hit sixty or seventy by the time he reached the intersection at the end, Hartmann leaning forward to see through the windscreen. Woodroffe was behind him, his hands gripping the rear of the passenger seat, and the nearer they got to Arsenault Street the more they realized that whatever was waiting there for them was not something they wished to see.

A hundred yards from the Field Office the smoke obscured everything. Schaeffer pulled to the side of the road, opened the door and started running immediately his feet hit the ground. Hartmann came up behind him, Woodroffe following, but within fifteen yards the pall of black and acrid smoke prevented them making any further progress. The heat was unbearable, like an inferno, and all Hartmann could think of was that they would have been within it had they left no more than ten minutes later.

Schaeffer was at the side of the road doubled up. He was gasping for air. Woodroffe dragged him back, shouting something unintelligible over the roar of flames, and when he turned Hartmann realized that he needed help bringing Schaeffer back to the car.

"Radio!" he was screaming at the top of his voice. "Gotta get back to the fucking radio!"

Hartmann could barely coordinate himself. He felt sick, not only with the smoke and the heat but with the import of what was happening around him. Then he remembered Ross and the other men, the men they'd left behind to take messages while they drove out to the restaurant. Impulse and instinct drove him toward the source of the heat, but survival inhibited him. He knew there was no way he would make it five yards closer to the Field Office.

Suddenly another sound, like something being wrenched wholesale from the ground, and Hartmann heard shattering glass, echoing all around him, and when he felt another rush of heat he threw himself to the ground and covered his head. It was like a hurricane passing over; he felt sure the hair on the back of his head was scorched. He lay there for a moment, and then he heard Woodroffe's voice again, screaming for him to get up, to get back to the car and call for help.

Hartmann rolled over. The sky was black above him. He lay on his side for a second, and then with every ounce of strength he possessed he forced himself up onto his feet and ran back toward the sedan.

The three of them made it back within seconds, and even as Woodroffe snatched the radio handset from the dash, even as he started shouting into the mouthpiece, Hartmann heart sirens. They were coming from his left, and he turned and saw flashing cherry-blue bars through the smoke. He could hear the thunder of flames behind him, relentless and deafening, and he sat down on the road, his back against the side of the car, and held his hands over his ears. His eyes were streaming with tears, a sharp burning sensation in his chest, and when he started to breathe deeply he felt the acidic smoke scorching the inside of his throat and nostrils.

Later, from evidence, from Crime Scene Investigation reports, from everything they could gather without any eyewitnesses, it seemed that a suitcase had been hurled through the door of the FBI Office on Arsenault Street. Forensics and Bomb Squad estimated there must have been eight or ten pounds of C4 plastic explosive packed inside that case. It was a simple detonation. The impact of the case landing in the foyer would have been enough to trigger it, and the force of the explosion took out the majority of the building's lower floor and much of the first. It also resulted in the deaths of Sheldon Ross, Michael Kanelli, Ron Sawyer and James Landreth. Every shred of evidence, every report, every document, every tape and transcript, every piece of recording equipment was destroyed too, but in that moment—as Hartmann, Schaeffer and Woodroffe watched flames bursting out from the back of the building—their only thought was for the men who had stayed behind.

None of them spoke. Dinner was forgotten. Medics came down from New Orleans City Hospital and checked each of them over. Hartmann suffered no burns or abrasions, but Woodroffe had skidded sideways into the car and bruised much of the left side of his body. Schaeffer was merely stunned into silence, and when the medics attempted to direct him away from the scene he told them to leave him alone. He was the assigned Duty Section Chief for the New Orleans FBI Field Office. This had been his territory, these had been his people, and something had torn his small world apart. The sole purpose of their being there— the investigation, the disappearance of Catherine Ducane, the details of

Ernesto Perez's illustrious history—was wiped clean in the face of the horror that had been perpetrated.

It would be more than an hour before the flames were finally extinguished, before Crime Scene and federal Criminalistics teams could enter the site, before anyone even began to ask questions about what had happened and why.

"Feraud" was Hartmann's first word. By that time they had made their way from the scene and were close to the Sonesta. Woodroffe concurred, Schaeffer also, but they knew that such an investigation took weeks, and evidence would have to be collected for days before anyone could even begin to understand how this had been done, let alone by whom.

Hartmann was incensed, angered beyond words, and yet he watched as Stanley Schaeffer's training kicked in. Hartmann's immediate response would have been to hit back at Feraud, hit back hard and fast, but Schaeffer kept telling him how such a thing could not be considered until they possessed direct and unquestionable authority to act. It was the same world of rules and regulations, the same command channels and disciplined rigidity that prevented them taking any steps toward investigating Ducane himself. The degree of corroboration they had already obtained regarding so much of what Perez had told them, the fact that everything pointed to a clear and undisputed motive for Perez's actions, nevertheless counted for nothing in the face of federal protocol.

Hartmann was beyond the point of questioning it any further and said nothing.

None of them spoke again until they reached the Sonesta. The second floor of the hotel was opened up and every agent was called back from the field. The atmosphere was one of disbelief and shock; men asking questions that could not be answered, men standing stunned and silent, their faces white, their eyes wide. Schaeffer stood before them, and to Hartmann's surprise he said some words for the four men who had been killed, and then he led the attendant crew in the Lord's Prayer. Some of them were not ashamed to show their emotions. Some of them could not stand, and so they sat with their faces in their hands, and all tried to reconcile themselves to the fact that such things could almost be expected, for this was their chosen life, this was the world into which they had walked, and some . . . well, some never walked out again.

Later—two, perhaps three hours—Hartmann went up to see Perez. The man seemed genuinely distressed and upset.

"How many?" he kept asking. "Four men . . . all of them young.

Families, with children also? Aah, such a waste, such an unnecessary waste."

And then he said something that Hartmann did not understand, and perhaps would not understand until this whole thing unraveled.

"This thing," he said. "This thing that Feraud has done . . . and I am sure, as sure as I am of my own birth and death that it was Feraud . . . this thing he has done has merely served to confirm that I have made the right decision."

And though Hartmann questioned him, insisted that he explain himself further, Perez would not divulge anything.

"Wait," he said. "Wait, Mr. Hartmann, and you will see what I have done."

Hartmann, Schaeffer and Woodroffe did not return to the Marriott. They stayed there at the Royal Sonesta, for this now had to be their base of operation, and while they lay, restless and afraid, in their beds, while they asked themselves if Feraud would also attempt to kill Ernesto Perez in the very hotel where they now were, Lester Kubis sat up until the early hours of Saturday morning preparing another room in which Hartmann could speak with Perez.

The following morning Feds would be stationed en masse in the foyer and around the Royal Sonesta Hotel. Less than a mile away three teams of Crime Scene investigators would pore through the rubble of the FBI Office's lower floor, and from the still-smoldering wreck they would salvage what little they could to help them understand what had happened. Schaeffer exercised a degree of self-control and military precision in everything he did, and he stressed time and again that they could not afford to lose sight of what they were doing and why. The investigation of the bombing was now someone else's problem; theirs was still the task of finding Catherine Ducane.

A report would come back from Quantico regarding the bombing in Chicago in March of 1991. Seemed that whoever had overseen the investigation had been in the employ of the Irish families, and with a word from their Italian counterparts the details had been "lost." Official documents acknowledged that a car had in fact exploded, but whether it was an intentional attempt on someone's life or a vehicular "accident" was never established. Two deaths were noted but there were no names, nothing at all to indicate who might have been in the vehicle when it exploded.

Sheldon Ross's mother would wake to find a representative of the Federal Bureau of Investigation on her doorstep, as would the wives of Michael Kanelli and Ron Sawyer. James Landreth had been orphaned at the age of nine, but his sister was still alive and well and living in Providence, Rhode Island. Her name was Gillian, her husband's name was Eric, and three weeks before they had been informed that there was a 95 percent possibility they would never conceive children. Gillian greeted the agent, a man called Tom Hardwicke, and while he told her of her brother's death she made coffee at the stove and cried without tears.

"Such a waste," Ernesto Perez kept saying as he sat facing Hartmann that Saturday morning. "Such an utter waste of life, is it not?"

And Hartmann—still shocked and horrified at what had taken place only hours before, still ragged from too little sleep and insufficient appetite to manage breakfast—looked back at Ernesto Perez and wondered when this nightmare would end.

The trick, he kept telling himself, *is to keep breathing.*

Ross, Kanelli, Sawyer and Landreth had missed the trick, it seemed, and so might Catherine Ducane if this went on much longer.

"Tell me," Hartmann eventually said. "Tell me what happened when you went back to Havana. Tell me what happened to your son."

And Perez, seated there in a room on the second floor of the Royal Sonesta, surrounded every which way by agents of the Federal Bureau of Investigation, leaned back in his chair and sighed.

"Okay," he said quietly. "I will tell you exactly what happened."

TWENTY-THREE

HAVANA. HOME OF my father.

Thirty-two years ago we had come here. Irony is sharp and relentless: he too was running from the murder of his wife.

Havana. Some imagined sanctuary perhaps. It had begun to show its age, to lose its charm and passion, but for me it had not lost its memories.

Losing also its Soviet patronage, but Castro was nevertheless still a presence everywhere I looked. American finance and influence had already begun to show, and as I walked my eight-year-old son through the streets of *La Habana Vieja* I could see where time had marked its passage through the city.

Three decades I had been absent, three decades of life with all its sharp corners and rough edges, but still the sounds and smells of this place returned to me as if it had all been yesterday.

I found the house where I had lived as a young man with my friend Ruben Cienfuegos, and for the first time I was truly aware of how much I had changed. Back then I had killed Ruben for the promise of something. Now I believed I would kill for two reasons alone: the vengeance of my wife and daughter, and to protect the life of my son.

There was no shortage of money, and I rented a small house on Avenida Belgica near the Old Wall Ruins. I hired a woman also, an elderly Cuban national called Claudia Vivó who was to stay with us to cook, to clean the rooms, to school Victor and care for him.

I was a man lost, a man without a soul, and often there would be afternoons when I would walk the streets without purpose or direction. Sometimes I would hear their voices, Angelina and Lucia, the sound of their laughter as they ran down the street behind me, and I would turn, my eyes wide with anticipation, and I would see some other child, some other mother, and I would lean against the wall, my breath shallow and fast in my throat, my eyes stinging with tears.

My heart was broken beyond repair. I knew it would never mend again.

I remember a day, perhaps a week or two after we arrived. Victor was home with Claudia Vivó; he was learning of Cuba and its history, for I had told him this was the country of his grandfather, and he wished to learn of it. Though it was only midafternoon, morning swallowed irretrievably in some vague wash of forgetting, the sky had deepened into incipient gray-green solidity. The air seemed thick, difficult to breathe, and I felt as if I could bear it only for moments. I wandered through the back streets, my shirt open to the waist, sandals on my feet, and at some point I stumbled toward a plankboard house with a veranda running the width of its frontage. I collapsed into a wickerwork chair, and I removed my shirt and used it to wipe the sweat from my forehead and chest. I heard voices behind me, someone calling for lemonade. Somewhere music played from an ancient phonograph, the bakelite records scratched and heavy, the sound like a chamber orchestra coming out through a maze of tunnels.

Sometimes I felt angry. Other times sad, alone, desperate, quiet. Sometimes I felt I could light the world with fire and watch everyone burn. And again, in that moment, I felt nothing. I was sick and weak and thin. I was fifty-three years old, and I felt eighty. So many things had changed, but changed for the worse, it seemed. People like me were no one at all, less than nothing, minus zero, and we had to carve our own way through life.

Often I wished I was someone else. Someone tall and strong. Anyone else. At least it would have been different.

The heat, the bruised and turgid air, made me feel nauseous. I took my damp shirt and put it on again.

Motivation came a little later, the sky darker, the promise of a storm pressing against the afternoon, some merciless and unforgiving invasion, and I rose from the chair and started walking the streets again.

I heard the absence of music. That had disappeared some time before. I could not remember when. My mouth felt stale and bitter, my muscles ached and I was hungry.

When I thought again I thought of Angelina. Real love meant touching without hurting, crying without pain, holding a heart in your mind, not in your hand. We were all children, it seemed, and those of us who learned of adulthood paid the price in forgetting how it was to be a child. We grew up, and childhood belonged to some part of history that never existed, and when I thought of those things, remembered what it was like when everything was so much larger than me, I sensed the loss of hope: I realized that those who had taught me about life had never really understood it themselves. They had pretended. They had cheated me. If a child is smart he gets what he wants. If an adult is smart he gets used. Betrayed. Abused.

And after that I thought of where I would go now, what I would do. It was safe here in Havana, but Havana was not where I wanted to be. I wanted to be home. I wanted to be in America. I wanted to be with my family. I could not stagnate here, could not dissolve and die here in this desolate quarter of the world, but I could not go back.

I thought of winter in America, the trees losing their leaves, colors that should have borne names like "cremona" and "anguish" and "eldorado," the scatterings of snow that you could smell in the air, the bitter wind haunting the eaves above the windows of the houses, ghosts of smoke from smoldering bonfires as people burned leaves in backlots and front yards . . .

And the hurt began again.

I retraced my steps to the house, where my son was studying. I stood at the back door, waiting for the sky to break open with the sound of rain. It came eventually, as I knew it would, and out beyond the limits of the house I could hear the lush vegetation stretching and yawning and swelling its leaves and stems and roots. Rain came like a waterfall, the rush of sound filling my ears, waves filling my eyes, every sense echoing the crescendo of nature as she burst and broke and bled. It was vast, immense, majestic. It represented everything, and yet nothing, and there were many things I did not understand.

Later, the air chilled and smelling of damp green destruction, I turned and walked back into the house. Upstairs I went into a small and immaculate room, the furniture not from this century, the counterpane covering the bed ancient and bleached with years of washing. I went through my dresser and found a white monogrammed shirt. I took a suit and other things from the wardrobe, silk and soft cotton and gaberdine pants with pleats and shoes with two sets of fastenings, buckles and laces, and over the laces a hand-tooled leather flap that prevented the cuffs of the pants from chafing. From beneath the pillow of my bed I retrieved my .38, heavy and solid, the handle pearled, threaded with lignum vitae beaded like marble. I hefted the weapon in my hand, tucked my finger behind the trigger guard, rolled it like a gunslinger, stepped back and aimed at the mirror, then turned and followed the lower edge of the windowsill with my eye along the sight. I smiled. I sat on the edge of the bed. I reversed the gun, touched my thumb against the trigger, lifted it, opened my mouth and felt the bottom of the barrel against my teeth. I smelled oil, cordite, saltpeter—blood, I thought—and when I pressed the trigger harder I could sense the internal workings of the mechanism preparing themselves for movement.

The sound of the hammer striking the empty chamber was almost deafening, as if the sound had echoed against the roof of my mouth, filled my head and then exited through my ears. I smiled again, withdrew the gun and turned it over in my hand. I replaced it beneath the pillow and crossed the room to the narrow bathroom. Inside, the white porcelain tiling and bathtub were hued green in the sallow light from the window. I opened the lower pane, looked out toward the road, and stood there for some small eternity listening for any sound within the house.

It was close to evening. Somewhere Victor was reading aloud to Claudia Vivó. I could hear the rain out there somewhere, hammering relentlessly on some other part of the world. Unbeknown to me it was raining also in Louisiana. Three hours and the Bienvenue would overflow its banks, the Mississippi–Lake Borgne tributary would burst its concrete stanchions and flood a town called Violet on Highway 39; the River Gulf Outlet Canal would swell and threaten the safety of the Intracoastal waterway running northeast out toward Gulfport . . . and a man called Duchaunak, a stranger to me, would run through the bayou at the edge of the Feraud territory. He would never make it home. He would collapse into the mud and drown, and his body would rest in eternity beside that of Carryl Chevron.

I understood the depth of losing. I saw the well of despair in which I could have drowned, but the one thing that floats us is hope. Faith perhaps. But what was faith if not in yourself? We believe we understand ourselves, but we do not; and perhaps if we did we would spend less time concealing from others that we were not who we appeared to be. We perform, you see, perform some drama for the world; we carry a case filled with faces, with words, with different scenes and acts and curtain calls, and we pray that the world will never see beyond the performance we have practiced for it.

I turned and looked in the mirror. My face looked old and lined, streaked with pain, it seemed.

"Who were you?" I asked myself. "What did you think or hope or pretend you were? Who did you think you had become?"

I reached out and touched my fingers to the cool smooth reflection.

My depression deepened, the urge for revenge gnawed at me, and somewhere in the small and narrow shadow of my soul I began to understand that my wife and daughter were dead, that Victor and I were alone in this world, and nothing would ever be the same again.

Later I went down for dinner. I sat beside my son as Claudia brought food for us. I listened to him talk excitedly about the things he had learned that day, and I sensed his perfect and complete desire to become a man.

One does not own one's life, I wanted to tell him. One borrows it, and if in the borrowing there is insufficient retribution made, then the life must be returned. This is the way of all things.

I did not speak; I listened. I did not see; I perceived. I did not clamor and plead for my own voice to be heard over that of my son.

He was what he was, and that was perfect enough.

As far as my own life was concerned, I had perhaps wishes for too much.

When my son was sleeping, I once again left the house.

I felt I was becoming something. I had walked out whatever thoughts had held me in the fine clothes, the buckled shoes, the gun in my hand, and I stood in the rain, water running down my face, a warmth glowing from within.

Je ne sais pas la vérité, seulement les mots du coeur, car ça, c'est tout que j'entends.

A voice inside my mind, a voice from New Orleans perhaps, rippling with echoes like a stone dropped into cool glassy water, spreading out through everything. The words of the heart: this was all I heard.

Blackness and rain and punctuations of silence, nothing but inter-mittent waves of water breaking up the dirt, flooding the riverbanks . . . nature crying her heart out . . .

I shed my skin like a snake, and if I believed, if I breathed and believed in all that I was I would eventually swallow my own tail and disappear. It was divine and preordained and complete in its simplicity.

There was a fluidity, a gracefulness in my motion. Like the birthing pain of some creature—unearthly, arcane, sliding through the walls of the chrysalis, splitting the cocoon and feeling it slip to the ground. I was everything, and yet nothing, and in my eyes was merely the reflec-tion of everything I was, everything I would become. If only for my son, I would breathe forever.

I stepped aside, I sank to the ground, I rolled in the soft and yielding dirt, water cooling me, washing the sweat from my skin, and when I stood I was black. I knelt, I cupped my hands, and from the rivulets that danced between the clumps of undergrowth I scooped a handful of liquid darkness. Against my face it felt smooth and forgiving, blending away the edges, the seams, the junctures between sound and silence, shadow and light, and when I ran my fingers back through my hair, feeling the mud on my scalp, I saw that I had indeed become something all-seeing, sensual and sublime.

Moving then, on the balls of my feet, stepping lightly, gathering speed, and soon I was running breathless and windswept through the trees, dancing between the trunks of moss-clothed trees, leaves against my face, against my skin. A ghost, a spectre, a haunting.

From the heart of this land, from the boundaries and limits I went like a wraith, my skin blended with nature so perfectly I was unseen. I was silent, and it seemed that I existed only in my own mind.

For miles it seemed, slipping through the night, the rain, the silence, until I came to a fence that ran as far as my eyes could see both left and right. I stepped back, and then with one stride I vaulted it, landing on bended knees on the other side, rain glancing off my sweated shoulders, leaning once again to refresh my face in the pools that had gathered.

I recognized myself as the creature who had surfaced from the swamps a thousand years before, who had padded silently into a motel room, who exorcised the sin from pale, weak bodies.

Poetry in motion, blessed and beautiful.

I assumed right of possession over my own imagination, my own faith and belief, and I saw that I could become anything I desired, and anything I desired I could have.

I believed that they were still alive—my wife and my daughter. I believed that they were somewhere waiting for me, and it was only a matter of time before we would be reunited.

I believed these things with all my soul, for to believe otherwise would have caused me to lose my mind. It ran like a wheel from beginning to end, back to inception again, and like a thread from a spindle it would draw us all together once more.

On the way back to the house I found a dog sleeping beneath a tree at the side of the road. With my bare hands I strangled it, and then carried its limp body to the edge of the woods and hurled it into the darkness.

I kneeled in the dirt and cried until there was nothing left inside.

Back inside the walls of the house, I stood motionless outside the door of Victor's room. I could hear him breathing, hear him murmuring as he slept, and I closed my eyes and prayed to a God I knew could not exist that he would survive these things.

I returned to my room; I lay on my bed; I closed my eyes

I slept like the dead, for that—at least within—was what I had become.

Of these things—these thoughts and feelings—I said nothing to Victor. He was a bright child; eight years old, eyes wide for the world and all it had to offer. Mrs. Vivó taught him well, even committing to his memory the basics of Spanish and the history of his grandfather's homeland. I watched as a man apart. I loved the child, loved him more than life itself, but there was something always in his eyes, something that told me he believed me responsible for the death of his mother and his sister. Perhaps it was my imagination, perhaps a projection of my own guilt, but each time I looked at him I could recognize his loneliness and confusion. He had lost his family in the same way I had, through the brutal actions of brutal men, and had I not taken such a path, had I been a man of learning and culture, had people like Fabio Calligaris and Don Alessandro not been part of my life, then none of these things would have happened.

One day he spoke to me of God. He asked me if I believed.

I smiled, I pulled him close, I pressed my face against his hair and I told him the truth.

"Some people believe in God, Victor, and some do not."

"And you? Do you believe in God, Daddy?"

I was quiet for a time. "I believe that there is something out there, but I cannot be sure what it is."

"Claudia believes in God . . . she prays every day before lessons, and then again before she leaves."

"It is good for people to have faith. Faith helps people make their way through life without fear."

"Fear of what?"

I sighed. "Fear of men, of the things that men can do."

"Like the men that killed Mommy and Lucia?"

I felt a tightness in my throat. It was difficult to breathe. Incipient tears stung my eyes. "Yes, Victor, like the men who killed Mommy and Lucia."

"Do you have faith, Daddy?"

"Yes, I do."

"In what? What do you have faith in?"

"In you, Victor. I have faith in you. Faith as well that one day we will see Mommy and Lucia again."

"Will that be soon?"

I shook my head. "No Victor, it will not be soon, but they will wait for us."

"I want to pray, Daddy. I want to pray with Claudia . . . for you and for Mommy and Lucia, and that we will see them again soon. Is that okay?"

I pulled him closer. "Yes Victor, that is okay. You pray with Claudia and have faith in these things."

"And what will happen to the men who killed them?"

"Perhaps God will make them hurt too," I said.

"He will . . . yes, he will," Victor said, and then he was quiet, and I laid him down on the bed, and I curled up beside him until his breathing slowed and he was asleep.

I did not need to work. The money that I brought with me would have kept us in comfort for a considerable time, but I was restless before long, agitated easily, and I understood this to be an indication that I could not exist without some purpose.

During the day, while Claudia was seeing to Victor, I would walk out among the people of *La Habana Vieja*. I would listen to them, watch them as they went about their business, trying to find something that would interest me. On the corner of Bernaza and Muralla I found an old-fashioned store that specialized in cigars and antique books. Here I would spend time talking with the owner, a man in his seventies by the name of Raúl Brito, and he spoke of the *revolucion*, of the days when Batista was in power, and the fact that on two occasions he had spoken with Castro himself.

Raúl was a man of education and literature and though he had at first begun his business dealing only in fine tobaccos and cigars, it was not long before he started to bring his own books to work in order to have something to occupy his mind. Customers would come, they would show interest in his reading, and soon he started to trade also in these. The store, known only as Brito's, became a gathering place for the elders of *La Habana Vieja*, and here they would smoke their cigars, buy and sell and read their books, and occupy their hours away from home.

I frequented Brito's more and more often, until there came a day in June of that year, a day no more than a week after Victor's ninth birthday, that Raúl asked me if I would be interested in managing the store once he had retired.

"I am seventy-four next month," he said and he leaned on a stack of battered leatherbound volumes that looked barely able to stand his weight. "I will be seventy-four, and as each week passes I wonder if I can manage to make it down here again." He smiled, the creases around his eyes causing them to almost disappear into the origami warmth of his face. "You are a good man, Ernesto Perez, a man of character, and I believe it would suit you to settle here and make your business."

I did not give Raúl Brito an answer that day, nor the next. I did not give him an answer until August, and then I told him I would be willing to manage the store, but I believed we should enact a partnership, that the name of the store should stay the same, and I should pay him a partnership fee to buy into the business.

"Money?" he said. "I did not suggest this because I wanted your money." He seemed slightly offended, as if I had made some improper suggestion.

I raised my hand in a conciliatory fashion. "I know, Raúl, I know you didn't, but I am a man of principle, and I feel it would be unjust to enter into this without making some contribution to the venture. I insist that it be this way, regardless of your viewpoint."

Raúl smiled. He winked. "Okay," he said. "If that is the case then we shall employ a lawyer and we shall draw up an agreement, a letter of cooperation if you like, and we shall have it sworn in and made legal,"

I held out my hand and we shook. I would give Raúl Brito ten thousand American dollars, and I would become his partner.

It was then that the difficulties began. My money was well-hidden in my house. I had no bank account, I had no records or registered assets. In organizing the legalities of our partnership I was required to provide a passport or some legal means of identification. These things I did not have, at least nothing current and admissible in a Cuban lawyer's office, and when the lawyer suggested I solve the problem by registering my name and place of birth at the local police headquarters I was caught like a rabbit in the headlights. I had made an agreement with Raúl to do this, but what was asked of me I could not provide, and no matter the attempts I made to construct this agreement based on a handshake and a word of trust, Raúl insisted that if we were going to do it then we would do it properly. It was, after all, my idea, was it not?

When I failed to appear at the police headquarters, not only on one occasion, but a second time also, the lawyer—a suspicious and invasive man by the name of Jorge Delgado—commented to the local constabulary that there was something unusual about the elderly man who lived in the house on Avenida Belgica. The constabulare, a card-carrying member of the Crusade for the Defense of the Revolution, an organization that was nothing more than the eyes and ears of Castro's secret police, was interested enough in me to ask details of Claudia Vivó, and she—loyal and reticent in her own way—merely served to awaken his further curiosity.

It was in the second week of September that he came to Brito's, and there he found me seated near the window, smoking a cigar and reading a magazine.

"Mr. Perez," he said quietly, and sat beside me at the narrow table.

I looked at him, and everything within me told me I was in for some difficulty.

"My name is Luis Hernández. I am the constabulare for this sector."

I held out my hand. "I am pleased to meet you, sir," I said.

Hernández did not shake my hand and I withdrew it slowly.

"I understand that you have been here in Cuba for some months?"

"Yes, I have . . . myself and my son Victor."

"And how old is your son, Mr. Perez?"

I smiled. "He is nine years old."

"And I understand he is tutored by Claudia Vivó?"

"He is, yes."

"I have spoken with her and she tells me he is a very bright boy indeed."

I nodded. "He is a bright boy, yes."

"And his mother?"

"His mother is no longer alive."

Hernández shook his head. "I am sorry. She has been dead a long time?"

"In March of this year."

"And she died here in Cuba?"

"No, she did not die in Cuba."

Hernández was silent. He looked at me and raised his eyebrows.

"In America. She died in America."

"Aah," he said, as if suddenly understanding something significant. "And may I ask how she died, Mr. Perez?"

"An automobile accident, she and my daughter, Victor's sister."

"And her name?"

"Angelina," I said reticently. I knew what was happening. I was caught between a rock and a hard place. Hernández was soliciting all the information he could with the appearance of concerned interest.

"Such a tragic thing, Mr. Perez . . . my condolences."

"Thank you," I said, and turned back to my magazine.

"And I understand that you have now come here to stay in Cuba?"

"Perhaps, I am not sure. After the death of my wife I wanted to be away from America for a while. Such a thing is very difficult to come to terms with, and I felt it would be better for my son to be away from any reminders."

"Of course," Hernández said. "If it were me I am sure I would feel much the same way."

I turned and looked out of the window. I could feel beads of sweat breaking beneath my hairline.

"And you came in with a visitor's visa or as a Cuban national?" Hernández asked.

"As a national," I said. "My father was born here in Cuba and I possess Cuban national status as a hereditary right."

"Indeed you would, sir," he said. "Indeed you would." He looked at me askance, and then he leaned back in his chair and stretched out his legs. "I have one question," he said, and he smiled like a man setting a trap for something he knew was defenseless.

I looked back at him and attempted to show nothing of any meaning in my expression.

"I understand that you are looking at the possibility of engaging in this business with Raúl Brito?"

"We had discussed such a thing," I replied.

"But the details of the agreement have not been worked out?"

I shook my head.

"It is not something you wish to do? You have changed your mind perhaps?"

"No," I said. "I have not yet made time to attend to the paperwork."

Hernández nodded his head. "So I understand. I happened to be speaking with the lawyer assigned to this matter, a Mr. Jorge Delgado, and he told me you have failed to make both of the appointments he has arranged with Mr. Brito and yourself to conclude the documentation."

"That is correct," I said. "I have been very busy with my son's schooling."

"But you are not so busy now," he replied, and once again he smiled his reptilian smile and looked at me through slitted eyes.

"I am not," I said, for there was nothing I could say in my defense.

"Then I think it would be a good idea, if only for Mr. Brito's peace of mind, that we conclude this matter this afternoon. I think it would be fair, in order to further prevent any inconvenience for both him and Mr. Delgado, that we go to your house now, collect your identification papers, and sign these partnership agreements."

I smiled. "Of course," I said. "I think that would be an excellent idea."

Hernández rose immediately. He looked very pleased with himself. I gathered my coat, threw it around my shoulders, and with a sense of ease and lack of concern I showed Hernández to the door and followed him out into the street.

We conversed as we walked, of nothing consequential—the weather, the shameful lack of care shown to some of Havana's more historic and beautiful buildings—and it was little more than fifteen minutes before we reached Avenida Belgica and the house I had rented.

The thoughts that passed through my mind were those thoughts one always encountered solely in hindsight. I had considered entering Cuba under an assumed name even as I left America, but I was so caught up in the necessity to leave that country, so unwilling to engage in any formal investigation of the murder of my wife and daughter, I had fled as I was. Of course I possessed a Cuban passport, and it was in my birth name, but that passport had been purchased for seven hundred and fifty dollars some years before from a skilled counterfeiter. In America I had carried no social security number, no formal identification, and the customs and immigration people at the Havana docks had no more than glanced at my documents as I entered. Leaving would have been different, a far more difficult enterprise altogether, as I knew from experience with my father so many years before. The passport I would show Hernández would be identified as a forgery under scrutiny, and that was a road I did not wish to travel.

I welcomed Hernández to my home graciously. I had prayed that Claudia and Victor would be away, and my prayer was answered. The house was still and quiet. I showed Hernández through to the main room of the house where Victor's study books were spread across the table, the room where he would sit with his tutor and learn everything he could of the world. I asked Hernández if he wanted a drink, and he accepted.

I walked back through to the kitchen and started to make some coffee. He called out questions through the half-open doorway. How long had I been living in America? What business had I been involved in there? Did I have any other living family here in Cuba? I answered tactfully, diplomatically, but I realized even as I was speaking that it made no difference what I said to him now.

I returned to the room bearing a tray, upon it two cups of fresh coffee. I asked Hernández if he wished for some warm bread, perhaps some cheese with his coffee. He declined politely, took his coffee, and then asked if he could see my papers.

I smiled, and said, "Of course, Señor Hernández," and once again left the room.

When I returned he was sitting quite relaxed in the chair. In his hand he held his coffee cup.

I walked toward him, my forged passport in my hand, and when he reached out to take it from me, as he closed his fingers around it, I lunged forward suddenly and buried a steak knife through his right eye. I jerked the knife upward and then down. He seemed transfixed, his other eye looking at me with such an expression of surprise I couldn't help myself. I started laughing, and it was almost as if Hernández smiled, as if this was some kind of practical joke, as if I had somehow managed to create the image of his impending death, and then would suddenly retrieve him from his fate. The smile did not last long. A second, perhaps two, and possibly it was nothing more than some involuntary reflexive action taken by the muscles in his face as they fought the intrusion of the blade. Perhaps, and this may be closer to the truth, it was nothing but my own imagination.

Hernández leaned forward as I released the handle of the knife. His hands clawed at his face, almost out of control, and then he rolled forward off the chair onto his knees.

There was little blood, almost none at all, and for this I was grateful. Visions of Carryl Chevron and the wide lake of blood that had pooled out of his body and across a dirty linoleum kitchen floor a thousand years before came back to me. I stepped away. I watched Hernández struggle with the pain, the shock, the agonizing disruption of all bodily functions, and then from his throat came a stuttering feral snarl like some wounded animal in its final death throes. And then he was still. I leaned over his body. With my right hand I pressed against the side of his throat. There was nothing. Constabulare Hernández was dead.

I removed my tie and jacket. I rolled up my sleeves. I dragged his body toward the edge of the rug and then I proceeded to roll him sideways until he centered it. I put my foot on his chest and used both hands to withdraw the knife. The muscles had already tightened around it and it took two or three sharp tugs to remove it. I walked to the kitchen, and with the remainder of the hot coffee I washed the knife thoroughly. I took a bottle of cleansing bleach from the cupboard, half-filled the sink with water, emptied the cleanser into it and then submerged the knife. I walked back to the main room and looked down at the cocooned body that lay there.

I was alert for any sound from the front of the house of Claudia and Victor returning. I had no idea where they had gone or when they would return. I contemplated the situation I had created. A body does not disappear. A body is a body. One hundred and sixty pounds of deadweight that will stay one hundred and sixty pounds of deadweight until it becomes something else. The house had no furnace, there was no rapid passage to the sea and, unlike Louisiana, there were no nearby bayous where such a body could be submerged and forgotten in moments.

I sat down where Hernández had been seated. The chair was still slightly warm from where he had relaxed. Through the end of the rug I could see the side of his face, the single open eye that seemed to look at me askance. I leaned down and closed it. He still seemed accusatory and suspicious even in death.

"You should not have been so interested in business that did not concern you," I told him, and "You should have attended to matters of greater significance and importance than this. This is your penalty for being too concerned with the details of other people's lives." I considered the perfect irony of the situation. After all the things that had been done, after so many lives had been abruptly terminated by my hand, this man had been perhaps closer than anyone to discovering who I was, and all because of some paperwork.

Having reprimanded him, in and of itself nothing more than a poor explanation to myself of why he was now dead, I was still faced with the grim reality: on my front room floor, wrapped in a rug, was a dead constabulare, and until I did something decisive he was going nowhere.

Fifteen minutes later I got up from the chair and started pacing the room. I walked around Hernández clockwise, and then counterclockwise. At one point I stopped near his head, leant down, peered into the hole where his face lay and said *"¡Hijos de puta!"* with such venom that spittle flew from my lips.

I felt vexed, angered by his silent presence, and though my first impulse was to take something heavy—perhaps a hammer, or a large stone—and beat his head to a useless pulp, I restrained myself. This matter was a problem enough without further complications to clean up. And then in back of that reaction was a sense of regret, a narrow sense of guilt perhaps. I felt a momentary panic as I considered the possibility that Victor might return and see a dead body in his house. I was not afraid for myself, but when I thought of my son my viewpoint changed. I wanted the past behind me, and yet here, even as I stood over the dead body of the constabulare, the past was making its insidious way toward the present.

I glanced at my watch. It was a little after two. I went out to the front and backed my car up as close to the house as it would go without attracting too much attention. I unlocked the trunk and propped it open with the edge of a blanket inside. I returned to the house, and from a strong cord I found in a drawer in the kitchen I cut two lengths which I used to tie up each end of the rug. Hernández was not as heavy as I had imagined, and I was surprised at the ease with which I hefted him up onto my shoulder. I stood within the doorway of the house until I was certain there were no passersby or people standing on their porches, and then I hurried across the few feet of pathway, used my knee to push the trunk upwards, and lowered Hernández's body into it. I had to bend Hernández at the knees to get him inside, and then I slammed the trunk shut and locked it. I drove the car down to the edge of the road and parked it once again. Visions of Carryl Chevron came back to haunt me. I remembered how the death of the salesman had started me along this path, how I had been a similar age to Victor, and the sense of coincidence was almost painful.

Claudia and Victor returned no more than half an hour later. I greeted them warmly. I had taken the steak knife from the sink, dried it carefully and replaced it in the drawer. I had warmed some bread, sliced some dried meat and eaten a sandwich. I felt levelheaded, altogether in control, and while Claudia prepared our evening meal I sat with Victor in the main room and listened as he read to me.

Later, evening closing up against us, I asked Claudia if she would be willing to stay with Victor for an extra hour or so as I had a small errand to run. Claudia was more than happy to facilitate me. I believed she was lonely perhaps, her husband having been dead more than three years, and the time she spent with Victor, the hours she spent in my house catering to us, seemed to give her purpose and respite from a world she felt no great desire to long inhabit. I took my car keys; I left the house. I let the handbrake off and rolled the car down to the end of the street before I started the engine. I did not turn on the headlights until I reached the intersection at the end, and then I took a route north along Belgica onto Avenida de las Misiones. I headed out toward the coast, to the Castillo de San Salvador de la Punta, and down there, down along the edge of the Canal de Entrada, I pulled the car to a halt above a dark gully that climbed down to the edge of the water.

From the trunk of the car I lifted the rug with Hernández's body inside and carried it to the edge of the high verge. I rolled him out from within, folded the rug and returned it to the trunk. I took a small can of gasoline from the back of the car and doused Hernández's body liberally. I stepped back and struck a match. I watched the flame for a moment, like a single candle against the night sky, and then I tossed it toward his body. The body ignited with a sudden *whoosh*, and flames swelled upwards. I was panicked for a moment. Such a fire would be visible all along the coastline, but by then it was too late. I hurried back to the car, started the engine without illuminating the headlights, turned around, and headed back to the road. At the top of the incline, perhaps three or four hundred yards from the fire, I killed the engine and sat watching for a while. No one came. There was no sudden alarm raised. It was as if the eyes of Cuba were turned the other way. How long the body burned I did not know. After thirty or forty minutes I started the engine once again and drove away. I was half a mile from Hernández before I switched on the headlights, and by the time I reached the house I had almost forgotten the man existed.

It was three days before Hernández's body was finally identified, more than a week before another constabulare came to Raúl Brito's shop to ask if Hernández had been seen there in the previous days. Raúl, forgetful at the best of times, said he could not recall the last time he had seen the man, and I acted patient and yet suitably ignorant of anything but books and cigars. I had already spoken with Raúl, told him that all necessary documentation had been signed, and had given him the first thousand dollars of the ten he was due. Raúl did not question me, I was his friend, and there was nothing requiring further discussion. I heard mention of Luis Hernández once more in the subsequent week, and then there was nothing. He seemed to have been a man of little conse-quence in life, and equally lacked consequence in death. The lawyer never contacted Raúl Brito regarding any incomplete documentation and the matter became unimportant. Each month for the subsequent nine months I gave Raúl a further thousand dollars, and Raúl—he of the old ways—never felt any need to consign the money to a bank. I was a partner in spirit, not on paper, and this arrangement served me well.

For three years my life with Victor became a simple and uncompli-cated matter of moving from one day to the next with merely the dark-ness providing the seam between. He was schooled well, and by the time he reached thirteen years of age I could see in him the wide-eyed longing for the world that had been present as a young child. He asked me of America frequently, of the things I had done, the life I had lived in the New World. I lied to him in small matter-of-fact ways. It seemed unnecessary to tell him anything he would not have been able to comprehend, and thus he heard what he wanted to hear and he imag-ined the rest. The better part of a year later, as we entered the fall of 1996 and I approached my fifty-ninth birthday, Victor came to me one evening and sat facing me in the kitchen. Claudia had long since left for the night, and the house was quiet. He brought with him a book filled with pictures, landscapes and nighttime horizons, and he showed me the towering image of Manhattan against a brilliant sunset.

"You have been to New York," he said, his voice almost a whisper.

"I have," I said. "I lived in New York for some years."

"Before I was born."

I nodded. "Yes, before you were born. I left New York in the spring of 1982 and you weren't born until the summer, and by then we had moved to Los Angeles."

"And you met Mommy there?"

"Yes, I met her at the beginning of 1974 and we were married in May of 1977."

"Where did you live?"

I smiled. I could remember the sounds and smells, the faces of the people in the street. I remembered almost word for word the discussion that was held regarding a man called Jimmy Hoffa.

"We lived in a small neighborhood of New York called Little Italy,"

"Italy? Like the country?"

"Yes, like the country."

Victor was quiet for a time, pensive almost, and then he looked up at me and said, "What was it like, Daddy . . . what was America like? I find it hard to remember much at all."

I leaned forward and took his hand. I held it as if it was my lifeline to something precious and eternal. "It is a vast country," I said. "Many, many, many times larger than Cuba. Cuba is just a small island near the coast of America. There are millions of people, tall buildings, wide streets, shopping malls larger than the Old Wall Ruins. Sometimes it is difficult to walk down the street because there are so many people coming the opposite way. It has everything good and everything bad that can be found in the world."

"Bad?" Victor asked. "Like what?"

I shook my head. "Sometimes it is difficult to understand why men do the things they do. Some men kill, some men take drugs and steal other people's property. Some men, out of desperation perhaps, feel that this is the only way they can live their lives. But against that it is possible for anyone to be happy in America. There is enough of everything to satisfy, and if a man works hard and keeps his word the whole world can be his."

Victor was quiet again. I watched his face. I saw the light in his eyes, and I knew what he would say.

"I want to go back to America, Daddy. I really want to go back to America and see it. I want to go to New York and see the buildings and the people. Could we do that?"

I sighed and shook my head. "I am old, Victor. I have come here to live the rest of my life. You are young, and when I am gone there will be all the time you need to see America . . . all the time you need to go anywhere you want in the world, and you won't have your old father slowing you down."

"I don't want to go alone, I want *you* to take me. I want you to show me everywhere you have been, all the places and the people—"

I let go of Victor's hand and raised my own. I shook my head slowly. "Victor . . . I don't know that you will understand even if I explain it to you, but I cannot go back to America. I am an old man now. I am nearly sixty years of age, and there is a great deal of America that I want to forget. We will stay here for a few years more, and then when you are eighteen you will be free to do whatever you wish and go wherever you might want to go. I will not stop you. I would not have it in my heart to stop you doing anything you wanted to do—"

"So don't stop me now," Victor said, and in his tone I heard that edge of fiery determination that I possessed as a young man. He was so like me in so many ways, and yet he was also innocent, and blind to the brutality of the world he desired.

"I cannot—" I started.

"You mean you *will* not," he retorted, and he snatched the book and slammed it shut.

"Victor," I said, my voice stern, unforgiving.

He glared at me defiantly.

"We will not talk about this any more tonight," I said.

"We will not talk of this ever again if you have your way," he replied.

"Victor, I am your father—"

"And I am your son. And I lost my sister and my mother too. I am lonely here. I spend all my time with Claudia, studying every hour of the day, and I cannot stay like this for the rest of my life."

"No one is asking you to stay like this for the rest of your life . . . just for a few years more."

"A few days more would be too long," he said, and he rose from his chair. He looked down at me, a young man defying his father, and though at some other time I might have raised my voice to him, though I might have sent him to his room for his lack of compliance and mis-behavior, I could do nothing but watch him silently as he spoke.

"I am fourteen years old . . . old enough to know what I want, Father, and what I want is to go to America. No, we will not talk about it any more tonight. But we will talk about it again, and we will keep on talking about it until you are prepared to see things from my point of view. Then you will make a decision, and if the decision is that you will not take me then I will find a way to go by myself."

He pushed his chair back with his knees, the sound like something ugly dragging itself across the ceramic tile, and then he turned and walked to the door.

He looked back as he stood in the doorway. "Goodnight, Father," he said, his voice curt and brusque. "I will see you in the morning."

I listened as he made his way up the stairs to his room, as he slammed his door shut behind him, and I leaned forward, my arms folded on the table, and I rested my forehead on my hands.

I imagined Victor finding his way to America alone. I imagined him reaching New York and wandering the streets alone. I imagined what might happen to him, who he might meet and what would become of him.

I felt tears in my eyes, a knot of twisted emotion in my throat, and I believed for a second that if he went he would become what I had become. Either that, or he would die.

I did not sleep that night, and when I heard him rise in the morning, as I listened to him prepare his own breakfast in the kitchen below me, I could not face the prospect of seeing him look so defiantly at me again.

I waited until Claudia arrived and his lessons began, and then I rose and showered. I dressed quickly and quietly, and left the house by the rear door and made my way to the store.

Victor did not so much withdraw from me as quietly disappear. I saw less and less of him, and this, I believed, was how he intended it to be. In the morning he would say little. He would prepare his own food and retreat to his room until Claudia arrived. Then he would join her in the main room and close the door firmly behind him. Though it was not locked it was obvious that he did not wish me to enter, and so I did not. I believed perhaps that I was allowing him some degree of control over his life, but all I was doing was allowing him to draw himself further away from me. In the evening when I returned from the store he would be upstairs in his room. I learned very quickly that he would arrange for the evening meal to be prepared before I came home, and he would eat with Claudia. This again was of his own devising, and it was evident in his manner and attitude that he no longer considered me a part of his life. I had refused him something that he longed for, and thus I had been summarily excommunicated.

On many occasions, too many to recall, I attempted to win him back, but he was stubborn, and as we entered October of 1996 I realized that he had chosen a path, much as I had done. Perhaps I consoled myself with the knowledge that where I had killed a man to gain my knowledge of the world, all my own son wished to do was visit America, the land of his birth, the home of his mother.

On the last Saturday of that month, a day that would mark the beginning of the end in so many ways, I went up to my son's room and sat on the edge of the bed. He did not look at me, he merely turned onto his side and went on reading his book.

"Victor, listen to me," I said calmly.

He did not respond.

"Victor, listen to me now. I am going to say something and you are going to listen."

Again he did not move or turn his head toward me.

"You want to go to America?"

There was a flicker of movement in his face.

"If you want to speak to me of going to America then you will turn and face me and talk to me like a man."

Victor moved sideways. He turned to look at me, his eyes almost without expression.

"We will go to America," I said quietly. "We will do as you wish and we will go to America, but you must understand something."

Victor sat up. He started to reach toward me. I raised my hand and edged backward. "Listen to me, Victor, and listen well. I will take you to America, but you must understand that I had a life there before you were born, and there were things done and things said that I believe you could never comprehend. If you happen to hear of these things then you should come and talk to me before you assume they are true, and before you make any judgment of me. I am your father. I am the closest person you have in this world, and I love you more than life itself. But I will not have you judge me, Victor. I will not have you judge me."

The fear was there, buried deep inside me, almost an integral part of my being. The fear of who I was, the fear of my son discovering the truth about his father. It was there, always had been, but I had been too afraid to face it.

Victor leaned forward and put his arms around my neck. He pulled me tight and hugged me. I inhaled slowly. I closed my eyes. I held him for some small eternity and I would not let go.

I did not want my son to see that I was crying.

The following day I made some calls to Chicago. I discovered that

Don Calligaris, Ten Cent, some of the others, had moved back to New York in the summer of 1994. I found Ten Cent without difficulty, and when I told him I was planning on returning to New York he told me that he could arrange a private charter out of Havana that would bring me to the mainland of Florida, and there I could take a train or drive up to New York. There would be no need for papers or identification. There would be no need for anyone but the Alcatraz Swimming Team to know that Ernesto Cabrera Perez was coming to America once more.

Five and a half years I had been away. My son, all of eight years old when we had left, was now a teenager with a mind and a character and a vision all his own. New York would be filled with painful memories, and I knew the time would come when I would walk those same streets where I had walked with Angelina Maria Tiacoli so many years before.

But that was a different life. That was a different man altogether, and I swore to myself that this time, *this time* it would be different.

I could not have been more wrong, but as I boarded that small aircraft, as we taxied along the narrow runaway and then watched through the windows as the ground was swallowed into obscurity beneath us, I imagined that I could return and still stay somehow disconnected from the past.

Truth be known the past had been there all along, and it was just waiting for me to come home.

TWENTY-FOUR

HARTMANN WAS NOT sure. Perhaps still stunned by the events of the previous night, perhaps frustrated at the fact that much of their evidence was now destroyed, and beneath that the feeling that whatever investigation might have been ongoing was bearing no fruit, it seemed that any sense of accomplishment or forward progress had been obliterated in one swift and effective act.

There was no way, at this early stage, to determine anything regarding the bombing of the Field Office, save that it had been done by someone who was aware of Perez's existence, someone who wanted Perez to disappear and did not care who might disappear with him. Hartmann himself suspected Feraud. The man had the authority, the wherewithal, and the people to carry out such an attack, and Hartmann also believed that Feraud would have seen the deaths of innocent bystanders and federal agents alike as merely casualties of war, even as some sort of bonus. And then there was Ducane. And if Perez's word was anything to go by, this man had been working hand-in-glove with organized crime for at least forty years. Ducane was now in his sixties, perhaps the same age as Perez himself, but had worked officially on the other side of the law, the acceptable side where everything as it actually was and everything as it appeared to be were very different. At least with people like Perez the world was black and white. What they did was straightforward: murder, extortion, blackmail, violence, drug-running, arms-dealing, pornography, prostitution, racketeering. In politics it was called public relations, fundraising, political leverage, lobbying, strengthening the vote and "exercising one's peccadillos." They were all the same thing, and Hartmann was not so naïve as to believe that people like Ducane were incapable of exactly the same things as Perez and his Alcatraz Swimming Team. It was not a difference of action, more a question of terminology.

That evening, the evening of Saturday 6 September, a day that marked the two-week disappearance of Catherine Ducane, a day that should have seen him in Tompkins Square Park with his wife and daughter, Ray Hartmann—he of the bruised heart and broken mind—lay on his bed in the Marriott Hotel. He could have transferred to the Royal Sonesta just as Schaeffer and Woodroffe had done, and it was not the threat of another bombing that had kept him away. It was simply the fact that he was attempting, seemingly against all odds, to maintain some distance between himself and what was happening. If he woke, showered, shaved and dressed in the same hotel where he had to speak with Perez, then it would feel as if that was all there was to his life. The Marriott was not home, could never have been anything even close, but at least it gave him the impression that there was a division between what he was doing and who he was. Now he believed that even if he had been given the choice to walk away he could not have done so. Even if someone had called and told him it was okay, that he could go back to New York and see his wife and daughter today, he imagined there would have been a question in his mind as to whether that was the right course of action to take.

Nineteen murders. Ernesto Perez had detailed to them nineteen different murders. Right from the encyclopedia salesman here in New Orleans to the Cuban constabulare who had been stabbed and burned in September of 1991, there were nineteen lives, nineteen people who no longer walked and talked, who no longer saw their husbands, wives, girlfriends, brothers, sisters, parents, children. Nineteen people who had vanished from the physical reality of life, who would never come back, who would never have another thought or feeling or emotion or passion. And beyond that, there were the additional eleven unnamed victims that had been summarily dispatched when Perez worked for Giancarlo Ceriano. All killed by one man. Ernesto Cabrera Perez. A psychopath, but at the same time strangely eloquent and cultured, considerate of feelings and the necessity for family, the power of loyalty and the giving of one's word. A paradox.

Hartmann found that all he believed in had been in some way challenged. The importance of his job, his so-called career. The value of friendship. The necessity to be trusted, to trust others, to make a promise and keep it. Just as Jess had asked him—would he now keep his promises? He believed he would. The deaths of Ross and the others, even the deaths of those who had been murdered by Perez, seemed to do nothing but highlight the importance of making every moment count for something, however insignificant it might seem at the time.

He had been an asshole, and it had not been because of his father, and it had not been because of genetics or some hereditary trait; it had been because of himself, he alone.

Perez had asked him whether circumstance governed choices, or if choices governed circumstance. Hartmann, now—perhaps in the most meaningful change of heart he had experienced since Carol and Jess had left him—believed it was the latter. He had made choices: to work, to stay late, to give too little credence and weight to the little things that Carol and Jess had considered important; and he had chosen to drink, whether it had been with Luca Visceglia or alone, he had nevertheless been in a situation where he could have said no. But he had not. Despite his word he had not. And this was the price he had paid. Choice governed circumstance, of that he was sure, and he knew that now, after all of this, his choices would be different.

During those early hours of Sunday morning, as New Orleans went through its routines; as people walked and laughed and danced down Gravier and through the districts of Arabi and Chalmette; as they ate at Tortorici's Italian and Ursuline's; as they drove along Chef Menteur Highway and the South Claiborne Avenue Overpass; as they talked their words out, expressing what was in their hearts and minds and souls; as they ran barefoot through Louis Armstrong Park, slowing down as they passed Our Lady of Guadalupe Church because they could not be sure, could *never* be sure that there wasn't a God, and God didn't mind the drinking, but the blaspheming and rowdiness around His house might just piss Him off enough to fly a thunderbolt through your heart; as they lived life in the vague hope that there might be something better just around the corner, and if not that corner then perhaps the next one, and everything came to those whose tongues were silent, whose hearts were patient, whose thoughts were pure and clean and simple; as people throughout the city went about the business of being frail and uncertain, impulsive and cautious, headstrong, passionate, unfaithful, honest, loyal, childlike, innocent and hurt . . . as all these things unfolded in darkness around him, Ray Hartmann believed that possibly—in some small and awkward way—what had happened here in New Orleans had been a second chance. If he came out of here alive, if he just remembered to keep breathing, then there might be a chance he could rescue his life from the depths to which it had fallen.

He hoped so. God, he hoped so.

And it was with that thought that finally, gratefully, he folded down into sleep.

Sunday morning Sheldon Ross did not come to collect him from the Marriott, because Sheldon Ross was dead.

That, above all else, reminded Ray Hartmann of the transient fragility of it all.

Hartmann arrived at the Royal Sonesta alone, but in ample time for his appointment with Perez. Yet even as he approached the front of the building he sensed that something was very different. There were cars outside that he had not seen before, men also—two of them, dark-suited, one with sunglasses—but there was something about their manner that told Hartmann they were not part of Schaeffer's little family. He paused on the other side of the street, intuition telling him that something was altogether awry. The taller of the two men watched him intently as he cleared the road and started down the sidewalk. When he reached the main entrance of the hotel a federal agent stepped out and raised his hand at the two men and Hartmann passed inside.

"New kids on the block?" Hartmann asked.

The agent smiled warily. "You don't even wanna know," he said, almost under his breath, and indicated that Hartmann should speak to a second agent at the reception desk.

"First floor, second room to the right," Hartmann was told. "Mr. Schaeffer and Mr. Woodroffe are up there waiting for you."

Hartmann paused once more. He looked at the man behind the desk but it was obvious there was nothing further to say.

Hartmann crossed the lobby and started up the stairs. He made it to the first floor landing, and as he turned he could hear voices. There was no one in the corridor, and he hesitated before making himself known.

"—don't know. That's the plain truth of it . . . we just don't know yet."

It was Schaeffer's voice—clear as anything.

"But Agent Schaeffer," another voice said, "you are paid to know. That is the entire purpose of your existence . . . to know things that no one else knows."

Hartmann frowned and took another step toward the doorway of the hotel room.

The second voice started up again, the sort of voice that belonged to someone who very much liked the sound of it.

"You have entrusted almost every chance of success to a burned-out alcoholic from New York—"

The hairs on Hartmann's neck rose to attention.

"—and this man, this Ray Hartmann, has already failed to secure a deal with this maniac Perez. I don't understand it, Agent Schaeffer. I just don't understand how a man of your background and experience could have entrusted the most important and delicate aspect of this matter to someone such as Hartmann."

"Because Ray Hartmann has earned Perez's confidence, Governor—"

Hartmann, standing there in the narrow hotel corridor, no more than three feet from the room where these people were speaking, realized who was inside. Ducane. Governor Charles Ducane.

"And when you are dealing with a man such as Ernesto Perez," Schaeffer went on, "you use whatever leverage or foothold you can find. We are not dealing with a rational man, Governor. We are dealing with a multiple murderer, a homicidal psychopath. The laws and rules and regulations that dictate the manner in which business is undertaken at Capitol Hill do not apply to situations such as this. What we have here is an entirely different world—"

"I do not appreciate the facetious attitude, Agent Schaeffer. I am here because my daughter has been kidnapped, and I am in personal communication not only with the attorney general himself, but also the director of the FBI. I can assure you that there will be no quarter given if it is discovered that any aspect of this operation has been mishandled by yourself or the men under your command—"

"And I can assure you, Governor Ducane, that every single thing that can be done *is* being done."

Hartmann, his fists clenched, his teeth gritted, took three steps forward and appeared in the doorway of the hotel room where Schaeffer, Woodroffe and Ducane had been talking.

Ducane was standing facing Schaeffer. Woodroffe was seated. Schaeffer appeared more vexed and agitated than Hartmann had ever seen him. There were dark circles beneath his eyes, and his hair was uncombed. Ducane, however, seemed the epitome of composure. He possessed the air of a man who always achieved his own ends and never had to explain either what he did or why he did it. His eyes were sharp and unforgiving. His hair—silver-gray and full—and his tailored suit: these things spoke of a man who had never envisioned the idea of going without. He did not, in Hartmann's estimation, appear to be a man deeply disturbed and distressed by the absence of his only child.

He turned as Hartmann entered the room. "Mr. Hartmann," he said slowly.

Hartmann nodded. "Governor Ducane."

"I have come to ensure that all progress that can be made is being made—"

"I understand," Hartmann interjected. The last thing he wanted was a lecture.

Ducane shook his head. "I am afraid, Mr. Hartmann, that I am not sure you *do* understand."

Hartmann opened his mouth to speak but Ducane raised his hand.

"You have a daughter, do you not, Mr. Hartmann?"

Hartmann nodded.

"How old is she? Eleven? Twelve?"

Ducane looked at Hartmann for an answer but continued speaking without waiting for it.

"Then you perhaps understand some small aspect of how this must feel for someone like me. My daughter is nineteen years old. She is barely more than a child herself. This man—" Ducane glanced up toward the ceiling; he knew Perez was in the building on an upper floor. "This animal . . . this insane criminal psychopath that you have secured inside this hotel . . . he has taken my daughter. *My* daughter, Mr. Hartmann, and I am in a position where I can do nothing but wait while you people fall over your own feet trying to find out what he has done with her. How would you feel if it was your child, Mr. Hartmann? How would you feel then? I am sure that there would have been an awful lot more progress in finding her. Where is she? No one knows but this man. Is she alive or dead? Huh? Is she dead, Mr. Hartmann? Well, whaddya know . . . the only person that knows is this man Perez."

Ducane glared at Hartmann, and then he turned and fixed Schaeffer and Woodroffe in turn with his gaze.

"To hell with this!" he suddenly said. "I am going up there to deal with this man myself!"

He made for the door.

Hartmann backed up a step, closed the door and stood in front of it.

"Out of my way, Hartmann!" Ducane snapped.

Hartmann said nothing.

Schaeffer looked like he was ready to implode. Woodroffe rose from his chair and joined Hartmann at the door.

"You cannot go up there, Governor," Hartmann said quietly.

Ducane grimaced. "I can do any goddamn thing I goddamn well please. Now out of the way."

Schaeffer stepped up behind Ducane and took his arm by the elbow.

Ducane turned suddenly. He wrenched his arm free and pushed Schaeffer back against the edge of the desk.

He started shouting, spittle flying from his lips. "You people!" he screamed. "You people think you can come down here and play with my daughter's life as if it holds no importance at all? You think you can do this to me? I am Charles Ducane, Governor of Louisiana . . ."

Ducane stopped suddenly. He turned back toward Hartmann. "You . . . you get out of my way right now!"

Hartmann shook his head. "No, Governor. I am not going to get out of your way. You are not going anywhere except back to Shreveport. You are going to leave us to handle this with the correct protocol and procedure. The director of the FBI has sent the people he considers best fit for this task, and they have done everything they are capable of doing, and will continue to do everything they can, until they have found your daughter and returned her safe to you. We have sixty men down here. Honest and capable men. They have spent every waking hour searching for any clue that might indicate where your daughter is being held. Already we have seen four men die as a result of this investigation, and we have no intention of adding your daughter's name to the roster of dead. I am not familiar with standard FBI procedure in these matters, I am not in a position to judge whether everything has been done to the letter, but I can guarantee that in all my years working in such situations as this I have never seen a more dedicated and committed group of people. These people have given up their own lives for the duration of this investigation, and nothing, absolutely nothing, has dissuaded them from doing what they believe to be right. Now you have to leave, because if I let you go up there then I can guarantee that Ernesto Perez will say nothing further and he will let your daughter die."

Ducane was silent for a moment, and then he backed up a step and looked down at the floor.

He turned and looked at Schaeffer. Was there a flicker of something apologetic in his expression? Hartmann could not be certain. He doubted Charles Ducane would ever allow himself to stoop so low as to apologize.

Clear in Hartmann's mind were the things Perez had said regarding Ducane. The young New Orleans old-money compatriot of Antoine Feraud. Did Charles Ducane have any inkling of who Perez really was, and why he had done this? Did Governor Charles Ducane in fact know exactly why Perez had abducted his daughter? Was he here for the reason he stated—to ensure that everything was being done to find her—or was he here to ensure that the things he did not want known stayed unknown?

Hartmann was exhausted—mentally, emotionally, spiritually. He did not want to fight this man, and even as he thought those words Ducane spoke again. His voice was cold and direct. There was nothing human within it whatsoever, and in that moment Hartmann understood that what Perez had told them about this man could very well be the truth.

"I will do as I wish, Mr. Hartmann, and what I wish is to see this man—"

Hartmann closed his eyes. He clenched his fists. "Governor Ducane," he said quietly. He looked up and opened his eyes. "There are a great many things we do not know about this man. There have been a great many things he has spoken about, and your name has been uttered on numerous occasions."

Ducane's eyes flashed. Was there a flicker of anxiety there?

"He has spoken of things that happened many years ago, in Florida and Havana, things that involved some of the most significant organized crime families in the country during the last fifty years. There has been talk of a man called Antoine Feraud—"

Again the flash of anxiety in Ducane's eyes.

"—and the killing of Jimmy Hoffa—"

Hartmann sensed Schaeffer go rigid. Woodroffe stepped forward. "Hartmann—" he began, but Hartmann raised his hand and Woodroffe fell silent.

"The killing of Jimmy Hoffa—"

Ducane raised his right hand and pointed at Hartmann.

Hartmann went cool and loose inside, like something had suddenly released the tension of every muscle in his body. What if he was wrong? What if everything Perez had told them was a complete fabrication?

"Don't you even consider threatening me," Ducane said.

Hartmann willed himself to keep it together.

Ducane seemed to take another step forward, despite the fact that there was almost no distance between them. "I don't know who you people think you are," he hissed, his voice growing more insistent and angered, "but—"

"But nothing," Hartmann interjected. His heart was trip-hammering in his chest. A thin film of sweat had broken out along his hairline. He felt nauseous and afraid. "We are doing our job, Governor, and our job is to listen to everything this man tells us and see if there isn't some clue, some thread of something that will lead us to your daughter. And if that means asking questions about Hoffa and Feraud and this Gemini thing—"

Hartmann was still talking, but even he did not register what he was saying, for the change in Ducane's color and demeanor was startling. The man seemed to step back completely without moving an inch. He stepped *down*, more accurately, and Hartmann knew that there were going to be no further challenges from this man. Governor Charles Ducane would not be visiting with Ernesto Perez today.

There was silence for some moments after Hartmann had finished talking, and Charles Ducane—his whole body tense, his face pale, his eyes wide like a man in shock—nodded slowly and said, "Find my daughter, gentlemen . . . find her and bring her back to me, and when that is done find some way to kill this animal for what he has done to me."

Hartmann wanted to say something but no words seemed appropriate. He watched as Ducane turned to look at Schaeffer and Woodroffe in turn, and then he stepped aside as Ducane came toward him.

Ducane left the room. Schaeffer went after him to ensure he did not try to go upstairs.

Hartmann walked forward and sat down at the desk. His hands were shaking. His whole body was covered in sweat. He looked at Woodroffe. Woodroffe looked back. Neither of them said a word.

Schaeffer returned within moments. He was breathless, red-faced; looked like a man on the verge of collapse. "I didn't know . . . didn't have any idea he was going to come down here," he started, but Hartmann raised his hand and Schaeffer fell silent.

"It doesn't matter," Hartmann said, the tension and fear audible in his voice. "It is what it is." He said nothing regarding his additional thoughts about Ducane's real motive for coming to New Orleans. He didn't say a word regarding his belief that Ducane seemed less like a grieving and distressed father than any distressed father he'd seen before. Such things were for himself alone, and no purpose would be served by voicing them.

Hartmann looked at both Woodroffe and Schaeffer in turn; neither of them were going to say a word about what had actually happened in that room.

An agent appeared in the doorway and nodded at Schaeffer.

Schaeffer nodded back. "He's gone," he said, the relief evident in his tone. "Let's get this done, okay?"

Hartmann rose from where he was seated and left the room. They went upstairs together—all three of them—and there was a moment's silence when they reached Perez's room.

Hartmann knocked on the door, identified himself, and the door was unlocked. Hartmann passed inside and waited for the outer door to be locked. He crossed the carpet, and without hesitating, opened the inner door and went inside.

"Mr. Hartmann," Perez said. He rose from a chair near the window. The room was hazy with smoke, and Hartmann noticed how tired Perez seemed to be.

"We are coming to a close," Perez said as Hartmann walked toward him. "Today I will tell you about New York, tomorrow how I came home to New Orleans, and then we will be done."

Hartmann did not reply. He merely nodded and sat down at the table facing Perez.

"It has been a long journey for both of us, no? And we have nearly come to an end that you might not have heard had the attempt on my life been successful. I have upset some people, it seems."

Hartmann tried to smile. He could barely manage any facial expression. He felt as if everything meaningful had been torn out of him and was being held in suspension somewhere. He might get it back, he might not: no one had told him yet.

"It has been a life of sorts," Perez said, and he laughed gently. "It has not been the life I perhaps imagined for myself, but then I imagine that this is the way it is for most of us, wouldn't you say, Mr. Hartmann?"

"I guess so," Hartmann replied. He reached into his jacket for his cigarettes. He lit one, set the box on the table, and leaned back in his chair. He wanted to tell Perez that Ducane had been downstairs only minutes before, but he did not. Every muscle in his body ached. His head felt like an overripe pumpkin, swollen with something acidic, ready to burst at the slightest provocation.

"You are not well, Mr. Hartmann?" Perez asked.

"Tired," Hartmann said.

"And this difficulty with your wife and daughter?"

"In limbo," Hartmann replied.

"It will go well, I am sure," Perez said encouragingly. "There is always a way through these things, of that I am certain."

"I hope you're right."

"So we shall begin," Perez stated, and he too lit a cigarette and leaned back in his chair.

From the other side of the room they would have looked like two friends sharing old times, perhaps having seen little of each other for years they were reminiscing, nostalgic half-memories creeping back toward the present as they talked through the years of their very different lives. Perhaps, despite everything, they could have been father and son, for their ages were a generation or so apart, and in the dimly lit hotel room it was difficult to distinguish their features clearly.

The last thing they appeared to be was interrogator and subject, for their manner appeared too relaxed, too friendly, too familiar altogether.

That was it surely. They were old, old friends, and after all this time they had collided in some unknown corner of the world, and for a few hours, no more, they had the chance to share their lives with one another and walk away enriched.

"Returning to New York after all those years," Ernesto Perez said quietly, "was like going back in time."

TWENTY-FIVE

EVERYTHING HAD CHANGED, and yet everything had stayed the same.

The house on Mulberry, the Blue Flame on Kenmare Street, Salvatore's Diner on the corner of Elizabeth and Hester. All these places were familiar to me, but the atmosphere was different. I had gained as many years as the city, but the city had lost its spirit.

It was October of 1996. I had left this place in November of 1982, with a wife and two small babies, almost fourteen years before; left this place for another city called Los Angeles believing that what I had found here in New York would always be mine.

Desire and reality could not have been more distant.

The people I knew here were gone also. Angelo Cova, Don Alessandro's boy Giovanni, Matteo Rossi and Michael Luciano. Carlo Gambino was gone, as were Frank Tieri and Anthony Corallo. Thomas DiBella, head of the Colombo family, had been deposed by Carmine Persico, and Caesar Bonaventre, the youngest head of the Bonanno family, had been replaced by Philip Rastelli after Rastelli's release from jail. Stefano Cagnotto was gone of course, because I had been the one to kill him.

Ten Cent was there to meet us at the train station, and I introduced him to Victor as Uncle Sammy. Ten Cent grinned and hugged me and kissed my cheeks, and then he did the same to Victor. Ten Cent had brought a toy bear with him, and when he saw the size of Victor and realized that he was no longer a child he laughed at himself. We all laughed, and for a moment I believed everything would be alright.

The Mulberry Street house was still there, and Ten Cent drove us down to meet with Don Calligaris. While his housekeeper fed Victor in the kitchen, Don Calligaris took me aside and sat with me near the window in the front room.

"We have become old men," he said, and in his voice I could hear the fatigue and broken promises. "I have come back to America. I cannot die alone away from my family. And this thing . . . this thing that happened with Angelina and Lucia—"

I raised my hand. "These things belong to the past," I said, and said it merely because I could not face talking of it. Despite the years that had intervened, it was still something that hung over me like a black shadow.

"It is the past, yes, Ernesto, but all these years you have been away I have carried a weight of guilt about that night. We still, to this day, have nothing more than rumors about what happened. It is clear that whoever killed your wife and daughter intended to kill me. Some men have died in our attempts to find out, and we are still looking. This thing was more than five years ago, but people like us never forget the wrongs that have been done to us. Now you are back we can work on this together, we can find out who was behind it and take our vengeance."

"I have come here as an old man, to have my son see America," I said. "I will take him places, show him some of the things that I saw, and then, more than likely, I will return to Cuba to die."

Don Calligaris laughed. He seemed out of breath for a moment and took some seconds to clear his throat. The lines and wrinkles in his face said everything that needed to be said. He was older than me by some years, and where a regular man would have retired—moved to Florida and spent his months fishing and walking and having his grandchildren visit him in the sunshine—Fabio Calligaris held onto his life with a vice-like grip. This territory was all he had, and to let it go would have seen him welcome the end of all that mattered. He was a tough man, always had been, and he would rather have died right there in the house on Mulberry Street than see his life's work passed over to someone younger.

"We do not talk of dying," he said quietly, and he smiled. "We do not talk of dying, and we do not talk of giving up. These are the subjects of conversation for weak and spineless men. We may be old, but we can still take what we want from this world for the years we have remaining to us. You have a boy, and he needs his father to be there for him until he is himself a man. He has lost a mother and a sister, and to lose you would break him before he has had a chance."

"I will be around for some years yet," I said. "There is no question about that. But with him beside me there is no way I can once again become part of this life."

Don Calligaris leaned back in his chair. He looked at me directly, and though there was warmth and friendship in his eyes there was also the cold determination for which he was renowned. "This life . . . this thing of ours, it is not something that you leave behind, Ernesto. You make your choices, you make your mark, and that mark will always be your signature. You have lived the life you chose to live and, though there will always be things that a man regrets, it is nevertheless a stupid man who believes he can undo what he is, what he has become as a result of his actions. I watch the TV now, I see movies about the kind of people we are." He laughed. "We are portrayed as a gang of thugs, mindless hooligans in silk suits who kill for no purpose. We are seen as vicious and unreasonable men, without hearts, but nothing could be further from the truth. More often than not people have died because it was a matter of life and death. It was a matter of you or them. And then there is the matter of honor and agreement. Men make promises on the lives of their families, and then they betray not only those they promised but also themselves. These are the kind of men that die, and these men deserve nothing better."

I listened to what Don Calligaris was saying, and I knew in my heart of hearts that it was true. Even as I had seen my own son drifting away from me and had contemplated the possibility of returning to America, I had known that if I returned it would not be because of his need alone. It would also be because of me. I was a man who had made choices which had involved the lives and deaths of so many people over the years. I knew that if I returned to New York, if I once again re-established my old friendships and bonds, then it would also mean once again wearing a coat cut from the same cloth. The man I was had been the result of what I had done, and what I had done could not now be undone. I was, and perhaps would always be, a part of this greater family. Just because I had a son did not change that fact.

I believed then that the difficulty I'd had in deciding to come back was not for fear of what Victor might find out, what he would see or hear, but my own unwillingness to resume my position in the grand scheme of things. I had a place, and in leaving I had left that place vacant. No one had come forward to take my mantle and assume my responsibilities, and no one ever would. No one but me. And now I was here, sitting by the window in the Mulberry Street house; my son in the kitchen; Ten Cent in the back room watching a ball game on the TV; Don Fabio Calligaris, old and gray and wrinkled, opposite me in his chair, and I realized that whatever I had left behind possessed the patience of Job. My clothes had been cut. I had worn them. I believed I could take them off and store them away somewhere in perpetuity.

This was not the case. They were the only clothes that had ever really fitted me.

"So you see," Don Calligaris said. "We are who we are, no matter what the world and all its voices might say about us. These things we have done are as much a part of us as our fingerprints, and they cannot be removed, they cannot be exchanged for something else. I know you well enough, Ernesto—" He smiled. He leaned forward and took my hand. I looked down at his liver-spotted skin and saw that his hand and mine were almost identical in their appearance. "I know you well enough to realize that you would never be happy crawling into some hole in Cuba and dying like some insignificant and inconsequential nobody. You are here. You have come home. The house where you once lived with Ten Cent is still there. The rooms are not the same—" He laughed. "At least we took the trouble to have the walls painted! But those rooms are there for you and your son, and while he goes to school, while he learns to be a good American citizen, you can be here by my side and help me straighten out the mess these kids have made of our city. The five families were here. They may be quieter now, they may have less influence than they did thirty years ago, but they are still alive and well and living in America. America was our country, and with the last breath in my body it will stay our country if it has anything to do with me."

He gripped my hand tighter. He was asking me to stay, to be one of the family again. I would return to a life I believed I had left behind. This time it would be different. This time I had a son of fourteen years old, and he would have to be protected from the truth of what I had done—and might yet do. This, of all things, would be the greatest challenge. And what was my other option? To visit New York, to see America for a handful of weeks, and then to return to Cuba, my son perhaps unhappy, homesick for the wide and awe-inspiring world he had glimpsed, and wait until I died?

I looked down at the floor. I closed my eyes.

I believed I had already made my decision as I sat on the edge of Victor's bed that night and told him we would come.

"Yes," I said, my voice barely audible. I looked up and cleared my throat. "Yes, Don Calligaris. I will stay here. This is my home, and I have returned."

Don Calligaris clapped his hands together. "Ha!" he exclaimed, his smile wide. He rose from the chair. I rose also. He reached out and placed his hands on my shoulders. He pulled me close and hugged me.

"My brother," he said. "Ernesto Perez, my crazy Cuban brother . . . welcome home!"

It began with the little things; always the little things.

We made arrangements to keep my life with Victor separate from my life with Ten Cent and Don Calligaris. He was enrolled in a good school, a Catholic school with family connections. Money changed hands and Victor did not need to provide identification or a Social Security number. He arrived on time, he worked hard, he showed great promise in his studies, and he seemed happy. After school he would return to the house where we lived, back a half a block or so from Mulberry on Baxter, and here he would watch TV and occupy himself as he wished when I was not there. Ten Cent lived there too, and I employed a woman much as we had employed Claudia Vivó in Havana. Her name was Rosa Martinelli, a middle-aged Italian widow with teenage sons of her own, and Victor fell in with them, good boys, honest and studious, and often he would stay over at their house or visit the movies with them. I did not worry for Victor, he was in good company, and for this I was happy.

So the little things began.

"Go and see Bracco," Don Calligaris would say. "Tell him we need the track money tonight. Tell him he has been late three weeks in a row and it will not be tolerated again."

And Ten Cent and I would go and see Bracco, the two of us—old men in our fifties—and we would scare up the neighborhood and remind people who we were.

"You're the one," they would say. "You're the one who clipped Jimmy Hoffa," and I would smile and say nothing, and they would read everything they wanted to read in that expression.

Sometimes we would meet at Salvatore's and discuss business, and in such moments I could have been twenty years younger and feeling that rush of anticipation knowing that I would be out in a couple of hours, out and down the street to call on Angelina Maria Tiacoli.

You're back again?

Yes.

You're not gonna give up, are you? How was the music show?

I didn't go.

You want me to pay for the tickets, is that it?

No, I don't want you to pay for the tickets.

So what do you want?

I want to take you out someplace nice, maybe see a movie—

And then the moment would pass, and I would look away toward the street and realize that, regardless of whether the past had waited here for me, there was no way I could find it again.

And then the little things became bigger things.

"That Bracco, he's got some kid called Giacomo something-or-other. He's making some noise downtown about how he does this and that for the family. Go with Ten Cent, go find the kid, bust his fingers or something and tell him he better keep his fuckin' mouth shut or next time you're gonna put some vents in his cranium."

And me and Ten Cent would go down there, to some broken-down warehouse on the south end of Bowery, and I would hold Giacomo in a chair while Ten Cent broke three or four of the fingers on his right hand with a monkey wrench. Stuffed an oily rag in the kid's mouth to keep him quiet, heard later that he got sick as a dog from whatever the fuck he might have swallowed, but sure as shit he kept his mouth shut from that point forward and we didn't hear another word.

I didn't kill anyone until the winter of 1998. A few weeks before Christmas it was, and the snow was thick and heavy along the sidewalks. I remember how much I felt the cold, something that had never bothered me before, and it came home to me that perhaps I should have been lying on a sunlounger near a pool outside of a rest home in Tampa Bay. I had smiled at that thought as I left the house on Baxter, as I walked half a block down and climbed into the car where Ten Cent was waiting for me.

"This is a fucking mess and then some," he said, and he clapped his gloved hands together and exhaled white mist toward the windscreen. "You ready for this?"

"As I'll ever be," I replied, and yet in my gut there was a cool sense of something unraveling. It was late evening, a little after nine. Victor was having a sleepover at Mrs. Martinelli's house, believing perhaps that his old father had already gone to bed with a mug of cocoa, but no—here I was, in a car on the corner of Canal Street with his Uncle Sammy, and me and Uncle Sammy were going to drive across to the Lower East Side and clip some asshole called Benny Wheland. Benny was a small-time loan shark, one of those assholes who charged a quarter on the dollar per week. Hit him for a thousand bucks and three weeks later he'd come looking for seventeen hundred and fifty and expect you to be real polite and grateful when you gave it him back. He didn't carry any muscle to speak of, just a couple of Irish fistfighters who fought bouts in the clubs around Water Street and Vladek Park. Meatpackers they were, nothing more than that, but they were big enough to intimidate the kind of people Benny Wheland lent money to. The problem with Benny—sweetheart though he was—was a mouth the width of the Williamsburg Bridge, and when he opened it you could have ferried three cars and a tow truck right down his throat. He had laid up a deal with a fight arranger called Mordi Metz, a decidedly dishonest Jewish businessman who was known as Momo. Momo governed the financial matters relating to all fights on the Lower East Side. He had a strong working relationship with our people, and when he needed a little heavy-handing on paybacks we were always happy to oblige. We took a 10 percent cut, we handed the cash clean and simple to Momo, and everyone was happy. Benny Wheland had welched on a payout to Momo, something in the region of thirty grand, and Momo called in a marker he was owed by the Lucheses. The Lucheses gave the job to Don Calligaris, and Don Calligaris gave it to us.

"Simple thing really," he told me. "He'll have the money, no question about it, and the deal is that whatever we get we keep all but a one-dollar token we give to Momo."

"One dollar?" I asked. "What the hell we gotta give him one dollar for?"

Don Calligaris smiled. "It's traditional. It's a Jewish thing. They gotta get their pound of flesh, you know?" He laughed, waved my question aside, and went back to business.

"It's worth it to us to keep Momo sweet," he said. "This guy Wheland is a fly in the fucking ointment as far as he's concerned, about as significant in the grand scheme of things as a heap of dog crap on the sidewalk. It means nothing to us to clip him, and this is what Momo wants. Besides, Benny Wheland has been known to open his mouth a few too many times, and things would be altogether quieter if he was out of the way."

I sat quiet for some moments.

"Hell, Ernesto, if I had someone else to send, someone I could trust, I would send them. You know that. This may not seem like a big deal, thirty grand owed to some Jewish guy running the fight circuit, but I got my orders, and orders is orders as you well know. Now, you gonna do this thing or do I gotta get some pimple-faced teenager with an attitude to go fuck it up for me?"

I smiled. "Of course I'll go," I said. I would not have questioned Don Calligaris's request. It was not in my nature to go up against him. He was in a tight spot. He needed someone to do the work. I agreed to take care of it.

And so we sat in that car as New York went on snowing down on us, me and Ten Cent in our overcoats and gloves, and when Ten Cent started the car and I looked at him I realized that he would do these things forever. Ten Cent was a soldier, he was not a thinker. He was a smart man, no question about it, but he had accepted the fact that he was not a leader. He was a man who made kings, not a king himself, whereas I had always questioned everything. I did not want to be a king, I did not want to sit in a chair someplace and give the orders to have men's lives ended, but at that point in my life I didn't want to be the emissary either. What I wanted I didn't know, but in that moment I had agreed, and once I had agreed there was no going back. That unwillingness to compromise my word had perhaps been the only thing to keep me alive that long.

We drove south toward Chinatown and then headed into the Lower East Side along Broadway. We had been given Benny Wheland's address, and we knew he lived alone. Apparently Benny had never trusted a woman enough to marry her, and the money that he had he kept beneath the floorboards.

"You gonna do this?" Ten Cent asked me as he pulled over to the side of the road and stopped the car. "I don't mind if you don't wanna do this, you know? You got a kid an' all, and I know that must change the way you think about things. I'm easy come, easy go on this if you don't actually wanna clip the guy."

I shrugged my shoulders. "We'll take it as it comes," I said. "Let's go talk to Benny and see what he has to say for himself, eh?"

Ten Cent nodded and opened the door. A freezing gust of wind and snow rushed in to greet us, and Ten Cent swore. He stepped out and slammed the car door shut.

I climbed out on the other side and walked around to where he stood. We looked up and down the street both ways. Smart folks were inside bundled up in blankets watching the tube. Only us—two old men in topcoats and scarves—were dumb enough to be out on a night like this.

Benny opened the door but it was held by two security chains. He peered out at us through the four-inch gap, his face screwed up against the cold wind that hurried in to piss him off.

"Benny," Ten Cent said. "How ya doin' there? You gonna open the fuckin' door and let us in or we gotta stand out here like a coupla schmucks freezin' our balls off?"

Benny hesitated for a second. It amazed me, never ceased to amaze me, that in situations like this people didn't realize what was going to happen. Or perhaps they did, and they knew there was an inevitability to it, and thus they consigned themselves to fate. Perhaps they would survive. Perhaps they believed that God might be on their side and see them through. I knew for a fact that God was the greatest welch-artist that ever existed.

"Whaddya want?" Benny growled through the narrowing gap between the door and the frame.

"Aah, come on for Christ's sake, Benny. We got to talk money with you. We got a means to work out this thing with Momo and it won't take more than a coupla minutes and then we'll be on our way."

I didn't know what Benny Wheland thought then, but his expression changed. Perhaps he believed that Momo, and whoever else Momo might have been connected with, wouldn't have sent two old men over to sort him out. Maybe he believed that if he was gonna get clipped it would be some wiseass kids who just muscled their way in and shot him in the face.

He hesitated a moment longer, and then he slammed the door. I heard the chains releasing, both of them, and then the door opened wide. Ten Cent and I went into Benny Wheland's house with gratitude and .38s.

There was a lot of talk, much of it from Benny, a little from Ten Cent, and after a while I got real tired of listening and shot Benny in the face.

When I walked over and took a look at him it was difficult to see anything but a whole handful of shit around his eyes and nose.

Ten Cent stood there with his jaw on the floor.

"Fuck, Ernesto . . . what the fuck?"

I frowned. "Whaddya mean, what the fuck?"

"Shit, man, you coulda told me you was gonna do that."

"What the hell d'you mean I coulda told you? What the hell did we come over here for? A cup of fuckin' tea and a chat with the asshole?"

Ten Cent shook his head. He lifted his right hand and massaged his ear. "No, I don't mean that. You know I don't mean that. I mean you coulda told me you was gonna just shoot the guy. I coulda put my fucking hands over my ears or something. Jesus, feels like I ain't gonna hear right for a fucking week."

I smiled and Ten Cent started laughing.

"You didn't wanna listen to any more of that horseshit, did you?"

Ten Cent shook his head. "Guy was a fucking radio station all by himself. Now, let's find this fucking money, right?"

We went through every room in the house. We prised up the floorboards, ripped open the backs of chairs and sofas. We found food cartons and dirty washing pretty much everywhere we went. We even found the remains of something that had been cooked black in the oven and then just left there because Benny hadn't been bothered to clean up after himself. The guy had lived like an animal. That said, regardless of his personal hygiene and housecare skills, we collected together something close to a hundred and ten thousand dollars, much of it in fifties and hundreds. It was a good take, better than Don Calligaris had expected, and as a show of good faith he sent a single dollar over to Momo in an envelope, and a further thirty grand in a jiffy bag.

"Straightforward enough?" he'd asked me when we'd returned to Mulberry Street.

"Straight as ever," I'd told him.

"Good job, Ernesto. Good to get the old juices flowing again, eh?"

I smiled. I didn't know what to say, and so I said nothing. I had done what was required, what was asked of me, and by the time I sat in my own room, a cup of coffee in one hand, a cigarette in the other, my feet up on the edge of the table and a movie on the TV, I felt distant enough from what had happened to feel absolutely nothing at all. I was numb, insensate to Benny Wheland and Momo and whoever else might have had a beef with either of them, and I just wanted a little time to myself to gather my thoughts.

It was then that I thought of Angelina and Lucia. I had not permitted myself the luxury of real memories since their deaths. After the shock, the horror, the pain and grief and crying jags that had racked my body for so many nights in the first weeks in Havana, I had separated myself out from everything that had happened and tried to start all over again. At least mentally and emotionally, or that's what I believed. It was not true. I had not overcome my sense of rage and despair about their loss, and though Don Calligaris had several times assured me that there were people still looking into what had happened and why, who had been behind the attempt on his life that had killed my wife and daughter, I knew well enough the way this family worked to realize that he was merely placating me. In this life of ours, things happened and they were forgotten. Within an hour, perhaps a day at most, Benny Wheland would be forgotten. The police would find him after some neighbor reported the smell of his decomposing body in a fortnight, and there would be a perfunctory investigation. Some eight-year-old kid two weeks out of detective school would come to the conclusion that it was a straightforward robbery and homicide, and that would be the end of that. Benny Wheland would be buried or cremated or whatever the hell was planned for him, and there would be nothing further to say. His death would be as insignificant as his life. Much like my father.

It was the same for Angelina and Lucia. Someone somewhere had ordered Don Calligaris's death, a bomb had been placed in his car, Don Calligaris had survived without a scratch. Someone somewhere would make a phone call to someone somewhere else, the differences would have been resolved in a handful of minutes, and the matter would have been closed. End of story. Evidently whoever had ordered the hit no longer wanted Don Calligaris dead or they would have tried again, and they would have kept on trying no matter how many attempts it took, and no matter who might have gotten in the way. Angelina and Lucia, well, they had gotten in the way, and had I been blood, had we been a part of this family for real, then perhaps someone might have done something. But I was Cuban, and Angelina had been the unwanted product of an unwanted embarrassment to the family, and it was not necessary for anyone to balance the scales in my favor. My connection to Don Calligaris had been enough to put my family in the line of fire, and though I bore no grudge against him, though I understood that he could do nothing directly to help me, I also knew that someone somewhere was responsible, and someone should pay.

That thought stayed with me until I slept, but when I woke it had left my mind. I did not forget, I merely changed its order of priority. It was there, it would never disappear, and there would come a time to do something about it.

The summer of 1999, and Victor's seventeenth birthday in June. It was then that I met the first girl he brought home. She was an Italian girl, a fellow student from his school, and in her deep brown eyes I saw both the innocence of youth and the blossoming of adulthood. Her name was Elizabetta Pertini, though Victor called her Liza and this was the name by which she was known. In some small way she was not unlike Victor's mother, and when she laughed, as she often did, there was a way she would raise her hand and half-cover her mouth that was enchanting. She wore her raven hair long, often tied at the back with a ribbon, and I knew within a matter of weeks, good Catholic girl or not, that she was the one who took my son and showed him that which had been shown to me by Ruben Cienfuegos's cousin Sabina. He changed after that, as all young men do, and he became independent to an extent I had not seen before. Sometimes he was gone for two or three days, merely calling to let me know that he was fine, that he was with friends, that he would be back before the week was out. I did not complain, his grades were good, he studied well, and it seemed that Liza had carried something into his life that had been altogether missing. My son was no longer lonely. For this alone I would have been eternally grateful to Elizabetta Pertini.

The discussion that took place between her father and myself in the spring of the following year did not go well. Apparently Mr. Pertini, a well-known bakery owner from SoHo, had discovered that his daughter, believed to be visiting with girlfriends, perhaps studying for her school examinations, had been spending time with Victor. This subterfuge, orchestrated no doubt by Victor, had continued for the better part of eight months, and though I was tempted to ask Mr. Pertini how he had managed to be so utterly unobservant of his daughter's comings and going, I held my tongue. Mr. Pertini was irate and inconsolable. Apparently, and this unknown to his daughter, he intended her to marry the son of a family friend, a young man called Albert de Mita who was studying to be an architect.

I listened patiently to what Mr. Pertini had to say. I sat in the front room of my own house on Baxter where he had come to find me, and I heard every word that came from his lips. He was a blind man, a man of ignorance and greed, and it wasn't long before I discovered that his business had been struggling financially for many years, that the intended marriage of his daughter into the de Mita family would reap a financial benefit sufficient to rescue him from potential ruin. He was more interested in his own social status than the happiness of his daughter, and for this I could not forgive him.

But there was a difficulty with whatever challenge I might have raised to his objections regarding my son courting his daughter. Pertini was a man of repute. He was not a gangster, he was not part of this New York family, and thus any issue of loyalty to Don Calligaris would carry no weight. Thirty years ago he would have been visited by Ten Cent and Michael Luciano perhaps. They would have shared a glass of wine with him and explained that he was interfering in the business of the heart, and sufficient funds to compensate for the loss of his daughter's "dowry" would have been delivered in a discreet brown package to one of his bakeries. But now, here in the latter part of the twentieth century, such matters could no longer be resolved in the old way. Any suggestion I might have made to Pertini about money would have been taken as offensive. No matter his thought or intention, no matter the fact that he knew I understood his motives, on the face of it he would have been insulted. That would have been his part to play, and he would have played it to the hilt. He professed an appreciation of his daughter's best interests. He knew as little of those as he did of my business. But had I insisted that there was a change in his plan, had I attempted to persuade him to reconsider who his daughter might marry, then Pertini—I felt sure—would have done all he could to raise questions about my reputation and credibility. That route would have been the route to his death for certain, and however much I loved Victor, however much I might have cared for his happiness and the welfare of his heart, I also felt that I could play no part in depriving Liza of her father.

The relationship was ended abruptly in April 2000. Victor, not yet eighteen, was inconsolable. For days he did not venture from his room further than the bathroom and the kitchen, and even then it was to eat next to nothing.

"But why?" he asked me incessantly, and no matter how many times I tried to explain that such things were often more a matter of politics than love, there was nothing I could do to make him understand. He did not blame me, merely resented my apparent lack of effort in preventing what had happened. Liza was grounded at home for those weeks, and on one occasion when Victor attempted to call her the attempt was cut short within seconds by her father. Moments later Mr. Pertini called me at the house and told me in no uncertain terms that I was responsible for my son, that if I did not ensure there were no further attempts to contact his daughter then he would seek an injunction against him for harassment. I assured him that no further attempt would be made. To me it was obvious why such a thing had to be prevented, but there was no way I could explain that to Victor. Again he saw me as failing to defend what he considered to be his God-given right.

It was not the only issue that contributed to my position in New York becoming untenable, but it perhaps marked a watershed. The matter that finally prompted our departure was far more serious indeed, at least for me, if not for Victor, though had we stayed there would have been questions asked that could never have been answered. The events of the early part of that year were perhaps indicative of how single-minded and relentless I had become in attempting to find some meaning for my own life. Back of all of it was the ghost of my wife, that of my daughter also, and though they were never far from my thoughts, it was in my actions that I recognized how unfeeling and brutal I would become if I did not assuage my sense of guilt about their deaths. That guilt could only be tempered by revenge, I knew that as well as I knew my own name, and it was in those weeks that my feelings of merciless rage were precisely demonstrated.

Where we had possessed strong ties with the Irish in Chicago, those of the Ciccro Crew like Kyle Brennan, Gerry McGowan and Daniel Ryan, it was not the same in New York. New York, Manhattan in particular, had become a playground for all who wanted a piece of the territory and what it had to offer. Street-gangs of Puerto Ricans and Hispanics had running gun battles with the blacks and Mexicans; the Poles and the Jews were attempting to milk the Lower East Side and the Bowery of all it could give them; East Village, the southern end of SoHo, and Little Italy had always belonged to us, a tradition as old as the Bible itself, but toward the end of the '90s the Irish, their leaders supported by the millions that had been invested in the construction industry, started to tread on our toes and demand a place at the table. Don Calligaris had no time for them—he had had little time for their ways and worries in Chicago—but here they served to remind him that things were changing, that things could not always stay the same, and that he too was approaching the end of his usefulness, and thus perhaps his life.

There were primarily two factions within the Irish community who held any kind of position: the Brannigans and the O'Neills. The Brannigans came from the construction background, their ancestors having built much of that part of the city at the turn of the previous century, but the O'Neills were new blood, the founder of their lineage a man called Callum O'Neill, an immigrant from the Midwest who believed he would make his presence felt in the capital of the world. There was no love lost between the two families and their bastard offspring. They would argue between themselves about the ownership of bars, bookies and boxing clubs. They were devoutly and vocally Irish Catholic; they built their own churches and turned up in their Sunday bows and brights to be as hypocritical as it was possible to be in front of their God and the Virgin Mary. After church was done they would drink until they fell down in the street, and then they would get up to knock each other six ways to Christmas just for the hell of it. They were like children, squabbling in the sandbox about who would win or lose which half of which street, but that did not make them any less dangerous. They were inbred and vicious, they did not have the class and intellect of the Sicilians and Genovese, and they didn't seem to care whose toes they walked on in order to get what they wanted.

Don Calligaris sent Ten Cent down to fetch me from the Baxter Street house. Victor was still bruised, but the wounds in his heart were healing and he was finding more time for his friends and the Martinelli boys.

"Sit down," Don Calligaris told me when I entered the kitchen. The room was filled with smoke as if he had been seated there for some hours contemplating some difficulty.

"We have an issue," he said quietly, "and was there any way to deal with this without you then I would take that route, but this is an issue of significance and it needs to be addressed quickly and professionally."

Someone needed to die; that was evident from his manner and the tone of his voice. Someone needed to die and he wanted me to kill them.

I respected Don Calligaris enough to let him talk, to hear him out, before I explained to him how this could not be done by me.

"We have the Irish problem knocking at our door and we need to send them a message," he said.

Ten Cent stepped into the room, closed the door and took a chair beside me.

"It needs to be a very clear and concise message, a message that cannot be misconstrued or mistaken for anything else, and a decision has been made that that message needs to be delivered by us."

"Who is it?" I asked.

"There is a history with the Brannigans," Don Calligaris said. "They are part of old New York. They have been here a hundred years or more, but this new crowd, these O'Neills, they have been here since last goddamn weekend and they are becoming tiresome. Our people have spoken with the Brannigans, we have drawn some lines in the sand regarding territories and dues, and it has been agreed that we will take care of the O'Neill problem so as to avoid an all-out war between the Irish factions."

"So who is it?" I repeated, knowing before Don Calligaris spoke whose name he would give.

"James O'Neill himself."

I exhaled slowly. James O'Neill was the godfather, the old man himself, the son of Callum O'Neill and the one who had brought the power and money to this part of Manhattan's Irish quarter. He was a heavily guarded man, a man treated like the Pope himself, and to be responsible for his death was to be responsible for my own. To kill James O'Neill would mean a retribution killing almost certainly, and to protect itself the Luchese family would have to give me up. They would not wish to, but that was the way of this world, and with Victor's life at stake also it would mean disappearing once again, disappearing somewhere where they would not think of looking.

"You understand what this means, Ernesto?"

I nodded. "Yes, I understand, Don Calligaris."

"And you understand what you would have to do as a result?"

"Yes, I would have to vanish into thin air never to be seen again."

"And this thing . . . you would be willing to do this thing for us?"

"There is no one else?" I asked, but in itself it was nothing more than a rhetorical question.

Don Calligaris shook his head. "There is no one else who could disappear as easily as you. There are other men who could do this, other men who would do it very willingly, but they have families here, parents and grandparents, wives and children and sisters. To make them disappear would be too difficult, and it's not as if we could enroll them in the Witness Protection Program."

Don Calligaris smiled, but his moment of attempted levity did not unburden the weight of responsibility I felt. What he was asking of me was perhaps the most difficult thing I had ever been asked. Killing O'Neill would be very difficult. It would be like killing Don Calligaris . . . no, more difficult than that, because Don Calligaris had only two people to look after him, myself and Ten Cent, and many were the days when we were in the Baxter Street house while Don Calligaris was in the Mulberry house alone. James O'Neill had at least two or three men with him at all times, men who would be all too quick to take a bullet for him and who would come after me unrelentingly until they saw me dead. If I did this I would have to make no mistake, and once it was done I would have to disappear immediately from New York and go somewhere where I could not be found. I had not only myself but Victor to think of, and to risk his life after all that had happened would be too high a price to pay.

"I would never be able to come back," I said. "I would have to leave New York and go somewhere . . . somewhere unknown even to you, and I would never be able to speak to you. If I was a younger man I could leave for ten years, perhaps more, and then I could return, but at my age—" I shook my head. "It would be the end of me as part of this family."

"I have been instructed to tell you that you will be given everything you ask for. I have been told that you will be paid half a million dollars and you will be respectfully and graciously retired from the family, and that no one will ever ask anything of you again. You will be treated as a made man, perhaps the first non-Italian made man in the entire history of the Luchese family. This is in itself a great honor, but I know you well enough to understand that money and status are not important to you. I know that the only important thing for you is the life of your son, but here is where you can take advantage of this. You can do this and then leave with Victor. You can go anywhere you want, and all the assistance you might need to accomplish that will be provided. Wherever you decide to go you can start a new life, Ernesto, a life without violence or killing . . . where people will not interfere with Victor's happiness; a life where there is no chance he will find out what you have done and the things that have happened in the past."

Don Calligaris understood me. He knew that the only way he would ever get me to do this was to present it in such a way as to benefit Victor. He was right. It was a clear decision. There was no question in my mind that at some point Victor would start to see things I didn't want him to see, perhaps hear things in error and begin to put the pieces of this puzzle together, and this I wished to avoid at all costs. Doing this would mean that any such eventuality would be completely avoided. There was a choice, of course there was a choice. There was never a situation in life where choices could not be made. But this time, and for the reason that had been given me, a reason I felt to be true, I believed that the choice was simple.

"I will do this," I said quietly. I could feel the tension within the room relax. Like the air released from a balloon. Don Calligaris had been charged with this task, and though Ten Cent would have given his life to honor Don Calligaris's request, though he would have taken a bus to O'Neill's house and waltzed in, guns blazing, with no concern for his own life, I could understand why Don Calligaris wanted me to see it through. No matter the past, no matter the years behind us, I was still an outsider, an immigrant from Cuba and the back end of the world. I could do this and there would be silence once I was gone. That was why it had to be me.

Don Calligaris reached out and took my hand in his. "You understand what this means to me?" he asked.

"Yes, Don Calligaris," I replied. "I understand what this means."

"You will have to prepare yourself in every way. Once this matter is dealt with you will have to leave without delay. It would be wise of course to send Victor on before you, perhaps some reason you could give him, somewhere he would be happy to go, and then you could join him afterwards."

"I will see to all the details," I said. "I won't speak of them to you, nor to Ten Cent, and therefore you will never be in a situation where you are required to give information you do not wish to. You can have the money ready for me?"

Don Calligaris smiled. "The money is already available for whenever you want it."

I tilted my head and frowned. "You were so certain I would do this?"

Don Calligaris nodded. He placed his hand on my shoulder. "Ernesto, you and I have been brothers for the better part of thirty years. I know you as well as any man, and I know that once you give your word there is nothing that can sway you from it. Who else could I trust with half a million dollars and my life's reputation?"

I rose from the table. I walked around it with my arms wide. Don Calligaris rose also and we hugged.

"We have had some life together," he said when he released me.

I stepped back. A tight fist of emotion lodged in my chest and I found it hard to speak. I looked at an old man facing me, an old man who had once been brash and arrogant and believed he would one day rule the world, and I realized that in some way he'd been more of a father to me than anyone else.

"Don Calligaris—" I started, but I could not continue.

He smiled and nodded his head. "I understand," he said, "and there is no need to speak. We have lived this life, you and I, and wherever we might find ourselves we will not be among those who will ask themselves what would have happened if they had sought such adventures. We sought them, we lived them, and now we are old we must look after ourselves, eh? There are people now dead because of us . . . but there are people who would not be alive had we not protected them. This thing of ours, eh? This thing of ours . . ."

I reached out my hand and took his arm. I held it tight and closed my eyes.

Don Calligaris closed his hand over mine. "For the rest of your life," he whispered, "I bless you and your son."

I was released, and then I turned and hugged Ten Cent. He said nothing, but in his eyes I could see that he would remember this day as something important and meaningful.

I stayed a few minutes longer. Don Calligaris told me to let him know when the money was needed and it would be delivered to the Baxter Street house.

I stood for a moment on the porch stoop, the smell of spring in the air, a cool breeze making its way down Mulberry Street, a street where once upon an age ago I had walked hand in hand with Angelina Maria Tiacoli, and then I turned and looked toward the sky.

"For your son, Angelina," I whispered, "and for your brother, Lucia . . . for you I will do this thing so he can begin his own life free from the past."

And then I pulled my collar up around my throat and started walking home.

That night I made my decision. To return to Cuba would have been madness. Chicago was out of the question also, for what was there in Chicago but the memory of a life I had chosen to leave? Los Angeles, Las Vegas, even Miami—all of them carried their own ghosts. It was when I thought of something Don Giancarlo Ceriano had told me so many years before that it came to me.

The thing that a man most fears will be the thing that eventually kills him.
And I made my decision.
My life would end where it had begun: New Orleans.
I broached the subject of a trip with Victor who seemed at once enthused.
"New Orleans?" he said. "But why?"
I smiled. "We are here in America, Victor. You said you wanted to see the things I had seen. I was in New Orleans for some years when I was a very small boy and I saw the Mardi Gras. It is like seeing the Pope address the people in St. Peter's Square, like being in Times Square when the New Year turns . . . there are some things that you must witness to believe it can happen."
"And when would we go?" he asked excitedly.
"Almost at once . . . a couple of days perhaps. I have planned for you to go ahead without me—"
Victor frowned. "You're not coming?"
I laughed. "Of course I will come. It will be a family holiday. But there is something I have to do that will take me a few days and then I will come down after you. We will meet there and stay for a week or so and then we will come back. Besides, there are so many things to do and see, so many places to go, I don't think I would find the energy to keep up with you."
Victor was nodding enthusiastically.
"So you are pleased with this idea?"
"Pleased? I think it's a fantastic idea. Let me go tell the Martinellis."
I shook my head. "Let me make arrangements," I said. "Until the arrangements are made I would ask you to say nothing of this to anyone, not even your friends the Martinellis."
"But—"
I raised my hand. "Remember the terrible trouble you caused for me in Havana when you wanted to come here?"

Victor smiled, looked a little embarrassed.

"Well, we did as you wished. We came here. I did that for you even though I did not want to come, and now I am asking something of you. I do not want you to tell anyone where you are going, okay?"

Victor looked confused. "Are we in some trouble?"

"No," I said. "We are not in trouble, but there is a reason I want this to be only between you and me, and I want you to give me your word you will keep it a secret."

Victor opened his mouth to say something.

"Your word, Victor?"

He nodded. "I don't understand, but if that's the way you want it—"

"I do, Victor."

"Then you have my word."

"Good," I said. "Now go and prepare some things for your journey."

And so it was done. I saw Victor board a train bound for New Orleans. He took with him clothes and money, one and a half thousand dollars in cash, and I had called ahead and made a hotel reservation for him in the center of the city. He would be there to see the beginning of the Mardi Gras. I prayed to a God in whom I did not believe that I would be there also.

I stood on the platform until the train had vanished from sight, and then I turned and walked back to my car. I drove to the Baxter Street house to collect my things, among them a suitcase containing half a million dollars in hundred-dollar bills. I carried my things to the car, stowed them in the trunk, and then I drove up through SoHo to the West Village, where I took a room in a cheap hotel, the fee paid in cash, a false name registered in the book.

I sat in the dank-smelling room for a little more than two hours. I waited until it was dark, and then retraced my journey back to the Bowery district.

At seventeen minutes past nine that evening, outside a small and fashionable Italian trattoria on Chrystie Street, eyewitnesses would say they saw a middle-aged man, graying hair, a long overcoat, step from the alleyway beside the building and open fire with two handguns. In a relentless hail of bullets three men would go down—James O'Neill, a second called Liam Flaherty, a third called Lonnie Duggan. Flaherty and Duggan were well-known boxing celebrities from the Lower East Side circuit. O'Neill was a multimillionaire construction heavyweight on his way to the theater.

The man, he of the graying hair and long overcoat, did not so much as run from the scene as expertly dodge between the passing cars and disappear down a facing alleyway on the other side of the road. No one could give a clear description, some said he looked Italian, others said he seemed more Greek or Cypriot. The guns were never found despite a three-day fine-tooth-comb scouring of the area by more than thirty policemen and a team from Manhattan's 7th Precinct Crime Scene Investigation Unit. The man disappeared also, like a ghost, like a vague memory of himself, and those that mourned the loss of O'Neill, Flaherty and Duggan were as nothing amidst the vast rush of noise that was Manhattan.

Had you followed me that night you would have seen me hail a taxi-cab three blocks away. That taxicab took me back to the hotel, where I collected my things and left immediately, taking another cab ride across the Williamsburg Bridge and all the way to Brooklyn. There I took a train bound for Trenton, New Jersey, where I stayed for a further two days before leaving for New Orleans.

As I departed, I tried not to think about where I was going and what it would mean to me. I was away, I had done what I had promised and I had escaped. Victor was safe. No one but I knew where he was, and that was enough for me. I knew I was entering the final chapter of my life, but I went without fear, without the sense of impending violence that had so often accompanied me, and safe in the knowledge that my son would survive me and know nothing of his father's past.

To me that was the most important thing.

It was what his mother would have wished.

TWENTY-SIX

"IT'S THE SON," Woodroffe said, once again stressing his certainty that Perez had not acted alone.

Hartmann turned at the sound of someone coming through the door of the hotel room. They had set up camp on the second floor, a suite of four rooms—one for Schaeffer, Woodroffe and Hartmann, another for Kubis and his recording equipment, a third for Hartmann to speak with Perez, the fourth to house the dozen or so Feds that always seemed to be on hand.

Schaeffer paused in the doorway. He looked confused, fatigued, worn around the edges.

"Whether it's the son or the Archangel Gabriel is the least of our worries right now," he said.

"What?" Woodroffe asked.

"Attorney General Richard Seidler has somehow managed to convince Director Dohring to go after Feraud."

"What?!" Hartmann said.

Schaeffer looked down at his shoes as if embarrassed to relay the message.

"Go after?" Woodroffe asked. "Go after, as in pursue a line of investigation, or go after as in arrest him and bring him in?"

"The latter," Schaeffer said, and then he crossed the room and sat down in an armchair against the wall.

"Bloodbath," Woodroffe said. "It'll be a goddamned bloodbath."

"Nothing, I mean *nothing*, goes out of this room, right?" Schaeffer said, and he looked at Hartmann as if Hartmann could not be altogether trusted.

"I don't believe this," Woodroffe said. "I understood that the policy decision regarding Feraud was to leave him be, let the old bastard croak and then take the family apart."

Schaeffer scowled at Woodroffe and shook his head, attempting to be discreet.

"Guys," Hartmann said. "I've been here right from the start of this. I am well aware of the fact that Feraud was a known quantity . . . I mean, for God's sake, you know how many times I came across his name over the years? The only thing that has come as a surprise is his connection with Ducane."

Schaeffer looked away for a moment, and then he turned to face both Hartmann and Woodroffe. His eyes said it all before he voiced the words. "Not Ducane," he said.

Woodroffe stood up and started pacing the room. "You gotta be kidding," he said. "You cannot be fucking serious. Seidler is not going after Ducane?"

"Seidler wants Feraud and Perez, but more than anything else he wants the girl back, dead or alive."

"So Ducane will just walk away from this?" Hartmann asked. "Despite everything that Perez has said?"

"Attorney General Seidler has received a transcript of every word that has passed between you and Perez," Schaeffer said. "He has tracked this every step of the way, first and foremost because of his responsibility to the system, secondly because we are dealing with the daughter of a United States governor. It is only recently that he has begun to appreciate how deep this might go, and that if any part of what Perez has said is true then they have someone within their own system that could cause them a great deal of trouble."

"Ducane will roll over on Feraud in order to save his own neck," Hartmann said. "No one, absolutely no one has been willing to testify against Feraud, but Ducane will . . . guarantee it. That's why they're not going to go after him officially. They will have him give confidential testimony to the Grand Jury—"

"The plea bargains that will go on I don't even wanna know," Schaeffer interjected, "and if that's what happens then all well and good, but the fact of the matter is that we still have Ducane's daughter missing, and whatever her father might be guilty of we still have a responsibility to find her. That has to be at the forefront of our minds regardless of whatever else might be taking place."

"Tomorrow morning," Hartmann said. "He said that tomorrow morning he will finish this. The deal was that we would hear him out, hear every word he had to say, and then he would tell us where he has the girl."

Schaeffer nodded. "And I hope to God she's still alive."

"But why?" Woodroffe asked. "Why all of this performance? What the hell has Perez actually gained by doing this?"

Hartmann smiled. "I think he wanted Ducane and Feraud taken out."

"For what reason?" Woodroffe asked. "What would he gain by having these two removed? These are people Perez has killed for. I mean, for Christ's sake, he killed three people here in Louisiana in 1962 at the behest of Feraud and Ducane, and then it appears that the death of Jimmy Hoffa, while not perhaps organized and ordered by Feraud, was certainly sanctioned or condoned by them both. This whole thing with the pattern that was drawn on McCahill's back. Surely that was nothing more than a reminder to Ducane about Hoffa? Ducane was willing to send McCahill to kill Hoffa, remember? Perez was an employee, that's the truth. These people were the ones who paid him, in effect. What on earth has actually been gained by doing this?"

Hartmann shook his head. "I don't believe we're gonna find that out until tomorrow."

There was silence for a moment, and then Woodroffe once again spoke of the son.

"What the hell is this with you and the son?" Schaeffer asked.

"It's the thing about family," Woodroffe said. "Perez was always an outsider. True, he might have worked and lived with these people for the better part of his entire life, but he was never really one of them. His wife and daughter were murdered and the families did nothing. They couldn't do anything, because of the nature of their relationship with Perez's wife, but primarily because Perez wasn't Italian. He was Cuban, an outsider, and really nothing more than a hired hand. Had he been Italian they would have taken their revenge. Of that I am sure."

"But they didn't," Hartmann interjected. "And so perhaps he has taken his own."

Neither Schaeffer nor Woodroffe said a word. The silence in the room was tangible, and when Hartmann spoke once more it was as if he was the only person present.

"Maybe all of this was about Feraud and Ducane. Maybe the girl is dead. That's the worst scenario, right? She's dead someplace, her heart cut out, or her body in pieces and thrown into the swamps for the gators. Maybe the son had nothing to do with it and never did. Maybe he was ignorant all these years to the kind of man his father was. Truth is, the only person who knows everything is Ernesto Perez, and come tomorrow—if he tells us everything—then we will know as well."

"You think she's dead?" Woodroffe asked.

Schaeffer nodded. "Yes, I reckon so. Statistically, a missing persons report is filed, and within the next twenty-four hours the leads stay live. After that they go cold, people make tracks across everything. Footprints, fingerprints, hair and fibers and Christ only knows what else get lost in the passage of humanity. Another three days and the likelihood is the person is dead. Give it ten and the odds on them being still alive are down to about 4 percent. That's statistics based on hundreds of thousands of missing persons reports, abductions, kidnappings, every kind of case where someone takes a walk and never comes home. The ones that are found, the ones that make it back alive . . . Well, they are home within forty-eight hours. That's just the cold, hard reality."

"So why kill her and go through all of this?" Woodroffe asked, knowing even as he asked the question that the answer was obvious, and voicing it for no other reason than grasping at straws, asking anything that might throw some fragile shadow of hope across the thing.

"So we would sit here patiently and listen to his life," Hartmann said.

"And that, simply enough, was the way he could make us hear the truth about Feraud and Ducane," Schaeffer said.

"Maybe," Hartmann replied.

"Right," said Woodroffe. "It's all a maybe."

Hartmann looked up at both of them. "Until tomorrow," he said, and rose from his chair. He walked along the hallway to the stairwell and made his way down to the foyer.

He believed he'd never been so exhausted in his life.

He was there on the street in front of the hotel when the FBI transporters came. There were two of them, an older man, tall and heavyset, almost too old to be in active service, and a much younger one, dark-haired, and had he been but a few years older they could have been stand-ins for himself and Perez. Agents such as these were specially assigned to tasks such as this—the passage of Ernesto Perez to Quantico, right into the heart of the Federal Bureau of Investigation Headquarters, and there—while he awaited whatever judicial procedure the Bureau had arranged for him—there would be a hundred profilers with a hundred different tests, all of them eager to ascertain the specific common denominator that linked all such people together. There was no one thing: Hartmann knew that from studying thousands of case files on all manner of killings. These people were human beings just like the rest of us, and Hartmann believed all people possessed the capacity and will to murder; it was merely a matter of environment, conditioning, *situational dynamics* as they were so often referred to, that precipitated that actual moment, the split-second heartbeat when the mind moved the hand and the hand pulled the trigger or buried the knife or tightened the cord around someone's unsuspecting throat. It was not complicated; it could not be filed or classified or cataloged or cross-indexed; it was what it was, and what it was would always and forever come down to people. Guns were never the cause of death; thoughts and emotions and reactions were the force majeure. People killed people, and that was all there was to it.

So Ray Hartmann sat smoking his cigarette while the transporters made idle talk with the other agents present, and no one seemed to possess the same degree of tenacity or drive about this thing. Perhaps they all subconsciously knew it was coming to an end. Perhaps they all believed that Catherine Ducane was dead, and thus there was nothing else worth fighting for.

Outside the hotel stood an armored four-by-four Humvee. Dark gray, mirrored windows, bulletproof tires, skirting between the wheels that was designed to prevent anything being rolled beneath the vehicle. It was in this vehicle that Perez would make his final journey from Louisiana. Once he climbed inside that car he would never come back. Of that Hartmann was certain. And himself? Would he ever come back? He believed not, for this had not only been a trial by fire, it had also served as some means of exorcism and catharsis. Perhaps Louisiana would always and forever hold his past, both his childhood, and this particular rite of passage.

He rose and crossed the foyer. He shared a few words with the transporters—the elder one, Warren McCormack, the younger one, David Van Buren. They were cold and businesslike; they were here to do something specific. They had performed this function a thousand times before, ferrying the worst the world could offer to their final destination, and they were hardened and matter-of-fact and eager to be on their way.

Hartmann left the Royal Sonesta and walked the long route back to the Marriott. He felt as if he were breathing New Orleans air for the very last time. Tomorrow he would be gone. Tomorrow he would fly back to New York and call Carol. He considered once more what she had said when he'd had Verlaine call her. That she'd expressed doubts. *Actions speak louder than words*, she had said, and he felt sure he could demonstrate the necessary actions if only he was given another chance. But how many chances had she given him already? And how many times had he let her down? He would speak with Jess again, he knew that, and it was something he could almost physically anticipate. He wanted that meeting so much, a meeting where they could talk about the possibility of making their lives together work. He felt the conflict then: the need to know about Catherine Ducane versus the desire to know nothing more. Perhaps that was the point he believed he could let go of it all. It was so much a part of him, as intrinsically his own as his fingerprints, the sound of his voice, the way his face looked when he stared at himself in the mirror. Perhaps he had let whatever held him within this go—finally, without question. Perhaps. Time would tell.

In his room he watched TV. Cartoons, ten minutes of some awful made-for-TV movie, a brief flash of news that reminded him that the world had gone on about its business without him. He'd been here eight days, all of thirteen or fourteen hundred hours, and whereas a week had just effortlessly slipped through his fingers in New York, this week had seemed like a hundred years all crammed together with no breathing space at all.

He turned the TV channel to the hotel radio and lay on the bed. Dr. John played "Jump Sturdy," and following on came Van Morrison singing "Slipstream." He remembered the record, the album he and Carol had bought together so many years before. *Best record to make out to,* she'd told him, and then she'd laughed and told him they'd wear the grooves flat by the time they were finished. It was all there just inches back of his forehead—the faces, the names, the colors, the sounds, the places—everything they had shared together for the better part of a decade and a half. And then there was Jess, all of twelve years old, nothing less than a woman in her own right, and how she had made everything they had worked for seem truly and eternally worthwhile.

He believed it was all there, every single moment of it, and now all he had to do was say the right thing at the right moment and he could take it all back.

And so he slept, once again fully clothed but for his shoes, and when he woke it was a little after six in the morning, and he stood on the balcony of his hotel room and watched as the sun rose and warmed and then bleached the landscape of shadows.

"So you're up for the last show," Schaeffer said as Hartmann appeared in the hotel room doorway.

Hartmann looked at Woodroffe and Schaeffer; they appeared as worn-out as he felt.

"What happens when he's done?" he asked.

"We got a couple of transporters who've come down," Woodroffe said. "Didn't catch their names but they're here from Quantico. That's where he's going after all is said and done."

"You were told that was gonna happen?" Hartmann asked.

"We were informed that people would be coming, of course," Schaeffer said. "They don't send names or dates or anything, just that people would be coming to take Perez."

Hartmann frowned.

Schaeffer laughed drily. "You don't work for the FBI," he said. "Everything, and I mean *everything*, is on a strictly need-to-know basis. We're just the babysitters. We're just here to make sure he sings like a canary and doesn't fly the coop. When our job's done we get to go home and someone else takes Perez wherever the fuck he's supposed to go."

"You'll go with him to Quantico?" Hartmann asked.

"Sure we will," Woodroffe said. "I ain't letting the guy disappear outta my life without saying goodbye."

"Me and Woodroffe will go with them," Schaeffer said, "and you, Mr. Hartmann, you get to go back to the real world and fix this business with your wife."

"Any more news on Feraud and Ducane?" Hartmann asked.

"I haven't heard anything else," Schaeffer said. "I imagine we'll catch something on the news sooner or later."

"A statement will come from Ducane's office that he has been taken ill and his doctor has consigned him to complete bed rest for a month. The month will pass by and another statement will come that he has been slow to recover, and this unfortunate situation has required him to graciously offer his resignation from the office of Governor of Louisiana."

"You are a dark-minded cynic, Bill Woodroffe," Schaeffer said.

"No, I am a realist," Woodroffe said. "Even in the face of something like this these people will protect their own. Indirectly, of course, they will in fact be protecting themselves."

"These people, as you so diplomatically put it," Schaeffer said, "are the same people that sign your paycheck."

Woodroffe shook his head and sighed. "I've had enough for one week," he said quietly. "I wanna go home and see my wife, eat a proper meal, watch a game on the tube, drink three cans of beer and sleep in my own bed."

Schaeffer smiled. He turned and looked at Hartmann. "You call me in a couple of weeks," he said. "Call me at my office and I'll tell you what I can about what happens with Perez, okay?"

"Appreciated," Hartmann said.

"And here we go," Schaeffer said, as a commotion of voices and noise was heard from the corridor.

Hartmann rose slowly from the chair. It seemed that every muscle, every bone, every sinew and nerve in his body was screaming at him to lie down. He fought the urge. He put one foot ahead of the other. He made it as far as the doorway, walked down the hallway and turned left.

He paused for a moment, closed his eyes for just a fraction of a second, and then he stepped into the room.

"Mr. Hartmann," Ernesto Perez said quietly.

"Mr. Perez," Hartmann replied.

"I believe this will be the very last time that we speak face to face."

"I believe so."

"It has been a fascinating week, has it not?"

"Not my choice of words, but I understand the sentiment."

Perez smiled and reached for a cigarette. He lit it, inhaled, and then allowed the tendrils of smoke to escape from his nostrils. "And you . . . you will be returning to New York?"

Hartmann nodded. "Yes. I plan to leave for home as soon as we are done."

"Home?" Perez asked, almost a rhetorical question. "I asked you whether you had managed to convince yourself that New York was your home, didn't I?"

"You did. Home is where the heart is, Mr. Perez . . . and my heart is in New York."

Perez looked down, and then turned slowly to the left. He spoke without looking directly at Hartmann, almost as if he was speaking to someone only he could see. "Age is a judge," he said quietly. "It is a judge and a court and a jury, and you stand before yourself and view your own life as if it was all evidence for a trial. You cross-examine yourself, you ask questions and wait for answers, and when you are done you deliver your own verdict."

Hartmann was silent. He waited for Perez to continue. He watched him almost without breathing, for he did not wish to disturb the man. It was as if Perez had slipped into a reverie, viewing all that he had done, all he had spoken of, and was now allowing matters to reach their own natural conclusion.

"I cannot say I have been right, and I cannot say I have been wrong," Perez said at last. "I find myself somewhere in between, and from this standpoint I can see how everything might have been different. Hindsight also is a judge, but he is biased and slanted toward a perspective that cannot be achieved without the luxury of hindsight. It is a paradox, Mr. Hartmann, indeed it is."

He turned back to face Hartmann. "We see everything so clearly once it has passed, do we not? I am sure there must be a hundred decisions you have made, and if given the time again you would have decided very differently. I am right?"

Hartmann nodded.

"So we live our lives for the moment, it seems, and we base our decisions on the information we have, but it seems that at least fifty percent of the time the information we are given is incorrect or false, or based on someone's opinion, someone with an ulterior motive or a vested interest. Life is not fair, Mr. Hartmann. Life is neither just nor equitable, and unfortunately we are not provided with a guidebook or a manual of rules regarding how it should be lived. It seems a shame, does it not, that in fifty thousand years of history we have yet failed to understand even the simplest aspect of ourselves?"

Hartmann looked away himself then. Perez was right, and despite the horrors that Hartmann had listened to, despite the violence and bloodshed that Perez had both instigated and condoned, there was something about the man that seemed to command an element of respect. Abhorrence and repulsion had in some small way become supplanted by a degree of acceptance. For all that had been done, Perez had never pretended to be anything other than himself. Unlike Ducane, unlike even Feraud, Perez had worn his heart on his sleeve; he had shown his colors; he had cheated and deceived and murdered, but never failed to recognize that that was what he was doing. Even his wife had been aware of the man he was, and though they had never spoken openly of his life he had never directly lied to her.

Perez looked across the table at Hartmann. Hartmann looked back. There was silence between them for some seconds, but that silence was neither awkward nor tense. It seemed, after all these things, that each had accepted the other. This thought did not disturb Hartmann. He did not question his allegiances nor his feelings. It was what it was. Perez had spoken the truth, and for this, perhaps this alone, he had earned Hartmann's respect.

"So," Perez eventually said, his voice clear and precise. "Let me tell you what happened when *I* came home to New Orleans."

TWENTY-SEVEN

AND SO AT last I had come full circle.

Ouroboros: the snake that devours its own tail, finally to disappear.

Here was everything I was, everything I became, everything I would ultimately be. Here was the beginning of every thought and deed, every action, every dream that soured and died some quiet and lonely death in the darkened shadows of my mind.

I arrived in New Orleans in early 2000. Mardi Gras was bursting the streets at their seams. The Vieux Carré was alive and throbbing with the sound of music and voices, the fireworks of color along rues d'Orléans, de Toulouse, de Chartres, de Sainte-Anne, de Sainte-Philippe, de Bourbon and de Bourgogne, the Halls of Preservation and Dixieland: the rolling syncopations of jazz blended with deep Southern gospel blues, and amidst all of this, my memories . . .

St. James the Greater, Ougou Feray, the African spirit of war and iron. Serpent and cross in the same cemetery on All Saints' Day, the spirited festival of Vyéj Mirak, the Virgin of Miracles, and her voodoo counterpart Ezili, the goddess of love. They drank to feed the spirit. Sacrificing white pigeons to the Petro loa. All Souls' Day, Baron Samedi, loa of the dead . . .

Carryl Chevron, gold and diamonds in his teeth, a car filled with wisdom—Aardvark through Aix-La-Chapelle to Canteloupe—and somewhere, perhaps even now, a brassy act in high heels with too much rouge and too little class, who waited hours in a dusty roadhouse asking herself whatever might have happened to the trick that never showed . . .

The smell of the bayous, the canal intersections, the wisteria and hickory and water oak; Chalmette District, the edge of the territories, the edge of the world perhaps . . .

The Havana Hurricane, his red-raw face imbued with alcohol and rage and the madness of sex alight in his eyes.

And she whose name I could even now barely utter without feeling the tension of grief in my throat . . .

And somewhere out there, in a world I had left believing I would never return, was my own son.

There—in a hotel on Lafayette Street, standing on the first floor veranda, behind me on the bed Victor's clothes scattered as if he had rushed to dress, to leave, to fill himself with the sights and sounds of this place—I stood quietly, my thoughts there for no one but myself, and I wondered how this would end. Seemed to me I had run from every place I had been; there had always been a reason to escape, behind me the deaths of people I had known and those I had not. Pietro Silvino, Giancarlo Ceriano, Jimmy Hoffa, Constabulare Luis Hernández; the dealers and druggies, the pimps and murderers and rapists and psychopaths. People whose lives had meant something of significance, and those whose lives had meant nothing at all.

I asked myself about my own life: if it had been something of value, or if I had truly been no better than those whose lives had been swiftly and expediently dispatched. I had never been one to rationalize and introspect, and understanding that nothing would be gained by such thoughts I closed them down quietly and stowed them away. Perhaps those thoughts would surface some other time, perhaps not. It did not matter, what was done was done, and there was nothing I could do now to change it.

I stepped back into the room to get a cigarette and returned to the veranda to smoke. I looked down into the crowd of swelling people, bodies pressed against one another with no spaces in between, and I knew I would not see Victor until he was ready to return. He was a young man now, seventeen years old, headstrong and determined and full of life. There was nothing I could do to contain his energy and neither would I try. He was *my* son, and so there would be something of me within him, but I prayed—once more to a God I hardly believed in—that he had taken from me only those things of worth. Some sense of loyalty, a respect for those who understood more of life than I did, an appreciation of the importance of family, and the knowledge that truth could be found no matter how much it might hurt.

I closed my eyes. My head filled with the sound of music, with the sound of the world and all it had to offer, and I smiled. I had been *someone*. That most of all: I had been *someone*.

I slept like a dead man that night, despite the noise, the heat, and the sound of the real world beneath me, and when I woke and put on my gown and walked through to the adjoining room, I saw Victor lying there on his bed, still fully clothed, beside him a girl, her skirt up around her thighs, her tee-shirt twisted almost to her neck. They were absent from this world, their faces flushed, their hair tangled from sweat, and I stood silently for a little while. Victor had not come back alone, and though my heart felt for him and I was in some way happy that he had found someone here, I also knew that this was the first sign of losing him. He was almost a grown man, and he would have his own dreams and aspirations, his own vision of how his life would be. And once he discovered that life, he would—inevitably—no longer be a part of mine.

I closed the door quietly behind me. I went back to the bathroom, I showered and shaved, and when I called down for breakfast to be sent up I once again returned to Victor's room to see if he and his friend had woken.

My son was still collapsed on the bed, but the girl was seated in a chair by the window. In the moment that she turned, the way her hair fell across her shoulder, the brightness in her eyes, she could have been Angelina. For a split second she looked surprised, afraid even, and then it was gone in a single, simple heartbeat. She smiled. She was someone different, and I wondered how I could have imagined she looked like anyone I had known.

"Hi," she said. "You must be Victor's dad."

I smiled and stepped into the room. "I am, yes," I replied. "And you are?"

She rose from the chair and walked toward me. She had on her skirt and tee-shirt, but her feet were bare, dirty from where she must have walked along the street, perhaps dancing, living life, loving all that New Orleans represented in this most passionate season.

"Emilie," she said, and then she spelled it for me. "Emilie Devereau." For a moment she looked a little awkward. "I met Victor last night. We were a little drunk." She laughed, and the sound was beautiful, a sound I had perhaps heard too little of in this life of mine. "I live upstate, quite a distance away. I was going to get a hotel room . . . we went every-where but they were all filled up to bursting. Victor said it would be okay if I just crashed here—"

I raised my hand; I smiled once more. "There is no explanation needed, Emilie. You are here with Victor and you are more than wel-come. Would you care for some breakfast?"

"Oh hell yes, I could eat a dead dog if it had enough ketchup on it."

I laughed. She laughed too. She was more than pretty. She carried herself with elegance and grace. She was about the same age as Victor, a little younger perhaps, and there was something about her that told me here was someone who could capture his heart effortlessly. Here was someone who would teach him to forget Elizabetta Pertini.

I turned back to my room. She followed me. Within a minute or two room service came with breakfast—fresh fruit, warm bread, some cheese and ham, eggs Benedict, orange juice and coffee. We sat facing one another at the small table by the open window, the breeze from outside lifting and separating the fine organdy curtains, and with it came the scent of bougainvillea and mimosa.

"So what do you do?" she asked as she poured juice into my glass.

I shrugged. "I am retired now," I replied.

"And before you retired?"

"I worked all across America, traveled a great deal."

"Like a salesman or something?"

I shook my head. "No, I was not a salesman." I paused for a moment. "More like a troubleshooter perhaps, a troubleshooter for businesses, you know?"

She nodded, "So you'd like go somewhere and if something wasn't working right in someone's business you'd fix it?"

"Yes, I would fix things, make them work again."

She nodded approvingly. "Cool," she said, and then glanced over her shoulder toward the door to the adjoining room. "You figure I should go call Victor or something?"

"He's okay . . . let him sleep. Seems you wore him out, young lady."

She looked at me askance, and then she blushed. "We didn't . . . we didn't . . . well, you know—"

I laughed. "Victor is not used to dancing for hours on end. He has come from somewhere where dancing was not his first order of business."

"He's cool though . . . he's a nice guy."

I nodded. "I think so, yes."

Emilie looked at me, her expression momentarily pensive. "Where's his mom? Is she gonna come down for the Mardi Gras too?"

"No, Emilie, she's not. Victor's mother died when he was a very young boy."

"Oh hell, that's awful. What happened?"

"A car accident," I said. "There was a car accident and his mother and his sister were killed. It was many years ago."

"Hell, I'm sorry, Mr. Perry."

I smiled. "Perez," I said. "It's Ernesto Perez," and then I spelled it for her which she found very amusing, and the moment of sadness was gone.

"So what you guys doing down here?"

"We came for Mardi Gras."

"Right, right," she said. "Me too. You been here before?"

"I was born here," I said. "A thousand years ago I was born right here in New Orleans, a little town outside of the city."

"And Victor was born here too?"

"No, he was born in Los Angeles."

"Like Los Angeles in California?"

I nodded. "The very same."

"Wow, that's cool. So he's like Californian, like the Beach Boys or something?"

"Yes, like the Beach Boys."

She nodded. She paused to eat her eggs. She glanced back over her shoulder toward the half-open door at Victor still collapsed on the bed.

"Go," I said. "Go wake him up. Tell him to come and have breakfast with the family."

She smiled wide. She almost fell off the chair and hurried back through to the adjoining room. She struggled to wake Victor, but finally he slurred resentfully into semiconsciousness, and when he realized that she was up, that I was right through in the next room sitting at breakfast, he rolled sideways off the mattress and hit the floor. She was laughing then, dragging him to his feet, pulling him across the room and to the table, where he sat down heavily. He looked as if he'd gone ten rounds with Slapsie Maxie Rosenbloom.

"Dad," he said matter-of-factly.

"Victor," I said, and smiled. "I think perhaps you should drink this." I handed him a bowl of hot black coffee. He took it, held the bowl between his hands, and then he looked sideways at Emilie and smiled sheepishly.

"You met Emilie then?" he said.

"That pleasure I have had already, yes," I replied.

Victor nodded, looking at me as if he figured I might need an explanation. I smiled at him. I sensed him relax. "I'm gonna take a shower," he said. "If that's okay with you guys."

"Sure," I said. "Emilie and I will sit here and talk for a little while."

I watched Victor head back to his own room. At the doorway he glanced back and smiled at Emilie. She waved him through the door and turned back to me.

"We went everywhere looking for a hotel," she said. "Everywhere was booked out completely and I didn't have anywhere to stay. My uncle is gonna be tearing his hair out."

"Your uncle?" I asked.

"Sure, my uncle. He brings me down here every year."

"And where is he?"

She shrugged. "Back at the hotel cursing me like God only knows what . . . probably have called the cops by now or somethin' equally stupid."

"He's at the hotel?" I asked.

Emilie looked awkward. "Well, er, yes . . . at the hotel. It was quite a way from where we were and there was no way we could have gotten a cab at that time."

"I see," I replied. "Of course not."

There was a moment's awkward silence between us.

"You should call him," I said, feeling the first sense of tension. The very last thing in the world I needed was to be tied up in some missing persons report with the New Orleans PD.

Oh sure, Officer, it was fine. I was over in the hotel with Victor and his dad. I slept there, and then I had breakfast. Sure, I'm telling the truth . . . go over there and ask them for yourself.

Emilie looked at me sideways. She smiled coyly. "Helluva liar I make, eh?"

I was silent for a moment waiting for her to explain.

"Okay, okay," she said. "I could have called my uncle and he would've come and fetched me, but . . . well, I like Victor, he's cool an' everything, and I figured what the hell, you know?"

"*Chi se ne frega,*" I said.

"Key senna what?"

I laughed. "It's an Italian expression. It means what the hell, who gives a damn, that kind of thing."

"Exactly!" she said. "I thought that very thing . . . not like I thought that we might—"

I raised my hand. "I believe your intentions were nothing less than honorable, Emilie."

She smiled. "Right, Mr. Perez, my intentions were honorable."

"Ernesto."

She nodded. "Right, Ernesto."

She reached for the coffeepot and refilled my cup. She was charming, bursting at the seams with life and energy, and I was pleased that Victor had found someone his own age here in New Orleans so quickly.

"So you should call your uncle," I reminded her. "Use the phone here. Give him a call. He'll be worried."

Emilie was hesitant for a moment and then she nodded. "I can use your phone?"

"Of course . . . over there on the stand."

She rose and padded barefoot across the carpet. She called information and asked for the number of the Toulouse Hotel. She scribbled the number on the jotter pad and then dialed.

"Mr. Carlyle, please."

She waited a moment.

"Uncle David? It's me, Emilie."

For a second she looked surprised, and then she held the receiver a few inches from her ear and looked across the room at me.

I could sense the explosion that was occurring at the other end and I smiled to myself.

"I know, I know, and you have no idea how sorry I am, but I'm okay . . . I'm fine, and that's the main thing—"

Another blast from the uncle.

"Okay, enough, Uncle David. I know you're pissed beyond belief, but the fact of the matter is that I'm okay and no one will be any the wiser. You let up on me and I won't tell Dad that you let me get away from you, okay?"

There was silence for a moment. The girl was bartering for her freedom.

"Okay, I promise."

Another few words from Uncle David.

"No, I promise, I really do. Cross my heart and hope to die . . . never again, okay?"

Uncle David seemed placated.

"Okay, I will. Maybe an hour or so. I'll get a cab and we can have lunch or something, alright?"

There were a few more words and then Emilie wished him goodbye and hung up.

"You were right," she said. "He was gonna wait another hour and then call the cops." She sat at the table, tucked her legs beneath her. "I'll go back in a bit and get the third degree for a while. Where was I? Who was I with? Where did I stay? All that kinda crap."

I nodded. I understood the third-degree kind of crap. "Your father?" I asked her. "He doesn't come down here with you?"

Emilie shook her head. "He's like the busiest guy on the planet. Meetings all the time, all sorts of important stuff. I think he's in the process of buying about eight trillion companies and if he leaves the office for like eleven seconds the world will end."

"A workaholic."

"A cash-aholic more like."

Emilie tore a thin strip of bread from a roll and dipped it in her coffee.

I looked toward the doorway and wondered what was taking Victor so long.

"So you guys here for a few days?" she asked.

I nodded. "Yes, we're staying for a little while. If Victor likes it here we might stay for some months."

"That would be cool. I could maybe come down and see you."

"Yes, that would be good," I said, and I meant it, for here I believed was someone that would give Victor all that he had become so aware of missing in Cuba.

The door opened and Victor walked through. His hair was wet, combed back from his forehead. He had on a pair of jeans, a white tee-shirt. Somehow he looked older, as if in one night he had gained a handful of years.

"Could I take a shower before I go?" Emilie asked.

I nodded. *"Mi casa su casa,"* I said. "Go ahead, take a shower, and then we will arrange a cab to take you to your uncle."

Emilie rose from the chair. She touched Victor's arm as she walked past him. "Your dad is cool," she said. "Hell, I wish my dad was more like yours instead of this Donald Trump thing he's got going on."

Victor smiled. He seemed pleased. He turned and watched her disappear and then came to join me at the table.

"Nothing happened," he said as he sat down. "I mean nothing happened between me and Emilie."

"But one day soon something will," I said. "And if it isn't Emilie then it will be someone else, and I want you to understand that such an event will be important and that it is natural and normal and the way life is. My first girlfriend was the cousin of a friend of mine. Her name was Sabina and her hair was longer than anyone's I'd ever known. It was perhaps the most important day of my young life, and it made me very happy."

Victor looked momentarily embarrassed. "You're not mad with me?"

I reached across the table and took Victor's hand. "You are happy?"

He nodded, "Yes, I'm happy. I had a great time last night, and I really like Emilie."

"Then I am happy too, and she said that if we stay here a while she will come down and visit with us."

"We could stay here awhile?"

"Yes, if that is what you want."

"For real? We could stay here?"

I smiled. "Well, perhaps not right here in this hotel but maybe we will take a house somewhere on the outskirts of the city and stay for a few months."

Victor smiled, seemed pleased. There was a light in his eyes, something new and youthful, something I had not seen the entire time we had been away from America. He was an American boy, perhaps more than I had ever been, and there were so many more things here that were right for him. Perhaps, truth be known, I had begun to realize that as my own life would come to an end so his would truly begin. Maybe that was now my purpose: to contribute to the life of another instead of contributing to their death.

Emilie reappeared. Her hair was wet, tied back with a colorful band, and she had on her deck pumps.

"A cab," I said. "We will send you back to your uncle and you will take whatever words he has to give you, alright?"

For a moment she looked irritated.

"If you are humble and tell him you are sorry then he will let you come back this evening and have dinner with us. Tell him he is more than welcome to join us if he so wishes."

And so it was done. Emilie Devereau was dispatched to the care of her uncle, and within an hour she called the hotel room to say that her uncle wished to speak with me. I introduced myself, told him that I was here in New Orleans with my son, and that his niece would be more than welcome to have dinner with us that evening. He seemed satisfied that it had not been some fabrication by Emilie to rid herself of her uncle for another evening. He apologized for being unable to join us but allowed that Emilie should come. Would I take care to see she was returned safely no later than eleven? I gave my word and the call ended.

Emilie came. We spent some hours together, the three of us, and it seemed for all the world that here were two young people, one of them my son, attracted to one another, enjoying each other's company, and perhaps, just perhaps, on the verge of falling in love. In Victor I saw myself, in Emilie I saw Angelina, and I vowed that I would do all I could to ensure this thing was preserved as long as it possessed a life of its own.

Emilie was in New Orleans another week. We saw her much of every day, and on two occasions I went with Victor to the Toulouse to collect her. There I met Uncle David, a remarkably serious man, and though he presented no opposition to his niece visiting with us I sensed an air of suspicion. I gave it no credence. It seemed to me that some people were born with such a slanted view of the world, and they were more than welcome to their fears and anxieties. Emilie was in no danger, for through her my son had found the greatest happiness I had witnessed, and for this I would be eternally grateful.

They stayed in touch once she returned home. He wrote often and she replied. On several occasions they spoke on the phone, and an arrangement was made for Emilie to visit once again nearer Christmas.

I rented a house on the western outskirts of New Orleans. I went about my days with nothing to concern me, and for some months it seemed sufficient that this was my life. Victor attended to the latter part of his schooling and enrolled at a college to study architecture. I supported him wholeheartedly, and he learned quickly and well.

Time unfolded quietly and without incident until the early part of 2001. It was then that I became aware of something that served to draw me back to my former life.

I was alone one afternoon. It was the second or third week of January. Victor was at college and I was eating lunch in a small restaurant. I had paid no particular mind to the people sitting at the adjacent table, but when I heard a name mentioned my attention was snapped toward them.

"Of course Ducane will shake things up. He's never been one to let these things go too easily—"

I turned and looked at them. I wondered if this was merely a coincidence, or if they were speaking of the same Ducane I had met so many years before.

I glanced toward them, and there, held up in the man's hand, was the front page of a newspaper. The face of Charles Ducane—so much older, but so unmistakably the same man—looked back at me. And the headline over it, DUCANE LANDSLIDES GOVERNORSHIP, almost took my breath away.

I did not eat anything more, but called for the check, paid for my meal, and left the restaurant. I walked half a block and bought a newspaper from a street vendor, and there, in startling black and white, the same face smiled back at me from the front page. Charles Ducane, the very same man who had stood beside Antoine Feraud nearly forty years before; the same man who had orchestrated the killing of three people whom *I* had murdered through his indirect command, was now governor of Louisiana. I smiled at the dark irony of the situation, but at the same time there was something about this that unsettled me greatly. I had not liked Ducane, there had been something truly sinister and unnerving in his manner, and I could only imagine that he must have risen to such a credible position through the sheer quantity of money that was behind him.

I walked the streets, unable to identify what it was that disturbed me so about this man: his manner, his conceited attitude, the feeling that here was someone who had engineered his way through life and arrived at a governorship through Machiavellian deceit and murder? And he had been the one, alongside Feraud, who had attributed killings to my name. The thing about someone having their heart removed: that had been Ducane and Feraud. It angered me that I was now in hiding somewhere on the outskirts of New Orleans, unable to engage in life the way I wished, and yet this man—guilty of the same deeds—was now proudly smiling from the front page of a newspaper with his public reputation intact.

At some point I tore the newspaper in half and hurled it to the sidewalk. I went home. I sat in the kitchen and considered my reactions, but I decided that I could do nothing. What was there to do? It would not have served any purpose to expose the man. In order to do that I would have to lay bare my own soul, and what would that have accomplished? Ducane was the governor. I was an immigrant Mafia hood from Cuba, responsible for the deaths of countless men. I thought of my son and the shame it would bring upon him. Whatever happiness he had now discovered here in America would be obliterated by one single action. I could never do such a thing.

After a while I calmed down. I had a drink and felt my nerves settle. True, I was here in this small house living my quiet life, but nevertheless afraid of nothing. Ducane, however, was up there in his governor's mansion, living with the ever-present possibility that someone might take an unhealthy degree of interest in his past. There would always be enemies, always be people who would find no greater pleasure than exposing the sordid details of some political figurehead's past, and money—no matter how much he might have—would only keep such things away for so long. Someone else, I concluded, could bring Charles Ducane down, and that someone would not be me.

Nevertheless I took an interest in the man. I watched him when he came on the TV. I went to the New Orleans City Library and learned something of his route to the governorship. He had been involved in state and city politics his entire adult life. He had worked alongside and within the bureaus that handled land acquisitions and property rights mergers, civil litigation, state legislature and union affiliations for industry and manufacturing plants. At one time he had spent six months as legal advisor to the New Orleans State Drug Enforcement Agency under the auspices of the FBI. The man had been busy. He had used his money and influence to carve out a position for himself within the political ranks of Louisiana, and for his efforts, for his undoubted generous contributions to many important funds and campaigns, he had been rewarded with his current title. In some ways he was a man not unlike me; he had used what he possessed to make something of his life, but whereas I had come from nowhere and ended up nowhere, he had started somewhere and wound up in an even more elevated position.

I collected newspaper articles about Ducane. I made an effort to see him when he made public appearances, and though there was even a moment when I approached him at the opening of a new art gallery and shook his hand enthusiastically, there was no indication of recognition. I knew who he was, I knew where he had come from and what he had done, but of me he knew nothing. I had been a means to an end forty years before, and beyond that he had even used my name to cloud the facts regarding several killings that had taken place. Whereas he was in the public eye, I remained anonymous, and that fact in itself became a source of particular enjoyment for me.

The following year Emilie returned once again for the Mardi Gras. The first week of April, and the streets of New Orleans exploded with life and color and sound. Once again her Uncle David brought her down, and once again he managed to be there without ever really being there at all. He was a strange man, quiet and aloof, and yet he seemed to have no difficulty permitting Emilie to spend much of her vacation with us. I believed that Emilie was more than a little responsible for his lack of opposition. We had seen her briefly a little before Christmas, but it had been a year since the previous Mardi Gras, and within that year she had grown. Victor would be nineteen in a few months, and in the following September Emilie would reach eighteen. She was a young woman, spirited and independent, and though I recognized her passion for life and all it offered, there was nevertheless an element of her character that I felt sprang from the strained relationship she seemed to have with her father. While she was with us she never called him, and he—apparently—never made any attempt to contact her. I questioned her one time, carefully, diplomatically, and her responses were dry and monosyllabic.

"He runs his own business then, your father?"

"And tries to run everyone else's as well," she replied, in her eyes an expression of sour disapproval.

"He is a driven man, it seems."

"By money, yes. By anything else, no."

I was quiet for a time. I watched her. She seemed at her most unhappy when the conversation turned toward her own family.

"But he cares a great deal for you, I am sure, Emilie."

She shrugged.

"He is your father, and despite the fact that he is a busy man I am sure that he loves you a great deal."

"Who the hell knows?" Again the sour expression, the flash of irritation in her eyes.

"All fathers love their children," I said.

She looked at me. "Is that so?"

I nodded. "Yes it is, and though there might be some people who find it difficult to express the way they feel it doesn't change the fact that they still feel those things toward their own blood."

"Well, maybe my father is the exception that proves the rule, eh?"

I shook my head. She was stonewalling me. "And your mother?"

Emilie smiled bitterly. "She left him, couldn't take any more."

"And where is she now?"

"Around and about."

"You see her?"

"Every so often."

"And she is perhaps a little more forthcoming in her affections for you?"

"She's as crazy as he is, but in a different way. She spends all her time worrying about what other people might think of her. She's possibly the most introspected and self-centered person I know."

I smiled. "Then tell me one thing?"

"Uh huh?"

"If your parents are so crazy, if they spend all their time either making money or worrying about what the world might think of them, then how come you turned out so good?"

She laughed, for a moment looked a little embarrassed. "Ernesto . . . stop it!"

I laughed with her. She relaxed. She asked me if we could go out, maybe see a movie or something, the three of us, and then have some dinner in a restaurant.

And we did, and there was no more talk of her crazy parents, and I knew better than to bring it up again. She was happy as she was, spending her time with Victor, the two of them like lovelorn teenagers, which is what they were, and I was happy for them both.

She left again the following week, and for a while it seemed that whenever Victor was not at school he was speaking with Emilie on the phone. I overheard a conversation. It was around the last week of May, and I was downstairs reading the newspaper. I went upstairs to use the bathroom, and as I passed Victor's door I heard him speaking.

"—like running away or something, right?"

He laughed as she replied.

"And you could rob his safe and come back down here to New Orleans and we could elope somewhere and get married in Mexico, and you'd never have to see either of them again."

Victor was silent again, and then once more he was laughing.

"I know, I know, I know," he said. "You don't have to tell me. I understand exactly what you mean."

I stepped away from the door to ensure I would not be seen.

"Aah, come on, I know that they're not involved in the same business, but can you imagine how it was for me? My dad was in the Mafia. He was a thug for the Mafia, for God's sake."

I felt the blood drain from my face. I felt my pulse quicken. Sweat broke out beneath the hairline above my forehead.

"I'm serious . . . no, it's not a joke. I'm telling you that's the way it was. Why the hell d'you think that we kept on having to move from city to city? He was a hitman for the Mafia, Emilie, I'm serious. He might seem like a friendly old man now, but that's because he's retired. Jesus, we went from Los Angeles to Chicago and then to Havana, and then we wound up in New York before we came here. I think something heavy happened in New York because we had to hightail it out of there so fast I couldn't catch my breath. I think he killed someone important. I think he killed someone really important for the Mafia, and they gave him shitloads of money and he came back here to New Orleans because he thought no one would find him here—"

I felt my world falling to pieces. I remembered things I hadn't remembered for years. I felt my fists clenching and releasing. My heart thundered uncontrollably in my chest, and for a second I believed I would keel over right where I stood. I took a step back and leaned against the wall for balance. I could not believe what I was hearing. Had I truly, honestly, imagined that Victor had been blind to everything that had happened around him as a child? Had I imagined that my life had been of such little consequence to him that he had never figured out anything at all? Who had I been fooling? Certainly not Victor—and in that moment I realized I had been fooling only myself. I was speechless, dumbstruck, overwhelmed with a sense of guilt the like of which I had never experienced.

"I mean, it took me some time, but I finally realized that my mom and my sister didn't die in an accident. They were killed in a car explosion that was meant to kill the man my dad worked for, this heavy-duty Mafia boss called Fabio Calligaris." Victor laughed. "I had an uncle of sorts, a guy I used to call Uncle Sammy, but everyone else called him Ten Cent. You tell me who the fuck is called Ten Cent apart from a Mafia hitman? Where the hell d'you get a nickname like that, eh?"

I took a step sideways and reached for the stair banister. I took another two steps, and with my left hand behind me I found the bathroom door. I pushed it open and stepped inside. I closed and locked the door behind me. I sat on the edge of the bath and started to breathe deeply. A wave of anguish overpowered me, and before I knew it I had grabbed a towel from the rail and buried my face in it. I started sobbing, a feeling of nausea tightening my chest and turning my stomach. For a moment I could see nothing but thick waves of gray and scarlet before my eyes. The tears rolled down my face. I wanted to retch but there seemed to be nothing at all inside me. I felt hollow. I felt broken, obliterated, and when I tried to stand it took every ounce of my strength and concentration not to fall backward into the tub.

I stood there for some time. How long I could not tell, but when I had finally managed to gather myself together I washed my face and combed my hair. I looked back at my own reflection and I saw a bitter and twisted old man. I was facing the truth, and the truth was ugly and distorted. How long had he known? Had this been some gradual accumulation of small things, like pieces of a puzzle that he had finally managed to assemble into a clear and evident whole? Or had there been one thing that had turned the light on in his mind? The death of Angelina and Lucia? How old had he been? Nine years old, all but three months. Had he known then? Had he been aware even then that there was something so very wrong about the business his own father was involved in? I could not bear to face the truth. My son, my only child, knew the truth about me. I was humiliated and distraught, crushed—much as my father must have felt when he realized he had murdered his own wife.

I stayed a minute longer and then I slowly unlocked and opened the bathroom door. I stood there silently, holding my breath. The house was silent. I edged along the hallway until I reached Victor's half-open door. I saw nothing. The bed where he had sat while talking on the phone was empty. I heard something downstairs. He must have finished the call and gone down. I didn't know how to face him. I didn't know how he would see me. But if he had known all along, if he had known these things for so long and still treated me as he had always done, then had anything truly changed? The only thing that had changed was that now *I* knew. Now *I* was aware that he knew of my past. Not the details, those he could never have guessed, but he knew enough to speak of how I might have killed people, how I might have been involved with organized crime, and how this involvement had brought the deaths of his mother and sister.

I took the stairs slowly. I had regained my balance, but still my chest was heavy and breathless. I reached the hallway below and heard Victor in the kitchen. He had switched on the TV, was watching some soap drama while he made a sandwich, and when I walked in and he saw me he did nothing more than smile.

"Making a sandwich," he said cheerfully. "You want one?"

I smiled back as best I could. I felt tension in the muscles of my face and imagined I must have grimaced. I shook my head, "I'm okay," I replied. "I'm not hungry."

"I gotta go to the library," Victor said. "There's some work I need to do, an assignment I have to get finished before the end of the week. We need anything? I could stop by the market."

I shook my head. "It's okay. We don't need anything, Victor. We've got everything we need right here."

I watched him as he ate his sandwich, as he surfed channels on the TV and drank a glass of milk, and then I sat for a long time after he'd left and wondered what I was feeling. Did I feel anything at all? I couldn't be sure, and to this day I cannot remember what, if any, decisions I made. I believed I had disconnected from my former life. I believed that Fabio Calligaris and Ten Cent, Slapsie Maxie, Jimmy the Aspirin, the Alcatraz Swimming Team, and everyone that had walked through these past years . . . I believed that I had left them all behind. But I had not, for they were there in my mind, and also—to my horror—they were in my son's memories as well.

Later he returned. It was dark. I had settled somewhat, had come to terms with some aspect of what I had discovered. I imagined that we could both survive this, that as time went by life would somehow become what it was in the present, and cease to be what it had been in the past.

I could not have been more wrong. I could not have been more wrong if I'd tried.

I did not speak to Victor of his phone call with Emilie. I did not question him as to what he knew, what he *thought* he knew, but I could not deny the fact that it was there, ever-present in the back of my mind. It was as if there was some closed box, and inside the box was all I had been, all I feared for what might happen, and only when I was alone, only when Victor was out, did I dare open that box and look inside. For the subsequent months, through his nineteenth birthday, beyond fall and toward Christmas, I wore a face for the world that was only half of my own. The man I had been was there, would always be there, but I did not let him loose. I could not dare to let him loose for fear of what might happen.

Emilie came down again after Thanksgiving. She and Victor spent a great deal of time away from the house, and only once was I aware of the fact that something more than teenage love occupied their thoughts and feelings. It was one evening, perhaps eight or nine, and she and Victor were downstairs in the kitchen. I had been upstairs reading and I came out of my room and started down the stairs as I was hungry. I stopped in the lower hall and could hear their voices. Perhaps it was innocent curiosity regarding what they might discuss when I was not present, perhaps a concern that once again Victor was detailing memories from his own past that involved me; whatever the cause I stopped there and waited to hear what they were saying.

"David has his own thing going on," Emilie was saying. "He has someone down here, some woman that he sees, I am sure, and so he doesn't really have a chance to complain about what I do."

"He has to call your father though?"

"Sure he does, but what happens and what he tells him are not necessarily the same thing. He tells my dad what my dad wants to hear, and that's the end of it. Me and David have an understanding. He knows I can take care of myself and he doesn't want anything to upset his own plans. That's why he's always so willing to bring me down here."

"And what about your mom?"

"Sometimes we tell her we're coming, like for a few days or something, and we stay maybe two weeks. I see enough of her. I mean for Christ's sake, all she does is spend her time telling me what an asshole my dad is, and there's only so much of that I can take. I come down here for a break from all that crap." Emilie laughed. "So David says we're with my mom and whatever, and my dad is happy with that because I'm not around the place bugging him while he's trying to work, and as far as my mom is concerned, as long as she sees me a few days of the year she doesn't complain. She's too busy arranging other people's lives to worry about what I might be up to."

"And your dad doesn't know about me?" Victor asked.

There was silence; I could only assume that Emilie was shaking her head.

"How come you haven't told him?"

"Because he'd be all over you like a freakin' rash, Victor. He'd have you investigated. He'd find out about your father. Before the week was out he'd know everything there was to know about you and that would be the end of my trips to New Orleans."

It was quiet for a few moments, and then Victor said, "We could take off somewhere. I know where my dad keeps his money . . . I mean, it's not like he puts the stuff in the bank or something. We could take some money and just disappear, vanish into the middle of America and no one would find us."

"You don't know who you're dealing with," Emilie said. "My dad's like this super-rich guy with all manner of contacts and your dad's a fucking Mafia hitman . . . you think between them they wouldn't have the wherewithal to find us if they wanted?"

Victor didn't reply.

"Victor, you gotta face the facts. My dad knew what I was doing down here he would have a coronary fucking seizure. I'm his sweet little teenage daughter, good grades, plays tennis, goes shopping in the mall with Daddy's charge card . . . he knew I was down here in New Orleans screwing a Mafia hitman's son he'd have me cut off from the family and put in a mental institution. We just got to accept the fact that it's gonna be this way whether we like it or not. We just deal with it. We see each other as often as we can, and when things change we can do what we wanna do."

"Things change? Whaddya mean, when things change?"

"Like when my dad dies or whatever."

"Dies? How the hell is he gonna die? You gonna kill him or something?"

Emilie laughed. "Hell, maybe I could steal some money off my dad and pay your dad to whack him!"

"No, Em, I'm serious. You're saying that to do what we want to do, to have people know about us, then we're gonna have to wait until your dad dies? For God's sake, that could be years and years."

Emilie sighed. "That's just the way it is . . . it's fucking Shakespeare, isn't it? The Montagues and the Capulets . . . the two families that could never be together. Romeo and freakin' Juliet, you know?"

I stepped away from the door and made my way back to the base of the stairwell. My heart was cold and quiet, like a stone in my chest. Sweat had broken out on the palms of my hands, and there was a deep pain throbbing in my head, stealing all my energy and my ability to think clearly.

My son and his girlfriend, nothing more than teenagers, had become the murderous star-crossed lovers. I did not believe for a moment that either of them had seriously contemplated any aspect of what they were discussing, but that was not the point. The fact was that they were talking about it, and thus such thoughts must have been in their minds. Emilie was a strong-willed girl, fiercely independent, and Victor was in love. There was no doubting that fact, and I knew how swayed he could be by someone such as her. She was, in her own way, quietly dangerous, and for the first time in my life I feared for him. Not as a result of something I had done or some element of my own past perhaps coming back to find us, but because of something *he* had done. He had known this girl a matter of two and a half years, they had seen each other perhaps a dozen or so times, but their separations seemed to have made them anxious to be together even more. I believed, certainly in the case of Victor and Emilie, that it was the fact that they could not be together all the time that made them want each other so much.

I went back upstairs. I sat on the edge of my bed. I asked myself what I was going to do, what I *could* do, and after some minutes I realized that I had no idea at all.

Emilie stayed until a week before Christmas, and then she returned to her father's home. She promised she would come back again for the Mardi Gras, and Victor made her swear that she would. They stood together in the front hallway for a small eternity, and Emilie shed some tears, and I believe Victor did also. It was as if I was watching two people being torn apart by nothing more than cruel circumstance and I asked myself why it always had to be so hard. Did we ultimately pay for what we had done? And, by default, by the mere fact that we were connected to those who had done wrong, did we pay for the sins of our fathers and mothers and brothers and sisters? In that moment I believed I would have killed Emilie's father. Without thought, without mercy, without compunction, I would have followed her to her house, waited silently until she left once again, and then stepped inside to murder him. He would be removed from the equation, and Emilie would have been free to choose what she wished to do. Perhaps Victor would go with her somewhere, out into the middle of America to lose themselves. Or perhaps she would have come here, and they could have spent the few years I would be alive living beneath this roof, aware of the fact that no one—but no one—would stand in the way of their happiness.

It was a crazy thought, a thought that belonged to the past, but the fact that I had even considered such a thing haunted me.

Victor let Emilie go, as did I, and we survived Christmas together. Once it had been enough that Victor was with me, but now I was so aware of how unhappy he was without her. It did not seem right. It was an injustice. I vowed that if there was anything I could do to redress the balance I would do it.

When Emilie returned after the New Year something had changed. There had been some difficulty between her parents, something that had rubbed off on Emilie, and for the first few days she seemed tense and quiet.

It was only at the start of the second week that both Victor and I understood what had happened, and how it was far closer to home than either of us had imagined.

"He doesn't want me to come down anymore," she said. We were seated at the dining table, eating dinner together as we had so often done before, and it was merely as a result of a comment that I had made that she finally broke down and told us the truth.

"I have thought about the summer," I said. "That we should perhaps arrange with your mother and father that you go somewhere other than New Orleans, perhaps a holiday in California?"

Emilie was silent; didn't say a word.

"Emilie? What do you think?"

"I think it's a great idea," Victor interjected. "We could go out to California and see Los Angeles." He turned and looked at Emilie. She had stopped eating. Her expression was distant and disconnected.

"Em?"

It was then that she said it: *He doesn't want me to come down anymore.*

There was silence for the better part of a minute, and then Victor said, "Who doesn't? Your father?"

She nodded. "My father."

I leaned forward. I felt concern and anxiety. "What did he say to you? Why doesn't he want you to come here anymore?"

She shook her head slowly and looked toward the window. "He said that I spend too much time away from home, that I am coming to the end of my studies and I should be working more and taking less vacation time. He said that he had spoken to my mother and they both agreed that it was time for me to grow up." She smiled bitterly. There were tears in her eyes. "I hardly see them, and yet they feel they have the right to tell me what I can do with my life."

"They are your parents, Emilie," I said, and even as the words left my mouth I knew I did not agree with nor condone what they had told her.

"Sure, they're my parents," she replied. "But that doesn't make me any less angry with them. What the hell do they know? What right do they have to tell me what I can and can't do? I'm nearly nineteen for Christ's sake! I'm an adult. I'm doing fine at school. I'll get the qualifications they want me to get, qualifications I never even wanted in the first place and only did because they insisted. I've done everything they wanted me to do the whole of my life, and just because they made mistakes doesn't mean they can force their opinions on me and make me do what they want me to do." She grabbed her serviette from her lap, bundled it up and threw it down on the table.

I looked at Victor. He was stunned into silence. I wanted to say something, anything that would make it alright, turn everything backward and give us all a chance to start over again, but there was nothing. My head and my mouth were empty.

"He said that this was to be the last time I could come down here until I finished school." Emilie said, and then once again she turned toward the window and fell silent.

"It will be alright," I said, believing at once that it would not. I wished in some way that she had said nothing. I wished she had perhaps left this until she was ready to leave. Then, at least, the time that we would spend together now would not be overshadowed by this revelation.

"He can't do that," Victor said, and in his eyes was the certainty that Emilie's father could do whatever he wished. He was a man of wealth and means, he could employ people to find her, he could have her grounded indefinitely, have her escorted to school and back again, and though in the process he might lose any remnant of love that his daughter might feel for him, the fact was that he could do whatever he wished and there was nothing Victor or I could do to change that. Emilie's father was in control. She was a part of our life, but she was not under our control.

"I don't know what to do," she said, and she turned back to me. She reached out and took Victor's hand. "I would ask you to come with me, but your life is here. You have to finish your own studies, and I know that my father would not approve of you."

She glanced at me nervously, and then she smiled as if making some attempt to lighten the atmosphere.

I knew it was coming. I knew what she would say, and in my heart I felt the rushing wave of horror at where we would go from here.

"I know my father would find out everything about you," she said. She looked at me. Her eyes were cool and emotionless. "I cannot make a judgment, but I know the truth, Ernesto. Victor has told me—"

"Emilie!" Victor snapped, but she turned and raised her hand and stopped him dead in his tracks.

"I am going to say what I'm going to say," she interjected, and once again there was that steely fire of determination in her eyes. Here was the fiercely individual Emilie Devereau; here was the strength of character that at once made her so attractive, and yet again made her someone you could not fool or deceive. "I am going to say it, and whether it's the truth or not doesn't matter." She looked at me once again. "You could be the richest man in Louisiana," she said. "You could own a hundred thousand businesses and donate millions of dollars to charity. You could have a spotless personal reputation and the best public relations people in the world, but still my father would not approve of my being with Victor."

I frowned. I did not understand where she was going.

She smiled. "But we all know that you don't run a business, and you are not the richest man in Louisiana, don't we? We know that there have been things that have happened in the past that none of us want to know the details of. We know that your wife and your daughter weren't killed in a car crash. I'm not going to pretend I know everything, and I'm sure there's a great deal more that Victor knows that he hasn't told me, but all of that is irrelevant. The truth of the matter is that my father is a bigot and a racist and a stupid and ignorant man. The simple fact that you are not American is enough. The fact that you are Cuban would be enough to convince him to never let me see Victor again. Like I said one time before, it all comes back to Shakespeare. Romeo and Juliet, the Montagues and the Capulets. We are destined never to be together if my father has anything to do with it."

Emilie turned and looked at Victor. "There have been things I haven't been able to tell you. There are things that I won't even tell you now. I love you. I want to be with you. But there is something here that is bigger than all of us combined and there is nothing I can do about it."

Victor was pale and drawn. His mouth was half-open as if he was trying to think of something to say but nothing was forthcoming.

Emilie raised her hand and touched Victor's face. "I didn't want to talk about this. I wanted to wait until I had to leave, but I cannot bear the thought of carrying this alone any longer. My father has forbidden me to come down here again and there seems to be nothing I can do about it."

Victor looked at me. He was waiting for me to say something, to make this terrible thing go away, but there was nothing I could do.

It was only later, after Emilie was asleep, that Victor came to me in my room.

"You have to kill him," he said matter-of-factly.

I raised my hand. "We will not—"

He stepped forward. "You don't think I know?" he asked. "You don't think I know who you are, what you have done? You think I have lived all these years without realizing what you did when I was a kid? I know who those people were, Uncle Sammy and Fabio Calligaris. I know that Mom and Lucia were killed by a bomb that was meant for Calligaris, and more than likely for you."

I sat silently. I watched my son vent his anger and pain. I could say and do nothing. How could I deny the truth?

"You don't think I know what you're capable of?" Victor went on. "I don't know all the details, and I don't pretend to know. Truth is I don't *want* to know. But I do know that men are dead because of you, and now . . . now when I need you to do something for me you cannot. I am your son, the only family you have left. I love her. I love her more than life itself, and now I need something from you you are going to tell me that it cannot be done. Emilie's father is nothing. He's a crazy person, someone who knows less about caring for his family than you do. Christ, of all the people you ever killed he probably deserves to die more than any of them—"

"Enough!" I said. "Victor, that is enough! You sit down. You sit down and listen to me."

Victor stood there, defiant and angry. I had never seen him so empowered with rage. He looked as if he would burst open at the seams.

"Victor . . . now!" I shouted, and hoped that my voice was not so loud as to wake Emilie.

He paused for a moment, and then sat down on a chair near the wall.

"You cannot ask me to do this," I said. "I am not going to deny what you say. I heard you talking to Emilie on the telephone long ago. I heard what you told her about me. I am not going to waste my breath trying to defend myself or my life, but the past is the past. I have left all those things behind. I made mistakes, big mistakes, and given the time again I would not make the same decisions. I lost your mother and your sister because of the decisions I made, and I know from experience that if I did this then I would lose you too. Not only that, but you would also lose Emilie. This is no simple matter of killing someone who stands in your way and that's the end of it. You go down that road and someone always pays the price. Look what I lost. The only woman I ever loved and one of my children. You think Emilie's father will not fight for her? And who's to say that with her father gone her mother would not feel the same way? These people, people with too much money and too little sense, they are perhaps the most dangerous people of all. You listen to what I have to say, you hear me on this. I am your father. I love you more than life itself, but I will not kill someone for you."

Victor looked back at me. There was honesty between us, true honesty for the very first time in all the years we had been together, and something had changed.

He leaned forward. He started to cry. I crossed the room and knelt before him. He rested his head on my shoulder. I put my arms around him and held him while his body was wrenched with grief.

"So what do I do?" he asked eventually. "What do I do? I love her, Father, I love her more than anything in the world. I have lost enough . . . I don't think I can bear to lose her as well."

"I know, I know," I whispered. "It will come right. We will think of something, Victor. We will think of something to make this right."

"Will we?" he asked, his voice cracking with emotion. "Will we make it right?"

"We will," I said quietly, and believed that I had never been more certain of anything in my life.

The two weeks that Emilie spent with us unfolded without further event. I said nothing, and neither Victor nor Emilie asked anything of me. They went about their business, they visited places together. They spent a great deal of their time in Victor's room and I respected their desire to spend their last days together and did not disturb them. I did not interfere in their life together, and I know that they were grateful to me for that. I did spend my time considering the problem. I looked at it from every angle and slant, and no matter the hours that I invested in this I could not think of a solution.

At last it was time for Emilie to leave. There were tears, of course there were, and both of them promised that they would speak and write at least once a day. I believed their feeling for one another was strong enough to see them through this, that the time would come when Emilie was old enough to make her own independent decision, her schooling behind her, perhaps her own career and home, and then she and Victor would be together once again. But I was also not so naïve as to dismiss the possibility that, separated from Victor, she would eventually miss the physical connection, that she would become a woman of means and methods, that she would perhaps find someone of whom her father approved, and then Victor would be left with nothing. He was loyal beyond question. Emilie Devereau was his first real love, perhaps the only one, and that was something with which I was familiar. After Angelina I could never have considered finding another wife. It had not been my age, it had not been the manner of her death; it was simply the fact that as far as I was concerned no one could ever have come close to being what she had been for me. She was alive in my thoughts, as was Lucia, and with them gone there was no thought that they could ever be replaced.

The subsequent weeks saw Victor burying himself in his schoolwork. He spoke with Emilie regularly, and I know that she wrote frequently because I was always there to see the mail arrive. But something was missing. The hope of when she would next come, the anticipation in our house as the weeks between her visits dissolved—that sense of promise had vanished. Victor was strong, and never again did he ask of me what he had asked that night. Nor did he question me about my past. It was as if we had all accepted the truth, and the truth—painful though it might have been—was now out in the open. It had evaporated, and there seemed to be no purpose in returning to it.

Toward the end of the year, my sixty-fifth birthday reminding me once again that time seemed to disappear effortlessly, more rapidly with each passing month, I resigned myself to the fact that the future of Victor and Emilie's relationship had been consigned to destiny. We shared Christmas together, Victor and I, but ever-present was the awareness that this was our first Christmas in New Orleans without her. It was different, but Victor seemed in good spirits, and it appeared he was coping reasonably well. On Christmas Day she called him, and Victor spent more than an hour talking to her. I did not listen to their conversation, but every once in a while I could hear him laughing and this pleased me. She had not found someone else it seemed, and perhaps her patience and loyalty were of the same caliber as Victor's.

I believed that everything would settle then. The New Year came, it was 2003; I was beginning to feel the weight of my years, that this life I had chosen could perhaps not have suited me better. I imagined that I would gradually fade out like a guttering candle, that I would be forgotten in the slow-motion slide of time and Victor would go on without me and find his own passage. He had done remarkably well with his schooling. He showed great promise and vision as an architect, and already there were possibilities opening up for him. He spoke of traveling to the east coast, that there were projects in Boston and Rhode

Island he was interested in, and I encouraged him to go out there and make his mark, to make his own individual presence felt in the world. He had not become his father, for this I was grateful, and though he knew more of me than I would ever have wished, it did not change the fact that he loved and respected me. Whoever I had been before, Victor had never considered me anything other than his father.

It was then, in the early part of June, that the ghosts came back to find me.

I was alone that night, Victor was away with friends at the cinema and I did not expect him back until late.

I was in the back room smoking a cigarette, and now I cannot remember what I was thinking about. I heard a car passing in the street beyond the front door, and then the car slowed and started to reverse. What made me rise and walk through to the front I do not know, perhaps some preternatural sense of foreboding, but I did rise, and I did walk through, and there I drew back the curtain and looked out into the street.

My breath caught in my chest. I could not believe that I was awake, that this wasn't some awful dream, some nightmare sent to punish me. Ahead of my house a car had come to a halt, a deep burgundy car, a 1957 Mercury Turnpike Cruiser, a car that had once belonged to Don Pietro Silvino and had been stored in a lock-up in Miami in July of 1968. A thirty-five-year-old memory surfaced like a dead body through black and turgid water.

The driver's door opened. I strained to see who was getting out of the vehicle. I could barely stand when I saw him. I leaned against the edge of the window and started to breathe deeply. There, on the sidewalk, no more than ten yards from where I struggled to maintain my balance, was Samuel Pagliaro, a man I had only ever known as Ten Cent.

He turned, and though he could not have seen me there behind the curtain, it seemed he was looking right at me. I felt a cold rush of fear pass through my body, and for a time I could not move.

He started walking toward the house. I backed away from the window and made my way to the front door. I opened it before he reached the end of the path. He stopped in his tracks. This old man, a man who made me see how far we had come, stood there for a moment and then held his arms wide and smiled.

"Ernesto!" he said proudly. "Ernesto, my friend!"

I felt tears in my eyes. I stepped out onto the path. I walked toward him. I hugged him. I held him for some small eternity and then I released him and stepped back.

"Ten Cent," I said. "Ten Cent . . . you are here."

"That I am," he said. "And as this is such a special occasion I have brought you your car!" He turned and indicated the Cruiser. It was the same as it had ever been. Three miles of silken paintwork and burnished chrome. My gift from Don Giancarlo Ceriano after the deaths of Pietro Silvino and Ruben Cienfuegos. I remembered everything, the past, all the things that had brought me here to this point, and I was overcome with emotion.

I started to cry, and then I was laughing, and then the two of us were walking into the house and closing the world out behind us.

We ate together, we drank wine, we spoke of things that had been, a little of things that were to come. Ten Cent asked after Victor; I showed him some of Victor's work and Ten Cent was pleased and proud like an uncle would be of a talented and bright nephew. Ten Cent was family, had always been, would always be, but at the same time he represented everything that I had so much wanted to leave behind. I realized then that such things could never be left behind. They were always there, and it was simply a matter of time before they found you once again. The present, even the future—these things were always and forever only a mirror held up to the past. The man I once was had now been reflected, and though time had passed, though the mirror was aged and spotted with distortions and discolorations, it was still the same man who looked back at me: Ernesto Cabrera Perez, killer, absentee father, indirectly guilty of the deaths of two of the people whom he had loved most.

Later, three, four hours perhaps, Ten Cent was quiet for a moment. He looked at me seriously and I asked him what was wrong.

"I came for a reason," he said. "I wanted to see you. I brought the car also. But there is another reason I came."

I fell quiet inside. I could feel my heart beating in my chest.

"Don Calligaris is dead," he said. "He died three weeks ago."

I opened my mouth to ask what had happened.

"He was an old man, and despite everything he survived all the world could throw at him. He died in his own bed, surrounded by the people who cared for him. It has taken me all this time and a great deal of money to track you down, Ernesto, but in his last moments Don Calligaris wished that I find you and tell you the truth."

"The truth?" I asked, fear roiling up inside me like a tornado.

"The truth," Ten Cent said, "about Angelina and Lucia . . . the night they died."

I felt my eyes widen.

"The bomb, as you know, was meant for Don Calligaris, and he did not tell you about it for fear of what you might do. But he is dead now, and before he died he wanted to know that you would discover the truth of who was responsible for their deaths."

Ten Cent shook his head. "It all went back to Chicago, the friends we made back then, the people we were involved with. There were disagreements, people in New York who were unhappy with the way things turned out, and the responsibility for resolving the differences was given to Don Calligaris."

"Differences?" I asked. "What differences?"

"The differences between those within the family and those outside who we were involved with."

"What people?" I asked.

"Don Calligaris was charged with the responsibility of closing down any business agreements we had made with Antoine Feraud and his New Orleans operations."

I looked at Ten Cent. I was struggling to understand what he was telling me.

"Don Calligaris, as he died, wanted me to tell you who was responsible for attempting to kill him . . . who was responsible for the murder of your wife and your daughter."

"Feraud?" I asked. "Feraud was responsible for the car bomb?"

Ten Cent nodded and then looked down at his hands. "Don Calligaris did not tell you, and made me swear that I would not tell you, because he feared that your vengeance might begin a war between the families that he would be held accountable for. Now he is dead, and he does not care what happens, and he loved you enough to want you to know the truth. He told me to tell you that you should take whatever action you felt was just in order to revenge the deaths of your wife and child."

I sat back in my chair. I was emotionally and mentally overwhelmed. I could not find any words to describe how I felt, and thus I said nothing. I looked back at Ten Cent. He looked back at me unblinkingly, and then I nodded slowly and lowered my head.

"You understand I will do what I have to," I said quietly.

"Yes," Ten Cent replied.

"And if I die doing this then it is not on your head."

"You will not die, Ernesto Perez. You are invincible."

I nodded. "Perhaps so, but this thing I am going to do will be the undoing of everything. It will mean losing Victor perhaps, and it will mean trouble for the families."

"I know."

"But even so, you tell me this and you are prepared to let the cards fall where they may?"

"I am."

I reached forward and took Ten Cent's hand. I looked up at him and saw the washed-out pale blue color of his eyes: the eyes of a tired man.

"You have done what Don Calligaris asked you to do," I said, "and for this I am grateful. Now I think you should leave, you should forget me and Victor and pay no mind to what happens now. This thing of ours is done."

Ten Cent nodded. He rose from his chair. "Give me your car keys," he said. "I am leaving the car I brought and I will take yours. You do what you have to do, and do it with the blessing of Don Fabio Calligaris."

"I will do this thing," I said quietly, and my voice was nothing but a broken whisper, "and that will be the end."

I watched him drive away. With him went everything I had worked to maintain; the falsity of my present situation dissolved beneath the weight of this knowledge.

I felt ageless and indestructible. I felt the years roll away from me and vanish into nothing. I wandered through my house, my thoughts racing in circles, and I found myself challenging everything I had striven to become.

I was a murderer. I had reached the end of my life but there was now one more thing that had to be done. I would go to my grave knowing that justice had been served.

Like the Sicilians had told me so many years before: *Quando fai i piani per la vendetta, scava due tombe—una per la tua vittima e una per te stesso.*

Yes, I would dig two graves—one for Antoine Feraud, and one for myself.

I slept well that night, secure in the knowledge that my life had turned full circle. I would swallow my own tail, and finally, silently, irrevocably, everything I had been, everything I had become, would magically disappear.

I would find Angelina and Lucia once more, and this thing of ours would be done.

TWENTY-EIGHT

WHEN PEREZ WAS done talking Hartmann leaned back in his chair and crossed his arms.

"What was the saying you used? The one about revenge?" he asked.

Perez smiled. *"Quando fai i piani per la vendetta, scava due tombe—una per la tua vittima e una per te stesso."*

Hartmann nodded. "But in your case the other grave was not for yourself, right?"

Perez nodded.

"One for Feraud and one for Charles Ducane . . . because these people were ultimately responsible for the deaths of your wife and your daughter."

Perez said nothing; he merely reached for a cigarette and lit it. There was an air of satisfaction about his manner, perhaps a sense of completeness, as if now he had said all he intended to say and his business was closed.

"It is some life you have had," Hartmann said.

"It is not over yet," Perez replied.

"You understand that you will spend the rest of your years in some high-security penitentiary facility."

"I imagine so."

Hartmann was quiet for a moment, and then he looked across at Perez. "I have a question."

Perez nodded.

"Your son."

"What about him?"

"Where he is, what he's doing . . . does he have any real idea of what has happened here?"

Perez shrugged.

"Does Victor know where you are, that you kidnapped the daughter of the governor of Louisiana?"

Perez shook his head.

"But he knows enough of the life you have led—"

"Victor knows that I was not prepared to kill Emilie Devereau's father," Perez interjected, "and though he believed his love for her was strong enough to have carried the guilt of such a thing, he is still in some ways naïve. He knew enough of who I was to understand that I would have been capable of such a thing, but when he finally realized that I would not commit this murder for him he decided that he would have no more to do with me." Perez paused and shook his head. "In his mind he managed to convince himself that somehow I had betrayed him."

"Do you know where he is now?"

Perez shook his head. "He is out there somewhere, Mr. Hartmann, and though I love him, love him more than any other person in the world, I am able to let him go. He will find his own way, I am sure of that, and though I will never see him again I know also that he will never become the man that I became."

"You're sure of that?"

"Yes, I am sure of it."

"You said something to me about Shakespeare, the two families that could never be together."

"I did."

"And this was what you meant . . . Victor, and Emilie Devereau?"

Perez nodded. "Yes."

"And when you could not give your son what he wanted you decided to seek revenge for the murders of your wife and your daughter."

"I did."

"Understanding that in closing that particular chapter of your life you would also see your own life come to an end?"

A hint of a smile from Perez, and then he closed his eyes for just a moment. He leaned forward, ground out his cigarette, and reached for another.

"They will seek the death penalty, you know."

"I know they will," Perez said, "but I am sure there will be many years of appeals and wrangling between the lawyers, and before they ever get to preparing my lethal injection I will die of old age." He drew on his cigarette; tendrils of smoke crept from his nostrils.

"And now?" Hartmann asked.

"Now I tell you where she is, right?"

Hartmann nodded.

"And as for me?"

"There are two men here from Quantico. They are going to take you to the FBI Behavioral Science facility where there are at least three dozen criminal profilers who want to pick your brains."

"The food will be good down there?"

Hartmann shook his head. "I have no idea."

Perez smiled. "Perhaps I will order take-out."

"Perhaps you will. And now, please, tell us where we find Catherine Ducane."

"You remember where you found the car?"

"Gravier."

"Just a little way from there you will find a place called the Shell Beach Motel."

Hartmann's eyes widened. "The Shell Beach Motel . . . that's no more than two or three miles from here."

"Keep your friends close, your enemies closer, that's what I was told," Perez said. "Cabin number eleven, the Shell Beach Motel. Go find Catherine Ducane and tell her it is over."

Hartmann rose from his chair. He crossed to the door, opened it, and beyond it found Stanley Schaeffer waiting in the hallway.

Schaeffer nodded at Perez.

Ernesto Perez rose slowly. He took one more drag of his cigarette and stubbed it out in the ashtray. There was an air of finality to this action, as if he understood that everything had now come to its own natural conclusion. He walked toward Hartmann, and then paused in the doorway. He reached out his hand. Hartmann took it and they shook. Perez then leaned forward and—with his hands on Hartmann's shoulders—he kissed each of his cheeks in turn.

"Live your life well, Ray Hartmann . . . go back to New York and make believe this thing never happened. Fix whatever differences you may have with your wife and make it work, if only for the sake of your child."

Hartmann nodded.

"So long, Ray Hartmann," Perez said quietly, and then he turned to Schaeffer and smiled. "Let's do it," he said, and when Schaeffer started down the hallway, Ernesto Cabrera Perez followed him slowly and never once looked back.

The FBI unit assigned to recover Catherine Ducane had already left by the time Schaeffer and Perez reached the street. Parked against the curb was the Humvee, beside it the two agents from Quantico, McCormack and Van Buren. Van Buren made his way around the back of the vehicle and handcuffed Perez. He escorted him to the side of the Humvee and McCormack opened the door. Van Buren climbed in beside Perez and used a second set of cuffs to manacle him to the arm of the seat. McCormack took the driver's side and Schaeffer sat up front beside him. By the time the engine had started both Hartmann and Woodroffe had reached the street outside the hotel. They watched as the Humvee pulled away, and as it passed the intersection Hartmann saw Perez turn and look at him. His expression was implacable and emotionless.

Hartmann lowered his head and looked at his shoes. He felt as if the center of his life had been pulled out and everything inside him was spiraling silently into the vacuum it had left behind.

"The son," Woodroffe said. "I still can't get my mind off the son."

"You were listening across the hall?" Hartmann asked.

"I was," Woodroffe said. "I know what Perez said, this thing about the son being pissed off because he wouldn't kill the girl's father, but I still feel there's something else. I'm gonna go inside and call Quantico . . . get them to run this Emilie Devereau through the database. If we can find her, we might be a step closer to finding where Victor Perez has been while his father has been with us."

"You still think he was involved, don't you?" Hartmann turned and looked at Woodroffe. Truth was he didn't care what Woodroffe thought; he didn't care what anyone thought in that moment. His mind was on Carol and Jess, how he would go right back into the Royal Sonesta and call them, tell them he was coming home, that he would meet them any time they wanted, any place they chose, and there were so many things he wanted to say.

"I think *someone* was involved," Woodroffe said. "The report said what it said . . . that it was improbable that one man would have been physically capable of lifting Gerard McCahill's body from the back of the car and into the trunk that night on Gravier."

"Go for it," Hartmann said.

Woodroffe turned and started back toward the hotel. He stopped and turned before he reached the door. "You didn't wanna go down and get the girl from the motel?"

Hartmann shook his head. "I want to call my wife. That's all I want to do right now."

Woodroffe nodded. "I'll come tell you when they pick the girl up, okay?"

"Sure . . . sure thing," Hartmann said, and then he watched as Bill Woodroffe turned and entered the hotel.

It was a good five minutes before Hartmann sat before a phone in the foyer of the Royal Sonesta. One of the Feds had hooked up an outside line bypassing the main switchboard. Hartmann dialed his own home number, the number that would take his call right across the East River into a two-bedroomed apartment in Stuyvesant Town. He could picture where the phone sat, right there on a small table in the front hallway. What time was it? Hartmann glanced at his watch: a little after two p.m. Carol would be home now; it would be another hour or so before she left to collect Jess from school. The sound of the line hummed in his ear, and then connection was made and he listened as the phone rang. He could almost hear Carol's footsteps as she made her way from the bedroom or the bathroom. Twice, three times, four times . . . where the hell was she? Why wasn't she picking up? Was she in the bath? Perhaps she was in the kitchen with the TV on and she couldn't hear it.

Hartmann willed his wife to pick up the goddamned phone. How many times had it rung now? Eight? Ten? He felt a tension in his lower gut. He was afraid, afraid that she'd had second thoughts, the very worst thoughts of all; afraid that she'd decided that his failure to arrive for their Tompkins Square Park appointment four days before was the little flag that told her nothing had changed. Ray had broken another agreement. Whatever the reason, the truth of the matter was that Ray Hartmann had added another broken promise to the vast catalog he had already accumulated.

Perhaps Hartmann would have hung on; perhaps he would have let the phone ring for another hour, would have sat right there with the patience of Job until Carol finally heard the phone, or Jess returned from school and picked it up . . . perhaps he would have done, but his plans were interrupted suddenly, abruptly, as three or four federal agents came rushing into the foyer of the hotel and began shouting.

Pandemonium broke out. It spread like wildfire through the lower floor of the building, and it seemed like minutes before Bill Woodroffe— the senior man amongst them—appeared in the entranceway, his face white and drawn, his expression one of complete shock and confusion.

"They got him," he was shouting at the top of his voice. "Oh my God, they've got him!"

Hartmann stood up suddenly. His chair tumbled over behind him and he almost fell across it as he started across the foyer toward Woodroffe.

"What?" he shouted. "What's happened?"

"For God's sake, they shot him!" Woodroffe screamed.

"They shot *who*?" Hartmann yelled back.

"Ducane!" Woodroffe said. "Someone just shot Charles Ducane!"

And in the confusion no one saw the radio light blinking at the main desk. No one—amidst the sudden rush of confusion and panic that swept through the Royal Sonesta—saw the light blinking or stopped to pick up the radio headset.

Had they done, they would have heard the Recovery Unit Chief's voice telling them to call Schaeffer in the transporter and get Ernesto Perez back to the hotel.

During the subsequent fifteen minutes or so, the few details they could gather regarding the shooting of Governor Charles Ducane came through to Bill Woodroffe. Simultaneously, the Recovery Unit was making its way back to the Sonesta, and out in Virginia, the FBI Identification Database was searching for the names of Emilie Devereau and David Carlyle.

A man had been arrested as he fled through a crowd gathered in Shreveport, Ducane's home city. Ducane had been speaking publicly, opening a new arts center in a local suburb, when a man had stepped from the crowd and shot him three times in the chest. Even as details were coming through, Ducane was being rushed by the emergency services to the nearest hospital. He was still alive but in a grave condition. It was believed one of the bullets had grazed his heart. The arrested man had already been identified as the eldest son of Antoine Feraud, and even as Hartmann picked up the few details of what was happening, FBI Director Dohring was organizing a task force to raid Feraud's property and take him in.

Perhaps because of all of these things together or the fact that no single man was directly assigned to cover unexpected eventualities, the Royal Sonesta became the eye of the hurricane and Ray Hartmann had no further opportunity to reach Carol.

The return of the Recovery Unit outside the building sparked a further wave of confusion.

Hartmann was out there to see them skid to a dead stop against the curb, and when the Recovery Chief stepped from the vehicle with nothing more than a bundle of clothes in his hands, Hartmann knew that something that could have been no worse had suddenly deteriorated into a nightmare.

Woodroffe appeared, and when he realized that Catherine Ducane had not been located, he ran back into the hotel to radio the transporter. Hartmann was there beside him as he tried in vain to raise a signal.

"Disconnected," Woodroffe kept saying. "They've disconnected the goddamned radio for fuck's sake!" and it was some time before Hartmann managed to get him to understand that the transporter radio had been disconnected intentionally.

"Oh Jesus Christ . . . Schaeffer!" he said, and then his name was being called and an agent was standing at the side of the stairwell waving his arms above his head to attract his attention.

Woodroffe forced himself through the crowd and reached the man.

"I've got Quantico on the line," the man was saying. "They've got an answer on your ID request."

Woodroffe pushed past him and hurried up the stairs to the second-floor room where Kubis had established a bank of computers with a direct and secure line to Quantico.

Hartmann followed at a run, all the while shouting above the noise from below.

"Schaeffer! What the fuck are you gonna do about Schaeffer and Perez?"

Woodroffe reached the second-floor landing and started down the hallway toward the room.

"Woodroffe . . . what the fuck are you gonna do?" Hartmann was shouting. "Catherine Ducane wasn't there . . . you understand what I'm saying? Catherine Ducane wasn't in the fucking motel cabin!"

Woodroffe stopped suddenly and turned on his heel. "Go down to the street," he said. "Go down there and tell the Recovery Unit Chief to go after the transporter. Take the clothes and give them to Forensics, and show this to the chief." Woodroffe handed Hartmann a single sheet of paper. It was headed with the FBI symbol, and beneath it was typed a concise route plan that the transporter would be taking back to Virginia.

Hartmann turned and ran back down the stairs.

Woodroffe entered the room where the computer system had been established and found Lester Kubis sitting there staring at the screen.

"What is it? What do they say?"

Kubis turned slowly and looked at Woodroffe over the rim of his glasses. "This," he said quietly, "you are not going to like."

Hartmann reached the street and found the Recovery Unit Chief. "Take this," he said, thrusting the sheet of paper at him. "This is the route plan the transporter is taking. Go after them and get Schaeffer and Perez back here."

The chief turned and started back to the vehicle at a run.

"Wait!" Hartmann called after him. "Where are the clothes you found?"

The chief indicated an agent standing on the sidewalk holding a plastic evidence bag containing a pair of jeans, some shoes and other items they had found in the motel cabin.

Hartmann raised his hand and the chief hurried back to his vehicle.

Hartmann took the clothes and went back into the Sonesta. He found someone from Criminal Forensics. "Take these," he said. "Get them to the County Coroner's office. Get hold of the coroner, a guy called Michael Cipliano, and find the assistant ME, Jim Emerson. Take whoever the hell else you need and get these clothes processed. We need the results of anything you find back here as fast as it can be done. Tell them it's for Ray Hartmann, okay?"

The agent nodded, and hurried away with the bag containing everything that remained of Catherine Ducane's stay at the Shell Beach Motel.

Hartmann stood on the sidewalk trying to catch his breath. Woodroffe was up on the second floor, the Recovery Unit was hightailing it down the street after Schaeffer and Perez, and Hartmann shook his head and wondered what the fuck was going on.

He went back into the foyer of the hotel just as the first radio calls came in for the remaining Feds to leave for the Feraud property. Units had been assigned from New Orleans itself, also from Baton Rouge, Metairie and Hammond. Among the wave of agents that would make their way out to Feraud's property were Robert Luckman and Frank Gabillard, men who had believed they'd seen the last of this thing a little more than two weeks before. Two units posted in Lafayette had been alerted, but they could not arrive for a further hour or more. It seemed that it was no more than a minute before the foyer of the Sonesta was cleared of people, and Ray Hartmann was left standing there, his heart thundering in his chest, his thoughts a whirlwind of confusion as he realized that everything they had organized was falling apart at the seams.

He watched people run from the building to waiting cars. He heard the cars leaving, listened as they vanished into silence, and then he turned and looked toward the stairwell. Woodroffe was up there with Lester Kubis. Hartmann snatched a radio unit from the main desk to receive any calls from the recovery guys, and started up the stairs to find them.

Woodroffe was standing in the hallway with a single sheet of paper in his hands. The expression on his face was of a man lost. Completely and utterly lost.

"What did Quantico say?" Hartmann asked.

Woodroffe looked up. "They were cover names," he said quietly.

"What were? Cover names for what? What in fuck's name are you talking about?"

"Emilie Devereau and David Carlyle."

Hartmann shook his head and frowned.

Woodroffe held out the piece of paper. "They were cover names assigned by the security office of the Governor of Louisiana . . . cover names for Catherine Ducane and Gerard McCahill."

Hartmann took a step back. There was something he didn't understand, something that didn't make sense. He opened his mouth to speak and silence issued forth.

"Victor Perez was in love with Catherine Ducane all along," Woodroffe said. "What did he say? The two families that could never be together? It was Ducane's family . . . his daughter was in love with Ernesto Perez's son, and Victor asked his father to kill Ducane—"

Hartmann snatched the piece of paper from Woodroffe. His mind was reeling. He couldn't grasp how this had been done. It was Perez all along. Perez had played them all. He had turned himself in to the FBI. He had shared his life with them, and in doing so had given evidence about Feraud and Ducane right to the director of the FBI. And Hartmann, in his eagerness to find the girl, had walked right out to Feraud's house with John Verlaine and inadvertently informed Feraud of Perez's location and intention.

Hartmann took a step back. He felt as if the whole world had tilted on its axis.

Antoine Feraud—believing perhaps that Ducane would be questioned and would implicate him—had sent his son to kill Ducane, and now Feraud himself would be taken in by the FBI. Both of the people responsible for the murder of Angelina and Lucia Perez would be delivered their own justice, and Perez . . .

"Call the Recovery Unit," Hartmann said, his voice short, desperate-sounding. "Call the Recovery Unit and find out what the fuck has happened to Perez."

"The daughter was in on it, wasn't she?" Woodroffe was saying. "Catherine Ducane was in on it all along, wasn't she? Wasn't she?"

Hartmann shook his head. "I don't know what the fuck has happened here," he said. "Right now I want to know what the fuck they've done with Schaeffer. Who sent these people from Langley? What were their names?"

"McCormack and Van-something or other—"

"Van Buren," Hartmann said. He turned to Kubis. "Call Quantico and find out if they sent people down to take Perez to Virginia."

Kubis frowned. "Did no one check already? Did no one check the requisition paperwork?"

Woodroffe turned and looked at Kubis. "You see how many agents we had down there?" he snapped angrily. "Did you see how many people were in and out the front of this building? This is one almighty fuck-up, I'll tell you that much for nothing. Someone's gonna lose their fucking head over this—"

"Well, let's hope to God it isn't Schaeffer," Hartmann said, and once again told Kubis to call Langley and find out the names of the agents sent down to collect Perez.

Within a minute he turned and shook his head. "They didn't send anyone yet," he said quietly, and then once again turned away from Woodroffe and Hartmann as if he did not wish to be involved in this any further.

Hartmann looked at Woodroffe.

Woodroffe stared back blankly, and then: "Schaeffer's dead, isn't he?"

"I'm going after them," Hartmann said.

"You ain't leaving me here," Woodroffe replied, and turning to Kubis he said, "We're going after the Recovery Unit . . . if there's any word on anything call me on the radio, okay?"

Kubis nodded, didn't say a word, and watched silently as Hartmann and Woodroffe left the room and started down the stairwell.

"This is beyond comprehension," Woodroffe was saying, but even as he said it he knew it was not. They had all been captivated by Perez's performance, and there was the girl, always the girl . . . the promise that if they listened they would find the girl and she would be alive, and within hours she would be returned to the care of her father.

But it had never been about that. It had been about revenge. Perez had dug two graves, and it seemed as if both of them would be filled one way or another.

They found the transporter and the Recovery Unit no more than five miles from the Royal Sonesta, outside of a small town called Violet on Highway 39. Hartmann skidded to a stop and he and Woodroffe went at a run toward the vehicles.

The Recovery Unit Chief was standing over someone, and for a moment Hartmann believed he would find Schaeffer lying there at the side of the road with a bullet hole in the back of his head, but as he came around the side of the vehicle he found Stanley Schaeffer standing there, speechless but very much alive, and he was looking down at something he held in his hand.

Hartmann walked over slowly. On the ground at Schaeffer's feet were torn strips of duct tape, tape that had been used to bind him, and to the side of that a canvas bag that—more than likely—had been put over his head.

Schaeffer saw Hartmann coming and held out his hand.

Hartmann approached slowly, almost afraid of what he might see.

Schaeffer's hand opened, and there within—small and silver, reflecting what little light was left in the sky—was a single dime.

Hartmann shook his head. "Ten Cent," he said.

"The older one," Schaeffer said almost disbelievingly, "and the younger one—"

"Was Victor Perez," Hartmann interjected.

He turned and looked at Woodroffe. Woodroffe shook his head slowly and looked down at the ground.

"There was someone here waiting for them," Schaeffer said. "There was a car here waiting for them. They taped my hands and feet, they put a bag over my head. I didn't see them, but it was definitely a girl . . . definitely, definitely a girl."

"Catherine Ducane," Woodroffe said. "They took us, didn't they? Perez and his son, the girl as well . . . they took us all."

Hartmann stood there, his heart like a cold stone in the middle of his chest. He breathed deeply. He steadied himself against the threatened loss of balance that assaulted him, and then he walked to the side of the road and sat down. He put his hands over his face, he closed his eyes, and it was a long time before he could even consider what he was going to do next.

Reports came later, inconsistent, inconclusive—but for one key fact.

Federal Bureau of Investigation agents, members of the ATF and DEA had raided the property of Antoine Feraud.

Daddy Always.

Men had been killed on both sides. There were numerous fatalities and woundings. Even as those reports came in, even as Hartmann listened to the words that were relayed back to the Royal Sonesta through Lester Kubis, men were being ferried to the Emergency Room in New Orleans suffering gunshot wounds. But one thing was known for sure.

Daddy Always was dead. Standing at the top of the stairwell in his own house he had fired on FBI agents as they came in through the front door. He went down in a hail of gunfire. He went down fighting back, and even as his body fell down two flights of stairs, even as his old and broken form lay spread-eagled at the foot of the risers, blood making its cautious way from his head and out across the deep polished mahogany flooring, Governor Charles Ducane's heart monitor flatlined while surgeons attempted to remove a third bullet from an arterial channel close to his heart.

They died within moments of one another, and had they known, had they been aware of that narrow coincidence, they might perhaps have been amused at the irony. As, undoubtedly, would Ernesto Perez, crossing the Louisiana stateline into Mississippi beside a tributary of the Amite River.

Night was closing in. The lights of the Royal Sonesta burned bright. Federal agents returning from the Feraud property were gathered and briefed. Even Verlaine was there, aware that all hell had broken loose and eager to understand what had happened in his territory.

And it was he who stood beside Ray Hartmann when Michael Cipliano showed up, beside him Jim Emerson and in his hand the report prepared from the clothes they had processed from the Shell Beach Motel.

"Her clothes alright, no question about it," Cipliano told Hartmann. "Nothing out of the ordinary, 'cept for this one little thing."

Hartmann, his mind too overwhelmed with all that had happened to cope with anything else, merely looked back at Cipliano.

"Back of her jeans we found some blood . . . tiny little spots of blood around the edge of the rivets—"

Hartmann knew what Cipliano was going to say before he uttered the words.

"Except it wasn't blood, Mr. Hartmann . . . it was burgundy paint, the kind you'd find on a '57 Mercury Turnpike Cruiser."

Cipliano was smiling, as if everything the world had to offer had now fallen into place.

"We estimated the carrier's height at maybe five-foot ten or eleven. Catherine Ducane was five-foot seven, but along with her jeans you brought a pair of three-inch high-heeled shoes . . ."

Hartmann closed his eyes. He stepped past Cipliano and Emerson and walked out into the street. He stood there on the sidewalk, the noise behind him blurring into nothing.

He inhaled, exhaled, inhaled once more . . . and then he found it: the ripe malodorous blend of smells and sounds and human syncopations; the heat of rare ribs scorching in oiled flames; the bay leaf and oregano and court bouillon and carbonara; the collected perfumes of a thousand million intersecting lives, and then each life intersecting yet another like six degrees of separation; a thousand million beating hearts, all here, here beneath the roof of the same sky where the stars were like dark eyes that saw everything . . . saw and remembered . . .

He thought of Danny, of looking out over the trees, out over the Mississippi to the Gulf of Mexico, a band of clear dark blue, a stripe through the earth, a vein . . . how they used to dream of sailing away, a paper boat big enough for two, its seams sealed with wax and butter, their pockets filled with nickels and dimes and Susan B. Anthony dollars saved from scrubbing wheel arches and hubcaps, from soaping windshields and windows and porch stoops for the Rousseaus, the Buies, the Jeromes. Running away, running away with themselves from Dumaine, from the intersection where bigger kids challenged them, tugged their hair, pointed sharpened fingers into their chests and called them weirdo kids, where they ran until the breath burst from their chests in great whooping asthmatic heaving gusts, turning down alleyways, hiding in shadows, the reality of the world crowding the edges of the safe and insular shell they had created for themselves. Danny and Ray, Ray and Danny, an echo of itself, an echo of childhood . . .

Ray Hartmann felt that vague and indefinable sensation . . . believed that each time he thought of these things he was younger for the duration.

And then he saw his mother's face, his father's too, and within a moment he had to wipe the soft salt-sting of tears from his eyes.

"It was always here," he whispered to himself. "Everything I ever was. It was always here."

And then he turned. Quietly, step by step, he turned and left. Walking slowly now, carefully, each chosen step a moment of thought in itself, and made his way down to the intersection.

It was there that he found a phone booth, and with his quarters in his hand he dialed the number, a number he could never have forgotten if his life had depended on it.

And he almost broke down in tears when he heard her voice.

"Ray? Ray, is that you?"

"Yes, Carol, it's me."

TWENTY-NINE

NEW YORK WOULD never be the same. At least not through Ray Hartmann's eyes. The eyes that looked out over the skyline as the plane banked and veered toward the airport were different eyes now. It was early afternoon, Tuesday 10 September. Eleven days had passed, during which Hartmann had lived two lifetimes, his own and that of Ernesto Cabrera Perez.

The world had fallen apart behind him as he'd left Louisiana. Ducane was dead, Feraud also; and though all efforts were being made by the federal and intelligence communities within the mainland United States, Hartmann truly believed that Perez, his son Victor, Catherine Ducane and Samuel "Ten Cent" Pagliaro had already left the United States behind. Perhaps they were in Cuba, or South America—it didn't matter. What mattered was that they were gone. And Ducane was a man who had died with his own reputation intact. He was acknowledged in the newspapers, on the TV; he was applauded as a man of vision, a man of the future. He went to his grave with his image unsullied by the ugly truth, for there were people above and behind him who knew that nothing would be gained by revealing that truth to the world. Charles Ducane had been murdered at the behest of Antoine Feraud, and now Feraud himself was dead. His son would be swiftly processed through the judicial system, and would irrevocably disappear. This was politics, the same politics that had given America Watergate and Vietnam, the deaths of two Kennedys and Martin Luther King. It was the public face of Charles Ducane that would be worn for the world: husband, father, governor, martyr.

These things did not concern Ray Hartmann. The sole and prevalent thought in his mind was his meeting at four p.m. in Tompkins Square Park. A little more than eight months he had been separated from his family. Jess would be different. It never ceased to amaze him how fast children ceased to be children and became young men and women.

Carol would have changed too. You cannot spend two-thirds of a year away from your husband, away from the familiarity of the family you have created, and not be somehow changed. But he had changed too; Ray Hartmann knew that, and he hoped—against everything that previous experience had taught him—that he had changed enough.

He had called Carol earlier, from New Orleans. She had said nothing for a good three or four minutes while he poured out every thought and feeling, every reason he believed they should meet again. He had apologized for Saturday ten, twelve, perhaps twenty times, and finally, exhausted perhaps, she had said, "Okay Ray . . . for Jess. Same place, Tompkins Square Park at four. And don't fuck this up, Ray . . . please don't fuck this up again. Right now I don't give a damn about how I feel, but I can't have Jess upset any more, okay?"

Earlier, still aloft, Hartmann had glanced at his watch: it was gone twenty after two. Fifteen minutes, and the New Orleans–New York flight would land; by three he would be on his way. He'd taken the earliest flight he could. There were questions to answer, even more to ask, and by the time John Verlaine had been given leave to drive Hartmann to the airport his nerves had been shredded.

"You gonna fix this for keeps, right?" Verlaine had asked him.

Hartmann had nodded but said nothing.

Verlaine had not pushed the issue. Everything that needed to be said would be said in New York. And so Verlaine had spoken of Perez, of the girl, of how everything they had imagined to be the truth had been nothing but a masquerade. They had been clever, they had planned everything down to the last detail, it seemed, and where the FBI had failed Perez had been quick to take advantage.

"You think they bombed the FBI office themselves?" Verlaine had asked. "You think the older guy and the son waited until Perez wasn't there and then bombed it just to throw as much confusion into the situation as they could?"

Hartmann had shrugged, his eyes on the signposts along the highway that told him the airport was fast approaching.

"It doesn't make sense that it was Feraud," Verlaine had continued. "Feraud's intelligence would have told him that Perez would leave the office during the day and would go back to the Sonesta."

Again Hartmann had been noncommittal in his response.

"I figure it was the son who bombed the office," Verlaine had concluded. "The son and the other guy . . . what was his name?"

"Ten Cent," Hartmann had replied, and when he'd said the man's name he'd felt as if he had known him, as if this character from Perez's past was now as much a part of his own. Perhaps all of them would reside somewhere three inches back of his forehead forever. It had been a journey, that much at least; he had done what he'd been asked to do and he could not have been faulted for his cooperation and willingness. But the thing was over. It was done. And if they found Ernesto Perez they would take whatever action was required and Hartmann would not have to be involved.

In some small and strange way he hoped that the man would never be seen again.

And then Verlaine had taken a turn into the airport sliproad, and before they knew it they were at the Louis Armstrong International Terminal and Verlaine was saying something about coming back down to New Orleans some time, that it had been good meeting Hartmann, that he should stay in touch, give him a call . . .

And Ray Hartmann, feeling some sense of kinship and fraternity for this man, had looked at John Verlaine and smiled.

"I won't be coming back," he'd said quietly.

Verlaine had nodded. "I know," he'd said. "But you gotta say these things, right?"

"Right," Hartmann had replied, and then he'd taken Verlaine's hand and shaken it firmly, and then he'd gripped his shoulder and said, "It was good to have you in on this, and hell . . . you'll have something to tell your grandchildren."

Verlaine had laughed. "As if," he'd said, and then he'd let go of Hartmann's hand and turned to walk back to his car.

"Remember the trick," Hartmann had called after him.

Verlaine had paused and turned. "The trick?"

Hartmann had smiled. "The trick, Verlaine, is to keep breathing."

The flight had been brief. New Orleans to New York. A handful of hours over Alabama, Georgia, South and North Carolina, and then the east coast across Virginia to Maryland, and then Hartmann could see the Atlantic to his right, and the flight attendants were giving them an ETA on their landing.

Ray Hartmann tried to remember how he had felt when he'd returned to New Orleans. He tried to convince himself that now he was *really* going home, but he knew he was not. Louisiana was there, there rooted in everything he was, and though he truly believed that he would never return out of choice, he also knew that he had those roots. Uproot, and the channels those roots left behind were still there, like fingerprints in the earth. The earth remembered, reminded you of your heritage no matter how far you traveled. He tried to persuade himself that home was not a location, but a state of mind. He tried to think of this a hundred different ways, but it would always stay the same. Perez had been right. New Orleans would always be a part of him, no matter where he went.

By the time he collected his bags from the carousel and made his way to the exit gates it was after two forty-five. He hurried out and hailed a cab, told the driver he needed to be across the Williamsburg Bridge and to Tompkins Square Park in East Village no later than ten minutes of four. The driver, whose name was Max, sighed and shook his head.

"You'll be wantin' a helicopter then," he said. "Williamsburg is jammed end to end. Truck took a spill about a third of the way down, took me the better part of an hour to make it across last time I tried. Might be better if we went up to the Queensboro and down Second Avenue through Stuyvesant." Max shook his head. "No, that way for sure will take us more than an hour. We'll take a risk, eh? Let's hope the Virgin Mary has a blessing for you today."

"Get me there before four and there's a hundred bucks in it for you," Hartmann said.

Max grinned from ear to ear. "Hundred bucks and I'll get you there last Tuesday."

The run was clear all the way to the bridge, and Hartmann looked at his watch every three or four minutes. By the time they hit the first slow it was twenty-five after three. He was nervous already, and the mere fact that time was against him made it all the worse.

Max was no help. He insisted on detailing the idiosyncrasies and eccentricities of pretty much every passenger he'd carried in the previous week.

Ray Hartmann heard the words as they battered each other out of the way to escape from Max's mouth, but what he was saying and whether it was of any interest was lost on him. It was just a noise, like the noise of car horns blaring at one another as the traffic ground to a halt at the entrance to the Williamsburg Bridge.

Hartmann looked at his watch for the hundredth time: three thirty-nine p.m. He swore under his breath.

"What was that?" Max asked. "You say somethin', mister?"

"The goddamned traffic!" Hartmann snapped.

"Told you so," Max said. "Took me near on an hour to make it across here last time."

Hartmann wanted to grab Max by the throat and shake him until he collapsed. He clenched his fists and gritted his teeth. He willed himself to believe that the traffic would suddenly ease up and start moving, that they would make it across the Bridge, that it would be nothing more than a right onto Baruch, left onto East Houston, right onto Avenue B and they would be there, pulling up alongside Tompkins Square Park, and he would be cramming Max's hands with grubby ten-dollar bills, and he would be running, and there would be minutes to spare, and Carol would know that he *had* changed because this time . . . *this* time he had not broken his word . . .

The cars ahead seemed to have parked up for the afternoon.

Hartmann wound down the window and took several deep breaths. He clenched and unclenched his hands. A fine gloss of sweat had varnished his face, and beneath his jacket he felt hot and cold flushes running alternately. He thought he might puke. He could think of nothing but this tight sense of nervous impatience, desperation almost, that seemed to have assumed complete control of his mind and body. He wanted to get out of the cab and start running. He wanted to hurtle full-tilt between the lanes of cars and make it all the way on foot . . .

At three forty-nine the traffic started moving. They reached the end of the Bridge and turned right onto Baruch at four minutes past four.

Hartmann had lit three cigarettes against Max's insistence that he not smoke in the cab, and each one had been left to burn almost to its filter before he threw it out of the window.

How much money he gave Max when the cab finally drew to a stop near the gates of the park Hartmann didn't know. It could have been his life savings and he wouldn't have cared. He even left his bag behind, and Max came after him, thrust the thing into his hands, and then stopped to watch as he charged across the grass toward the bandstand.

By the time Ray Hartmann reached his agreed rendezvous point with his wife and daughter it was thirteen minutes past four.

The bandstand was deserted.

Hartmann stood there, pale and drawn, covered in sweat, his bag dropped at his feet, everything inside him tightened up like a fist, ready to explode at the slightest provocation.

He swore three or four times. He scanned the people nearby. He started walking one way, and then he turned and walked the other. He saw a child with a woman, he opened his mouth to speak, and then he realized the child was a boy and the woman was old and gray-haired and walking with a cane.

He backed up against the cold concrete base of the bandstand. He felt his knees giving beneath him. He felt the sting of tears in his eyes. He couldn't breathe. His heart was trip-hammering like it intended to overload and stop and send him crashing to the ground . . . and some-time later someone would find him and call the police, and the police would call the emergency services, and they would come down and find him dead and cold and stiff and . . .

Ray Hartmann started to cry. He went down on his knees, his face in his hands.

This is what you get for everything you didn't do, his inner voice told him. *This is what you get for being a lousy father and never paying attention, and never helping Jess with her schoolwork, and drinking when you said you wouldn't. This is what you get for being a loser, born and bred, and no matter what you do now you will always look back at this moment and beat yourself to death about it, because this is everything that your life will ever be, and there's nothing, absolutely nothing you can do about it . . .*

And then there were footsteps, the sound of someone running, and for a moment he paused, instinct like radar tuned to every sound around him, and Ray Hartmann looked up, and through his tear-filled eyes he saw her . . .

"Dadddeeeeee!"

EPILOGUE

HE STOOD UP slowly.

He surveyed the faces before him. He took one step forward and gripped the edge of the lectern.

It's not here for notes, he thought. *No one brings notes to say what they have to say here. They put this here so there's something between you and them . . . something for you to hold onto if you feel you're going to lose it. If you feel just like I feel now . . .*

"Hi," he said.

There was a murmur from the gathered ensemble of people. Men, women, young and old, dressed every which way, nothing similar between them, except one thing, and that was something you could never see, and in most cases would never have guessed, but they were all here for the very same reason.

"Hi," he said again. "My name is Ray."

And there are times when he finds it hard to believe that he ever jeopardized what he possessed, as if only a crazy man could have failed to recognize what was here.

They came back at him then, a chorus of acknowledgments and nods of approval.

"My name is Ray. I am a father. I am a husband. I am an alcoholic, and until a few months ago I was drinking."

And there are times when he looks at his own reflection in the mirror and asks himself if he ever really knew himself, or anyone else for the matter.

There was a murmur of sympathy, and then beneath that a ripple of applause, and Ray Hartmann stood there, his heart beating, and he waited until the crowd had settled down before he spoke again.

"I blamed my wife, I blamed my job. I blamed my own dad because he was a drunk too. I blamed it all on the fact that I lost my younger brother when I was fourteen years old . . . but the truth of the matter, and this was the hardest thing of all, was that I was the only one to blame."

Time, he knows now, does not heal. Time is merely a window through which we can see our own mistakes, for those seem to be the only things we remember with clarity.

Again there were murmurs of consent and agreement, and once again a ripple of applause that spread through the crowd.

"Some time ago I went home to New Orleans, and there, again because of my job, I met a man who had spent his life killing people."

Jess speaks to him, and in her voice is the same feeling, the same emotion that she always possessed. She does not care to remember the time he was away, as if that was merely a blip on the heart monitor, and now it has passed it can be forgotten so easily.

Ray Hartmann paused and looked at the faces watching him. He wanted to be outside in the car with Carol and Jess. He wanted to be anywhere but here, but he knew, knew with all of his being, that this time he was going to keep his side of the agreement.

"See it through, Ray," Carol had told him. "See it through this time . . . start it and finish it, no matter what it takes, okay?"

And he watches Carol. This is the girl he fell in love with, the girl he married, and in her he finds everything that he knows he could ever want, and in some small way he believes he will spend the rest of his life measuring up to that.

"And I listened to this man, and despite all the terrible things he had done, all the lives he had destroyed, there was one thing that he taught me. He taught me that the strength of family is the only thing that can really see you through."

In the early hours of the morning he will wake, and there will be a sound within, and the sound will be something like a heart beating, but now it is not the heart of a frightened and desperate man; it is the heart of a man who believed he had lost everything, and then somehow retrieved it.

Later. Christmas Eve.

Ray Hartmann stands in the kitchen doorway.

The phone rings.

Carol is out back somewhere bringing groceries in from the car.

"Jess!" Hartmann calls out. "Can you get the phone, Jess?"

"Aw Dad, I'm busy."

"Jess, please . . . I gotta help your mom with the groceries."

He listens for her footsteps on the stairs, and when the phone stops ringing Ray Hartmann walks through the kitchen to the back door and takes a bag of groceries from Carol. He sets it down on the worktop, and then he pauses as he hears Jess's voice from the hallway.

And the heart beats with a cautious sound, as though there are still a great many lessons to learn, but his eyes are open, his mind is willing and, if anything, he has learned the greatest lesson of all: that of humility, that he was not always right, that the complexities of life cannot be avoided or denied.

"Jess? Who is it, honey?"

Jess doesn't answer.

He leaves the kitchen and walks toward the front of the house, and then he slows as he hears what she is saying.

It is the same world now, and yet somehow different.

"I don't know . . . of course I don't know. It's supposed to be a surprise."

She is silent for a moment.

"What *would* I like? Oh, I don't know. I could use some more make-up, and I need a new purse, and there's a couple of CDs I'd like. I've hinted enough times to Mom so if I don't get those then I'll know she's really lost the plot—"

"Jess?" Hartmann asks. "Who's on the phone, honey?"

Jess turns and smiles. "Some friend of yours," she says, and then she adds, "Here's my dad . . . nice to talk to you, and have a good Christmas yourself, okay?"

Jess holds out the receiver and he walks toward her and takes it.

"Hello?" Hartmann says. "Who is this?"

He sees it for what it is; an endless stream of circumstance, coincidence, of decisions and choices.

"Mr. Hartmann."

Ray Hartmann feels his skin go cold, as if someone has doused him with ice water. The hairs on the nape of his neck stand to attention and he knows all the color has drained from his face.

"Perez?"

"You have a bright daughter," Ernesto Perez says. "I am sure with your care and guidance she will grow into a fine young woman, Mr. Hartmann."

"Wha—"

"You do not need to say anything, Mr. Hartmann . . . nothing at all. I just wanted to make sure you were okay, and that you had worked things out with your family. It seems you have, and here we are, Christmas Eve, and you are all together."

"If you think—"

"Enough, Mr. Hartmann. It was merely a social call. A call to wish you well, to give you my blessing at this special time of year. I wanted you to know that I appreciated all you did for me, the way you listened, the time we shared, and to make sure you were back on the right track. My mind will rest now, because I think you understand this as well as I. If you can't give your children what they want, then what is the worth of your life?"

Hartmann doesn't speak; cannot say a word.

"I called to make sure that something good came from all of this. Aside from the death of your people . . . that was never meant to happen. There was never meant to be any more killing, Mr. Hartmann, but the men that died in New Orleans, that was an error in judgment. People were still in the building when it was believed the building was empty—"

Hartmann closes his eyes; he can see the face of Sheldon Ross.

"Such is the way of war, Mr. Hartmann, but I am sorry for their deaths, sorry for their families and how they must have grieved. And perhaps I called also to answer a question for you . . . a question you asked me a very long time ago."

Perez pauses again as if for effect, and it was almost as if Hartmann could *hear* him smiling at the other end of the line.

"You asked me why I chose you, remember?"

Hartmann makes a sound, like a murmur.

"There was a case," Perez continues. "A very interesting case, and you had a witness. It was November if I recall correctly, a cold November some time ago. It was the night before your witness was to be presented before the Grand Jury, and she was found in a motel on Hunters Point Avenue near the Calvary Cemetery."

Hartmann feels the tension rising in his chest. Even as Perez speaks he can see the scene unfolding before his eyes, the way the woman had been found, the sense of complete despair that had accompanied him and Visceglia as they'd realized their entire investigation was undone.

"There was a certain element of creativity to her demise, don't you think, Mr. Hartmann? I can now assure you that that was something of which I was aware, and though not directly involved in her departure from your case, it was nevertheless something I followed with great interest. Let us say that my advice was requested as to how to resolve that particular detail."

Hartmann can see the woman's spread-eagled form across the cheap motel bed, the way her arms and legs are bruised, the cocaine around her nose and mouth, the way one hand is tied and the other left free to create the possibility that she could have self-administered the lethal quantity of drugs.

And then, after that, Hartmann remembers the very moment he broke his promise to Carol and Jess, how he had assuaged some small aspect of his rage and frustration in the company of Jack Daniels, how he'd staggered home and fallen through the front door of his Stuyvesant Town home, as drunk as a man could be and still conscious, how he'd collapsed in a heap on the kitchen floor and lain there until Jess had found him.

Perez speaks again, and Hartmann tenses every muscle in his body. It is everything he can do not to hurl the receiver against the wall.

"Remarkable that no matter her life beforehand, no matter how respectable and well-mannered she had been, she will always be remembered as a woman with a penchant for gang-bangs and nose-candy."

Hartmann cannot say a word.

"I was there, Mr. Hartmann . . . there in a car across the street watching as you and your friend came away from that motel. I can recall, almost as if it were yesterday, the expression on your face, the sheer horror and disillusionment you carried as you walked away from that building. It made me stop for a while, Mr. Hartmann. It made me think of things I had not considered before . . . and, curiously, after all I had done, after this life I have led, that single incident made me feel as if I owed something to you."

There is silence for a second. Hartmann wants to say something—*anything*—but there is absolutely nothing he can say.

"I wish you all a good Christmas, Mr. Hartmann, you and your very special family," Perez says quietly. "And this thing . . . this thing of ours is done."

The line goes dead.

Ray Hartmann stands there for some moments before he gently replaces the receiver in the cradle.

He walks out back to the kitchen and stands there for a moment watching his wife and his daughter unload groceries.

He sees it in a different light, and this time his eyes are open.

Carol looks up at him and frowns. "What is it?" she asks.

Hartmann smiles and shakes his head. "Merry Christmas," he says.

"Merry Christmas to you too."

"I love you, Carol."

Carol Hartmann pauses with a watermelon in her hand. She looks at Jess. Jess is frowning and smiling at the same time.

"What the hell's gotten into you?" she asks. "You gone soft in the head or what?"

Hartmann shakes his head. He looks down at his shoes, and then up at his wife and his daughter.

"So you gonna stand there like a retard or you gonna help us with the groceries?"

"I'm gonna help with the groceries," Ray Hartmann says, "and then maybe we go see a movie together and bring some pizza home."

"Good deal," Jess says.

"Good deal," replies her father, and believes that life defines itself in circles, and where we start, there we also find our own conclusions, and this is the nature of the world we have created and all we have become.

He steps into the kitchen and lifts a grocery bag from the floor.

He watches his wife, and when she turns toward him he looks away. He smiles to himself. He feels complete; perhaps for the first time in his life he feels complete.

There are things done, and things said, but somehow all these things are lost in the slow-motion manic slide of time. Lost, but never truly forgotten.

Ray Hartmann believes in faith, and faith—perhaps after all this time—finally, unconditionally, believes in him.